of the Mountain Men

Books by Tony Moyle

'The Circuit' Series
MEMORY CLOUDS
MEMORY HUNTERS
(Pre Order – Release Date Nov 2020)

'Ally Oldfield' Series
THE END OF THE WORLD IS NIGH
LAST OF THE MOUNTAIN MEN

'How to Survive the Afterlife' Series
THE LIMPET SYNDROME
SOUL CATCHERS
DEAD ENDS

Sign up to the newsletter
www.tonymoyle.com/contact

Last of the Mountain Men

TONY MOYLE

Copyright © 2020 by Tony Moyle

All rights reserved. This book or any portion thereof may not be reproduced or used in any manner whatsoever without the express written permission of the publisher except for the use of brief quotations in a book review or scholarly journal.

First published: February 2020

ISBN 9798609085573

Limbo Publishing, a brand of In-Sell Ltd

www.tonymoyle.com

Cover design by Damonza

For…

Sara

"For in the final analysis, our most basic common link is that we all inhabit this small planet. We all breathe the same air. We all cherish our children's future. And we are all mortal."

John F. Kennedy – June 1963

... and very brightly the men of the mountain will burn.

- Chapter 1 -

A Person of Interest

The only item Mario Peruzzi left behind following his untimely death was a tatty plastic bag full of letters. Not one of them was a suicide note. Neither did any of the carefully handwritten envelopes contain useful directions for family or friends to carry out his last wishes. The future recipients of the letters weren't even people he'd met personally. Yet each one had the individual's name and address neatly annotated on the front of the crisp, white paper in black ink. Each one had the precise postage neatly stuck to the front based on the length of its journey to destinations dotted in every corner of the globe. They were seemingly insignificant obituaries to mark the passing of one extraordinary life.

Leaving so few possessions was an extraordinary achievement for a man reported to be worth the equivalent of Mozambique's Gross Domestic Product. That's twelve point three four billion dollars, in case you're interested. Yes, the envelopes he'd used were certainly of a higher quality than the ones that normally hit people's doormats every morning sometime around eleven. Yes, he'd splashed out on an expensive black fountain pen to get the calligraphy on the front just right. Yes, postage was more expensive these days and many of the letters had more stamps on them than the face of a football hooligan's victim. But none of this meagre expense explained where the remaining twelve point three billion dollars had gone.

Simply no one knew.

Rumours persisted that a fortune existed on a scale unimaginable to anyone outside of the investment banking

A PERSON OF INTEREST

fraternity. When there's money, rumoured or real, there will never be a shortage of people or institutions determined to locate it. News of Mario's demise would seep out into the murkier corners of the internet and every would-be treasure hunter or conspiracy theorist would want in on the action.

Mario had no formal next of kin. His was the last branch of a family tree that could be traced back to the sixteenth century and one notorious ancestor, Nostradamus. So far no one had come forward to make a claim on his wealth because in truth there was no proof that any actually existed, and boy, had people tried. A court of law had proved beyond doubt that Mario was responsible for the Oblivion Doctrine, a highly complex online network of websites and companies that two years ago had dominated the internet like Google did before it. Its ability to generate revenue was legendary but following the trial none of its funds could be legally traced back to him.

There was a time when the Oblivion Doctrine made money faster than a seven-year-old YouTuber unboxing new toys, but the exact extent of its earnings was still a mystery. If the money did exist then highly paid, talented accountants had squirrelled it away in murky trust funds, dubious investment vehicles and unregulated tax havens. Tracing the money would be more complicated than working out why God saw fit to give the Tyrannosaurus Rex ridiculously small arms when clearly the rest of its torso had been designed for something much more fear-inducing. What's more, at no time had Mario attempted to access any of the money, either before or during his forced residence within the French justice system. There was even less chance of him doing so anytime soon because he'd drawn his last breath yesterday, sometime around noon.

If the money was out there, as everyone believed, then the letters must hold the key to finding it.

The last two years of Mario's existence were spent as prisoner 76230 in the company of other high-profile felons

A PERSON OF INTEREST

in the 'special area' of Clairvaux Prison near Troyes, France. His life sentence had been secured by proving his part in organising, and almost causing, the Apocalypse. Two years ago, the Oblivion Doctrine had purposely combined a newly discovered Nostradamus prophecy and a mildly contagious flu pandemic to feed the population of the world with an unhealthy dose of panic and paranoia via its internet chatrooms and online media outlets. As a result, humanity descended into an act of collective self-harm that only ended when three unlikely saviours successfully proved that the prophecy was a fake. The Oblivion Doctrine was tarnished, and Mario was apprehended, charged and sentenced for the hoax and his part in the murder of Bernard Baptiste, a well-known Nostradamus scholar. Mario had gone almost unnoticed by the rest of the world since, a notorious bit part in an interesting chapter of recent history that no longer made the headlines.

Until today.

People who die at fifty-five usually do so because some underlying genetic condition, poor lifestyle choice or catastrophic accident insists upon it. That was not Mario's fate. Everyone, including Mario, predicted he was going to die young. His immune system had been compromised after contracting N_1G_{13}, the flu strain that people feared would bring about human extinction that he'd done so much to propagate. The flu didn't kill him immediately, but when pneumonia entered his body without a suitable immune system to fight it off, the writing was on the wall, and subsequently on dozens of sheets of the prison's official headed notepaper.

In interview room two the contents of the plastic bag full of letters lay spread out on a steel table that had been buffed to within an inch of its life. On one side stood a scruffily dressed man with his arms crossed. Impatiently he glanced to the equally buffed silver-framed analogue clock that adorned the wall next to the only exit. If you were going to catch any diseases in the prison it definitely wasn't

A PERSON OF INTEREST

going to happen here. The surgically sheened room had been evacuated of all known germs and had all the hallmarks of the quarantine area in a zoo. The man looked at the clock once more and offered the empty surroundings of the room a deep and disgruntled sigh.

Americans were always late, thought Timon.

In the Frenchman's cultural perception, Americans had a tendency to show up towards the end of an event in a tornado of exuberance and noise. They'd offer no apology for their lateness, take over whatever it was that you'd been doing for the entirety of the time they'd been missing, before convincing you that success had only been achieved as a result of their late intervention. Then, they'd sell their version of events for the rest of time until everyone believed it wholeheartedly, partly because they'd already optioned the publishing rights for the book, taken out full-page adverts in the national newspapers and repeated it on social media until everyone got bored. Not everyone in the world felt this way, but the French had more reason than most for disenchantment when it came to their cousins from across the pond.

In the last two decades the Americans had tried to remove the words associated with 'France' from public consciousness because of a perceived lack of solidarity. This resulted in a campaign to rename everyday items that previously had a relationship with the country. Which was a shame really because France didn't have many cool words that were synonymous with it in the first place.

The Germans were associated with efficiency, the British had empire, the Spanish had Inquisition, and the French had... toast. French people were resolutely proud of the fact that their nation was mostly synonymous with items that related to food, fashion or furniture. Whether it was fries, baguettes, doors or knickers the Americans had the gall to rename all of them, usually with the word 'freedom' in its place. This gave 'French knickers' a completely new connotation right across America.

A PERSON OF INTEREST

The peace of interview room two was expunged by a stocky man moving through the shiny metal door as if it had never made its acquaintance with the door frame. The Governor immediately regretted his irritation at the man's tardiness. Now he'd have to deal with other character flaws that he believed the American would unquestionably bring in with him.

"Is this his bag?" asked the newcomer forcefully.

Before receiving the answer, the man immediately moved towards the table and polluted its immaculate metal surface with large, sweaty fingerprints.

The Governor nodded with a cringe.

"Have you opened any?"

The Governor shook his head. He'd not opened any, but he certainly knew who they were addressed to which presented him with a short-term advantage over his brash guest.

"Well, let's hope they're full of cheques, ones with lots of zeros!"

The man riffled through the contents of the bag and spread the letters precisely across the table top. Timon Ortiz had no prior experience of dealing with the FBI, but he correctly guessed that they normally didn't ask or need anyone's permission to do anything. The moment they entered a room any responsibility or authority that had once belonged to you was immediately and effortlessly transferred to them. There wasn't much he could do about it, other than break out a big dollop of intolerance for all things American.

"I didn't know he was one of yours?" said Timon in a doubtful tone.

"One of ours?"

"American."

"No, Mario's not an American citizen but that doesn't really matter. You see, they're all ours, if we decide they are," replied the man, fixing his stare on Timon in a threatening manner that suggested there was only one boss

A PERSON OF INTEREST

in the room, and it was no longer the Governor of Clairvaux Prison.

The American casually threw a black wallet onto the table which sprang open like a cheap magic trick. A small, square photo of himself looking more manicured but equally disconsolate gazed out of its laminated home. On one side it simply read 'FBI' and below the photo on the other it announced to the reader its owner, 'Daniel Hudson'.

"Was this all he left?" demanded Hudson.

"That and a few items of clothing," replied Timon, looking up from the wallet.

"Odd, though, wouldn't you say?"

"Not really. People generally don't die naked unless they slip in the shower."

"The letters," said Daniel pointedly.

"It might be strange in this digital age of ours, but people are still allowed to write letters, or has your President made that a criminal offence, too?"

"Not since this morning," replied Hudson coldly.

It was mid-afternoon so Timon wasn't confident the situation hadn't changed, such was the impulsive nature of the White House these days.

"Mario wasn't a normal prisoner," added Hudson. "Everything he does, or did, should I say, must be viewed as suspicious, given his past crimes."

"Have you heard of rehabilitation?" asked Timon. "I know it's originally a French word but I'm guessing you're still using it?"

Daniel nodded almost imperceptibly, perhaps under orders not to overly agree with anything.

"In many ways Mario was a model prisoner. I see no reason why he remains a person of interest."

"Governor, you run one of Europe's most secure prisons, which holds some of the world's most notorious criminals of the last fifty years: each and every one of them is a person of interest to us. Given that fact, it baffles me why you chose to place the most high-profile criminal of

A PERSON OF INTEREST

the last decade in the middle of your collection of dangerous killers, terrorists and traitors. Of course, Mario's a person of interest, more now than ever."

"But he's dead!"

"So what?"

The Governor shrugged in a way only a true Frenchman can. He had to deal with this type of negative attitude from the local police force: it just went with the territory. Anyone who worked in the criminal justice system the world over had a shared culture of suspicion towards anyone outside of the ropes. Harboured within their DNA was a deep-rooted prejudice that everyone they met was guilty of something. In their eyes it didn't matter if you were a baby in a pram, you were still capable, and probably culpable, of whatever crime they'd been sent like bloodhounds to investigate. At this moment those suspicions rested on Mario. Apparently even the dead couldn't be trusted.

It had already been proved that Mario was an exceptional criminal with a genuine intent and track record for causing public mayhem at every feasible opportunity. That might be unusual on the outside of these walls, but here at Clairvaux characters like him were two a penny. In Timon's professional opinion Mario was way down the pecking order of possible malcontents compared to the VIPs that resided here. Mario had approached his incarceration with a humility and genuine will to rehabilitate that was uncommon compared to his fellow inmates. Timon's overriding mentality was that everyone could be rehabilitated. Governors like him were keen not to see prisoners return, whilst policemen like Hudson were convinced they should.

"Let's see what Mario's been up to, then, shall we?" whispered Special Agent Hudson under his breath.

"I believe you're wasting your time," replied Timon picking something from his ear that was probably more interesting. "Prisoners who know they're dying often write to all kinds of people. Sometimes it's to express remorse for

A PERSON OF INTEREST

past crimes, and sometimes it's to offer words of peace to family members. It's even been known for them to write to the press in an attempt to justify their misdemeanours."

Three dozen standard-sized envelopes lay spread out over the table. Hudson picked up the nearest one and held it up in front of Timon's face like a dog being forced to acknowledge the illicit excrement recently deposited on the living room floor.

"Victim, friend or journalist?" grunted Hudson.

Timon Ortiz shrugged again when he saw the addressee on the front of the envelope, a Mr J. Johnson.

"None of the above," clarified Hudson. "Over the last two years, Governor, we have been monitoring Mario Peruzzi's personal network and business empire in order to locate a vast sum of money that he generated through illegal activities. Money that the US government would like to seize for other purposes."

'Other purposes' was code for 'purchasing a massive arsenal of lethal weapons capable of eviscerating an innocent Pakistani yak herder from the safety of a small office in Omaha'.

"I can also tell you," continued Hudson, "that there is no 'Mr J. Johnson' within his network, so why would he be writing to him or any of these people?"

"Why don't you open one and find out?" replied Timon desperately hoping that the contents were no more sinister than a thankyou note to Mr Johnson for his recent letter, part of the prison correspondence scheme that Timon himself had been responsible for creating.

Hudson needed no further prompting. He held the letter up to the light to confirm it only contained a piece of paper and not contents of a more sinister nature. In the past letters like this one had been known to contain small traces of white powder, dangerous substances like anthrax, although Daniel thought the chances of Mario being able to smuggle that in here were pretty remote. He slid his thumb under the flap and gently ran it along the edge of the envelope, prising it open with the least amount of

A PERSON OF INTEREST

disruption to the contents inside. His enormous, hairy fingers eased the one-page letter from the envelope, and he tried unsuccessfully to make sense of it.

"I don't get it," said Hudson passing it over to Timon for confirmation. "It's blank."

"It isn't blank," said Timon curtly, wondering how on Earth someone like Hudson managed to get a job in the FBI when he couldn't identify the simplest of con-tricks. Each page was essentially blank other than a two-digit number at the top and a number of small cuts in the paper that left a series of holes in an irregular pattern.

"What is it, then?"

"It's obviously a cipher," replied Timon, rather intrigued by the finding.

"Oh, rehabilitated, is he?!" offered Hudson aggressively. "You've done a super job."

"It could mean anything. Maybe it's an elaborate treasure hunt to help you find the missing money," smiled Timon, instantly regretting it.

Special Agent Hudson didn't do humour. He'd voluntarily had it surgically removed twenty-one years ago as part of his FBI induction programme. It was part of a package deal that also wiped out other important human characteristics such as fear, empathy and self-doubt.

"Mario's up to something. What's the number two at the top mean?" he said to himself.

"You'd need to find the book that relates to the cipher or none of it will make sense."

Daniel wasn't big on reading. Not books at least. Emails and memos took up enough of his time without adding to them. What he did know was that there were more books in the world than there were dollars in Mario's bank account, and there was no way anyone might guess which one it was. A new angle was required. When Hudson needed answers, he preferred to extract them from people rather than from paper.

"Who did he bond with?"

A PERSON OF INTEREST

"Everyone. The special area is a community in its own right, and he took a keen interest in everyone who's housed there."

"I want to interview all of them. Today. I want to know what he was planning and why he was sending these codes to these people," replied Hudson.

"And what should I do with these?" replied Timon, pointing to the letters. "Shred them?"

"Of course not! You don't work out a secret by cutting it up into tiny strips. Once my people have copied the contents and listed the recipients they must be sent out as planned. We may never know what his intentions were until we do. Every one of these people is a person of interest to the American government until proven otherwise."

"What if, by sending them out, we inadvertently set in motion exactly what Mario was planning? Then we'd be complicit in a crime, wouldn't we?"

"I wouldn't worry, my peculiar French friend, we'll soon have our people in close pursuit. Actually, we'll have someone watching these folk before they even receive their letters."

"There is one letter that Mario didn't put any postage on," added Timon, finally unleashing his short-term advantage.

"I'm sure the prison can afford a stamp."

"There's no need. I think Mario was expecting me to hand-deliver it."

Timon stretched out his arm, picked up a letter and handed it to Special Agent Hudson. It was addressed to him. Like all the others his name was scrawled in black ink, although the handwriting on this one was more hurried than the others. Hudson wiped the sweat from his bald head with a handkerchief and stared at the letter in disbelief. He was no longer a member of the *secret* service. Mario had not only known of Daniel Hudson's existence, but also foreseen his visit.

A PERSON OF INTEREST

"It looks like Daniel Hudson is also a person of interest to the American government," said Timon childishly, revelling in Hudson's obvious discomfort.

"I am the American government; how can I be a person of interest to myself? I know everything about me!"

"Surely in your line of work no one should be above the law. I can't wait to see how you get on trying to interrogate yourself," laughed Timon.

The Governor had pushed his luck too far. There are some people in this world you just shouldn't fuck with. Alongside bailiffs, men who own dogs with square faces, anyone with the prefix 'Don' before their name, and all females over the age of eight, people employed by the FBI were definitely part of that list. A hand jumped out from Hudson's side and grasped Timon by the throat. His body was lifted from the floor up to the agent's eyeline.

"Listen, you little French turd, I know seventeen ways to kill and dispose of your body using only the meagre objects contained in this room. No one would find a trace of you. No forensics, no evidence, no Timon. I'm particularly effective at killing someone with a clock. I'd be happy to demonstrate it for you, it's rather impressive."

Timon's head rattled around his shoulders like a rag doll. "Sorry," he gulped.

"Apology accepted! Now, how about you drop the anti-American bullshit and start being helpful?"

Timon's face turned a deep shade of purple before Hudson dropped him back on his feet with a splutter and a cough. Hudson immediately returned to the envelope that had his name on it and proceeded to open it in the same manner he'd done with the last one. There was no cipher inside his letter. Just three names he didn't recognise.

Ally Oldfield, Gabriel Janvier and Antoine Palomer.

- Chapter 2 -

Diego

Daniel Hudson's head hit the table in synchronicity with the thud of the door of interview room two closing again. All day he'd been here, and he had nothing to show for the effort. A procession of scumbags and reprobates had been escorted in turn to the room where Daniel had attempted to seek the answers to his questions. He wasn't asking for much. All he wanted to know was what Mario's inmates knew about the letters and, if possible, shed any light on the lives of Janvier, Palomer and Oldfield. Sadly for him, each of the interviewees arrived with ulterior motives and their own objectives.

Interrogating convicted criminals is very different from interviewing suspects. The motivation of a suspect is rooted in a desire to avoid being caught, whether they happened to be innocent or guilty. This modus operandi tended to work against them if they were culpable of the crimes they'd been accused of. A suspect is often a virgin to the process of being questioned. They aren't aware that their bodily movements, choice of language or the congruence of their deeds might actually highlight their guilt, at least to the expert eyes of someone like Hudson. So keen are they to maintain their well-rehearsed stories that they often walk blindly into Daniel's hands. That made interviewing suspects easy.

That's not the case with convicts, particularly those 'life-termers' like the ones that occupied the special area of this prison. They had nothing to gain from telling the truth, and nothing to lose by maintaining their silence. Whereas a suspect might positively influence the length of

DIEGO

their sentence if they're coerced into co-operating, a convict was going back to their cell forever, whatever they said or did.

Dozens of prisoners had already been in for their friendly 'chat' with Daniel Hudson and not one had co-operated, even under the pressure of the countless techniques that he applied without thought or effort. They revelled in the opportunity to goad the authorities or spin another layer of lies to a story that had accumulated more layers to it than the ash that falls on the slopes of an active volcano. It was hard for Daniel to assess whether any of them knew anything about Mario's plans but weren't telling him, or actually didn't have the foggiest idea in the first place. Either they were unwilling to divulge it or just happy to watch the FBI squirm: after all, entertainment in jail normally involved a massive shift in sexual orientation or rather limited games of I spy.

Over the past nine hours Daniel had questioned two corrupt politicians, a member of the Spanish ETA organisation, three Algerians separatists, and four rap artists, all of whom insisted on being referred to by their artistic pseudonyms. It didn't matter how many times Daniel asked Mr Boo-ya what he knew about the letters, the response was always something about, 'the music's gonna get ya'.

Daniel finally lifted his head from the smooth metal table and glanced at the door. He'd been told before the last prisoner entered that there was no one left to question. According to Timon these were all of the people Mario had associated with in the last eighteen months who still remained within the confines of the prison. Daniel wasn't so sure. He knew there was one individual held here that he'd not spoken to.

He picked up his phone and sent a one-line text. The response came moments later in the form of the door opening. Timon stood at the entrance hoping for a sign that the FBI might have exhausted their interest in his little kingdom.

DIEGO

"All done?"

"Not quite. Is there anyone else that Mario spent time with?"

"No. You've seen them all," replied Timon, unconsciously demonstrating to Daniel the irrefutable signs of guilt that all suspects failed to hide. His eyes wandered from direct contact: he hid his hands behind his back and responded slightly more quickly than normal.

"I'll ask you that question again, and this time I want you to think very carefully about your answer as it may affect the future prosperity of your family. Is there anyone else he spent time with?"

Daniel fixed the Governor with an expression of distrust that made Timon's nerves shake. Policeman just had a knack of knowing a lie when they heard one.

"Yes," replied Timon reluctantly, crumbling under the heat of his own examination. "But it's not possible."

"Everything is possible when you work for the FBI," exclaimed Hudson.

"It's complicated."

"Well, *he* is complicated," replied Hudson, "but that's not going to stop me talking to him. It's no secret that he's here."

"You don't have sufficient training or experience to deal with him. It's much too risky."

"I appreciate your concern for my well-being."

"I'm not worried about you, I'm worried about the rest of us."

"Just bring him to me."

"Maybe we're both thinking about different people," replied Timon hopefully.

"Ilich Flores Navas."

A lump formed in Timon's throat. The job of a prison governor wasn't an easy one. There were constant threats to the lives of his employees, potential for violence amongst inmates and a shitload of paperwork. Every prison had 'A-listers' that required special management to ensure they weren't responsible for any of these eventualities. In all of

DIEGO

France's many prisons, no other Governor had an Ilich, and everything about him required thought and preparation.

"Maybe tomorrow, if I can organise it in time."

"Organise it! Just go down there, grab him by the balls and drag his sorry arse up here."

"Impossible! With Ilich there are forms to fill in, calls to make, processes to follow, Presidents to inform…"

"Crap to that. I only need ten minutes with him."

"But he will want to take a lot more of yours. He'll use it as an opportunity to manipulate you. He has a talent that people find hard to resist."

"Let's start again," replied Daniel with a fake smile that almost cracked his square-chiselled jawline. "My name is Special Agent Daniel Hudson and I've worked for the FBI for over twenty years. In that time, I've had the misfortune to share a room, much like this one, with some of recent history's biggest shitheads. Amongst others I have successfully interrogated: Charles Manson, Whitey Bulger and Martha Stewart. Not one of them has successfully manipulated me."

"Martha Stewart, didn't she make cakes?"

"Yes, and she was a lot tougher to work out than Charles Manson. Now, if you weren't sure until now, while I'm here I own this prison and everyone in it, including you. Bring me Ilich Flores Navas NOW!" he shouted, slamming his fists on the table and making it rattle and shake.

"It's on your head," replied Timon.

"Fine."

The Governor stormed to the door but halted before he went through it, seemingly remembering some important advice that was vital to the agent's survival.

"Right. There are a few things you need to know about Ilich. Don't mention the class system or ask him to remove his glasses. Oh, and don't whistle."

"Don't whistle?!"

DIEGO

"Yeah, it's like he's allergic to it, drives him into a complete rage. Oh, and the most important thing of all, under no circumstances mention the name Radu Goga. The last time that name came up in conversation it almost triggered a mass uprising and one of the guards lost an ear. Nasty business."

Daniel wasn't a fan of ignorance. In general, to protect his ego and limit the power of his adversary, he'd pretend to know all information even when it wasn't the case. On this occasion even a random guess wouldn't help him. "Who is Radu Goga?"

"Ex-Russian diplomat and the subject of Ilich's attention back in the seventies. Ilich didn't fail too often but he did when it came to Radu Goga."

"What happened to him?" asked Daniel.

"He defected to the West. Some say he was crucial in winning the Cold War after he co-operated with the Americans for over a decade. Then he vanished out of sight. No one has seen him since the late-eighties. Best not to mention him."

"As I didn't know who he was until you just told me I think it would have been highly unlikely that I'd have mentioned him. I mean it's hard to say Radu Goga by accident, isn't it?" replied Daniel sarcastically.

Daniel might be a highly skilled interrogator with multiple awards and accreditations, but he also liked nothing more than competition. A worthy opponent made the job more interesting and allowed him to pit his wits against the greatest minds from the criminal community. Part of that game meant adding a bit of needle to proceedings to make the opposition feel uncomfortable, knock them off their stride and chip away at their defences. What he always needed was a button to press that would trigger the advantage. Radu Goga was it, and there was no way Daniel wasn't going to use it.

"Go on, then, go get him," demanded Daniel bossily.

Timon shook his head and tutted loudly as he left the room. Prisons ran on procedure and discipline, and

DIEGO

Hudson demonstrated neither quality. The faster the American finished his enquiries, the sooner Timon could return to a normal pattern. He sent one of the guards to retrieve Ilich and have him escorted through the grounds of the converted eighteenth-century abbey. An hour later the door opened to interview room two and a short, plump man with receding hairline, silver pencil moustache and dark glasses casually entered the room like he owned it.

"Take a seat," offered Daniel as he remained motionless on the other side of the table massaging a pen between his fingers. "I'm Special Agent Daniel Hudson. I have a couple of questions for you."

Ilich stood firm as the door closed behind him with a loud clang. Behind the round thick, dark glasses his eyes panned the room analysing every feature. They came to rest on the unknown middle-aged man holding court a thousand miles from his castle. He didn't recognise him, but he instantly knew whom he represented. Only the FBI would have the balls to drag him away from a crossword without prior warning.

"Ilich Flores Navas, or would you prefer me to call you Diego? After all, that's what everyone else calls you, isn't it? The general public associate that name with a seventies freedom fighter who evaded capture for two decades, but they don't really know the terrible reality of your crimes. I know who you really are, Diego. I know what you've done and there is nothing romantic or glorious about it. Sit down," snapped Daniel, pointing at the empty seat.

Finally, Diego dragged the metal chair from under the table and plonked his portly frame on it without uttering a word.

"How well did you know Mario Peruzzi?" asked Daniel, advancing immediately to the central point of the interview.

Diego didn't reply.

"What did the two of you talk about?"

Still no comment. Diego sat vacantly, his gaze piercing through the agent and into the background.

DIEGO

"You helped him, though, didn't you? Gave him the information he was looking for? Helped him hide the money?"

Diego's tongue briefly emerged from his mouth and licked his hairy top lip.

"Are you only talking with body language, is that it? You should know I'm trained in it. I know what those signals mean."

Diego was certain the agent didn't, because it was simply an indication that his lips were dry.

"Licking your top lip reveals signs of nerves, Diego. Did you know that?"

He did, and it wasn't.

"Unless it's the 'sexual lick' which means you're attracted to me," replied Daniel, looking for any way of goading a response.

It wasn't that either.

They sat in silence for a few minutes like a pair of chess players waiting for the other to take the next turn. Daniel scanned his back catalogue of interrogation techniques to decide which tactic in the playbook he was going to use next.

"If you co-operate with me, Diego, I can make it worth your while, you know. I can make life more comfortable for you here in prison. If you don't, I can make it worse, too. What is it that you want?"

The interviewee remained passive. There was nothing that Diego wanted from this man. Fifteen years spent in jail under the protection of the French government had the effect of immunising you from the luxuries that people on the outside took for granted.

"Shame. We might have helped each other out, but nevertheless I'll still get what I came for. What do you know about these people?" asked Daniel, sliding the letter that Mario had sent him along the table until it was right under his nose. "Did Mario mention Oldfield, Janvier or Palomer to you?"

DIEGO

It was no good. Whatever Daniel tried it was met with the same consistent benign reaction and unshakeable lack of co-operation. Threats, bribes, kindness, anger and gentle suggestion were absorbed like a brand new sponge. In twenty years of interrogation Hudson had never failed to find an angle, a pressure point that would unlock the information he wanted. There was only one thing left to do. The very thing he'd been told to avoid.

"How does it feel to be a failure, Diego? Only one failed mission in all that time, and now you're stuck in here with no way of completing it," he said, pointing out the room unnecessarily. "People always get caught in the end, even those who have been on the run or disappear for thirty years. After all, we caught up with you, the mighty Diego, the inconspicuous phantom who became a legend. No one can stay invisible forever. Not even Radu Goga."

Slowly and calmly Diego raised both hands to his face and removed his glasses. Wrinkled skin encircled bright blue eyes that shone brightly like diamonds. Diego's reign of terror may have ended years ago but his face showed no limit to the potential mischief he was still capable of.

"And very brightly the men of the mountain will burn," he whispered in a softly spoken South American tone, all the time fixing his eyes firmly on Daniel's.

"What does that mean, Diego? Is it a warning? Is that what you told Mario?"

"No... he showed it to me... and I explained what it meant."

"Explained what it meant?" replied Daniel, a little confused.

"Yes."

"The men of the mountain will burn," Daniel repeated. "Burn what?"

A knowing smile crept over Diego's face as if nostalgia had washed through him. Then after a moment of self-reflection he answered the question casually as if it was no more than a courtesy.

"Everything."

DIEGO

It wasn't immediately obvious to Hudson whether the quality of the communication had improved since the silent stage had given way to the verbal one. The information was complex, like a riddle with no sign of obvious clues.

"What does 'everything' mean exactly? You can't burn everything, Diego. Try burning the sea, or rocks, or flame-retardant fabric," replied Daniel, becoming more exasperated by his lack of understanding. "You're just playing with me, that's all, aren't you? Trying to steer me off-track with your gibbering nonsense."

"Just wait and watch."

"How do we crack the cipher?" asked Daniel, holding up another of the letters. "That's got something to do with it, hasn't it?"

"You haven't found Radu Goga," Diego replied with certainty, ignoring the original question and turning the interview around. "I doubt you even know who he is."

"Who are these people?" Daniel continued, grabbing a couple of random letters from the bag on the floor beside him. "Mr Catesby, Mr Percy, do you know who they are?"

"If you had found Radu, *he'd* have killed him already. He only has one mission, and no one will stop him from completing it. I may be here for the rest of my life, but my eyes pierce these walls. I am still watching him."

"That's not how it works, Diego, you have to answer my questions!" shouted Daniel, losing his temper and rising from his chair. "You know what we are capable of. Everyone you have spoken to since you arrived here is on our radar. Every visitor you've ever had is subject to our surveillance."

Hudson pulled out a laptop from his bag and within minutes had accessed FBI files relating to his infamous adversary. He turned the screen around.

"This was the last person who came to see you, just two weeks ago. You recognise him, don't you? Thanks to you, he now has a tail on him."

"But that's not Radu Goga," replied Diego coolly.

DIEGO

"Don't worry, I'll find him, too! That'll wipe that fucking smile off your face."

"Mr Hudson, I've been in jail for fifteen years and I haven't committed a crime in nearly thirty years. I accept that I will die here. Shouting at me is unlikely to help you. I've known far more frightening men than you, Mr Hudson. Chávez, Guevara, Arafat, Gaddafi, Haddad, to name just a few. You have no power to keep me in this room, and I have no reason to stay. Old age has mellowed me, and my rehabilitation has taught me to humour angry men like you. I am tired of this. I will allow you one final question but only if you answer one of mine. One question each, nothing more, and then I will return to my cell."

Hudson felt momentarily disarmed. It had taken persuasion and skill to encourage Diego to talk at all and it was clear he meant everything he said. Having already asked so many questions he was being forced to choose one, but which one? It would have to be a question that might allow him to follow the answer further through other people, like finding the corner piece of a jigsaw in order to build the foundations for the edges. Should he ask about the money? No, if he found out more about Mario's intentions surely the trail would lead there eventually. Should he push Diego on the three names in his letter? Which one, though? What if he picked the wrong one? Maybe it was best to pick up on something Diego had said without being asked; after all, if he'd already mentioned something without pressure that must be a clue in itself.

"You mentioned that you explained to Mario about 'the men of the mountain'. What did you tell him?" asked Daniel enunciating every word slowly and clearly to ensure his question came out exactly as he intended to avoid any attempt that Diego might duck or twist it.

"A good choice. I explained to Mario how the Mountain Men have been in the background for four hundred years unknown, unseen, quietly reshaping the path of human history. I explained how he might use this knowledge to achieve his own goals," answered Diego.

DIEGO

"What goals?"

"One question, that was all I offered you. Now you must answer mine."

"Ok, shoot," he said, probably an unwise choice of words when you're talking to one of the most talented assassins of the twentieth century.

"Which country offered Radu Goga sanctuary?"

It was true to say that Daniel didn't know the answer. He'd not even heard the name until an hour ago, so there was little chance he'd know the details. He'd find out for himself in due time. Even if he had known the answer, he wasn't going to tell Diego who had played him with his silent treatment and personal demands. Now it was his time to fight back. He pursed his lips and whistled the French national anthem. Diego jumped from his seat and kicked it over, grabbed his ears with his hands and screamed obscenities at the top of his voice.

"Hmm, what do you know, you really don't like whistling," said Daniel, continuing with even more vigour.

- Chapter 3 -

Ripples

Spring 1603. The Royal Palace of El Escorial. Forty-five kilometres north-west of Madrid. Tuesday. Just after lunch.

Entry to El Escorial, the magnificent palace of Philip III the Spanish King, was only possible via one of three massive doors that stretched the height of the huge outer walls, and one of them had just been closed securely behind him with a loud thud. His elaborate hat was ruffled violently by the wind that swept up the hillside on a seemingly unstoppable advance only curtailed by the steep and newly built sandstone walls of the palace. As he turned away from the door stunning views stretched out in all directions. Sweeping hills, blanketed with scorched beige grass encircled the hill where the castle had been built elevated above all else. It was the perfect position for defending against an attacking force but a bugger on the knees if you had to walk it.

As meetings went, it wasn't the best. Although it certainly might have been worse. It had been known for audiences with the King to end with the invitees leaving in a very different state to how they'd arrived, and often they never left at all. He still had all his limbs and fingers but not the one thing he'd come for.

If a passer-by had been on this exact spot about an hour ago, they'd have witnessed a man, dressed exactly like John Johnson, approaching the door that now separated him from the interior courtyard of El Escorial. They'd have noted that both men wore the same military garments, carried the same sword housed in its scabbard, and walked

RIPPLES

confidently to, and then from, the palace. But if they had the opportunity to be in very close proximity indeed, they'd also have noticed one tiny but significant difference.

His face.

An hour ago, John Johnson wore a wide smile that brimmed with expectation and offered gracious welcome to his host. One hour later that expression had completely vanished, replaced by one tinged with disappointment and regret. Much had rested on the result of the meeting and much had not been achieved. Just securing a meeting with the King had been a minor miracle. Very few requests to meet Philip were granted, particularly when they came from those lacking significant title or regal standing. A lowly military captain like John would need more than just rank and a cheesy grin to secure such an opportunity, even if he was fortunate enough to own both. A network of contacts also helped. Powerful friends who were on first-name terms with Philip had endorsed the quality of his character and the purpose of his visit. A purpose that John was assured Philip would subscribe to. A purpose based on one simple truth.

The Spanish hated the English.

Fifteen years ago, the Spanish had been the proud owners of a spectacular fleet of galleons which controlled the oceans. They were the envy of every nation the world over. Not even the British, a mighty and renowned seafaring nation, competed with the majesty and power of the Spanish Navy. Not until recently, that was. The power balance had somewhat changed because now most of the Armada Española was being sailed by a diverse collection of molluscs in a variety of locations somewhere on the bed of the North Sea following a series of catastrophically poor decisions and a ruthless Queen of England. As a result, the current Spanish fleet consisted of a small number of very thin, blue canoes, seventeen two-man dinghies, a number of poorly converted fishing boats and an emergency fleet of knackered galleons originally decommissioned in the fifteenth century and lacking anything more frightening to

RIPPLES

the enemy than some poorly whittled figureheads of a rather busty señorita.

The sinking of the Armada was just the tip of the iceberg when it came to the Spanish hatred of all things English.

The English worked too hard, ate dinner in the middle of the day when everyone else in Europe knew that was the ideal time for a nap, had skin whiter than albino ghosts, had a dislike for anything foreign, and were generally difficult company at parties. Added to that their royal family had a history of divorcing Spanish princesses and believing that the Protestant faith was a much better religion as a consequence.

Yet none of these circumstances had been enough to compel King Philip to act.

John had been led to believe that their idea would be more exciting to Philip than a dog discovering its tail for the first time. It would be the ideal opportunity for Philip III to make his mark and avenge his father's naval losses. Philip III, though, was no Philip II as John discovered almost immediately. The current King had none of the ambition or determination that his father possessed. None of the ruthlessness or inbuilt sense of leadership. John's immediate assessment of this King had been one of disappointment. Philip III was a miserable man whose only redeeming feature was a total lack of charisma. If only someone had warned him. 'Philip the Pious' was all they'd said when mentioning him. John hadn't bothered to check the meaning of the word 'pious' because he was pretty certain it meant 'full of holes'.

The purpose of his meeting was simply to gain Spanish backing for their campaign. What he left with was the King's blessing, an offer of 'good luck' and a raised thumb. Not a bean of extra funding, no highly trained Spanish archers, and no offer of counsel as to how they might achieve their objectives. Nothing. Now what? King James wouldn't accidentally fall from power by deciding he was rubbish at it. He had to be removed: the tyrannical establishment had to be dismantled. James's unbreakable belief in his faith and the cruelty towards those who did not subscribe to it was severing John's country in half.

Someone had to stop him.

Whatever it took.

John gave the sandstone wall a petulant kick with his right foot and immediately regretted it. The pain reverberated through his toes and up the back of his leg like an instant outbreak of sciatica.

"There's no point kicking new stone."

John followed the source of the advice to an elderly gentleman slumped against the same wall some twenty feet away. John nodded in a style that beautifully balanced acknowledgement with a lack of enthusiasm to extend any potential conversation.

"They only finished it twenty years ago," the man croaked. "Proper craftsmanship, that."

John nodded more gently this time in case *it* happened again.

"If you really have to kick a wall, I'd recommend somewhere like Pompeii. No one would care much: the Italians have a total disregard for history. I'll warn you, though, you'd probably put your foot straight through a wall there. Very weak masonry, don't you think?"

That was proof. *It* was happening again. He'd caught a nutter. If a complete stranger talked to you only once it was officially and rightfully labelled as a normal human pleasantry. If, however, you'd offered them clear facial signals that you'd rather rip your own ears off than continue with the social interaction, and yet they'd continued blindly marching on towards it, then you'd snagged yourself a bona fide nut job.

It didn't seem to matter where he travelled in the world or what he did, John had a face that encouraged weirdos to talk to him, or at him, depending on how you viewed it. Why he owned such a talent had always been a mystery. He could be sitting in a tavern minding his own business, quietly supping on a mug of mead and it was almost

RIPPLES

guaranteed that some mindless, drunk idiot would disrupt his peace by forcing John to listen to their views on the merits of cod liver oil and its use as a lubricant. If he was walking through the streets of London the odds of some feverish old woman launching themselves at him to offer some ludicrous service, like the reading of his dog's palms, were about evens. Nutters stuck to him like fluff collects inside the belly button.

"Thank you," he said raising a gloved hand in the man's direction and whispering, "random old loony."

Many centuries later modern behavioural scientists would discover that the chance of a nutter strike increased exponentially if you directly engaged with them. Sadly, scientists in the seventeenth century consisted of a small group of people whose only application of so-called science included: 'stick a leech on it', 'remove it with a sharp object just below the knee', or a simple philosophical debate which asked people to speculate which came first, the chicken or the nutter. John wasn't a scientist, he was a freak magnet.

"Interesting building, this," said the decrepit old man. "Did you know it was built to commemorate the Spanish victory at the Battle of St. Quentin in fifteen fifty-seven, more than forty years ago?"

"Was it?" said John curtly, trying to remember what else he had planned today other than being distracted by pointless beggars.

"Strange really, because the outcome of that battle was as much to do with French incompetence as it was Spanish bravery. If only we'd put the bloody boats at the front of the troops," he chuckled.

"We?" said John, allowing some of the man's innate babbling to infiltrate his thought-process and settle at the front of his mind.

The old man smiled to himself under his hood. After all these years he was still able to draw people in when they were least inclined to.

RIPPLES

"Yes indeed. I was there, I'll tell you the story for one escudo."

"Not just now, I'm a little busy. Anyway, it was, um… nice… talking to you."

It hadn't been nice. It had been awkward, irritating, distracting, frustrating, and pointless, but John was English and, in his language, 'nice' was the right adjective to use for all of those alternatives in situations like this. Even nutters could be offended and that would be very un-British.

"It wasn't nice," replied the old man.

"I beg your pardon, are you suggesting I'm the one who's irritating…"

"What happened to you in there? Not nice at all, but it happens to all of us," said the old man, maintaining a conversation only he knew the subtext of.

"What are you talking about?" asked John.

"Rejection."

"I've no idea what you mean."

"Yes, you do… John."

"What the… How do you know…"

"Come a bit closer, I can't hear you from over there with these ancient ears," said the man, beckoning him over with a single finger.

When John got within a couple of feet, more of this strange character's features came into focus. Under the man's tatty cloak and hood hid a more presentable gentleman. Fine garments woven from expensive fabrics were loose-fitting against a body that had shrunk several sizes since the day the clothes were fitted. Frizzy, silver hair receded from the top of his brow, and short, white stubble clung to the worn skin of his chin. A silver chain circled his neck and disappeared beneath his shirt. The old cloak hid the real character underneath, but no costume could cover up the man's obvious health issues. Milky white clouds consumed eyeballs that hadn't seen the beauty of the world for a good few years. The skin on his hands was blistered

RIPPLES

and his yellow face was a clear sign that the liver no longer functioned at peak performance.

"Old age," replied the man, guessing John's facial reaction. "It's not much fun, I can tell you."

"I guess not."

"This King is not as bold as the last one, I'm afraid. Your offer was always going to be dismissed."

John brandished his blade and held it to the blind man's neck, so the metal tickled the hairs on his chin. "One of Robert Cecil's men, are you?"

"No," the old man replied, unflinching. "Cecil couldn't find a horseshoe in a blacksmith if he was covered in magnets… and I never work for anyone other than myself."

"Then how do you know who I am?"

"Because I have sought to know."

"For what purpose?"

"The very same purpose you presented to Philip. You seek support to overthrow the King of England. Philip refused to help you, but you have other options. There are people who might assist you."

"What a tramp!" he laughed cynically.

"I've always preferred to call myself a wanderer."

The afternoon sun rebounded fiercely against the sandstone where small brown lizards scuttled from the gaps in the brickwork to bask upon the hot surface. The old man, unfazed by the dazzling sun, stared into the distance, unmoved by the blade threatening his neck.

"Perhaps you might put that away before you cause an accident."

John replaced the sword inside its scabbard.

"I'm seeking an apprentice," said the old man confidently.

"Ha! You're a little too old to break one in, wouldn't you say? What are you, sixty-two?" asked John, still perplexed by this odd weirdo offering him assistance. Over the years he'd got quite good at humouring their bizarre suggestions, but somehow today the situation felt different.

RIPPLES

"Seventy-one and it's never too late for anything."

"Wow, I'm not sure I've ever met anyone in their seventies. Are you sure?"

"Of course I'm sure! What do you want me to do, chop an arm off so you can count the rings?"

"No, obviously not. It's just unusual, that's all."

"I'm unusual."

"Who are you exactly?"

"I have owned many names in my long life, but now I am simply called the Mountain Man."

"The Mountain Man," repeated John, rolling his eyes and wondering what terrible deeds he must have been responsible for in a past life to suffer such mentally disjointed individuals on such a frequent regularity. Maybe he used to be Genghis Khan, or the man who told Moses there was no way on Earth he was giving up the massive bull statue that everyone had always prayed to before Moses got overexcited about a talking bush catching fire.

"The first," added the old man. "But not the last."

"Ok grandad, whatever you say," John replied, slowly taking backward steps as quietly as possible. "Oh, look, my friends are waving at me from the road, I'd better…"

"No, they're not," replied the Mountain Man. "I might be blind, but I'm not stupid. Sit down."

Strangely something about the man's voice made it impossible for John to disobey. He sat cross-legged a few feet in front of him.

"Can you guess why they call me the Mountain Man?"

"First person to scale Mont Blanc?"

"No."

"You have the stability of a goat?"

"No."

"Enlighten me, then," replied John, convinced he wasn't going to be.

"People like us, John, live at the bottom of the mountain, while people like your King sit perched upon the top surrounded by the ill-gotten gains achieved by the ruthless bloodshed meted out by their forefathers and the

RIPPLES

oppression of the masses. I have made it my life's mission to help others climb that mountain, to burn down the established order of the world."

"Not been very successful, have you?"

"It's a struggle that cannot be achieved in one man's lifetime. It will take centuries. I once told the Queen of France, Catherine de' Medici, that I was the first ripple, but that others would follow until eventually her Kingdom would be overcome by the flood. My time is drawing to a close, but the ripples must continue until they turn into a wave. I have chosen you to be the next Mountain Man."

"Have you now, and why would I want to do that?"

"Because you need funding."

"Don't tell me, you're also a banker."

The man took out a small sack and tossed it on the ground where it rattled from the noise of coins colliding with each other inside. On inspection the pouch contained enough gold coins to set one man up for life. John's amusement towards the situation spun on its head.

"Are you giving me this?"

"No, I am paying you to do a job."

"I could just take it."

"Yes, but ask yourself something: would a wealthy man in my current state of health really engage with a notorious traitor like you without some form of protection? I've reached the age of seventy-one for a reason. How far do you think you'd get? Cecil might be useless but others I know are not."

John glanced nervously over his shoulder, doubting whether the man was blind at all. In the background the only obvious signs of backup consisted of a spindly man remonstrating with a donkey over a static cart and two plump women hanging their washing up on the King's manicured topiary that bordered the open-sided courtyard. Two soldiers in full military regalia were currently losing the argument as to whether they should be allowed to continue.

RIPPLES

"A job?" said John questioning his current life's purpose. He thought he had a job: it was the very reason for visiting this remote part of Europe in the first place.

"It's more of a calling, really. I'm paying you to carry on my mission and Chambard's memory."

"Who's he?"

"Chambard was my mentor. He made the ultimate sacrifice so that I could live. Millions will make similar sacrifices before the prize is won."

"Don't you have children? Can't you pass it on to one of them?"

"They have other duties and I'm keen to distance my name from this. It must be the people of the world that win, not some distant historical figure."

"What is it you want me to do exactly?"

"Exactly what you have been trying to do without success. Disrupt the oppression of the British royal family."

"How?" asked John.

"That's up to your imagination but there are three rules we Mountain Men must always abide by."

"Go on."

"You must only use the wealth I provide you to aid the poor to climb the mountain."

John mentally weighed the small sack of coins in his palm. At most it might help the population of the small village of Wetwang in West Yorkshire have a better than average Christmas, but it certainly wasn't going to make much of a dent in global poverty.

"There's not much I can do with this!"

"That's only a deposit. If you accept my offer, I will grant you access to a secret bank account held in Lyon under the careful watch of the powerful Fugger family. My own family will continue to oversee these funds, although not the reason for them, in case something should happen to you before you're able to pass on the responsibility. Until that moment the funds are yours to use as you see fit."

RIPPLES

"But you don't know me! I might have a horrendous drink problem or be hopelessly addicted to buying small Scottish islands."

"I'm no fool, John. I have already vetted you thoroughly. You were born under another name in the North of England. You became a Catholic when your mother remarried when you were eight. You've had a distinguished military career fighting for the Spanish in the war against the Dutch, and have recently been recommended for the rank of Captain. Last year you met a man called Robert Catesby who convinced you to make this journey to seek support for his plan to displace the King."

"Who told you all this?"

The Mountain Man appeared to know almost as much about John's life as he did. There were details from his early years that even he found hard to remember. This was no random stranger sent to pick away at John's sanity. This was someone purposeful and well informed.

"It doesn't matter who told me, it's enough for you to understand that I know."

"But where did all the money come from?"

"Wandering, as it happens, can be a rather lucrative career path. Let's just say I have acquired some objects of value over the years."

John recognised doublespeak when he heard it. It was obvious to him that these items had been acquired through nefarious means. Whether that was by theft, deception or trickery didn't really matter. In fact, the truth was all of them and a lot more.

"Shall I go on?"

John nodded and then realised that wasn't an effective way of communicating with a blind man and quickly rectified his mistake. "Yes, of course."

"As well as the rule about how you use my money, any objectives you set out on must be achieved through non-violent methods only."

"Seriously!"

RIPPLES

"I'm very serious."

"You're aware that the authorities that you want me to overthrow have these objects called swords and cannons, aren't you?"

"Of course."

"Then you must also be aware that it's just these weapons of death that are used almost exclusively to keep said rich people in power."

"Life's nothing without a challenge."

"A challenge! How am I supposed to disrupt the system if all I'm doing is waving a fly swatter and asking them politely to 'move on please, it's someone else's turn'?!"

"Your wits, John. There's no point climbing the mountain if the people scaling it use exactly the same tactics as the ones at the top. Such tactics will only result in turning those rebelling into the very people they sought to overthrow. Power corrupts absolutely, and all that follow you must remember this."

Pacifism was an honourable position, it just wasn't very popular or effective for many reasons. People fighting with weapons against people that didn't have any exclusively came out on top.

"I hate to ask but anything else?"

"Yes, you must pass this responsibility on to the next worthy person. This ascension must continue until equality has been achieved."

"Who do I pass it to?"

"That's entirely up to you, but it must be someone who seeks as you do to topple those that corrupt and subdue mankind. It is an important decision. If our campaign is passed into the wrong hands it might have dire consequences for the future."

"This is ridiculous, you're a nutty old man with a small bag of coins demanding that in some way I redirect the path of human history, and yet you've been doing it for decades and by all accounts all you've achieved is blisters and insanity," chortled John, raising his hand to point at

RIPPLES

the recently completed El Escorial, probably the most ostentatious building in history, to demonstrate his point.

"That's not true."

"Look around you!"

"Are you trying to be funny?"

"Oh... sorry."

"I've been focusing on the French campaign," he replied calmly.

"What have you achieved there, then?"

"I've been quietly turning the French people against the royal family."

"How?"

"A combination of highly sophisticated sit-ins, peaceful rallies, inciting rebellion in busy taverns and printing highly critical posters."

"They must be quaking in their boots. It's hardly a revolution, it's more like a quarter turn of a nutter with some loose change."

"I also blew up the young King Charles's bed using gunpowder," replied the old man, quickly sensing he might be losing his audience.

"Now that's more like it. Did the boy die?"

"Oh no, non-violent, don't forget, we just managed to blow his bed clean out of the window and scare the wits out of him... At least we would have done if he'd been in bed."

"But he wasn't?"

"No."

"So, in fact all you did was destroy a bed."

"It's the intention more than the execution that's important."

"I suppose. Still it's an interesting idea," said John, the cogs of his mind rotating over to the next one to crank up an idea. "Where did you get the gunpowder from?"

"Oh, it's easy if you know the right people. Merchants don't care who they sell it to as long as you have the money. There's a company in... Hold on a minute, why are you asking about that?"

RIPPLES

"No reason," replied John, looking guilty, and pleased to get away with it in the current circumstances. "If I do take your offer, I need to know who you really are."

"Fine. I have owned many names over the years, but most people know me as Philibert Lesage."

"Never heard of you."

"Exactly my intention. I chose my name to be as forgettable as possible. Unlike yours which is just plain silly."

"What are you talking about?"

"John Johnson, I mean how did you come up with that?"

"My father gave it to me," said John, looking sheepish.

"Really! What was his name, then?"

John paused for a moment, proving without doubt that the words about to leave his mouth were definitely a lie. "James Johnson."

"Your family were big fans of alliteration, then?"

"Oh yeah, it's a tradition. I have a sister called Jane."

"John, there's a group of people in life that you really shouldn't try to con and that's conmen. I know that your father's real name was Edward Fawkes and your papers state your real name is Guido Fawkes."

- Chapter 4 -

The Bodleian

In the corner of an expansive wing of the Weston Museum, part of the famous Bodleian Library in Oxford, a middle-aged woman in a plain, dark dress was putting the finishing touches to an exhibition she herself had organised. Immediately in front of her a single scrap of paper, no bigger than a Post-it note, had been sandwiched between two panes of glass and mounted several feet from the four edges of a huge, wooden frame. In turn the frame hung on a plinth in the very centre of the room so no visitor missed what might at first sight appear to be an empty exhibit. To further ensure people's attentions were drawn to it, a multimedia screen stood in front exclaiming, 'The genius of Philibert Lesage'.

Dr Ally Oldfield gave the glass another rub with her cloth to remove the invisible smears that only she could see. It had become a rather compulsive act. The more she buffed, the more convinced she was that her own efforts to achieve crystal-clear perfection were in fact adding further blemishes to the glass. It had to be right. This was her first official test since landing the plum job. The big one! Professor of Medieval Languages at Oxford University, a place where the subject had been taught since the early eighteenth century.

It wasn't usual university procedure for a new member of staff to be afforded the honour of curating their very own exhibition in a library that had more books than some Third World countries. As a copyright library the Bodleian had the right to demand a copy of every book ever published, a right that it invariably invoked. This further

THE BODLEIAN

enhanced its status as one of the best libraries in the world but became a nightmare when it came to storage space. Five thousand new books arrived every day. No sooner had you found a place to stack them than another five thousand arrived. There are only so many bookcases you can own, only so many ways you can squeeze books together. Once the main libraries filled up, predominantly with the older books that were the most precious, new books had to be accommodated elsewhere.

Fifty years ago, the capacity issue was solved by building tunnels for the storage of newer editions. A five-mile network of tunnels went under the library and beneath the road to connect the Bodleian to the Weston Library at the other end. Those filled up almost as soon as the work was completed, and the university immediately commissioned the construction of a humongous warehouse just outside Swindon. This wasn't a prestigious setting to rival the other locations dotted around this illustrious campus.

Swindon was famous for… Actually it wasn't famous for anything. The only helpful information to be found on TripAdvisor was 'don't go'. The only tourists who ended up there did so as a consequence of poor map reading and only stayed because they got stuck on a road system the locals called the 'magic roundabout'. In Swindon the word 'magic' was a euphemism for 'ridiculously confusing and likely to land any driver incapacitated and absurdly angry'. Ally Oldfield went once and hadn't liked it much, marking it out as one of the only occasions she agreed with popular opinion. If there was a pecking order for the library's collections, she hoped the Swindon site housed all the cheap, romantic smut whose paper pages seemed to have reproductive properties.

In total the Bodleian's collection was twelve million items strong, but it didn't own everything. There was one treasure which Dr Oldfield donated personally, which explained why she'd managed to jump the queue of disgruntled 'dons' who'd waited several decades to get their

THE BODLEIAN

own exhibition. It hadn't made Ally popular, but she liked it that way. Even when she wasn't trying to be obnoxious, she wasn't popular, so on balance she felt it might speed things up if she tried all guns blazing to be a pain in people's arses.

The Lesage prophecy on its own wasn't reason enough for the honour of an exhibition to be bestowed on someone. It mattered that she was regarded by almost all her peers as an exceptional researcher with an astonishing level of intelligence and a brilliance with languages that most people couldn't comprehend, let alone actually grasp. Obviously, along with those positives it was common knowledge that the woman was also a total bitch. They were right on all counts. Ally found this last personal attribute to be the easiest to pull off. It was instinctive and required about the same effort level she applied to blinking.

Not even Ally could explain why she acted this way or why it didn't bother her in the slightest. If there was a time when she'd got on with people, she certainly couldn't remember it, but then again, she tried extremely hard not to. Her formative years had been at best problematic and at worst psychologically scarring. Mostly the memories had been consigned to a part of her brain she no longer had the capability of accessing. Adulthood hadn't come quickly enough and provided her with the legitimate mindset of not caring very much about other people. It was just payback for how they'd not cared much for her during childhood. In recent times she'd attempted to change this, but when you had forty years of demons it was easier said than done. Change meant confronting her past and that was a strand of history that not even her skills could unlock.

She took a step back from the glass convinced for the moment that no more effort was required to further aid the glass to gleam from the intense lights being emitted down on it by a countless number of bulbs. This wasn't the only exhibit, but it was the most important. It would be the first time the Lesage prophecy was presented to the public, and

THE BODLEIAN

given the familiar recent circumstances it related to, people were clamouring to see it. Everyone knew about the prophecy that ended the panic.

The Lesage prophecy was encircled by other priceless works, each encased in their own personal vacuums, protected behind case and barrier. They were all highly interesting works of literature, but as proof to some prophetic genius they were as worthless as low-grade toilet paper. The Lesage prophecy was unique amongst so-called equals. Not only was it the only authenticated example of the writing of Philibert Lesage, as priceless and rare as Percy Shelley's *Poetical Essays* also here in the building, but it was the only one amongst the thousands in the exhibition that actually came true.

This unquestionable truth had temporarily altered Ally's views on the subject of predictions, for a few weeks at least. That was all thanks to the four lines of the prophecy and one Antoine Palomer, its last owner and a distant relative of the great Lesage himself. Antoine was an elderly man in whose company she had fought to disprove the Oblivion Doctrine's attempts to persuade the world that Nostradamus had predicted the imminent end of the world. Antoine had more influence on Ally than most people she'd met, but being open-minded to new concepts had not stretched to his suggestion that she should let other humans into her life more.

In the distance behind her the sound of metal bouncing off stone tiles shook her back into the present. Seeking out the source of the noise, she turned her head to witness a chain of metal crowd barriers hitting the ground one after another as a lanky, tweed-wearing idiot desperately chased the tail of these interlinked dominoes, always arriving just after the next one fell or clumsily knocking them over in his attempt to stop them falling in the first place. The final metal post fell inches from Ally's feet and in one final act of sabotage whipped its pursuer to the floor with its red velvet barrier cord like a wayward skipping rope. The young man

THE BODLEIAN

crashed to the deck, sending his unfashionable glasses skating along the polished floor.

This was Lance Carter. A postgraduate who officially owned the worst job in the history of Oxford University, and very possibly the history of education in general. All universities employ a vast army of staff members, most of whom go unseen and unnoticed. But not all jobs are made equal. Outside of the mostly unrewarding duties offered by jobs in bars, cleaning and security, all of which involved dealing with the decidedly indifferent personal hygiene habits of the average undergraduate, none even came close to the very worst jobs on offer.

On the Oxford campus there was one member of staff whose only duty was to patrol the campus's statues in order to ward off any pigeon intrepid enough to attempt to defecate on them. If he arrived too late, the second task of his job description was to meticulously clean up the aftermath. This eventuality was most likely given the maths. There was one of him, hundreds of statues, thousands of pigeons and no other place they enjoyed doing their business.

Another poor sod had the responsibility of adjudicating over the bewilderingly complex array of rules that all students and personnel had to abide by while at Oxford. Most of these archaic rules dated back to a time when shoes were only just becoming popular and no one had yet bought a postage stamp. There were thousands of these rules that included, amongst many other ridiculous instructions: ensuring all gowns were precisely nine and a half inches above the ground at all times, even during the process of walking, which made the job of measurement that much more difficult; enforcing the rule that only professors were allowed to walk on the grass; and the eradication of any angle found to be less than forty-five degrees. Unsurprisingly staff turnover for this role was high on account of all the insanity it was responsible for.

Then there's the poor bastard that had to teach organic chemistry, a fate worse than cleaning up pigeon poo for a

THE BODLEIAN

living. However, none of these travesties of human suffering came anywhere close to the emotional trauma of being Ally Oldfield's intern. Officially the worst job on campus.

"I'm so sorry, Dr Oldfield," replied Lance, scrambling around on his hands and knees to find his glasses and rejoin the world of the sighted rather than slipping around on the polished floor like a broken otter.

Ally simply stared at him when his obvious suffering might be eased by a kindly outstretched hand.

"Knew it was you," she grunted.

"I don't quite know what happened," he offered, finally locating his thick-rimmed spectacles and replacing them on his head.

"You happened!"

Lance had what most people described as an 'unfinished look'. Unlike his much wealthier and esteemed peers he was one of a rare group of students who'd earned his place at Oxford on academic merit rather than financial superiority. His clothes were stylistically too old for a man barely in his early twenties and all of them looked like they'd recently been donated to Oxfam by a rather portly gentleman with a penchant for paisley. It was also immediately clear on first meeting Lance that he flatly refused to recognise the rumour that someone in the Egyptian period had invented a simple device called a comb.

"I can fix it," he replied energetically.

Before he could launch himself into a frenetic period of correction, a bony hand caught him around the collar.

"No. Stop, you'll only make it worse. In all my years I have never met anyone with such a natural talent for clumsiness. It's like a superpower. It's not normal."

"I can't help it."

"I think you can," replied Ally beginning to believe that Lance might have been sent to annoy her. "Who put you up to it? Tell me that. No one wants to work for me. Was it Jenkins, that useless excuse for a human?"

THE BODLEIAN

"Jenkins?"

"You know, Jenkins, Professor of eighteenth-century Studies. Walks around pretending to have arthritis and when challenged on the details of his own subject matter can only respond incipiently with the phrase, 'it's all conjecture,' before pretending to be lost."

"I wasn't put up to anything, Dr Oldfield. I'm here because I applied to be your intern."

"Specifically, mine or just an intern in general?"

"Yours specifically."

Ally looked at him suspiciously. Apart from being greener than the untrodden university lawns, by all accounts what he lacked in common sense and physical stability he made up for with an exemplary academic record. Surely, though, he'd done his research; it wasn't difficult to find out that she was notoriously difficult to work with and had pints of milk in her fridge that had lasted longer than most understudies.

"Have you been tested?" asked Ally pointedly.

"Every semester, ma'am."

"I mean for disorders."

This was just the type of insensitive questioning that Ally was famous for. If she thought it, she said it. There was no point beating around the bush or worrying about people's feelings when all she really wanted was the answer.

"Do you mean…"

"Dyspraxia, Guillain–Barré Syndrome, early onset Parkinson's, Unexplained Stupidity Condition…" she said, interrupting him.

"No, I've not been 'tested', and I believe you made that last one up. I'm just clumsy and inquisitive, that's all. No underlying problems that I'm aware of."

"Why, then?"

"If you want to learn the most you have to work with the best," he replied.

"You're aware that I'm impervious to flattery on all levels, aren't you?"

THE BODLEIAN

"I worked that out on my first day, but thanks for confirming it for me."

"Looks like I'm stuck with you, then," she said disappointingly. "If you could restrict your carnage for the next few hours, we might just be ready to open the exhibition."

Ally left the Lesage plinth and approached a section laid out inside a slanted glass case that jutted out of the wall. A large, colour-printed board on the wall highlighted the work within. 'Nostradamus, history's greatest fraud'. In the centre of the collection was the copy of *Les Prophéties* discovered in Lyon two years ago and purchased quite cheaply from the Museum of Printing. The last owners weren't overly keen to hold onto it once part of it had been verified as a fake. In truth, Ally knew the prophecy in the preface, the page that was open inside the case for the public to read, wasn't even by Nostradamus, but as it would never be known who wrote it, she'd decided to keep it in this part of the exhibit.

"I never did understand the last line of this," said Lance, leaning around her shoulder.

"It doesn't matter, it's a fake."

"But why write only part of a fake? The first three lines did have some basis in the actual events that occurred a couple of years back even if they didn't fully come true. Why not the last line? And the men of the mountain will burn," he muttered. This was another one of Lance's idiosyncrasies. He was prone to saying things out loud rather than keeping them in his thoughts, as if only saying them would demonstrate to others that his brain was working correctly.

"Who cares!" said Ally abruptly. "I think your main duties as my intern are to lift, shift and try not to break anything. You're not here for your critical thinking or unqualified opinions, you're here to watch and learn."

"I just find it interesting," whispered Lance under his breath.

THE BODLEIAN

"I think it's nearly finished," said Ally, scanning around the room one last time. Tomorrow the general public would be allowed in and only people's ignorant reviews on the internet stood between her and success. "Right, let's get coffee."

"I don't drink it, bad for your teeth."

Ally huffed and stormed off towards the exit which was reached by meandering through a preordained route through the special collections, like being trapped in a Swedish furniture store. Lance followed a few paces behind but stopped frequently to gaze at some of the magnificent pieces on display. Lance was a bookworm. There was something incredibly magical about the anatomy of a book even before one considered the dedication and creativity that had been poured into the contents by the author. Some young people liked roller coasters: his buzz came from paper and ink.

"What does this say?" asked Lance, pointing to the front of a book written in a foreign language he didn't recognise.

Ally glanced at it briefly, more interested in caffeine than literature.

"Poems of Love and Life," she said instinctively.

"What language is it?"

"Not sure."

"Then how do you know what it says?"

"I can just read it alright," she snapped angrily. "Languages just make sense to me, even those I haven't studied."

"That's incredible!"

"No, it isn't. It's logical. All languages are derived from others. Latin, Slavic, Romani – the list goes on. If you know those then it's easy to read ones derived from them."

"How come I can't read it then?" replied Lance who spoke more languages than he had digits.

"Because you're not me! Let's go, don't you have young people stuff to do?"

"Young people stuff?"

THE BODLEIAN

"Don't you go out on a Friday night to drink, dance and steal traffic cones?"

"No. I'll probably just read."

"You're single, right?"

"Wait!" he said, stopping at another glass case. "This one is my all-time favourite piece."

Ally reluctantly stopped again. She couldn't really leave until he'd been escorted from the building. This wasn't because of security clearance; it was simply part of her risk assessment that if she didn't, he might knock it all over again.

"You have expensive tastes," she said, staring down at a fragile manuscript wrapped in old leather and stitched in blue thread. "The Shikshapatri. It's worth about twenty million quid, although it's not likely to be sold anytime soon. It's not even the Bodleian's, it's on loan from the Indian government."

"It doesn't seem very well protected for something that important."

"Don't you believe it. This place has the most up-to-date security systems money can buy. Pressure plates, closed-circuit monitoring, around-the-clock security guards, microchips and sensors everywhere. It would be easier to rob a bank vault than steal from the Bodleian, and pointless anyway."

"Why?"

"Because this piece is unique. It would be almost impossible to sell. There would be only two reasons for taking it."

"What would anyone want with it other than the money?" asked Lance.

"Only if someone wanted it for their own personal collection or they were hell-bent on creating an international incident. If anything happened to this book it's anyone's guess how the Indian government would react. This book is sacred. Every year the library has to allow special religious ceremonies to take place with it. If someone stole the Shikshapatri it would be the equivalent

THE BODLEIAN

of the Russians nicking the American Constitution or the Germans stealing our Magna Carta."

"It's a good job it's safe, then."

"Quite safe. Come on, I've been here for hours, and I have stuff to do. If you want to spend more time gazing at the exhibits then come back tomorrow and buy a ticket. That way, I won't have to suffer your incessant questions."

- Chapter 5 -

The Furlong Nursing Home

The Furlong Nursing Home was no better or worse than any other property that housed those approaching the end of life. How could it be? They all looked and felt the same. In the United Kingdom they were almost exclusively Victorian buildings with dull grey façades and wide bay windows accessorised with slightly yellowed net curtains that clung to plastic rails with the same tenacity as the human occupants clung to life. Nursing homes were generally situated in the middle of towns, or near seafronts, the view from the windows being totally irrelevant as not one of the residents could see through the net curtains, and almost none of them had left their seats or beds since the moment they were deposited there, mostly against their will. A large sign was always erected somewhere in the garden or car park to ward off even the bravest graffiti artist or would-be burglar.

Like all care homes, the Furlong was staffed by people born with a different genetic make-up to the rest of humanity. Every one of them an absolute hero. Genome scientists were still trying to establish which chromosome was missing from these people, but it was definitely the one that governed the reaction the rest of us had to random acts of aggression, soiled sheets, wrinkly skin and sponge baths. It was also linked to a bewildering level of positivity to the calling and an utter acceptance to being paid a horrifically puny amount of money to deal with the latter on an exhausting shift pattern five or six times a week.

THE FURLONG NURSING HOME

Other than these thoroughly decent humans no one else really wanted to go anywhere near nursing homes, including the people who'd been responsible for picking it out for their own family members. Visiting wasn't something most people wanted to do, it was something they had to do – at least that was Ally's view.

Oldfield sat in a crumpled ball in the driver's seat of her Rover car, head stuck to the steering wheel, lungs hyperventilating. Steam condensed on the inside of the windscreen and a couple of people had already knocked on the window to check she wasn't trying to perfect a slow version of carbon monoxide poisoning. She couldn't sit there forever. Eventually she'd have to pull the plaster off and get it done. She stepped out into the car park which was situated just off the main road and immediately in front of the Furlong Nursing Home. A woeful figure gazed forlornly out of the net curtains in a vague hope that she was either the rescue party or Death himself. Her black outfit probably didn't help clarify it.

It was like this every Friday.

A build-up of anxiety increased through the course of the day and led to the construction of a list of fictitious excuses she might use to cancel, followed by guilt, followed by thirty minutes sitting in the car contemplating self-harm, before the ultimate walk of doom. She knew she shouldn't feel like this. After all, it wasn't his fault he was here. It was hers. Her recent relocation from Warwick to Oxford meant his last nursing home in Blackburn was just too far away for regular visits and she was the only one left who did. She'd made the logical decision to move him from the comfort of the 'North' to the unfamiliarity of the 'South' at the age of eighty-eight.

It hadn't been a popular move.

Those who tell you elderly people don't like change are wrong. There are as many young people in the world immovably stuck in their comfort zones as there are old people with a similar mentality. It wasn't the move from one home to another that led to the arguments; after all,

THE FURLONG NURSING HOME

he'd hated the home in Blackburn. The staff there had an overzealous desire to keep their residents' minds and bodies active through daily doses of circuit training and mandatory Sudoku tournaments when all the residents really wanted was tea, morning television and hard-boiled sweets. The real reason for his intransigence had everything to do with the word 'South'.

England, like many nations, has a reasonably small geographic area and a million different cultural identities. Anyone driving 'North' from the 'South' will notice a spectacular change in attitudes, accents and habits somewhere around Derby. Where the exact divide between 'North' and 'South' was had been debated long past closing time had sounded with no agreement. If you were born in Newcastle, people from Derby were as soft as margarine and lived much too close to London: 'South' for them meant Middlesbrough. If you lived in Brighton, people from Birmingham lived in the 'North' and Newcastle in their minds was practically Iceland. Wherever you lived, though, no one would argue that Blackburn was in the 'North' and Oxford most definitely 'South'.

If you'd lived in the 'North' for as long as he had, everything about the 'South' was different, intimidating and frankly wrong. No one down there referred to you as 'duck' or 'love' unless you were in fact an actual duck or someone they were in love with. Everything you bought was at least fifty percent more expensive and it appeared to be a criminal offence to be nice to other humans. The transition from one state to another might be the equivalent of moving to Mars, and Ally knew she was responsible for it.

Ally trudged up to the front door of the Furlong Nursing Home to discover what challenges she might encounter today. Inside, as normal, a collection of smiley-faced women in stained white jackets were busy taking tea orders or redirecting little old ladies back towards the lounge area.

"Oh, hello, Ms Oldfield."

THE FURLONG NURSING HOME

"Doctor."

"Are you?" said a bleached blonde nurse trying to do several tasks at once. On every visual part of her body other than her face she sported elaborate and colourful tattoos, all of which moved in a blur as her body never seemed to come to a standstill. She scurried behind the reception area where a visitors' book lay open on the desk. Another nurse emerged from a door clutching six mugs of steaming tea in one hand and a tray of biscuits in the other. Evolution had been working at high speed in Oxford by the look of her hands. She had a grip like a vice but a body that was smaller than most primary school children.

"Sheila, did you know Ms Oldfield was a doctor?" said the peroxide blonde, who wore a badge announcing herself as Kay.

"Well, I never, he's never mentioned that before, Ms Oldfield," replied Sheila the tea juggler, who gave Ally a wide smile and a wink.

"DOCTOR Oldfield," Ally snapped in response, "and he's not likely to mention it, is he, not in his condition?"

"He talks about you all the time, Ms Oldfield, he's very proud of you."

"I doubt it. In there, is he?" she replied, extracting herself from another round of pointless human small talk.

The world outside filtered through the net curtains and bathed nine styles of armchair, each in a different state of disintegration, in grubby sunlight. Collectively the chairs formed a semicircle around the living room. In the centre a television that would have been the peak of technological innovation in nineteen eighty-nine shrouded the room in a synthetic glow and talked to itself at full volume. Of the nine people that occupied the chairs, four of them were definitely sleeping; either that or they'd each swallowed noisy traction engines. Two of them might be dead, if the smell was anything to go by. Two were having conversations with themselves, even though each would politely wait for the other to stop talking before continuing on their own topic of interest. The final chair dweller was sitting wide-eyed with a newspaper spread out across his formal trousers.

Just for a moment Ally hoped that Horace was one of the sleeping ones, or even one of the corpses. It wasn't a nice thought, but Ally didn't care. Anything to get her out of here and back to something in life more vital. One of the nurses came in behind her with a chair which was placed at the side of the only occupant in the room who appeared present. He looked up from the black and white broadsheet.

"Hello, Dad," offered Ally coldly, as if she'd rather be meeting Jack the Ripper.

The old man's eyes sparkled as they rested on the visitor and an internal engine somewhere behind them spat out a name to go with it.

"Audrey, what a lovely surprise."

"Ally."

"It's been such a long time."

"I was here last Friday."

"No, that can't be. I haven't seen you since, now when was it exactly, Audrey?"

"Ally," she repeated. "And it was last Friday."

"Nineteen ninety-seven. The Workington Cricket Club annual awards dinner."

"Was that a Friday?" asked Ally sarcastically.

"No. Awards dinners were always on a Saturday. I remember that one very clearly because Trevor scored fifty that very afternoon."

"Who's Trevor?"

"Your husband," he replied after an uncomfortable pause as his mind caught up with his mouth.

"Dad, I'm not married."

"He had a little dog called Bing... great voice... I remember buying the single. What was it called, Audrey?"

"Ally."

This was how it was every Friday. One week she'd be Cathleen from the corner shop, other times Brenda from number fifty-three, and on one memorable occasion Eva

THE FURLONG NURSING HOME

Braun from Nazi Germany. She couldn't remember the last time she was Ally the daughter, at least not since the move down 'South'. It was almost as if the tiny change in latitude had scoured away his memory. The only way to have a reasonable conversation with him was to go along with the alias. That had been particularly difficult on the day of the Eva Braun incident when any of the residents with the ability to use their legs had started a mini-riot after insisting that she be returned to Nuremberg for trial.

At no point did Ally find her father's slide into dementia funny. All it did was move her further away from a man she'd never been that close to in the first place. And crucially further away from any chance of discovering the answers to the questions about her upbringing that only he might provide. In truth she knew very little about her father, and nothing at all about her mother. When she was six years old, she'd been removed from their care without warning and explanation. Only hazy memories of her life prior to that upheaval would occasionally be unlocked by a comment or emotion. Most of those early emotions were positive and happy, unlike the rest of her childhood which she did her best to lock away in a dark memory vault entitled 'Keep out'.

She'd spent the rest of her childhood in the company of cruel adoptive parents. It was only in adulthood, in the mid-nineties, that Horace her genetic father sought her out, and by that point the damage had already been done. Forming any kind of relationship beyond a polite and civil one had been almost impossible.

Whether it was fair or not to do so, she ultimately blamed her father for her childhood trauma and how it had affected her character later in adulthood. We are all the product of our upbringing. If you screw over a child's early years or adolescence don't be shocked if the end result is someone bitter and twisted. Whatever the reasons for her abandonment, in her eyes it was his fault. Ally's inability to trust other people, her difficulty in expressing

THE FURLONG NURSING HOME

empathy, social awkwardness and lack of friends were all a direct result of her childhood, or lack of it.

The only person whom Ally counted as a friend was Antoine Palomer, an eccentric Frenchman. It wasn't a friendship in the traditional sense. They didn't visit each other regularly or call each other up to see how they were doing. They didn't share many interests or ideals. They didn't send each other birthday or Christmas cards, but of all the people Ally had met she didn't hate him even half as much as the rest of humanity. In her book that made him a friend.

Their meeting had happened quite by accident and they'd spent less than two weeks in each other's company. In that short time, they'd shared the unique experience of stopping the end of the world, and that does tend to be more memorable than meeting someone on holiday or a long transatlantic flight. At their last meeting Antoine had advised her to let people in more. Spending more time with her father was just part of that process, that's if he ever recognised who she was.

Today she would have to be Audrey, but it didn't really matter. She was only really here out of a sense of duty to her own genetics. Plus, he never really wanted to talk about her, much to her irritation. Politics was the only subject he seemed able and keen to debate, and it didn't matter if she was Ally, Audrey or Attila the Hun.

"I see Labour won the Carlisle by-election," she said, offering up her only piece of preprepared political insight.

"Fascinating contest," he replied, sitting forward in his chair and becoming more animated. "It was the local issues that swung it. I read that the candidate from the Green Party was gaining momentum after the flooding that happened there a few years back. Ultimately, she lost out because she's a vegan and there's a large farming community in the area."

Ally couldn't really explain why Horace's coherence improved to the level of a healthy person when he got on to the subject of politics. Maybe it was his daily

THE FURLONG NURSING HOME

consumption of the national newspapers. Perhaps there was something locked away in that brain of his that made the retention of the subject easier when everyone else in the country did their utmost to stop it entering their heads in the first place. It certainly wasn't a subject that Ally had much interest in, but if he was happy and talking it meant she didn't have to.

"Audrey, did I ever tell you about meeting Edward Heath?"

"Ally! Yes, only once or twice."

"Heath was a great man. He wouldn't have wasted money like the present lot do," replied Horace, wagging his finger in the air as if he'd been standing in a Cabinet meeting.

"I've got a new job," replied Ally, desperate to get the conversation back to the real world.

"Don't you like working at the chemist's anymore?" asked Horace sympathetically.

"Professor at Oxford University," she continued.

"Audrey, have you seen how much they are spending on renovating parliament, it's a disgrace."

"Ally," she replied pathetically.

"Billions, that's how much. They're going to use some…" He paused as he struggled to formulate the next word, not from a lack of memory but genuine disgust. "… Foreign company to do the refurbishments, some French lot."

"Right," she replied, secretly pleased it wasn't being completed by a British firm as it might not be finished in her lifetime.

"I read it in the papers," he said, pointing to the table in front of him.

A picture of the Houses of Parliament was spread open on the coffee table and the headline caught Ally's attention.

'The Mountain Plc Win Parliament Contract'.

She reached forward and brought the broadsheet closer to feign interest. The Mountain Plc meant nothing to her,

THE FURLONG NURSING HOME

but as she scanned through the article the comments from some of the executives of the company piqued her interest like a suppressed form of déjà vu. The names seemed familiar. The CEO was a man called Catesby and their chairman was a Mr Percy. She'd heard those names appear together somewhere before, but she couldn't put her finger on where.

"Someone should put a stop to it," said Horace, redirecting her back to the conversation.

"Were you active in politics when you were younger, Horace?" asked Ally pretending not to be herself in order to unlock just one clue to his past.

The question triggered the metaphorical walls to go up.

"They don't make peppermints the way they used to. Too small and soft."

In Ally's opinion it often felt like Horace wasn't just affected by his deteriorating mind, but might be consciously avoiding certain subjects. Even before the steep decline in his mental dexterity he'd always steered her away from knowing more about his history.

"I've brought you some Turkish Delight," said Ally, attempting a new line of conversation. "Your favourite and better than peppermints. What were Mum's favourite sweets?"

Horace's body immediately tensed up and his eyes welled with tears on hearing the question. His immediate and visible discomfort deteriorated into anger as his arms swung wildly in the direction of his guest and he started to wail uncontrollably. Some of the sleeping congregation were woken and started to mimic Horace's behaviour. The growing commotion, though, wasn't enough to shake the two unresponsive guests from their comas.

"Nurse!" shouted Horace at the top of his voice.

"You don't have to get agitated," replied Ally coldly.

"Nurse, I want to go to my room. I don't know who this woman is," he said, shaking his finger in Ally's direction.

"I'm Audrey," replied Ally, firmly maintaining today's character.

THE FURLONG NURSING HOME

Horace's eyes fixed on her, his hands shaking on the arms of the chair, face grey and frightened. "Audrey's dead!"

"I know the feeling," sighed Ally, getting up from her chair and leaving the room.

Until next Friday when events would repeat themselves all over again.

- Chapter 6 -

Neighbourhood Watch

Most of the university's professors lived near their colleges somewhere in the city, another benefit of reaching the zenith of their academic achievement. The city wasn't just famed for its historic buildings and illustrious past. The city of Oxford had a renowned reputation for stimulating learning on and off the campus. Professors were known to meet each other socially to debate their newest theorems over a frothy-headed pint under the low-beamed ceilings of pubs that could date their origins to Tudor times. Inspiration was accelerated by the thought that the greats of science and literature had sat in the same seat before you as they'd figured out some great, beer-fuelled discovery.

Nostalgia for the old times, though, can end up being an excuse for procrastination and drinking on a Wednesday evening. Little these days was actually achieved in the pursuit of the 'light bulb' moment and Ally certainly didn't need buildings or peers to motivate her into work. Other than sleep and drink coffee, it was all she did anyway. People generally stifled her innovation rather than enhanced it, and if you wanted to avoid crowds the best decision was not to be there in the first place.

Ally had secured a small cottage in the quaint and picturesque village of Stanton St. John, fifteen minutes outside of the city. She'd been forced to rent, quite against her will, because the last affordable property to go on the market in the village was some time before the turn of the last century, such was the intransigence of the locals.

NEIGHBOURHOOD WATCH

Like most small villages, Stanton's spidery arms spread out from a central church in a mildly chaotic style that only took account of the geography for its design rather than some poorly considered town planning bill. Most new arrivals were attracted to the village by its strong sense of community spirit and local amenities, so often threatened with closure in places like this. There were two pubs, neither of which Ally had been in, a small convenience shop that sold items only pre-war veterans would either want or recognise, a village hall that held regular events that ranged from pottery classes to jujitsu for the over-sixties and, as far as she was concerned, only one significant problem.

The locals.

The upside of living in a small village deep in the countryside was a lack of company, but that didn't mean no company. On the downside those that did live there had a deep sense of ownership over everything that happened, and everyone that lived, within the village boundaries. It wasn't acceptable to be a recluse when the place functioned as a community that supported each other. At least that's how they liked to describe it.

Really, they were all just nosy bastards.

Sheltered from the real world, which was somewhere on the other side of the A24, everyone who strayed off the beaten track needed to be interrogated relentlessly, and boy, could the locals talk. No one ever wanted to just offer a pleasant 'good evening', they wanted a deep and meaningful download on every subject from marigolds to meningitis. The majority of the locals were old or retired and didn't see another human all day, so when they did, they made up for it. If you were caught in their tractor beam you were going talk to them whether you liked it or not. It was Ally's worst nightmare. Over the months she'd made a detailed analysis of the villager's movements to work out the perfect time for returning home from work.

The answer was night-time.

NEIGHBOURHOOD WATCH

Ally drove her dark green Rover Series 3 discreetly into the village so that it made as little noise as possible. A difficult task for a vehicle that had the reliability of a paper golf club. It had seen better days but, a little like Horace's mind, it couldn't actually remember when they were. Driving it was like playing Russian roulette. Ally never knew from one day to the next what might greet her when she turned the key in the ignition. It might run like a charm or just as easily make a loud, grinding noise before farting out fumes that smelt like the inside of an incinerator. Today her luck was in.

No one noticed as she glided quietly into the village. The clock on the dashboard silently clicked to eleven in the evening, signalling a slender fifteen-minute window before the unwanted attention of the late-night pub dwellers. Only one more corner to navigate before her pretty little cottage would come into view. Home and dry. Another day of avoiding contact with the neighbours achieved. As she rounded the church her heart sank.

People.

Lots of people.

Striking a variety of unusual poses and poor fashion choices, they were loitering in the grounds of her cottage. Some wore expensive dressing gowns with tassels that dragged through the grass, some had fishing waders up to the crotch, and one was wearing a balaclava. All of them wielded torches which were being pointed at various parts of Ally's cottage like a poorly organised geriatric rave. Ally turned off the road and up through the opened light green gate to park on the grass alongside the house. Whatever was happening there, any attempt to avoid the neighbours was now dead. A wrinkled face, still showing signs of a hastily removed face pack, appeared at her window, torch illuminating her face like an ancient trick-or-treater.

"Ms Oldfield, thank goodness you're safe," said the voice partially muffled by the glass. Ally attempted to wind it down, but the car decided this was the moment to not

NEIGHBOURHOOD WATCH

co-operate. She was being forced to leave the protection of the Rover if she wanted to get rid of them.

"Doctor," she replied while unconsciously locking the car and marching to her front door. "I'm very safe, thank you, Ms Honeywell."

"Stop, me darlin', you can't go in!"

"Why ever not?"

"Too dangerous," said Ms Honeywell overdramatically as if the house was about to be bombed or had recently been infested by zombies.

"Listen," said Ally, turning to Ms Honeywell aggressively. "I've had a very disappointing day. I've already had to put up with all sorts of mental people and I have no desire to add to that list."

Ms Honeywell had thick skin. If she'd believed for a moment that Ally was referring to her, as was the case, she'd still have ignored the suggestion. Everyone knew everyone in Stanton, but people knew Ms Honeywell better than most and not through choice. Of the half-dozen neighbours currently circling the cottage pointing flashlights through the windows, most of them lived in the immediate vicinity of Ally's cottage. Ms Honeywell lived about a mile away, yet it was always guaranteed she'd be the first on the scene of any event or incident.

"There's been a break-in, me darlin'!" she said in a manner that suggested such a thing hadn't happened in Stanton for over a hundred years. It was highly likely she'd been the first on the scene then, too.

"A break-in?"

"Yes, horrible, isn't it? Can you imagine, me darlin'?' Here in Stanton! I'll be writing to the MP first thing in the morning. I told him last year this would happen if they cut the police budgets. They never listen, if only they..."

"How do you know there's been a break-in?" asked Ally using her usual tactic of bulldozing someone else's sentences before they'd finished them.

NEIGHBOURHOOD WATCH

"There was a smash," she replied. "Melvyn heard it… didn't you, me darlin'?" she shouted in the direction of the house.

"Yeah," came a muffled and shaky voice from behind the rose bush which sat under the living room window. The only obvious sign of Melvyn's whereabouts was the sleek brown tail of his Labrador dog that was wagging furiously from behind the bush.

"What sort of smash?" Ally asked impatiently.

"A big one."

"Describe it."

"Melvyn said it was like glass breaking."

"Maybe it was just a gust of wind that came through the window and knocked a glass off the sideboard," offered Ally much more concerned by the unwanted attention of the neighbours than any potential intruder.

"Oh, you shouldn't leave the window open when you're not here, Mrs Oldfield."

"Doctor. Why not? These buildings get freakishly hot."

"Burglars, me darlin'" whispered Ms Honeywell as if it was prohibited to use the word.

"And when was the last burglary in Stanton?" asked Ally.

"Nineteen eighty-three."

"There you go, then, nothing to worry about."

"That's because no one leaves their windows open," replied Ms Honeywell judgementally.

"Anyway, I'm sure there's a simple explanation for it, no need to get involved. You must be tired, all this excitement?" said Ally hopefully.

"There is a simple explanation, me darlin'. Your kitchen window is broken," replied Ms Honeywell who made it her business to know everything before anyone else did and then offering a cast-iron explanation before you had time to react. "Someone threw a brick through it. I mean, what's the world coming to? Youths, that's who it'll be. Noisy, unruly brats with nothing better to do than run

NEIGHBOURHOOD WATCH

around like hooligans, me darlin'. They should all be enrolled in the Army."

Ally left Honeywell's rant mid-monologue and walked along the narrow, moss-covered path to assess the damage to the window for herself. She was greeted by Melvyn who had reappeared from behind the bushes sporting the world's only Burberry balaclava. Spencer, the Labrador, who was always one step in front of him, bounded up and sat politely at her feet waiting for permission to maul her. She liked Spencer and wished that humans were as well trained.

"Hello, my dear," said Melvyn. "Nasty business, this."

It was clear to Ally that neither Melvyn nor Ms Honeywell had ever lived, or possibly ever even been to a place, where crime was a daily occurrence and was frequently more severe than a brick through a window. If only she could send them on an exchange programme for a week to toughen them up. She'd lived in the inner cities up 'North' for years and this kind of thing happened most days in most neighbourhoods.

"Nothing to worry about," replied Ally. "You can go home now, thank you. I'll deal with it."

"We were just about to call the police," exclaimed Ms Honeywell who'd quickly followed in Ally's slipstream, desperate not to miss anything.

"No! Don't do that, I'll never get to bed."

"But there's been a crime, me darlin', it's our duty to report it."

"No, it's not *your* duty, it's mine."

"Here, you can use my phone," said Melvyn, holding out a television remote control, which probably explained why he was constantly complaining about the terrible mobile signal in the village, an issue he'd raised with the local councillors on nineteen occasions this year alone.

"I'll do it in the morning. Goodnight," she said sternly, offering a little wave behind her as she placed the key in the front door.

NEIGHBOURHOOD WATCH

"What if there are intruders inside?" said Ms Honeywell who shuddered in horror when the word passed her lips.

"Then they'll probably be better company than you two," said Ally under her breath.

Ally disappeared into the darkness of the hall. She stared through the peephole in the front door. It was plain to see that none of the neighbours were moving on anytime soon. They were probably waiting for her to scream in horror or come running back out again. Even if intruders had entered the building, which Ally very much doubted, she certainly wasn't afraid of them. She'd grown up with worse people in her life and had never relied on anyone to fight her battles for her.

She moved casually into the kitchen, flicking the lights on to see the extent of the damage. The top panel of the sash window had been shattered and the catch had been opened. Fragments of glass filled the sink, sideboard and across the floor's ceramic tiles. She bent down to get the dustpan and brush from under the sink and emerged to find Melvyn's face pressed up against the non-broken pane of glass.

"Anyone in there?" he asked with a thumb in the air.

"Yes, me! Go home."

She drew the blinds, which rustled from the breeze passing through the damaged area. Quickly she swept up the loose glass and deposited it into the bin. There were definitely small shards that she'd missed but there always were when glass broke. After a week or two of daily hoovering she'd probably still find a wayward piece in a mug or under the doormat.

She searched around for the object that had transformed the normally overheated kitchen into the much-improved cooler one. A regular-sized house brick was retrieved from under the breakfast table. There was nothing particularly unusual about it other than someone had seen fit to lob it into her kitchen. Maybe it was youths, just as Ms Honeywell had suggested. She certainly couldn't

NEIGHBOURHOOD WATCH

think of anyone she'd annoyed enough to receive such treatment. Presumably the locals were already in the early stages of planning a major neighbourhood watch meeting to discuss the worrying level of antisocial behaviour. By the end of the week they'd be out on patrol interrogating anyone showing interest in bricks. Housebuilding would be delayed for months.

Several objects that had once been positioned purposefully around the kitchen had been disrupted by the passage of the brick through the window. She picked up a picture frame that had been knocked off the windowsill and laid face-down on the draining board. The glass in the frame was still intact and behind it was a black and white picture of Horace. She replaced it in place and subliminally gave it a gentle clean with a J Cloth.

After a brief search there appeared no further reason for alarm, so she poured herself a glass of water and headed to the living room with the intention of reading, but fully expecting to be asleep before she made it to the end of the first page. As she approached the living room door a faint noise of talking was seeping through the closed door. Had she left the television on? She barely ever turned the thing on, so she thought it unlikely. Placing her ear to the wood it did sound like the television was entertaining itself. She placed her hand on the handle and gently pushed it open, flicking the light switch with her other hand.

The small television in the corner of the room was pumping out some brainless reality show that seemed to centre on attractive people running around in skimpy clothing in an attempt to prove who had the best body and the smallest brain. This wasn't the type of programme that Ally watched, and it was soon obvious who had been. A young woman, wearing the most ridiculous and elaborate disguise imaginable, was asleep on the sofa. A bottle of one of Ally's expensive red wines was sitting empty on the floor along with a selection of her fridge contents mostly half-eaten.

NEIGHBOURHOOD WATCH

To Ally's disappointment the young woman wasn't really an intruder. If she had been Ally would have had no qualms about calling the police and having her carted off, hopefully to get what was coming to her. Instead the sleeping offender was someone she knew. It'd been a couple of years since she'd last seen her and even with the ineffective disguise she was wearing for unknown reasons, it was unmistakably Gabriel Janvier.

Gabriel was many things to Ally, but a friend wasn't one of them. They had nothing in common other than fate placing them together in a small forest in Limonest at the height of the N1G13 outbreak. Although Gabriel had been vital in helping them loosen Mario's grip on the panic sweeping the world at that time through her mastery of all things electronic and online, Ally had nothing in common with her whatsoever. Plus, she'd made it perfectly and overtly clear that she didn't like Gabriel much.

Gabriel wasn't very good at reading the signs.

Ally marched over and shook her violently by the shoulders. The young woman's dark wig slipped over her eyes and she came to with a scream, believing she'd gone blind in the night. Ally quickly placed a hand over her mouth to avoid further interest from the busybodies out in the garden.

"I was sleeping, you know," yawned Gabriel.

"Oh, I do apologise," replied Ally with a little bow. "I didn't realise I was in your house. Please feel free to drink my expensive wine, watch my television and take over my life!"

"Ok, thanks," said Gabriel, completely missing any sense of sarcasm in Ally's voice. "I hope you don't mind, I let myself in."

"Gabriel, you didn't 'let yourself in', you threw a brick through my window. It's not the same thing."

"Isn't it?"

"No, its official name is trespass."

"Shit, they still have the death penalty for that, don't they?"

NEIGHBOURHOOD WATCH

"That's treason. I hope you know I have a horde of neighbours outside because of you? Why didn't you just text me if you wanted to visit?"

"You didn't give me your number," replied Gabriel, "and you'd have said no if I had."

She was right. Ally didn't have house guests. She didn't know anyone well enough to invite them and no one she did know would want to stay if she did.

"Gabriel, what are you doing here dressed… like that?"

"They haven't called the police, have they?" she said nervously.

"Not yet, but I wouldn't be surprised if they did. What's happened?"

"I'm on the run from the FIB!" sobbed Gabriel.

- Chapter 7 -

Three Rings

The birds outside her window chirped an improvised concerto, each feathered musician desperate to announce the arrival of morning in their own unique key. Ally normally welcomed it, even on a Saturday, but today she dragged the duvet further over her ears to muffle the chorus. It wasn't just the birds that hastened her retreat. Unless yesterday had been a terrible nightmare, the arrival of morning and her unwelcomed guest were bound to bring further disappointment.

Last night she didn't have the mental energy to deal with her surprise visitor and the no doubt idiotic reasons behind her decision to break into Ally's house. She'd metaphorically pointed the evening to the exit door, reluctantly made up the bed in the spare room for Gabriel, and retired to her own. In the morning there would be no motive for avoiding it. She'd have to find a more permanent solution.

House guests weren't something she was used to. What did you do with them? Did they feed themselves? Were you supposed to entertain them? The thought sent a shudder through her body. Endless small talk, a lack of peace, people potentially breaking her expensive antiques, and complying with a false routine sounded about as enjoyable as having your ears syringed. The general thought of being a host was bad enough before considering that her current house guest was someone she had a general dislike for. Maybe, she prayed, Gabriel had decided to leave in the night, concerned that the authorities were closing in on her. Luck didn't really work like that, not for Ally at least.

THREE RINGS

As she pulled the duvet further around her body to cocoon herself from the increasingly dazzling sunlight that had joined the birds in their incessant campaign to force everyone out of bed, the doorbell decided to join in. Two seconds later it rang again. Her house had one of those bells that was so quiet the person ringing it might mistakenly believe that they hadn't pressed it hard enough the first time. Either that or someone impatient was on the other side.

Ally slid out of the side of the duvet like a corpse escaping from a body bag. She flailed around in the gloom to locate her dressing gown before heading for the front door. The bell rang for a third time. Her pace quickened down the stairs, even though she had no real interest in greeting whoever stood on the other side.

"The bell works fine," barked Ally as she swung the door open. Peepholes in doors were invented for moments like this and she hated herself for not using it. "Oh bollocks."

"Just wanted to check on you, me darlin', after your terrible ordeal last night," replied Ms Honeywell, desperately trying to look past Ally to see what might be happening within the confines of the cottage.

"Why?" she snapped in response.

"It's our neighbourhood duty, me darlin'," replied Ms Honeywell. "We all look after each other."

"I don't need anyone to look after me, thank you, I've been doing that since I was six."

"Well, you don't need to anymore, now that you have your guest with you."

Ally stopped in her tracks. Had this elderly do-gooder rigged up bugging devices in every property in Stanton? Ally had only discovered Gabriel at about midnight, and she guessed at most it was now about six-thirty in the morning. Maybe Honeywell hadn't left the garden. Perhaps she'd spent the night staking out the house, listening for every sound and watching every movement. How she managed to do this whilst simultaneously knowing what was going on in every other property in the village was beyond the processing capacity of the most powerful computer ever built.

"How did you…"

"Arrived about an hour ago, me darlin'. I thought it was strange for someone to have guests arriving so early. After last night's problems I thought I'd investigate and check you were alright."

"No one arrived an hour ago. I was in bed so they can't have."

"Young lady let him in," said Honeywell authoritatively.

"Let who in!?"

Ms Honeywell reached into a tatty handbag and pulled out a tiny notepad that looked like it had been thoroughly chewed at the edges by Melvyn's dog. She licked her fingers and flicked speedily through the pages. Holding the page close to her face, she squinted her eyes and screwed up her face like a prune being squeezed by a vice before reading out her hastily scribbled notes.

"Five foot nine, skintight white T-shirt, jogging bottoms, muscly, dark hair, early thirties, olive skin and… foreign-looking," she said disapprovingly, as if foreign was a byword for 'deeply suspicious'.

As she put away her notepad Ally noticed she'd also written the word SHIFTY and underlined it three times.

"Ok, Ms Honeywell I'll look into it."

"Does your landlord know they're staying, me darlin'?"

The door closed firmly in her face as Ally retreated into the cottage.

"Gabriel!" she shouted at the top of her voice up the stairs. There was no response. "Don't make me come up there."

Saturdays weren't supposed to be like this. They were supposed to start around eight in the morning with a pot of strong Italian coffee boiling on the Aga, its nutty smell taking the kitchen hostage and instigating the first gentle steps into morning rejuvenation. Once properly brewed it

THREE RINGS

would be enjoyed in the back garden with the newspapers spread out over the table. Not the tabloids: they weren't aimed at intelligent adults like Ally. It was the broadsheets or nothing. If the weather permitted, she'd slip out the back gate and disappear into the Oxfordshire countryside for a gentle stroll before returning refreshed around lunchtime.

Saturdays definitely shouldn't start with her shouting up her own stairs at an uninvited French millennial with an amazing ability to annoy her host with every word uttered and every action taken. A few minutes after Ally's demands, Gabriel appeared at the top of the staircase scantily clad and rubbing her eyes. Ally didn't know what the garment Gabriel was wearing was called but if she had to name it, she'd have called it slutty chic.

"Morning," yawned Gabriel innocently.

"Do you have a man up there?"

"Obviously. I'm on the run, I'm not celibate."

"Don't you think you should have asked me?"

There was an awkward moment as Gabriel reflected on the question. Her English was good, but it had been a while since she'd used it in conversation and wanted the extra moment to make absolutely sure she hadn't misinterpreted what Ally meant.

"Um… I didn't think you'd be into that sort of thing to be honest."

"Owwww, no! That's not what I meant. Come down here, we need to talk."

Gabriel stumbled down the stairs half-asleep and half-dressed. Where last night a wig had hidden it away, today Gabriel's newly dyed hair was trying to remain in a ball, even though most of it hung limply over her shoulders. It had been blonde the last time they'd met and, although the colour had been changed to black it had little effect in changing the stigma associated with blondes of a certain age.

"Got any vodka?" she said as she passed Ally and made her way into the kitchen.

THREE RINGS

"No! It's seven in the morning, Gabriel."

"So?!"

"This time of the day is normally associated with breakfast."

"I know. I like it on my cornflakes."

"I don't have any of those either."

"Toast?"

"Yes, I have bread."

"It's good on toast, too."

Ally wondered if even the wild antics of the legendary rock bands of the nineteen seventies included vodka on toast. It was a mystery how she'd survived to this tender age the way she went through booze. It didn't seem the right time for counselling: there were more pressing issues to deal with.

"Who is he?" said Ally, pointing up through the ceiling.

"Buff."

"Is that a name or a description?"

"Both," she grinned.

"What sort of a name is Buff?!"

"What sort of a name is Ally?" she replied defensively.

"A real one. It's short for Alison."

"Is it?"

"Yes. What's his short for, Buffalo?"

"I haven't really asked him. I only met him the other week."

"What!? Do you mean you've gone on the run with a man you barely even know?"

"Sorry, Mum! I didn't know you cared."

"I only care because you're both inexplicably in my house. Once that isn't true, you can be assured I won't be in the slightest bit bothered. In the last six months I've managed to avoid even the neighbours getting past the front door and yet here you are. I must have smashed a lot of mirrors when I was younger."

"I didn't know I was likely to be on the run when I met him. Then, when I had to leave France, he said he wanted to help me escape."

THREE RINGS

"And did you think that was normal behaviour?"

"Normal when you're in love."

Ally's mouth dropped open. This was typical Gabriel. Naïve and corruptible. What Ally didn't know was quite how predictable this pattern was. The young woman's love life had a tendency to repeat itself. A good-looking guy in a bar would buy her drinks, shower her with affection, proclaim his undying love, and within hours she'd be on all fours offering the only thing they were really interested in. A week later they'd be controlling her every move and appearance, before shattering her self-esteem, borrowing her car and seducing all her friends. That was Gabriel's version of love and no dictionary definition was ever going to back it up. Ally knew she wasn't going to convince her of this mistake either, so she avoided opening another can of worms.

"Why are you here?"

"I told you last night, I'm on the run from the FIB."

"And, as I told you last night, it's not called the FIB, it's the FBI, but why do you think they are interested in you?"

"I was followed. Last week everywhere I went this car was always behind me driving like a lunatic."

If she had been followed it was certainly plausible that any pursuer would have to drive like a racing driver to keep up with her. Gabriel's driving style, which Ally had experienced first hand, was at best described as reckless and at worst described as death-defying.

"By any chance did this car make a really irritating noise and have a flashing blue light on the roof?"

"No, it was just a normal car with two normal-looking men in it. I took a photograph of it when it was parked outside my house and that's how I know it was the F…"

"B.I.," added Ally. "How did you work that out?"

"Traced it."

"How?"

"Don't you remember, I'm an internet Ninja."

Ally nodded. In truth it was the only thing Ally respected her for. She had an uncanny ability to interrogate all things digital and technological. Given Ally's opinion of Gabriel's general intelligence level she still struggled to understand how it was at all possible.

"Anyway," added Gabriel as she nibbled away at a piece of bread she'd helped herself to. "I hacked them, so I know who they are."

"You hacked the FBI."

"Yeah, it was easy."

"And stupid. If they weren't monitoring you before, then they certainly are now."

"They can't, I left all my tech behind when I went on the run."

"Phew, that's a relief. You've outwitted them," replied Ally sarcastically. "Obviously the FBI are screwed if they can't find someone using the internet as they're all manacled to their desks. Quick history lesson. There was a world before the internet and the FBI were pretty successful then, too. Why did you come here? Why didn't you go to Antoine for help, he must have been closer?"

"I tried. He's gone missing. I'm not surprised really. They have a file on him, too."

"The FBI have a file on Antoine?"

"Yes."

"Why?"

"Because they have one on all of us?"

"What!? I can understand why they have one on you, you're a notorious computer hacker, but why do they have one on me?"

Gabriel shrugged. None of this information seemed to bother her greatly because in truth she didn't really know anything about the FBI. To her the letters were no more dangerous than BMW or FCUK. What had affected her most was not being able to get money out of the ATM. That really was the end of the world as far as she was concerned. It was like they'd taken the air from her lungs.

Ally did know who the FBI were and that they didn't keep files on people without good reason. If you had a file, you were a person of interest, but why would she be one?

THREE RINGS

Her involvement with the authorities had only ever been positive. After all, she was one of the people who'd helped the police bring Mario to justice and return order to the world. Since then she'd pretty much become invisible to anyone outside of her own lectures, the people that work at the university and the staff at the Furlong Nursing Home.

The fact that the FBI had a file on Antoine, Gabriel and herself meant only one thing. Something was happening. Why hadn't Antoine warned her? He wasn't a selfish man. If he'd gone into hiding after discovering his own file, why hadn't he got a message to her? Maybe he couldn't. Maybe his communications were being watched. Maybe hers were. She visualised the image of Ms Honeywell wearing an FBI bulletproof vest under her Marks & Spencer pastel cardigans, and a revolver hidden amongst the contents of her tatty handbag. A moment later she shook the idea from her mind. Only foolish people did paranoia.

The kitchen door swung open and a man wearing a towel around his waist sauntered in as if he lived there. Wet footprints squelched on the grey ceramic tiles as he padded to the fridge, took out a carton of milk and started to drink directly from the plastic bottle. Once his thirst was quenched, he advanced on Gabriel, milk still dripping from his lips, and commenced an inspection of the inside of her mouth with his tongue. It was an investigation that seemed extremely thorough.

"STOP!" shouted Ally, as the voice that she thought she'd been using the moment he entered the room finally located the frequency needed for humans to hear it.

"This is Buff," replied Gabriel.

"Oh good, because I thought you might have stashed more than one man in my tiny cottage without my knowledge."

"Gorgeous, isn't he?" Gabriel squealed as a wandering hand took a pinch of an arse cheek.

"No. I'd rather date a beetroot. You can't stay here. You'll have to leave."

THREE RINGS

"Why?"

"I don't have the space."

"You live on your own."

"My landlord is coming around today, and I'm not allowed to sublet."

"We're just visiting."

"Oh good. It was lovely to see you, goodbye!"

"We have nowhere else to go and you owe me a favour," begged Gabriel.

"How do you work that out?" asked Ally.

"I once let you stay in my caravan."

"Only after Antoine paid you ten thousand euros. I'll accept the same fee."

"Duh, didn't you hear me? I said I can't get to my money."

"What a shame… goodbye," repeated Ally as she motioned for them to leave like a marshal directing a jumbo jet into its hangar.

"Please, Ally! We need your help," added Gabriel with one final desperate plea. Her eyes welled up and her bottom lip started to wobble uncontrollably. Ally presumed this was fake and she wasn't going to be even slightly convinced by it.

"What about him?" she said, pointing at the semi-naked bodybuilder. "Doesn't he have any money?"

"No. His accounts have been frozen, too, and it's all my fault," she sobbed.

Buff's appearance remained calm and composed. His attention was never in the present: always his eyes rested on everything but the people who were talking, like he didn't care much or was distracted by more important stimuli.

The doorbell rang again and almost immediately came the customary second ring. Ally wondered if the day could get any worse. She stomped to the front door where the bell rang for the third time before she reached it. She swung it open fully expecting to see the withered frame of her most annoying neighbour on the hessian doormat.

THREE RINGS

"Ms Honeywell, please fuck off!"

It wasn't her. Not unless she'd gone through a rapid sex change in the last twenty minutes and had transformed into a tall, silver-haired gentleman with a bushy beard, and a full policeman's uniform.

"Ms Oldfield."

"Doc… yes," she replied, deciding when to pick her battles.

"It's a good job swearing at a police officer isn't a criminal offence, madam," said the warm, smiling figure towering over her. "Although having met the infamous Gladys Honeywell I'm sure we could build an effective defence founded on retaliation for her being a public nuisance."

Ally found herself smiling which under the circumstances of the morning was a big surprise. Probably in his late-fifties, the policeman had a nostalgic quality about him that reminded her of how policeman used to be in the old days. Back then your local constable appeared friendlier and more supportive than today's career-focused crime fighter who was more interested in statistics than having a genuine desire to help the public.

"PC Dearlove," he said in introduction. "Is this a good time?"

"Not really but as I fully expect the day to deteriorate over the coming hours, talking to you might be a blessed relief."

"Sounds like a long story!"

"The longest and I won't bore you with it. What can I do for you?"

"We've had reports of a break-in at this property last night."

"Just a broken window, nothing to worry the police about, I'm sure."

"No job too small, madam."

"I thought you were under-resourced and didn't have time to deal with this sort of incident?" she asked, remembering a recent conversation with Horace where he'd again bemoaned the policies of the current government.

"We don't, but it's nothing compared to the manpower required to deal with Honeywell's mailbag. Plus, I'm local, as it happens."

"Stanton?"

"Yes."

"I've not seen you around," said Ally honestly.

"That's probably because you don't mingle with the rest of us," he said knowingly.

"I've been busy," she lied in response.

"How did the window break?" he asked, moving back to work subjects.

"Probably falling debris."

"I don't recall a brick storm last night, Ms Oldfield."

Ally offered a horrible fake laugh. Just ten minutes ago she'd had no cause to feel nervous around anyone connected to law enforcement, but that was before she'd found out the FBI had a file on her, and before she was harbouring a known criminal.

"Would you like me to investigate it?"

"No! Everything here is fine. I appreciate your concern, Officer."

"It's no trouble. I like to be out in the community as much as I can and with Honeywell on point that's quite often, I can tell you. If you don't want to report it, I'll tick it off my list. Another statistic towards the key performance measures," he added, pretending to strangle himself to demonstrate his feelings towards them. "What about these reports I'm hearing of a couple of suspicious-looking characters around the village last night? Have you seen anyone sinister?"

"Only the neighbours."

Dearlove nodded in agreement. If this was as difficult as his job got, God help the locals if anything serious ever happened in the village.

"Well, if you do see anything you can call me on this," he said, passing her a little card with his number scrawled

THREE RINGS

on it. "That's my personal number: be quicker than calling 999."

The radio mounted on PC Dearlove's trousers crackled into his crotch as an announcement from someone fighting static electricity barked orders into the airwaves. At the very same time Ally's dressing gown made a ping noise. She reached inside to retrieve her phone and the text message that had just made its noisy interjection.

"Tango four nine, tango four nine, this is Oxford Central, over."

"Oxford Central, Oxford Central, go ahead, over," replied Dearlove, holding a button down but not lifting the radio from its belt. He smiled at Ally, making an eye-rolling motion to suggest whatever it was would be entirely unfulfilling.

Ally read her text message and the blood drained from her face. It was from Ernest Culpepper, the Museum Librarian and one of her bosses at the university. Ernest was an old school type who normally refrained from using anything with buttons that didn't involve clothing. A text message from him was always serious and urgent.

"Possible robbery reported at Broad Street, Oxford, over," crackled the radio.

"Understood, on my way, over and out," replied Dearlove. "Must be going, duty calls. Have a good day, madam."

"Any chance of a lift?" Ally asked quickly.

"A lift?"

"I think we might be going to the same place. I've just received a text message. There's been a robbery at the Bodleian's Weston Library... on Broad Street."

- Chapter 8 -

The Root of the Mountain

After his difficult conversation with Diego, Daniel Hudson spent the night in the Hôtel de l'Abbaye across the road from the prison. From his second-floor window the grounds of Clairvaux, suffocated by a twelve-foot-high wall, spread out into the distance and up to the feet of the impressive eighteenth-century building. It seemed perverse to him that some of France's most dangerous villains were afforded such comfortable surroundings.

There were suburbs of Paris where colonies of people lived in squalor, deprivation, and the constant fear from the dangerous drug gangs that patrolled the streets threatening lives and livelihoods. Through no fault of their own they eked out a modest existence from the ruins of run-down high-rises in dire need of modernisation. Yet here in the splendid tranquillity of the French countryside another property provided by the state was occupied by murderers, rapists and terrorists living in relative comfort. As Hudson watched the sun rise up behind the prison, he thought society had got it wrong somehow.

The village of Clairvaux was like a thousand others dotted around the French countryside. Elderly, flat cap-wearing men on antique bicycles with cigarettes dangling precariously from the corners of their mouths rode to the boulangerie to pick up bread. Cars were parked chaotically wherever they'd commandeered enough space, whether there was another car on the inside of them or not. Intricate webs of washing partially camouflaged old

THE ROOT OF THE MOUNTAIN

women in their daily pursuit of watching the world go by from first-floor windows, desperate to catch a neighbour's inappropriate behaviour and fuel the day's gossip.

Daniel allowed the strange atmosphere to breeze in through the open window for a few minutes before reluctantly lifting himself from the armchair and grabbing the gleaming black suitcase from the bed. It looked no bigger than a weekend bag, but its contents had kept him going for weeks. After all, he had a flight to catch and those bastards charged a fortune if your bag didn't fit in the overhead locker.

His superiors, of which there were too many to remember, had determined that his next stop would be England. It wasn't an easy decision for them to reach because many of those superiors fiercely disagreed with each other. After all, Mario's letters had been sent to every corner of the globe and any one of them might turn out to be the next-best lead. Local agents had already been positioned to stake out the addresses those letters were sent to, and so far, all of them had reported the same problem.

The addresses didn't exist.

It's possible the locations existed at some point in history but the relentless sprawl of mankind's desire to redevelop to meet the demands of the public meant they weren't there now. An address that had been listed in the City of London was now a large office block. An address listed in Boston was a car park, and an address in Geneva had been rebuilt as a children's soft play area. When you're a local FBI agent told to watch over a location until further notice it's not long before suspicious mothers wheeling prams get concerned by a shifty-looking man in a sharp suit hanging around by the swings.

Daniel had allowed Timon to send out the three dozen letters because he knew his agents would get there first. Now the letters were in the system and there was no way of tracking them down because there was no way they could be delivered. They had copies of the contents but what good was that if you could neither understand the meaning

THE ROOT OF THE MOUNTAIN

of the cipher, nor predict who they were really intended for? The whole situation wasn't going to look good at his annual appraisal. There were twelve billion dollars at stake and he'd not found even a cent of it. The letters were the clues, and now they were lost in the postal system.

The only country in the world that doesn't have a traditional postal service is Guatemala. Even when it did have one, the likelihood of you receiving your annual birthday card and enclosed money were close to zero. Almost anything sent by mail would have been opened, pilfered and damaged, and might finally arrive with you some time after your next birthday or even the one after that. The suspension of the service in Guatemala meant it was also the only country in the world without a 'Dead Letter Office'.

Not every country gave it the same name, but they all had one. Any letter that can't be successfully delivered or returned to its sender is stored in the DLO and has been since the invention of the stamp. What happens to the mail after it arrives there really depends on the country in question. If the items are valuable, they might be auctioned; if unclaimed they might be recycled; and on occasions they might be acquired by a philatelist, a person who studies postal history. There's only one philatelist in the world currently. His name is Clive.

Tracing Mario's letters had become much more difficult. Although the process had already begun it would take weeks to identify all the DLOs, access them legally and locate those individual letters amongst the huge archive of lost mail that ran into the hundreds of thousands of items. In the meantime, Daniel would have to follow up on the other leads that he had.

Daniel's immediate instincts told him that Diego had some involvement in what Mario was planning, through either direct support or the offer of valuable information. Diego was a renowned terrorist and had multiple convictions for extortion, just the sort of accomplice Mario might use to hide his moncy. What most intrigued Daniel

THE ROOT OF THE MOUNTAIN

was what Mario had been planning to use the money for. Given his past crimes it wasn't a big stretch to imagine that the money would be used to fund criminality in some way. The mystery of the letters only suggested it further.

Then there was Radu Goga.

That name had been the key to unlocking Diego's silence but how did it relate to finding the money? Why was it important at all? Daniel had very quickly mined the FBI archives for more information, whether it was relevant or not. Radu, it transpired, had been a rising star in the Russian Communist Party during the sixties and seventies. His high-profile defection caused outrage across the Eastern bloc and several notorious dictators offered millions for his assassination. Diego was just one of those equipped to find and kill him, but he never even got close.

In the early years of his asylum Radu had been compelled to work for the Americans, passing on his secrets from the Communist bloc thereby eroding the capabilities of the Russian KGB. Once that period ended Radu was surplus to requirements and the authorities almost completely lost track of him. Where he was currently living or whether, indeed, he still was had so far been impossible to verify, at least through any of Daniel's sources. The last photo of him, taken in the late nineteen eighties, was all he had to go on. All other files were classified.

Of the three people listed inside his own letter only one had been tracked down and that happened two weeks ago. Unknown to him until yesterday, Gabriel Janvier was already a person of interest to the FBI. The reason for the bureau's interest was linked to their own interest in Mario: it appeared they were both looking for the money. On top of that, Gabriel had been conducting a series of hacks against the FBI itself. This activity had not gone unnoticed. A local French office of the Bureau had been notified, and after a short period of success, Gabriel Janvier had given them the slip. She'd resurfaced yesterday when her passport was flagged travelling across the English Channel, and she wasn't alone.

THE ROOT OF THE MOUNTAIN

Antoine Palomer was no more than a ghost. No one had seen him, no one had called him, and no money had left his accounts. His house was not just lacking human activity, it was lacking anything at all. In the last year he'd sold all his businesses, bequeathed his foundations to other charities, and closed all his bank accounts except one. The one he hadn't closed was the biggest mystery of all. The account had been active for hundreds of years and had been managed by some of the oldest banks in history, yet Antoine had never made a single withdrawal. Not once.

The final name in his letter would be the easiest to trace: they just hadn't bothered yet because it wasn't interesting enough. Ally Oldfield was a professor in a renowned university, made no attempt to hide her identity or endeavours, and had almost no networks. Her movements and spending weren't suspicious. Her mobile phone was barely used and when it was, only to shout at a bloke called Lance. All in all, she was the least likely criminal you could ever imagine, which was exactly why Daniel and the FBI thought she was definitely up to something. This hunch pointed him towards England, the home of Ally Oldfield and the last known location of Radu Goga.

*****

It was the worst possible day for all this to happen. Today was supposed to be the opening of Ally's exhibition and now it was ruined. Everything had been organised down to the very last detail. The PR people had made a buzz across social media, local personalities had been booked to open the collection, and even the local radio station was going to interview her. She'd thought that if anything was likely to go wrong today it would probably have something to do with Lance, but she was wrong. No level of contingency planning would have prepared for this.

The scale of Ally's trauma had not been picked up by her chauffeur. PC Dearlove drove with more care than

THE ROOT OF THE MOUNTAIN

haste, hummed annoyingly to himself and attempted to make light conversation as if he was on a first date. Ally felt more compelled than usual to join in: after all, he would be able to take her closer and quicker to the scene of the crime than her own driving might.

"Don't you just love this countryside?" asked Dearlove.

"It's alright," answered Ally.

"I've lived here my whole life, couldn't think of a nicer place to be."

"The Lake District," answered Ally truthfully, feeling he was probably being a little short-sighted.

"Is that where you're from?" asked Dearlove.

"No. Do you think you can drive a little faster? Maybe put the flashing lights on."

"It's a burglary, Dr Oldfield, and it'll still be one when we get there. Where are you from, then?"

"Hard to say really."

"Surely you must know where you were born?"

She didn't.

Ally had never seen her birth certificate and didn't really want to. Wherever she'd lived before arriving in the custody of her adoptive parents in the mid-seventies it was no longer important, if it ever had been. Horace had never felt inclined to shed light on it either. The 'North' had always felt like home.

"Somewhere in the North," she replied finally.

"You're foreign, then," chuckled Dearlove.

"You should try it, PC Dearlove, you might like it."

"Norman, please," he replied with a smile.

The sedate pace of travel gave Norman plenty of time to lay out his life story and Ally did her best to fake interest. Norman was a divorcee with two grown-up children who both lived abroad somewhere, although it didn't seem clear whether he knew exactly where. He explained that being in his late-fifties he was way beyond the police's recommended retirement age but had nothing else to do to stimulate himself other than work. Ally could empathise: she certainly wasn't considering retirement in the future

THE ROOT OF THE MOUNTAIN

unless they forced her to do so. Surprisingly from first appearance and his gentle manner, it also transpired that Norman was quite the rebel.

"This is against procedure," he said with a grin.

"What is?"

"Me giving you a lift when you're not under arrest."

"Why are you doing it, then?"

"Because I think we should be helping the community and you are part of that. Plus, I don't like stupid rules."

Modern life was all about rules. It's apparently the only answer to every question, particularly when an exception occurs that no one expects. If someone foolishly uses a hot iron to take the creases out of their clothes while they're still wearing them, the manufacturer is compelled to publish a warning in their warranty. DO NOT IRON THE CLOTHES YOU'RE WEARING! In the past Darwin called this 'the survival of the fittest', a natural selection process where inferior genetics aren't given the opportunity to multiply. Not now. Now we have to protect them from themselves while forcing everyone with an IQ higher than fifty to read the same stupid rules.

It's mostly these exceptions that provide the rule book these days. Teachers aren't allowed to hug children when they're upset, couriers aren't allowed to carry heavy boxes in case they hurt themselves, music lovers aren't allowed the tops of drinks bottles at gigs in case they throw them at the band, and in some places the phrase 'Easter Eggs' has been replaced by 'Spring Spheres' on the off chance someone gets offended. Norman grew up in the sixties when rebellion was a popular concept. His generation protested against nuclear weapons, ill-judged wars and the oppression of minority groups, and was in favour of free love. Rebelling against a rule only in place to protect idiots was easy after all that.

It took twice as long to get to the museum as it normally took Ally. Dearlove stopped at traffic lights, slowed down if someone looked like they wanted to cross the road, and kept the vehicle below the recommended speed limit. Ally

THE ROOT OF THE MOUNTAIN

wondered if he demonstrated this restraint for all of his call-outs. What if a terrorist attack was in progress or someone was threatening violence? Dearlove would only get there to clean up the mess and take witness statements.

A queue had formed outside the Weston Museum two hours before the museum was due to open which was about the same time four police cars pulled up outside the main entrance and cordoned it off. By the time PC Dearlove's car arrived the line of people had mostly been encouraged to disperse, clear that nothing would be opening today other than a case file. Several of the museum's staff were loitering on the steps outside the building, including the museum's librarian, Ernest Culpepper.

PC Dearlove pulled up alongside the other patrol cars and dragged himself gingerly from his seat. There was a collection of popping sounds and creaking joints as his body refamiliarised itself with being vertical again. Ally joined him on the pavement with much less discomfort.

"Right, Ally, it's time I did some work," said Norman, fixing his police cap in position and climbing the half-dozen stone steps up to the museum entrance.

Lance Carter was standing behind the police cordon, craning his long neck to get a better view. A length of police tape was wrapped around his leg and some of it was even lodged in his trouser flies. Ally had no interest in asking how it got there.

"What's happening?" said Ally as she joined the small congregation of staff members.

"Something has gone missing?" replied Lance.

"Please tell me it's not the Lesage prophecy," asked Ally desperately. Material objects weren't generally that important to her but, along with her Ram locket, the prophecy was something she cared deeply for. Not only did it have significance in her own life, it was also a unique piece of history.

"I don't think so, it's a bit vague at the moment, there's a rumour the Shikshapatri has been stolen."

THE ROOT OF THE MOUNTAIN

The Bodleian and Weston Libraries had state-of-the-art security systems. CCTV cameras covered every inch of the building's floor space, most books were tagged, access to the most valuable items was restricted, and everything was patrolled by a vast team of security guards working around the clock. On first view there seemed no obvious signs that a break-in had even occurred. None of the glass panes were broken and the alarms weren't blaring. If she was going to find out more it wasn't from Lance. She moved over to speak with the librarian.

"Ernest, what's happened?"

"Doctor Oldfield…"

"Doctor," she replied spontaneously.

"Yes… I know," said Ernest, looking irritated by her interruption and lack of perspective.

"Right, force of habit."

"It's a shame this has happened on your big day."

"It's sort of the way my day is going, to be honest. What's the situation?"

"I received a call from one of the security guards walking his patrol. He reported that the Shikshapatri was no longer in its case, but there was no sign of any interference with it."

"How is that possible?"

"I guess that's what the police are trying to understand. I haven't had time to check the CCTV yet, but from what I saw inside it was almost as if the book had vanished. Whoever did this must be a genius with technology, that's all I can say."

"A genius," muttered Ally, joining up the coincidental dots of the last twelve hours. "An IT ninja perhaps."

"They haven't allowed anyone to go in yet. It's so frustrating they might be damaging my priceless collection," bleated Ernest.

The small crowd preoccupied themselves with fanciful rumour-mongering and fresh cups of coffee, most of which Lance was sent to buy and only some of which returned in the plastic cups rather than down his trousers. After several

THE ROOT OF THE MOUNTAIN

hours of police 'comings and goings', with the removal of evidence and equipment being fetched, PC Dearlove exited the building and approached Ally.

"The Chief would like to see you," said Norman, looking glum.

"Me!?" said Ally.

"Yes."

"She's not going in without me," huffed Ernest in a tone of superiority. "They're my babies!"

"Who are you?" asked Norman gently.

"Ernest Culpepper, the Librarian, I was the one who made the call."

"Then I think you'd better come in, too."

Norman lifted the police tape so the two of them could limbo under it. Ernest and Ally followed him up the steps and into the main building, a journey Ernest had taken a dozen times a day for the past ten years. Inside, a series of police employees wearing white overalls, goggles and masks were busy with their own forensic worlds. Bags of evidence, each tagged in minute detail, were piled up on the floor by the entrance. In the special collections room, a gruff-looking, overweight man stood over a raised glass-topped case looking vacant.

"That's the Chief," said Dearlove, pointing him out unnecessarily. "DCI Bolton."

"Is this her?" said Bolton without offering introductions or pleasantries.

"Yes, sir," replied Norman.

"Mrs Oldfield?"

"Doctor!"

"I only recognise doctors if they're holding a scalpel or shoving a finger up my arse to squeeze my prostate," replied Bolton graphically. "You aren't allowed to do either."

"Sadly, I don't have a scalpel with me this morning or you might be investigating a very different crime scene."

"Threats of violence are taken very seriously," he replied curtly. "Can I ask you to explain your movements over the last twelve hours?"

Ally glanced at her watch. "Yes, I've been consistently moving from one idiot to another for more than twelve hours. Mostly in my cottage fifteen miles away."

"When was the last time you were here?"

"Lance and I left here at about five o'clock last night."

"Who's Lance?"

"My intern."

"We'll need to talk to him later. I wonder if you can explain this," said Bolton, encouraging her to approach the exhibit case.

"I thought that was your job," replied Ally, ready to take the fight to this egomaniac chauvinist.

"What do you think I'm doing exactly?" snapped the senior officer. "Come a bit closer and see for yourself."

Ally moved up to the glass case and peered inside. The priceless piece of literature that once lay on a plinth displaying its ancient Sanskrit text to the world had been replaced by a small piece of white card. There was a short message written neatly on the front.

You are not the beginning. T.M.M.

"Right," said Ally. "What's the pay like for doing your job for you?"

"Better than you might think," replied Bolton. "What do you make of it?"

"Why do people keep confusing me with some legendary criminal investigator when my actual expertise is deciphering sixteenth-century texts written in Old Prussian!?"

"Pick it up and look at the back," suggested Bolton firmly.

"But that's evidence, you're not meant to contaminate it surely?"

THE ROOT OF THE MOUNTAIN

"We've taken all the prints that we need. Pick it up," he repeated more aggressively.

Cautiously she leant over the opened case and lifted the card up. She turned it over, expecting to see more information from the perpetrator written on the back. It would have been a lot simpler for her if that had been the case. Instead the back was much more familiar. It was one of her own business cards.

"Now how did the thief of a priceless manuscript get hold of your business card?" said Bolton in full-on accusation mode.

"Clearly, it's a doddle to pinch the Shikshapatri compared to getting hold of my business cards. I keep them in Fort Knox, after all! I suspect, Detective, it might have been quite an easy task for anyone with the expertise to steal the book."

"Hmm, you're not helping your case, you know."

"What case!? Are you really that stupid? The thief probably got them from a stationery cupboard or had some printed. It's not difficult these days. You can get anything you want printed online. Even 'DCI Bolton, World's Greatest Policeman', anything you want."

Bolton's expression was unaffected by her taunts. In his experience coincidences were always significant. The thief hadn't left this randomly, there must have been a motive for it. The business card wasn't the only evidence that could be attached to her either. Oldfield worked there and by the look of the crime scene it had to be an inside job. No forced entry. No alarms. No security breaches. CCTV footage wiped.

"What do you make of the note?" asked Bolton.

"Nothing," she said untruthfully. It was extremely interesting to her, but she wasn't going to share that with him.

"Don't you think it's strange that it says, 'you are not the beginning' and not 'this is just the beginning'?"

"Maybe the thief's dyslexic."

THE ROOT OF THE MOUNTAIN

"Please don't fuck with me, Oldfield, anyone would think you had something to hide."

"If it helps," added Ernest, "she's always like this. Officer, if I could butt in for a moment. All of our rare books have a tracking device, a small microchip that acts as a beacon for its whereabouts. Have you tried to locate it?"

"Yes, we're not stupid, you know."

Ally let out an involuntary noise of disagreement.

"We've already talked with your security team who've looked into it."

"And what was the outcome?" asked Ernest eagerly.

DCI Bolton pointed to the case. "It says the book is still here."

Ernest leant over the glass to have a closer look. Other than the stand and the air it was empty. "I can't see it."

"Obviously not. The thief must have removed the microchip and left it in here."

"That's what I mean. I can't see the chip: against the white fabric it should be easy to spot. Did you have that removed, too?"

"No," replied DCI Bolton. "Maybe the chip has malfunctioned."

"Or maybe the thief made the book invisible," added Ally sarcastically. "I'm leaving."

"Not unless you want me to arrest you."

"For what?"

"Let me tell you my theory," replied Bolton in a way that made it clear there wasn't really a choice. "I think the note does refer to you. Ally Oldfield is not the beginning, but the beginning of what? I believe that this event is just the start of a series. Which makes me believe that you are involved or connected to these crimes in some way."

"Amazing! By the way, how's your first week on the job going?"

"I wouldn't be laughing if I were you. A business card with your name on it, a crime clearly carried out by insiders and your access card used to enter the building in the middle of the night. No other suspects on my list at the moment."

"I didn't use my access card last night," she replied.

"But someone did. Can you prove it wasn't you?"

She could, but not without confirming her alibi was someone currently avoiding the attention of the FBI. She only had one access card, all members of staff did, and it was in her purse, so how could anyone use it in the dead of night? It didn't really matter right now. The evidence wasn't enough to justify an arrest and there were far more concerning aspects to this chain of events. Who wrote the note? What did she have to do with the beginning? And then the biggest question of them all. Who or what was TMM?

- Chapter 9 -

Vikings and Indians

The Shikshapatri was far more than just a book. It was a religious manifesto. It contained two hundred and twelve verses of sacred text written by Swaminarayan who was considered by his followers to be the manifestation of God. The manuscript was adopted by his Hindu followers as a social handbook on how to live a moral and religious existence. It chronicled everything from promoting non-violent behaviour, veganism, respect for others, celibacy, and abstinence from liquor and drugs. Everything that Gabriel frowned upon.

The copy of the Shikshapatri housed in the Bodleian was the oldest copy of the text known to exist and was the last copy presented by Swaminarayan himself to the British Raj in the early part of the nineteenth century. The impact of its theft wasn't purely just a problem for the library's insurers. The news of its loss was about to put British colonial history under the microscope and piss off about half a billion Hindus. Imagine the uproar if the Indians borrowed the Ten Commandments chiselled on two tablets of stone but carelessly left them on the bus on the way home.

It was clear to the investigation team, who spent the rest of the day forensically sweeping the building, that the book was gone. In situations like this the police moved out and the politicians moved in. By four o'clock the Foreign Secretary was photographed looking grave and serious on the steps of the Weston Library. Shortly afterwards a statement was issued by the Indian Prime Minister. Its contents were direct and unambiguous. They held the

VIKINGS AND INDIANS

British government directly responsible for the theft and expected immediate answers.

By five o'clock the Indian Ambassador to Britain had been given his orders and was seen marching down the pavement of Downing Street to lobby the Prime Minister into action. It was bad enough that a piece of Indian heritage was being housed in the hands of its colonial oppressors and quite another for them to lose it completely.

The British response was not altogether surprising.

Politicians hated being accused of inactivity, it made them look weak and ineffectual. They didn't really care what actions were taken as long as they could lay claim to them if it turned out to be successful, or completely dismiss them if they didn't. India was a close ally and major trading partner which meant jobs and prosperity, which also meant votes. Their alliance could not be jeopardised. On top of that over a million citizens with Indian heritage called Britain their home and collectively they might decide to make life complicated.

The evidence from the crime scene was sparse. No group had claimed responsibility and few clues suggested any obvious suspects. There had been no demands made for its safe return. There was no motive and no likelihood that the thief might profit from their crime. There was a market for everything these days but there was almost no way to sell the manuscript without drawing the attention of the authorities. Highly paid advisors scratched their heads to understand why someone would steal it in the first place. Creating disruption was their only conclusion.

The Prime Minister summoned his closest confidants around the Cabinet table to debate their next action and review the evidence. The only clues pointed loosely to a middle-aged member of staff with no police record. No one truly believed it was her, but it was her name at the scene of the crime and her security card last used on the premises before the incident.

It was enough. Enough at least to appease the Indians for a couple of days. By the end of Saturday afternoon, a

VIKINGS AND INDIANS

warrant had been issued for Ally Oldfield's arrest, and minutes later a network of international institutes had been notified.

*****

It was rare for Oxford students to own a car, but a lack of funds was rarely the reason. The majority of graduates had enough family wealth to drive around in brand new Ferraris. Sports cars might be good at helping secure a date, but they were useless in a city of pedestrian walkways and bicycle lanes. As a consequence, most students decided to trade in their expensive wheels for… expensive wheels. Who'd have thought that a collapsible pushbike might be a babe magnet?

As normal when it came to comparisons, Lance was among the exceptions. Following his graduation, he'd moved out of the city centre to an area that was far more car-friendly. He generally only used it when he was moving items to the library or traipsing back and forward to his family's house in Kent, which he did most weekends. Today it was the single reason why Ally liked him, a situation he was completely unprepared for.

After the grilling by DCI Bolton her head was spinning with questions. Who would want to steal the manuscript? Why would they use her business card? How had they done it? Who'd stolen her security pass? What did TMM mean? How did she get here? The final question received an immediate answer from Lance who reminded his boss that she'd arrived by police car and quickly offered to drive her back home. She had little choice but to accept. It felt like time was ticking and something bigger was afoot.

"How do you think they managed it?" asked Lance as they sat in the never-ending traffic that seemed to permanently encircle Oxford and quite possibly the entire country.

"No idea," she said bluntly. "The bigger question is why?"

VIKINGS AND INDIANS

"You said it was priceless. Seems a reasonable motive."

"Not when you consider the message."

"What message?"

Ally reached inside her bag and pulled out her phone. She'd secretively taken a photo of the front of the card that the thief had left inside the display case. She turned the phone around so Lance could read it.

"What do you think it means?" he asked.

"I have no idea at the moment. It's not a coincidence that it's on my business card, though."

"TMM…" Lance whispered to himself as he was prone to do when thinking. "Initials? Acronym?"

"Who knows?"

"Maybe it's text speech," said Lance who wasn't in any way cool enough to know how most of it worked. "Too many mouths?"

"What?"

"Um… take my monkey."

"Yes, that'll be it, 'you are not the beginning, take my monkey'! You've solved it," she replied sarcastically.

"Not that, then. Teach me Mandarin."

"No… I think it's more likely to be initials."

"The Mickey Mouse."

"Please stop talking."

Lance knew compliance was a good reaction to staying on the right side of his cantankerous boss, but it didn't stop him coming up with a plethora of further examples in his head. Lance loved nothing more than solving problems. Crosswords, Sudoku, treasure hunts and puzzles were all nightly hobbies even if they weren't likely to get him a date with the opposite sex anytime soon.

Finally, the traffic lights turned green long enough for two or three more cars to continue their journey another hundred metres before the next set of lights enforced the next roadblock. Lance slipped the car back into neutral and gazed out of the window towards a retail complex that dominated the landscape. A large advertising board loomed over the pavement to brainwash trapped drivers

VIKINGS AND INDIANS

into wanting to eat pizza, go bowling, shop, or jump up and down on a trampoline. Almost without thinking about it his lips moved unconsciously as the subliminal advertising snared its next victim.

"I need some crampons," muttered Lance.

"What?"

"Crampons."

"What's one of those? A crap tampon!?"

"They're spikes you fix to your walking boots."

"But what's that got to do with anything?" said Ally forcefully.

"Oh, nothing. Just didn't know there was one on this retail park."

"One what?"

"A Mountain Warehouse, it sells stuff for outdoor pursuits. I like to hike, I think I told you."

He had but she wasn't the faintest bit interested then and wasn't likely to change her opinion now.

"Mountain," said Ally slowly.

"Mountain Warehouse," repeated Lance slowly.

"The Mountain Men."

"That's a bit sexist, women enjoy hiking, too, you know, and they cater for everyone."

"No, not that, I'm talking about TMM. What if it means 'The Mountain Men'?"

"Who are they?"

"I'm not sure but I'm guessing they like to burn stuff."

"And the men of the mountain will burn," said Lance in response.

"Pull over!" she shouted.

"Um… I'm in traffic, no one's going anywhere."

They waited impatiently for the next set of lights to momentarily switch to green before turning into the retail park.

"Lance, I need you to get on your phone. Look up a company called Mountain Inc."

"Sure, but why?"

VIKINGS AND INDIANS

"Since yesterday the word 'mountain' has come up in conversation twice. Its appearance coincides with the discovery that the FBI have a file on me, Gabriel's surprise visit and one of my business cards turning up at the scene of a crime. I have a strong hunch that something peculiar is happening."

"Who's Gabriel?"

"An idiot. You'd like her. Now, get going, you're apparently good at research, or at least you should be."

"But what am I looking for?"

"Anything unusual."

The pair assaulted their phones with their fingers in the search of any information about the 'Mountain Inc.' There were thousands of pages that made reference to the business. According to the company's own website they'd been around for over a hundred years, mainly working on infrastructure projects in the United States. In the last year the company had been bought by a hedge fund operating from an office in Bermuda. From that point in time onwards any meaningful information was much harder to find. Acquisition by a private company had meant a reduction in the transparency the previously public company was obliged to publish.

"There doesn't seem to be anything unusual," said Lance, whose interests didn't stretch to the corporate world or the construction industry.

"This is why you're my intern, this is teaching right here," exclaimed Ally. "You're missing the obvious, not asking the right questions. Why would a company, who has always worked in the US, suddenly decide to branch out into projects over here? The parliament refurbishments are worth billions, you'd think the government would be desperate to award it to a British firm?"

"I guess the new owners decided on a different strategy. I still don't see what they've got to do with the theft of a valuable Indian book."

"Not just a different strategy... a different everything," replied Ally. "Look, the whole board of directors was

VIKINGS AND INDIANS

replaced only a few months ago and there's something familiar about these names."

"Familiar?"

"Catesby, Percy, Wright, Wintour, Keyes, Bates, Rookwood... I've seen them listed together before."

"Me, too," replied Lance. "There's only one name missing."

"Missing? Who?"

"Guy Fawkes."

"That's it! All of these people were co-conspirators in the Gunpowder Plot of sixteen hundred and five."

"Wow, what are the chances of that?" said Lance quite inconsequentially.

"None."

"Right, now we've worked that out, shall I take you home?"

"You're not getting it, are you?"

Lance's face confirmed his answer.

"The men of the mountain will burn. The Mountain Inc. The Gunpowder Plot. This company isn't planning to refurbish parliament... they're planning to blow it up."

"What? But why?"

"I'm not sure, but I bet it's got something to do with Mario Peruzzi: he's the only person who connects Gabriel and myself."

"But what's that got to do with the theft?"

Ally couldn't answer the question because it was the one part that made no sense. It didn't seem to have anything to do with it, other than that TMM might referring to the Mountain Men. And she didn't really know who or what they were or whether she'd made up the concept in her mind.

"It's been a long day, why don't I drive you home?"

"Don't patronise me, I have more caffeine running through me than a Colombian coffee farm. We need to contact the police."

VIKINGS AND INDIANS

Ally quickly remembered that she'd put PC Dearlove's personal number in her phone case. She immediately rang the number and only reached his voicemail.

"Bollocks, no answer. There's a police station not far from here, isn't there?"

Lance nodded.

"Let's drive," demanded Ally. "Step on it, Lance!"

It was the only time in her entire life she wished Gabriel was there. Lance moved away from the parking lot like a short-sighted eighty-year-old pensioner. Mirror, signal, manoeuvre and they were off, sort of.

*****

The flight touched down on the tarmac and immediately set into motion a now familiar race. Who would be the first person on the plane to get a signal on their mobile phone? A series of harmonious 'pings' ran through the economy section to proclaim the winners. The flight had taken less than two hours, yet people jumped to their devices like they'd been trapped in a cave for a week.

Daniel Hudson was no different, even if it might be argued that the contents of his texts and emails were more important than those of the people around him. The quantity of notifications would also exceed anything his fellow passengers had to contend with. Daniel scanned through the fifty or so new messages that had been trapped in stasis while he was whizzing along at thirty-five thousand feet. Most took up only a fraction of his bandwidth as his filtering skills skipped over pointless internal memos and useless junk to locate more substantial subject lines.

One grabbed his full and immediate attention.

It wasn't easy for the FBI to act unilaterally outside of the United States. The Bureau was, after all, focused mostly on managing threats within its own jurisdiction and only operated outside of its territory if significant external threats existed. Although it had offices in most European countries most of the bureau's work was done supporting local security agencies with intelligence or resources. It was rare for the FBI to take a direct lead in an ongoing investigation outside their borders. Daniel's current brief was one of these and there were more than twelve billion reasons why. If Mario's money was going anywhere it was going back into the US Federal Reserve where it would be immediately swallowed up by the gargantuan national debt pile.

Local countries weren't keen to be seen by their voters to pass responsibility to the 'Yanks', however strong the FBI's reasoning was. Daniel had to jump through hoops to be here at all and there were always conditions attached. He'd have to work with the local law enforcement and national security services, and keep a low profile. He had no jurisdiction to make arrests or to bring charges unless it had been signed off by the Senate or there was an immediate threat to life.

All these steps of bureaucracy had been completed to allow him to be in England legitimately and for only one reason. To question the very person mentioned in the email grabbing his attention. While everyone else clambered to be the first to squeeze their bodies into the aisle with the world's largest hand luggage, Daniel sat immovable, carefully consuming the details in the email. According to Interpol an arrest warrant had been issued for Ally Oldfield. It looked like his next destination was going to be Oxford.

*****

A dilapidated inkjet printer vibrated violently and with a mighty jolt came to life. The drive belt whirred desperately in an attempt to reach the necessary velocity to push the sliding rod across and allow the ink cartridges to deliver their streaky message onto an even more ancient invention, paper. Slowly the black and white picture crept out of the machine to the noise of tortured cogs and worn circuit boards. The table under the machine danced along to its

VIKINGS AND INDIANS

unorthodox samba beat as the roller finally released the paper from its clutches and the whole operation fell silent until the next time it was called into action.

Jim, the custody sergeant, lifted the paper from the printer and analysed its contents. The grainy picture of a middle-aged woman stared out of the page. She didn't look particularly dangerous, but then again, they rarely did in their pictures. Crime wasn't the exclusive pastime of those born with faces only mothers could love. Jim thought she looked like a rather sullen character. Black, frizzy hair drooped around a face full of worry lines that lacked the layers of cosmetic enhancements almost all women of a certain age applied religiously.

He laid the arrest warrant on the table and went hunting around his desk for some Blu Tack. This mugshot had been fast-tracked which meant it had to be actioned as a priority. Soon a dozen police teams would be heading out to arrest Ally Oldfield for the most notable robbery in British history since the Great Train Robbery. In the meantime, everyone else would have their eyes peeled in case they happened to see or hear any reports of her. The public would soon see this very picture appearing on their social media feeds and local television news programmes. If Ally Oldfield had any sense, she'd be miles away by now, Jim thought.

Other than the reason for the arrest warrant the page contained a few additional facts. Weight, height and age were described rather matter-of-factly and at the bottom of the page, along with the phone number to call should anyone spot the fugitive, it read, 'Do not approach, may be dangerous'. Jim knew this was code for 'She wasn't coming quietly'.

The station had been unusually quiet for a Saturday night. Normally by this time of the evening it would be crowded by a collection of damaged souls waiting to be processed. Tonight, there was only one and he was drunk. The best remedy for those arrested while inebriated was to keep them occupied in the reception area until they

VIKINGS AND INDIANS

sobered up. The alternative involved lots of forms and cells full of puke.

"Can... hic... I go now?" asked the drunk politely. "I... honestly feel... I feel fines."

"No, you're not," replied Jim. "You've just spent the last five minutes trying to tie your shoelaces."

The drunk tried to look at his feet but found it impossible to keep his head from wobbling in all directions like a weeble man.

"How'd I do?" he slurred.

"Not well. One of your shoes is under the chair over there," said Jim, pointing at it. "The others on the wrong foot."

"Oh... blah. Shoes... funny things, though," said the drunk who fell onto his knees and was encouraging the lost shoe to come out of its own accord like a lost puppy under a bush. Jim watched with both amusement and something bordering on paternal concern.

"Fancy dress night, was it?" asked Jim conversationally.

"Nooooo," replied the drunk indignantly.

"You normally dress like a Viking when you go out, do you?"

"Nooooo. Sometimes... hic... I go as a Roman."

"I guess the sandals are easier to do up compared to those Viking boots when it comes to laces," Jim replied with a grin.

"Yeah. Av you got... my helmet?"

"Yes, Mr Catchpole, but I think we'll keep hold of it, and you, for a little longer. We'll probably keep the broadsword indefinitely, though."

"No, sir," he muttered, looking in the wrong direction. "You can't do that. It's... hic... from the Battle of Stamford Bridge."

"Chelsea fan, are you?"

"No! Viking battle... old days... ages ago. Took it from a Cossack."

Mr Catchpole gripped the counter to aid his legs, which were desperately attempting an uncoordinated campaign

VIKINGS AND INDIANS

of not falling off the floor. Drool cascaded down the side of his mouth and collected in the matted mass of a fake beard while both of his eyes were exploring the insides of his eyelids. When the door to the police station opened and two people rushed in, he attempted to turn to face the enemy but the tiny change in air pressure was enough to send him plummeting into a heap somewhere out of Jim's vision. The custody sergeant immediately dragged himself over the top of the desk to see what damage the drunk Viking had sustained and whether he'd have to spend the next week completing an injury report. Fortunately, Catchpole's body had decided the floor was as good a place as any to aid sobriety. He raised a shaky thumb to confirm it.

"I have important information," said Ally, defiantly tapping on the desk to get Jim's attention. "You must act immediately, or you'll find me a rather unpleasant visitor."

Jim looked up from the crumpled drunk lying in a pile on his reception floor and into the eyes of an angry-looking woman not much taller than the counter. Instinctively he glanced at the warrant still in his hands and then back at the woman. It was her. Maybe she'd decided to come quietly?

"Oh. Right, good choice," said Jim. "It's a lot easier for everyone this way."

"There's nothing easy about it. People are going to die!"

"Die?" replied Jim, double-checking the warrant which he'd placed on the desk out of her eyeline. There was nothing about that on there. What terrible deeds had she been responsible for over the last couple of hours?

"Yes, I expect hundreds of people will be annihilated," she barked.

"Not just a thief, then?" Jim mumbled to himself under his breath. Her demeanour looked anxious and a fire of intent burnt in her eyes as if possessed.

"No, not just a thief. A mass murderer, too."

VIKINGS AND INDIANS

Jim considered the distant past when they might have trained for situations like this. It certainly wasn't business as usual. A normal day consisted of some mild cases of antisocial behaviour, the occasional domestic disagreement, and drunk Vikings. Actually, drunk Vikings were less common, but people suspected of mass murder and thefts that resulted in major diplomatic crises were almost unprecedented. What was he supposed to do? Could he handle it on his own? Everyone else was out of the station... looking for her. Maybe the best thing was to keep her calm and try to get an arrest done before she bolted for it.

"These are very serious crimes," said Jim calmly.

"You're telling me! Parliament's about to be blown up."

"Terrorism!"

"Of course. What would you call it?" said Ally, not entirely sure why the man wasn't writing more of the details down or asking more pertinent questions. Just her luck to find the only police station where the custody officer was working his first day.

"Is he involved, too?" asked Jim, pointing at Lance whose lanky frame was looming over Ally's diminutive figure.

"Yes, he did the research."

"Brains of the operation, is he?"

"Has anyone... hic... got a fag?"

"I've told you, Mr Catchpole, it's no smoking in here."

"I'll take... harrumph... an e-cig."

"Also not allowed."

"Are you going to do something or not?" demanded Ally, smashing her fist on the counter.

"When is this going to happen?" asked Jim.

"It's probably happening right now and yet you're stood here doing nothing. Call for reinforcements, alert the authorities."

"I'm more than capable of dealing with two suspects already on the premises with the doors locked," he replied,

VIKINGS AND INDIANS

pressing a button under the desk that automatically sealed the only exit.

"This is ridiculous!" shouted Ally. "If you don't call in the counterterrorist team right now, I can't be held accountable for my actions."

"You looking... hic... at me!" the Viking shouted aggressively.

"Right, that's it," said Jim, panicking. "You have the right to remain silent..."

"I don't... hic... like being trapped. Makes me angry."

"That goes for you as well, Mr Catchpole. Anything you do say..."

"Bollocks!" shouted Ally.

"Will be taken in evidence..."

"You stupid man, they're out there right now about to cause havoc across London and you're busy arresting a Viking for being drunk."

"I'm not reading him the caution, I'm reading it to you, too," replied Jim, slightly confused as to what was happening.

"Us! We've just come in to report a possible crime and you're trying to arrest us. No wonder the police have a bad reputation in these parts."

"He's a big lad..." stammered Catchpole pointing into the sky at Lance. "Nice shoes. Saxon, are they?"

"Slush Puppies," replied Lance who was feeling uncomfortable by the whole situation.

A moment later his shoes were a mass of suede and vomit as the drunk Viking unloaded an evening's consumption over them. In the commotion Steve slipped a pair of handcuffs over Ally's wrists and repeated his initial reading of the caution.

"Ally Oldfield, you are under arrest. You have the right to remain..."

"Silent! I won't!" she shouted. "The Mountain Men are coming whether you arrest me or not."

- Chapter 10 -

Confession

England, 1605

A dirty linen curtain twitched uncertainly before finally being dragged gently to one side. Behind it sat a flustered-looking priest on a small stool. The wooden confessional around him had seen better days, but its condition was no real surprise. In the past sixty years, since the death of Henry VIII, Catholicism had been outlawed, reinstated, promoted, banned and finally, with the Act of Settlement, officially tolerated but unofficially persecuted. Even the most ardent Catholic worshipper wasn't quite sure what the rules were from one day to the next. In recent history most of the faith's churches had been burnt or sacked, and most preachers killed or banished. Those that remained resolute to the old religion, most of whom were from the North East of England, had to make do with whatever facilities they could find. Like this one, most were hidden away in rural homes or down quiet, secluded streets.

What had once been the beating heart of society was now nothing more than a faint pulse. Father Tesimond had no church to be proud of. No stained glass to beckon in its worshippers. No sanctuary for those in need. Services would be delivered wherever there were Catholics, rather than calling them to him or attempting to convert them. Like a travelling salesman he roamed from safe house to safe house supporting all those trustworthy enough to listen.

Today's location for carrying out God's work was Gayhurst Court in Buckinghamshire, home of Everard

CONFESSION

Digby. The confessional booth here had been rescued fifty years ago when the local Catholic church suffered at the hands of Protestant violence. It had scorch damage, chips in the wood from wayward blades and only three original legs. Its condition was symbolic of the faith it stood for. Sometimes you had to manage with less and this was certainly better than conducting a confessional on a park bench.

"Forgive me, Father, for I have sinned," said a voice from the other side of the curtain.

"Well, that's a given, you're practising Catholicism," replied the priest.

"Yes, I'm aware of that, but that's not why I'm here to confess."

"How long has it been since your last confession?" asked the priest in a tired voice.

"I'd say it was about… thirty minutes ago," guessed the man.

"If that!" replied Tesimond who had met this particular man approximately half an hour ago in the same beaten-up booth wondering when he might get back to some good, old-fashioned Jesuit praying.

"I've thought of something else…" explained the man.

"What is it this time, Guido?"

"Don't call me that, you know I don't like it. It's like having my mother behind the curtain."

"Alright, Guy, don't get touchy. Let's hear it," sighed Tesimond.

He'd heard enough confessions that day to last a lifetime. Each one had challenged his faith, his position amongst the Jesuit clergy and the strength of the religious seal that conjoined the confessor with the priest. First Robert Catesby had dropped the revelation that they were planning to blow up the parliament building and wanted to know if it was morally acceptable. The moral dilemma hinged on whether it was alright to kill lots of people you didn't like even if you killed a couple you did. In normal

CONFESSION

times this would have been met with a straightforward 'no', but these were not normal times.

To some people, Catesby's cause was justified.

When 'some people' just happened to be the Pope it did have a habit of swaying pronouncements in your favour. Robert Catesby's plan was to remove King James and his ministers and replace the monarch with someone of a Catholic persuasion. They'd identified James's daughter, Elizabeth as the right fit, even though she actually had no Catholic persuasions whatsoever. Catesby felt because she was young and innocent, she might be persuaded to have the right persuasions if they held her captive and threatened to kill her favourite pony.

This plan, although not without its ethical challenges, was very much in line with Papal policy, and in the name of God pretty much anything could be approved. This information had forced Father Tesimond to seek his own confession in order to review his own personal feelings towards it. Then shortly afterwards, Guy Fawkes had appeared to seek advice on whether he and the other conspirators should write a letter warning any Catholic Lords to call in sick on the fifth of November, the day parliament was due to be opened and sent skyward.

Father Tesimond's conscience had barely got a breather before Fawkes was back for a second time.

"I'm worried," said Fawkes.

"I'm pretty sure 'worried' doesn't count as a sin. Guilt, yes. Envy is definitely in, I might even let you get away with mild annoyance but…"

"Oswald, this is serious."

"I get it, I'm wearing a stupid hat, aren't I? It's not just for show."

"I can't see the hat, it's behind the curtain."

Why was he wearing the hat? He immediately took it off and felt a lot more comfortable.

"I've come to you not just because you are a man of God," said Guy tentatively, "but also because you are my friend and I have known you since school."

CONFESSION

"Ah yes, the Royal School of William and Mary in the Horse Fayre, happier days when boys sought nothing more than a peck on the cheek from a maiden or squabbled in the grass over a dropped farthing. A time of innocence before adulthood brought tougher choices like which religion should I worship, what do I believe in, and should I stack thirty-six barrels of gunpowder under the seat of the establishment and trigger genocide?!"

"I think we've already been through that one thirty minutes ago," replied Guy bitterly. "You said on balance it was probably alright to do it as long as all of us dedicated our lives to pure thoughts and deeds."

"Then what else is there to be worried about? Isn't that enough!?"

"There is something else."

"Are you also secretly planning to steal the moon, or melt the King of Sweden? There's a limit to God's leniency, you know."

"No, nothing like that. I was given a great duty and I'm worried that if our plot should fail, I may not be able to fulfil it."

"What great duty?"

"I am the Mountain Man," said Guy grandiosely.

"You're the what!?"

"I have been granted great wealth and knowledge in order to stimulate the rebalancing of the establishment's grip on power. It is a calling and those who are chosen, as I was, are known as the Mountain Men. It is my duty to pass it on to the next in line. Someone who is worthy of the responsibility."

"Right," said Tesimond uncertain as to whether Guy might have been sniffing too much gunpowder and had inadvertently caused himself a minor brain seizure. "Have you got anyone in mind?"

"Yes… you."

"Me?! Why me? I'm not a freedom fighter, I'm a man of the Church."

CONFESSION

"You don't need to kill anyone, it's one of the rules, actually."

"What rules?" sighed Tesimond, desperate to witness his very first miracle, preferably one that made him disappear without warning.

"Three of them, you need to listen carefully."

"Guy, I'm not an imbecile. I'm sure I can remember three simple pieces of information."

"Um, you know what they call you?"

"No."

"Father Forgetful?"

"Who does?"

"Almost everyone."

"Why?"

"Well, once Rookwood told you in confession that he didn't want anyone to know that he'd given his wife syphilis and then later that week you told me in the tavern."

There was a long, thoughtful pause from the priest. "I don't remember that."

"There you go, exactly my point."

"Ok, so I sometimes I forget things. Anyway, what were these five rules?"

"Three rules."

"Whatever," huffed Father Tesimond, losing interest.

"The first rule is to only use non-violent rebellion. Number two is only to use the wealth for…"

"Let me stop you," said Tesimond, leaning into the curtain, not convinced he'd heard him correctly. "You're about to plant enough gunpowder under parliament to blast it to the sun and you're telling me your mission is non-violent! That's like pretending that adultery is non-sexual or that bowel surgery is non-invasive."

"It's a one-off. Even the first Mountain Man used gunpowder: he told me himself, so I think it's allowed."

"Oh, so I'm guessing your definition of non-violent is a little different from mine. I think non-violent means 'no one gets hurt', while your version is more like 'no one gets

CONFESSION

hurt as long as they're not within a one-mile radius', something like that?"

"Rule two," said Guy, attempting to move the conversation on, as it was getting harder to justify it even to himself. "The funds that I have left you must be used for this cause only."

"Guy, do you know what vows Jesuit priests take?"

"Not really. Something like 'Thou shall not touch people inappropriately'?"

"There are four vows we commit to: poverty, obedience, stability and chastity."

"The non-touching part is in there, then," added Guy, making a mini-celebration with his arm and clenched fist.

"Yes, it is, and as much as I'd love to spend all of your money on a nice summer retreat, I'm not allowed."

"Good, then I've no need to worry that you might misspend it. I've left instructions for how the money will pass to you if anything happens to me. Sign here please."

Guy slid a roll of parchment under the curtain. It wasn't very complicated, partly because lawyers weren't so keen on terms and conditions in the seventeenth century as they would be in the future. Tesimond quickly scanned the page and before he could open his mouth a quill dripping with ink also came under the curtains.

"I'm guessing the third rule is to pass it on to someone worthy?" stated Tesimond, pushing the signed document back to Guy.

"Precisely."

"Do I get any clues on what 'worthy' means to you, as we seem to agree on so little else today."

"A man of honour, stature and suffering oppression. Someone with leadership skills who can muster others to action. Most importantly someone who won't be corrupted by the power itself."

"Right. You know I'm only doing this because I'm a friend. I don't really want anything to do with it."

"I appreciate it."

CONFESSION

"And what happens if you get caught with a pile of gunpowder and the King's men come after me?"

"I'm sure they don't execute priests," said Guy confidently.

"Have you walked down London Bridge recently?"

"No, I've been in Spain."

"Then next time have a look at some of the decapitated heads on the ends of pikes: quite a few priests up there. What's left of them at least."

"We'll do everything we can to protect you," added Guy.

"I feel immensely reassured," lied Tesimond.

"But will you do it?" asked Guy desperately.

"Yes, allegiance to friendship is more important than allegiance to the Crown, particularly one that no longer recognises my religion."

"Great, if the worst happens to me, you are the next Mountain Man. Good luck," said Guy, jumping from his chair and having lifted a load from his chest.

"Hold on!" shouted Tesimond. "You've only told me about three of the five rules!"

- Chapter 11 -

Boom!

In the last twenty years the advancement in scientists' ability to accurately forecast biological eventualities is nothing short of remarkable. There are tests to predict which of us will suffer some terrible genetic disease, which of us is predisposed to obesity, and the probability of a given couple producing offspring with blue eyes. All of this is possible because a group of highly dedicated geeks mapped something called the human genome. It's like a Haynes manual for building a human, but, like all instruction manuals, it's not always easy to decipher. Occasionally pages will be lost or skipped, or the reader will simply lack the understanding to follow. Even within the vast gigabytes of the Human Genome project some unusual characteristics of human behaviour can't be explained.

Deep inside all of us, dodging in-between the double helix of life like a racing driver navigating a chicane, are attributes that wear a cloaking device and can't be explained by counting the pairs of nucleobases. However much the chain is assessed it will never explain why incredibly attractive women date ugly men, why anyone might voluntarily eat a durian fruit, or why someone would attach a piece of elastic to their feet and jump from a tall building only to bounce halfway back up again.

They will also never develop a test to explain why people with absolutely nothing to hide will feel an immediate sense of guilt the moment they come into contact with a blue flashing light or a policeman. When this occurs the instinctive response within every human

BOOM!

being is to convince themselves that they've secretly stashed half a kilo of cocaine up their arse, are knowingly holding fourteen illegal immigrants in their basement, and have recently fiddled their tax return to the tune of six million pounds. Hands will sweat like sprinklers at the thought of the polygraph test that will clearly prove their guilt, their eyes will find it impossible to look at their accuser, and even light questioning will bring a full and lengthy confession for every unsolved crime from the last fifty years.

On this particular Monday morning it was Ally's turn to engage the paranoia. Over the last thirty-six hours, held captive in a soulless room with only a small window and a metal door with a wide cat flap that only opened from the other side, these doubts had festered. It didn't matter that Ally was a resolute character known to stand up for herself in the face of anything life threw at her. This was a new experience, or at least she thought it was. The longer she'd sat there, the more a vague sense of familiarity tried to invade her soul like existential rising damp.

The intense claustrophobia, the lonely isolation of being separated from the people you relied on, the fear of not knowing what came next had all joined forces to infiltrate her psyche and play tricks on her mind. A distant, hidden memory wedeled through her subconscious like a slalom skier trying to dodge the gates of truth. It wasn't a recent memory, if it was a real one at all. It came from somewhere deep and forgotten. Locked away in her memory banks to be ignored, hopefully forever. But now the solitary situation of her cell was encouraging her to release it. Struggling to decide whether the thought frightened or intrigued her, finally she closed her eyes and attempted to block out the present and allow it the freedom to speak to her.

The relative comfort of the grey-daubed prison walls faded from her vision and her memories propelled her backwards in time to chase a wispy and faint vision. She physically shuddered as the haze cleared and she was

BOOM!

placed in the centre of a dirty basement devoid of natural light. A biting breeze assaulted the crack under the heavy door and whistled through the gaps in the shoddy brickwork. Her head rested on her chest and was surrounded by matted, dirty hair that drooped down like a curtain. Like the first drops from a rain cloud just breaking, a single trail of tears ran off her face and bounced off her shoes. Pretty shoes. Shiny red with a strap and buckle that extended over the top of her feet to stop them falling off. Underneath the leather, speckled drops of blood contrasted against the white cotton of her stained socks.

A sobbing sound bounced off the walls of history like a voice concealed in a box, finally released after forty years. How old was she? Five or six? Maybe younger. Where was she? Why would anyone leave a young girl there to face such horrors?

Suddenly she was consumed with a fear she'd consigned deep within her soul at the same time as the memory itself. It was an uncontrollable panic, visceral and malicious. It carried a clear message: nothing would ever be the same again. The memory drew the young girl's attention to the other side of the door where a conversation in an alien language was taking place between surly, harsh voices. Animated and angry, their intentions belied any ounce of humanity towards the youngster. Panic increased a further notch.

They were coming for her.

The cat flap in the door to her prison cell opened and Ally leapt out of her bed. She let out a blood-curdling scream that she didn't know she was capable of as the past was substituted by the present. Two seconds later the door creaked open and a giant of a man cast the room in shadow. The light from the corridor skipped off his bald head where a generous amount of sweat was doing its best to cling to the slippery cone of his crown.

"Doctor Oldfield, I'm Daniel Hudson," he stated sternly. "You need to come with me."

BOOM!

Guilt returned. Whatever had happened in the past was catching up with her. There was so much of her early life she didn't remember, or didn't want to, that it would be impossible to defend distant crimes once committed. Clearly if the vision was anything to go by, she'd been a master criminal toddler no doubt responsible for some heinous crime that was only now coming to light. It was no wonder she didn't remember it. Maybe this was the real reason the FBI had a file on her. Maybe they'd had one for decades.

Meekly she followed Hudson out of the cell in a manner uncharacteristic for a woman who only did what she wanted with little concern for the wishes of others. A journey of only ten or twenty feet brought them through the internal corridors of the small-town police station that seemed quite unprepared for the magnitude of the event. Daniel entered a small room that only differed from her own cell because of the table in the middle and the tape recorder that sat on it. In one corner of the room stood a man with his arms crossed. It was clear that these two weren't local law enforcers. The absence of official uniforms was enough to tell her that.

Daniel pointed to the other seat and settled into his own. His immense frame, which would have looked more at home in the defensive line of an American football team, levitated miraculously over the edges of the chair. Ally took a breath to encourage the oxygen to stimulate her back into the here and now. Whatever she'd remembered about her past would have to wait: she had to remember why she was here in the present.

"I understand you have refused to call your legal representative?"

Ally nodded.

"Your funeral."

Daniel leant to one side of the table and removed a brown file from a briefcase that was out of Ally's eyeline. He placed it respectfully on the table in front of him and opened the front cover. He pressed play on the tape recorder and started to read.

"Doctor Alison Oriana Oldfield, Lecturer in Medieval Languages at Oxford University, resident of Stanton St. John, born October the second, Nineteen Sixty-Nine. Adopted by Derek and Martha Brownlee in May of Nineteen Seventy-Five. Attended St Andrew's School for Girls in Lincoln before graduating with distinction from Durham University. After graduation you took several jobs working as a waitress: several of those establishments were closed down because you complained about hygiene," said Daniel, looking up from the file. "You must have been popular!"

"Do I look bothered?"

"No. From there you started and completed a PhD for which you are now rightly referred to as Doctor Oldfield, before gaining your first post as a professor. Wrote your first book about Nostradamus in the mid-Nineteen Nineties for which you were paid a decent advance before writing several more where you weren't so fortunate. After the millennium you wrote further books on other notable historical figures and unexplained events that weren't successful enough to be listed in your file and are now out of print. I think that probably sums up most of your life... Sorry, hold on, this is important... Two years ago you saved the world from Armageddon and last week you stole an incredibly valuable manuscript from your own museum. Anything to add?"

As Hudson correctly summarised the highlights of her life, until the last line at least, Ally's granite-thick exterior, which had momentarily crumbled into dust back in her prison cell, was being hastily rebuilt complete with turrets and a miniature catapult. Ally licked her fingers and mimicked the opening of her own file and pretended to turn the pages.

"I don't seem to have much on you," she glared across the table. "Maybe you're so insignificant it's not worth knowing."

BOOM!

"Today I'm the most significant person in this building, probably the whole city," bragged Hudson. "Even a woman of your renowned research skills couldn't compile even the simplest of résumés on me. All you need to know is that I am here to find out what you know."

"Your accent is rough, but still quite easy to place," she continued. "American obviously, but more specifically from the hoarseness in which you pronounce vowels it's from North Indiana, although unquestionably you've spent much of the last twenty years in other parts of the country. The accent has been softened and you've picked up some of the verbal traits of those born on the East Coast, so I'd say you now live around Philadelphia. The accent, attire and cockiness mean you work for the FBI. You may be very proud of your file on me, but as I already knew you had one and don't dispute the contents other than the last sentence, you may as well drop the smugness. You see, some of us don't need computers to do our research."

"I only have one question for you, Dr Oldfield," replied Daniel, ignoring her attempts to rile him. "Where is it?"

"How should I know?"

"Because I think you've always known where it is."

"I've always known where it was, I don't know where it is now."

"So, you confess you had knowledge of its whereabouts," said Daniel, sitting forward awkwardly, slightly surprised at his speed of progress.

"Of course. It's been in the same place for decades. People come from all over the world to see it."

"Hang on," said Daniel pensively. "What are you talking about?"

"The Shikshapatri, the reason you're holding me here under some crazy theory that I would steal from my own employer with zero motive and even less experience."

"I'm not interested in the book! Do you think they'd draft the FBI in for a minor theft and some pointless bilateral disagreement? I'm talking about the money."

"What money?"

BOOM!

"Mario's money."

"Peruzzi! I haven't thought about that idiot for more than two years. I don't know anything about his money. You're wasting my time."

"I never waste time."

"Money is the last thing anyone should be thinking about. I came to the police station because I wanted to warn the authorities about a potential threat to the British government. In return for my civic duty, I'm arrested and questioned by an accountant pretending to be a law enforcer."

Daniel's thought-process stopped dead in its tracks. Inside the four walls of Ally's cell the last sixty-six hours had passed by very differently for her than it had for anyone with access to a television or mobile device. She'd had neither. Life had effectively been frozen and there was no way she'd know what had happened.

"What threat?" asked Daniel going with his instincts to learn more before revealing what he and everyone else on the outside knew to be true.

"Someone is planning to blow up parliament."

"I see. Who exactly?"

"I believe they're called the Mountain Men. I'm not sure who or what they are right now but I believe they were also behind the theft at the Weston."

"The Mountain Men," mumbled Daniel incoherently as if the name was stuck on his tongue forever. "What's the connection between the Weston and parliament?"

Ally explained how she'd made a link between the note left at the scene of the crime and the company recently employed to renovate the heart of British democracy. She rattled through the names listed on the company's website and the correlation to those who tried to carry out the Gunpowder Plot more than four hundred years ago. With every name Daniel's eyes widened until they almost fell out onto the table. He carefully wrote the information on a pad in pencil. When she'd finished, he grabbed his tablet from his case and opened a photo app. He turned it around so

BOOM!

Ally could see the screen. Swiping to the left like an impatient Tinder subscriber, pictures of envelopes flashed in front of her.

"Catesby, Percy, Rookwood... they're all here," he said.

"What are they?"

"Letters sent by Mario a week ago."

"Maybe you should arrest him, then, rather than me," huffed Ally.

"We would, if he wasn't dead. This was all that he left after passing away but every one of them is addressed to a location that no longer exists. I think they have something to do with your Mountain Men."

"Was there one addressed to Guy Fawkes?"

"No."

"There's a letter addressed to each of the conspirators but not to the person most associated with the plot. Why?" said Ally mostly to herself. "What's inside the letters?"

"That's classified. I'm doing the interrogation, not you."

"What you need to do is alert people to the threat, investigate the Mountain Inc and check for massive piles of gunpowder under the floor of parliament."

"There's no need," replied Daniel passively.

"Of course there is. Don't you see the link?!"

"Yes, but it's too late," explained Daniel, turning the tablet around and logging into the national news feed before passing it over to her.

"Shit!"

The photo that leapt out of the screen was the very definition of chaos. Ally was immediately cast back twenty years to the skyline of New York after the terror attacks that hit the Twin Towers. Smoke and dust blocked the autumn sky, flames licked the horizon and a colony of human ants scurried for safety. The tower of Big Ben no longer stretched into the sky, instead it lay semi-submerged in the filthy waters of the Thames, crushed and smouldering. Down the length and breadth of Waterloo

BOOM!

Bridge lumps of rock, chiselled by masons hundreds of years before, had impaled the roofs of cars or crashed and tumbled onto the road like giant wayward bowling balls. Molten stained glass streamed down the side of the building from the inferno that still glowed like a volcano in the guts of the building. The roof of the Palace of Westminster had been eviscerated by the force of the explosion. Nothing of it was left in place.

For a moment Ally forgot where she was, absorbed by the live coverage streaming out of every web page from every angle around London's broken heart. Reports were updating the situation minute by minute and mercifully at this stage it appeared fatalities were low as a result of the building being mostly unoccupied at the moment of the explosion. On the bridge a line of the wounded were propped up against railings, bloodied and bruised from the debris that had showered down on anyone in the vicinity of Westminster. A cavalcade of ambulances stretched out in every direction.

"Is that what you were expecting?" said Daniel calmly.

"No. I think it's just the beginning."

"Don't you mean 'you' are not the beginning?" replied Daniel with reference to the note at the museum.

"You're not suggesting I had anything to do with this, are you? I've been stuck in here, for a start."

"You're not a suspect, but yes, I do think you have something to do with it," replied Daniel, presenting Ally with the hard copy of the letter Mario had written to him. Inside were written the three names that at the time were unknown to him. "He sent me this."

"Mario?" she asked pointedly.

"Yes. It appears he wanted to place the three of you at the centre of this chaos."

"Now I know why you have a file on me and why you have been driving around after Gabriel."

"Driving around after her?" said Daniel quizzically.

"Yes, she went on the run… so I'm told."

BOOM!

As much as Ally found Gabriel to be a vain and pointless blot on her otherwise tranquil existence in Stanton, she had no desire to drop her in the hands of the FBI, whatever she might have done. If they were going to catch her it would be a good, clean fight and Ally didn't believe the authorities needed extra help to do it. Gabriel would probably get caught buying clothes at a shopping centre.

"I've no record of that," said Daniel, checking through another file. "She's not high-profile enough for that level of attention. She's only a hacker."

"And prone to histrionics, it would appear."

"What do you make of this sentence?" said Daniel writing on a piece of paper in a rather rushed and illegible style.

'and very brightly the men of the mountain will burn'

"Just look at the news," replied Ally. "There's your answer. Clearly Mario is using the prophecy to get his revenge on us after the other parts of it were proven to be fake."

"I think it goes further than that. What if these Mountain Men are real and have always been there?" said Daniel, careful not to reveal too much of his conversation with Diego.

"What do you mean?"

"A secret society bent on disrupting the established world order by passing their knowledge down a chain through history. What if Fawkes was one of them?"

"Then why isn't Guy Fawkes on one of the letters?"

"Because Mario is playing a game. He's challenging us to understand the rules."

"Pretty sick game. I always thought that it was the Mountain Men themselves who were going to burn, but it seems these were instructions left for others. But who? Show me who else was sent a letter," demanded Ally, holding her hand out towards the tablet.

BOOM!

"You're a suspect."

"According to your file I also 'saved mankind' and it looks like I might have to do it again. If you want to solve this, Agent Hudson, you'll have to show me what you know or risk seeing another national landmark go up in flames. What if they strike elsewhere? Washington perhaps?"

What harm would it do? thought Hudson. If she was involved, she'd know who they were anyway, and he might notice a change in her body language which might implicate her. If she wasn't, she might just provide the breakthrough needed to identify the real perpetrators. Hudson opened his Camera Roll on the tablet and started to scroll through all the letters that had been left by Mario.

Ally had an amazing capacity to remember facts. Others had often commented that she had a photographic memory, although she'd often respond that it was simply about having something most people lacked, concentration. The names flashed momentarily in front of her and she repeated each one as many times to herself as she could before the next name appeared. Giulio Genoino, Philip Beaumont, Voltaire, Georges Couthon, Arnold Ruge, Élie Marion, Christopher Wren, Alberto Bayo and Jules Guesde. The final picture that scanned past her was one of Daniel dressed as a superhero, possibly Iron Man.

"What do you make of it?"

"I think men of a certain age shouldn't wear fancy dress," replied Ally disdainfully.

Daniel turned the tablet and frowned. "Office party, sometimes you have to act like everyone else does. It's not something I'm keen on doing."

"At least we agree on one thing."

"What about the names, do you recognise any of them?" asked Daniel.

"No," she lied. "But I think you and your team might need a history lesson. If this is not the beginning, then those names hold the key to what happens next."

BOOM!

More than one of the names on the list was familiar to her and, although she wasn't able to place all of them immediately, it wouldn't take her long to do so once they saw fit to release her. Then all she'd have to do is work out the sequence of the Mountain Men.

"We know that the Oblivion Doctrine had a massive network of unnamed collaborators working on its content through open-source software," said Daniel. "There might be thousands of people out there ready to act on Mario's behalf and he might have set this in progress years ago."

"Then we need to work out the pattern before they try to re-create history again."

Daniel nodded. He wasn't ready to trust Ally yet, but it wouldn't hurt if she was using her own skills to figure out his problem.

"I only have one further question for you at this time, Dr Oldfield. Are you familiar with the name Radu Goga?"

"No, was it on one of the letters?"

Daniel ignored her response. "I appreciate your mild co-operation, now I have to interview your accomplice."

"Accomplice?"

"Yeah, the lanky kid with the specs. Apparently, he's set fire to his cell twice, even though there's nothing combustible in there."

"At least you don't have to work with him."

- Chapter 12 -

The Reign of Terror

The longest the police were allowed to hold Ally and Lance without charge was forty-eight hours. Once that point had elapsed late on Monday evening and no extension was approved, they had no choice but to release them. Ultimately the only evidence the police had was a business card, Ally's authorised access to the museum and no forensics. No fingerprints, no footage of any suspects, no trace on the book and no witnesses. If Ally had been responsible for the theft, she'd done an excellent job of hiding her tracks. Although there wasn't enough evidence to make formal charges that didn't mean it would be the end of the matter. Ally knew that before the day was out it wouldn't just be Ms Honeywell staking out her small, picturesque cottage.

Ally was led from her cell to the reception room at about eight o'clock in the evening. Lance was already there signing the paperwork to have the possessions taken from him after his arrest returned. Some of his clothes had clear signs of flame damage and his body swayed even more erratically than usual. The bags under his eyes suggested he'd missed the fortnightly bin run. As he caught sight of Ally a shudder ran through his body as if permanently scarred by the experience. The custody sergeant behind the desk pulled out a plastic zip bag of Ally's possessions and placed it on the desk.

"Sign," he said gruffly in a manner that suggested giving items back meant the person had in some way 'got away with it'.

THE REIGN OF TERROR

The friendly face of PC Dearlove appeared from a back office.

"I'll give you a lift home," he said. "After all, I know where it is."

Another officer encouraged Lance to follow him, but the discombobulation of the last two days had settled on Lance like dust on an old picture frame. The only thing he was capable of was incoherent mumbling and delirious tremors. In the end the officer grabbed him by the hand and led him away like a chimpanzee being escorted onto the set for the filming of a PG tips advert.

The city of Oxford was a much less impressive sight at night than it was in daylight. Its famous architecture was mostly in shadow and only the lamp-posts and passing headlights illuminated their way through the darkness. By the time they broke through the suburbs and plunged into the countryside, only the first fifty feet were visible in front of the car. The journey passed without conversation, but it was far from silent. In a manner that Ally was now used to, PC Dearlove talked endlessly, frightened by the thought of a pause extending for longer than a second. All Ally did was think and occasionally nod, mostly as a result of the countless potholes that bounced both of them up and down.

Dearlove gibbered on about the state of the roads, the state of the police force, the state of Oxford City Football Club and the State of Alaska, where he was planning to go on a cruise. Occasionally he offered some words of encouragement regarding the state of her own case and the likelihood that everything would 'blow over' whilst being careful not to give too much away that might affect any trial against her if it didn't. Ally didn't care about any of it. All she cared about was the list of names she'd seen on the tablet and repeating them, so she didn't forget any.

As the police car approached the cottage the figure of a wrinkled, nosy pensioner unsurprisingly blocked access to the driveway. Ally nodded her appreciation for the lift before quickly alighting from the car with the intention of

THE REIGN OF TERROR

trying every tactic she knew to avoid contact with the one-person picket line.

"Police car, me darlin', not good for the village, you know."

"Not good for the village!" replied Ally angrily.

"Village of the Year competition soon, me darlin', very important."

Ally stopped what she'd planned would be an unabated dash for the front door.

"No, it's not important."

"It's good for the community."

"A group of pompous fossils with double-barrelled names measuring the colour spectrum of the rhododendrons, the quality of butter in the local scones, and counting the number of Kings who've stayed at the Inn over the past thousand years. Why would any of that matter?"

"Tourism, me darlin'."

"You hate tourists. You said they made the place look messy!"

"They don't have to come just because we win."

"Then what's the fucking point!?" replied Ally, losing her cool after what had been a rather difficult few days.

"Pride in the village. Won't look good if we have..." She paused. "... A felon living here."

"I haven't been charged, so you shouldn't worry."

"No smoke without fire, me darlin', is there?"

"Then you've obviously never heard of a smoke grenade. Now if you don't leave me alone, I might be forced to buy one and lob it out of my window to ward you out of my garden. Goodnight."

Ally left Ms Honeywell to stew in the garden. Inside the sanctuary of the cottage the lights were off, and a soundless tranquillity filled the air. This was how coming home should feel like. Whether permanent or temporary, Gabriel had gone. The first irritating domino, which had kicked off an otherwise perplexing long weekend, was no longer primed and waiting to knock over a load more trouble. A

THE REIGN OF TERROR

weight lifted and tiredness suddenly crept through her mind and muscles. Since waking on Saturday morning, the best solid stint of sleep she'd had was about an hour. On the pad in the kitchen she wrote down the names she'd seen during her interview with Daniel before dragging herself up the stairs to her bedroom. It was Tuesday tomorrow and the university would expect her back at work.

Ally was woken by the smell of coffee. She'd experienced a bout of deep sleep that had the effect of questioning whether she'd slept at all. No sooner had her head hit the pillow and her functions had gone into shutdown than an aroma of coffee was dragging her away from it. It must have been later than normal because her morning alarm call of the dawn chorus had finished, and the birds had flown off to concentrate on lunch rather than breakfast. Although almost impossibly short she still felt rested and cleansed from the strife of the preceding days. Maybe today would bring better times. She opened her eyes and all hope was shot down by a wig-wearing French girl wielding a cafetière.

"Morning."

"God!" swore Ally before trying to suffocate herself with a pillow.

"No," replied Gabriel in case Ally was in any way confused. "Didn't think you believed in God?"

"I think your existence is enough proof that He doesn't exist. I thought, hoped even, that you'd left."

"I did leave for a while. Went shopping. Bicester Village. Got some amazing bargains."

"People on the run don't go shopping at one of the busiest shopping centres in the country. Hold on, you said the bank had frozen your accounts."

"Well, I thought they had because I couldn't get any money out, but then I remembered another reason why that might be."

"You didn't have any money in your account, did you?" replied Ally.

THE REIGN OF TERROR

"No."

"How did you go shopping, then?"

"I borrowed some."

"Who from?"

"You. There's a pot in the kitchen full of notes."

"Yes, I know, that's where I put it."

"Well, I borrowed some."

"You didn't borrow it, you stole it."

"Tomato, tomato."

"Kitchen, five minutes, we need to talk," growled Ally.

Once Ally had showered, changed and consumed the entire contents of the cafetière she marched down into the kitchen. Gabriel was on one of the stools against the kitchen bar fiddling with her hair and staring vacantly out of the window. Waiting for things to happen used to be easy. You just took out your phone and surfed the internet until the next stimulus arrived. Without it, Gabriel had no fallback plan and she wondered how people managed boredom before the arrival of technology.

"Where's Buff?" asked Ally as she entered the room.

"Out."

"Where?"

"He never says, but I expect he's gone for a run."

"Good because I need to talk to you about the FBI."

Gabriel pulled a face that gave a perfect resemblance of someone who didn't have a clue what the initials meant.

"The FIB," repeated Ally who had more important tasks to complete today than educating an imbecile. "When did they start following you?"

"Don't know really, might not have noticed them at first."

"But when did you first notice them?"

"Probably the first time Buff came to my flat. I drove him home and I noticed them behind me."

"Did they follow you home?"

"No, I think I lost them in the lanes."

"I suppose that's possible. You could lose Lewis Hamilton in the lanes."

THE REIGN OF TERROR

"Who?"

"Never mind. I met with the FIB yesterday and they told me they weren't following you. The only reason they have a file on you is because Mario Peruzzi wrote your name in a letter."

"Who's he?"

"You're kidding, right?!" said Ally in exasperation.

Gabriel looked at her blankly and shrugged.

"Megalomaniac, head of the Oblivion Doctrine, big château in Marseille, we arrived in a helicopter, you punched his assistant in the face…"

"Oh, yeah, I remember. I thought his name was Marcel Marceau."

"Marcel Marceau is a mime artist… and very much dead."

"I'm not very good with names," replied Gabriel unapologetically. "I was looking at the list of names on your pad here this morning and I only recognised one of them. It's one of the reasons I like Buff, easy name to remember. It's not just the name, though, obviously I like other things about him. He's macho, fit, and has a massive…"

"I implore you not to finish that sentence."

"… social media following."

"Back up a minute," replied Ally grabbing the notepad and holding it up to her. "Did you say you know one of these names?"

"Yes."

"Which one?"

"Georges Couthon."

"How?"

"He's French!"

"But so is Voltaire and he's also on the list!"

"Never heard of him. I thought Voltaire was a brand of make-up."

Ally bit her lip. "How do you know about Georges Couthon?"

"The reign of terror."

THE REIGN OF TERROR

"What?"

"Duh, keep up. Everyone who went to a French school learnt about the Revolution."

"I'm sure that's true… but I didn't go to one."

Ally knew about the 'French Revolution' but not about some of the people that were responsible for it. The Gunpowder Plot was a singly British affair and wouldn't have been taught in schools on the other side of the Channel, and the same was true of the French Revolution. Other than the highlights, the specific details were left out of lessons in English schools.

Ally grabbed her laptop from the shelf and immediately searched for more information about Georges. In the latter part of the eighteenth century following the execution of the French monarch Louis XVI, the country was gripped by a battle over power, ideology and the policies of the fledgling Republic. The opportunistically named 'Committee for Public Safety' was set up by Maximilien Robespierre with the sole purpose of arresting, processing and executing anyone found to be working against the new state. This 'reign of terror' lasted for over four years and resulted in over three hundred thousand arrests and more than seventeen thousand executions.

In minutes the full horrific details of Georges's activities were scrolling down the screen in front of her until she stopped on one significant word.

Mountain.

"Tell me about the mountain," asked Ally.

"Which one?"

"The one from the French Revolution."

"There aren't any mountains in Paris."

"It's not a geological feature, you airhead, it says here that Georges was part of a movement called the Mountain."

"Oh, that Mountain. I seem to remember that it was a political party run by four people who were responsible for the removal of the monarchy during the Revolution."

"Was Georges one of the four?"

THE REIGN OF TERROR

"No, I think he worked for Maximilien Robespierre."
"Was he part of it?"
"Oh yeah, major player."
"Why did they call it the Mountain?"
"No idea," said Gabriel, popping a piece of gum in her mouth. "Is it important?"
"It's important if you believe in coincidence. The list of names on my notepad are all accomplices to people who attempted or succeeded in bringing social upheaval and the destruction of the establishment. They tried in London in the early seventeenth century and succeeded in France in the eighteenth. It's all connected to the same word. Mountain. The men of the mountain will burn."
"Burn what?" asked Gabriel casually.
"Burn anything that they perceive to involve the oppression of the masses. Just like parliament went up in smoke two days ago."
"Did it?"
"You are aware that information isn't just available through a smartphone, weren't you? Try the watching the news on television!"
Ally grabbed a piece of paper out of a kitchen drawer and wrote the numbers of the centuries down the left-hand side of the page, sixteenth at the top and twenty-first at the bottom. She wrote Guy Fawkes first and then Robespierre somewhere in the middle. Almost one hundred and ninety years separated the two. If Hudson was right and the Mountain Men were a secret group passing their knowledge and ideas down through the generations, then there had to be half a dozen people between Fawkes and Robespierre. The culprits would be linked in some way to the names on her list. All she had to do was work out who and what they'd been responsible for.

Mario had decided to stage a re-enactment of history for his own purposes and it wasn't just out of revenge. Parliament's destruction was just the beginning, but what came next?

THE REIGN OF TERROR

*****

Throughout history most wars had something to do with religion. It's curious, really. It would be hard to find a religious book that advocates such action. The Ten Commandments don't include a line about 'killing anything that moves in the name of God'. They tend to steer people away from violence and more towards kindness. Yet there have been hundreds of wars in the name of Christianity from the Crusades to the Holocaust.

It's not just Christians either. Almost every religion has been responsible for waging war and every time it happens, they pronounce that 'God is on their side'. What if your opponent also believes this? God can't be on both sides surely? Not unless you believe in multiple gods like the Greeks and Romans who could legitimately argue they all had one or more gods on their side. Then the argument was about which God you had. Good if you bagged Zeus, but useless if you only had Dionysus, the God of Decent Wines.

Of all the religions, only Buddhism and Hinduism had any right to claim 'clean hands' when it came to religious warmongering. When was the last time you heard of a Hindu issuing the equivalent of a fatwa, burning other nations' flags or threatening to invade Jerusalem? Hindus believed in karma and intentional action, and only acted as a response to something else. But not just any type of action. Their beloved Shikshapatri was very clear when it came to matters of war. Violence in all forms was unacceptable. Which meant followers had to find alternative ways of displaying their displeasure.

Since the theft of the book last week millions of Hindus were gradually being persuaded to participate in a slow and intentional campaign against the British government. The early protests, which involved disgruntled individuals with nothing better to do with their afternoons, were gaining momentum. Up and down the land, in every city and large town, groups were engaged in peaceful

THE REIGN OF TERROR

campaigns outside churches and town halls. 'Don't buy British' and other slogans were chanted and were having an economic impact. Understandably the largest protest was outside the Weston Museum itself. What started as a small gathering had grown to the point where hundreds gathered every day.

The Indian government had reacted by suspending co-operation with the Brits on a number of key initiatives until there was progress on recovering the book.

Progress, though, had been non-existent.

When your own parliament had just been blown from the face of the Earth very few diplomats and politician were concerned with an ancient stolen book. Their attention was simply focused on identifying which organisation or state was responsible. The secret services were left wanting. There had been no indication or intelligence that the strike was coming. No group had taken responsibility. Every country around the world, both allies and historic opponents, had all universally offered their help and denounced the perpetrators. The ferocity of the explosion and resulting fire had left little evidence for the investigators to go on.

Unscrupulous commentators even had the gall to suggest the bombing had been carried out by the Indians in retaliation to the theft. More informed experts pointed out they believed in karma not kamikaze. Wild speculation will always consume the vacuum evacuated by a lack of explanation and evidence. Unsurprisingly the Mountain Plc had been implicated. Their offices were raided and found to be empty, nothing more than a shell organisation run by ghosts. The press was quick to turn their attention to the government. Yet again politicians had focused on profits above people. There had been a shocking lack of due diligence in the procurement process. Bribes had been paid to anyone with pockets. No one was surprised. Capitalism had form.

The Prime Minister called an emergency security meeting. Ministers, officials and diplomats were all

THE REIGN OF TERROR

summoned and not just from the United Kingdom. Any country able to provide intelligence was invited. Daniel hadn't even been in Oxford twenty-four hours before he was being driven at speed to the capital and an audience with the government. Soon they would know about the Mountain Men and, like Ally, that was about the sum of the knowledge available.

- Chapter 13 -

Fish Boy

Naples, 1637

When the King decides he wants you dead he's normally going to get his way. You only have two choices. Run or hide. Hiding can be tricky. Hiding in the house next to the palace because it's the last place they'll think to look is plain foolish because it's actually the first place they'll look. Seeking refuge with known accomplices might feel safe for a day or two, but when fifty percent of the country were actively hunting you it would be like waving the world's largest white flag. Running is also less than ideal when the fastest mode of transport is by horse. There is a third option to running or hiding. Running and hiding. If Father Tesimond wanted to have any chance of survival he had to run and hide somewhere far away and in a big crowd. There were worse places than Naples.

Crammed onto a narrow stretch of coastline in the shadow of the mighty Vesuvius lived a vast community of two hundred and fifty thousand people. It was a diverse, multicultural city where no face seemed out of place. Italians, North Africans, Ottomans and Slavs lived, traded and fought over its identity. Anyone could fit in unnoticed. It was a thousand miles away from the people who wanted him dead and, unlike England, Naples was a place where Catholics were not just tolerated but protected. As the last decade had already proven, finding Father Tesimond here would be like locating a rare penny in a massive bank vault.

FISH BOY

More than thirty years had passed since the fateful day when King James had signed his arrest papers, an event that was no more than a distant memory, like the recollection of a passage read in a book. When the noose had tightened around the gunpowder plotters, Guy Fawkes had been true to his word. None of the conspirators implicated the priest, and as all of them had been executed almost immediately there wasn't much chance they were going to go back on their word. Within days of Guy's own brutal demise Tesimond had been smuggled to Calais by boat amongst a cargo of dead pigs.

Once there, he'd retraced the steps he'd taken as a younger man while studying theology in the iconic religious centres of mainland Europe. He moved slowly through France, earning a meagre living in any way he could before finally arriving some years later in Rome where he set about writing his own account of the Gunpowder Plot and secured work as a teacher. The longer and deeper he immersed himself in the sanctuary of Catholic countries, the more difficult it became to track his progress. Although elderly in years by the time he reached Naples rumours still persisted in England that Tesimond planned to kill the British monarch. There were fanciful conspiracy theories doing the rounds in the royal court that he planned to send King James a gift laced with poison.

The truth of his exploits was far more interesting.

The weight of Guy's mission had lagged on Father Tesimond's mind for years. Although he'd influenced many to the causes the 'Mountain Men' stood for through his teaching and the charity he offered to help release people from their impoverished condition, he knew what Guy really wanted was a rebellious hothead with no thought for their own welfare. Someone who would create their own noise to match the mighty Mountain rumbling on Naples's horizon. In the thirty years since his escape no such candidate met the criteria.

Now time was running out.

FISH BOY

Age had rapidly eroded both the quality of his life and his ability to carry it out. Moving more than a few metres required a Herculean effort and because that power was no longer within him the old preacher was forced to rely on the support of the community who lived around the square in the Pedino quarter of the city. It was an area famous for its fish markets. Fisherman lived, traded and paid their taxes within this claustrophobic and ramshackle district. At least they were supposed to pay their taxes. If you didn't want to the only alternative was to secretly offload your morning catch to characters like Tesimond before an official-looking gentleman with a ledger got out of bed.

Smuggling was normal. If you wanted to stay alive it was as essential as eating or breathing. The Habsburgs who reigned over most of Europe had waged a catalogue of disastrous wars against neighbours, which in turn forced the people to put their hands in their pockets to pay the bill. Every year the tax on fish increased, and every year the impact was felt most fiercely amongst the modest folk of Naples. The only way to avoid it was to conduct secret trades to avoid the taxman's share. Tesimond had checked the Ten Commandments and was reassured that none of them made any mention to buying 'hooky' fish.

A gentle tap struck Tesimond's door almost faint enough to go unnoticed. Dawn had not yet crept over the horizon, but Naples's fishermen had been awake since they saw it set yesterday evening. After several minutes' delay a slither of candlelight peeked out along the edge of the door and an old, wrinkled face peered out into the alleyway.

"Morning, Father," whispered a voice on the other side.

"Francisco. It's a little early, even for you."

"Got to stay one step ahead," replied the man with a wink. A large, wooden crate overflowing with writhing fish was held firmly in the man's muscular arms. The fish were so fresh most would have survived their morning trauma should anyone decide to throw them back in the sea. Behind Francisco's stocky frame a young boy was biting his nails and staring at his feet.

FISH BOY

"Got some help today, I see."

"My son, Tommaso," said Francisco, "old enough to earn his keep, and by God, we all need to."

Tesimond beckoned them in and both fishermen, old and young, sidled through the crack in the door and closed it behind, checking the alley for prying eyes as they went. The penalty for being caught selling product before the duties had been paid was severe and frequently resulted in torture, death or worse. Francisco had always had a soft spot for Tesimond. He was an outsider and, unlike his other customers, no one would suspect a priest to be anything other than whiter than white. Plus, if he'd given his approval even God couldn't judge them.

"If you don't mind, Father, I'm going to leave young Tommaso here to deal with your order today so I can get around to the others. He needs the training and out of everyone I trust you the most."

"Certainly, Francisco. I was a teacher, don't forget."

The priest gave the young boy a kind smile and painfully shuffled towards the chair by the cold fireplace.

"Just do as I told you," demanded Francisco sternly.

The boy nodded unconvincingly.

"I'll be back in ten minutes," added Francisco as he headed back out into the alleyway that led off Pedino's main square.

Tommaso's blond hair cascaded down the sides of his tanned skin and in the centre of his face small, black eyes like empty wells pierced the floor tiles. His expression was about as far from enthusiasm as it was possible for a face to be. Work experience sucked. Career options were limited when everyone in your family had done the same job since the invention of the fish hook. If your dad was a fisherman, you were destined to follow and so was everyone who came after you. Suggesting that you quite fancied a career in flour trading because the smell of fish made you retch and sand gave you a rash was more controversial than saying you wanted to wear frocks on a Saturday night, excel at needlework and have everyone call you Karen. The seventeenth century wasn't the right time or place for experimenting with personal life choices.

Tommaso's social awkwardness was poisoning the atmosphere of the small, bare room. Two complete strangers faced off in opposite chairs while a collection of fish flapped uncontrollably in a shoddy, wooden crate on the floor between them. Eventually the old man would say something surely, Tommaso thought to himself. Come on, do you want fish or not? Tesimond waited, as he always did, for the salesmen to sell. Francisco would always give him a steer on the best 'fish of the day' or advice on what might be a little cheaper because it wasn't selling very well that week. Selling was an art form the boy clearly hadn't mastered yet. Maybe he needed a little push.

"What's good today?" asked Tesimond, breaking the deadlock.

"Fish," replied Tommaso plainly.

"Yes… but which ones?"

"Those ones," he said, pointing at the box of fish as if the decrepit old man might have missed it.

"I can see you still have a lot to learn, young man. Normally your father will tell me about the fish, help me choose. I'll help you out a little. Can I have two sea breams please?"

Tommaso peered into the box and picked up two slippery specimens at random. He held them in the air for Tesimond's approval.

"Those are lobsters."

Tommaso shrugged as if it didn't seem to matter.

"The biggest difference between the sea bream and the lobster," added Tesimond kindly, "is the absence of legs and pincers."

Tommaso dropped the two crustaceans back in the box and grabbed the first thing he saw that lacked legs.

"No. Those are scallops," said Tesimond calmly before the boy had even removed them from the box. "Bream don't come in a shell, they're fish not… shellfish."

FISH BOY

The youngster's hands returned to the writhing, fishy bodies with a squelch for a third time and removed two non-shelled and non-legged items.

"You're getting much closer, but those are called anchovies and, although rather delicious, they don't make much of a meal unless you're on a diet."

Tommaso sighed in a way that suggested the customer was being unfairly picky about tax-free fish.

"Why don't I point a bream out to you… just this time?"

The boy nodded but even his own head wasn't convinced it cared very much. Father Tesimond's body creaked out of his chair and a shaking finger pointed to two medium-sized fish with black and silver scales. Tommaso leant forward towards the two fish and lifted them about an inch in the air into the elderly priest's hands. He then held out his own to receive payment as his father had instructed.

"I'm not quite done," replied Tesimond. "I think I might also take a couple of sea bream as well."

"You said they were sea bream," chuntered the young boy, pointing at the two fish in the old man's hands.

"Oh, yes. My mind isn't as sharp as it once was. Do you have any mackerel?"

The boy rolled his eyes. What he saw in the crate was fish. Not sea bass or bream or mackerel or swordfish or gurney or whiting. Just fish. Horrible, stinky, slimy, smelly fish. In thirteen years, he'd survived on a diet almost exclusively based on fish and he'd never noticed a difference in any of them. They all tasted like fish. Why were other people so bloody picky? He pointed to a selection of different-shaped fish in the crate and watched carefully for a subtle change in the priest's facial expression.

"Nope. No. Not that one. Warmer. That's a crab. Almost. Nearly. That one!"

Tommaso slopped two more fish onto Tesimond's lap and again put his palm outwards.

FISH BOY

"Coins!" demanded the boy, desperate to bring the transaction to a close.

"You don't like fish much, do you?"

The boy shook his head.

"Why not?"

"Boring."

"What would you rather be doing than selling fish?"

"ANYTHING."

A spark of an idea formed inside Father Tesimond. For thirty years he'd prevaricated over who to pass the responsibility of the Mountain Men on to and now he was running out of time. If he died without doing so it wouldn't matter if he'd made a wrong choice. The only wrong choice would be not choosing at all. This boy was young, strong and had no hope. What he needed was a purpose that didn't involve spending most of his life floating around in a boat.

"Do you love your King, boy?"

"No. I love coins," he said, his hand still outstretched.

"What about power, do you love power?"

"COINS!"

"How do you feel about taxes?"

Tommaso's attention span wasn't great at the best of times but he'd tried hard to follow his father's instructions to the best of his ability. As far as he remembered, the process was fairly simple. Show the customer the fish, let the customer choose the fish, collect the customer's coins for buying the fish, and leave with the rest of the fish. Easy. At no stage did he remember any instructions about identifying types of fish, receiving careers advice, or dealing with questions about his belief system. Maybe this was his dad's idea of a joke. An initiation test to challenge him and give everyone down at the dockside a really good laugh at his expense. He wasn't falling for it.

"If I answer will you pay me?" asked Tommaso desperately.

"Yes."

FISH BOY

"Dad says taxes are stupid because the people are starving."

"And would you like to help?"

"Not really. I'm only thirteen."

"Why should that matter? Ever heard of Joan of Arc?"

"No."

"Led the French Army and defeated the English… at thirteen years of age."

The boy's eyes widened. "Wow."

"Don't you want to be someone like that?"

"Dad says I have to be a fisherman."

"Do you always do what he says?"

"Pretty much."

"Authority figures aren't always right, you know. Sometimes people have to stand up against tyranny. I can help you do that."

"Like John of Arc?"

"Joan."

"A girl led an army!"

"Yes," croaked Tesimond. "Anyone can achieve greatness if they have the heart and will."

"If a girl can do it then I certainly can," replied Tommaso, puffing out his chest. "What happened to her?"

"Oh, they burnt her alive."

"COINS!"

"Hold on," replied Tesimond, dragging his withered body over to a chest that sat by the side of a rickety, old bed. He removed a small bag of coins and returned to the boy after several minutes of awkward dexterity. "There you are."

The boy opened the pouch and searched amongst the gold coins for something small enough to pay for a pair of sea bream and a couple of mackerel.

"Got anything smaller."

"Nope."

"I'm not a bank, you know. Can't give you change from this lot."

"It's ok, it's all for you."

"Father said I shouldn't take advantage of the customer."

"You're not. I have an exciting job for you."

"Does it involve being burnt alive?"

Tesimond reflected on the treatment that had befallen the last Mountain Man. From the accounts he'd received, Guy Fawkes's execution involved being hanged, drawn and quartered. At no point in this excruciating ordeal had fire made an appearance.

"No."

"What's the money for?"

"I'm offering you a job."

"Does it involve fish?"

"It involves freedom: how you achieve it is very much up to you."

"Freedom from what?"

"Tyranny."

"Who's he?"

"He's the man on top of the mountain."

"Doesn't all the smoke get in his eyes?"

"It's not Vesuvius. The mountain is a metaphor for the minority who increase your taxes, tell you what to do, and suppress your rights."

Tommaso looked confused. He'd created a vision of some bloke up a mountain demanding taxes while he ran up the side lobbing halibuts at him. "What can I do about it?"

"With the right guidance you can lead the people against it. Help the people take back power."

"What guidance?"

"All you have to do is follow two important rules."

*****

The call from Ernest Culpepper came at eight o'clock on Tuesday morning. It wasn't good news. In it he explained that, due to the ongoing investigation into her possible involvement in the theft at the Weston Museum, Ally was being suspended until further notice. Access to the university's buildings had been restricted and her lectures would be delivered by Jenkins. In better news, at least from Ernest's perspective, the Prophecy exhibition had finally opened, and Lance had been placed in temporary charge of its success. Which meant it was only a matter of time until it wasn't.

Ernest hadn't sugarcoated the news. Ally suspected he was secretly pleased by the university's quick reaction to events. After all, he was just one of many colleagues who had expressed resentment at her being awarded the honour of organising an exhibition in the first place. He'd been applying to run his own without approval for years. It wasn't enough for him just to be the Librarian, an honour that only a few dozen people had held before him. Much had changed in the ten years since he took the role and much of the library's success was down to him. He'd fought hard to secure the funding needed to expand the facilities, but there was never enough investment to manage the vast task of housing every book ever published.

The more the library grew, the more money it absorbed. It was hard for an academic like Ernest to understand the brutal economics of the situation. In his mind money was secondary to the preservation of history. Oxford University might be one of the richest institutions in the world but there were still choices that had to be made. Imposters like Ally didn't have the library's best interests at heart, as this incident had proven. Maybe now they'd listen to him. Maybe now they'd take his ideas seriously.

Ally took the news of her suspension pretty well. Nine dinner plates smashed into a thousand pieces on the kitchen floor weren't keen on agreeing with her. It would not stand. No one stopped her from doing the one thing that truly satisfied her. No one was going to get in the way of her projects and the pursuit of learning. If she wanted her job restored it would be up to her to figure out all this Mountain Men nonsense. The only way to do that was to discover the whereabouts of the book and that meant breaking out one of her greatest strengths, research.

She ran each name from the front of Hudson's letters through an internet search engine as well as scanning through her own sizeable library of books. A few of the names were complete dead ends, sometimes only producing a single reference from the billions of searchable pages, sometimes not even as much as that. The oldest name on the list was a priest called Giulio Genoino, who'd lived in Italy in the early part of the seventeenth century, but as far as she could establish there was no obvious link between him and Guy Fawkes. If the Mountain Men had always been there, they must have been passing on the task from one candidate to another. As Fawkes had never even been to Italy and Genoino had never been to England, why was the name on the list? It was a total puzzle. The only obvious link was the date: they were both alive at the same time.

The back door opened, and Buff walked casually in. If he had been for a run, as Gabriel had suggested, he certainly wasn't dressed for it, and neither was he showing any of the common signs of having done so. No sweat, no fatigue, just a bulky man in blue jeans and a T-shirt.

"Make yourself at home," said Ally sarcastically as he helped himself to some cereal from a container on the sideboard.

"Yeez," he mumbled in a thick French accent.

It was hard for her to admit it, but she had to agree with Honeywell: there was something shifty about him. In the four days since he and Gabriel had arrived, this was only the third time she'd even seen him. He spoke rarely and had a disengaged attitude that made it look like he was either preoccupied or uncomfortable being in the company of others. Gabriel had remarked that he was just nervous about being in another country for the first time, but Ally's instincts told her otherwise. As this was the first time she'd been alone with him, now was the moment to seek more answers.

FISH BOY

"Enjoying England?" she asked in the friendliest tone she could muster.

"Yeez."

"Different from your country?"

"Yeez."

"Where is it that you're from?"

"Potato."

Ally opened a search engine and brought up a map of the world. "Point to it."

He pointed at France. "Potato."

Gabriel ran in from the living room and threw herself at him as if he'd just returned from a three-month stint on manoeuvres in Afghanistan. Ally shielded herself from the onslaught of affection. They exchanged a few words of French that Ally immediately knew were slang expressions for things couples did to each other in the privacy of their own homes.

"We were just having a chat. Getting to know each other," said Ally. "Something you clearly haven't done yet."

"Not true. We know everything about each other."

"Ok, so when's his birthday?"

"Easy. Easter Sunday."

"Which is a different date every year," replied Ally.

"What's your point?"

"Well, he can't have been born on, say, the ninth of March and the twelfth of April, can he!? Unless his poor mother went through the longest labour in history."

"I know the sixteen digits of his credit card, what more do I need?" offered Gabriel. "And I know all about his hobbies, family and favourite food."

"Is it potatoes?" suggested Ally.

Buff nodded excitedly, even though he thought they were talking about football.

"Where did you meet him?" asked Ally, still suspicious that anyone in a two-week relationship would voluntarily go on the run with someone they'd just met.

"Nightclub. He came over and chatted me up."

FISH BOY

"And is that normal?"

"It is if you're as hot as me," grinned Gabriel, pouting. "Said he was a fan of mine."

"A fan?"

"Said he saw the press coverage back in the day, you know when I saved the world."

"Helped to save it," added Ally in order to bring some elements of truth to her claim.

"Do you get many fans chatting you up?" asked Gabriel brashly.

"Hard to say," replied Ally. "I've normally kneed them in the bollocks by the third or fourth word."

Ally rarely frequented places where anyone might foolishly attempt to chat her up, libraries, antiques shops and her own cottage not being places where single men tended to congregate. Where most single women made an effort to attract the opposite sex, she made a point of actively repelling them. She wore plain clothes that made her look frumpy, never wore make-up, and maintained a scornful expression that was more effective than a chastity belt. On the very rare occasions that a mature, single, antique-loving, short-sighted amnesiac happened to offer a smile or wayward chat-up line they were soon doubled over clutching their crotch and screaming several octaves higher than they thought they were capable of.

"What do you do for work?" Ally asked Buff directly.

"He's an entrepreneur," replied Gabriel proudly.

"Let him talk for himself," snapped Ally angrily.

"Doggies," replied Buff.

"Is he talking about sex again?"

"Kind of. He breeds dogs for a living," replied Gabriel. "I'm afraid his English isn't very good."

"You don't say!"

"Big doggies," said Buff, adding a visual mime and some barking noises.

"Shaggy ones if you ask me," muttered Ally. "Right, well, if you wouldn't mind taking your pet away, I can get on with some work. Go watch some television or something."

"I have been," replied Gabriel. "Took your advice and watched the... news... is that what it's called? I'll be honest, not a big fan. They keep talking about some uprising that happened in Nepal last night. Wherever that is."

"The only thing likely to be rising up in Nepal are the mountains."

As the last word left Ally's mouth a bell rang inside her like a burglar alarm and she immediately rushed into the living room slowly followed by the other two.

"It's not Nepal... it's Naples," murmured Ally as she watched the coverage of mayhem unfolding in the heart of the famous Italian city.

Crowds of masked vigilantes had terrorised the town centre, Molotov cocktails had been hurled and shop windows smashed. The Regional Assembly was still ablaze, and a group of protestors had barricaded themselves inside. Street battles had erupted between thousands of demonstrators and lines of heavily armoured police. Anything and everything not permanently attached to the ground had been used as a projectile. Bricks, traffic barriers, plastic chairs and glass bottles had flown across the sky. Ally even spotted one strange hoodlum throwing fish. On one side of the court building someone had graffitied the letters TMM in black paint so that it covered the whole of one wall. Ally hurried back to her computer and typed 'Naples uprising' into a search engine.

- Chapter 14 -

Pudding Lane

It didn't take long for Ally to make the connection between the past and the present. The current uprising against the authorities in Naples was a carbon copy of an incident that happened in sixteen forty-seven. A rebellion that loosely involved Giulio Genoino, one of the names on her list. An octogenarian preacher, Genoino, had been a thorn in the establishment's side for more than four decades. He'd fought stoically for the rights of the common man and in doing so inspired many of them to follow his ideals. In sixteen forty-seven when a crippling tax increase was enforced on the fruit sellers of Naples, the collective resignation of the people finally broke down. Blacksmiths, tanners, farm workers and fisherman had had enough.

One of Genoino's trusted agitators, Masaniello, led a thousand men in revolt against the Customs Office and razed it to the ground. This unexpected success emboldened the wider population and soon the town's disquiet was unleashed. An almost unstoppable anger gained momentum and Masaniello led his men to the Viceroy's palace, where they ransacked its armouries and opened its prisons. Within days the city's administration crumbled in chaos and Masaniello was effectively left in charge of the city. Recognising their initial defeat and waiting for the Holy Roman Empire to send reinforcement, the Viceroy played for time. He invited Masaniello to the palace where he heard and agreed to all of his demands. Taxes were cancelled, rebels were pardoned, citizens were granted additional rights, and Masaniello himself was appointed 'leader general'. Finally,

PUDDING LANE

after hundreds of years of Habsburg rule the people had finally scaled the mountain and brought down their oppressors.

It lasted about a week.

The Viceroy placed a gold chain around Masaniello's neck, and he was seduced by the offer of a pension and wealth beyond measure for a modest fisherman from Pedino. Whether poisoned by the administration or as a result of the power that rapidly went to his head, he began to display frenzied and irrational behaviour. Days after his meteoric rise he was placed under house arrest, but Masaniello was a wily and strong adversary. He escaped his confinement and in an act of insanity stormed semi-naked into the cathedral in the middle of the Archbishop's service. In a crazy tirade of blasphemy, he denounced his fellow citizens and all they had accomplished. He was immediately arrested, removed to a nearby monastery and executed by a group of flour merchants.

Masaniello would become a legend. In the centuries to follow he would be commemorated in song, paintings and statues, but his name and nature would be almost completely lost to history. Masaniello had been born Tommaso Aniello, the once young and disaffected fisherman who achieved more in a week than all of the Mountain Man who'd gone before him. But, as Philibert had warned, he'd become the very thing they'd sought to overthrow.

When Ally woke up on Wednesday morning, she again read through the story of Masaniello and wrote his name down on her chart. The pictures from current day Naples and the TMM imprinted on the wall were proof that he'd followed in Guy Fawkes's footsteps even if there was a gap in the number of years between them. She made the conclusion that not all the members of this mysterious group were as proactive as others. There would be gaps in the chain between seismic events. Where would they strike next? Masaniello's uprising had briefly brought fire and revolt to the streets of Naples, but which event in history came next? She looked again at her list of names but was interrupted by her phone ringing. Lance's name appeared on-screen and she answered it immediately, fearing the worst.

"What's gone wrong?" demanded Ally immediately.

"Nothing," he replied innocently.

"I don't believe you."

"I was just ringing you to say everything here was going well," replied Lance who appeared to be speaking to her from the side of a road.

"What's that noise?" she asked suspiciously.

"Cars."

"Not that noise, the shrill repetitive ringing I can hear in the distance."

"Oh that. That's just the fire alarm."

"There's a fire!?"

"No, it's fine, there's not an actual fire, I just leant on the glass and accidentally set it off. I was just ringing to let you know it's a false alarm in case anyone calls you first."

"I don't really know how you've survived this long. Isn't the point of natural selection to weed people like you out?"

"Just lucky, I guess," replied probably the unluckiest man on the planet. "Did you see what's been happening in Naples?"

"Yes."

"Is it them?"

"Absolutely."

"Do you know where they are going to strike next?"

"Not yet. I just have to find a name on this list that links Masaniello to the middle or late part of the seventeenth century and involves a revolution – either that or a massive amount of burning."

"That should be pretty easy. Just look on the list for a Thomas Farriner."

"He wasn't on the list... but then again he wouldn't be," said Ally, rapidly analysing her own words. "The Great Fire of London started in his bakery, so he was responsible. It seems like Mario has only addressed his

PUDDING LANE

letters to accomplices of these events to make it harder for me to work it out. Bastard."

"The Great Fire was hardly an act of rebellion," replied Lance as the noise of the fire alarm finally stopped in the background behind him, making him momentarily shout down the phone and then immediately restrain the volume of his voice.

"Actually, that's not necessarily true. There were many people at the time who believed the fire was started deliberately. There were more people rounded up for being foreigners than there were people fighting the flames. They even executed a random Frenchman for the crime, even though he wasn't even in London on the day of the fire. Many academics defended him. Hold on," said Ally as she gave an off-the-cuff history lesson. "Christopher Wren! He was on Hudson's list."

"But Christopher Wren wasn't involved in the fire, was he?"

"It depends how you look at it. Wren ended up rebuilding most of the city: think of all the money he must have made from it. Why would he be on Mario's list if he's not got something to do with it?"

"Seems a bit thin to me."

"That's rich coming from you."

"I do have feelings, you know," replied Lance who absorbed much of the jibes at his own expense but couldn't help thinking his unnatural height and width weren't really fair targets.

"Don't care. Come and pick me up immediately, you're only doing damage there and my car isn't likely to get all the way to London in one piece."

She cancelled the call and moved back into the living room where Gabriel was still trying to follow the news feed. Buff had disappeared once again.

"Gabriel, I need to go to London to…"

"I'll get my coat," she interrupted without flinching.

*****

PUDDING LANE

Travelling long distances in a confined space with one idiot was bad enough, but putting up with two at the same time was purgatory. What made it worse still was Lance's inability to function the moment he set eyes on Gabriel. This was definitely not a mutually held connection: she barely noticed he was there. Lance was transfixed by her the moment she'd gracefully tiptoed down the garden path, flicking the hair of her overbearing wig and pouting like a model on a catwalk fashion shoot. He'd tried hopelessly to act less like a postgraduate geek and more like a cool and relaxed alpha male.

He failed miserably.

When Ally introduced her squatter, he attempted to shake her hand but realised at the last moment that her culture of greeting tended to involve a kiss on both cheeks. The resulting confusion that followed involved him butting her in the head and partially shaking one of her boobs. From that faux pas any semblance of social normality left the building and turned out the lights.

In a panic to regain his reputation he tried to open a door for her and pulled the handle clean off the car. She ignored the chivalry and casually went around to the other side. Gabriel had no interest in skinny, geeky men who drove to the speed limit and wore a shabby collection of charity shop cast-offs. To her, Lance wasn't really a guy at all, not in the sense of being an eligible one at least. Not quite invisible but not quite fully visible either. A ghostly apparition of the opposite sex that had been fully screened in seconds and found not to conform to her extremely narrow dating criteria.

Lance's criteria, on the other hand, were so wide you couldn't see the sides. He'd be happy to date any woman who noticed his existence without the incentive of future payment. He found most women almost impossible to engage fluently with but meeting an actual 'pretty girl' was a complete brain fuck. The entire two-hour journey to London was consumed by Lance's attempts to bridge the

PUDDING LANE

gap between his meagre experience with women and an attempt to somehow connect with someone way out of his league. This predominantly involved Lance asking questions that generally didn't make sense and Gabriel ignoring them anyway. The best examples of these included:

Did she eat cheese?
How many times had she seen the film *Jaws*?
Which smell did she prefer, grass or pine needles?
Had she ever been to Iceland?
What did she think of unicycles?
How many 'keepie uppies' could she do with a football?
Had she ever seen a wart in the shape of a walnut?

She declined to answer any of these oddly wayward questions, which was a shame because Lance actually did own a wart in the shape of a walnut.

"Weirdo," she muttered more loudly than most might if they were looking not to offend.

Having never actually been in a real relationship herself, Ally was no expert in the process of wooing the opposite sex, but it was her opinion that Lance's approach was not likely to result in him beating her to one. It was actually a mystery to her why anyone would want to spend a single evening with another human, let alone the rest of their miserable life. It was just another behaviour that the majority of people agreed on that she didn't fully understand. She'd logged it in a category that included streaming services, Nando's and body piercings.

Gabriel wasn't much better company than Lance. Then again it was hard to take her seriously at all today given she was sitting in the back seat chewing gum and wearing a huge, bushy wig in some vain attempt at anonymity. It never passed her mind that fake hair, a neon catsuit and bright, shiny pink latex boots might in fact draw attention rather than reflect it. The FBI didn't need to follow her, they just needed to wait until it got dark and then followed the dazzle. They'd be able to pick her up from satellites orbiting the globe several miles away.

PUDDING LANE

Ally preoccupied herself by blocking out the two external nuisances and focusing on the task at hand. If her hunch was right and the next target was a repeat of the Great Fire of London, it meant this was potentially the third attack by the Mountain Men. If true it meant, by her calculation, there might be as many as a dozen more attacks to bring the chain up to the modern day. But what was the motive? If Mario wanted revenge against her there were far easier ways of achieving it. The disruption had already robbed her of the only thing she cared about, her work, so why did it have to continue? Mario had failed to bring the world to its knees once: maybe this was his posthumous attempt to finish the job.

The chain had to be broken. If they solved it before the next incident occurred, they might work out who was responsible and bring it to a speedy end. It was impossible to know when it would happen, though. Since Saturday three events had taken place in four days and yet the robbery was still the one that made least sense. The book had never been stolen in the past, so it didn't fit the formula of the other two.

Following the events that had destroyed the Houses of Parliament late on Saturday night, there was an understandably high police presence throughout the centre of London. The government had raised the threat level to 'Critical' which meant an attack was expected imminently and required a higher number of checks, resources and security. On almost every major street corner a police van was parked up and armed officers patrolled the vicinity. Surely even the Mountain Men wouldn't have the audacity to attempt something under these conditions, thought Ally, as she observed the police numbers through the passenger seat window.

The nearest place that Lance found to park the car was on the South Bank of London Bridge. From there they'd have to proceed on foot, an action that was a lot easier if you weren't walking in four-inch heels and wearing a wig

PUDDING LANE

that made you look like Diana Ross had just been electrocuted.

"Which way to the shops?" asked Gabriel, revealing her real motivation for joining the excursion.

"About two miles that way," pointed Ally. "This is the financial centre of London."

Gabriel looked crushed.

"I can take you later if you want," added Lance helpfully.

"No thanks, dweeb boy. I'd rather be seen without make-up on than spend another minute with you!"

"If you change your mind…" offered Lance, completely overlooking the rejection.

"Where are we going anyway?" said Gabriel, oblivious to his attempt at a response.

"Pudding Lane. That's the starting point."

"Pub crawl?" asked Gabriel.

"Great Fire!"

They headed across London Bridge dodging in and out of the dawdling tourists and sharp-suited executives walking at pace. A selection of beggars had secured the best residencies on every lamp-post and were perfecting their own unique approaches to gain favour from the passing masses. Some asked politely, some tried to make a joke, some had dogs, some tried to sell street-made trinkets from discarded rubbish, and one went with tradition and did his best to look near death's door. Quite possibly this was his natural state.

Their grey faces were perfectly camouflaged against the murky waters of the Thames that flowed some metres below them through the gaps in the bridge's barrier. The clouds added their own palette to the scene of foreboding that seeped through the very psyche of the city. As the bridge transformed itself into the main road, Ally took a right turn. A gold tower stretched into the sky, a beacon of colour breaking through the gloom.

"Monument," she said, confirming her own navigational skills.

PUDDING LANE

"What's it called?" asked Gabriel.

"I just said… Monument."

"That's not very original, is it? They could have given it a decent name. They could have called it the Big Gold Thingy."

Ally actually agreed with her for once, although not with her spontaneous alternative. Monument was not only the name for the two hundred and two-foot gold-coloured tower that loomed in the sky over them, but also the name for the area of London they were currently in. Monument was significant today for two reasons. It was erected to commemorate the Great Fire and its height was the exact distance between its roots and the bakery where the fire had first started in Pudding Lane.

"You know who designed this, don't you?" said Lance, reading some of the signs that were placed around its curved walls.

"Yes. Sir Christopher Wren. That's why I think it's linked. Now we just have to find the bakery. If they're going to re-create it, that's where we need to be."

Today's Pudding Lane was quite a different place from the one of the seventeenth century. Surrounded by high-rise office buildings and cornered by the rear entrances to hotels, it was the sort of narrow road mainly used by delivery vans or talented taxi drivers who used it to wind their way through the constant traffic. It was certainly not somewhere you'd walk at night unless you were up to no good, and even then, you'd think twice. It was dark and steep, and, as they walked from the lower end to the top, noticeably lacked one critical feature.

There was no longer a bakery there.

They walked up and down it twice in case it was hidden behind a shutter or offset from the road itself. The only shops of note were a troubled-looking travel agency and a plush sushi deli.

"That's disappointing," said Lance.

"Telling me," replied Gabriel. "Of all the places you could have brought me in London you brought me here."

PUDDING LANE

"We're not tourists, Gabriel. We're here to stop a crime."

"Then you should storm the travel agency: look how much it is to fly to New York, criminal."

"Did you know there wasn't a bakery anymore?" asked Lance gently.

"Obviously not," snapped Ally. "But that doesn't matter. Most of the letters I saw on Hudson's tablet were for addresses that no longer exist. The attack will happen here even if there isn't a bakery."

"Where?" asked Lance.

"Two hundred and two feet from Monument. Lance, work out on your phone where that might be?"

He nodded, quickly opened his phone and set the map to draw a circle of two hundred feet from the base of the tower.

"Where's the closest point?" asked Ally.

"Here," he said, pointing at the sushi bar.

"Right, that's where the fire will start."

"Do they bake sushi?" asked Gabriel vacantly.

Ally ignored her.

"Right, this is the plan. Lance, you stay by the door and look out for anyone suspicious. Gabriel and I will go inside and put a stop to whatever they are planning."

Londoners are accustomed to seeing peculiar things. A city this big will always draw colourful characters with unusual behaviours. Nothing is really a surprise and odd becomes the norm that folk who live outside the city would be immediately drawn to. The two female Asian servers standing behind the counter of the sushi bar didn't even blink when a fluorescent-clothed, wig-wearing twenty-something and a plainly dressed, frizzy-haired woman entered the establishment together. Just two more customers in search of a mid-afternoon salmon fish roll. Normal, though, quickly ended when the older woman grabbed a chair and secured the door from the inside.

"NOBODY MOVE!" shouted Ally.

PUDDING LANE

One of the servers slowly raised her hands while the other folded hers together and stared defiantly at the apparent multi-coloured daylight robbery.

"Where are they?" said Ally advancing on the counter.

"There's some in the fridge over there and some more here on the counter," replied the less flustered of the servers who was pointing at a now depleted late lunch collection of plastic trays.

"I want the Mountain Men," added Ally sternly.

"We have some volcano rolls left," she replied, pointing down at the trays.

"Hmm, they look good," replied Gabriel. "I'll take two."

"No, you won't," huffed Ally. "Look, we know what you're planning, where is your kitchen?"

"We don't have one."

"Then how do you make the sushi?"

"The fish is raw, and the rice is cooked on a metal hotplate. We don't really need a kitchen."

"I don't believe you," huffed Ally walking behind the counter and opening a door in the wall immediately behind it. Inside was a rather small and hectically organised stockroom and no obvious incendiary devices.

When Ally lurched towards the door, the more composed server had lifted an empty saucepan ready to protect herself and her shop from the clearly disturbed intruder. As Ally turned away from the stockroom in confusion a metal pan struck her square in the face and Ally slumped to the ground.

When she returned to consciousness some minutes later, she was propped up in a plastic chair with a painful thudding sensation trying to escape through her skin and a bag of ice held up to her head by Lance. In the seat opposite Gabriel was tucking into some volcano rolls.

"Good job I was here," said Gabriel between mouthfuls of spicy mayo, rice and tuna. "They wanted to call the police, but I told them you'd pay for the leftover stock if they didn't."

PUDDING LANE

"What…"

"You're welcome."

"I think you might have got this one wrong," offered Lance.

"I'm never wrong."

Before Lance could point out the obvious facts against that position his phone rang. After a few seconds of conversation, he offered the phone to his boss.

"It's for you."

"Me. Why would someone phone you if they wanted me?"

"Maybe because you never answer your phone."

Ally had a habit of screening any calls that did not show the person's name on the screen when it rang. The chance of this happening was about three in seven billion. There were only three people in her contacts: Ernest Culpepper, Lance and her father's home. Only one of these people rang regularly and he was currently nursing the bump on her head. Everyone else got screened and might get a return call in the weeks to follow when she could be bothered to check her voicemail.

"Who is it?"

"Antoine."

She immediately grabbed the phone out of his hand.

"Where the fuck have you been!?" she hollered down the phone.

"There's not much time, Ally, they'll be tracing my call. I have left something for you in a safe deposit box in a bank on Oxford Street. It contains important information that might help you. You'll need the following number to access it."

Ally quickly searched in her bag to grab a pen and write down the twelve-digit number and exact address on the back of her hand.

"Good luck, it's down to you now."

*****

PUDDING LANE

Paris, Louvre Palace, 1652

John Evelyn gazed in quiet contemplation at a stylish oil painting that depicted a battle scene of epic proportions. A sea of horses and human bodies filled two-thirds of the canvas, while the other third featured a crumbling stone arch framed against ominous black clouds. In the background standard bearers held aloft ripped flags frozen in mid-flutter while the soldiers in the foreground fought for supremacy in hand-to-hand combat as they trampled over the broken corpses of friends and foes alike. It was hard to say who was fighting who. Were there two armies or more? Or was every man fighting for his own cause? Maybe all of these conclusions were being left to the viewer to decide. Although he knew this was a relatively new painting, the battle scene it portrayed was a historic one, although no less brutal or barbaric than the perpetual skirmishes that erupted regularly in every corner of Europe at the moment.

John wasn't much of an artist but, like most born into relative wealth, he'd spent many hours trying to perfect the art form. Artistry just wasn't a talent he carried. He'd compensated for this deficiency by spending many enjoyable hours visiting the great collections in Venice when he'd travelled there in his youth in an attempt to find himself. What he actually discovered on the journey was an acknowledgement that he was more accomplished in the written word as a method of conveying his beliefs, although as yet none of his musings had reached the lofty heights of this magnificent painting. Whoever the artist was who'd painted it must have held an immense standing or notoriety for Louis XIV to hang it there amongst his personal collection in the Louvre Palace. John felt extremely fortunate to be able to appreciate it now and that was only possible because his new father-in-law, Sir Richard Browne, was the British Ambassador to Paris.

The painting next to it, which he casually moved to after deciding he'd spent enough time not understanding

PUDDING LANE

the meaning of the first one, also featured an unknown battle scene. This canvas focused on one central warrior who stood in profile to the viewer. The soldier stood slightly stooping and gazed forlornly over the destruction of battle that he'd either created or suffered. As John leant closer to explore the soldier's facial expression to contemplate the answer for himself, he was aware that a presence was hovering behind him.

"Do you like it?" said a gruff voice.

"I do," replied John, pausing. "Lovely brushstrokes."

He actually had no idea if this was true or not but having spent hours in the company of the famous art dealer Thomas Howard this was exactly the type of response his friend used to express praise of an artist's work. Other phrases he'd picked up included 'I love the way it captures the light', and 'you can almost feel the artist's pain in this piece'. He never really felt confident about some of these critiques fearing he might get caught out so tended to resort to 'brushstrokes' like a drunk returning blindly to the bottle.

"Aren't they?" added the man who moved forward to stand shoulder to shoulder with John. "What does this piece say to you?"

That was it. He was out of his depth. Why hadn't he kept his bloody mouth shut about the quality of the brushstrokes? In fact, why couldn't people just appreciate the painting for what it was, just a nice picture? This old intruder to his appreciation, dressed rather shabbily considering the company he was keeping today, was clearly one of those oversensitive types that needed to connect with the painting on a different level than him. He'd met plenty of these pompous, ethereal navel-gazers during his tour of Italy and had learnt precisely nothing from any of them, other than that they were overimportant idiots.

"Very interesting piece," said John stalling for the right words. "I guess for me it portrays the hostility and futility of war."

PUDDING LANE

"Well, obviously!" said the man disparagingly. "But what do you feel?"

Feel? He didn't feel anything, other than the honest answer which was hunger and mild pressure from being asked to critique a rather nondescript painting. Not answering wasn't really an option, though. He was in the palace of the King and amongst people of a higher standing. Fitting in was all part of the game. He had to say something, something intelligent.

"I think mostly I feel… sadness," he lied, pulling a glum expression to help back up his emotion.

"Is that it?" said the man, sounding rather offended.

"Um… lovely brushstrokes."

"Yes. You said that already."

"May I ask what you feel about it?" asked John turning the tables to see what he might extract from the old man's answer.

"When I gaze upon it, I feel the soldier's terror, his panic, his ambition for revenge, and mostly I'm filled with a visceral sense of sonder."

"Sonder, yeah, I get sonder, too, I was going to say that earlier," bluffed John, not having the first idea what 'sonder' meant.

The old man gazed at the painting longingly for a while, brow furrowed and deep, heavy breaths wheezing in and out of his lungs uncontrollably. Finally, he connected to what he wanted to say.

"What the artist has captured here, with effortless ease, is the ability to bring all five human senses leaping out of the canvas, grabbing the viewer and surrounding them with stimuli that raucously infect the soul. I have a tingling sensation through my body as his hand touches his blade, I can hear the din of the battle still ringing in the air, I can smell the blood oozing from his wounds and taste the bitter pallet of death that hangs in the air."

John's stomach rumbled embarrassingly, momentarily distracting the geriatric art critic.

PUDDING LANE

"It's an incredible window on history, the artist has built a bridge that connects two different time periods but has still managed to mirror the human condition of then and now."

"I couldn't agree more," nodded John, desperately trying to experience any of what the man had just described and failing utterly. "You must have been schooled in one of the great renaissance colleges of art to be such a master at translating the intentions of the creative mind and to understand the subtleties of his craft."

"No, never studied it."

"Then how are you able to get into the mind of the artist so effortlessly."

"Easy, really. It's one of mine."

"You own it!" said John, casting the old man up and down again.

"No! I painted it, Aniello Falcone," he said with an elaborate bow that he struggled to return from.

"John Evelyn," he replied with an outstretched hand and no such histrionics. "You painted this?"

"Yes, all of these are mine," he said, pointing at several other paintings that hung along the wall of the raised balcony which traversed the large dining hall where the King and his guests were enjoying their extravagant meal.

"Impressive. I have to say they look particularly good hanging here in this magnificent palace."

"You're right!" replied Aniello. "The Louvre would serve the people better as a gallery than it ever will as a palace for a King with too much power and not enough sense."

"I don't think that's very likely, do you?"

"No, not really. Although I wonder how long this royal family can cling to power before the common man rises up in a bid for freedom."

John felt uncomfortable. He was not born into high society, but neither did he come from impoverished roots. His father had made his living selling gunpowder to the very same people that Aniello seemed to despise. A background of moderate wealth had given John a chance to study and seek the sort of professions usually limited to those on the higher rungs of the social ladder. But rebellion, that wasn't something he'd even considered legitimate. He believed in time that equality would be gained peacefully through the enlightenment of the masses and the meritocracy that went with it.

"You like battle scenes, don't you?" said John, looking to change the subject from insurgency to imagery.

"They are my forte, but I have done portraits as well. Come and look at this one," he said, beckoning John to follow.

Falcone edged slowly down the walkway and pointed with pride at the picture of a young man painted from the neck up. It was unlike the other work that John had been reviewing. The exquisite precision and vivid colours of the oil paintings had been replaced by simple red and white chalk work, drawn on a piece of paper rather than an expensive canvas. The face of an attractive young man stood in profile, his strong jawline open, as if shouting a command, and, although it was a simple composition compared to many John had witnessed today, it captured the honest and steely perspective of the subject. Other than the head, the only feature of note was a simple cap that covered almost all of his hair. John knew this marked him out as someone who probably came from humble beginnings.

"What do you think?"

"Um, lovely… brushstrokes."

"It's chalk!"

"Chalk strokes," replied John tentatively. "Who is he?"

"This is my friend, Tommaso, known to many as Masaniello."

"It's very unusual for a commoner to be the subject of a portrait like this."

"True, but he was much more than a simple fisherman. Six years ago, he overthrew the Viceroy of Naples in a bloody rebellion and momentarily reached the summit of the mountain. My 'company of death' fought by his side against the oppressors until we, too, were defeated."

"You fought the authorities? What are you doing here, then?"

"Art is nothing without an audience and I have other reasons for being here."

"I suppose," replied John, not convinced by the argument. "What happened to Tommaso?"

"Murdered before he could complete his mission."

"What mission was that?" asked John.

"Standing up for the common man. Tommaso is proof that rebellion by force is a battle that peasants cannot win."

"Is that why you painted these battle scenes?"

"Nah, not really, I'm just rubbish at doing bowls of fruit."

They stood silently for a moment staring at a drawing that John considered to be substandard to the artist's other compositions but didn't like to say, given his close proximity to the creator.

"What do you do?" asked Aniello to break the silence.

"I write, diaries mainly, but I'm also a leading expert in silvology."

"Trees!"

"Yes."

"What have trees ever done for us?"

"Trees are an essential part of our ecosystem and we cannot thrive without them."

"They're not essential. Can a tree write a sonnet?"

"Um no."

"Can a tree paint?"

"It's not really what they're there for."

"Can they lead an army into battle."

"No. What have you got against trees?"

"Trees don't need protecting, people do."

"Not true, it is my belief that trees are critical in helping humans to breathe."

Aniello doubled over in laughter, desperately trying to stop himself from damaging his already frail body by reaching out to the wall for support. "That's the most ridiculous thing I've ever heard."

John folded his arms angrily. No one ever took him seriously. The people he spent his life with had all achieved their life goals in diplomacy, artistry and war. Deep thinkers were always victimised. "Mark my words, without trees there would be no humans."

"Pfft, trees will always be there. A lack of trees will never be a cause for human anxiety."

"We can learn much from our shared ecosystem and I intend to write all about trees when I get back to London."

"What about mountains, are you interested in those?"

"I suppose so, trees grow on mountains, don't they?"

"Indeed, and what do you hope to achieve from your writing endeavours?" asked Aniello composing himself.

"Progress, education and understanding."

The old man rubbed his scraggly beard and considered whether now was the right time to pass on the mantle.

"You are not a poor man," said Aniello accurately having observed the obvious evidence in his attire and speech. "What does progress mean to you?"

"Equality and a chance for everyone to exceed their own horizons."

"Tommaso believed in those same principles but it corrupted him. I have come to realise that a thousand words in the right ears will have more impact than a thousand weapons. It is through the arts that social change will be instigated."

"You're so right. Lucky for you then that you have an affluent sponsor in King Louis."

"I don't need him, I pay my own way."

"I didn't know the arts paid so well."

"They don't. I think you generally have to die to make any money. My funds come from a different source. What if I offered you a type of bursary in return for you carrying on my work?"

"Oh, I don't know, paintings aren't really my thing. I've tried still life, but the people all come out looking like

PUDDING LANE

deformed vegetables and my horses end up having massive bodies and legs that all appear to come out of their arses."

"I'm not asking you to paint. I'm asking you to write, teach and inspire. I'm inviting you to be a Mountain Man."

- Chapter 15 -

The World's Oldest Bank

Realistically there are only three ways to move across a city as big as London. Tube train, walking or taxi. None of these are foolproof. Taking the tube requires the traveller to squeeze their body mass into an impossibly shaped space no bigger than a rabbit hutch in sweltering temperatures never experienced on the surface of the Earth, even with the increasing threats of climate change. Whilst moving from station to station it's almost certain that the traveller will have to suffer biochemical warfare from the unrestricted body odours that only tube travellers seem to own.

Unique to London's tube network are a couple of extra treats that you don't find in other First World countries. Staff members have specifically been recruited for their dislike of other humans and the infrastructure itself will only work to its intended timetable on the second Monday in May and only then if the external temperature is exactly sixteen degrees centigrade. At every other time the overall service and punctuality will be officially measured by the London Transport authority as 'shit'. Ally had experienced it once before and as a consequence had a new level of empathy for battery hens. She swore never again.

Walking was certainly less stressful and often quicker. The main barriers to walking the city were the other people who also walked in it. City folk have an inbuilt code for how they should get from one point to another which they learnt from crows. They never deviate from their line of travel, even if something else appears to cross it. If you're not a city dweller it's impossible not to weave in and

THE WORLD'S OLDEST BANK

out to avoid being trampled on. This in effect doubles the total distance you were originally planning to walk. Collisions generally only occurred when two city people enter the same flight path, which often leads to an excellent range and pitch of local expletives. In London, if you're really lucky, you might even witness some good, old-fashioned cockney rhyming slang which might include someone being called a Brighton Rock, a Friar Tuck or a Kuwaiti Tanker.

This would have been Ally's preferred option if she hadn't been travelling with Gabriel. Not only was she unwilling to walk the mile or two to Oxford Street, but also her latex boots had incapacitated her from moving more than a few feet without moaning or making a scene. A London taxi was by no means perfect, particularly as they were entering rush hour, but it was a decent compromise.

"I still don't know how he got your number," insisted Ally, referring to the call that Antoine had made to Lance.

"I'm guessing he got it via the university."

"They don't print interns' personal mobile numbers in the campus directory or on the 'contact us' page of the website. I mean who would want to ring you?"

"Apparently Antoine Palomer."

"It's suspicious, that's what it is. This whole fucking week is suspicious. It's like God Himself has decided to piss me off," she said, momentarily and uncharacteristically shaking her fist at the sky.

"Let's hope he's sent us something useful," replied Lance.

Their taxi, driven by a man who had a general aura that suggested he'd only just been released, followed the contours of the Thames. At times it moved at top speed, and at others lay at rest with regular blasts of the horn. The average speed of a London taxi was officially thirty miles an hour. Averages can be misleading. No taxi in London ever travelled at that speed. They travelled at sixty or zero.

THE WORLD'S OLDEST BANK

"Where's Big Ben?" asked Gabriel, who had been ignoring the conversation between the others and was taking in the sights of the city when they weren't in a blur.

"Please watch the news," beseeched Ally with a sigh.

"Oh yeah, silly me. Big Ben is always on the news, it's on the opening credits. That must be where it's gone," she replied vacantly.

"Gabriel, that's just a video of it! The real tower is currently lying horizontally in the Thames, having been blown up by the Mountain Men... the reason we are here in the first place."

"Oh yeah."

After ten minutes of traffic-restricting travel, they reached their destination and were deposited at one end of Oxford Street for a fare that would easily buy you a small bungalow in Hull. Ally wondered why taxi drivers moaned so much.

There was a steady stream of eager shoppers bustling up and down Oxford street desperate to spend their money on any old bargain, desired or not, that screamed out from the posters in every shop window. The security box that Antoine had described in his call was located in a branch of the Halifax bank only a few hundred feet away if the directions glowing out of Lance's phone were to be believed. The bank was one of the few buildings that the hordes seemed uninterested in. They entered the large reception area and were met with a sense of calm sheltered from the exterior by large glass doors.

The process of retrieving the security box was far less taxing than Ally imagined. Normally interactions with a bank, even one you were a customer of, required intense scrutiny of your existence. Four-digit codes, multiple sources of identification, secret words that you'd set up decades ago and completely forgotten were all essential for the simple act of withdrawing a small sum of your own money. Then if that didn't meet the bank's rigorous procedures, a barrage of difficult questions was unleashed. What did you spend four pound sixty-three on a week last

THE WORLD'S OLDEST BANK

Thursday? What was the name of your neighbour's budgie when you were six? How many pairs of socks do you own? If you can't answer these your bank will freeze your account indefinitely or until you provide thirty-four separate proofs of who you are, in person but only in a remote branch in Stoke. Apparently, fraud in Britain was worth billions of pounds every year, presumably perpetrated by individuals who knew a lot more about people's lives than they did.

Today it was mercifully different. A rather pleasant tiller asked for a driving licence and the identification number. That was it. Once approved, the three of them were escorted to a back room where they watched through a glass screen as a robot fidgeted to and fro until it located the box they needed.

The robot arm slid a small metal box through a hatch and returned slowly with an electronic whirl to its idle position. Ally opened the box, still unsure as to what she might find inside. It was a letter. There was no address, just her full name. Antoine had either visited the branch in person to store it here or had engaged another to do so. How long it had been there was a mystery, as were Antoine's whereabouts. Ally put the letter in her bag, and they returned to the street.

Gabriel was almost beside herself with excitement. This was Oxford Street, London's premier shopping centre, just too tempting for a shopaholic of her reputation. Ally gave her permission to explore and sent Lance off to keep an eye on her. Ally, meanwhile, made a beeline for the coffee shop across the road. Nursing a double shot of expresso and a latte chaser she made herself as comfortable as possible on a cheap, tacky sofa surrounded by mothers with babies and overly loud teenagers shouting at each other, even though they were only inches apart. She pulled out the letter and opened it. It was beautifully handwritten and stretched to several pages.

THE WORLD'S OLDEST BANK

Dear Ally,

As I'm sure you're already aware I, like you have become a person of interest to the FBI, although, unlike you, I was aware of it sometime ago. I hope therefore you understand the need to act in such secrecy. Any contact with you via phone or email would have drawn the authorities to my position. I'm writing this to you following the bombing of parliament and have now made some connections that might help you. I'm sorry I'm unable to do so in person.

Two years ago, following our successful co-operation to stop Mario's organisation creating mayhem, I decided it was time to retire. My life has always been focused on helping others, but I felt it was time to concentrate on my own welfare. The Countess would not have wanted me to die at my desk. I set about selling my business interests and charities to those whom I felt would be able carry on my family's legacy. I kept only one member of staff to help me, someone whom I have invested time and money in over the past few years as part of the bursaries that we offer talented individuals who are unable to achieve their potential without a little support. I'm glad in this moment that I did. He has been most useful. In the process of selling these concerns I discovered two revelations, one sadly too late for me to stop it.

All the companies that I sold, I discovered later, were purchased by phantom holding companies all loosely connected to our old friend, Mario Peruzzi and the Oblivion Doctrine. I couldn't understand at first why he wanted to buy them. Was he trying to hurt me? Was it spite? Did he want to buy them so he could destroy them? Was he trying to sully my good name? The answer was quite different, as I have come to understand. Mario was looking for something in particular, and he wasn't the only one.

This brings me to my second revelation. Whilst auditing my affairs I discovered a bank account linked to

THE WORLD'S OLDEST BANK

me that I had no knowledge of. Although I was the executor of the account it was not mine and nor was it in my name. I could not withdraw money from it, change it or deposit anything in it except in very specific and pre-agreed circumstances. The account was not with my normal bankers and was registered with a bank I didn't even recognise. After doing a little research I discovered that the bank is one of the oldest in the world, having been set up over four hundred years ago.

In that time the bank had been acquired by bigger competitors but continued trading under its original name. Through history, as other account holders have died or changed their providers, the number of accounts has decreased. My account is the very last one associated with the Fugger Brothers who officially stopped trading in the late-seventeenth century.

The balance in the account runs into the tens of millions, but I'm sure Mario was not interested in the money. After all, he's reported to have access to much more than that. I dug a little deeper to see what I could find out. The account has changed hands around twenty times in the last four hundred years. I haven't been able to identify all of the account holders as most of the records have been lost or kept secret. The names of those who I can identify would blow your mind. Benjamin Franklin, Karl Marx, Lenin and Che Guevara, to name just a few!

I'm sure you've made the connection already that if I'm an executor and the account is that old it's clear who set it up in the first place. Philibert Lesage was a man determined to make a difference. The charities that I've run for most of my life are all examples of a legacy that ran through my veins even before I knew who he was. What if he had other methods for instigating change? What if he was behind the Mountain Men?

The recent incidents that you have been caught up in are all connected, although how much they relate to the real Mountain Men is unclear. Mario must have discovered them somehow and tried to buy my businesses in order to

THE WORLD'S OLDEST BANK

learn who they are and were. Which brings me to the other people who are looking for answers. The FBI have been drawn to this mysterious account because they suspect that the funds have been used for activities that Philibert may not have initially desired or condoned. No doubt they are already following your activities closely: be careful, they are only interested in one thing.

Although I've tried hard to piece together the whole list of previous owners, the bank would not or could not tell me who they all were. I can, however, tell you who the current one is. The name meant nothing to me, but perhaps it will be more familiar to you. His name is William Haggar. I've been unable to locate more information about him as my use of technology is limited as I attempt to avoid the attentions of the state. Given Philibert's propensity for hiding his identify it's very possible this trait has continued in his apprentices and William may go by other names.

Whoever he is, it's clear to me this William Haggar is the latest Mountain Man. However, I don't believe he is responsible for these attacks. History is in the past and William is very much in the present. When I look at the evidence, I can only conclude that Mario is in some way behind the attacks and he is using the Mountain Men for other purposes, in some part to wreak revenge against us. What William's part in all this is, is still unclear and very possibly not connected at all.

I'm sorry I cannot be more useful or support you in person. I hope that you have managed to get closer to others in order to form bonds of friendship and connections so that you are not in this mess on your own. Remember, not everyone is an enemy, there is much to learn about ourselves and others if we take the first step.

Your friend, Antoine Palomer.

Ally folded the letter and placed it in her handbag, removing as she did so the research she'd been

THE WORLD'S OLDEST BANK

documenting on the Mountain Men. The last of the known attacks was Masaniello's in the middle of the seventeenth century. The earliest name in Antoine's letter was Benjamin Franklin who was active in the middle of the eighteenth century, a hundred years later. What she'd hoped for from the letter was answers, not more questions. None of Antoine's letter had identified the next target or who might be behind it. Pudding Lane had been a hunch that had backfired on them spectacularly and yet she was convinced another historic event would soon be replicated and carried across people's television screens.

The other new information was the name of William Haggar, whoever he was. So many names cartwheeled around in her head. The names on the letters, most of which related to mildly famous names from history, the names related to some ancient bank account, Radu Goga whom Hudson was so keen to learn about, and now Haggar. She traced her finger down the list. She knew the origins of the Mountain Men. Philibert had passed it to Fawkes who somehow passed it to Masaniello, and she now knew who was last on that list. It was all the people in the middle that stumped her.

- Chapter 16 -

Dead Letter Office

Their return to Stanton St. John came just after the sun had disappeared from view and the congestion between London and Oxford had relented. It had been a frustrating day for everyone. Gabriel's ridiculous clothing had been photographed multiple times and had already been turned into a meme and shared a million times. Lance's attempts to endear himself to her had failed miserably and Ally was simply exhausted by all the questions circling around her head. Wednesday was about to disappear and stand aside for its replacement, but she wasn't hopeful Thursday would bring any significant improvement in her mood. All she wanted was a good night's sleep.

When Lance's car finally chugged into the village, Ally was relieved and somewhat surprised to see no welcome party at her door. There were no neighbours besieging her cottage, no Ms Honeywell waiting to greet her with some village emergency, no police barricade waiting to cart her back to jail and, to Gabriel's disappointment, no Buff waiting inside the home. Before any of this changed, Ally dismissed Lance and headed up to bed.

Six hours later the doorbell rang.

Twice.

Thursday wasn't making a good first impression.

Ally reluctantly dragged herself down the stairs where not even the sunlight was ready to illuminate whoever might be on the other side. She swung the door open where the looming figure of Daniel Hudson consumed the doorway, dressed as he always was in his unruffled, perfectly crisp, dark suit.

DEAD LETTER OFFICE

"Good morning."

"It's neither good nor morning," replied Ally pointing out the darkness that still filled the sky.

"But morning starts at midnight."

"Not for normal people it doesn't. What do you want?"

"Help," replied Hudson honestly.

"Are you offering or asking?"

"A little of both. Can I come in?"

"Do you have a warrant?"

Hudson unleashed a croaky chuckle as if the very concept of the FBI needing any document for anything was somewhat farcical. "I'm not doing a search, but if you'd like me to produce some meaningless piece of paper to brandish at you, I can have it with you in five minutes. I'll go to the car and write it out on a Post-it note. The FBI don't really need permission to go anywhere."

"Were you a bully at school?"

"Yes," he replied without any sense of irony in his voice. "Anyone else at home?"

It was an interesting question. Asked a week ago, the answer would have been immediate and unequivocal. These days it was harder to tell. People moved through her cottage like it was a busy international airport terminal. Sometimes people were there, sometimes they weren't and there was no 'in/out' board notifying the actual homeowner of the truth.

"Does it matter?"

"Only if they happen to be on the FBI's Most Wanted list."

"Apparently I'm on it, does that count?"

"Don't flatter yourself, you're no way near the most wanted. I'm not here to arrest you: as I said, I'm here for help."

Ally reluctantly waved him in and headed for the kitchen where she felt it necessary to offer her so-called guest something hot in a mug. It was apparently what normal people did, even when they didn't like the person visiting. Hudson followed her in, subconsciously analysing every feature of the cottage as he went. This was how special agents were whether on duty or not. They'd been trained to notice the absence of normality and the abnormal itself which meant nothing was left lacking scrutiny.

"Nice place," he offered quite genuinely.

"I didn't know the FBI had an interior design department?" huffed Ally, filling the kettle with water and placing it on the hob.

"It's called small talk."

"You can call it small, long, tall or big, I still don't give a shit. Tea or coffee?"

"Coffee, black."

It was the correct answer because she didn't actually have any tea. She filled the cafetière with fresh coffee and waited for him to open the conversation around his real reason for being there.

"How was your trip to London?" he asked casually.

"Disappointing."

"Great Fire of London, it was a reasonable guess, but ultimately wrong. Our analysts had already dismissed it. Although sadly we failed to identify the correct target. That happened overnight."

"Another attack, where?"

"Somewhere called Occitan in France. A thousand farmers attacked an Army barracks and a church. They've caused havoc overnight, spreading through the valleys and gaining popular support as they went. It appears under control now."

"Why did they do it?"

"I guess it's similar to the 'gilets jaunes' protests, but more random and violent."

"What makes you think it's connected?" asked Ally.

"They very purposely set up three haystacks and set them on fire as a message. Want to guess what it read from the sky?"

"TMM."

DEAD LETTER OFFICE

"Correct. We did some research into similar historic events and identified a name that might have inspired it. He was called Jean Cavalier. In seventeen hundred and three he led something called the Camisard rebellion against the Catholics in exactly the same region."

"Was he on your list?"

"You know that's not how the list works."

Ally immediately felt foolish. It wasn't an emotion she was used to feeling and generally pointed it out in others. Of course, he wouldn't be on the list. Mario hadn't wanted it to be easy for any of them.

"A predecessor and ally of Cavalier's, Roland Laporte was on the list, though. He died at the very start of the Camisard conflict, from what we can piece together, but there's almost no information about him."

"Did the original uprising succeed?" asked Ally.

"It depends on your definition of success. It got further than most uprisings around that time and set a benchmark for later events. This was only eighty years before the French Revolution. Skirmishes like this went on for years until people started to believe that they might just succeed in their ultimate aim."

"Full-blown revolution," answered Ally. "We know the French Revolution features on Mario's list. If he re-creates that part of history, we're all in big trouble."

She didn't disclose it, but the news of Benjamin Franklin's name yesterday suggested the American Revolution, which came just ten years earlier, might also feature on the list of the Mountain Men's accomplishments. Antoine, though, had cautioned her about the FBI's intentions, and she was more guarded than usual.

"Then we'd better work out the sequence fast before that happens."

"We! I don't work with others. It disagrees with me, just ask Ernest Culpepper."

"You work with Lance and Gabriel, though."

DEAD LETTER OFFICE

It shouldn't have surprised her that the FBI knew her every move – after all, they were the FBI. They didn't have a reputation for being slapdash. It didn't stop it being a rather disconcerting feeling for someone as ferociously private as she was. In future she'd have to remind herself that they were always watching and listening.

"I'd describe my involvement with those two as community service rather than work," she replied. "If you know all this, what do you need me for anyway?"

"We don't know what will happen next."

"And you think I do?"

"Yes, with help I think you might be the only one who can work it out. When we last met, I refused to show you the contents of the letters Mario sent out. Now that I'm satisfied you are not connected to these crimes and that someone is using you as a diversion, I'm willing to show you, if you agree upfront to assist me."

"Assist you?"

"Help me stop these bastards and help me to locate Mario's money."

"I will help with the first part, but I have no interest in supporting the US government in their pursuit of capital gains so they can use them to further oppress poor people around the world. It irritates me that your only motivation is to find the money."

"It's my job, Ally. You can understand the importance of that to someone like me?"

"Not if the reasons behind the instructions are morally misguided. I may work for others, but I choose why I do it. All that's important to me is to stop the carnage and to solve the puzzle, the moment the money comes into it I'm done with it and you."

"Fine."

Hudson removed the tablet that Ally knew held the photos of the letters. He slid it forward so she could get a look at the contents. The letters on-screen had no writing on them other than two numbers at the top and consisted of small holes that had been cut out of the page in a

DEAD LETTER OFFICE

seemingly random pattern. They were only visible because of the silver metal table underneath. Ally knew immediately that if the reader of the letters had the correct book and page number, they would be able to place the letter over its text to reveal a hidden message.

"What do you make of it?" asked Daniel.

"Not much," said replied. "What you've effectively got here is a picture of a Scherenschnitte."

"A what?"

"Scissor cuts. It's the art of cutting paper to form a symmetrical design. Do you have the originals?"

"No, just the pictures."

"Then you're screwed."

Ally pressed the plunger down on the cafetière and poured two cups of strong coffee into the waiting mugs. She passed one to Hudson who was staring out of the window deep in thought. He'd been too hasty in sending the letters to their intended destinations. He'd acted without the intelligence needed to make the call. It was a rookie error for such a senior agent. Doing so had made the situation more complicated and only he was responsible for fixing it. As he gazed out of the kitchen window to the gentle dawn light that was framing the autumnal sky against the bare apple trees out in the garden his eyes landed on the frame of a black and white photograph. It leant up against the windowsill just below a piece of wood that had been used to board up the smashed glass. The picture featured an elderly man with wispy, white hair holding a stern yet wise expression. He got up to take a closer look. He'd seen this face before somewhere.

"Family member?" he asked casually.

"Yes."

"Who?"

"None of your business frankly," she replied angrily. It was one thing to allow the FBI into your home; it was quite another to reveal your backstory. She steered the conversation back to the letters. "Doesn't look like you can offer much help, after all."

DEAD LETTER OFFICE

"Can't we still use the picture of the letters?"

"Of course not. Why do you think Mario sent them in the first place? Only the holder of the letter can access the cipher because only they know which book to use. Plus, the letters are exactly the right proportions to read the message. Even if you printed them out and made the cuts yourself, it wouldn't fit perfectly. If you have neither you're basically stuffed."

"Stuffed?" replied Hudson, quite unclear as to what she meant.

"Screwed, poleaxed, nobbled, up the creek, basically you're fucked."

"What if we could find the letters?"

"Then you'd need the book."

"We both know which book it is," replied Hudson.

The revelation hit Ally's synapses like a thunderbolt. The Shikshapatri. It was rarer than hen's teeth, and Mario would know that using any other book that had thousands of versions in circulation would make it easy for the FBI to solve the puzzle if they got hold of one of the letters. Finally, the bits of the jigsaw were falling into place. The Mountain Men had stolen the book from the Weston, found the letters addressed to the gunpowder plotters and other infamous people, and followed the instructions presented by the cipher. Presumably the book would then be passed on to the owner of the next letter where a new set of instructions would be laid out.

London, Naples and Occitan had been hit in a matter of days, so it made sense that they weren't dealing with one suspect but multiple offenders possibly all over the world. A network of people who'd engaged with the old Oblivion Doctrine perhaps? It could be absolutely anyone. The ringleaders, whoever they were, would broadcast the instructions specifically designed to inspire the uprisings of others. That way it would become almost impossible to identify who was leading and who was following amongst all the chaos. She'd been so tied up in tracing the next target she'd almost completely forgotten about the book.

DEAD LETTER OFFICE

"Any news on the recovery of the Shikshapatri?"

"Nothing. The Indian government have given their British counterparts until Friday to return the book or at least make progress towards doing so. The Brits are still convinced that the blowing up of the Houses of Parliament was in some way retribution for the theft and have accused the Indians of covert involvement. Each day the Hindu mass protests outside the Weston gains more followers and attention. There were over two hundred there yesterday. It's becoming almost impossible to enter the building. I think they may decide to close it tomorrow. The whole thing is a total mess."

"Back to square one."

"Square one?" replied Daniel vacantly.

"First base," she added, quickly remembering as an American he might need a more familiar reference point. "No letters, no book, no progress."

"Let's find the first on that list."

"How?"

"By going to the Dead Letter Office."

"Where's that?"

"Belfast."

The door to the kitchen swung open and a bleary-eyed Gabriel sauntered in with almost no care for who else might be in there. The make-up on her face, which had been dutifully applied yesterday, was now smeared over her face like a Joker tribute act. She held her head with one hand and used the other as a guide as she stumbled through the room in search of some paracetamols or, failing that, more vodka. Ally and Daniel watched with interest as she fumbled through cupboards becoming more and more desperate for a pharmaceutical solution to her hangover. Each cupboard was left open when her search resulted in failure. Within minutes she'd turned the kitchen into the scene from a burglary.

"Second drawer under the sink," said Ally before she started ripping out the fitted kitchen.

DEAD LETTER OFFICE

She tried to raise a thumb but struggled with the overwhelming advantage of her foe, gravity. She grabbed two tablets, threw them down her throat, and leant over the sink to drink directly from the tap and wash them down.

"They can really drink, these locals. I've never done a yard of ale before, thought I might explode from…" said Gabriel turning from the sink and finally realising it wasn't only Ally she was talking to.

"Gabriel Janvier, meet Daniel Hudson."

"Oh hello. I didn't know Ally had friends."

"I don't think that would be a good description for it. I'm with the FBI."

"The furniture store?" asked Gabriel. "What have you ordered?"

"Gabriel, he's with the FIB."

She froze solid. "Merde!"

"Don't worry, Miss Janvier, we have bigger fish to catch than you at the moment. Even though you successfully hacked our computer systems, which was rather impressive, by the way. I'm granting you immunity until we can stop the Mountain Men."

"Does that mean that I can't catch measles?" she said vacantly.

"Immunity from prosecution, not immunity from infectious diseases," explained Ally. "You'll have to excuse her, she's a simpleton."

"You mean I can do whatever I like?" Her eyes gleamed through the haze of her hangover. "I can even murder someone."

"No! Of course not. Who would you want to murder anyway?" asked Ally in dismay.

"I can think of one person."

"I'm giving you temporary immunity against any crimes you may or may not have committed up to yesterday," corrected Hudson. "If you help us, I'm confident we'll overlook the hacking offence that it would be simple to convict you of."

DEAD LETTER OFFICE

Hudson took a mobile phone from the inside pocket of his jacket and held it up towards Gabriel. "This is for you: I'm sure you've missed having one."

"I've coped. It's not the first time that I've lived without one, you know. I used to be a prepper, didn't have one then. Olds always think us youngsters can't survive without a phone, yet I notice you lot seem to use yours just as much as we do. Hypocritical, really. Maybe you should try going without one, too."

However well you think you know someone, they can still surprise you. Ally had seen this wisdom in Gabriel before, yet it always came out of the blue like a summer thunderstorm. Ally wondered where it came from and whether Gabriel was even able to control it.

"You don't want it, then?" said Hudson, about to replace it in his jacket.

"Don't be stupid. I'd happily rip it off your dead corpse if you don't give it to me!"

Just like that the transformation vanished.

"It's yours. I think you'll need it if you're going to help us."

"And you're sure they're not going to be able to trace me?" asked Gabriel, moving forward, hand outstretched to take it from him.

"That's what immunity means, yes."

Ally wasn't convinced Daniel was being genuine. The FBI used any means at their disposal, and they'd have no qualms in double-crossing a millennial computer hacker.

"We were never really that interested in you anyway," replied Daniel. "It's your boyfriend we're more interested in."

"He's not my boyfriend anymore," Gabriel snapped in reply.

*****

Of all the things Ally expected Thursday to throw at her, Northern Ireland wasn't one of them, but by mid-

DEAD LETTER OFFICE

afternoon she and Daniel had landed at Belfast International Airport. An hour later they were standing on the banks of the Lagan River in the shadow of the nine-storey, red and grey exterior of the National Returns Centre. Any letter that entered the postal system in the United Kingdom, whose sender or recipient couldn't be identified, ended up here.

Behind these walls three hundred 'letter detectives' scoured through the millions of items in search of a clue that might help them identify the intended recipient. It wasn't normally a place the general public were allowed to visit, but as usual the FBI appeared to have an 'access all areas' pass. Ally and Daniel waited in reception for their scheduled appointment.

"Mr Hudson, welcome to the DLO," said a kindly-faced gentleman whose cheeks shone with a red glow. "My name is Seamus Cafferty: I understand you are searching for a letter."

"Yes," replied Daniel.

"Shouldn't be too hard, only two million for us to look through!" he replied jovially. "Please, follow me."

On the other side of the main double doors they were escorted to a lift where Seamus pressed number three on the wall panel. The lift crept slowly up through the floors with a creak as Seamus whistled away to himself completely out of tune but in total contentment. The smile on his face never budged an inch. Seamus was the type of person who struggled with any other emotion than complete bliss. He could receive news that his dog had died, his wife had left him, and his car had been stolen, and you'd barely notice a difference in his demeanour.

The lift doors eased open and the third floor stretched out in front of them. It was a huge, open-plan space, dotted here and there by small cubicles in a totally irregular pattern like the owners had complete freedom to decide on their own rules. Rows of people sat on swivel chairs in front of huge piles of mail. Stacks of pigeonholes extended from the floor, up behind their desks, and loomed high above

DEAD LETTER OFFICE

them. Further sacks of envelopes surrounded them like flood barriers.

"This floor is dedicated to our lost mail," said Seamus proudly. "Anything that can't be delivered comes here. Everything has to be opened so we can identify where it belongs, in fact this is the only place in the country where we are allowed to do that. We get all sorts of treasures here. There's an annual competition for the strangest item."

"Who's winning?" asked Daniel politely.

"Difficult to say, it's been a very good year. So far, we've had a mummified hand, a set of traffic lights, a dead rat and a thousand pounds in cash addressed to Admiral Nelson. That was one of our success stories, actually."

"How can you call that a success? He's been dead for two hundred years," replied Ally sharply, getting irritated by Seamus's relentless positivity.

"We found out it wasn't the real Nelson, obviously that would be ridiculous. It was actually meant for a pub called the Admiral Nelson. Someone was trying to pay the bill for a party but wrote out the wrong address. We always say that the clues to finding the answers are usually in plain sight. If you can't find the answer you're just not looking properly," chuckled Seamus.

"Fascinating," answered Hudson, considering his own case. "I think you're probably right."

One of Hudson's great skills was his ability to alter his character to the situation he was presented with. It was a vital part of the job. If you wanted people to open up, so you might learn from them, then you had to gain their trust. From Ally's perspective it looked very much like arse-kissing. The sight of him doing it made her actually feel a little sick. It was one of the characteristics that separated them. Much of the rest of their personalities matched rather well. They were both ruthless in pursuit of their goals, disliked histrionics, tended to lead a solitary existence and were confirmed workaholics. She hadn't voiced it, but she had a niggling respect for him, when he wasn't kissing people's arses.

"What chance of finding one of our letters?" asked Ally forcefully.

"If your letter still exists, then it's somewhere here," he said, waving his arms at the room.

"Why wouldn't it exist?" asked Hudson.

"Unless it's been claimed we only keep stuff for two months. Then, unless it's valuable, we destroy them. I was told in your original request to come here that the letters you are looking for were only sent a few weeks ago, so they should be here. You just have to look in the right place."

"You're not expecting us to look, are you?!" replied Ally indignantly.

"No, of course not: we have an excellent record system. All we need is a date and the location you think it was sent to. What date do you think the letter went out?"

"Two weeks ago, but there were several sent to the UK so there might be more than one still here."

Hudson detailed the addresses and recipients he was looking for and Seamus sat down at a computer terminal and started to enter the details. The first two searches returned negative results. If the letters had been here, he explained as he typed, then they'd already been accounted for.

"Nothing so far. It's very possible that someone has claimed them," said Seamus.

"Who?" asked Hudson.

"We don't keep any records about that information, sadly."

"Try Philip Beaumont," suggested Ally.

"We've struggled to place that name," said Daniel. "Who is he?"

"A pseudonym used by Oswald Tesimond, a friend and associate of Guy Fawkes's. I believe from the research I've done he might have passed the mantle on to Tommaso during his travels to Naples at the end of his life. He was never part of the Gunpowder Plot and seems to have had

DEAD LETTER OFFICE

no involvement in anything violent. It's possible that the Mountain Men were not just men of action and may have included men of thought. Christopher Wren and Voltaire, for example, had no links to anything sinister but yet their names are on the list. The only people they associated with were men who developed theories on social reforms or were involved in education."

"I never thought of that," said Hudson. "That means there may be big gaps between the more active characters."

"Yes."

"We do have an item with that name," replied Seamus excitedly. "It's addressed to a Hindlip Hall but was returned to us."

"We must see it," demanded Hudson.

Seamus strolled off to the location indicated by the computer system and returned ten minutes later holding an opened envelope. Ally quickly snatched it from his hand and carefully removed the letter from within. She held it up and the light pierced through the holes cut into the paper. This was it, they were one step closer.

"Hudson, let's go," demanded Ally. "No time to lose."

"I thought the Brits had manners?" he replied coldly.

"What?"

"This man has just spent time helping us and you're treating him like an object."

"Ah it's ok," said Seamus who'd still be smiling if you hit him repeatedly over the head with an iron bar.

"No, it's not," said Hudson. "Say thank you."

"Get some perspective, Hudson," barked Ally defiantly.

Quite unexpectedly Hudson drew a gun from around his waist and held it threateningly at her. It was a tactic he'd been considering using ever since they left Ally's cottage, but needed the right opportunity. A specific theory about Ally's background was running through his head and he needed to test it.

"We're not leaving until you say thank you," he said clicking the safety catch off the weapon.

DEAD LETTER OFFICE

Ally peered down the barrel of the gun and her spine tingled. It wasn't the first time she'd faced one, but it was only now as the fear overcame her body that she knew it for certain. A memory looped up from her guts, dragging a distant long-lost emotion kicking and screaming with it. The distress made her hands shake and propelled her body involuntarily to her knees, hands covering her head, tears streaming down her face. The circumstances of the past weren't visual, but the feeling of nostalgia was as clear as the laminate floors below her. Had he lost it? Was he really going to shoot her over this?

"Thank… you," she stuttered desperately from her huddled position on the floor.

"Now, that wasn't hard, was it?" replied Daniel, replacing the gun out of view. The reaction was exactly the one he'd expected and proved his hidden theory perfectly.

Seamus nodded his acceptance completely unfazed that a man had brandished a gun in his place of work. When you were in your late-fifties and spent your entire life in Northern Ireland, the past was a place where guns were a regular feature of life. He held out his hand to Ally and escorted them back to the lift and eventually out of the building itself. Out in the autumn air, Ally regained her normal granite composure.

"What the fuck was that about?" she said through gritted teeth.

"I was testing a theory," he replied calmly.

"What theory?"

"Why you're so angry at the world."

"Lots of practice," she replied, turning her back and storming off.

- Chapter 17 -

Karma

It was the first time in her life that Ally Oldfield had been to Northern Ireland. She'd had longer baths. By Thursday evening their Aer Lingus plane was about to touch down at Heathrow Airport surrounded by thick, grey clouds. The one-hour flight had barely got off the ground before it was going through its landing procedures. Daniel and Ally didn't speak for the entirety of the flight for very different reasons. They were both certain that the other was withholding information from them. How could she trust someone who pulled a gun out to make a point? Had he guessed, or hoped, that she'd react in the way she did? What was he trying to prove? What did he know that she didn't?

Daniel squirmed uncomfortably in a seat designed for a midget. His knees were pressed together in such a way that blood had stopped flowing to his toes. Normally he'd distract himself from the discomfort by working, but having his laptop open so close to her might be a mistake in the current circumstances. They might be working together but there was still information he was not authorised to reveal. Classified documents that might well explain her reaction back at the DLO. There would be a time for disclosures, but it wasn't now. Lines of enquiry had to be opened first.

There were actually two vital avenues he wanted to explore and the order in which he navigated them might turn out to be crucial.

The Mountain Men incidents had occurred every two days. Saturday night had seen parliament burn, on

KARMA

Monday Naples went up in smoke, and on Wednesday it had been Occitan's turn. Tomorrow was Friday and they still had no idea where the next attack would be.

FBI agents were taught to interrogate all possible avenues of intelligence before making their decisions. When lives were at stake errors were costly to reputations and individual lives. Data in the right hands, assessed by the right people, was a wonderful weapon, but it wasn't always the answer. Daniel had always been encouraged to make judgements based on instinct when the evidence was lacking or took too long to establish. This felt like one of those moments.

The plane bounced erratically a number of times as it struck the tarmac of Heathrow's second runway before being forced to decelerate like an owner furiously pulling on a lead to stop a rabid dog chasing a neighbour's plucky cat. Evening had passed into night-time and the turgid November clouds had broken out into rather unconvincing rainfall.

"Call Gabriel," said Daniel.

"I've had enough disappointment for one day, thanks."

"Do you want to work out who the Mountain Men are or not?"

"Obviously. Flying to Northern Ireland for two hours isn't my idea of fun, you know."

"And do you want to know who you are?"

For almost the first time in twenty years, Ally was lost for words. There was no pithy comeback or sarcastic taunt. No defensive rebuke or intellectual challenge. Just silence as his words pierced her ears and kidnapped her ability to react. Did she want to know? She wondered if it would make life better or worse. There was nothing frightening about knowing who she was today. That could be controlled and manipulated. History wasn't that flexible. It had a tendency to be obstinate and unavoidable. Learning about history was one of her only joys in life, yet she knew almost nothing about her own.

KARMA

"What do you know of it?" she snapped, turning her internal frustration outward as her mouth caught up with the idea of her being cornered like a frightened animal.

"Just a hunch. I'll know soon enough. That's why I need you to call Gabriel. Meet her at the Weston tonight and work out where the book is so we can stop the next attack. Go into the museum after they've closed the exhibitions for the night. I'll meet you there later."

"But the book isn't in the library, they've searched high and low for it."

"But have they?" replied Daniel. "Something that Seamus said got me thinking. The clues are often in plain sight as long as you know where to look. The tracking microchip for the stolen book was still there in the museum, and I think the book is, too."

"High and low... why didn't I think of that? But if it's there I'll go and look for it alone. Why would I possibly need Gabriel to help me?"

"Because she's a genius."

"Being good once in a hundred attempts doesn't make someone a genius."

"Let's just hope she's due one, then."

The plane pulled into the gate and as normal a stampede of self-important businessmen and drunken holidaymakers fought over the narrow space in the aisle. Daniel and Ally left them to it.

"You do know I'm still the main suspect in the robbery. I can't just walk into the Weston and use my access card: there will be a SWAT team up my jacksie before I opened the front door."

"Use this," said Daniel, passing her a white plastic key card. "It'll give you access to almost anywhere."

*****

Karma, they say, is only possible for those who can discern right from wrong. Small children, animals and politicians are therefore excluded. Hindus believe that everything we

KARMA

have ever thought, spoken, done or caused is a result of karma either from this life or a past one. Unkindness yields spoilt fruit and good deeds bring forth sweet ripened fruit. When bad deeds are committed it's only a matter of time before the Universe pays you back.

All you needed was a bit of patience.

Ok, a lot of patience.

Karma isn't great at keeping time. The reward for good deeds might not even happen in your current lifetime, but rest assured somewhere down the line if you play your cards right and are exclusively nice to other people, a future you will probably win the lottery. The opposite is also true. Which meant a future Ally Oldfield was likely to have a thoroughly miserable time unless her attitude changed, or possibly a past Ally Oldfield was already responsible and was repaying her for past misdemeanours. Of course, Ally didn't really go in for that sort of thing, but there were a large number of people who did.

They happened to be extremely committed to the ideology and on this particular occasion were also somewhat in the way.

Even at ten o'clock in the evening the protest outside the Weston continued unabated. Today was Thursday, the fifth day since they'd started to assemble. Now a crowd of about two hundred people stood between Ally and the main entrance. Their collective chants drifted through the city centre muffled by the din of chattering revellers and noisy buses. Their traditional religious clothing added a well-needed splash of colour to the grey façades of the historic buildings. In the centre of the group a young woman wearing a flower garland around her neck was putting the finishing touches to a poorly planned placard.

"What are you doing?" asked Ally sternly.

"Protesting!" replied Gabriel without shifting her concentration from finishing the message in shaky red paint.

"Against what exactly?"

"Um… not sure exactly. It just looked like fun."

KARMA

"Show me," said Ally pointing at the placard.

"It's not quite finished…" she tried to reply, but Ally's hands had already grabbed it from her.

"Save our shoes!" read Ally aloud. "I'm not sure where to start. So many questions."

"That's why all these people are here," said Gabriel doggedly. "They've all had their shoes stolen and they're protesting against it."

"Look at the other placards," responded Ally. "You might notice a complete lack of shoe references."

Gabriel glanced around at the other signs being held up by the mostly Hindu congregation. 'Our sacred book' was a popular phrase, as was 'Boycott Britain'. There wasn't a huge amount of creativity on show other than a small sign that read 'If Karma doesn't get you, we will'.

"Why do they want us to follow Steve?" asked Gabriel, pointing to a sign on the edge of the group.

"Student prank probably. Listen, I called you here against my better judgement because, apparently, I need you to help me. I didn't call you here so you could join a hippy commune. Come on."

She grabbed Gabriel by the arm and led her towards the museum, although they weren't planning on going through the main entrance. Even with Daniel's special key there were still security measures in place that would alert people to their presence. Those would have to be disabled before they could start the search for clues to the book's whereabouts. That's where Gabriel came in. They entered via the staff entrance at the rear of the building, Daniel's card giving them instant access.

"Time to earn your rent," said Ally. "I need you to disable as many of the security systems as you can."

"What do they have here?"

"Cameras, sensors, magnetically sealed doors, and pressure plates. They also have a team of guards who monitor the place on an hourly cycle."

"Want me to knock them out?" said Gabriel clicking her knuckles.

"Do whatever you have to."

A number of offices lined the corridors where they'd entered the building. Ally knew them well. Ernest's was two doors down the left-hand side and opposite that was the room that housed the computer servers. Ally opened it with the skeleton key and Gabriel disappeared inside. Twenty minutes later she returned, smiling.

"All done," she said, holding a laptop in one hand.

"Where did you get that from?"

"It was in there. I've set it up via Wi-Fi to their security systems so we can see what they can see."

"Can you get a reading for the Shikshapatri's microchip?"

"Easy!"

She opened the lid of the computer and went to work. Two minutes later she turned the screen around. A small red light was flashing intermittently on a detailed map of the Weston's special collections room. Ally could get there with her eyes closed but knew there wasn't much point. She'd seen into the exhibit case on the day the book was stolen and knew the book wouldn't be there now.

"Is this like Pokémon GO!?" asked Gabriel curiously.

"What the hell is that?"

"It's a game. You use your mobile phone to find little virtual creatures."

"What's the point in that?"

"It's makes going outside fun."

"You know if you go for an actual walk, in the actual countryside you can see actual creatures all over the place."

"But they might bite you! Better to look for virtual creatures. I once found a Pikipek in my garden. It was cute."

"I knew this was a mistake," sighed Ally. "Let's stay in the real world, shall we? What we are looking for is the book that your friends out there have been protesting about for the last few days. It has a microchip on it to track its position."

KARMA

"It's there, though," said Gabriel, pointing at the screen.

"But it isn't there, that's just the point. The police looked for it, but couldn't find it."

"Did they have their eyes closed?"

"No."

"Where is it, then?"

"Have you ever heard the expression to look for something 'high and low'?"

"Yeah of course."

"Well, the police didn't. Come on, follow me."

The further they walked, the darker the network of passageways became. Eventually after several minutes of gloom, Ally stopped next to a large, metal door distinctly different to the others they'd passed. This one appeared wider and more secure. Ally had only been through it once and her normal security access didn't open the lock. Ernest had taken her through it as part of her tour of the facilities when she first joined the university staff. It had left her breathless and she only wished she could have stayed there longer. It was time to see if Daniel was right about his skeleton key card opening almost any lock. She pressed it against the security plate and the light turned green. The clanging sound of a lock turning proved it further.

Ally swung the door open and advanced into a large cage lift big enough to hold a small van. There weren't many options for this lift's destination. You either went down or you stayed here. The lift crept downwards so slowly that it was hard to know if it was moving at all. Only when they'd reached the bottom did a bell chime to indicate their arrival. Through the door the soft glow of emergency lighting lit their way. The air was cold and musky with a disconcerting feel about it. Ally turned her phone's light on and pulled the cage open. In front of them a network of tunnels stretched out into the distance.

"Where are we?" asked Gabriel.

"Under the museum. Seventy years ago, they excavated this area so they could store more of the library's books. Is the tracker still working down here?"

"Yes."

"Then lead on."

"It's a bit creepy."

"What are you more frightened of, the tunnels in front of you, or me behind you?"

"I'll get a move on."

They followed the red dot as well as they could. Unlike the map of the floor above, down here there were access issues. It wasn't possible to walk in a straight line so they had to identify the tunnels that would take them to the point closest to the red light. On either side of them lines of bookcases stretched up the walls from floor to ceiling crowded with leather-bound volumes not important enough to be housed anywhere more meaningful.

"Why would it be down here?" asked Gabriel as they inched along in the bitterly cold air.

"To keep it safe. Whoever stole it knew that removing it from the museum would be too difficult, so they just made it look like they had. Since they opened the large warehouse in Swindon very few people use these tunnels now."

"But how did the thief get it here?"

It was an excellent question and one that Ally had only one possible answer for. An insider must have been involved. If the stolen book unlocked the cipher as she believed, then they must have translated all of the letters at once before leaving it here, or they'd have to come back here every time a letter was discovered.

"Here," said Gabriel stopping with a jolt. "We're right over the red dot."

Ally shone her phone over the bookshelves on either side. "Help me look."

"What picture is on the cover?"

"Picture?!" exclaimed Ally desperately.

"Yeah. Romantic fiction, battle scene, spacecraft… ?"

KARMA

"It was written two hundred years ago, it doesn't have a picture on it!"

"No wonder there aren't many copies, then. Must have bombed without some decent cover art."

"Gabriel, we're not looking for a copy of 'Harry Potter and the Corridor of Uncertainty'…"

"That's not one of them," she interrupted angrily.

"What we are looking for is a sacred text. Like the Bible. Do you see many Bibles with cover art? No!"

"Kids' Bibles have pictures."

"But they're not two hundred years old, are they!? What we're looking for is about the size of a wallet, bound in light brown leather with blue stitching. Its pages are really fragile so be careful. You look that side, I'll look on the other."

Moments later, a thud hit the bookshelf just to Ally's left ear. It was followed by another. Then a book struck her on the shoulder blade. Any book that wasn't bound in fragile brown leather with intricate blue stitching was being hurled over Gabriel's shoulder with the same manoeuvre she used every morning to find the right clothes to wear.

"STOP!" shouted Ally, turning to berate her for a lack of respect.

Gabriel stopped in mid-throw.

"Don't move!"

"Why?"

"That's the one."

Ally rushed forward and gently prised the book from Gabriel's grasp before she was able to jettison two hundred years of history down the tunnel. She gently untied the leather strap that kept the book protected inside its case. The pages hadn't been damaged by its short holiday underground.

"Right, let's get this back upstairs."

- Chapter 18 -

Gobbledygook

Ally slid a pair of protective gloves over her fingers, carefully removed the Shikshapatri from her bag and laid it out on the desk in her office. It wasn't the oldest book she'd ever handled but it was definitely the most important one right now. Given its unusual treatment over the last week it was in a reasonable condition. None of the pages had been torn or removed and importantly it had been kept dry and away from any chemicals that might have reacted with the delicate pages and damaged it irreparably.

Finding it was a big deal. Any remaining doubts the authorities had over her own involvement in its theft would finally be dispelled and hopefully by tomorrow she would be reinstated to her job. Then life could return to her version of normal. The Indian government would cease their rather irrational sabre-rattling that had the potential to spill out into further violence and economic uncertainty for both nations. The crowd a few metres outside the front door would celebrate, pack up their things, put their shoes back on and go home happy. Most importantly, finding the Shikshapatri would lead to the unlocking of the code to Mario's Mountain Men.

The book was the missing link.

They had one of the letters, they knew who the others had been posted to, and Ally had at least some clues as to which event was likely to happen next. The most recent incident in the French Occitan region was the re-enactment of Jean Cavalier's rebellion of the early eighteenth century, and Ally knew the trail pointed from that skirmish right up to the doorstep of the French

GOBBLEDYGOOK

Revolution some ninety years later. Up to that point the original Mountain Men hadn't accomplished much. A failed gunpowder plot, a minor and short-lived rebellion in Naples, and a skirmish in an insignificant region of the French countryside. What it did demonstrate, however, was that they were learning. Experience and failure had been passed from one member to the next, each achieving a higher level of success than the man that preceded them. It only took them another eighty years to get it right.

If Mario managed to instruct his vast army of online miscreants to re-create the French Revolution, things would get really spicy.

Time was ticking.

Ally still firmly believed that there must have been other attempts at rebellion in the eighty years between these known events. The Mountain Men would have needed to hone their abilities in order to overthrow a whole nation state. The problem was that she'd been through the history of Europe at that time and there didn't appear to be any. If she was going to discover what it was, she needed to crack the code before they handed the Shikshapatri back to the police and the ever-anxious Ernest Culpepper. To do that they needed the letter they'd retrieved from Belfast, currently in Daniel's possession.

After their exploration of the tunnels and once they'd returned to her office, she'd immediately dialled his number. There was no answer. She'd left a voicemail, but an hour had passed and there was still no response. The early hours of Friday morning had crept into the clock face above her desk and it might be several more hours before any news reached them. In the meantime, Gabriel had fallen asleep on the comfy swivel chair and Ally was forced to make do with the less comfy floor and wall. Soon she, too, drifted off.

A muscly hand gripped her shoulder and shook her violently. Only darkness flooded through the window as she peeled her eyes open and pulled her hair free from the cabinet next to her desk which had snared it when her body had slipped sideways into sleep.

"Wake up."

"I'm awake," she replied bitterly, rubbing the tiredness from her eyes and struggling to focus on Daniel's huge presence looming over her. "Where have you been?"

"I've been busy," he replied plainly.

She wondered if he ever slept? Did FBI agents have special, super powers or were they just bred to survive without rest? He regularly seemed to make an appearance at times that coincided with the peak productivity of binmen and foxes. In reality, Daniel hadn't slept, but nothing about his attire or expression suggested it. He, too, had been busy seeking answers.

"You found the book?" he said flatly.

"Yes. Where's the letter?"

Hudson reached inside his jacket and passed her the letter.

Gabriel woke with a start and leapt out of the chair like a cat had been threatened with a cucumber. It was quite obvious she had no recollection of where she was or, more disconcertingly, how it felt to wake up without having previously drunk her body weight in schnapps the previous night. Her body twitched, she scratched her head and forensically analysed parts of her body like they'd only just been reassembled in the correct order.

"Gone again," she stuttered under her breath as she glanced around the tiny office.

"Who has?" asked Ally.

"Buff. Told me he loved me. Liar," she barked. "Left me without even saying goodbye."

"I think my presence might have more to do with it, I'm afraid," said Daniel rather sympathetically.

"How come?"

"We don't have time for sob stories," said Ally, butting in. "In the list of today's priorities your love life ranks slightly below the contents of my fridge or Lance's academic prospects."

GOBBLEDYGOOK

"You are a very mean woman," said Gabriel starting to well up.

"Boo fucking hoo," snapped Ally.

"You… you know who you are going to turn into… if you're not careful, don't you?" sobbed Gabriel.

"Who?" replied Ally with a huff of insignificance in her response.

"Ms Honeywell."

Ally hadn't seen it coming, but Gabriel was right. Ally viewed Ms Honeywell without considering the woman's backstory or possible motives for why she behaved the way she did. All she really saw was a nosy busybody who cared about no one other than herself. Honeywell was apparently friendless, purposeless and isolated. A set of characteristics that might be laid over Ally's own like a piece of tracing paper. Only one of those attributes was left unfulfilled, but give her time and she'd catch up. Was that what she wanted? Did she want to end up like Honeywell? No, but somehow she felt like it wasn't within her power to avoid. She couldn't escape who she was, and breaking that pattern wasn't easy. She searched her soul and found another part of her personality that she often relied on, the ability to go on the defensive when pushed like this to consider her fate. Rather than face up to the reality of Gabriel's point it seemed like the right moment to unleash it.

"At least I won't end up like a washed-up bimbo. An Instagram reject, whose looks will have eroded and left nothing under the foundations to prop up your miserable reality. I'm seeing multiple failed marriages, several kids and no prospects," she replied, pretending to look into a crystal ball. "That'll be you. A tragic alcoholic living in a shabby bedsit and living off handouts!"

"Ladies, this isn't the time," said Daniel. Breaking up catfights had not been in his FBI training manual.

"Bitch!"

"Trollop."

GOBBLEDYGOOK

"Pompe à chiasse!" erupted Gabriel completely forgetting her adversary spoke perfect French.

"I'm a diarrhoea pump, am I…? Well, Gabriel, if your brain was made of dynamite there wouldn't be enough to blow your frankly laughable wig off. You useless, cheap, weak ninnyhammer!"

"ENOUGH!" shouted Daniel standing between them before the claws came out. "This is not the time. You need each other, even if you don't see it yourselves: right now you are both alone."

The two women analysed each other for a moment. He was right, they were. At that moment they both relied on each other in some form or another.

"I'm sorry," mumbled Gabriel under her breath.

"Apology accepted," replied Ally. "Now let's look…"

"You, too," said Daniel forcibly.

Ally's mouth dropped open and both eyeballs rolled in their sockets at the preposterous nature of his instruction.

"Do it," he barked more fiercely.

"Sorry," she mumbled, only just coherently while looking at her feet like a scorned child.

"It'll do, now let's take a look at the letter," replied Daniel as he unfolded it and held it up to the light that was beating down from the ceiling.

"Why has it got holes in it?" enquired Gabriel.

"You'll see in a moment," he replied.

Ally fished the book out of her bag again and once more placed gloves over her hands. She took the letter from Daniel and placed it over one of the pages in the book.

"All we have to do now is find the right page," she said. "My guess is that each Mountain Man had a separate letter and a separate page in the book. Tesimond must have been the third Mountain Man after Philibert and Guy Fawkes so let's try that page first and see if it makes any sense."

Ally gently laid the A4-sized letter horizontally over the manuscript with one hand and wrote what she saw through

GOBBLEDYGOOK

the cuts in the letter on a separate piece of paper with the other. The Shikshapatri was written in Sanskrit, an ancient Indian language that had a history that stretched back over three and a half millennia.

"Looks like gobbledygook to me," said Gabriel.

"Imagine it's a line of computer code," said Ally disdainfully. "It's as easy for me to translate this as you can read those."

When she'd written down each word separately, she started to translate what they meant in English. Although like most other languages she was fluent in Sanskrit, she'd not studied it for some time. If she really struggled, she could always just look it up on Google Translate or check the various translations of the Shikshapatri which were available in every modern-day language.

"I think we must have the wrong page," she said after double-checking a few words online.

"What makes you say that?" asked Hudson.

"Because based on this page the cipher says, 'my left bosom shall meet with great miseries and shall never kill goats'."

"Are you sure you've translated it correctly?"

"Oh, I'm sorry, did you want to do it?! I forgot you FBI types are experts in everything," snapped Ally, giving Hudson her most evil-eyed look. "I'll just try a different page."

Ally gently turned the book to the next page and repeated the exercise with the same level of patience and precision.

"What does it say this time?" asked Gabriel, craning her neck in an attempt to see for herself.

"Bugs obtaining women through anger shall sacrifice limbs as firewood without their permission," read Ally despondently after she'd finished the new interpretation.

"I suppose it does mention fire," replied Gabriel unhelpfully, "maybe it's still a clue to the next attack?"

GOBBLEDYGOOK

"It's a clue… that we haven't identified the right page again," replied Ally with a frown. "Why don't you both shuffle off and give me some space to work?"

They didn't need to be told twice. Hudson pulled up a chair and buried himself in the mass of emails that had arrived since waking up this morning and Gabriel went to the gift shop only to be left disappointed when she found it was full of mainly educational items and… closed.

After two hours they returned from their other distractions to find a rather flustered Dr Oldfield. Piles of paper, rolled up hastily into balls, lay scattered around the table and across the floor. The book was only just visible under the mess.

"Any luck?" asked Hudson.

"Loads," she said sarcastically. "I cracked it ages ago, I just thought I'd build some tension."

"Are you always like this?"

"Yes, she is," interceded Gabriel.

"What do the other pages say?"

"Lots of bullshit. There's 'No one shall grab the attachments of Krishna or pass urine through a door', or my personal favourite, 'a King shall never wear clothes for fear mental widows made them from fruit or leaves'. It's a waste of time."

"I don't get it," said Hudson, scratching his bald scalp. "It must be the right book. There was the business card with 'TMM' inscribed on it and the letters must have a text to break the code."

"What a very modern way of thinking," scoffed Ally. "Everyone believes something even when the overwhelming evidence suggests otherwise. The cipher is connected to a book, but it's not the Shikshapatri. I have been through every page and approached it from every angle and not one line of it suggests anything that might help them or us."

"Why would they steal it, then?" asked Hudson.

"Presumably for reasons other than this one. The Mountain Men are all about helping the meek to rise up

GOBBLEDYGOOK

against their masters. The theft did that. Millions of Hindus around the world are protesting and demonstrating their discontent. Not just about the book. The theft of the book has created a mistrust in the establishment and further eroded their belief in the system. It was a catalyst for something else, that's all."

"Shit," said Daniel. "So, it was a waste of time?"

"I'm afraid so. Mario did love to play games. Yet again he's made us follow the queen while all the time he was hiding it somewhere else."

"Follow the queen?"

"It's a card game that I have no time or desire to explain to you. It's time we took this back to Ernest and the police," said Ally, holding up the priceless Shikshapatri in her gloved hand.

Hudson grabbed an evidence bag from his case and carefully allowed it to slide inside, sealing the top with the Ziploc.

"You realise without the correct book we have no idea where the next attack will be."

"Then it's time for you to be an investigator and for me to be a lecturer once more. I'm done with all this," sighed Ally.

"People are going to die, Ally," replied Hudson desperately.

"They do that, but then you don't really care anyway because the only thing that's important to you is finding the money."

"I'm sorry that you think that's all I care about."

Hudson placed the jiffy bag in his case and stormed out of the door. Ally hoped it was the last time she had to deal with the FBI and that her records would no longer be of interest to them, but she doubted it. She glanced at her watch. It was creeping towards seven in the morning and soon the doors to the Weston Library would be flung open and a horde of visitors would swarm in pretending to be interested in history. Almost all of them would ignore the educational boards, take one look at the visuals before

GOBBLEDYGOOK

moving on to the next with almost no memory of any of it, only proving their visit had happened by buying some tacky plastic from the gift shop.

*****

London, 1767

The café house culture first became popular in London in the middle of the sixteenth century when Pasqua Rosée, the Greek servant of a coffee-loving British merchant, opened the first coffee shack against the stone wall of St Michael's churchyard in a labyrinth of alleyways just off Cornhill. Before long, coffee was so popular it became a genuine alternative to beer consumption. Coffee in those times was consumed 'black as hell, strong as death and sweat as love'. Ally would have approved.

When one person breaks the mould and succeeds in the face of everyone's initial disdain and scepticism, soon the rest follow suit like lemmings, all of them pretending falsely that they'd always been supportive. By the middle of the seventeenth century a coffee house stood on every road in London. Almost exclusively attended by men they were meeting places to discuss the news of the day, debate, share and learn. The most famous of all of these was the Rainbow Coffee House on Fleet Street.

The Rainbow was a famous meeting place for Freemasons, French refugees and authors. On this bright April morning two of its patrons nursed mugs of thick, black coffee and engaged in a deep and meaningful conversation about art, philosophy and science. At least they would have been if one of them wasn't a massive narcissist.

"It can't be as bad as you make out, surely?" said a smartly dressed, portly man with an unusual accent and a receding hairline.

The man opposite continued to sob uncontrollably, blowing his nose into a rather tatty-looking handkerchief.

GOBBLEDYGOOK

Although dressed formally it was in a rather bohemian style as if he was desperate to send the world a message that he was unmistakably a 'creative' type. A ruffled, colourful scarf billowed dramatically around his neck like he'd been molested on the way there by a haberdashery. His trousers were red, he wore a white shirt with hand-stitched yellow embroidery and carried an old umbrella with a duck's head handle, even though it hadn't rained in the city for days.

"It is that bad," he snivelled in a broad French accent. "They all 'ate me!"

Jean-Jacques Rousseau had always been a rather anxious individual prone to exaggeration. In a time when men of his talents were two a penny, the rush for acceptance was that much harder for him than the luminaries who scorched a path. Voltaire and David Hume, to name two, were people lorded for their modern take on social matters, their successful plays and intellectual books. Jean always felt less than exceptional and as a result was prone to overdramatising his feelings.

"They don't hate you. Why would they?" said the calmer of the two men.

"It's because I'm foreign!"

"Then they must hate me also. And Voltaire, he's French don't forget."

"And they don't take my work serious either," sniffed Jean-Jacques.

"I can assure you that I do. Your *Letters Written from the Mountain* is an exceptional piece of work and as for your work on the 'Social Contract', I think it might be the most powerful plan for the emancipation of man I've ever read. I've already sent a copy to Washington."

"Where's that?"

"Oh, it's not a place. George Washington, he's a friend of mine. Ha, imagine if they named a place after him! He'd find that quite amusing. Washington thinks your work might be the perfect model for a future constitution if independence is secured."

GOBBLEDYGOOK

"Voltaire said it was shit," blubbed Jean-Jacques.

"Well, he can be rather cutting with his critique in my experience."

"At least I can always count on you, Benjamin. You're my closest friend."

"Right…" Ben replied awkwardly. "You know this is only the second time we've met, don't you?"

"No! It can't be."

"Yes, I think you'll find it is. David Hume introduced us at his house last year before the two of you fell out, remember? We only met today by accident. I was supposed to be meeting Andrew Kippis, but when you saw me you grabbed hold of me, started crying and haven't stopped since."

"Well, it still counts because I don't have a single friend other than you in the whole world. No one to share my terrible news with."

Benjamin Franklin was one of the most intelligent men of his generation. Not only was he well thought of as a diplomat representing his homeland in London, but he was also an inventor, entrepreneur and member of the Royal Society here in England. The Royal Society didn't suffer fools or charlatans. Only the most exceptional minds were invited to join. Sir Christopher Wren, Sir Isaac Newton, Nicolas Fatio and John Evelyn had all been members. It didn't take a huge amount of brainpower to know that Jean-Jacques was luring him in for sympathy. Even the intelligent can be susceptible to a sob story.

"Terrible news?" said Benjamin.

"Yes… I'm dying!" screamed Jean-Jacques to ensure the whole of the coffee house was fully informed.

"Dying?"

"Yes."

"What's wrong with you?"

"Leprosy."

Franklin's main areas of expertise did not include anatomy or medicine, but even he could very quickly work out with a casual glance with the naked eye that his

GOBBLEDYGOOK

companion didn't have leprosy. His skin had no lesions, all his limbs were still functioning adequately, if his overexuberant mannerisms were anything to go by, and there were no obvious signs of damage to his eyes, one of the sure-fire symptoms.

"Jean, you don't have leprosy."

"I do! One of my fingers fell off this morning."

"Which one?"

"This one," he said, pointing to the pinkie on his left hand.

"But it's still attached."

Jean stared at it quite shocked that it appeared to have returned to his hand during the night without informing his brain. Realising his misdiagnosis, he quickly changed tack.

"Dropsy!"

"Not leprosy, then."

"No, I got them confused."

"Why isn't your body swollen up? When fish get dropsy, they blow up like balloons."

Jean-Jacques puffed out his cheeks to make his face look bigger.

"I don't mean to pry," asked Benjamin delicately, "but do you take a lot of drugs?"

"Nuh," he mumbled still trying to keep his cheeks full of air and continue to talk to Benjamin without him noticing the farce. "Only laudanum."

"That's an opium!" exclaimed Franklin. "That drug is a killer."

"There you are, told you I was dying."

"You look perfectly fine to me, many good years ahead of you. Now, I must be…"

"On top of dropsy, I also have pleurisy, diphtheria, earache, a chronic bowel disorder and… botulism."

"You do know that most of those are highly contagious, don't you?"

"Yes! How do you think I got them?!"

GOBBLEDYGOOK

"What I meant by that was, you probably shouldn't be in a coffee house spreading them around."

A few of the patrons closest to the pair had raised their cloaks to their mouths and were gently shuffling their chairs to get as far away as possible.

"Did I also tell you I have smallpox?"

"I think I know what you really have," said Benjamin.

"What? Tell me."

"Hypochondria."

"Oh God! That's the one where your toes turn black and fall off one by one every other Monday, isn't it?"

"No. That's the one that affects the brain and means you think you are unwell when you're not. There's nothing wrong with you, Jean-Jacques. What's this really about?"

"I'm really dying!" he repeated. "I need to pass it on before I shake off life's mortal coil. It might happen today!"

"Pass what on?"

Jean-Jacques scanned the room, leant forward and encouraged Benjamin to come closer to him. Then in a whisper he said, "A secret."

"A secret. I'm starting to understand why Hume fell out with you. What do I want with a secret? I have enough going on in my life without clinging onto some madman's baggage."

"You could use it, it's a very powerful secret," Jean-Jacques continued to whisper. "Down the years it has expanded like a rolling snowball. Soon it will be so big it will break through the chains of imperialism and change the world for the better."

"Unless it can have some influence on the despicable Tea Act that the British continue to force upon my countrymen, I think it's unlikely to be of much interest to me."

"Oh, but in the right hands it can. In the hands of the Mountain Men, anything is possible. Even revolution," he whispered nervously.

Benjamin Franklin's ears pricked up. He lifted his mug and drained the last drops of coffee into his mouth. In

GOBBLEDYGOOK

recent weeks it had been tea, not coffee, most on his mind. The British colonialists had allowed the East India Company to sell tea in the Americas without any tax duties. This had flared up regional tensions around his home city of Boston. Choosing to use diplomatic routes here in London had no influence on a change of policy. There had to be another way of changing the outcome. Maybe this was it?

- Chapter 19 -

Every Trick in the Book

There seemed little point in going home. By the time she got there she'd just have to turn around and come back again. At least she hoped so. Once Daniel had returned the book to the authorities, theoretically clearing her name, he'd promised to text her with confirmation. As far as she was concerned that would be the end of it. Then all she'd need was confirmation from the university that her suspension had been cancelled. She sat patiently outside Ernest Culpepper's office awaiting his arrival.

The last seven days had been a complete waste of time and effort. One of the biggest achievements of her life, the exhibition she'd been preparing for months, had been taken from her. There has been no time to receive the accolades, academic plaudits or inner self-congratulations she knew it deserved. She'd been robbed of the moment by a masked and secretive society intent on dragging her into their chaos. On top of that she'd been unable to identify who they were in order to put a stop to it. She hated losing battles of intellect. It made her rather obnoxious to be around, even more so than usual. She'd had to suffer Gabriel, Daniel, jail, Belfast and a ridiculous French bodybuilder whose vocabulary was limited to the word 'potato'. She exhaled a deep sigh as all of this information whirled around her mind.

At least she didn't have to suffer Gabriel this morning. She'd got bored and tagged along with Daniel hoping that he'd either give her a lift or happened to pass a bar or a shop, not that either was open at this time of the morning. Ally had no idea when the irritating snowflake would see fit to move on to other poor sods she could annoy. Gabriel was intrinsically linked to the Mountain Men conspiracy, and until that was solved, she'd probably linger like an incurable form of cancer.

Behind the panelled walls in front of her was Ernest's office, which was much nicer and plusher than her own. To her recollection she'd only ever been inside it once, and that was barely further than sticking her head around the door. Crowded with mementoes of his career and bursting with shelves stuffed with books as if the problem with library space had initially been tackled by the Librarian single-handed. If librarians had man caves, this was his. A place that was always locked and few were ever invited to enter. Outside it, in the gloom of the corridor, a couple of antique, worn leather chairs awaited whichever misbehaving student had been called to see him. Today it was her. There was no reason for her to feel guilt, yet it ran up and down her veins like the traffic of a free-flowing six-lane motorway.

Ally's phone buzzed in her pocket. The blunt text from Daniel confirmed the book had been returned to the police investigators as planned. The noise of approaching steps echoing around the dog legged corridor pulled her from her thoughts. Dressed as usual in his over-elaborate corduroy suit and offensively coloured bow tie, he turned the corner and immediately froze as his eyes settled on Ally.

"Dr Oldfield, you've been suspended, you're not supposed to be here."

"Good news, Ernest. We found the Shikshapatri."

Ernest's face remained sombre at the revelation, something Ally was a little surprised by given how he'd reacted quite hysterically when he'd first heard about its theft.

"Right. That's good. It doesn't change the situation, though."

"Yes, it does. It means I'm not suspended."

"That's for the board to decide, it's not down to me."

EVERY TRICK IN THE BOOK

"Then go tell them," implored Ally.

"There are processes. We do things right here at Oxford. We'll need proof and evidence before we exonerate you."

"Evidence! The book wasn't stolen so there is no evidence that I was involved in stealing it," said Ally, pausing as the situation suddenly caught up with her. "Hold on. You didn't even ask me what happened to it."

"I only have your word that it has been recovered."

"Look, here's your evidence."

Ally stood up, clutching her phone, and showed Ernest the pictures she'd taken of the book and the text she'd recently received from Hudson.

"That does seem conclusive," he replied tentatively.

"Good, then I'll go back to my exhibition," replied Ally, picking up her bag and attempting to march past her boss.

"No," said Ernest, sternly holding his arm out to block her progress. "Go home, Ally. Let me talk to the board, smooth things over with them."

"When?"

"Today. I'll go today. I have some meetings, but I'll see to it. We can get you back in your post by Monday."

"What?!"

"Due process."

"Fine. Well, I might still be suspended from my job, but I'm not banned from the museum, am I?"

"No, of course not."

"Then I'll just spend the day here anyway."

"You'll need to buy a ticket."

"You're kidding me! It's my exhibition!"

*****

The only area of the Weston Museum that wasn't free to enter was the Prophecy Exhibition. Squeezing her ten-pound ticket in her hand with the force of a million pistons she stropped from the ticket office to the exhibition room keen to assess how much of it was still standing since it had

EVERY TRICK IN THE BOOK

fallen under the curation of Lance some days ago. When she reached the room there was no one there other than the smartly dressed woman standing guard over the entrance, hand outstretched to receive people's tickets. She took Ally's without a second thought.

Ally weaved her way carefully through the different exhibit stands. After detailed assessment she was surprised to find that the painstaking work of recent months was almost exactly as she'd left it. The Lesage prophecy was still mounted and untouched, pride of place in the centre of the room. The educational boards were still in their rightful places and none of the cordons, that kept sticky fingers from priceless works of art, had been moved. The outcome seemed so impossible she felt herself fighting the inclination to accept what her eyes were showing her. Against all expectations and hampered by the challenge of his own spatial awareness, Lance had succeeded. She was glad he wasn't here. No doubt he'd be fishing for some form of acknowledgement. Doing your job right, she thought, was not enough reason to be offered recognition, only relief.

She approached the famous, yet wildly misleading, edition of Nostradamus's *Les Prophéties,* still protected behind its sealed glass case. The book was open so the public could view one very specific page, the one with its unique and fraudulent preface. That's how she'd left the book the last time she saw it.

It wasn't the case now.

Instead the book had been laid open to the first full page of quatrains, the four-line verses that Nostradamus was keen to make up with a bewildering regularity. Who would change the page on display? Had Lance messed around with it? She searched around in her bag but soon remembered that she no longer kept the keys to the cabinet. She'd been forced to relinquish them to Lance when Ernest suspended her from duty. She glanced at her watch. Just after nine. Surely Lance would be here soon.

EVERY TRICK IN THE BOOK

"Dr Oldfield," called Lance from a distance as he rushed through the museum tucking his ludicrously bright orange shirt into his unrivalled mauve trousers as he ran. There was no excuse offered for why he was ten minutes late, but it was perfectly conceivable, having witnessed how he'd dressed himself, that someone from the medical community had attempted to return him to the safety of whichever institution he'd escaped from.

"What are you doing here?"

"It's a long story," replied Ally abruptly, suggesting it wasn't one she wanted to share. "Do you have the key to this cabinet?"

"Yes, it's in your office."

"Run along and get it, then," she demanded.

When Lance returned five minutes later, Ally had rigged up a barrier of red velvet ropes and golden stands around the Nostradamus exhibit to keep either a now plentiful number of visitors away from it, or possibly her. Ally was already breaking out her world-famous customer service tendencies by telling anyone who even slightly nudged the barrier to 'bugger off'.

"Here it is," said Lance, holding the key in his palm.

"Why is this book open to the wrong page?" she barked as if the fault lay solely at her young intern's feet.

"Is it? I didn't notice."

"And that is why you fail. An academic leaves nothing to chance and notices everything. We look for the abnormal and the absence of normality. You see only what is on the surface."

As the words left her lips, she realised the similarities between her job and that of an investigator like Hudson. They were both seeking evidence, only his was generally a lot fresher than hers ever would be. They both had to connect the clues to work out the answer.

Lance unlocked the display case and Ally immediately grabbed the book. There was no need for gloves: this was not a prized, sacred piece of history like the Shikshapatri. She turned the pages to the preface in order to replace the

EVERY TRICK IN THE BOOK

book on its plinth in its planned position. It was an impossible job. The preface had no prophecy, fake or otherwise. Hysterically she flicked through the pages in case it had decided to relocate itself.

"Shit."

"What is it, paper cut?" asked Lance.

"No. Bruised ego," she replied with a sigh. "This book is not our version of *Les Prophéties*."

"What? It has to be. No one has opened the cabinet since the day before the exhibition was due to open."

"Then where is the prophecy?" she screamed, grabbing Lance by the hair and forcing his head towards the book. "Every copy of *Les Prophéties* is unique and no other version has a prophecy in the preface. Someone has switched it. Someone who had access to it."

Like sun piercing through cloud her mind cleared. Synapses fired and a million commands were sent around her body for her brain to process, which it did with ease. The revelation came back in nanoseconds. The thieves never intended to steal the Shikshapatri, they just wanted her and the police to believe they had. Amongst the distraction, political crisis, false accusations and restricted access, no one would notice when they switched Nostradamus's book. Even without all the distractions they'd know that the only person with keen enough eyes to notice the deception would be her. They'd framed her for the robbery in order that she couldn't be there to notice. All along it was their copy of Nostradamus's book that was being used to decipher the letters. Not even this replacement would give precisely the same answer if the letters were placed on the right page. But where, then, was the original?

She examined the lock on the display case. There was no sign anyone had forced it open and there was no evidence that it had been picked. Whoever switched the book must have had access to the key. Which narrowed the list of possible culprits down to the people she worked with.

One in particular.

EVERY TRICK IN THE BOOK

"Who put you up to it?" she said to Lance, as a finger leapt out to accuse him.

"Put me up to what?" he replied innocently, having not made the connection yet.

"Everything."

"Um, ok. Can you at least narrow it down a little?"

"I should never have believed it. You specifically applied to be my intern. Mine. No one has ever done that before. Usually they get dragged to me kicking and screaming like boisterous infants. Not you. You came here voluntarily, or you were put up to it. Now I know why."

"I'm not with you," replied Lance, face screwed up like it had been squeezed in a vice.

"You had the keys, Lance! You had my security pass to come and go as you pleased. My business cards are all over my office. It would have been easy enough for you to pick one up, write a message and frame me. You know how this place works. It would have been simple for you to disrupt the security systems, avoid the guards and hide the Shikshapatri in the tunnels. I thought it was an inside job, and it was. It was you. How much did they offer you? Someone with your lower-class background would have found it impossible to avoid the temptation. What have you got to say for yourself?"

"I didn't do any of that. I wasn't even here the weekend of the robbery. Ask my parents. I was in Kent with them like I am every weekend. I only came back when I heard what had happened."

"But you were outside when I got here, and it was early in the morning."

"Check with them. I left Friday after work and came back as soon as I heard the news."

"Rest assured I'll check your alibi. Even if you ignore the robbery it still doesn't explain why you applied to be my intern."

"No, it doesn't," sighed Lance like gas escaping from a popped balloon. "Someone asked me to apply."

"Who? Mario?"

EVERY TRICK IN THE BOOK

"No. Antoine asked me."

In this context it wasn't a name that Ally ever expected to hear.

"What? Why did he put you up to it?!" shouted Ally, grabbing Lance by his tie and dragging him down to her eye level.

"I guess he was worried about you."

"Worried. No one has to be worried about me. I'm a survivor. Always have been."

"He felt you needed someone in your life."

"Oh, and a lanky twenty-something buffoon was the best he could come up with, was it? He could have bought me a dog."

"You hate dogs."

"A lot less than I hate you at the moment."

"He felt you might need some help adjusting to your new approach to life."

"What new approach to life? Antoine appears to have gone totally mad."

"Didn't you talk to him about opening up more, letting people in, connecting on a human level?"

"Yes. I thought he was talking about getting therapy, not adopting a walking occupational hazard with the combined talents of a geriatric bobsleigh team. I can't believe Antoine would do this to me. I think you're trying to cover up your crimes."

"No. Why do you think I received Antoine's call when we were in London? How else would he have had my number? You said so yourself at the time."

Ally reflected on her reaction at the time. It had seemed unlikely to her, but with everything that was going on, and having recently been concussed by a large frying pan in the hands of a small Asian woman, she'd overlooked it.

"Ok. Let's say hypothetically Antoine did send you, then why did he pick you?"

"Because I was the last."

"The last what?"

EVERY TRICK IN THE BOOK

"The last of his scholarships. Antoine's family have been sponsoring all kinds of worthy causes for generations. His foundation helps poor but gifted students around the world by sponsoring them through their education. I was the last one that he invested in before he sold or closed his businesses. The only way I could continue my education was if I managed to secure an internship. He suggested you were unlikely to have many offers and it suited his plans to have someone who was in contact with you. I suspect he knew he would have to go underground, and that Mario would not know about me."

"The only thing that seems implausible here is that he thought you were gifted," she replied bluntly.

"My gift isn't gymnastics, you do know that, right? Don't judge me on my faults, Dr Oldfield, judge me on my strengths. My exams results speak for themselves."

She silently conceded that was true. Antoine was constantly reminding her to see the best in people, when she so often immediately identified the fault. Perhaps this was part of her process of adapting to other people in a more natural way. She couldn't completely dismiss Lance's claims of innocence, yet when judgement had already been made on the basis of preconceived bias it was hard to shift positions.

"If you weren't behind the theft or switching the book, who was?"

"No idea," replied Lance honestly.

"I'm going to give you the benefit of the doubt for now."

"Antoine would be proud of you."

"But I've got my eye on you until we can find the other book. It must be here somewhere."

"There are twelve million books linked to this place, the chances of finding it on our own will be tiny," replied Lance.

"You're right. We need help. We need a librarian."

*****

EVERY TRICK IN THE BOOK

"He's really protective of his personal space," said Lance as he watched Ally wage a full-out assault on Ernest's office door.

"I know. I wonder why," she said under her breath as the hairpin continued to probe around in the lock. "How many times have you been inside?"

"Never. He always meets people out here in the corridor."

"I've only ever peeped through the door. It's curious. I'm a staff member and even I haven't been in there. This is Oxford University, it has a culture of openness and yet this room is permanently closed off."

"But why would Ernest get involved in something like this?"

"I don't know but until he explains himself, I'm keeping an open mind. There aren't many other people who could have opened the cabinet. Damn it, this isn't working," she said, standing up and stretching out her back from the pain of spending too long hunched over the door handle.

"Where does he keep the key?" asked Lance.

"Probably on him. I actually wish Gabriel was here: she'd probably find a tech way to get in."

"Doubt it, looks like an old-fashioned lock."

An idea spontaneously launched itself out of Ally's mouth. "Have you and the librarian actually met?"

"Oh yes, lots of times. Usually as a result of health and safety violations, to sign the first aid book or help assess any structural damage caused."

"Hmm. Good. Well, we're not getting in here anytime soon. What say we play a game while we wait for him to come back?"

"A game? You don't like games."

"It's more of an intellectual problem," she lied.

"Oh, in that case."

"I read recently that you can snap a dictionary in half by kicking it with force in just the right place. Jenkins said he didn't think it could be done and I disagreed. I'd love to

EVERY TRICK IN THE BOOK

prove that snivelling little git wrong," she said sliding a copy of the *Oxford English Dictionary* off a shelf in the corridor.

"Where did you read this?" said Lance sceptically.

"*New Scientist*," she lied. "Let's see if they were right."

"Ok, well, happy to oblige if it's in the name of research."

"It is. Now, I'll hold the book open in both hands and I want you to kick it as hard as you can down the spine. Give it a good kick mind, as much effort as you can."

Lance took a few paces backwards, rocked back and forth slightly as if he was about to set off on an Olympic long jump record. His pointy leather shoes clawed at the floor like an angry bull before a surge of energy burst out of his knees. Just as his foot was about to land on the dictionary Ally jumped to one side and Lance's foot and most of his upper leg crashed through Ernest's office door.

"Accidents will happen," smiled Ally as she pushed the door open and sent Lance hopping half in and half out of the office.

"What if he comes back?"

"He said he had meetings."

Ally helped Lance extricate his leg from the door and both of them entered a place of mystery. It was hard to identify an office at all, there were so many books piled up. It reminded Ally of the DLO in Belfast where the employees worked in the shadows of huge stacks of letters surrounded by sacks full of more. There was no daylight in the room, although she suspected that somewhere behind the columns of books were windows that had long since forgotten to worry about how clean they were.

A large, old-fashioned desk was just about visible against the nearest wall. It was covered in chaotic paperwork and a plethora of charming ornaments from far-flung places of the world. None of these seemed out of place, their collective sense of oddness making them perfectly suited to each other. There was a small, wooden pygmy warrior sitting on a half coconut plinth. A samurai

EVERY TRICK IN THE BOOK

helmet peeked through the reams of admin like a hidden assassin waiting to pounce. A rather tacky, self-assembled Eiffel Tower lay against the back wall with its top half bent at an angle.

"Now we know who picks the stock for the gift shop," whispered Ally.

"We need to leave," replied Lance nervously. "We shouldn't be here."

"I wouldn't be so hasty. If he hasn't got the book, then you're definitely my number one suspect. Spread out and look, but be careful."

Asking Lance to be careful was like asking a bee to be less buzzy. The two aren't easy to separate. Wisely he decided that looking only with his eyes, hands behind his back and legs in a fixed standing position was the best pose to minimise damage. Ally, in contrast, went in hands first, moving anything that might conceal what she needed. Quickly she riffled through the contents of the desk without luck. She opened the first drawer, glanced casually in, as if it might be an unlikely place to hide something secret, and there it was. Sitting completely alone, the only place in the whole room devoid of clutter.

"Got it," she said, flicking to the preface to validate her find.

"Brilliant. Does that mean I'm off the hook, then?" asked Lance hopefully.

"I'd say you're very much still on the hook," came a stern, posh voice from the doorway. "Both of you."

- Chapter 20 -

The Sequence

It's hard to know how long the subject of the weather has been a universal talking point for British people. It's as much of a mystery as why a bunch of Neolithic gentlemen decided to drag a bunch of massive stone blocks a couple of hundred miles from Wales to the middle of a field in England and erect them around a henge, presumably moaning and grumbling as they went about the 'bloody weather'. The Brits just can't help themselves. It's like social Tourette's.

It doesn't actually matter what type of weather is being experienced on the day in question or whether it's noticeably different from what happened yesterday, the topic is still the only conventional talking point when two people's paths cross. It doesn't seem to matter if this happens to be two perfect strangers or friends who have known each other for decades. Favourite opening lines for the average Brit include: 'cold, isn't it?', 'terrible weather we're having' and 'I think it's going to rain?' Notice how none of these snippets of small talk include anything remotely positive.

There are two excellent reasons for this.

Even though the scientific doubt about global warming can no longer be disputed, the sun shows up in Britain about as frequently as the monster appears in Loch Ness. Secondly when it does have the cheek to be sunny it takes the average Brit nine minutes before they're complaining about being 'too hot'.

Which gets to the real heart of the matter. The weather is just a convenient reason to moan and that's far more

THE SEQUENCE

important to the British sentimentality than whether it's raining. It also acts as a convenient crutch to avoid them talking about anything remotely personal or interesting. In the week since Daniel arrived on these shores, he'd learnt almost nothing interesting about most of the everyday people he'd met other than they thought it might 'drizzle tomorrow'. None of their meteorological insights were remotely helpful because he had perfect eyesight and was capable of looking out of a window to ascertain it for himself.

Right now, he was witnessing irregular drops of precipitation bounce off the windscreen of his rather pathetic hire car. Car, he thought, was a rather misleading description. Where he came from, only supercars had three doors and even those were longer, wider and taller than this piece of shit. He'd shot bigger raccoons. Children had more advanced pedal cars. Getting in the driver's seat, if you were the volume of Daniel, involved a level of contortion yoga masters had yet to perfect.

He peered through the steamed-up glass and drops of irritating rainfall at the grey-coloured building he was about to visit. In the distance a desperate, wrinkled face stared out of the dirty blinds of a bay window at his car, parked thoughtlessly at a forty-five-degree angle and on a slight incline. Here it had passed lunchtime, but the warm sun was only just climbing out of its pyjamas and into morning on the other side of the pond where the focus of his attention now rested.

Daniel had been forced to delay his next appointment as the result of what was happening on the other side of the Atlantic. The Mountain Men had struck again, and for the first time in his own country. Boston, to be precise. As the news alerts came thick and fast out of his phone, shortly after his arrival in the car park, he immediately logged onto the news to witness the shocking details for himself from the cramped confines of his automotive coffin.

No doubt within minutes he'd get the call.

THE SEQUENCE

On his mobile phone the video footage from the media helicopters told their own story. On a large, concreted area next to the Boston dockside the letters TMM had been inscribed on the ground and were being broadcast to the world. Every American would immediately know what they were written in. Loose tea. In the waters of the harbour dozens of colourful containers had been unloaded into the ocean, some floating, some semi-submerged, and all dispensing their contents into the Atlantic. Nearby several of the depot buildings were ablaze and probably smelt rather appealing given the produce inside.

The original Boston Tea Party had been the precursor to the revolutionary war that started eighteenth months later: the first of many successful revolutions against the establishment over the following century and a direct influence on the French Revolution just a decade after. The Mountain Men were learning fast and their next member would go further than just making a big cup of tea in the Atlantic Ocean.

As expected, his phone rang.

"Yes, sir," answered Daniel after one solitary ring.

"Are you watching?"

"Yes, sir."

"And?"

This was how Jeff McNamee spoke. Never more words were used than entirely necessary and the ball for explanation always firmly placed at the other person's feet. It was hard to know if this was because McNamee didn't know a huge amount about a given subject, or whether he was using it as a tactic to understand what you knew before he'd reveal it. It didn't really matter either way because McNamee had risen to the level of Assistant Executive Director, and the last time Daniel looked, he hadn't.

"It's unfortunate," replied Daniel a little too casually.

"Unfortunate!"

"Yes. Any casualties?"

"No."

"At least that's something."

THE SEQUENCE

"I only wish you had given me 'something' over the incompetent length of your current assignment."

McNamee was an intensely humourless man whose dedication to the Bureau was second only to a dedication to his own ambitions. Jeff would never be happy in middle management. It was the top or nowhere. The two men were of similar age and joined the Bureau around the same time. This was when their career curves diverged. Jeff's rise up the ranks had been assisted by a warm jet stream marked 'arse-licker'. Daniel didn't mind. He was more than happy in the field getting his hands dirty with the real work. What he did mind, though, was having to report to a man for whom failure was unacceptable not because of the importance of the mission but because it restricted his chance of another promotion.

"I'm dealing with a highly complex and fluid situation here, sir," replied Daniel.

"Am I supposed to care?"

"No."

"Where's the money, Hudson?"

"I'm working on it."

"That's not good enough. We're not talking about twenty bucks here, it's twelve billion, for God's sake. Not easy to hide."

"We're getting closer. We've recovered one of the letters."

"A letter!" replied Jeff sarcastically.

"Yes."

"Two weeks ago, you had all of the letters in your possession until you decided in poor judgement to post them around the world. That's hardly progress, is it?"

"But we are close to breaking the code," he lied.

"My patience with you is running thin. The situation in Boston has turned up the heat on both of us. The Administration don't care what happens in London or Naples, but they do give a shit when it strikes the homeland. I'm giving you forty-eight hours to achieve some real progress or I'm removing you from the case. Is that understood, Agent Hudson."

"Yes," replied Daniel tersely. There was little point in arguing.

"Good."

"Have you acted upon my request, sir?" asked Daniel.

"Yes."

"And?"

"I struggle to see what an old Russian defector has got to do with this case," replied Jeff.

"I think it has everything to do with it. Radu Goga connects a lot of the other clues. Did you get what I need?"

"It's not been easy. His case file is entwined in Cold War politics and the paranoia that went with it. They've released his file for me, but it has so many redactions it's like trying to read a crossword."

"Send it anyway."

"Fine, but don't let it distract you from the main goal here. I'll be in touch Sunday night and I expect some results."

The phone went dead but was quickly resuscitated by the ping of an email. Daniel immediately scrolled through his mailbox to find what he'd requested. Jeff was right about the redactions. There were more blacked-out words in the file than there were visible ones. It looked like a cipher all of its own. He read through the pages at speed, seeking one particular piece of information he hoped it might contain to further prove his theory. He found it. A single word was all he needed.

Daughter.

*****

Ernest Culpepper stood in the doorway of his office to block their escape. Having spent the last two unplanned hours convincing the board to overturn Oldfield's suspension and allow her to return to work, he felt a little

THE SEQUENCE

aggrieved she'd spent the same time breaking into his office.

"To think that I believed your stories?" he said with a sigh. "Only to catch you red-handed in the middle of another burglary."

"This isn't a burglary," snapped Ally.

"Did someone invite you in?" he replied gently. "The state of the door would argue otherwise."

"Don't turn this round on me!" barked Ally. "You're the guilty one here."

Lance edged out of view, hoping that the Librarian might not notice he was there. In the process he stumbled on a book and fell face first into a bookshelf.

"I'm disappointed in you, Mr Carter. I thought you had more sense than to get embroiled with a felon. You have your whole career in front of you. At least you did until now. No one will ever employ you after this. Your life is ruined. If you avoid a criminal conviction, you'll certainly have to drag with you an employee report that will put off every university, academic institution or private company in the Western world. You'll probably end up being a primary school teacher: they'll take anyone."

Lance stared at his feet. What would his parents say? How would this look to his friends? Not well, he guessed. He'd been given an opportunity that few others were afforded. An education in one of the finest universities on the back of a distant backer's charity. A man who trusted Oldfield. Lance trusted her, too, even if she was the most cantankerous and difficult person he'd ever had the misfortune to meet. Yet the rest of life before this job had been rather dull, and that accusation was not possible when it related to his employment with her.

"It's not about him," snapped Ally. "It's between you and me."

"This is about you, Ally, not me. I never studied law. I actually wanted to at one point in my educational journey, but the length of study put me off. I've certainly read a lot of books on the subject, though. One of the perks of the

THE SEQUENCE

job," Ernest said, pointing out the many piles of texts propping up the room from certain structural collapse. "What I have pieced together from the subject, though, is that guilt is proven by evidence. I have plenty. Motive, witnesses and a repeat offender. No doubt your fingerprints are also plastered all over my office door."

"Not unless my fingers were attached to the bottom of Lance's shoes," Ally replied petulantly. "I also have my own evidence."

Ally held up the copy of *Les Prophéties* and grinned like she was holding the winning lottery ticket. If she was hoping for a sudden confession, she was going to be disappointed.

"It's a book," replied Culpepper innocently. "Not unusual for a librarian to be in possession of one."

"It's THE book," she snapped. "It's the book that unlocks the cipher and stops the Mountain Men and it was here locked in your office."

"Says who?"

"What?" replied Ally, starting to lose her accusatory footing.

"Who's to say that you didn't have the book in your possession when you broke into my office?"

"My witness," she croaked, pointing at Lance.

"You mean your accomplice."

Ally was getting tired with being manipulated into thinking she'd got the wrong man. Would her accusations stand up in court? Probably not, but she had the book and the letter, and it was time to prove that they belonged to each other. She casually sat down at the desk, opened the book to page three and laid Tesimond's letter across the top. Bingo.

"What are you doing?" said Ernest, his voice rising unaccustomedly from his usual soft-spoken lilt.

"Finding out what these letters mean."

"I'm calling the police."

"Fine. I've met most of them thanks to whoever's behind all this. Let's see if they arrest you or me."

THE SEQUENCE

Ally scribbled down the message from the letter on a loose envelope that had been discarded on the desk with many other paper sacrifices. The resulting code simply read: Naples-Fisherman-Paris. Most of it made sense to her. The first two words described the location and profession of the Mountain Man who'd followed Father Tesimond. It proved in her mind that Masaniello was the fourth in line. This letter, though, was a hoax. It was never meant to be used, it was only ever designed to keep them guessing. It was less clear what the reference to Paris meant.

"What does it mean?" asked Ally, turning to Ernest.

"I think it's time you left my office and faced the music. To think that I have bent over backwards for you. It was I who argued for you to have your exhibition. It was I who backed your integrity in front my bosses, only for my own reputation to be sunk by your treachery."

Ally wasn't really listening. If she was about to be sacked or arrested it didn't matter. The scent of victory pierced her nostrils like a bloodhound tracking a fox. She was close, she was certain. She held the envelope in her hands staring at the three words she'd just deciphered. If she could work out the third part of the code, then the picture would be clear. As she transfixed her eyes on the back of the envelope, she realised there was something inside it. Instinctively she lifted the flap to remove it.

"Don't touch that!" hollered Ernest, lunging forward to take it from her. "That's my property!"

"Lance," demanded Ally.

As if an invisible programme had been set off inside him sometime over the last month, Lance grabbed the Librarian in a rather unorthodox bear-hug.

"Let go of me, boy," growled Ernest.

Inside the envelope was a blank piece of paper which featured familiar cuts across it. On the top of the page, just like the others Ally had seen both in real life and on Daniel's photos, was a two-digit number. One zero. Ally quickly opened Nostradamus's book to page ten and laid

THE SEQUENCE

the letter over it. The resulting code read: New World, Politician, Paris.

"Now I'd say that was pretty strong evidence, wouldn't you agree, Ernest? Definitely wasn't me that placed this here."

Culpepper's expression changed. What had been a strong and disciplined defence of the situation was replaced by a sullen, frightened one.

"I think it might be best if Mr Carter left us for a moment," he added nervously, still being manhandled by the postgraduate.

Ally nodded for Lance to loosen his grip and confidently indicated for him to leave them. This situation didn't feel particularly dangerous to her given past experiences. Ernest was a softly spoken, rather weakly built fifty-nine-year-old who probably didn't have the strength to step on a spider, let alone cause her any danger. Once Lance's clumsy footsteps were no longer audible in the distance, Ernest slowly pulled out a chair and flopped down into it. Something about his mannerisms suggested he was under more pressure than he'd originally made out. His immaculately smart suit hung uncomfortably on his ageing frame as he removed a silk handkerchief from his waistcoat pocket and blew his nose. On closer inspection Ally could see tears welling in his eyes.

"Do you know how much it costs to run a place like this?" muttered Ernest, as if to himself.

"Not really, but Oxford is one of the most prestigious universities in the world, it's hardly got a funding crisis."

"That's true but other universities do not own a copyright library. The costs required to maintain such a thing rise exponentially every year. There was talk amongst the board of reducing its scope. As you know, we do not have to take every book published but we endeavour to do so. In the world of higher education, we have to compete."

"A very big part of me doesn't care right now."

"Oh, but you should. Books are everything. They document our history, enrich our present and secure our

THE SEQUENCE

future. They capture humanity's progress in the fields of the arts and sciences. They reveal who we were, are and want to be. Without books humans lack knowledge. Books are a tangible proof of human progress. I know how important they are to you also, Dr Oldfield."

"You know there's this thing called the internet, don't you?"

"It will never be a worthy substitute. Buildings like this one are a beacon of learning. I will not allow lesser men of apocryphal technology to diminish their purpose."

"It's been quite a few days since I last slept in a bed, I'm dangerously caffeine-deficient and frankly feeling a little murderous. Where are you going with this?"

"I was offered an investment."

"Good. Take it, then."

"I did," he said, pointing back to the book in her hands.

"Mario! How?"

"A month ago, I was approached by one of his representatives who informed me that if I helped them, I would share in a vast sum of money that would safeguard the future of the Bodleian for decades."

"But why you?"

"Because I was the only one who had access to the books. We bought this version from Lyon and I used my connections to get Vienna to loan me their copy. There are only three first editions in the world: now two of them are here. Plus, he was keen that you should be involved somehow. It was important, in their eyes, that you were kept out of the way, even implicated if at all possible."

"Is that why you stole the Shikshapatri?"

"No. I had nothing to do with that. It was not part of the plan, although it was a rather useful distraction."

Something still didn't make sense, thought Ally. In all of her investigations the one event that seemed to link to her most was the book that no one was willing to own up to stealing or hiding.

"Who stole the Shikshapatri, then?"

THE SEQUENCE

"It wasn't stolen, you said so yourself this morning. It was always here. If it hadn't gone missing, they had other ways to remove you from the scene; because of its disappearance they never needed to."

"What was your involvement with the letters?" asked Ally, holding the one she'd just found aloft.

"Not much. I'm simply the Librarian. When they locate a letter, the Courier pays me a visit, and uses the book to decipher the code. That then sets the ball rolling for the next Mountain Man."

"There are no Mountain Men," replied Ally sharply. "These events are not being perpetrated by lone wolves, they clearly involve a vast network of people. I suspect the whole concept of the Mountain Men is nothing more than a fabricated conspiracy designed by Mario."

"Perhaps. The money, though, is not fabricated."

"Why confess all this now?"

"Because I know how much you love this place and your job. If you don't let events run their course, I will ensure that everything you cherish is taken from you. The institution is more important than the individual."

"You don't really know me, do you?"

"No one here does."

"Then what you need to know is that I'm allergic to following orders and find it impossible to let greedy, two-faced bastards win."

"Shame. You can't stop it now, Ally. The only way to recover the money is to complete the sequence. Only then can the funds be accessed."

"I don't care about the bloody money, you snivelling bookworm. I care about answers. Where and when will you meet the Courier next?"

"Why would I tell you that? All of this is still only your word against mine, and if I don't meet the Courier soon a series of revolutionary uprisings will happen all around the world anyway. No one will get any money, but a series of Western societies will fall into turmoil. These people have been waiting for decades to rise up against their oppressors.

THE SEQUENCE

Some don't care about the money either. They care about havoc and fire. They care about climbing the mountain. Mario has given them the route and means to scale it."

"This is not about freedom. This is about greed and you are going to lose everything unless you co-operate."

"You'll just have to call the police and see which one of us they arrest then, won't you?"

"I'll save you the time," came a voice from the door.

*****

Ernest was led away from the building securely detained in Daniel Hudson's handcuffs. Parked at the rear entrance waiting for them was a police car. Daniel only recognised it as one because it said 'police' down the side. Everything was small in this country. Police cars in the US could easily been seen from space.

DCI Bolton, stern-faced and grumpy as always, held the door of the car open as if it was the entrance of a high-end hotel.

"Dr Oldfield, don't think this changes my opinion," he said aggressively. "You are still a person of interest."

"Whatever. You have nothing on me. The Shikshapatri has been returned and if you still believe I have anything to do with any of it then come pay me a visit in Stanton," she said slowly and loudly as she announced her intention to leave. "Be nice for someone other than Honeywell to haunt my doorstep."

"I might just do that," he replied with a heavy nod.

It went unnoticed.

"What do you want me to do with him?" asked Bolton as Daniel unceremoniously bundled Ernest into the back seat.

"Read him his rights and then you can take both of us to your nearest station. I have some questions for him which he isn't going to like. Then, when he refuses to answer them, I'm going to beat the shit out of him,"

THE SEQUENCE

replied Daniel, leaning down to the height of the car window and offering the Librarian a rather manic grin.

"This is my jurisdiction. I call the shots here. You might get away with behaviour like that in the States but it's not appropriate here."

"I'll give you twelve billion reasons why it is. I also have more powerful friends than you. Be under no illusion who is in charge here. I might have to abide by some of the local processes, but this is my rodeo. Capeesh? Now get in the car," added Daniel forcefully. "I need a moment alone with Ally."

The disgruntled detective retired to the driver's seat after a short attempt at arguing his position failed to make any impact. Outside the car Ally quickly briefed the Special Agent about everything she'd learnt from Ernest and his office and made it clear that his interrogation needed to focus on the next meeting of the Courier so that the sequence could be broken.

"It's been one hell of a week," said Daniel as the late November air of early evening circled around them. "I think you deserve a Friday night drink."

"Friday!" mouthed Ally realising how much of the week had passed her by unnoticed. "I completely forgot."

"Forgot what?"

"Dad," she said, turning immediately on her heels.

"Wait!" shouted Daniel. "There are things I need to tell you."

She was gone before the words left his mouth.

- Chapter 21 -

The Passing of Horace Oldfield

The rain pelted down on the taxi's windscreen like the sound of overhead gunfire. Drowned pedestrians huddled under cheap umbrellas and crept through the floods of water building up on the pavements. Bedraggled dogs, ears drooping limply over their faces, sought shelter under hedgerows as their obedient owners attempted to drag them home. Through the steamed-up window and furious wiper activity, Ally noticed little of it. She was late and the only thing she paid attention to was seeing the sign that identified their arrival at the Furlong Nursing Home.

It didn't matter who she ended up being today, her father would still complain she was late. He might not remember who people were, but he never failed to know what the exact time of day was. Punctuality would put up a stiff fight against the relentless march of dementia.

The taxi aquaplaned into the steep car park and came to rest with a jolt outside the front entrance. There was no time for the normal pre-visit routines. No time for the prevarication, guilt or despondency that preceded these Friday evening pilgrimages. Visiting time would soon be over and her duties would lie unfulfilled. So far nothing this week had been routine: at least this would be. She hurled some money at her driver, dived out into the rain and made a dash for the warmth of the reception.

The atmosphere inside the home was at odds with the normal chaos and positive determination shown by the staff. Glum faces and furrowed brows seemed the order of

THE PASSING OF HORACE OLDFIELD

the day. Maybe one of the residents had recently died? Surely that was a relatively frequent event, though, she thought. The conveyor belt to the afterlife was a constant stream of in- and outpatients in a place such as this.

When Ally reached the reception desk, Kay, the peroxide blonde who seemed to live permanently on the premises, had an expression markedly different from the one she normally wore. The overworked mascara had been ruined further by a bout of tears that were still visibly welling in her eyes.

"Mrs Oldfield," she said with a pause. "Didn't you get our messages?"

"Doct…" she almost replied instinctively but stopped herself. "What messages?"

"Voicemail, texts, home phone and emails. We've been trying to reach you for hours. Even left a message with a man at your house. Although I'm not surprised that one didn't reach you as he only responded with the word 'potato'."

The content of the news that had yet to reach her seemed, in her mind, to be obvious. Their tears backed it up. It was the inevitable truth that every family member had to face eventually. Horace had passed on. She hadn't prepared herself for it. Sadness wasn't her first reaction, not in the conventional way at least. A better description would be remorse. History, hers at least, had died with him. Now she would never know the truth of where she came from and who she really was. His dementia had made it difficult but not impossible. She always hoped that one day he would eventually give her a clue, an accidental crack in his memory that might allow some of the truth to escape.

"Did he leave peacefully?" asked Ally in a more sensitive manner than she thought she was capable of.

"Not really," replied Kay, shaking her head slowly. "There was a terrible racket."

People who haven't witnessed death imagine a natural passing to be a rather peaceful process. 'They slipped off

THE PASSING OF HORACE OLDFIELD

into sleep' was etched on many a gravestone in every cemetery in every corner of the country, but was it really like that? It appeared not. Rather morbidly, Ally wondered what it was like. After all, she lived for learning and this was just research. She couldn't bring him back now.

"What happened?" she asked.

"It started with the fire alarm."

"He made a sound like a fire alarm?"

"No. He set the fire alarm off."

"Spontaneous human combustion is a myth," added Ally curtly.

"Yes... obviously," stammered Kay.

"What's the fire alarm got to do with it, then?" replied Ally, swimming in confusion.

"We think he opened the fire escape."

"Why didn't someone restrain him?"

"It was three o'clock in the afternoon and everyone else apart from the duty nurse was busy doing the afternoon tea."

"Hold on. Back up a minute. You say he departed at three in the afternoon and somehow set off the fire alarm by going through the fire escape. Right?"

"Yes."

"So where did you find him in the end?"

"That's just it, we haven't yet."

"Then how do you know he's dead?"

"Dead!? He's not dead, or at least let's hope not," said Kay nervously. "Although a man of his age and in his condition is certainly in a lot of danger."

The momentary relief that rushed through Ally on discovering the news that her father wasn't dead was immediately replaced by a new wave of anxiety. Having a father with dementia stuck in a home was difficult enough but to think he was loose out in the wider world on his own was terrifying.

"Have you called the police?" Ally demanded.

"Yes, he's in the lounge taking witness statements as we speak."

THE PASSING OF HORACE OLDFIELD

Nursing homes called it a lounge, when everyone else in Britain called it a 'living' room. Lounges were resting places between destinations, like the ones in airports or train stations. A living room was only accurately labelled when it exclusively had 'living' people in it, which on any given day in a nursing home might only refer to fifty percent of those inside. Hence the suitability of using a different word. Ally left Kay mid-sentence and burst into the lounge. An elderly PC was shuffling from chair to chair trying to establish if any of the occupants were conscious and whether they could shed light on the recent disappearance.

"Dr Oldfield," said PC Norman Dearlove brightly. "How are you?"

"What?!" she snapped.

"Are you well?"

"Does that really matter right now?" she mumbled innately, quite unused to answering such pointless questions.

"It does to me," he replied with a cheeky wink.

It went unnoticed.

"No, then, if you really want to know," she answered finally. "Obviously my father is missing. In which universe is that ever going to put me in a good mood?"

"Of course," he said sympathetically but continued to smile warmly like a lunatic. "Sorry to hear about your father. Don't worry. We'll find him."

"What can you tell me?" she said focusing on the solution and feeling less confident about the competence of the local police force.

"Not had much luck with these folks, I'm afraid. Doris over there," he pointed to a withered figure whose head was drooping almost into her lap, "tells me she's soiled herself again. Pat thinks she heard an owl, and Walter is convinced that Horace was planning to join the French Foreign Legion. I'm not sure they're still a thing."

THE PASSING OF HORACE OLDFIELD

"I think your immense talents are wasted here," she added sarcastically. "I know he didn't like the home, but I had no idea he'd try to escape."

"Do you have any thoughts about where he might go?" asked Norman, forcing his body out of its crouching position next to the now sleeping Walter.

"Yes. There's only one place."

"Well, tell me and I'll get a patrol car over there immediately."

"The North," added Ally. "I'm not sure one car will be enough."

"Frightened," said a croaky, muffled voice on the other side of the room.

Ally and Norman scanned the lounge to identify the possible life within the alternative 'living' room. In the far corner an immaculately dressed pensioner with shiny silver medals pinned to a lapel was wrapped to the waist in a layer of blankets. Wrinkled eyelids occasionally parted to reveal deep blue eyes underneath, while the croaky, heavy breathing gushed in through a mouth that gasped for every ounce of oxygen.

"Hello," said Norman softly. "Can you help us?"

"Lieutenant Stanley Packer," replied the man, attempting a salute through the layers of insulation. "Got spooked."

"What do you mean?" asked Ally.

"Someone came… asked questions," added Stanley.

"Who?"

"Serious-looking. An Army man, no doubt about that, seen thousands of them down the years. You can always tell a military man by his shoes. Look at my shoes," barked Stanley as if ordering a platoon of troops. The force of the command sent both of their attentions down to the floor.

"You're wearing slippers," said Ally correctly.

"Liar! A soldier never wears slippers. I polished these myself just this morning. Look at them and tell me what you see."

"Paisley swirls," replied Ally.

THE PASSING OF HORACE OLDFIELD

"Your reflection! That's what," he insisted. "All proper soldiers have shiny boots, just like Horace's visitor."

"When was this?" asked Norman, interjecting.

"What day is it today?" asked Stanley.

"Friday," said Ally and Norman in unison.

"In that case," he paused for longer than a human normally needed to in order to massage memory back into place. "June."

"June was months ago."

"Then it was July."

"What else do you remember?" asked Ally, trying to redirect the man's mind to something useful.

"It was quite hot."

"Not July, what do you remember about Horace's visitor?"

"Who's Horace?"

"My father. You said he had a visitor."

"Father never had visitors, he had a gun, you see. Lived on a big squirrel farm."

"I'm not listening to any more of this nonsense," growled Ally. "My father is out there somewhere, and I need help to find him."

"I'll see if I can get a description," said Norman. "Why don't you see if the nurses know more about this visitor, if indeed there actually was one?"

Ally returned to reception and was immediately offered tea. It was like offering garlic to a vampire. She never drank tea and couldn't understand why the answer to almost every crisis experienced by English people was to stick a bag with the tips of a bush into boiling water and then add cow juice to it. How did that solve someone being burgled, being fired from their job, coping with the news of a terminal illness or bad exam results? If the crisis happened to be mild thirst it might be a decent remedy, but that was about it. Even more extraordinarily people actually said, 'Oh I do feel better,' after drinking it. Were people really that easily pleased?

THE PASSING OF HORACE OLDFIELD

"I don't want tea. I'd like answers. Did someone come to visit Horace recently?"

"We've been very short-staffed this week," said Sheila as if in defence of a crime. "You can check the visitors' book, we might have missed it."

"Missed it!"

"It's not a high-security prison, Mrs Oldfield."

"DOCTOR… I'm a fucking doctor. Is that so hard to remember!"

Both women froze to the spot not quite sure how to respond. It didn't really seem important in the circumstances.

"Dr Oldfield," replied Sheila, pulling herself up to her full height of five foot two. "People come and go as they please around here. Sometimes charity workers come in to talk to lonely residents, sometimes relatives we've not seen before visit them. We don't ask for their passports. We're just happy that someone remembers who they are. It's not easy working here, you know. How much do you get paid as a so-called doctor? I bet you're rich, aren't you? Try living off minimum wage and then see if you worry about what someone calls you. Do you have to deal with random acts of violence in your job? Do you have to clean up pensioner's piss morning, noon and night? No! Didn't think so. I'll tell you why that is, DOCTOR Oldfield… you don't have the character for it. You don't have the kindness for it."

Both women stormed into the back office and left Ally alone. Around her the gaudy nineteen seventies wallpaper was peeling off the walls. The carpet was frayed and bare under her feet. A musty smell of doom clung in the air. Maybe this was her own destiny. Who would visit her when she eventually arrived here or somewhere like it? No one. There wouldn't be anyone because no one visited her lovely cottage in Stanton unless they were on the run from the FBI.

Loneliness was acceptable when you had something to distract yourself from acknowledging it. That didn't stop it

THE PASSING OF HORACE OLDFIELD

being there, lurking in the background waiting for its time to consume you when you were least prepared to overcome it. What would distract her when she had no work to do? When her body held her hostage to a thread-worn armchair in a dimly lit room surrounded by a wall of dirty net curtains, what then? The thought lingered and she shivered from it. She'd never invited loneliness into her life. It invited itself in while she'd been busy alienating those that tried to block it off.

It had grown inside her like a cancer from a young age. When other children were protected by their parents, she'd provided for herself. When the shield provided by most adults had been lowered, only her tenacity and independence kept her alive. Loneliness had been the drug that healed her wounds and now it was an addiction that wouldn't let go. She had to break free of it or accept the fate that awaited in a not-too-distant future. Once she found Horace, she would have to find something almost as important. The kindness that Sheila had correctly identified was missing. Kindness for herself and kindness for others.

She opened the leather-bound visitors' book and flicked through to the last few pages. There were far more entries on any given day than she'd expected to see. Everyone had someone. They hadn't visited under some guilt trip or genetic duty, they came because they missed their loved ones or appreciated the joy their visit would bring. Some of the visitors' names appeared almost every day. Sometimes for hours at a time. She drew her finger down the page seeing some names so often she felt she knew them. Then suddenly she stopped on today's list.

Horace Oldfield did have another visitor today.
Radu Goga.

- Chapter 22 -

The Eagle and Child

It didn't take Daniel long to get the answers he was looking for. After all, he no longer had the luxury of time. In less than two days he'd have to convince McNamee he was on top of things. Daniel had twenty years of experience of extracting answers from people. Ernest had no chance. Ultimately, he was just an unfortunate bystander in a much wider network of perpetrators. In the right place, right time and with the right pressure applied. Daniel felt rather sorry for him. He wasn't really being selfish. He'd acted with good intentions but nevertheless still illegally. The justice system would reward his cooperation with leniency. It was his first offence and the charges against him no more severe than one of obstructing justice.

There was much that Ernest didn't know about the Mountain Men, Daniel was certain of that. He didn't know where the money was, or what the code meant, or how its message was delivered to the people responsible for carrying out the events of the last week. Neither could he shed any light on the pattern that linked each of the Mountain Men. It made sense that this was the case. The less he knew, the less he might reveal. Ernest wasn't a hardened, experienced criminal willing and able to resist someone like Daniel. The people behind the uprisings knew this, too. Ernest was there for only one purpose. To allow easy access to the only book that deciphered the code, and no one was likely to suspect him of that initially.

What Ernest had been able to relay to Daniel was the location and time of his next meeting with the Courier. The same location they'd met on four previous occasions

THE EAGLE AND CHILD

in the last week, always two days apart. The Eagle and Child public house in the centre of Oxford. Their next appointment was tomorrow lunchtime. Although Ernest couldn't identify the man's name, he had given Daniel a detailed description.

Probably French, but certainly with a deep French accent, the Courier stood around five feet seven inches tall, had brunette hair, brown eyes, thirty-something, broad in stature and almost always shabbily dressed. Rarely did the meeting take longer than a few minutes. Ernest illustrated how he would always sit in the back room of the narrow bar at a table next to the open fire. The book would be concealed from view until the Courier arrived. He'd take a seat directly opposite the Librarian, often with his head and face hidden under a hood. Once the man revealed the presence of the letter to Ernest, the Librarian would pass him the Nostradamus book and the Courier would go to work. As soon as the code was deciphered the man upped and left with barely a word exchanged.

Daniel left the interview room and made his way through a network of corridors to the rear entrance of the building. A dingy courtyard cluttered with debris and large, colourful bins greeted him. The night had stealthily set in while he was cooped up inside the plain walls of the enclosed interview room. He reached into his jacket and produced a cigarette which he lit with a small strip of matches similar to the type handed out by hotels and restaurants in the days when smoking was more accepted. It was rare these days for him to partake in such a self-destructive habit.

A decade ago it was as regular an act as talking, such was his need for the addictive lure of the thin, white sticks. These days it wasn't the nicotine he needed. That desire had long since been supplemented by a stronger willpower and an unrelenting struggle against weight gain. The habit which had for so long been associated with eating, driving, waiting, socialising and waking up had been subdued by

THE EAGLE AND CHILD

other distractions, but there was one activity that he'd never managed to disassociate with smoking.

Thinking.

No matter what the challenge his brain was trying to solve, it was always made clearer by walking away from his desk, sparking up a cigarette and taking one delicious, extended drag. Almost immediately the solution presented itself. It wasn't clear whether it was the act of smoking that helped focus his mind or just the distraction from all other stimuli. Certainly, he tried just standing outside and not smoking as an alternative, but that had about as much success as mowing a lawn with a comb.

Something about Ernest's description of the Courier bothered him. The visual representation of the character sounded familiar and if Daniel did know who it was it might not be the cleverest idea for him to replace the Librarian for the exchange. The Courier was organised and secretive. If he suspected or discovered any change to the normal routine, it might scare him off and they might never get another opportunity. They couldn't risk using Ernest either in case he gave the game away. The smoke filled up Daniel's lungs and his brain instinctively picked two names.

Over the next hour Daniel made several attempts to the reach the first name on his list. Every time he tried, he reached her voicemail. He glanced at his watch to see the analogue hands stretching north. It was late and she'd had a rather challenging few days. Maybe she'd turned in for the evening. He left the third voicemail message before turning his attention to the second name on his list. The preparation for tomorrow's exchange had to happen now: it would be too risky to wait until morning. He dialled a second number.

"Yes," yawned a voice after a dozen rings had droned through the mobile network.

"Lance Carter?" asked Daniel.

"Ah ha," he mumbled in confirmation.

"This is Daniel Hudson from the FBI."

THE EAGLE AND CHILD

There was an extended silence as Lance recalled an uncomfortable interrogation that had been the feature of last Saturday. Was this going to happen every weekend? he thought.

"Are you still there?"

"Yeah. Do you know what time it is?"

"Time you got your arse over to the police station."

"What have I done this time?"

"Nothing, yet. The FBI needs your help."

"But I'm in Kent, only just got here."

"Then you'd better get back, immediately."

"Why?"

"Because I say so."

"I think, if I'm being arrested, you have to come to me."

"No. Look, do you want to prove your worth to Ally Oldfield or not?"

"I'd rather sleep and have a weekend off," replied Lance honestly.

"Let me put it another way, then," added Daniel, changing his line of attack. "How would you like the FBI to be a constant shadow over you for the rest of your life?"

"I'll get my keys."

*****

The Eagle and Child, better known to the locals as the 'Bird and Baby' had many claims to fame. It was in the 'rabbit room' at the back of this small, end-of-terrace, magnolia-painted pub that the 'Inklings' met most Monday or Tuesday lunchtimes during the nineteen thirties. Future literary superstars such as C.S. Lewis and J.R.R. Tolkien would gather to discuss their fantastical ideas or to read excerpts from their latest manuscripts over a warm, frothy pint of local ale. Just like the coffee houses of London a century or more before, places like this were the epicentre of enlightenment and learning. It's quite possible that a baby Gandalf or a lion cub called Aslan took their first

THE EAGLE AND CHILD

tentative steps amongst the felt-covered bar stools under the Eagle's sixteenth-century beamed ceilings.

Much history had travelled through it. Soon it might capture some more.

Lance looked tired. Not only had he spent much of yesterday evening and this morning completing a seemingly pointless three hundred-mile round trip from the Kent coast, where he'd been seen off quicker than the Luftwaffe, he'd also endured an unexpected shopping trip. Lance's fashion style, which was best described as eccentric aristocracy meets certified lunatic, was deemed to be inappropriate for a covert FBI mission. Mustard-coloured slacks, a luminous psychedelic shirt, and welly boots might, Daniel concluded, result in either the target going blind, or the locals being hypnotised.

Daniel's plan required something a little more traditional. Lance had to act as a legitimate stand-in for Ernest, which meant he had to look more like a librarian and less like the member of an exclusive hippy commune. It wasn't just the new, light brown, conservative-styled mohair suit that Lance was wearing, though. Underneath he'd been wired up to allow Daniel to hear everything that was happening from his position in the 'rabbit room'.

The whole of the pub had been requisitioned for the benefit of the FBI. Staff had been replaced by undercover policeman, punters were no longer the normal delinquent late-morning lost souls seeking liquid solace. They, too, were now members of Daniel's team. Only Bill, the pub's landlord, was allowed to remain active in case any local knowledge might be called on. It couldn't be guaranteed that regulars wouldn't call in, but most of those that Bill knew normally frequented it this early had been tracked down and encouraged to stay away.

In less than twelve hours every detail, every scenario and every circumstance had been prepared, tested, considered and checked. Everyone was ready. Almost.

"I'm not sure I can do this," said Lance anxiously as he took up position next to the welcoming, crackling open fire. Sweat was already trickling down his brow from the intense heat and his own nerves.

"Don't worry. You'll be fine and I'm just in there through that door," said Daniel, pointing it out a few metres away.

"Wouldn't Ally have been a better choice?"

"Yes, but I can't get hold of her and you were second on my list. Just be yourself, act naturally."

Acting naturally had never really worked out for Lance that well. 'Natural' usually meant an intense level of social awkwardness, spatial awareness reflexes that created destruction with every move, and a propensity to fart uncontrollably when he was anxious. If Lance ever did secure a date with the opposite sex, and the odds of that were equal to finding the Crown Jewels in your cereal box, the smell would most certainly make it the shortest date in recorded history.

Daniel passed Lance the copy of *Les Prophéties* that was central to the meeting. He placed it on his lap.

"Nearly time. We'll be listening the whole time. Remember once you've seen that he has the letter, use the agreed signal."

"Ok. Could I get a pint to settle the nerves?"

"Bill, pint of beer please!" hollered Daniel in his deep, booming voice.

"Thanks," replied Lance.

"Now let's get this bastard," added Daniel, before departing from the main bar and retreating to his secretive position.

Lance took a gulp of his beer as his shaking hands propelled much of it over the surface of the oak table. He glanced at his wristwatch obsessively. No matter how many times he stared at the face it resolutely refused to move forward. Had he been frozen in time? The more he fixated on it, the more his stress levels rose. He could feel the sweat oozing through his pores and his heart rate rose exponentially. How had he got here? He just wanted a good education. Antoine never suggested his internship

THE EAGLE AND CHILD

might include being an FBI stooge, breaking and entering, being arrested for acts of terrorism, or acting as his boss's personal chauffeur. Was this the beginning or the end of the surprises? he wondered. His guts grumbled at the possibility it might be the former.

The main door of the pub opened silently and a man in a hooded jumper walked casually into the warmth of the pub and out of the elements hounding the town centre of Oxford. As his head carefully scanned the interior his eyes rested on the table they normally used. His body noticeably jittered for a second as his brain analysed the lanky occupant supping from a pint mug. Instantly the newcomer was left with a decision. Approach and interrogate, or retreat and escape. Delay would cause him embarrassment and produce unwanted anger from his employer. The meagre expression on Lance's face coupled with a dress sense typical of an academic swung the pendulum towards engagement.

The man swiftly moved forward, immediately taking a seat on one of the low bar stools on the other side of the table. He leant forward so his features were concealed by his hood. Lance, trying to remain 'himself', as Daniel had advised, sprang forward with his arm outstretched in welcome, the custom he always used when greeting people. On this occasion, due to his mind being befuddled by everything that was going on, his hand collided with his mostly full pint of beer, knocking it with a decent velocity towards the target who, doing his best to remain anonymous and unsighted, didn't see it coming. The frothy, brown liquid splattered the man's hood and flowed over the table into his lap.

"Oh God! I'm terribly sorry."

"Idiot!" growled the man, unable to move out of the wet patch in case it blew his cover. "I'm totally soaked."

"Let me get you another one," replied Lance apologetically, his mind desperate to find a way to appease the situation.

"It wasn't mine, you cretin."

THE EAGLE AND CHILD

"Oh yeah. Would you like one any…"

"No. Who are you? Where's the Librarian?"

"Lance Carter," he replied, gently holding out his hand again but realising that the chances of the man shaking it were now minimal as his hands were currently occupied in the job of bailing out his trousers. "Ernest has been taken ill. I work for him at the Weston and he instructed me to meet with you."

"Prove it," grumbled the man.

Throughout the interaction the man kept his features from view by mainly looking at the edge of the table rather than up. Lance reached inside his jacket to retrieve his wallet. The fabric was rather tight still and he struggled to release what he needed. Finally, with a heave the wallet came free, slipped from his grasp, flew across the table and struck the man on the top of the head before landing in the pool of beer.

"What the…" screamed the man, instinctively looking up so that Lance caught sight of his face.

"Sorry, let me just take that back."

Lance rescued the wallet, unclipped it, removed his Weston Library ID pass and slid it nonchalantly back across the table.

"It doesn't look much like you."

"Yeah, I had longer hair back then and, as you can see from my photos, I was going through my lime green phase." The photo of Lance had a passing resemblance to a leprechaun that had been passed through a pasta machine. "It's definitely me, though."

"What has Ernest told you?"

"Nothing. Just to meet you here so you could borrow the book."

"Show me."

"Show me the letter first," said Lance overeagerly. The whole experience was making him squirm like a toddler in a ball pit.

"That's not 'nothing', is it!?"

THE EAGLE AND CHILD

Lance's stomach made an audible grumbling noise as his nerves spread through his duodenum, ricocheted around the small intestine, barged into the large intestine, and joined a sizeable queue just inside his colon. Only one stop left on that route.

"Oh. Jesus. What in all that's holy is that?"

"Sorry. I'm having a bit of a crisis," offered Lance.

"My fucking eyes are watering. Pass me the book," the man barked, waving his arm furiously in front of him.

"Ernest said only to lend you the book once I knew it was you, and the only way of knowing that is to see the letter," lied Lance, rather convincingly.

In the two minutes since this shadowy character entered 'The Eagle and Child' he'd been subjected to floods, physical assault and chemical warfare. If he wanted to leave in one piece, he felt it might be best to give Lance a flash of the letter.

"Right, good enough? Where's the book?"

Lance held it up so he could see it, but that was as close as the man was getting to it. Lance knew how much this book meant to Ally and there was no way he'd be responsible for putting it in any potential jeopardy. He wouldn't have to. He'd done what had been asked of him and now all he had to do was make the signal. The FBI were listening, but they weren't watching. The signal would tell them when to strike.

That's if he could remember it.

"Pass it over," said the man eagerly.

"I can't yet," hesitated Lance.

"Why not?"

"Just hold on, I'm trying to remember."

"You're trying to remember why you can't pass me the book!?"

"Yes."

"What's wrong with you? Have you been tested?"

"You're not the only one who's asked me that."

"Quelle surprise," replied the man effortlessly in his own language and matching accent.

THE EAGLE AND CHILD

It didn't matter how much Lance squeezed on his synapses the answer wasn't coming. The stress hormones were zooming around any channel available and had completely kidnapped other functions. Fortunately for him, more experienced and balanced members of the team had been listening to every part of the conversation and had decided now was the time to pounce on their prey.

Daniel, with the poise of a jaguar, had quietly left his shelter, shuffled slowly to a position directly behind the target and immediately in front of Lance, who let out a relieved sigh. Daniel reached forward and pulled the hood back to reveal a mop of neatly combed hair.

"Don't even think about moving," whispered the FBI agent leaning, forward to speak into the man's left ear. "The whole place is teeming with my people."

Daniel unbuttoned his jacket, allowing his gut the freedom it desperately needed, before squeezing his body into the chair between the two men. For the first time he was face to face with the Courier, so far the most important conspirator in this vastly complicated case.

"You!" said Daniel, his hand spontaneously leaping to his mouth in horror.

- Chapter 23 -

Radu Goga

The search for Horace continued through Friday night and well into Saturday morning without even a hint of his whereabouts. In the normal circumstance of someone going missing, those searching would check all the places the individual might be familiar with. Their workplace, their friends' houses, local clubs or family members. Horace had none of these. In the short period he'd lived in the 'South' the only place he really knew was the Furlong Nursing Home, which was the one place Ally was sure he wasn't. The clues were sparse.

There was no evidence, according to Norman at least, who'd offered to help Ally with the search, that Horace had been abducted. There was no sign of a struggle and his disappearance had happened in the middle of the afternoon when even the other residents would have noticed. The only solid information they had was that 'someone had come', according to Stanley and, although he'd not managed to verbalise anything more substantial it did seem authentic. The name in the book confirmed it further but didn't explain it. What interest did Radu Goga have in a man like Horace?

Ally had only heard the name once before and that was a cursory mention last weekend in an Oxford prison during Daniel's interrogation. Now the name stared out of a shabby visitors' book in an even shabbier old people's home. What did Radu Goga want with her father? Did they know each other? Was it the reason for her father's retreat? Had Radu helped him escape? None of these questions had answers. She could only hope that Horace might be able to shed some light on it, if she ever located him.

Whatever had happened at the home it was enough to scare Horace into a retreat that was very much out of character. Horace's physical condition normally meant unaccompanied trips to the bathroom were strenuous enough and yet he'd managed to leave the lounge, open the fire escape, presumably unaided, and leave the building without support or being noticed. That was as far as the trace went. Had he booked a taxi? It seemed unlikely given his mental frailty.

Norman's small police car had spent the last twelve hours escorting Ally to various dead ends. Local churches, a homeless refuge, several pubs and even a Labour club, which was basically a small shed where the entirety of Oxford's Labour movement could assemble. All twelve of them. Now the car was back at the care home to double-check he'd not returned. Ally trudged back to the car, her shoulders slumped and her face glum.

"No good?" asked Norman kindly.

Ally shook her head.

"What about your place?"

"He never went there," replied Ally.

"Might he have been able to find out where it was?"

"Potentially but it's fifteen miles away, how would he get there? None of the local taxi companies have seen him and the buses are woeful."

"Maybe that's all we can do for now. When was the last time you went home, Ally?"

"I think it was Thursday," she said unemotionally.

"Now might be time to get a good night's sleep?"

"It's daytime!"

"Nice cup of tea, then."

"No," she scowled.

"Lift? It's about time I went home as well," said Norman who'd exceeding his normal working hours sometime last night.

"Yes, ok."

RADU GOGA

"Jump in, we'll be home in no time."

"Not the way you drive, we won't."

As usual, Norman completely overlooked the veiled insult like nothing she said would shift the smile from his face or the bounce in his heart.

*****

For nearly thirty years, Radu Goga had been a ghost. The name, and whoever it once belonged to, had passed into myth. That wasn't true for anyone who'd lived during the tumultuous nineteen sixties and seventies. Back then people on both sides of the Iron Curtain knew his name. In a time when 'East' and 'West' were engaged in a Cold War that spanned every element of people's lives you couldn't avoid the name of Radu Goga. Although few knew much more about him than that.

During the Cold War both factions worked tirelessly to encourage defections from the other. It was one of many strategic threads in a ball of bewilderingly complex initiatives spun to defeat the ideology of the other that included propaganda, misinformation, the funding of terrorism, support for sympathetic nations, and the insatiable desire to outbuild the other in the size of its nuclear arsenal. Both sides achieved stunning successes when it came to the poaching of the other's intellectual assets. Nuclear scientists, Army officials, diplomats, journalists and even Olympic athletes moved from one side to the other as if the Iron Curtain was actually suffering metal fatigue. Some were more useful than others and all were lauded by the victors, but none had the impact of Radu Goga.

His was the highest profile defection of the entire Cold War because it offered proof, if any were still needed in the West, that Communism had failed. A member of the Politburo's inner circle, a man of status and power, had wilfully broken free from the shackles of Communist oppression and moved into the light of capitalism at great personal expense.

Radu's disaffection had accumulated gradually. Like millions of other people, he'd grown up under the brutal totalitarian influence of Joseph Stalin. Like many people in the region, particularly if your community was not being brutally persecuted, the worst parts of the state were ignored in an act of collective amnesia that only saw the ideological seeds of progress and not the shocking abuse and hardship which were happening all around them.

Radu was a political scholar as much as a Communist convert. As the despotic leaders that followed Stalin continued to deviate from the chapter and verse of ideological utopia, so did Radu's loyalty. The breaking point came when the Soviet leadership ordered him to assassinate a journalist who'd expressed discontent at the regime. In Radu's opinion this crossed a line. The founding fathers of Communism, people like Karl Marx and Lenin, had themselves fought against the authorities by expressing their controversial views. Now they, the movement for change, had become the oppressors of expression. It was time for Radu to act on his conscience.

Defections weren't easy. You couldn't just walk to the border and hop across, not unless you wanted to do it with more holes in you than a Swiss cheese. Detailed planning and just the right opportunity had to present itself. Radu's chance came during an official Soviet trip to Germany. Sent with a message to the East German Chancellor, Radu took a detour and walked confidently into the American Embassy where plans had already been drawn up to safely escort him to the United States. Over the coming years the Americans learnt much from Radu, but there was one secret he always kept to himself.

The cost of his defection was felt most acutely by his family.

The challenging circumstances of his transition from one side to the other meant his wife and daughter were trapped in his native Romania. The Americans insisted it

RADU GOGA

would be impossible to intervene and too dangerous for them to be extracted. In retribution for Radu's treachery his family were subjected to imprisonment and torture, and treated as traitors. His wife, Elena, was never seen in public again and rumours circulated that she had taken her own life under the immense strain of her husband's disappearance and her own brutal treatment. His daughter's body, like millions of others living in the regime, was never recovered. Over the decades Radu's guilt grew, ultimately mutating to create a bitter and angry collaborator. His anger towards both 'East' and 'West' was equal only to the one he held against himself.

Over the following decade the Soviets authorised countless attempts to assassinate Radu, but none succeeded. Some assailants came close but ultimately all of them failed. The information he held went beyond secrets of national security; for some people his knowledge would remain dangerous until his dying day.

As the world passed through the nineteen-eighties the hostile climate warmed and Radu's use to the West diminished. Less was asked of him, and his whereabouts and actions were scrutinised infrequently. Until he disappeared completely, coincidentally on the same day the Berlin Wall fell. No one believed he was dead. No one believed he was acting alone. People didn't just leave the clutches of a corrupt system. The conspiracy theories raged. Had he returned to post-Communist Romania? Had he been granted a new identity as a reward for his part in ending the Cold War? Had he been a double agent all along?

The truth had been hard to pinpoint, but Daniel Hudson had discovered enough to rule out some of those theories. The rest would only be revealed when Daniel found him.

*****

RADU GOGA

The trees of Stanton St. John had shaken off most of their leaves, forming an autumnal blanket of orange and brown over the paths and bridleways of the village. At the entrance to the village a white sign with black writing confirmed its identity. After several hours of exertion, the elderly cyclist stopped briefly to take it in and take a deserved rest. This was where the man had told him to come. This was where it would happen, although no one knew when. He'd need to be patient and he'd need somewhere inconspicuous to wait.

Comfy loafers, caked in dirt and mud, pushed down on the pedals as the antique bicycle trundled along the main road, dodging the large stones that poked out of the surface like granite icebergs. In the distance the steeple of a church was nestled amongst a row of thatched roofs attached to stone cottages. To his right a narrow driveway, carved by a tractor taking its daily route across arable land, weaved its way to a picturesque house on the edge of the village. Unlike the other houses, this building lacked the comforting plumes of smoke that spiralled from the tops of chimneys.

He turned off the main road and carefully skirted the watery potholes for fear of damaging the fragile and borrowed bike permanently. At the end of the drive the white-painted house was clad in wisteria bushes which would make the house beautifully photographic in spring but gave it a more haunted quality during autumn. The old-age pensioner gingerly dismounted from the pushbike and approached the front door slowly. As he peered through the small window in the front of the black-painted, wooden door there was no obvious activity inside. No car was parked in the drive. No lights were on to overcome the late Friday afternoon gloom. It seemed, on first appearances, that the property was empty. Maybe it was a holiday cottage only inhabited during the peak season? It didn't matter, it was empty now, and it would do as a place to regroup and plan his next move.

RADU GOGA

Carefully the octogenarian bent down to look through the letter box in order to establish an easy way of breaking in. Along the narrow hallway vibrant plants in plain, grey, plastic pots suggested this was no holiday home. The pristine interior must have been cleaned every morning and then left in lonely perfection. Whoever lived here didn't spend much time inside by the looks of things. He moved his attention to the lock. Nothing serious, a simple catch that opened the door from the inside. A lack of deadbolt or chain gave the impression that the owner didn't have much fear of being burgled.

The old man slowly returned to what he thought of as upright, but what most of us would call hunched. He moved towards the wisteria bushes and dug around behind the branches, removing a long stiff piece of wire designed to keep the tree growing in exactly the way the owner intended. He manipulated one end into a hook shape before feeding it through the letter box. Holding the other end in his hands he pushed his ear to the door. After only two attempts the hook made contact with the catch and the door clicked open.

In the hallway he politely wiped his feet on the mat. On a small table next to the door a stack of unopened mail, mostly with notable brand names printed on the envelopes, waited to be opened or thrown immediately in the bin. The man picked up the first to see who it was addressed to.

Ms Gladys Honeywell.

*****

Norman pulled up next to the church in an unintentional lay-by which had been eroded into the bank over the years as every day vehicles were forced to take evasive action from oncoming tractors. Across the road Ally's tatty green Rover car sat in semi-retirement on the driveway penned in by the light green fences which cordoned off her small, attractive cottage. When she left it on Thursday, on a rather unexpected trip to Belfast, she had no idea it would be Saturday before she returned. It was a good job she didn't have pets.

Imagining the comforts set to greet her inside its ivy-covered shell released a valve that drained her adrenaline and swamped her body with emotional fatigue. Coming home shouldn't cause anyone anxiety. It should be a place of personal sanctuary protected from the strains of the modern world and the challenges faced in pursuit of one's purpose in life. Recently there had been more of modern life's strains inside the house than outside it. Today her guard was down. Whatever unexpected surprise lay inside she was just going to ignore it, kick off her shoes and sleep for as long as the bloody birds left her be.

"I'll ring you as soon as I've heard any news about your father," said Norman, gently placing his hand on her thigh in comfort. It probably wasn't wise.

"What the hell are you doing?" snapped Ally sharply.

"Just being kind," said Norman, a little taken aback by the dismay in her voice.

"You don't need to sexually harass me at the same time!"

"My deepest apologies, Ally," said Norman, removing his hand as if her legs were the jaws of a rabid dog. "I was just trying to be your friend."

"I only have two friends. They're called coffee and bed. I don't need any others," snapped Ally as she swiftly exited the car and slammed the door in protest.

Norman chuckled to himself. He always liked the fiery ones. He turned the ignition again and slowly weaved through the village to about two hundred yards away where his own house hid in the shadow of the village pub.

Ally crossed the road and violently pushed open the squeaky gate. She got as far as the door before she noticed something was out of place. Today was the first time in the year since she'd first moved in that she'd managed to get from the road to the door without being interrupted. She stopped to gaze around the area from the raised level of the front step. There was no sign of her. Had she died?

RADU GOGA

Had she got bored of Ally's absence and decided to double up her patrols of Mr and Mrs Sanderson across the road. The lack of interrogation should have been welcomed but it was the absence of the normal that sometimes set her intellectual antenna racing.

Maybe there was a logical explanation for it? Ally hadn't seen Gabriel since the early hours of Friday morning and felt certain she'd returned here in the meantime. Maybe Gabriel had been Ms Honeywell's arch nemesis? Someone who could reach a higher plane of crazy. Maybe even Honeywell couldn't deal with the incessant madness of Ally's millennial intruder.

Ally pushed the key into the lock and opened the door quietly. The house was in chaos. Furniture had been tipped up, vases smashed and scattered over the floor in a thousand pieces, pictures hung to their hooks for dear life and were left at acute angles. Most disturbingly a trail of blood ran down the side of a once pristinely painted white wall. The blood led down the corridor and into the living room where bloody hand marks were visible on the frame of a door that hung limply on one hinge.

Ally's adrenaline soared. Silently she crept down the hall on tiptoes to avoid pressing the noisy ceramic shards down on the exposed wooden floor. There were no sounds in the house, which suggested that whatever had happened here was well and truly in the past. At the living room door, she peered around the corner and was greeted by an even more worrying sight.

In the middle of the room, tied to a chair by her legs, waist and arms, was Gabriel. Her head was slumped backwards where her black-dyed hair, rather than her crazy wig, draped down to the floor. A scarf had been wrapped around her mouth before being tied somewhere around the back of her neck. She was completely motionless but strangely there was no sign of the blood that had been so prominent on the walls in the corridor. Ally moved into a room that had suffered the same rough treatment as the hallway. She leant down and placed her finger on Gabriel's throat to check for a pulse. The warmth of human contact triggered the captive into life.

Gabriel responded hysterically. She screamed through her gag, swung her head around wildly, and struggled to free herself from the ligatures cutting into her skin.

"Control yourself," snapped Ally as if she'd experienced nothing worse than a splinter. "What have you done to my house?"

She removed Gabriel's gag and the young woman gasped for air.

"Run, Ally. He's gone completely mad."

"Who has? Where's the blood come from?"

"It's mine," said a male voice behind Ally's head.

Instinctively she swivelled around to find, for the second time this week, the barrel of a gun directly in her eyeline. This time the effects had more impact, as if the first time had merely loosened the memory, and the second had released it to the surface like the breaking of an elastic band. The identity of the marksman, lurking in the alcove behind her living room door, was shrouded by the sudden recollection and weight of her own traumatic past.

Once again, a six-year-old version of herself swamped her thoughts and emotions.

Her heart thumped in her chest so rapidly she thought it might burst through her chest. Her feet felt sore from running too far and too fast. The red shoes were being scuffed as she dragged them on stone and tree root, desperately looking behind in the distance to see who was chasing her. The shoes were special, almost as important as holding onto life itself. They had been a gift from her father, the only physical reminder of a man not seen for months. Behind her bolts of lightning pierced through maleficent clouds like intermittent searchlights. The bolts of electricity framed the eerie turrets of the château that still loomed on the hill behind her.

The château's basement prison lay behind her, but freedom was far from certain. She darted towards a small orchard of apple trees at the bottom of the hill that might

RADU GOGA

offer shelter from the mounting rain and her noisy and motivated pursuer. The six-year-old girl slumped behind the trunk of an apple tree, her loud panting a beacon to her exact position. In the darkness she closed her eyes and prayed. Those prayers were only partially answered. The crunching noise of twigs breaking under heavy boots dragged her eyelids open. The barrel of a gun greeted her and set off her frantic screams. On the other end of the gun, somewhere out of focus, a bitter voice was shouting obscenities in a harsh foreign language. Fear took hold as she curled into a ball to await the end. A deafening shot echoed down the valley before a body slumped on the mud.

She opened her eyes. Forty years had evaporated but her position was identical, upturned furniture rather than apple trees the only protection against an armed assailant. As her visual focus expanded from gun, to hairy hand, to muscly arm, finally the owner's full identity came into view. The man's free hand held his chest, unable to prevent the blood oozing from a deep wound painting his white T-shirt with blood red motifs.

"Where is Radu Goga?" demanded Buff in perfect English.

- Chapter 24 -

The Courier

Mistakes are inevitable and, as it happens, necessary. Everyone makes them. Unless of course you happen to be a hormonally supercharged teenager. Then apparently you get a pass and everything you do is totally without question or error. If you're everyone else, though, mistakes are an essential mechanism to help us develop. We learn as much from our mistakes as we do from our successes, although clearly it does depend on what you're doing at the time.

If your mistake occurs at thirty-eight thousand feet while you're in control of a jumbo jet with five hundred passengers on-board you might not get a chance to learn much from it, particularly if as a consequence of the error bits of you are scattered over a four-mile-wide radius. If your mistake takes place while you're free climbing the Burj Khalifa, it might not be possible to have a second go at it. Fortunately, most of us aren't hindered by life and death-scale events when we make errors. Often the only side effect is a bruised ego, inventive use of language and a slightly higher than usual blood pressure.

The human ego's reaction to mistakes can generally be separated into two polarised categories: 'Fuck it' and 'Go again'. The first might not be a permanent state of being, although the more frequently the same mistake repeats, the more likely that outcome becomes fixed. Occasionally, after a brief period of 'Fuck it', the emotions might relent, the mind might clear, and the right support might be offered to engage the 'Go again' instinct. There's a small fraction of people in the world who only know 'Go again', but they're freaks and aren't to be trusted.

THE COURIER

Daniel Hudson was not one of these people.

Sure, he was dedicated, motivated and conscientious, but that didn't mean he lacked emotion. Right now, he was firmly entrenched in the 'Fuck it' camp. Some mistakes hurt more than others. Particularly ones that you realise some time after the event were completely avoidable if you'd had the foresight to see them. That was the problem with foresight, it was much easier to appreciate after the event and devilishly difficult to predict beforehand.

After his initial and spontaneous reaction, brought on by realising who the Courier was, abated it was followed by an unnaturally long period of silence. This was followed by Daniel's incoherent babbling and the rapid expansion of his jawline. This state continued for what seemed like hours. Even Lance was getting concerned by the total lack of composure shown by the lead agent in an FBI assignment.

Even though it was clear to anyone present that the Courier was completely surrounded with no chance of escape, he appeared to be the only one enjoying it.

"Surprised to see me?" said the Courier with a grin.

"Timon Ortiz," said Daniel struggling to form the words in case they had secret hypnotic powers. "I can't believe I missed this."

"And yet we knew you would."

"What did I overlook?"

"Your own arrogance," replied Timon boldly. "That was your mistake, Agent Hudson."

"Who is he?" whispered Lance, desperate to catch up.

"He's the Governor of Clairvaux Prison where Mario was held before he died," replied Daniel without moving his head, as if he was communicating with his own altered state.

"You should have listened to me. I said we would end up being complicit in the crime," taunted Timon. "You thought that was a warning, while all along I meant it as an instruction."

"What are you on about?" said Daniel.

THE COURIER

"None of the events over the last week would have been possible without you, Daniel. You're more of a Mountain Man than anybody!"

Two weeks ago, unknown to him at the time, Daniel had everything he needed to solve the case all in one place. The Courier, the motive and the letters: three elements he'd chased across Europe with limited success for the last week.

"You wrote my name on the letter," he said in sudden realisation. "I thought the handwriting looked a little more rushed than the others."

"Yes, of course. Mario didn't know you were coming. He knew the FBI were, but not you. Your desperate ego wanted you to believe that you, Daniel Hudson, were notorious. That your name was in some way important. That's your blind spot and it clouded your judgement and sucked you into his deceit."

"You wanted me to focus my attention on Ally, Gabriel and Antoine."

"Yes."

"But why?"

"I'm afraid that will remain with me until I die."

"Might be sooner than you think," growled Daniel.

"We'll see. You might have more important things to focus on."

"How could you betray the responsibility of your office?"

"We French have always found it difficult to do what we're told. There are beliefs in life that come before reputation or status. Maybe you should try and experience some of them, rather than just following orders."

"Money. That's all it was about for you."

"No. It's about freedom. The Mountain Men represent centuries of revolutionary spirit, an age-old struggle of the people versus the system. A broken system. There were times in the last one hundred years when it looked like that system would be rebuilt to work for everyone equally, but the rich and powerful are hard to shift. Resolutely they

THE COURIER

manipulated the masses to believe in their version of truth and opportunity. Compliantly the population slid further down the mountain because they became distracted by materialism and false security. New approaches are required. They have always excelled at innovation."

"Who have?"

"The Mountain Men of course. Every person to hold that position has evolved, learnt from the mistakes of the last, and taken their purpose to the next level."

"You've been brainwashed."

"Have I indeed?" said Timon.

"The Mountain Men are a relic," said Daniel bluntly. "A shadow from history that's no longer relevant. Replaying their endeavours hundreds of years later is pure fantasy. A twisted cult played out for the purposes of chaos to gain notoriety and power for yourselves. That's not what they stood for."

"You still don't know what's happening!" chuckled Timon at Daniel's assessment. "How would you know what they stood for, you know almost nothing about them."

"You're just Mario's patsy."

"My orders don't come from Mario. The real Mountain Men are much harder to resist. I told you that. Not even you were able to resist him."

"Diego!"

"Yes."

"Bollocks. He had no influence on me whatsoever. Quite the opposite, he gave me everything I needed."

"Really! Then why have you been trying to track down Radu Goga? For your purposes or his?"

Timon grinned in deep appreciation of his own part in the deception. Daniel had walked straight into it. Timon had planted that name in his head and Daniel had used it to goad Diego into answers. They knew the FBI wouldn't be able to ignore the mystery surrounding the Russian defector. They knew Daniel would look for him and they knew if anyone had the means to find him it was the Americans.

"But what interest do you have in Radu Goga?" bleated Daniel.

"Unfinished business," replied Timon.

"Your business here is finished, Timon. You'll take no further part in it. We have cracked your code, caught you and stopped the sequence in its tracks."

"No, you haven't," he laughed. "It can't be stopped."

"What are you talking about? We have you. Without you the chain is broken. The chaos will end."

"No, it won't. Quite the opposite. What you've witnessed this week is just the start of the chaos. If I don't decode this letter and pass on the information, anyone associated with the Oblivion Doctrine will rise up against their oppressors in an organised and collective mass action that will make the Arab Spring look like a tap with a faulty washer. Whatever you do next, chaos is coming."

"You're bluffing."

"And yet maybe I have a pair of Queens. Ready to it, Agent Hudson?"

"I don't chase Queens, I chase money."

"Which is why your actions are so important. The money represents the system, the greed, the summit of the mountain. Your deluded responsibility to retrieve it makes their victory inevitable."

"Where is it?" barked Daniel aggressively.

"It will only be revealed at the end of the sequence. It's decision time, Hudson. Either you allow mass revolution to spread over every major city in every Western country all at once or you allow a small fraction of them to proceed so you can attempt to recover the money."

There was no escaping the fact that Timon and his organisation had covered up the bases. If what he said was true, Daniel was being asked to choose between a small set of terrorist attacks and the threat of worldwide revolution. There had to be a way to end both eventualities, but for

THE COURIER

once he was working on his wits, rather than highly considered and pre-planned strategies.

"What can I offer you to make it stop?" asked Hudson tentatively.

"Nothing. This is what I want. Change."

"Anarchy, more like."

"When did real change occur without it?"

"I'm done listening to your bullshit. Tell me where I can find the money, or I will be forced to rearrange the way your face looks."

While Hudson and Ortiz engaged in a rather testosterone fuelled stand-off, Lance was focused on the letter that lay on the table slightly damp from the earlier beer spillage. He'd seen the letters before, but he'd not had time to consider them fully. Puzzles were, after all, his thing. After his tenure with Ally he'd thought about applying to work at GCHQ, the government's code crackers. He'd already completed most of their online tests in preparation for it. They were designed for only the very brightest academic minds and he'd flown through them with hardly a second thought. This, though, was the Holy Grail.

Suddenly, unburdened by the expectations Daniel had placed on him, Lance's natural talents were rising to the surface. There was one feature of the letters he'd previously paid little attention to: the two-digit numbers printed on the top of each one, the only visible writing on any of them. The one on the table had the number eleven on it. The one Ally had in her possession showed zero three on the top. It was this recollection that got him thinking. It didn't say three, it said zero three. Why zero three? If this was the third of the letters, addressed to the third of the Mountain Men, why did it need to have a zero in front of it? Maybe it had some other meaning that wasn't immediately obvious.

"I'm losing my patience with you, Timon. Tell me how these letters lead me to the money?"

THE COURIER

"They're bank account numbers," Lance blurted out with a snap of his fingers. "Sort codes and bank account numbers come in pairs even when they include single digits."

"Smart kid," offered Timon, genuinely impressed. "If only he could hold his beer."

"Is this true?" said Daniel, grabbing Timon by the collar.

"Yes. You had it right in front of you weeks ago. If only you'd had someone smart like this kid on your team."

Lance couldn't help but blush. People weren't generally nice to him. He knew Timon was the so-called 'bad guy', but he couldn't help warm to him.

"It's a shame you don't know the sequence, though," added Timon.

"That bit is easy," said Lance, grabbing the pen from his jacket that had already leaked ink down the inside pocket after being nervously chewed earlier in the morning. He pulled the letter over to him and started to note down a list of names quite similar to the one Ally had started earlier in the week. "Lesage, Fawkes, Tesimond, Masaniello were one to four, and we know the second and fourth had their activities re-enacted. We also know Boston came from the letter with zero ten on it. The only other event that we know occurred recently happened between the fourth and tenth, which leaves only one number in the sequence so far unknown. Five, Six, Seven, Eight or Nine."

"What about the sequence from here onwards?" asked Daniel.

"That's easy, too. This letter leads to the next one."

Lance took out the book and placed the letter over page eleven to produce the code: Paris, King, Red, Mountain, Geneva.

"What does it mean?!" Daniel shouted at Timon with a growl.

"Don't spoil the kid's fun."

"We know the first two words are about the next event which we already know is a re-creation of the French

THE COURIER

Revolution because we have the name Georges Couthon. That only leaves three words to work out," said Lance as if to himself. "If they call you the Courier then that means you don't just bring the letters to be decoded, you also retrieve them, and the only information to help us here is Geneva. The next letter is at the DLO in Geneva."

"Very good," said Timon. "Are you looking for an apprenticeship?"

"Not just at the moment."

"Whose letter is in Geneva?" asked Daniel.

"I guess it doesn't really matter," replied Lance. "As long as you use it to find the next letter, and so on."

"What about the Red Mountain?"

"Not sure on that part," replied Lance.

"Don't look at me," huffed Timon. "You'll find out eventually when the world burns, won't you?"

"Not if I get to Geneva first and put a stop to it."

"You'll need to get a shift on: if the information in this letter isn't posted on the Oblivion Doctrine's dark web by the end of Sunday evening, every single one of its users will rise up in unison. You can't stop that, even if you do find the letter."

"Unless I find all of the letters," said Daniel.

"It still won't help you. You can't stop the chaos unless you have a genius on your team that can hack the Dark Net and reach the Oblivion Doctrine's army."

"Oh, don't worry. I've got one of those," replied Daniel, signalling his team to move in by casually raising his hand. "Take him away."

Timon was placed in handcuffs and escorted away. From here he'd be transported to the type of facility he'd so long been a part of, but this time it would be in a very different capacity.

"Can I go back to Kent now?" asked Lance with a hand raised meekly.

"Kent?" asked Daniel, unfamiliar with the word.

"Home," added Lance. "I might still catch Saturday night board games. We're playing Monopoly tonight."

THE COURIER

Many activities in the modern world took less time than a single game of Monopoly. Redecorating a house, scaling Kilimanjaro, learning Hebrew from scratch, repainting the Sistine Chapel, and what Daniel had in mind for him.

"No, I'm afraid it'll have to wait. You're part of my team now."

"Maybe I don't want to be."

Daniel's expression darkened and his stare pierced Lance's brief defiance. Lance averted his eyes.

"Obviously I want to be, though," he corrected himself.

"That's better. We must act quickly. We have less than thirty-six hours before we lose control. I'm going to Geneva to find the next letter, and once I have that one, I'll move to the next. Let's hope they're not spread too far apart."

"You'll need the book," said Lance.

Daniel held out his hand, but Lance unconsciously tightened his grip on the book and squeezed it into his belly protectively. "Does she trust you?"

"Who?"

"Dr Oldfield."

"I doubt it. Does she trust anyone?"

"No."

"Then what's your point?"

"This book means a lot to her. If I give it to you it'll be on my head if something happens to it."

"I give you my word I'll return it to her. There are much more important things than this book that I need to give Ally Oldfield. Trust me."

Lance reluctantly passed it over. "What do you need from me?"

"Find Gabriel. She's the only one who has the skills to infiltrate the Oblivion Doctrine's dark web."

"How do you know that?" asked Lance.

"Why do you think the FBI was interested in her in the first place? She was already trying to hack it."

"What should I tell her?"

THE COURIER

"When I've found the money, I will send you a photo of the account and she can post it to prove that the sequence is complete. That should put an end to it."

"Ok. What about Dr Oldfield?"

"Tell her that we've broken the sequence and we'll never know who the other Mountain Men were. Tell her there will be no more Mountain Men."

- Chapter 25 -

The Red Mountain

Paris, 1895

At the end of the nineteenth century, Europe was in flux. Competing ideological and philosophical ideas were challenging the conventional way of life. Most of the continent still cowered under the ever-expanding empires of Britain, Germany, Austro-Hungary and Russia, whose imperialistic families, encircled and protected by a watertight moat of the bourgeois, had largely ruled for centuries. Change, though, was coming. A foul smell hung on the breeze and infected the nobility's nostrils. It differed from the normal 'odour of peasant' they were so accustomed to smelling. It was the stench of revolution and its source was some distance away.

The fledgling United States had thrown off its colonial oppressors and taken its first baby steps towards autonomy. Their blazing trail produced a domino effect that millions in the old world had yearned for, and fewer, but more powerful, people had feared. France, inspired by, and allies to, their American brothers, rose up against their monarchy only to foolishly replace it with the autocratic Napoleon dynasty. France rebelled for a second time: by then they were getting pretty good at it.

Then the pattern stopped. The European Imperialists tightened their grip by ruthlessly trampling any minor insurrection with callous brutality. The pressure of discontent grew with mounting fear.

It was only a matter of time.

THE RED MOUNTAIN

After a hundred years of relative normality where the minority masters drove the majority to their ends, the mood was changing. Soon the pressure would burst. An undercurrent of dissatisfaction swelled in the factories, farmyards and streets from Liverpool to Leipzig. It was the fuel that drenched the soil under their feet, but who or what would add the essential spark? Particularly when the establishment worked so tirelessly to hide the matches through their increasing use of violence, false imprisonment, censorship, executions, misinformation and fear. A thousand years of authoritarian tactics were dusted off and reused in a desperate attempt to continue the suppression of the masses.

A man can be killed.

An idea, though, that was impossible to destroy.

Being a member of a Socialist party brought many occupational hazards. The most likely being prison. A futile act on the part of the establishment because it did not act as the deterrent they'd hoped it would be. The number of times you'd been arrested and jailed acted as a résumé of your Marxist credentials. If you hadn't spent time in jail you weren't viewed as clever or sneaky, you were simply seen as lacking commitment.

In the forty years since his birth, Paul Lafargue had been incarcerated almost as many times as he'd had birthdays, some of which he'd celebrated behind bars. It was not the only reason he was a leading figure in the French Workers' Party, but it was a reputation that certainly hadn't hurt.

Being Karl Marx's son-in-law probably helped a smidgen, too.

Lafargue's most recent stint in prison had been a watershed moment for their cause. Not only had he been elected as the very first Socialist politician in France, he'd achieved the feat without his knowledge, because as usual he was in custody. That made him the first Socialist politician to be elected and imprisoned all on the same day.

THE RED MOUNTAIN

He'd arrived in jail as just another irritating, noisy activist and left it as a politician and a figurehead of Communism.

And that created a paradox.

The rich and powerful are always drawn to those with influence and fame. Socialist or not, Paul Lafargue was a celebrity and as a result the bourgeois government attempted to cosy up to him, businesses tried to employ him, and the press wanted to illuminate him. Marxism was about the people, not the individual, but how could Socialist ideology be promoted without charismatic individuals and funding? It was a huge ideological dilemma. Paul didn't want power, he wanted revolution.

The baton would have to be passed.

A short, spindly man entered the office clutching a bowler hat around his midriff as if he was trying to hide his awkward and embarrassing excitement. He looked more like a monk than a freedom fighter. A crescent moon of hair circled from one ear to the other and a beautifully trimmed goatee beard bristled on his chin. His plain brown suit was modest but perfectly creased in all the right places. He lingered at the door of the office not confident enough to break his host's obvious concentration, and not scared enough to run away.

"Sit down, man," said Lafargue curtly, briefly looking up from the article he was in the middle of writing.

The monk sat down and fidgeted into position on the rigid, unwelcoming chair. On the walls around him black and white faces sneered down in judgement from their celluloid prisons. A series of well-fondled books lay open on the desk in front of him, all of which he'd read in his pursuit of meaning.

"I suppose you're here for the prize?" demanded Lafargue, lifting a lit cigarette that smouldered in the ashtray before taking an extended drag.

"Yes."

"Many have come but none have succeeded in convincing me they are worthy of it. I warn you now, I don't suffer fools, I can spot an imposter from two hundred yards and may terminate this conversation at any time based on any factor that I decide makes you unsuitable."

The monk gulped anxiously.

"Name?"

"Vladimir Ilyich Ulyanov."

"Oh dear. You're not making a very good start, are you?" tutted Paul, pulling a face that suggested the monk had insulted his mother.

"I'm not with you."

"I'm looking for a Socialist hero. A leader of the masses. A figurehead who will lead the people to their emancipation. Our followers are simple folk with minimal education. Most are illiterate."

"Yes, I know."

"And can you really see them chanting that? Hmm? Give me a V, give me an L, give me an A… It'll take them forever. By the time they've chanted it, the Army will have shot them all."

"But… that is my name," replied Vladimir timidly.

"Then there's the placards. They'll have to be massive to fit it all on. Where will they get the materials from? Hmm, tell me that? You going to open a stationery shop?"

"Oh. Yes, I see what you mean."

"Didn't think it through, did you?" replied Paul.

"I wasn't really responsible for it," added Vladimir meekly.

"That's not my fault, is it?"

"No… I've been working on an alias, though," added Vladimir trying to rescue the process.

"Good, good. What were you thinking?"

"I was thinking it would have to be a strong but humble name. One that people can connect with, but not a name associated with any historic monarch or regularly used by the aristocracy. A name of the people and for the people."

"Very good. Thought of one?"

"Yes. Steve."

"Steve?" replied Paul disconsolately.

"Yeah."

THE RED MOUNTAIN

"Hey, everyone," mocked Lafargue, "lay down your tools, sacrifice your lives for the greater good, tear down your establishment oppressors and follow 'Steve' to freedom. They might even rename a city after you, St Stevesburg."

"Not Steve, then?" replied Vladimir.

"No."

"What about Dave?"

"I have plenty of other people to see today."

Vladimir started to sweat. He hadn't expected it to be this hard.

"Maybe I'll name myself after a natural feature of the land to demonstrate my nationalist belief in the fatherland and to associate with those that I seek to inspire to freedom."

"You're not going to name yourself after a tree, are you?"

"No. I was thinking maybe a… river," replied Vladimir, tentatively seeking approval.

"Ok. Well, I suppose there is a symbolism in that of our struggles. On the one hand, you have the power of the water gushing towards the sea, and on the other, the image of stillness and peace. The rejuvenating properties that are needed to cleanse the land. I like it."

"Right. Then from now on call me Volga."

"Not that one."

"Really?"

"Why don't you have a think about it? All that matters to me is that you are committed to changing your name."

"Definitely," replied Vladimir sighing with relief.

"Fine. Now tell me what you have done so far to promote the cause of Marxism?"

"I started by setting up a Marxist workers' circle in Saint Petersburg, encouraged revolutionary cells in industrial centres, and wrote a book."

"A book? I've not read it."

"It's very good."

"How many copies did you print?"

THE RED MOUNTAIN

"Two hundred."

Paul did a quick mental calculation in his head.

"So that's approximately one copy for every six hundred thousand Russians, then! I do hope they get passed around. Which century are you planning the revolution to start?"

"A journey of a thousand miles starts with a single step."

"It does. But you'll never get anywhere if you stop to take a breather after the first one."

"It's a start, though," replied Vladimir confidently.

"Barely," replied Paul. "How many times have you been in jail?"

Vladimir paused. Was it a trick question? Was Lafargue testing his rebellious nature or his moral standing? It was time to break out the debating skills he'd spent years developing at university and in revolutionary circles across the country to find out.

"How many would be good?"

"Someone your age, I'd expect it to be in double figures at least."

"Twenty," he replied instantly, even though the answer was less than two and more than none.

"Impressive. What for?"

Vladimir did his best to feign recollection while desperately trying to ensure his answers were appropriate.

"Two counts of harassment, three for inciting riots, a couple of convictions for public order offences, and a couple for cow tipping."

"Cow tipping?"

"It's when you push a cow over when it's asleep."

"Which isn't actually a criminal offence, it's just very childish."

"Yes, I suppose so," replied Vladimir, who hadn't actually ever pushed a cow over but was running out of ideas. "All the others are serious, though."

"Hmm, I guess. I expected a bit more, though, if I'm honest."

THE RED MOUNTAIN

It felt like the interview was slipping away from him. Vladimir had spent years roaming around Europe seeking learning and influence. He'd tried and failed to rally other Marxist groups to him and all he'd achieved in the last few years was an extended stay in a Swiss health farm, and even then, his mother paid the bill. Nobody took him seriously. He just needed a break, the help of a luminary who believed in what he was capable of and willing to condone his methods. This was his moment and he needed to rescue it.

"I've heard about this prize, Comrade Lafargue, but very little about what it entails exactly."

Paul calmly pulled himself out of his chair and peeked through the curtains of the second-floor room. It was just after lunch on a mild October morning and only a few people were milling about in the road below. Once he was certain the building wasn't being watched he drew the curtains and plunged the room into gloom.

"The prize," whispered Paul mysteriously, "is an offer to join an elite group of servants to our cause."

"How many people are in this group?" asked Vladimir.

"You would be the thirteenth."

"Isn't that unlucky?"

"Marxists don't believe in religion, so it can't be."

"Right, of course. Thirteen people is quite small but it's enough to stimulate debate and new ideas. Is it like a Politburo?"

"Kind of."

"Who's in it?"

"Me and you… the other eleven are dead."

"So, actually, it would be just us… hanging out?" replied Vladimir, not entirely sure if he was being invited into an exclusive club or being groomed.

"No. I won't be around for long either, so I need to find a new member."

"Really? Are you ill?"

THE RED MOUNTAIN

"No, I'm just going to choose the time and manner of my passage from this world, and when I do you will be the only member of the group left."

"I thought Marx was against elitism? This sounds more like Blanquism."

"Marx was against it in principle."

"But not in practice?"

"No, not really. All sorts of people write down their thoughts, but how many really believe them? I mean, did Jonathan Swift really believe there was a land full of little people?"

"That's a book of fiction, though."

"Is it? Well, I'll be... " said Paul, distracted for a moment as an image of Gulliver being mugged by a load of miniature pygmies ran through his mind.

"But your father-in-law believed in some of it, right?"

"Hmm, oh yes, I'm sure he did," replied Paul, being dragged back from his daydream.

"And you believed in him?"

"Very much so."

"So how can you justify an elitist group, like the one you mention, being set up to promote and achieve freedom for the masses?"

"Because Karl Marx was in it."

"Oh. Did he start it?"

"No. It's a network of luminaries that goes back three hundred years. Karl had a thirst for knowledge and spent his whole life learning from others. The Mountain Men taught him much."

"If it was ok for Marx, then it's ok for me," replied Vladimir who had to accept that Paul was Marx's son-in-law and someone who'd actually spent time with him. "Who were the others?"

"Marx received the honour from Bertrand Barère who left the title in his will. He indicated that he received it from Maximilien Robespierre, another of the architects of the French Revolution. Before him came Benjamin Franklin and the Socialist writer Jean-Jacques Rousseau,

THE RED MOUNTAIN

whose writing inspired Washington and Robespierre. After Jean Cavalier died in Dublin the title briefly went missing, before it came to Rousseau, but I haven't worked out how. Cavalier received the honour from Nicolas Fatio, who apparently stole the prize from John Evelyn because he thought he'd been corrupted by the aristocrats and achieved little with the prize other than writing about the Great Fire of London and a very detailed thesis on the impact of trees."

"That's quite a list."

"Every Mountain Man has evolved the struggle to achieve the main goal either through armed conflict or the pursuit of knowledge. Their three hundred-year fight will culminate in the next recipient. Finally, the time has come when the great class struggle will climb the slopes of progress and rebuild society."

"I believe you are right, but why do I need a title? What's needed is a great strategy, provocative pamphlets and organised action, not some antiquated ceremonial position that sounds suspiciously similar to those that we are trying to remove."

Paul was stumped. He hadn't really considered it this way. The Mountain Men were a noble group with no intention of holding onto any power. Yet it did go against Marxist thinking.

"It's not just about the title," said Paul. "The prize comes with a sizeable fund. There's a couple of million in the account."

"A couple of million! Where has that come from?"

"Mainly from the activities of past members. Sales of books, paintings, interest paid on the account and the remains of their estates."

"Which sounds a lot like capitalism?!" said Vladimir, looking horrified.

"No, not at all. Rebellions aren't free, you know."

Down the ages many of the fathers of Socialism spent much of their time promoting the idea of land reform and the share of wealth equally amongst the proletariat.

THE RED MOUNTAIN

Ironically most were funded by wealthy capitalist benefactors. Marx himself was connected to the famous Dutch company Philips and was often funded by his compatriot Friedrich Engels, himself part of a wealthy company of cotton mills. Marx left more than two million dollars in his will but interestingly none of it was 'left to the people'. Socialism has always been misunderstood, but it's not the theory that should be lambasted, the focus should always be on those who execute it. Power always corrupts, whichever ideology you follow. Even the Chinese have realised that Communism without some form of international market is unworkable.

"Are there any rules on how this fund is used?" asked Vladimir.

"Not that I'm aware of."

Vladimir considered his position. He was skint, unsuccessful and broadly ignored by the world. This might be his big break, and just because the other Mountain Men had used their wealth for dubious purposes, it didn't mean he had to. This was his opportunity to put it right, to put a pure form of Marxism into practice.

"In that case I accept the prize."

"I haven't offered it to you yet," said Paul scornfully. "I haven't seen Emile Vandervelde yet."

"Isn't he from Belgium?"

"Yeah."

Vladimir raised an eyebrow.

"You're right," replied Lafargue. "Be a total waste, they can't even agree with themselves. Sign here, Steve."

*****

Cuba, 1966

The Tricontinental Conference was the biggest gathering of anti-imperialist leaders in history. Over five hundred delegates from Asia, Africa and South America gathered on the island of Cuba just ninety miles from their

THE RED MOUNTAIN

greatest enemy, the United States of America. In normal circumstances the Americans would never have allowed it, but there was nothing normal about the nineteen-sixties.

The Bay of Pigs, the Cuban Missile Crisis, the Kennedy assassination and the Vietnam War had all made any intervention impossible. They would be listening but anything more than that would bring the world closer to atomic annihilation. Which was a shame really, because how often in history do you have all of the leaders of Communist countries and terrorist groups, including Salvador Allende, Fidel Castro and Malcolm X, all in the same place.

The delegates, representing more than eighty countries, met with a simple aim. To blend the two great currents of world revolution: the one that began in Nineteen-Seventeen with the Russian Revolution, and the current anti-imperialist liberation movement gaining traction off the back of Cuba's success and supported by the Socialist giants of China and Russia. Imagine an eighteen-thirties holiday for certified fundamentalists, rebels and lefties.

The highlight of the conference was the closing session delivered by Castro himself. There were many themes. The conflict in Vietnam and the support that would be offered. The mysterious disappearance of Che Guevara, Trotskyist distortions in Mexico and the revolutionary campaigns sweeping Indonesia. Most of this is well documented because a hundred foreign journalists were invited and encouraged to report back what they heard. Which mainly they didn't. Choosing instead to cherry-pick the contents in order to scaremonger the citizens of an already petrified and paranoid West.

What is less well known is what happened after the closing session.

"Comrades, thank you for delaying your departures," announced Castro grandly to the dozen hand-selected delegates huddled around a board table in a small syndicate room. The iconic Cuban cigar stood to attention out of the corner of his mouth, slightly impeding the clarity

THE RED MOUNTAIN

of his words and the quality of the air. A thick plume of smoke spiralled across the heads of the group.

"Did you forget to announce something?" asked Virgilio Shuverer, one of the Panamanian diplomats.

"An addition," choked Castro.

"But your closing speech went on for two hours," huffed another disconsolate voice from somewhere around the table.

"Not everything I say should be shared openly. I only want the foreign journalists to report what I want them to," he replied mysteriously.

"Fat chance," someone whispered.

"We have some important decisions to make and you have been chosen to be here because I trust you above all others."

"About what?" asked Nguyen Van Tien, the delegate from the National Liberation Front of South Vietnam.

"I mentioned in my closing remarks that comrade Guevara has been dispatched on a very secret mission to support revolutionary action in Bolivia. It is a campaign neither of us believe he will return from."

"So! Dying isn't that unusual. You said in your speech that a hundred thousand people have been killed in Indonesia fighting against their oppressors."

"No, you're right. We are all prepared to make the ultimate sacrifice. It is Che's destiny, but he must be replaced."

"Replaced? There are plenty of people who can take over his mantle, that's the beauty about Communism, no one's above anyone else," added General Enrique Líster a veteran of the Spanish Civil War.

"Che wasn't just a freedom fighter against the Yankee imperialists."

On hearing the word 'Yankee' the entire collective spat on the floor like a swarm of flies had entered their throats in unison.

"He is a Mountain Man," added Fidel when the guttural noise of phlegm had ceased.

THE RED MOUNTAIN

"I should think so if you've sent him to Bolivia," replied Virgilio. "Not a flat bit anywhere!"

"It's not meant to be taken literally."

Castro took a moment to describe the secretive organisation that for four hundred years had been underpinning the movement of the masses against the system and how it had been central in the successful revolutions in the US, France and Russia, as well as providing most of the essential reading on Socialist ideals over the past two hundred years.

"How did he get it?" asked Van Tien, sounding a little put out that the honour never came to him.

"The honour was bestowed on him by Vittorio Vidali, the Italian revolutionary who was instrumental in the Spanish Civil War, the first attempt to kill Trotsky and the guerrilla war we successfully waged throughout South America. Vittorio told Che it was passed down to him by Lenin himself, although he was a compulsive liar and there is much speculation that Lenin disliked him because he kept having sex with married members of the Comintern. Italians! Like all of the Brothers that went before him, Vittorio realigned its purpose and methods to take into account the ever-changing landscape that we are faced with. He knew that traditional uprisings are no longer effective. He understood that sometimes the only thing the Yankee dogs understand are acts of terror."

More spittle sprayed around the place.

"Vittorio was a great warrior," croaked General Líster. "Fought with him back in the day. A little unorthodox but rather effective."

"We're rebels. Unorthodox is essential," replied Castro.

"Who will take Che's position now?" asked Líster.

"That's why I have gathered you. I require your nominations."

"Hold on a second," said Van Tien sternly. "Was there a change in our ideology whilst I was away? I mean, I know I've spent much of the last twelve months underground shooting out the legs of the Yankee invaders,

THE RED MOUNTAIN

but last time I looked we were still following Marxism-Leninism?"

"Yes, Brother, no change there."

"Then I refer you back to one of the key principles of Communism that 'all rights to inheritance should be abolished'."

In the last century a mostly right-wing media, influenced by their capitalist political masters, had tried to paint anyone with Socialist ideals as simpletons. Accordingly, Socialists were uneducated, unconnected, unpleasant and dangerous. The bogeyman got off lightly in comparison. The truth, of course, is often misinterpreted. Some of the greatest minds have had Socialist ideals, and even those with less intelligence could still read. In a room of this many people there was always someone with diehard theoretical beliefs they could recite faster than a Shakespearean actor quoting Macbeth.

"That is true, Comrade, but technically no one has the right to inherit this title, that's why we are here to choose."

"Seems a little convenient."

"Yes, it is," said Castro, blowing a massive smoke ring. "The person we need will be a beacon for our struggle for decades to come. It will be vital that they embrace new approaches and strategies to overcome the gathering clouds that are set to rain on us in the years to come. They must be without weakness."

"What about Guido Gil?" suggested Virgilio.

"Who?" sneered Castro with a grimace.

"Member of the Dominican Republic delegation. He's an excellent strategist, always compassionate, and a really deep thinker."

"Compassionate! I said no weaknesses."

"Euclides Gutiérrez Felix," suggested General Líster.

"No! Man's scared of his own shadow. I once saw him jump out of his skin when a cork flew out of a champagne bottle."

"Castellón from Panama?"

THE RED MOUNTAIN

"Not mad enough," added Castro before a full résumé was reeled off.

"Who, then?" said Van Tien. He'd seen this sort of game played before. The leaders feigned interest in other people's views just so they could insist on their own choice. Castro already knew who he wanted, and it would be someone best placed to advance Castro's aims.

"Well, as you've asked, I do have someone in mind."

"Funny that," huffed Van Tien.

"General Alberto Bayo."

"Wasn't he your mentor?" asked Virgilio.

"I think we should vote on it," replied Castro, ignoring the previous response and knowing all too well that he was, and he didn't want it to look like a whitewash.

"Vote on it!" replied a shocked-looking Van Tien as if someone had snapped his favourite AK-47. "That's democracy!"

"How else are we going to decide?"

"The way Communists always decide. We'll have a huge fight and the one that's least dead can choose."

A collection of miniature weapons, previously concealed about the bodies of each of the attendees, were silently unleashed and brandished under the table, waiting for the first move. Flick knives, small revolvers, a grenade and throwing stars were all ready to go. Initially, Virgilio went to the wrong pocket and aggressively pulled out a packet of cigarettes.

"I've heard enough."

The collective turned in the direction of the man sitting quietly at the other end of the table. Dressed in full military uniform and sporting more medals on his jacket than a decent-sized battalion, the man scribbled on a notepad with an elegant, expensive fountain pen. He was a rather thin, weedy-looking man quite atypical for someone of his creed. They all knew where he came from, even if some were unable to associate him with a name. None of the last two weeks would have been possible without the support of his nation.

THE RED MOUNTAIN

"The Soviet Union will decide," he said calmly. "On the craggy slopes of the Urals, through the gruelling tundra of Siberia and along the muddy banks of the Volga the revolutionaries have struggled. They held back the Mongols, the Kaiser, and Hitler. The Mountain Men belong to the motherland and the motherland will choose."

"I think they started in France," said Castro gently.

"SILENCE!" bellowed the Soviet General.

"Sorry," everyone replied harmoniously while silently concealing their weapons again. Even freedom fighters didn't argue with the Red Army.

"Who is the Soviet's choice, Radu?" asked Castro.

"The candidate will be," Radu Goga paused and his eyes scanned the contingent before a finger extended and pointed, "You!"

All eyes descended on José Flores Navas.

"First Secretary Goga, I hold you and your nation in the highest regard, may they long remain strong and resilient to the imperialist scum, but I'm not sure you know who he is."

"It matters not. The Soviet voice will be heard."

"But he's a lawyer."

"I am," said José, nodding vigorous reinforcement.

"Bloody good at counterarguments, paperwork and legal jargon but probably not good at infiltration, espionage and rallying swaths of the populace in rebellion. After all, everyone hates lawyers, even in Communist states. No offence," offered Castro.

"None taken."

"Then he can choose an alternative," barked Radu.

"I very much doubt that Navas spends his social life surrounded by vicious freedom fighters."

"I know one," replied José.

"Really, who?" asked Castro.

"My son. He's been at the conference the whole time and is further inspired to join our struggle for freedom."

"What's his name?" asked Radu Goga.

"Ilich Flores Navas."

- Chapter 26 -

Chaos for Hire

Clairvaux Prison, France, three months ago.

Everything generally fits into an order, for better or for worse. Just as Darwin concluded in his book, *The Origin of Species*, natural selection creates and is often responsible for this order. The strongest, quickest and smartest will win out against those less genetically capable. It seems counter-intuitive, then, that Darwin's writing had a positive influence on Karl Marx given his teachings about the Socialist principles of fairness and equality. The answer to this is simple. Socialists believe in materialism. Only 'things' exist, not ideas, magic or religion. Like John Lennon, they just didn't believe in them.

Karl Marx believed that the world was full of material contradictions which required resolution through social organisation, but there was one big problem with his theory. Most people were resolutely convinced in their belief in Gods. Enter Mr Darwin, the unexpected saviour of Communism. Suddenly Marx had scientific proof that the natural world complied with his philosophical model without the need for intervention from divine powers. Just like the natural world, societies corrected themselves, usually violently when a contradiction or imbalance existed.

This natural selection created a pecking order. This was true in businesses, communities, societies and even prisons.

In Clairvaux Prison the top dog was called Ilich Flores Navas, or Diego as he was known to the rest of the world.

CHAOS FOR HIRE

Below him were the highly dangerous inmates housed in the 'special area'.

Below them were regular prisoners.

Right at the bottom were the prison guards.

The arrival of a new inmate often changed the balance within the highly organised structure of the prison population. Sometimes that new arrival would try to challenge the historical order like a young stag attempts to usurp the alpha male. When that imbalance occurred in Clairvaux a big fight usually broke out to see who remained at the top of the pyramid. It didn't happen often. The last challenger to this potential imbalance left the prison in a series of rather inexpensive, plastic containers. Like Stalin, Mao, Jong-un and other notable figures of Communism that went before him, Diego wasn't going to be forced out. It would take someone of even greater notoriety and power to depose him.

Twelve months ago, a new inmate might have provided that challenge, if Diego hadn't been wise to it, and having the Governor in your pocket helped in that regard. Timon's sensibilities towards the principles of rehabilitation had a tendency to make him easy to manipulate but that wasn't the main reason for his close relationship with Diego. Timon wasn't a fool. He knew what Diego was capable of if he, too, tried to disrupt the pecking order. Through a combination of fear, admiration and strong Socialist beliefs, Timon worked with Diego to keep the peace and provide him with information about new arrivals.

That's how Diego first heard about Mario Peruzzi's arrival even before it occurred.

Everyone knew about the Oblivion Doctrine, even those who'd been behind bars at the time of its greatest achievements. There was no escape from the chaos it had briefly spread across the four corners of the world. Its anarchy had been total. Society had lost its composure and had descended into carnage. Fear rather than ideology had been the catalyst for change, something Diego had

CHAOS FOR HIRE

understood and nurtured himself over the four decades of his tenure as the Mountain Man.

Everyone who'd occupied the role before him had their idiosyncrasies. Che Guevara had approached change through guerrilla-style action. Lenin had used oratory skills and ideology to achieve his aims. Marx, on the other hand, had used the position to establish academic arguments to the change that would be achieved. Each had learnt from the last in choosing their own path. Diego had sold his Mountain Man to the highest bidder, while remaining true to the notion of disrupting the pillars of the establishment. Chaos for hire.

Mario had been cut from similar cloth, which meant another stag was entering his turf.

While everyone in the world was familiar with the prophecy that Mario tried to use to bring the world to an end, only two people were in a position to understand what the final line meant.

... and very brightly the men of the mountain will burn.

The one line of the prophecy that had yet to play out in real life was all about Diego. There seemed no way that Mario might know, and that became his advantage. Twelve months passed and Mario seemed more than happy to fit into the normal order of things. Diego kept him in his sights and assessed who he fraternised with. If Mario was happy to see out his time as a model prisoner, all the better for him.

Then the mood changed.

Mario's behaviour crossed the boundary of compliance into an erratic, even rebellious character. His demeanour became agitated, and whispers circulated of a secret plan to depose the top dog. Diego did the only sensible thing. When a potential enemy appears, the best ploy is to invite them into your circle so that you are well placed to crush them completely. A tactic straight out of the Communist playbook.

CHAOS FOR HIRE

Timon provided the intelligence, and Diego provided the perfect vehicle.

An exclusive poker night took place in the 'special area' every Tuesday evening. Six players maximum, always by invite only. Chips were exchanged based on a system of assets and favours that would be realised after your release. These often included cash, access to criminal networks, assassinations, ill-gotten gains from past thefts, and the promise of some deed completed on behalf of the other. In order to stay in the game add-ons were possible but had to be suitably attractive to the remaining players. As all six players wanted to be active participants in the game, Diego drafted in Timon Ortiz to act as both croupier and an extra pair of eyes.

Tonight's game featured Diego, Mr Boo-ya, Mustafa Suter, an Algerian dissident, Michel Boudain, a master thief, William Haggar and, for the first time, Mario Peruzzi. Mr Boo-ya went out early, relinquishing his stake of a three-album rap contract in the process. Mustafa went next, but less quietly. Although he was in debt to Diego to the tune of 'three assassinations of his choosing', he left the table insisting that they were all going to die horribly in their beds before the week was out. It was like this every week. Finally, Michel lost a bluff and reluctantly accepted that his offer of a two-week, all-expenses-paid holiday with his mistress might not go down well.

Three men remained.

"Three of hearts," announced Timon as he placed the river card face-up on the table and looked over at William to see what his move might be.

William had nothing. Actually, less than nothing. A pair of nines wasn't going to cut it. Sometimes waiting for the river card rescued you, sometimes it buried you. All his chips were on the table and Mario had more than enough to match anything he might add in.

"There's no shame in folding," offered Mario. "You're due for release next week, aren't you?"

William nodded.

CHAOS FOR HIRE

"Do you want to add in?" asked Timon.

"You're already in debt to Diego here, you don't want to be in my debt as well, do you?" added Mario, trying to manipulate the outcome.

William shook his head.

He gazed at his cards once more but to his disappointment they hadn't changed. He'd played enough poker to know that this arrangement of cards would only win if Mario was bluffing and, so far, that hadn't been his style. One of the secrets to playing a good game of poker was to separate emotion from maths. It was much easier said than done, particularly when you were playing people you were desperate to beat. After a further five minutes of reflection finally William folded his cards.

"No shame in it," said Mario coldly.

Without the histrionics that characterised some of the other players' exits this evening, William casually stood up, gave Diego a knowing nod and returned to his cell accompanied by a waiting guard.

"Good kid," said Diego. "Rubbish poker player."

"One on one now," replied Mario.

"Indeed," smiled Diego who'd worked hard all night to ensure it was so.

Timon dealt out the cards one more time. Mario looked emotionless as he carefully lifted the two cards from the table to see two Queens hiding under the green felt of the poker table.

"So, is tonight luck or skill?" asked Diego.

"A little of both."

"You like games, though, don't you?"

Mario nodded gently, aware that Diego was seeking more than just the answer. He was searching for his 'tell'.

Before the three-card flop hit the table, Diego pushed half his huge pile of chips into the centre. "Raise."

"Blind bet. Either you have a pair of aces or you're bluffing," remarked Mario.

"Or maybe I like games, too."

"I don't have enough chips to call you," said Mario.

CHAOS FOR HIRE

"Then fold or add on," said Timon in response.

"I'll add on," said Mario confidently.

"And what will you use for the exchange?" asked Diego. "There's only one thing I want from you."

"How about twelve billion dollars?"

The other two fell silent. The unofficial rules of their game allocated chips based on the agreed value of the asset on offer. A fortnight with Michel's mistress, after what may have been some rather unbelievable descriptions of what the winner might expect, was agreed to be worth ten chips. Cash was a little easier to categorise and this amount was certainly worth more than Diego's stack. Timon wrote twelve billion on a blank black chip and flung it over to Mario who placed it immediately in the centre.

"That wasn't the exchange I was seeking, but I'll accept it anyway."

"Looks like you might be short of chips yourself, Diego?"

"I have something to add in that might interest you?"

"What, more valuable than the money?"

"To you it's priceless."

"What?"

"I can tell you what the last line of your prophecy means."

A smile crawled slowly across Mario's face. "Yes, I know you can."

The wind was momentarily taken from Diego's sails.

"I see you don't just bluff in poker. There's no way you can know what I know."

"That's true but I do know about the secret bank account held in your name. I tried to buy it from Antoine Palomer with the rest of his assets and companies."

"I can see I have underestimated you. But it doesn't tell you anything about the prophecy. Only I can tell you what that means."

"Why would I care?"

"Because the Governor tells me that your recent change in mood is because you've received some bad news. Less than three months, he tells me. Those facing their own mortality often seek closure."

"I have already planned for it. They are just waiting for the rules of the game."

"Interesting," replied Diego. "What are you going to do?"

"I wouldn't want to spoil it for you. The information you have won't change anything?"

"Play the game and see."

"Will you accept the add-in?" asked Timon, wondering what time the game might end so he might get some sleep.

"No, it's not enough compared to twelve billion," replied Mario sternly.

"Then I'll have to fold, and we deal again," said Diego, trying to goad Mario. "Then you'll never know if you might have beaten me. Unless there's something else you want from me?"

The corner of Mario's lips curled further, a certain 'tell' that he got what he'd come for.

"There are some people that I need dealt with."

"Ok. Revenge?"

"Yes. Everyone knows your track record and what you are capable of."

"You're too kind. Who are they?"

"Their names are Ally Oldfield, Gabriel Janvier and Antoine Palomer."

"Do you want them killed? I have three assassinations in this pile somewhere," he said, referring to his earlier wins.

"No, I could arrange that myself."

"What, then?"

"I want you to humiliate them," replied Mario aggressively. "And keep them out of the way. If I arrange that it may disrupt my plan should they make the link to me."

"Easy. Add it."

Timon wrote the words 'Mountain Men' and the three names on the back of blank chips and threw them into the

CHAOS FOR HIRE

pile. With both players effectively 'all in' Timon dealt the five cards without the need for the rounds of betting that normally accompanied the flop, the turn and final river cards. Diego assessed the outcome. Poker was mathematical and he knew his hand gave him an eighty percent chance of winning.

"Diego, you're first," instructed Timon.

Two Aces were turned.

"Good hand," replied Mario. "But I always find the Queens."

The two Queens in Mario's hand and the one on the table confirmed his improbable victory. Mario might have the Queens, but Diego was still the indisputable King. Diego grinned, an atypical reaction for someone in defeat, but that was because losing had been his plan all along.

"Well played. Let me tell you about the Mountain Men and you can tell me about these three," he said, pointing at the chips featuring the newly written names.

Mario listened intently to Diego's history lesson that he traced almost unbroken back to the sixteenth century. The more he described the acts of the Mountain Men, the more Mario's mind schemed. It might provide the perfect cover for what he'd got planned, as well as being a suitable way of bringing his story full circle. If Diego could add to it by destroying the reputation of Ally, Gabriel and Antoine, then his revenge would be complete.

Diego's trap worked perfectly. Mario would use the history of the Mountain Men within his chaotic swansong, and in turn it would act as cover for his own plans. Their reappearance would force Radu out of his hole, and all he had to do in return was help Mario frame three ordinary members of the public.

*****

Clairvaux Prison, France, three weeks ago.

"How are you finding life on the outside?" asked Diego casually through the telephone that hung limply from the side of the glass window.

"Boring," came William's honest reply.

"Patience. Mario's death means that life is going to get much more interesting for you soon. What have you got for me on the three names?"

"Antoine Palomer has gone to ground following the hostile takeover of his businesses. I believe he suspects something."

"Don't worry about him. Mario already mentioned his name during our little game, and I suspect Antoine is already connected to us somehow. Mario's already taken everything from him, there's not much more we can do. What about the other two?"

"I've found Gabriel Janvier near Lyon. She's a self-employed 'IT Ninja', whatever that means. Appears to be an easy target. She's been secretly trying to track down Mario's money herself over recent months."

"And the other one."

"Easy to locate. She's a Professor of Medieval languages and quite a prominent academic."

"Have you found her pressure point."

"Yes, it's all about work for her."

"Where does she work?"

"Oxford University," replied William.

The cogs of Diego's brain ceased up as he attempted to identify the best way to carry out his commitments to Mario.

"It's not enough. We need something else. What about family?"

"She's a loner. Adopted when she was six by a Mr and Mrs Brownlee, both deceased. There are no known siblings and she's not married. Just an elderly father in a home."

"Did you say Brownlee?" replied Diego sharply.

"Yes."

"Did you get the woman's full name?"

CHAOS FOR HIRE

"Yes, it's here somewhere," replied William, searching through a folder full of paper. "It's Alison Oriana Brownlee."

Diego dropped his phone. The name Oriana would stick long in his memory. The frightened little girl with the distinctive shiny, red shoes.

"Boss. You ok?"

"Find her," he growled. "Find her and then we'll find him."

"Who?"

"Radu Goga, of course. He's the only other person who knows about the real Mountain Men. The only man I ever failed to kill. That responsibility falls to you now. Mario's plot will no doubt bring him out in the open as I initially expected, but she can help bring him down. Find her."

"How?"

"You must work that out for yourself. Over the last two years I have prepared you for this moment. I have taught you all I know about our people and their history. Now it is your future. There are no rules. Help people scale the mountain in any way you see fit. The only thing I ask of you is that you complete the task I was unable to finish."

- Chapter 27 -

William Haggar

Ms Honeywell's greatest ability was knowing everything that was going on in the village of Stanton. What people did. Why they did it. Where they went. Who they knew. When, and quite often before, they did it. Many people accepted her as an eccentric member of their community, a topic of harmless debate or at the very least an extra level of security. Many, like Ally Oldfield herself, labelled her a nosy busybody who had little else in life to distract her than other people's business. Neither of these descriptions was accurate.

The truth was far more interesting.

Since the war this region of the country had always been associated with the practice of snooping on others. Bletchley Park, home to the World War Two code-breakers, was only thirty miles away. Gladys Honeywell knew it well. Her mother had served there under the watchful eye of Alan Turing in ninety forty-four. As a child she'd listened excitedly to her mother's stories of what happened within the secretive walls of 'Hut Eight'. It was no surprise to anyone that she followed in her mother's footsteps in joining Bletchley's successor, GCHQ, which was thirty miles in the other direction. Stanton St. John sat in-between like the epicentre of a spy map.

A spinster, long since retired, she found old habits were hard to kill. When you saw patterns in events and people's actions it's hard not to follow your nose. Now her once full-time job had been relegated to a hobby, but not just any old, boring hobby like needlework or renovating old cars.

WILLIAM HAGGAR

This one made her responsible for the safety of the people of Stanton, should the sleepy, rural village ever need it.

Today some of them did.

PC Dearlove might be the regular 'bobby on the beat' but she made sure he was kept up to speed with anything suspicious around the community. New residents were afforded particular scrutiny in case they turned out to be troublemakers determined to shatter the utopia of this award-winning village. Conformity was the name of the game and if you didn't, then Honeywell was hot on your heels. Her natural gift, government training, forty years of dedicated experience and an abundance of free time made her almost unbeatable. Overconfidence and arrogance can be hard to separate.

A lack of crime, partly as a result of her tireless routine of sticking her nose in where it wasn't invited, lowered people's defences. The safe environment of the village was one of its main selling points as a result. Until today, the last burglary in the village had been last century. The last abduction didn't even feature in official records. Today Ms Honeywell found herself on the receiving end of both, and even she hadn't seen it coming.

"It's preposterous, me darlin'," she said defiantly.

"What is?" replied the old man.

"We don't have burglaries in Stanton!"

"I'm not a burglar."

"But you're in my house, me darlin', uninvited!"

"True."

"Then you're a burglar."

"No. If I wanted to get my hands on an antique blender, some floral curtains and a menagerie of cat ornaments I'd have gone to my nearest car boot sale," replied the man honestly. "I have no interest in stealing from you."

Other than being gaffer taped to a kitchen chair her treatment since returning home to find it not empty had been more than courteous. If he hadn't been a felon, she probably would have approved him as a future resident purely on the basis of the man's rather polite demeanour and old school manners.

"Abduction, then. I know your sort. You're planning some sexual depravity!"

"I'm really not that sick," he replied, sitting calmly on the other side of the table more interested in the pages of the village magazine.

"What is it you want with me, then?"

"Information."

"No. My lips are sealed."

"You've not stopped talking since you got back. In fact, I'd wager you haven't stopped talking in some considerable time. Nineteen Eighty-Three would be my best guess."

Honeywell pursed her lips and looked up to the ceiling overdramatically as if she was completely in control of the situation. When Honeywell moved there was always one part of her that remained static, her hair. Every morning it was subjected to an hour-long regime of attention that involved unloading two cans of hairspray on it. The fumes seeping out of her barnet were enough to keep the fire in the kitchen raging for hours without ever adding any wood.

"I mean you no harm, madam," he said, trying to force a smile through his wrinkled skin. "My name is Radu Goga and I need someone with local knowledge to help me with a couple of things."

"You promise you're not going to try to have your wicked way with me?"

"At our age, Ms Honeywell, I think it's entirely unlikely. Even if the desire was there the physical probability has long since emigrated. I'm looking for someone."

"I know everyone, me darlin'."

"Good."

"Why are you looking?"

"Unfinished business."

It was just the sort of gossip-like phrase that drew Honeywell in. Any whisper that went around the village grabbed her attention, mainly to ensure nothing illegal was afoot. At least that's how she justified it.

"Unfinished business, with whom?"

"Ally Oldfield."

"Doctor Ally Oldfield," Honeywell added in a gesture that never seemed to feature when Ally herself was around.

"I also need to locate a gun."

"A gun! Do you have a licence, otherwise it's against the law, me darlin'?"

"My intentions to use such a weapon probably go beyond the legalities of needing a licence, don't you think?"

"Murder! No. Not here. I won't have it, I tell you. This is Stanton, those types of things don't happen here. Not on my watch. Boarstall yes, Oddington maybe, even Horton-cum-Studley there might be a slim chance, but not here. Not in Stanton St. John!"

"Fear not, Ms Honeywell, I did not say I was going to murder anyone. Self-defence counts as manslaughter normally."

"Is Ally going to attack you, then? I always thought she was a wrong 'un. You can see it in her eyes. Vicious, dangerous eyes devoid of kindness. I told Norman he needed to keep a close eye on her. I said she was going to be trouble, me darlin', but do they listen…"

"No need to hyperventilate. I do not fear Ally Oldfield, only who she mixes with. Now where would I find a gun around here?"

"Nope, not saying."

"I could just burgle every house in the village until I find one. Imagine the crime figures? You'll be swamped by hordes of police and local journalists walking on the pristine lawns and littering the streets. The place will become a circus. In the weeks to come homeowners will erect unsightly cameras on every wall and lamp-post. Your crusade will be over."

WILLIAM HAGGAR

The corners of Honeywell's eyes started to twitch uncontrollably at the thought of her village being infiltrated by outsiders and modern technology.

"Mervyn," she said reluctantly after a period of internal struggle. "He's got a couple of shotguns."

"Great. Lead the way," said Radu getting up delicately and helping Gladys out of her chair. "Then we need to find a quiet place to hide that overlooks Ally Oldfield's house."

"It would have to be the church. That's the only building overlooking it."

"Perfect."

*****

"Where is he?" barked Buff again.

"How should I know?" rebuffed Ally. "I didn't even know the name of Radu Goga until last week, and out of all the people I'm keen to see right now he isn't one of them."

"Liar! You're protecting him."

"Call me whatever you like, I have no idea who he is, let alone where he is."

"You are so DUMPED!" screamed Gabriel, still weeping uncontrollably from the confines of her chair.

"I've already dumped you and I was only dating you in the first place to get to her," laughed Buff.

"Owww, you're sick, sick, sick!" she screamed.

"As usual you've got the wrong end of the stick," mumbled Ally from the corner of her mouth. "Buff, I don't know who the hell you are, but it appears you've learnt English since Wednesday."

"I know who he is!" shouted Gabriel hysterically. "His real name is William Haggar. Apparently, Buff is a nickname!"

"No!" gasped Ally sarcastically. "There was me thinking his parents were big watchers of vampire-based television."

"I know, it's shocking," replied Gabriel, missing the sarcasm completely. "I heard what Hudson said about him so I hacked into his FBI file so that I could find his real name. I was planning on rubbishing him on social media before posting lots of revenge porn! But when I came back here to confront him, he assaulted me and tied me up to a chair. I just thought he was being kinky at first but then he pulled a gun!"

"Only after you stabbed me in the boob, you mad bitch!"

William Haggar, one of many names that Ally had heard over the last week that didn't own a home, until today. This character was the owner of Antoine's mysterious bank account and if his conclusions were correct, he was a Mountain Man.

"So, you're responsible for all of this madness over the last week?" asked Ally.

"No," said Buff. "We only serve the pursuit of progress. To help the weak and powerless break the shackles of their oppressors."

"Bullshit," added Ally before he could continue. "Tell me one thing you've done to help the oppressed?"

"I rallied the Hindus to action."

"You stole the Shikshapatri!?"

"Yes."

"How?"

"I have a history of getting into places you're not allowed to be in," he said, making it clear he was a burglar when he'd intended quite the opposite. "All I needed to do was take your access card, business cards and convince Gabriel to disrupt their systems for an hour."

"What?!"

"In my defence," replied Gabriel innocently. "He said it was part of an online game he was playing, and he needed the points."

"I'll deal with you later."

"Neither of you is leaving until someone tells me where Goga is."

"You're not very quick, are you? Why did you steal the book?" she asked.

"Partly as a distraction to other events, and partly because the book is sacred and does not belong to anyone other than those who follow its teachings. The Hindu race have been emancipated."

"No, they haven't, you imbecile. Since I returned the book yesterday morning they've broadly gone back to their lives. Hold on," she said, pausing. The facts were coagulating to reveal a very different picture. If it was Buff who'd stolen the book it didn't explain why Buff left her business card in its place. "Why include me in all this?"

"Because Mario wanted you out of the way. To implicate you in his scheme. I needed you for another reason."

"What reason?"

"Because you are not the beginning," he replied cryptically.

Not for the first time she considered what it meant. If she wasn't the beginning, the inference was clear. She was the end, but the end of what?

"I think I see what's happening here," said Ally.

"Me, too!" screamed Gabriel again. "He's only been dating me to get to you."

"No, that's not… actually, you're right," said Ally unexpectedly agreeing with Gabriel for one of the first times ever.

"You sick bastard!" Gabriel sneered, while a spontaneous shiver reverberated up her body at the thought of it. "You like wrinkly, old women, do you?"

"I'm not wrinkly!"

"You're not smooth like me, though, are you?"

It wasn't the right time for petty catfights. Buff was getting agitated and Ally needed to retake control.

"You sought Gabriel out so she would lead you to me. The FBI weren't following Gabriel before she tried to hack into their systems to look for Mario's money. They were following you. You left my business card in place of the book to draw their attention to me. But it wasn't just to get me out of the way. You thought their attention on me would identify Radu Goga, but why?"

"Because until recently Radu Goga was the only other living person who knew about the Mountain Men. My predecessor tried to kill him after he defected to the West thirty years ago, fearing he might tell the Americans all about them. He knew while Goga lived he might bring down four hundred years of history. He has to be eliminated."

"But I don't have anything to do with him."

"Yes, you do, you just don't know you do. My master saved your life so you might eventually lead us to him. You were too young to remember. Just a little lost, orphaned girl."

Ally closed her eyes. The hazy visions from the past, that had desperately tried to force their way through forty-five years of granite like resistance over the past week finally burst, fully formed in front of her eyes.

Ally cowered under the dripping branches of an apple tree. Above her the muscular military man with thick, dark straggly hair, an unshaven face and piercing black eyes raised his arm and aimed his revolver. He chuntered angrily in a language which she couldn't fully decipher. As she connected adult life with infant memory the words revealed themselves. Romanian. Ugly, angry words of threat and doom. She closed her eyes and hugged herself into a ball. As the final moment crept its icy fingers of fear over her small body a shot rang out across the dark skies. When she opened her eyes, the bulky soldier lay in a heap by her side, a bullet hole in the back of his head and blood soaking into the rain-sodden ground.

She looked up at a second man.

He was shorter and rounder. His appearance and clothes suggested he wasn't part of the armed guards that had kept her prisoner for the past few weeks. The small pencil moustache bristled on his top lip as he let out a comforting smile. His hands dropped down and gently lifted her off the mud.

"I do remember," she croaked, finally allowing the truth to seep out into the open world. "I'm not the beginning, I'm the end."

The doorbell rang.

Twice.

*****

Lance was always nervous about calling on people unannounced, particularly if that person happened to be Ally Oldfield. Experience had taught him that, irrespective of the nature of his visit, whatever she was doing was more important. Ally summoned you, you never called on Ally. Lance stared at the doorbell on the left-hand side of the little cottage door and hoped that it might ring itself and he could blame it on the local 'youths' playing pranks. There was no one around, just him. Only he could press it.

It wasn't even Ally he wanted to find. Daniel had been very specific in his instructions. Find Gabriel and tell her to infiltrate the Oblivion Doctrine's dark web and put an end to the impending global uprising. Once Daniel Hudson had retrieved the letters, worked out the numbers and secured the money the rebels would have nothing to motivate them. Not everyone was an ideologist. Most were just greedy. It was clear to Lance that the thousand insurgents primed and ready to revolt had been sold the idea of a share in the money. A capitalist present wrapped up with a big Socialist bow.

His arm got halfway to the bell before it leapt back into his pocket. Saturday afternoon was struggling to give way to Saturday evening and the cold and dark were settling in around him. Maybe Gabriel wasn't even here, he thought. After all, it wasn't her house. Maybe she'd gone back to France or was out for the night. The fate of the world was in the hands of a prevaricating, anxiety-ridden buffoon. He shook it off. Today he'd already proven his worth. He'd shown what he was really made of in 'The Eagle and Child' pub. Perhaps it was time to stand up to his boss as well.

Finally, he rang the bell.

He rang it again, unsure as to whether it made a sound the first time.

As he was about to ring it a third time, he heard a chain being secured on the other side. The door opened a fraction.

"What do you want?"

"Ally, it's Lance."

"Fuck off. I'm sick," she added.

"Ok, I'll be…" He paused, before his mouth forced his feet to retract their immediate desire to retreat. "No, this is important."

"Do what I say, you stupid idiot."

"No. I won't be pushed around anymore. I'm not your slave to direct at your leisure. I'm a strong individual. I have attributes, strengths and my own opinions and… I will be heard!" he bellowed down the street.

"I did warn you!"

A revolver peeked out from behind the crack in the door and the entire contents of Lance's confidence subsided. He dropped to the floor in a scared heap, but the timing of his fear was never better. A loud shot rang out over his head and a bullet obliterated the porch light that hung on the wall just above the doorbell. The door quickly slammed shut and the people on the other side retreated into the safety of the cottage.

Lance slithered down the pathway like a disorientated anaconda desperate to get away from the scene. At the end of the path he cowered behind a boxwood shrub. The shot had come from across the road and the only building opposite was the church. Which meant he was directly in the middle of two people carrying guns. This hero lark was harder than it looked, he thought. Panting for breath he reached inside his jacket and removed his phone.

"What service do you require?" came a voice on the other end.

"Police!" exhaled Lance with a nervous quiver. "Stanton St. John is under siege!"

- Chapter 28 -

Stand-off in Stanton

Within the hour Stanton St. John was devoured by flashing blue lights. A dozen police cars descended on the sleepy village and tried desperately to find suitable places to park. Norman Dearlove, who was first on the scene, having wisely decided to walk, was acting parking attendant. It might be his village, but it certainly wasn't his authority to command the whole operation. That responsibility rested on the shoulders of DCI Bolton who marched from team to team with a grave look on his face and tried to demonstrate he knew what he was doing.

Few believed him, least of all Bolton.

No one had any past experience of something as serious as this.

Armed stand-offs didn't happen in places like Stanton. They didn't even happen in nearby Oxford. The local police authority was furiously checking the procedural manuals to discover the right protocol, while the fifty strong gang of police officers loitered vacantly at the scene awaiting further instructions. Police dogs barked insatiably at the rather perplexed local cat population who continued to do whatever the fuck they wanted, as usual. A van, packed to the ceiling with heavily protected and armed men hiding serious faces under Kevlar helmets, screeched into the midst of the confusion.

Lance, quite against his will, had been wrapped in a silver foil blanket and dumped in the back of an ambulance to guard against shock. DCI Bolton stomped up to the back of it, clutching resolutely to his air of importance.

"Did you make the call?" he said abruptly.

STAND-OFF IN STANTON

"Yes."

"Where's the shooter?"

Lance pointed in two directions with both arms.

"Working in teams, are they?"

Lance shook his head.

"It appears, sir," said Norman, interrupting the unfair interrogation, "that one shooter is holed up in the church, and a man with a gun has taken hostages in the cottage opposite."

"Hostages?"

"Yes. Ally Oldfield and possibly one other."

"That woman just can't keep her nose out of it," huffed Bolton.

"Bit unfair, sir, it's her house!"

"What do we know about the shooters?"

"They don't like each other much," added Lance. "One's already opened fire."

"Right!" shouted DCI Bolton to anyone who could be bothered to listen. "I want firearms officers covering both these properties and someone bring me a megaphone immediately."

*****

Inside the cottage, Buff extinguished the lights and took both women up to the first-floor bedroom that looked out on the road. Taking a sheet from a cupboard he tore long strips off it to bandage the stab wound on his chest. It was still bleeding but it wasn't enough to stop him now. Not after everything he'd been through in the last few weeks. The scene outside did complicated matters a little.

"It looks like you're trapped," added Ally unhelpfully.

"Not while I have hostages."

"Oh, how the mighty fall," she said snidely.

"What do you mean?"

"The Mountain Men. Do you think this is what they had in mind? Trapped by a mildly inoffensive police force

STAND-OFF IN STANTON

inside a small cottage in an insignificant rural village with a famous historian and a slut for hostages."

"That's not true," replied Gabriel indignantly. "You're not famous."

Ally ignored her: it came naturally these days.

"Every one of the Mountain Men have drifted further from their ideals before their inevitable corruption by its legend," continued Ally.

"Nonsense," barked Buff. "The course of human history has been in our hands."

"Not done a great job, then, have they?"

"They've brought freedom to the people of the world."

"Didn't someone once say that history is always written by the winners? Which of your predecessors succeeded exactly?"

"Most of them," replied Buff, one eye still watching the build-up of adversaries outside the window.

"Guido Fawkes executed, Masaniello murdered, Jean Cavalier corrupted by power, Robespierre deposed and killed…" listed Ally before he interrupted her.

"… Franklin, Marx, Lenin, Guevara and Diego Navas all achieved greatness," Buff snapped angrily.

"Thank you," she smiled. "I didn't know who some of them were."

"It doesn't matter now," replied Buff unmoved.

"Yes, it does. You think these revolutionaries won great victories for the equality of the common man, but you are deceived by your own blindness. The American Revolution only liberated white rich men and produced the capitalist monster we see today. They, too, are looking for the Mountain Men, but not to preserve them. It's just about the money, an instinct deeply rooted in a system your group helped create. Lenin's thugs killed anyone who didn't agree with his ideology and your own master, Diego Navas, was little more than a political terrorist, more interested in his own status and wealth than the rise of the masses. You've been duped. I'm sure this is not what Philibert Lesage imagined."

STAND-OFF IN STANTON

"How do you know what is right and wrong? They are just opinions, not facts. No system is perfect, and change takes time. Each step has taken us closer to the summit."

"That's just the point, though, isn't it? Not everyone can, or wants to, reach the top of the mountain, there's just not enough room."

"We'll see. Our intentions can't be any worse than the inequality in the world today."

She had to agree on this point. When humans and power were involved, no system would truly reflect the collective will of the masses because as soon as the masses had power, they would adopt the very same attitudes they'd been fighting against. Masaniello and Cavalier had proved it beyond doubt. If Hudson found the money, he'd show the modern-day equivalent of it. Power corrupts absolutely whatever system you followed.

"Who fired at us?" asked Ally.

"Radu."

"I understand why you might want to find him, but why does he want to find you?"

"He doesn't want to find me," said Buff casually.

A searchlight illuminated the bedroom window and the crackle of a loudhailer boomed around the village.

"Identify yourself," came the echo from down below.

"You speak to them," demanded Buff, hiding behind the window frame for fear that the next bullet zooming across the road had his name on it.

"What if someone shoots me?"

"He won't."

Ally tentatively lifted her head above the radiator bolted to the wall under the window frame and slowly revealed herself to the posse down in the street.

"Mrs Oldfield," confirmed Bolton as the searchlight dazzled the figure in the window.

"Doctor," she replied indignantly.

"What's the situation?" came the booming response.

STAND-OFF IN STANTON

"There's a body-building nut job up here who until Wednesday had a vocabulary restricted to the words 'dog' and 'potato'. Oh, and he's got a gun!"

"What does he want?"

"Hold on!" she shouted down to the road.

"They want to know what you want?" asked Ally, ducking back to the floor again and finding the gun yet again trained on her.

"Radu Goga."

"Is that it? Don't you want global liberation or something?" she sneered.

"Ask for loads of money and a helicopter," blurted Gabriel.

"Whose side are you on?" replied Ally.

"It entirely depends on the outcome," she replied, winking at Buff.

"You can stop that," snapped Buff. "I never fancied you."

"Arsehole."

Ally returned to her audibly imbalanced conversation with a megaphone.

"He wants Radu Goga."

DCI Bolton looked bewildered. He turned to Lance who was still huddled under his cheap blanket like a late finisher in the London Marathon.

"Apparently he wants Radu Goga. Isn't that a type of Mediterranean dip? Right, somebody call Waitrose."

"On it," replied a nearby constable.

"Wait. Does he want carrots or crisps with his Radu Goga dip?!" shouted Bolton, relaying his question back to Ally through the device.

"Radu Goga is a man, you dipshit!" growled Ally.

"A man? Where is he?"

The large searchlight splintered into pieces as a bullet struck the middle of the glass and the light immediately went out. The armed officers lost their minds and started strafing the fourteenth-century stonemasonry of the church quite at random.

STAND-OFF IN STANTON

"STOP!" shouted Bolton.

"I think he might be over there!" shouted Ally. Only her hand was visible above the window frame as it pointed the answer across the street. The rest of her body was undercover in case the trigger-happy police marksmen got her before Buff did.

The siege continued through Saturday night and into Sunday morning. A catering van was called to supply the countless, and mostly pointless, contingent of police officials, constables and hangers-on that had swelled in size by the hour. The normal population of Stanton was two hundred, but that had almost doubled overnight. The locals, most of whom were more fascinated than concerned, went to the pub for a lock-in. Smokers were given the task of reporting updates to the rest of the bar every time they went out for a fag.

TV and radio news crews picked up on the ongoing hostage situation and were buzzing around in helicopters or arguing with the police stationed at the cordon to let them through. Lance got a couple of restless hours of sleep in the back of the ambulance. The adrenaline of being fired on had almost waned. Today was Sunday. Today was the day that this small patch of chaos was going to pale into insignificance with the simultaneous revolts about to descend on an unsuspecting Western world. He had to get to Gabriel somehow. He went to find Bolton, a germ of an idea creeping through the grey matter and into the light.

"Excuse me."

"Not now, boy, there's adult work being done," said Bolton without looking up from the map that was the subject of his and his team's interest.

"Sorry, didn't mean to…"

"Speak up, Lance," said Norman Dearlove who had been his shadow for much of the stand-off. "If it's important."

"DCI Bolton, I must get inside that house," added Lance forcefully.

STAND-OFF IN STANTON

"Be my guest. I'll need you to sign the disclaimer, though, in the likely event of you being shot."

"You don't understand. If I don't get to Gabriel more chaos will be inflicted on the world. If he wants Radu Goga let's give him what he wants in return for Gabriel."

"But we don't have Radu Goga."

"We could pretend," replied Lance.

"What good will that do?"

"Um... it might stop the impending erosion of Western society!"

"I think you're exaggerating."

"Do you have a better plan?"

The answer was no because they didn't have any plan at all. Staring at the map was mainly an attempt to create the illusion that they might have one.

*****

Ally woke from a fractured, nervy nap with only one thought on her mind. Horace. Through all of this discord her ageing father was still out there somewhere lost and confused. That's if nothing more serious hadn't happened to him. The longer she remained there the longer his agony continued. The dawn of a new day hadn't brought any certainty to how her own situation might be resolved, but as soon as it was, she could get back to searching for him. Hopefully she'd think of a quick way out of this.

Buff remained alert, gun still fixed on her position. His wound was under control, but the blood loss had affected the colour in his face. Gabriel lay on the bed snoring like someone had released the kraken.

"Oldfield," came a blast from the megaphone.

Buff nodded for her to answer.

"What?"

"We have an offer for your captor. We will allow him safe passage from the house and the use of a vehicle if he releases the young woman in return."

STAND-OFF IN STANTON

"Oh thanks," she replied, aggrieved at her own place in the deal. "You'll have to bring a foghorn to wake her up, but I'll tell him."

"They're offering safe passage from the house if you give Gabriel her freedom," she confirmed.

Buff had always intended to wait until morning before making his move. As long as he had one hostage, that would protect him. He had no illusions the police truthfully intended to allow him safe passage but that didn't concern him. He had his own plan and that required him to be out of the house and preferably not in a body bag. Buff nodded his agreement.

"He agrees, although I'm not sure I do!" bellowed Ally out of the window.

"Tell him to come down!" shouted the megaphone.

"Lead the way, Dr Oldfield," replied Buff, shaking the gun at her.

"At least you know what to call me."

Ally made a walk she'd made hundreds of times before. Out of the bedroom, along the hall and down the staircase, although it was the first time she'd done it with a gun positioned between her shoulder blades. She pushed open the front door and a hundred faces stared back at her. At the end of the small, descending path that led from the house down the shallow slope and onto the road a car was waiting for them with its doors open. Several armed personnel did their utmost to focus their sights on the man firmly pressed against her for cover.

"Move further away, or I'll shoot!" shouted Buff.

The ensemble crept backwards, most comically losing their footing on the shabby condition of the road or bumped into the various obstacles in the way. Lance watched carefully. Buff pushed Ally around the car to the other side and continued to march her across the road.

"What's he doing?" said Norman in a whisper.

"Exactly what I expected him to do," replied Lance. "It's all about Radu Goga."

STAND-OFF IN STANTON

"You do realise that you've now placed your boss in a place where two people have guns rather than one?" replied Norman nervously.

"It's for the greater good, but think of it this way," said Lance. "Now both of them have to deal with Ally Oldfield."

"Everyone turn around or you're going to have a corpse on your hands!" shouted Buff. "Do it!. DO IT NOW!"

"Do what he says!" bellowed Bolton.

Everyone complied apart from Lance. While everyone looked away from Buff, he bolted for the slowly closing front door, sneaking in just before it slammed shut.

After no further instructions were offered by the assailant one by one the contingent swivelled round to their original positions. They just managed to catch sight of Buff and Ally as they disappeared into the church.

"At least we only have to look in one direction," replied Bolton.

Lance scurried up the staircase and darted into all available rooms in search of Gabriel. After a few wrong turns he located her lying angelically on the spare bed. Lance forgot for a moment why everything had been so urgent. She was the most beautiful woman he'd seen, or at least one who didn't scowl back at him. Under all the make-up, fluorescent clothing, hentai tattoos and giant, plastic earrings was this Aphrodite of imperfection. He knew she was beautiful the first time he'd seen her, but the passage of the last week had installed a confidence sadly lacking at the time. Maybe his newfound self-esteem would appeal to her more?

Reality returned.

She hated him.

He was a geeky postgraduate who had the charm and appearance of a kitchen mop. In many ways he was way out of his depth, new confidence or not. He gave her a gentle shake to wake her up. It went unnoticed because it was less fierce than the shaking the bed demonstrated as a result of her own snoring. He tried again. Nothing. He

STAND-OFF IN STANTON

grabbed her by the shoulders and shook with all of his might while shouting aggressive demands for her to rise.

"Don't shoot!" she screamed, as a wayward fist swung out and caught him square in the face.

Lance was susceptible to nosebleeds at the best of times. He'd never quite worked out why it was. The explanation many had given him was some farcical-sounding blood clotting abnormality. It certainly wasn't that today. His nosebleeds never came on like this, although it was the first time he'd received someone's right hook square in the face. Blood gushed out of both nostrils and ran down his new suit.

"I've come to rescue you," he gurgled painfully.

Gabriel had never been rescued before. All that most of the boys she met wanted to do was control her. Subconsciously she was attracted to good-looking bad boys that fitted a pattern which failed so miserably time after time. Ally was right. Maybe she also needed to change or end up in the situation Ally had so painfully framed for her. She looked beyond Lance's laughable exterior. The bloodstained, goofy features, the streak of piss stature and ridiculous combination of what some might call fashion. Under it all was kindness. Under it all was a man resolutely and unashamedly being himself. She flung herself at him before he ran away.

"I wasn't expecting that," gasped Lance somewhat quizzically.

"I've always fancied you," she replied, kissing his neck passionately.

"You said I was a weirdo!"

"I love weirdos."

"No, you don't. You're just in shock," he replied. "And right now, I need you to focus and get to work."

"Work! I need therapy after what I've just been through. It's going to take weeks to sort my brain out."

"You'll have to suck it up, I'm afraid. Where's the nearest computer?"

"Ally's is downstairs."

STAND-OFF IN STANTON

Lance grabbed her firmly by the hand as they rushed down the stairs and into the kitchen where Ally's rather archaic laptop sat neatly next to a pile of books regimentally filed in alphabetical order.

"You can hack, right?"

"Of course. I'm one of the best."

"Good. Get us on to the Oblivion Doctrine's dark web. We need to send them a message."

- Chapter 29 -

Last of the Mountain Men

Even though it was only across the road, it was the first time Ally had ever been inside the local church. In general, the only time she ever ventured inside any church was to conduct historical research. It wasn't religious buildings themselves she had a problem with. The architectural structures were often fascinating and contained significant artefacts or stories of interest. Her problem centred on what they were used for. A deeply passionate atheist who possessed challenging arguments and a sarcastic tone on the subject of the existence of God might be welcomed by the local vicar, but they weren't remembered fondly. A lack of genuine friendships also meant she wasn't invited to many christenings, weddings or funerals, not that she would go if she were.

Stanton's church had a gloomy, forgotten quality about it. Although it was the middle of the day, and the many colourful stained-glass windows surrounding them were doing their best to let the light in, it still had an atmosphere that felt devoid of attention and love. From their position at the rear entrance a series of arches carved their way down the belly of the nave like the jaws of an alligator in dire need of dental assessment. On the floor a dirty, blue carpet separated the lines of pews that queued patiently for the next service to commence.

At the far end of the church was the unmistakable figure of Ms Honeywell bound to a chair in front of the altar. To Ally's great relief her mouth had been suitably

LAST OF THE MOUNTAIN MEN

gagged to segregate her voice from everyone else's ears. Honeywell squirmed awkwardly to release herself from her enforced state with little success. It was clear that if she was being held against her will someone else was also there, somewhere in the shadows.

Buff nudged Ally forward with the barrel of his pistol. They walked slowly down the blue carpet until a hand rested on Ally's shoulder for her to stop when they approached the halfway point along the nave. Buff knew a trap when he saw one. Radu Goga had survived being hunted by various former paymasters for more than forty years. He'd escaped the Communists, survived his confinement at the hands of capitalists, and disappeared into obscurity without trace for over three decades. KGB-trained, CIA-instructed, state-sponsored and a first-class honours degree from the school of hard knocks.

Buff couldn't compete.

His own qualifications, for the unique position he found himself in, were based on a criminal record that included petty squabbles, armed robbery and grievous bodily harm. The weight of history sat uncomfortably on his shoulders. Each of the Mountain Men, whether notorious failures like Fawkes or legends of popular culture like Che Guevara, had made their mark on the world. What would his legacy be? How would he meet the expectations placed upon him?

There was only one way.

Kill Radu Goga.

If he succeeded where his predecessor had failed, then that at least would be enough for him to leave his mark. It was likely he'd get caught as a result, but as Diego had already proved, being arrested did not curtail your ability to carry out the deeds that came with the title. Buff's eyes scanned the scene ahead. One old woman strapped to a chair, a simple altar and a number of tatty curtains hanging down the chancel on the left and right sides of it.

LAST OF THE MOUNTAIN MEN

"That's far enough," came an old, gargling voice over the church's microphone before Buff's considered next step had time to hit the carpet runner.

"Show yourself," growled Buff.

"Take one more step and the old woman dies."

"Which one?" asked Buff.

"I'm only just in my fifties," muttered Ally, pointing at Honeywell to reinforce the point.

As ever, Ally's deep desire for answers reduced the feeling of fear that should have rightfully taken priority. The visions of her past demonstrated being aimed at wasn't a unique occurrence. Had that experienced also reduced her general fear over the years? Had it been responsible for a reckless lack of care and the tough fearless exterior she'd carried through her life?

"What do I care if she dies?" replied Buff. "She means nothing to me. I only want you, Radu."

"Then release Ally and let's deal with this ourselves."

"Why, so you can shoot me from your hide? Not happening."

He knew her name, thought Ally. How? Who'd told him and why would he want to know? If Radu Goga had been in hiding for thirty years, why would he reveal himself now and here? Was he trying to help her stop the Mountain Men or was there some other plot running underneath?

"How do you know who I am?!" shouted Ally, receiving a jab in the back for her insolence.

"I've made two major mistakes in my life," said Radu, his voice echoing off the nave's arches. "I regret both very deeply. In nineteen sixty-six I rashly chose Ilich Flores Navas to take up the role of the Mountain Man. At the time I did not fully understand the true purposes of that secretive group. I do now. I'm certain the instigator of the Mountain Men never envisaged they would morph into the violent, brutal, corrupt and power-obsessed brand of dissidents they are today. Unintentionally they have created the unrelenting elitism of Western capitalism and the corrupt oppression of Eastern Socialism. The mountain is still there, very few have reached the summit, but many have fallen trying."

"Lies. We work for the people!" shouted Buff angrily. "You've been brainwashed by those holding their ground at the top, you traitor!"

"Traitor," said Radu, considering the word reflectively for a moment. "I certainly was, yes. I believed that my commitment to the USSR's ideology was both noble and just. It clouded my judgement. I was rash in my decision to choose Diego. I lacked the foresight to see what he might become. The CIA helped me understand the errors, not just in my system but unwittingly in theirs also. I assisted them in finding and capturing Diego and then, when it was safe to do so and the opportunity arose, I escaped from both systems. While the Mountain Men could no longer cause global catastrophe, I retired in peace."

"But you knew we'd come again!" shouted Buff.

"Yes."

"Then why didn't you act when they blew up the Houses of Parliament?" interceded Ally, aggrieved that anyone should know everything she'd struggled to understand over the past week but did nothing to stop it.

"Because I knew it was a hoax."

"It's no hoax, I saw Big Ben floating in the Thames!"

"It wasn't a real event from history, though. I knew someone was pretending to be the Mountain Men, but at the time I had no idea the real one was pulling the strings in the background. Not at least until I discovered Ally had been dragged into it."

"What have I got to do with any of this?" huffed Ally, listening carefully to the argument.

"Because you were my second mistake," came Radu's emotionally charged response.

*****

LAST OF THE MOUNTAIN MEN

"What is the dark web exactly?" asked Lance as Gabriel struck the keys on the computer with a speed and precision that seemed barely credible.

"It's like the normal worldwide web but secret and harder to access," replied Gabriel robotically, unable to draw her eyes away from the screen.

"What's on there?"

"Very illegal porn, drug dealers, terrorists and international crime syndicates."

"Oh right," replied Lance uneasily. "You can't be on it very much, then."

"Boom, I'm in!" giggled Gabriel.

"That was quick," said Lance suspiciously. "It only took you about thirty seconds… and by the looks of it you have quite a few messages in your inbox from someone called darkscreamqueen?"

"I've been very lonely," she said, turning to him. "I'm going to give it up, babe, promise."

Lance hadn't officially had a girlfriend before unless Libby Ansell counted when he was six. He didn't think it was officially registered as they'd only held hands for nine seconds and exchanged notes with hearts scrawled in crayon. If Gabriel was his first girlfriend, and the jury was still out on that, from the subject lines of these messages she'd exchanged quite a lot more than love letters with some of these dubious online strangers.

"What does S&M stand for?" asked Lance, innocently scrolling down some of the messages.

"Oh, don't worry, I'll show you!"

"Sausage and mash?"

"No. Isn't there something we needed to do?"

"Yes, you're right, let's get the message out to the Oblivion Doctrine."

"What do you want me to write?" asked Gabriel.

Daniel had been a little vague on this point before he raced off to find the last of the letters.

"Write, 'Mountain Men code broken, money found, call off your action'," he replied.

LAST OF THE MOUNTAIN MEN

"Ok."

It didn't take long before the responses came through. Hundreds streamed in to the dodgy inbox from countries all over the world. From Albania to Zaire, the alphabet of world disorder was primed and ready to act. It was happening today and, although some of the replies were foreign, Lance understood most of them. The return messages were simple and similar.

Prove it.

"They don't believe us," said Gabriel.

"I can't blame them really. A sex addict and a lanky academic posting from a sleepy village in a backwater of England with zero internet history in this group isn't that convincing if you're a hardened money-hungry nut job desperate to cause someone else's chaos. What would you do?"

"Rebel," she said a little too emphatically.

"We need to show them the money," added Lance.

It was less than twenty-four hours since he'd last seen or heard from Hudson. It had seemed an impossible task. There was no way of knowing how many letters there might be in the sequence after the one he was chasing in Geneva. If the next in the chain was on the other side of the globe, he'd never make it in time. Even if it wasn't somewhere remote and he'd managed to retrieve all the letters, that still didn't indicate which bank was holding the money in its vaults. Without that a blizzard of terror was about to be unleased on the cornerstones of civilisation.

Lance reached for his phone and dialled the number Daniel had given him during his own police interview last weekend. It seemed to ring for an age before the agent answered it.

"What?" grunted Daniel as if he'd been distracted from a much more important task.

"Mr Hudson, I'm with Gabriel but the message isn't working. They don't believe us. Where are you?"

"I'm doing some banking," replied Daniel, sounding exasperated and worn out.

LAST OF THE MOUNTAIN MEN

"Which bank?"

"It's the one the hedge fund that owned the Mountain Inc uses. It's offshore in Bermuda."

"You're in Bermuda!"

"No. It's the twenty-first century and they've got internet banking these days. Plus, twelve billion dollars in notes is a bit too much to carry out in bags."

"I see your point," replied Lance, feeling foolish. "Then where are you?"

"London, but I'm struggling. I've used two of my three guesses to access the bank account already, but they've both been declined. I only have one chance left. I need to know the missing number in the sequence. I have 02, 04, 10, 11, 15, and 17, but I'm missing one."

Lance knew this already. It had been in the back of his mind like the name of a song you knew but couldn't remember. Which Mountain Man was Jean Cavalier in the sequence? Compared to the other Mountain Men there was almost nothing written about his achievements or history to offer him any clues. All he really knew was the date. Seventeen hundred to seventeen forty-five. They knew Masaniello was the fourth and was active in the middle of sixteen hundreds, so there was no way Jean could be the fifth: he hadn't been born.

Masaniello was killed in the rebellion he'd created so he must have passed the title to someone also involved. The letters had all been posted to contemporaries or co-conspirators, Lance knew that much. Sir Christopher Wren's name, which had originally led them on a wild goose chase to Pudding Lane earlier in the week, must have been associated with one of the Mountain Men. Lance considered whether either John Evelyn or Samuel Pepys might have been the sixth candidate: both men were friends of Wren's. If that hunch was correct it meant Jean Cavalier came after that. But was he number seven or number eight?

"If only Ally were here," mumbled Lance.

"She's not with you?" replied Daniel in surprise.

LAST OF THE MOUNTAIN MEN

"No, she's being held hostage in the church by William Haggar and Radu Goga."

"Oh shit. Lance, I need that number so I can get to you as soon as possible. Hurry."

Seven or eight. Lance scoured his mind. Images from the last week which were photographically imprinted on his memory flashed through him. Even the merest fraction might contain the answer. Regimentally he scanned his memories for answers. He pictured himself in the Weston, then in his car, the police cell and then the interview room. Just as Daniel had done with Ally an hour earlier, Lance's interrogation included the image of the FBI agent holding up his tablet and swiping through the letters. They shot in front of his eyes. Then he froze on a picture with the name Élie Marion scrawled on the envelope. The number on the letter was zero seven.

"It's zero eight," he bellowed down the phone.

"Are you sure?"

"Completely. Élie Marion was involved in an attempted uprising in London with a scientist called Nicolas Fatio. He must have gained the title from the Royal Society where he'd have met Pepys and Evelyn. Jean Cavalier came after them, he's number eight."

"Lance, your mental dexterity is quite breathtaking," replied Hudson.

"Thanks," replied Lance.

"There's only one problem."

"What?"

"I've already tried zero eight in my last guess. Maybe it's zero seven, I haven't tried that combination yet. Should I try it?"

Lance's ego deflated like a burst Zeppelin. What had he missed? Puzzles required your full attention, an open mind and access to all of the facts. He'd scanned his mind from beginning to end and missed something. Then it hit him like a ninety-mile-an-hour yorker from a Caribbean fast bowler.

LAST OF THE MOUNTAIN MEN

"You are not the beginning," breathed Lance down the phone. "It's not just about Ally, it's about the money. Enter the numbers in reverse, using zero eight as before."

The line went quiet. Gabriel and Lance waited patiently for Daniel's voice to break the silence.

"I'm in," replied Daniel calmly. "It's all here. All twelve billion and change."

"Send a screenshot," replied Lance.

*****

"I'm a mistake!" screamed Ally. "What mistake?"

Somewhere out of sight to the left of the altar a door creaked open and an elderly gentleman with thinning, silver-grey hair emerged holding a shotgun resolutely in front of him. Thin and withered in stature, he strode confidently out into the light and aimed the gun at Ms Honeywell's shaking frame.

"Dad!" gasped Ally in astonishment. "What are you doing here?"

"That's Radu Goga," replied Buff, repositioning the gun from Ally's back to a position hovering over her shoulder.

"Bollocks! His name is Horace Oldfield," she offered in rebuttal. "You've got the wrong man."

"It's both," replied Radu softly.

"What!?"

"Like Philibert Lesage, who you're so interested in, I have had many masks down the years," answered Radu gently.

"But why didn't you tell me?" moaned Ally.

"Deep shame and fear," he exclaimed, holding back his own tears. "My biggest mistake was leaving you and your mother to the mercy of men like this."

"Men like this saved her life," argued Buff. "She'd be dead if it wasn't for the Mountain Men."

"You only did that so you could get to me one day."

LAST OF THE MOUNTAIN MEN

"You lied about having dementia!" added Ally disdainfully, not focusing on the most relevant revelations. "I bet you're not even Northern!"

"I've lied about many things," replied Radu. "You must have so many questions. I'm sorry I've never had the courage to answer them. Today, I promise you'll get those answers."

Ally experienced a powerful vibration on her shoulder which was accompanied a split second later by a loud explosion that deafened her left ear and forced her to the ground. The acrid smell of burnt charcoal wafted through the air and a small cloud of grey smoke floated maliciously above her head. Through her hazy vision the figure of an old man lay crumpled against the foot of the altar, arms outstretched in the sign of the cross, blood streaming from his chest.

"Dad!"

She struggled to her feet and rushed forward before Buff's voice interrupted her.

"Stop. There's nothing you can do for him."

"You bastard!" she shouted. "He was the only one who knew the truth."

"Not the only one. Now you and the old woman know the true identity of the Mountain Man," he replied, fixing his gun once more on Ally's position a few metres in front of him. "You're not the beginning, Ally Oldfield… you are the end."

It might have ended forty-five years ago in a small orchard on foreign soil in shiny, red shoes. Now it would end in an empty church, in a village largely ignored by the outside world, wearing shabby flats. The gun fired again and, just like the memory that felt so real it could have been yesterday, she cowered in fear. The sound of another body hitting the carpet-lined flagstones of the church floor filled the nave. After it was obvious the bullet hadn't struck her, she opened her eyes, half-expecting to see Honeywell's body next to her father's.

LAST OF THE MOUNTAIN MEN

The shock of the last few minutes had rendered Honeywell speechless for the first time in her life, but the shaking through her body proved beyond doubt she was still alive.

Behind Ally, in the doorway of the church, Norman Dearlove was shrouded in a plume of grey smoke. Buff's body lay on the floor, blood seeping onto the now purple carpet. Norman stood resolutely, gun gripped firmly in his hand and the ubiquitous smile still clinging to his face despite the moral gravity of his actions. Seconds later a mob of police officers burst into the building wielding firearms incompetently and shouting at anyone who'd listen to 'get on the floor'. The cavalry was here but the damage had already been done.

- Chapter 30 -

Post-Mortems

Ally watched from a solitary bench at front of the church next to the graveyard as they wheeled out two black plastic-coated bodies. History had died with Horace, and both he and it would be buried out of reach. Ally found her emotions hard to place. Ultimately her father had been living a lie that had directly influenced the pattern of her life. He had ample chance to make it right but hadn't found the courage to do so. A lack of answers had always been difficult for Ally to accept, and she'd made a successful career out of ensuring she generally didn't have any.

The emotional cocktail shaking through her had a base ingredient of fury, a dash of anger all mixed together with a generous measure of grief topped off with a slice of loss. Horace had been her only real family for the last thirty years. His arrival helped release her from the false and humiliating abuse inflicted by an adopted family who never truly accepted her as one of their own. Now she was truly alone. Often our worst fears are hidden under the surface, contradicted by our own verbal denials. Loneliness wasn't her wish, as she made people believe: it was her inevitable destiny.

The image of loneliness was further compounded by the delicate removal of Ms Honeywell from the church strapped down in a wheelchair. They might as well have been removing a mirror, such was the symmetry of the path Ally found herself on. Honeywell's face was pale and gaunt from her ordeal but none of it had negatively affected her indestructible vocal cords.

POST-MORTEMS

"Scandal, me darlins', here in Stanton!" she screamed indignantly to anyone within earshot. "It'll never be the same again. Scared forever. It's her fault, me darlins'. Bloody newcomers."

"Stay calm, Ms Honeywell," replied one of the paramedics checking her blood pressure as they trundled down the uneven path towards Ally.

"Arrest her!" screamed the old woman.

"Not today," said DCI Bolton who'd moved silently behind Ally's bench. "But maybe one day."

"What happened to Norman?" asked Ally keen to thank him for his bravery and unable to pick him out of the crowd.

"Removed from duty pending an internal enquiry."

"Why?"

"He's not licenced to carry a firearm," replied Bolton sternly. "When we heard the first shot go off and were discussing how to storm the church, he took a gun out of the van without our knowledge. He broke the line of command and every rule in the book."

"Norman doesn't believe in your rule book. He prefers to use his instincts and it's a good job for me that he did. Maybe he deserves a medal rather than an enquiry."

"Procedure is…"

"Screw procedure. Do you always do what you're told?"

"Yes. It's how you get to become a senior officer."

"Then thank God Norman isn't a brown-nosing pedant like you. The world needs rebels who are willing to see past rules to reach the right outcome."

"These so-called Mountain Men were rebels, too: didn't really work out for them, did it?"

"Rebellion isn't the problem, integrity is."

"Maybe you've been on their side all along," replied Bolton, considering whether to go back on his original remark about not arresting her.

"I admire them for one thing: they work mostly on their own."

POST-MORTEMS

"You may wish to review that policy given your escape today, don't you think? You definitely had some help. Anyway, it's time we sent you off with Honeywell to get checked over," said Bolton, pointing to the ambulance that had just received a rather talkative octogenarian with anger management issues.

"Will you heck. There's nothing wrong with me that a strong mug of coffee won't fix. I'm going home."

Ignoring Bolton's remonstrations and so-called 'procedure', Ally shook her legs into life and scurried between the squad cars, dodged the police tape and frenetic activity to greet the other side of the road. Through the gate, up the shallow bank and in through the front door. On the other side a jubilant party was in full swing and it had nothing to do with her escape to safety.

Heavy, thumping music roared out of the kitchen, making the pictures in the hall vibrate in their frames. Gabriel occasionally came into view dancing around the house like a raver on a speed overdose, while Lance desperately tried to follow in her wake, occasionally receiving a tight embrace or tongue down his throat in reward for the effort.

"What the fuck are you two doing?!" shouted Ally, enraged by the insensitivity being displayed.

"We won!" shouted Lance. "We've stopped the Mountain Men!"

"No, you didn't! Norman just shot him in the back of the head."

"No, the other ones. We just stopped world carnage," added Gabriel. "Isn't it great!?"

"No, not really I've just lost my father."

"That happened on Friday," replied Gabriel in response to what was old news. "Stop milking it and stealing our thunder."

"He's dead!" she confirmed bluntly.

Gabriel and Lance's impromptu dancing ended abruptly.

"I'm really sorry, Dr Oldfield," said Lance.

POST-MORTEMS

Gabriel reluctantly turned the music off as the sombre homeowner was led into the kitchen. Lance made Ally a coffee and the three of them congregated around the kitchen table to share their stories. Ally described the events in the church and the end of Buff. Gabriel didn't even flinch. Lance updated Ally on the last few days. Finding the Courier, working out the sequence, locating the money and stopping the uprising.

"Once we shared a picture of the account balance," finished Lance, "everyone online started to panic. I think they realised it was over and they'd never get their hands on the cash. Chaos has a price, it would seem."

"Where's Hudson now?" asked Ally.

"On his way here from London," added Gabriel.

"Arrived from London," said Daniel, who was consuming the doorway to the kitchen and made the others jump. "Door was open."

"Mission accomplished," replied Ally bitterly. "No need to stay, you have your money. Don't you have a flight to catch?"

"I'm not quite finished here," he added. "Perhaps you kids can give us some space."

Lance and Gabriel glanced at each other and grinned knowingly. Unfortunately, they weren't thinking the same thought. Gabriel envisaged a booze-fuelled afternoon at the 'Twilight Alehouse', in the village followed by some sordid sexual experimentation, while Lance was wondering if his parents were free so he might introduce them to his first-ever girlfriend. Somehow, they'd work out a compromise that involved getting Lance's parents shit-faced.

The youngsters giggled their way down the hall and out into the hubbub of the street, still a mass of police activity and ambulances.

Hudson helped himself to a mug from the kitchen sink, poured out a measure of coffee and perched awkwardly on a stool.

POST-MORTEMS

"Quite a fortnight. I think next time I come to England I'll try to see more tourist attractions."

"I would normally recommend Big Ben, but you might need to bring diving gear. Unless your government is feeling generous and offer to pay for its rebuilding from the cool twelve billion dollars they've just stolen."

"You never know," said Hudson unconvincingly. "Ally, they told me what happened to Radu Goga on the way in. I'm sorry."

"Don't you mean Horace?"

"Which do you prefer?"

"I'm not sure yet."

"Give it time."

"Time's the one thing I no longer have."

"It's not just time you need, though, is it?" said Daniel softly.

"No, but some things can't be bought," she said, referring to the only motive he'd displayed throughout the whole time she'd known him.

Ally popped the kettle back on the hob and waited in silence for its steam to whistle out into the kitchen.

"What will they do with the money?" she asked.

"It'll be used wisely."

"No, it won't," she huffed desperately. "The US will invest it in new ways to suppress personal freedoms. More security, more surveillance, more weapons to frighten poorer, less advanced nations."

"Do you hate my country, Ally? Do you believe that we are a force for good or evil?"

"I hate what we have all become, irrespective of which land mass you happen to call home. It runs against everything that the Mountain Men were built for, and they've ended up funding the very people they wanted to change. Ironic, isn't it?"

"It wasn't their money, it was Mario's."

"It's the people's money. It was the common man who blindly invested in the Oblivion Doctrine or were scammed by Mario's vast empire of misinformation. It should go back to the people."

"Let's see what happens."

"Don't you feel disgusted by it?"

"I'm just doing my job, Ally. Like you, I take pride in doing it well."

"But that's where we differ. I do it right, not well."

Daniel took a long gulp of his hot drink and reflected for a moment. He'd made plenty of mistakes this week. His blindness had made the authorities dance to the enemy's tune. An insatiable desire to discover the identify of Radu Goga had led them to him and ultimately his death. Those facts were inescapable. Collateral damage happened, Hudson knew that, but he didn't have to like it.

"What will you do now?" asked Hudson.

"Prepare for a funeral no one will attend and go back to work, if they let me. What else can I do?"

"Whatever you want to do," replied Hudson. "Our lives are not anchored by our history."

"I'll never know my history," she growled.

"Did Radu tell you that you'd get the answers today?" asked Hudson in an eerie flashback to events only a few hours ago.

"Yes. How do you know that?"

"Because he told me," said Hudson firmly.

Ally froze solid, unable to think clearly or grasp the right question. "When? Where?"

"I went to see him on Friday at the Furlong Nursing Home, around lunchtime, a few hours before I expected you'd go there."

"It was you who wrote Radu Goga's name in the visitors' book? I've been trying to figure out, if Horace and Radu were one and the same person, why that name would appear."

"I wanted the nurses to announce me to him, I wanted to see his reaction. I also thought it might give you a clue."

"You could have just told me."

"Things were moving so fast that day."

POST-MORTEMS

"But how did you know that Horace was really Radu?"

"Initially it was that photo," said Daniel, pointing to the black and white picture on the windowsill. "The FBI provided me with a photo of him from the nineteen eighties, and when I saw your photo, I knew the two of you were connected somehow. The rest of the story took quite some time to piece together. I didn't know much about him, but I suspected there was more to him than I was being allowed access to. It was only when McNamee relented and sent me further information, just before I went to see him, that I discovered he had a daughter. The conclusion had to be she was you. The rest of the story I received first-hand."

"He told you his story!"

"Yes."

"Why you and not me? I've been trying to get him to open up for years."

"Because my visit confirmed to him that the Mountain Men were back and that their actions and my errors had unwittingly put them onto your scent. He knew if they identified you, eventually they'd be able to get to him. I didn't know what he was going to do next, but he wanted me to know his story in case he wasn't able to tell you personally. Would you like to know it now?"

When you've searched your whole life for meaning, being offered the truth can be terrifying. Ever since Antoine had encouraged her to let people in, she'd hunted for the answer: now all she had to do was say yes and that quest would be over, but it would change her forever. She'd no longer be able to hold onto the shroud of history like a comfort blanket.

"Tell me everything," Ally choked.

Daniel spent the next hour trying to recount Radu's story amongst the constant interruptions of Ally's questions. He described how Radu reacted when a split-second opportunity to pursue a greater moral purpose was presented to him and how the consequence of leaving his family tore him apart. It was months later that he learnt of their fate, although it came as no surprise. The family of defectors were always treated as traitors themselves.

"I'm only now recounting those terrible days," said Ally with a shiver. "I'd suppressed them away only for them to be triggered over the last few weeks. Is that why you pulled the gun on me in Belfast?"

"Yes. It was just a hunch. If you were directly related to him then I believed, from what I'd read, that you'd have suffered because of his actions. I'm sorry. It was a cruel thing to do but it was necessary to understand what was going on in your mind."

"I certainly know now. I don't think I'll ever be able to wear red shoes again. What happened to my mother?"

Daniel gave more details of what Radu knew about his wife and how he'd first learnt of her fate but wouldn't believe it until he discovered the truth decades later.

"What about me? Why didn't he come for me earlier?"

"He said there was no news of you, so he assumed you'd been killed by the KGB in retribution. It was only when Diego tried to have him killed a few years later that he learnt what happened to you. Diego was desperate to gloat about how he'd saved Radu's daughter from death. That's when Radu knew he could never mention what he knew about the Mountain Men for fear that Diego would kill you. That's why he kept the truth from you. He'd left you in danger once; he wasn't going to do it again. When he travelled incognito to the UK in the early nineties, around the same time that Diego went to prison, he sought you out. When he found you, he again falsified his identity and subsequently so did you."

"What do you mean, my identity?"

"Your name isn't Alison Oldfield. Your adoptive parents decided to retain your first name as your middle name, which gave me another clue to your identity. Your real name is Oriana Goga."

"Doctor Oriana Goga," she corrected him instantly.

"I guess it must be."

POST-MORTEMS

"If I was originally born in Romania, why did I end up being adopted by a British family?"

"I think only Diego can answer that fully, but my guess would be for purposes of secrecy. I assume the Brownlees weren't just your adoptive parents. I suspect they were also working within Diego's circles. There's no way the KGB would have allowed Diego to remove you from them, so it's likely he didn't want anyone to find out. The best place was the last place anyone would look, the West."

"At least that explains why I can read Romanian: seems I've retained some of my early learning."

Daniel drained his now cold coffee and shifted his body position as if to leave.

"Where are you going?"

"Home. I've given you everything he told me."

"Oh, there's a lot more that you know that doesn't concern my father. You knew who Buff really was, didn't you?" asked Ally.

"No, not until the end. We knew that he'd visited Diego in prison, that's why we were following him. He didn't strike us as a particularly interesting suspect."

"You could have arrested him anyway."

"On what grounds: weak vocabulary or poor choice in girlfriends?" he chuckled.

"Sometimes people aren't all they seem, are they?"

"True." He certainly wasn't who Gabriel thought he was. "Anyway, thanks for the coffee."

"Where are you going?"

"I think I've earned an expensive holiday," he replied with a wink. "Let's hope the FBI can afford to pay for it."

As Daniel got to the kitchen door, he remembered something important. He reached inside his leather holdall and removed a carefully wrapped object. "I promised to bring this back."

After Daniel had left, Ally gently lifted the paper on the parcel and the unmistakable cover of Nostradamus's book peeked back. She quickly removed it to check the preface.

POST-MORTEMS

There was the unique prophecy and now all four lines of it had come true one way or another.

- Chapter 31 -

New Beginnings

All she really wanted to do was sleep, but when did she get what she wanted? How much slumber she'd missed out on was measured in days rather than hours. Just for once she hoped the Universe would ignore her for a good eight or nine hours.

Fat chance.

It was Monday morning and the Universe's harpies, those feathery, little arseholes outside her window, were determined to remind her it was supposed to be a workday. Finches, sparrows, chiffchaffs and a distant cockerel weren't familiar with the concept of pulling a 'sick day'. Ally had never taken one before. The very thought of not going to work for any other reason than death would have been an abomination just last week. Today it was necessary. The last week had left her mentally and physically exhausted. It was time to enjoy a day of peace, and for once the house was empty.

Gabriel had dragged Lance away in a frightening act of sexual aggression. Presumably they were holed up in the nearest hotel where Gabriel would be completing Lance's final leap into manhood. The poor guy was probably as petrified as he was exhilarated. If they were still together by morning the relationship would officially be regarded as one of Gabriel's longest.

Ally gave up. Sleep would be just another of life's luxuries afforded to those who could afford double glazing or their own sparrowhawk. She slipped out of bed and removed the eye bogeys from impeding her vision. Now that sleep had been removed a different plan formed in her

NEW BEGINNINGS

head. It included coffee, Mozart's piano concerto number twenty on her hi-fi, and a good book. Failing that, a bad book, it didn't really matter: today she needed to escape into someone else's world. The doorbell's chime immediately destroyed any hope of it.

She almost reached the door by the third ring. It would have been a personal record if she had. At least that was something to look forward to. Her hand rested on the catch as she visualised the potential occupants on the doorstep. She could ignore it? Pretend it never happened. She peered through the spyhole, deciding the door would remain firmly shut if Honeywell was on the other side. She wasn't. She didn't recognise who was.

Reluctantly she released the catch.

"Good morning, ma'am," said a serious-looking American wearing an expensive, dark suit and holding an umbrella to shield against rain that wasn't falling.

"Is it absolutely urgent?" expired Ally desperately. "I mean, surely I can have one day off. I'm perfectly prepared to return to the disappointment and chaos on Tuesday if you'd like to bring your obvious drama back here then."

"Sadly not."

"Right," sighed Ally.

"My name is Jeff McNamee: you may already know who I am."

"Nope."

"I'm Daniel Hudson's boss: I thought he might have mentioned me."

"Nope."

"Is he here?"

"Nope."

"Do you know where he is?"

"Nope."

"You're not being very helpful," huffed McNamee.

"Aren't I? Shame."

"He hasn't returned for duty. I wondered if you could shed any light on that?"

NEW BEGINNINGS

"Nope," she said, finding her responses were boring herself. "How did you end up as his boss?"

"What do you mean?"

"Oh, so you do know how to ask a good question. I wondered if you did. Is this going to take long? It's just I'd planned to count my coffee beans today."

"The money, Dr Oldfield, where is the money?"

"I assume it has been consumed by your vast national debt."

"No. I thought you might know where they both were."

Ally had seriously misread Daniel Hudson. It wasn't all about the money, or about the dedication to the corrupt system he represented. If McNamee's inference was anything to go on, Daniel hadn't returned the money as she'd accused him of last night. If he hadn't, then where was it? He wasn't stupid enough to keep it and greed wasn't his motive anyway. Like Ally, what Daniel cared most about was the answer. Solving the riddle to prove he was worthy enough of the challenge. He'd done that and yet still stopped long enough to give her some closure over her past.

"Have you checked down the side of the sofa," replied Ally sarcastically.

"It's quite hard to hide twelve billion dollars, no thoughts on where it is?"

"Are you imagining Daniel's on the run with the world's biggest suitcase! It's all electronic these days."

"That money belongs to the state."

"No, it doesn't. It belongs to the people. It was never yours to take back. You represent greed. A modern system that rewards a policy of 'everyone for themselves' and step on your neighbour in the pursuit of ever-increasing wealth. The Mountain Men stood for something purer. They stood for the will of the people, not the pursuit of profit. Yes, sometimes they got it wrong but good intentions poorly executed are always worthier than bad intentions executed well. I don't know where your money is, Mr McNamee,

NEW BEGINNINGS

but I do hope you and your paymasters don't find it. There are enough rich and powerful men in this world."

She attempted to slam the door, but a size ten shoe disrupted it.

"I will be watching you, Dr Oldfield. I never fail. This is not the end of the matter."

"But I'm not the end," replied Ally. "I am the beginning."

The foot was removed, and the door continued its original journey to the frame.

For an hour peace returned to her world. The first cup of coffee went into her system so quickly she couldn't be sure if it had happened at all. She poured a second cup just in case and sank her body into the deepest and most comfortable of her three-piece suite. No sooner had she reacquainted herself with her own leather arse groove than the doorbell chimed. She ignored it, and the two follow-ups. The only thing that might extract her from this sofa right now was a nuclear strike. Down the corridor a key turned in the front door lock. Who had a key other than her? The landlord? What would he be doing here? Maybe Honeywell had already got started with a petition to turf her out for turning the village into a humongous crime scene.

The catch on the door clicked open and the breeze rattled in through the open door.

"Ally!" came a familiar voice down the corridor.

"Shit."

She was back.

Gabriel burst into the living room with the force of a jet fighter. The random, blinding colours of her normal fashion sense were absent, replaced by a formal more English countryside get-up. Her hair was tied back in a conventional fashion and she was wearing almost no make-up. If it hadn't been the familiar voice and brash entrance, Ally would have confused her for Lady Muck.

"Why do you have a key?" demanded Ally.

"It's so I can open the door," she replied honestly.

NEW BEGINNINGS

"I know what the function of a key is, I'm asking why you specifically have one for my door. Where did you get it?"

"Buff had one."

"Brilliant," she huffed. "I wonder what else he stole from me."

"Do you like my new styling?" said Gabriel, pirouetting to give Ally every angle.

"No."

"Oh thanks. It's lovely, isn't it?" replied Gabriel, demonstrating that nothing had changed about her ability to listen poorly. "It's all thanks to Lance. God, I love him. He's made me realise that I've been trying to be someone I'm not."

"And to prove that point you've dressed like a person… you're not… again!"

"It's not important…"

"Correct. Now go away. I have some important solitude to get on with."

"Not today. I've brought someone to see you."

"If it's anyone other than Bishop Desmond Tutu, I'm not interested," she answered, waving Gabriel away from her and closing her eyes in a hope that magic spells were still a thing.

"Better than him," said an old man's voice at the door.

"Antoine! Where have you been?"

"Here and there, but definitely here now. Can I come in?"

"Of course, there's a fresh pot on the counter, grab a mug and make yourself comfortable. It's good to see you," she replied truthfully.

"Thanks. I see you're making good progress."

Soon the three old acquaintances were fully charged with caffeine and sitting in a circle around the roaring wood-burner. They exchanged stories from the past few weeks and reminisced on what others called memories, and Ally called nightmares, of their shared past. It hadn't been the morning Oldfield had hoped for but there was

NEW BEGINNINGS

something unique about it. The last week had changed her perspective and washed away much of the trauma she'd carried through her adult life. Now here she was socialising and actually enjoying it.

"This isn't just a courtesy call," said Antoine, bluntly cutting through the warmth of their company. "There has been a development."

"A development?" asked Ally.

"Yes. You'll remember I sent you a letter about the strange bank account that was in the name of William Haggar?"

"Yes," replied both women.

"The account has been transferred to me. It appears Mr Haggar did not make arrangements for the next Mountain Man to take up his post before he died."

"Does that make you the next Mountain Man?" asked Gabriel.

"No. The account has always been in my family's name as a backup in case such an eventuality occurred. It happened once in the eighteenth century from what I can see. At that time the executor passed the title on based on who they believed to be the right candidate. That's not my main news, though. Yesterday the account received a new deposit."

"Let me guess," said Ally reflecting on the morning's first visitor. "Twelve billion dollars."

"Twelve point three four billion, to be precise."

"You're rich!" shouted Gabriel, returning to her former persona that valued materialistic gain above right and wrong.

"No. The money belongs to the Mountain Men. Philibert's vision was to protect mankind from the worst of the establishment. He wanted to give society hope from the pressures placed upon them. There is much work still to do."

"Then who are you going to choose?" asked Ally.

"I think there is a reason why so many of the Mountain Men failed," said Antoine. "Men have always been the

NEW BEGINNINGS

establishment. Men have consistently shown down the centuries that they are susceptible to the corruptibility of power. Therefore, Mr Haggar will be the last of the Mountain Men. It's time for change."

"Oh no. Not me. I'm done with mountains," said Ally, wagging her finger defiantly in the air.

"I wasn't talking about you. I've already formally made the account transfer. Gabriel," he said with a smile, "you will be the first of the Mountain Women."

Antoine passed her the details of her new responsibility.

Gabriel gazed in wonder at a bank statement that featured more noughts than she'd ever seen. An intense energy rose inside her gut, did cartwheels through her chest and burst out of every available orifice. The sound resembled a squirrel exploding.

"Seriously!?" said Ally in dismay. "Have you lost your tiny little mind!"

"Now that doesn't sound like the new Ally to me. Show more faith."

Gabriel clattered onto the carpet and started praying to the log-burner.

"What are you going to do first with this burden?" asked Antoine as she flopped on the floor.

"Buy lots of shoes."

"See what I mean?" exclaimed Ally. "You've created a monster."

"It was a joke, Ally," rebuffed Gabriel. "It's time that the Mountain Women saved mankind from themselves. We will be a force for the protection of the environment because if we don't there will be no more mountains to climb. We'll take on and beat big business. We'll change politics. We'll save cute animals, particularly the really fluffy ones."

"A noble cause," said Antoine. "I'm sure Ally will be right behind you."

"I'll be hiding, but yeah, right behind you."

"What about you, Antoine?" asked Gabriel. "You'll be there to help, won't you?"

NEW BEGINNINGS

"I'm retired."

"Lucky bastard," whispered Ally.

*****

The doorbell chimed once more.

Since Antoine and Gabriel left just after lunchtime, Monday had conformed with her initial wishes. Dinner was in the oven and she was looking forward to eating it. Cooking wasn't a great love but eating never got old. Surely, this time it had to be Honeywell at the door? If you'd had two sets of visitors in any one day and neither of them had been her, it was just a matter of time.

The doorbell rang again.

What could she replace it with? she thought. Maybe a nice, shiny door knocker with a silencer on it. Perhaps nothing at all. Let them use their scrunched-up fist and beat on the door like the old days. Then there was always technology. If she bought one of those fancy contraptions that videoed who was at the door and alerted your mobile phone, she'd be able to ignore Honeywell from a safe distance. If it had a two-way transmitter, she might be able to haunt the old witch? Her lips curled into an evil grin.

The bell went for the third time and Ally's fantasy evaporated. She launched up from her seat angrily.

She flung the door open and a preformulated sentence of the most despicable collection of profanities seamlessly tripped off her tongue.

"Piss off, you rancorous, pus-ridden, arsed-faced harpy."

"Fruity."

"Norman!" she said in surprise. "I was expecting…"

"Honeywell, I hope!"

"Yes."

"She's bedridden after her ordeal. I've never seen the village so relaxed."

"Give her time. How are you?"

NEW BEGINNINGS

"I'm great. The investigation into my conduct starts in the morning but do you know what, I'm not bothered what happens. I'm just glad I could make a positive difference."

"Thank you, bravery isn't a common trait. What are the flowers for?" she said, noticing the bouquet of lilies under his arm.

"They're for you."

"Why?" she said suspiciously.

"Why not?"

"Because it's weird."

"Women usually like flowers."

Her face suggested she might be the exception.

"What do you want?" she said returning to the abruptness she was famous for. "I've just put dinner on."

"Would you like to go to the pub?"

"The pub?"

"Yes. It's this building in the village that serves drinks and acts as a sort of meeting place for friends and members of the community," he replied sarcastically.

"I've never been."

"I know, that's why I'm asking you."

"I have dinner on."

"Then turn it off."

Ally was torn. A man, whose company she actually enjoyed, was asking her to do something that normal people did. Was this the future? Was it better than the past? The junction was open, and the two options were highlighted by synaptic neon signs. Was she going to be brave, like Norman had been in the church, and go forward to something new, or retreat to something safe, which happened to be a shepherd's pie? She stalled at the neuropathway traffic lights.

"What's that?" she pointed to an object peeking out from under the bunch of flowers.

"One of your books. I was hoping you'd sign it for me," he said, holding it out to her. "Big fan."

NEW BEGINNINGS

"I didn't know this was still in print," she said assessing the slightly worn cover and tracing her finger over the title, *The Truth about the Voynich Manuscript*.

"It isn't," blushed Norman. "Took me quite a while to locate a copy."

"I'm not surprised. Unfortunately, it didn't have the success that my Nostradamus books had. Maybe one day people will appreciate it."

"What about that drink, then?" asked Norman, who was nothing but persistent.

"Is it a date?" replied Ally uncertainly.

"Yes, I suppose so."

One of the synaptic neon direction lights illuminating her two choices flickered and went out.

"Why not?" she smiled. "It's only shepherd's pie."

THE END

Dr Ally Oldfield will return…

Sign up to the newsletter
www.tonymoyle.com/contact/

- Fact or Fiction -

The History of the Mountain Men

Although *Last of the Mountain Men* is primarily a work of fiction, there's a huge amount of factual history featured in it. The main focal points in developing the story were to understand what happened to Philibert Lesage after the conclusion of *The End of the World is Nigh* (*TEOTWIN*) and to explain what the final line of the original prophecy meant. In truth 'and the men of the mountain will burn' was a line I'd originally intended to have a different meaning but after reviewing my notes for the last book I couldn't remember what it was!

That created its own mystery.

I couldn't stop thinking about it.

Who were these Mountain Men?

Philibert's story was in essence about the underdog taking on the establishment. Like the majority of the people living in his era, life was almost impossible. Only the very smallest minority of people had power and wealth, often achieved through the persecution of those who didn't. We view those times with a sense of disgust and think ourselves lucky that we are not subjected to such inequality. Although much has changed in our standards of living, maybe we should also stop and compare the reality of our own times.

We live in an age where the wealthiest eighty people collectively have more affluence than four billion people, half of the planet's population.

THE HISTORY OF THE MOUNTAIN MEN

If you're not angry about this, then you're not paying enough attention. Perhaps equality has not advanced as much as we think?

The process of change is often a slow one. Real change is not achieved in one lifetime but often over many. It was this premise that got me thinking about Philibert's desire to be 'the first ripple striking the banks of the establishment'. When I first wrote that line in *TEOTWIN* it was always meant as a reference to the French Revolution that would partly realise the prediction some two hundred years on from Phil's own story.

There have been hundreds of revolutions down the centuries, from changes in technology, ideology and political systems. Not all of them, including those that involved the toppling of governments or sovereigns, have been violent. Neither have all of them been successful. But they are not events that spark from a vacuum. They develop over time with the slow erosion of people's tolerance to the status quo. They sometimes appear to be random, but if you track their causes they rarely are. They are dominoes set up by the passage of history and the events of others. But what if past events weren't just inspirations for future ones? What if these seismic developments in history were directly and purposely connected to each other?

It was this thought that stimulated my desire to research and learn more about rebellious events. I went first to the French Revolution, an event I knew little about. What I discovered made my mouth drop open. I only needed to see two words to know I was on the right track to a story.

The Mountain.

One of the political groups responsible for the downfall of the French royal family was called the Mountain. It perfectly connected the prophecy and Philibert's words.

I'm often taken aback by the randomness of chance. It's not the first time one of these writing schisms has appeared through my books. Part of me feels that sometimes the story itself is leading me blindfolded in a direction of its

THE HISTORY OF THE MOUNTAIN MEN

choosing. Equally part of me feels that if you've written four hundred thousand published words the chance of these schisms occurring is greater than you might imagine. Nevertheless, the discovery of these two words, related to the subject I was researching, instantly compelled me to want to write the story. If a book wants to be written, you shouldn't try to stop it.

What I didn't realise at that point was how much more research I'd need to do!

The challenge now was to connect four hundred years of human progress through the same broad purpose. If this was only done by exploring historical figures and their influences, it would have been easy. One person's successes and actions have always had an influence or created inspiration in others. Just look at music. Where would modern popstars be without The Beatles, and where would they be without Black American pop music or Elvis, and where would they be without the Blues? However, I wanted my Mountain Men to be physically connected to each other, not just inspired by them.

I began at the end.

I'd always wanted to explore the fate of Mario Peruzzi. How would he cope with losing his status and empire? How would he feel about Nostradamus's legacy being ruined? How would he try to reap his revenge? It was logical to me that the events of *TEOTWIN* would land Mario in jail. As a French resident it also seemed reasonable to assume he'd end up in a French prison. I researched some of the more famous ones and their more notorious inmates.

In Clairvaux Prison, one name jumped out of the page.

Ilich Ramírez Sánchez.

Carlos the Jackal. A Mountain Man?

Writing about living people, as I've come to learn, is a recipe for litigation, so after much deliberation I decided to base the character Diego on Carlos rather than use the actual man. Of course, this paragraph has now made it

THE HISTORY OF THE MOUNTAIN MEN

more likely he'll sue my arse or have me silenced! Let's hope he doesn't read the appendix.

I'd always liked the idea of using Guy Fawkes in the story because his timeline crossed over with Philibert's and partly because he was a famous failure. There's a lot more comedy in heroic failure than there ever will be in success.

The challenge was set. Physically link Guy Fawkes to Carlos the Jackal through four hundred years of history. Every step would have to include notorious figures who were involved in the pursuit of social progress for the right or wrong reasons.

Easy. Right?

No.

Very, very difficult!

Just for fun here is the whole list of the Mountain Men and their connections, motivations and outcomes. Think of it like a game of Socialist Top Trumps!

The First Mountain Man – Philibert Lesage 1564–1603

Motivation – Climb the Mountain.
Outcome – Unknown.
  Fact. None whatsoever.
  Fiction. Everything. I made him up!

The Second Mountain Man – Guy Fawkes 1603–1605

Motivation – Religious freedom and the removal of the Protestant King James I.
Outcome – Failure. Executed.
  Fact. Guy Fawkes was sent to Spain in 1603 to seek support from the King of Spain to overthrow the English monarch King James. He did travel under the alias of John Johnson. The Gunpowder Plot was ultimately unsuccessful after the plotters wrote a letter to the Catholics who might have attended parliament on the day of the bombing, November 5th, 1605. Fawkes was not actually the main conspirator in the plot but was discovered at the scene with

THE HISTORY OF THE MOUNTAIN MEN

the gunpowder by the authorities. This act alone has made Fawkes synonymous with the event and the date ever since.

Fiction. Obviously he didn't meet Philibert Lesage because I made him up!

The Third Mountain Man – Oswald Tesimond 1605–1636

Motivation – Jesuit priest.
Outcome – Died of old age in Naples.

Fact. He was known to use the alias Philip Beaumont. Father Tesimond did take the confessions of Guy Fawkes and Robert Catesby prior to the plot. It is said that he also sought confession from his own priest. Central to these confessions was the need to challenge whether it was legitimate to kill in the name of God. Tesimond did escape to the continent when the authorities attempted to arrest and execute him for his part in the planning of the Gunpowder Plot. After travelling through France and Italy he settled in Naples.

Fiction. Did he meet Tommaso Aniello, aka Masaniello? Well, there isn't any evidence to conclude this either way. Tommaso was thirteen in the year Tesimond died and it's highly likely that a boy of that age at that time would have already been sent to work with his father who was indeed a fisherman. The priest Giuliano, instrumental in the uprising, may also have known the priest Tesimond.

There's no evidence to suggest Tesimond was forgetful.

The Fourth Mountain Man – Tommaso Aniello 1636–1647

Motivation – Repression of the masses.
Outcome – Mostly failed. One week of success before madness and execution.

Fact. Tommaso Aniello better known by history as Masaniello, did lead an uprising against the Viceroy of Naples due to high taxation on the common folk. There is little known about his life, most of which is only captured in paintings. It is said that the Viceroy accepted

THE HISTORY OF THE MOUNTAIN MEN

Masaniello's demands and through either poisoning or sudden dizziness from the speed of his ascent up the 'mountain' Masaniello went mad. A week later he was brutally murdered.

Fiction. He actually loved fish. (This may also not be true.)

The Fifth Mountain Man – Aniello Falcone 1647–1652

Motivation – Repression of the masses.
Outcome – Unsuccessful. Died of the Plague.

Fact. Not the most obvious candidate for someone to become embroiled in armed conflict. Falcone was a painter who took up arms with Masaniello against the ruling Spanish Empire to avenge the deaths of a nephew and a pupil. He formed an armed group called 'The Company of Death' which included other well-known artists. After the brief Naples uprising, he travelled to Rome and later to Paris where Louis XIV became his patron. Two of his pieces of art are still in the Louvre, which opened to the public as a gallery around a hundred years after Falcone's death.

Fiction. There is no concrete evidence to suggest Falcone met with John Evelyn, but they were certainly in Paris at the same time and moved in the same circles, so it's perfectly possible. Falcone never was good at painting bowls of fruit!

The Sixth Mountain Man – John Evelyn 1652–1690

Motivation – Trees.
Outcome – Died of natural causes.

Fact. John Evelyn was married to the daughter of Sir Richard Browne, the British Ambassador to France in 1647 and remained in Paris until 1652. Evelyn, the son of a gunpowder merchant, became a botanist and diarist. His diaries of the Great Fire of London were overshadowed by those of his peer, Samuel Pepys. Along with Sir

THE HISTORY OF THE MOUNTAIN MEN

Christopher Wren he was responsible for submitting plans to rebuild London after the Fire. All were rejected by King Charles II. He wrote many books over his lifetime on various subjects from horticulture, the education of children, air pollution, human culture, and his 1661 blockbuster, 'Instructions concerning erecting of a library'. Evelyn was an early member of the Royal Society, the oldest scientific institution in the world. Other notable members were Sir Isaac Newton, Wren, Pepys and Nicolas Fatio.

Fiction. He was a better painter than I gave him credit for. There's no evidence to suggest he personally erected any libraries.

The Seventh Mountain Man – Nicolas Fatio 1690–1701

Motivation – Science and social mobility.
Outcome – Died of natural causes.

Fact. Nicolas Fatio is a little remembered scientist from Switzerland who was overshadowed by his friend and colleague Sir Isaac Newton. He was appointed to the Royal Society at the age of twenty-four. His many achievements include the 'jewel bearing' which is still used in watchmaking to this day. His career was overshadowed by his involvement with the 'French Prophets' who came to London after the Camisard uprisings. These prophets included Élie Marion and Jean Cavalier. Both Jean Cavalier and Nicolas Fatio were in Geneva in 1701.

Fiction. There is no evidence to suggest that Jean and Nicolas met in 1701; however, there is much evidence of Fatio's involvement with the millenarian group that Jean Cavalier was part of. In fact, the scientist was convicted of associating with them in 1711.

The Eighth Mountain Man – Jean Cavalier 1701–1740

Motivation – Religious freedom.

THE HISTORY OF THE MOUNTAIN MEN

Outcome – Partial success. Led the Camisard rebellion but was seduced by the power offered by the authorities.

Fact. Jean Cavalier was a young and talented leader who won many victories in the battle against the French Monarch in the mostly Protestant region of Cévennes. His troops were often referred to as the 'mountaineers' on account of the geography of the region. The Camisards fought a guerrilla war against foes that were normally many times bigger in number. Like Masaniello before him, his success forced the King to negotiate. Cavalier was offered a position, his battalion of men recognised as an effective fighting force and granted pensions. He accepted the offer and some of his followers turned against him. Jean travelled to England in 1706 with other 'French Prophets' and formed a regiment of refugees that fought with British troops. In later years he wrote his autobiography and became Lieutenant Governor of Jersey. He was known to drink in the Rainbow Coffee House. He died in Chelsea, London.

Fiction. There is very little written about Jean Cavalier. There are some stories that exist that represent him as the love rival to Voltaire for the hand of Olympe. There is also a chance that two men called Jean Cavalier existed at the same time and their stories have been confused with each other.

The Ninth Mountain Man – Jean-Jacques Rousseau 1754–1767

Motivation – The Social Contract.
Outcome – Influenced the US and French revolutions.

Fact. Rousseau was a giant of philosophy and his work was a great influence for both the American and French revolutions. He studied the work of the 'French Prophets' that Cavalier was a part of and was friends with many other notable scholars. His most famous work, *The Social Contract*, argued against the idea that monarchs were divinely empowered to legislate, work that would later influence Karl Marx. Rousseau asserts that only the

THE HISTORY OF THE MOUNTAIN MEN

people, who are sovereign, have that all-powerful right. In 1764 he wrote *Letters Written from the Mountain*, the last published work in his lifetime that outlined his views on censorship, religion and politics in both theory and practice. In 1766 he formed a friendship with David Hume who invited him to London. They soon fell out. Rousseau was an anxious man who worried constantly about his status and legacy. It's not known if he was a hypochondriac, but he was certainly a drama queen!

Fiction. There is no clear way of saying how Jean-Jacques became the ninth Mountain Man, as there is a fourteen-year gap between him and Jean. I believe he acquired it on his trip to London in the 1760s through the people he met at the Rainbow Coffee House, a stomping ground for the French Prophets. It's also possible that Montmorency's family assigned it to him when it became vacant, as Antoine suggests at the end of the book.

The Tenth Mountain Man – Benjamin Franklin 1767–1785

Motivation – American Independence.
Outcome – Successful (if you happened to be white and rich). Died of natural causes.

Fact. Franklin spent a large portion of his life in London between 1757 and 1775. In that time, he was made a member of the Royal Society, became involved in radical politics through gentlemen's clubs, and represented American interests in the British parliament. He was known to be a friend of David Hume's who associated with Rousseau. Both Rousseau and Franklin were in London at the same time. Franklin opposed the 1765 Stamp Act that gave tax breaks to the East India Company for imports of tea into the United States. He was instrumental in the leak of the Hutchinson Letters in 1773 which proved the British were cracking down on Bostonian dissent. This expose led directly to the Boston Tea Party and the American Revolution. Franklin was inspired by Rousseau's 'social contract'.

THE HISTORY OF THE MOUNTAIN MEN

Fiction. There is no written evidence that Rousseau met Franklin in London, although they moved in the same circles and were both there in 1766. They were known to Voltaire and David Hume, so it would be amazing if they did not meet at some point.

The Eleventh Mountain Man – Maximilien Robespierre 1785–1794

Motivation – French Revolution.
Outcome – Partial success. Executed by rival political factions.

Fact. Benjamin Franklin was American Ambassador to France between 1776 and 1785. Robespierre, who was a judge during 1783, wrote to Franklin about a case involving an experiment concerning a lightning conductor. Robespierre was a keen student of Rousseau and unquestionably met Rousseau's friend René de Girardin at the Jacobin Clubs that cultivated the derision against the monarchy. Robespierre was one of four key members of the 'Mountain', a radical political party that believed in the execution of the Monarch, land reform and price controls. Maximilien was instrumental in the 'reign of terror' following the revolution. This campaign created the blueprint for future genocides when it came to popular uprisings.

The Twelfth Mountain Man – Bertrand Barère 1794–1841

Motivation – French Revolution and staying alive.
Outcome – One of the few instigators of the French Revolution who died of natural causes.

Fact. Barère was another prominent member of 'The Mountain' and one of the only members to survive execution, having escaped from prison and retreated to Bordeaux. In the following years he became a spy for Napoleon before being sent to prison from which he again escaped. Banned from France he lived in Belgium before

THE HISTORY OF THE MOUNTAIN MEN

returning to Paris in 1830 to serve Louis, the new monarch. In later life he was a journalist, although there are few details of this. He died in Paris in 1841, the sole survivor of 'The Mountain'.

Fiction. There's no evidence to suggest he met Karl Marx.

The Thirteenth Mountain Man – Karl Marx 1841–1883

Motivation – Philosophy and social revolution.
Outcome – Marxism.

Fact. Marx moved to Paris shortly after Barère's death to become editor of a Franco-German newspaper. In 1848 he wrote the pamphlet 'The Communist Manifesto'. His political and philosophical thoughts had enormous influence on subsequent intellectual, economic and political history, and his name has been used as an adjective, a noun and a school of social theory. His work is equally lauded as criticised but his position as one of the world's most influential thought leaders on social science cannot be doubted. It's also true that Darwin's work on *The Origin of Species* that included the process of natural selection was fundamental in Marxist ideas being legitimised.

The Fourteenth Mountain Man – Paul Lafargue 1883–1895

Motivation – Activist, politician and writer.
Outcome – Committed suicide.

Fact. Paul Lafargue was the son-in-law of Karl Marx. Born in Cuba, he spent much of his adult life in England, France and Spain. Amongst his achievements include being a physician and writing the book *The Right To Be Lazy*. He was the first Socialist politician elected in France. Lafargue did meet Lenin in Paris in 1895 along with a number of other prominent Socialists.

The Fifteenth Mountain Man – Vladimir Ilyich Ulyanov (Lenin) 1895–1923

THE HISTORY OF THE MOUNTAIN MEN

Motivation – Revolution.
Outcome – Successful. (If you agreed with him; if not, then death.)

Fact. Ulyanov changed his name after his arrest and extradition to Siberia in the early 1900s. He took his name from the Lena River. His Bolshevik uprising was the second of the Russian Revolution, having been upstaged by the Petrograd strike and military rebellion of February 1917. Against popular belief, the October 1917 uprising was not the bloody affair it is made out to be. It was also not a popular uprising like the February event. Actually, only about a hundred people stormed the Winter Palace and there was very little violence. Lenin wasn't even there as he was 'in hiding'. Most of the uprising was managed and co-ordinated by Trotsky.

Fiction. He never considered calling himself Steve.

The Sixteenth Mountain Man – Vittorio Vidali 1923–1956.

Motivation – Chaos and sex.
Outcome – Assassinated.

Fact. Born in the Austro-Hungarian Empire, he was one of the founders of the Italian Communist Party before Mussolini expelled him. In 1922 he joined the Bolshevik Party and relocated to Moscow where he was constantly accused of having affairs with the wives of other members. He was again expelled, this time to Mexico, where he murdered a colleague over his love for his wife. He fought in the Spanish Civil War and was implicated and very likely involved in a failed assassination of Trotsky in Mexico. He often travelled through Cuba before and after Castro's Communist party came to power.

Fiction. There is little written about the relationship between Lenin and Vidali. Vidali went on to be an anti-Trotskyist which was very much Stalin's position rather than Lenin's. Vidali marked a change in the activities of the Mountain Men into terrorist activities.

THE HISTORY OF THE MOUNTAIN MEN

The Seventeenth Mountain Man – Che Guevara 1956–1967.

Motivation – Revolution.
Outcome – Cuban revolutionary success. Killed in Bolivia.

Fact. A young medical student born in Argentina, Guevara joined Castro's July 26th movement that led to a popular uprising against Cuba's Batista government through two years of guerrilla-style tactics. After serving several posts in the new Cuban regime he travelled abroad to instigate revolution from imperialists abroad. He was captured in Bolivia by the CIA where he famously said before being executed, "You will only kill a man."

The Eighteenth Mountain Man – Ilich Flores Navas 1967–2017.

Motivation – Political terrorism.
Outcome – Imprisoned in Clairvaux, France.

Fact? Based on Ilich Ramírez Sánchez who did attend the Tricontinental Conference in Cuba, January 1966, with his lawyer father.

Fiction. All of it, I promise…

Last of the Mountain Man – read the book!

Printed in Poland
by Amazon Fulfillment
Poland Sp. z o.o., Wrocław

67303915R00226

GW01157489

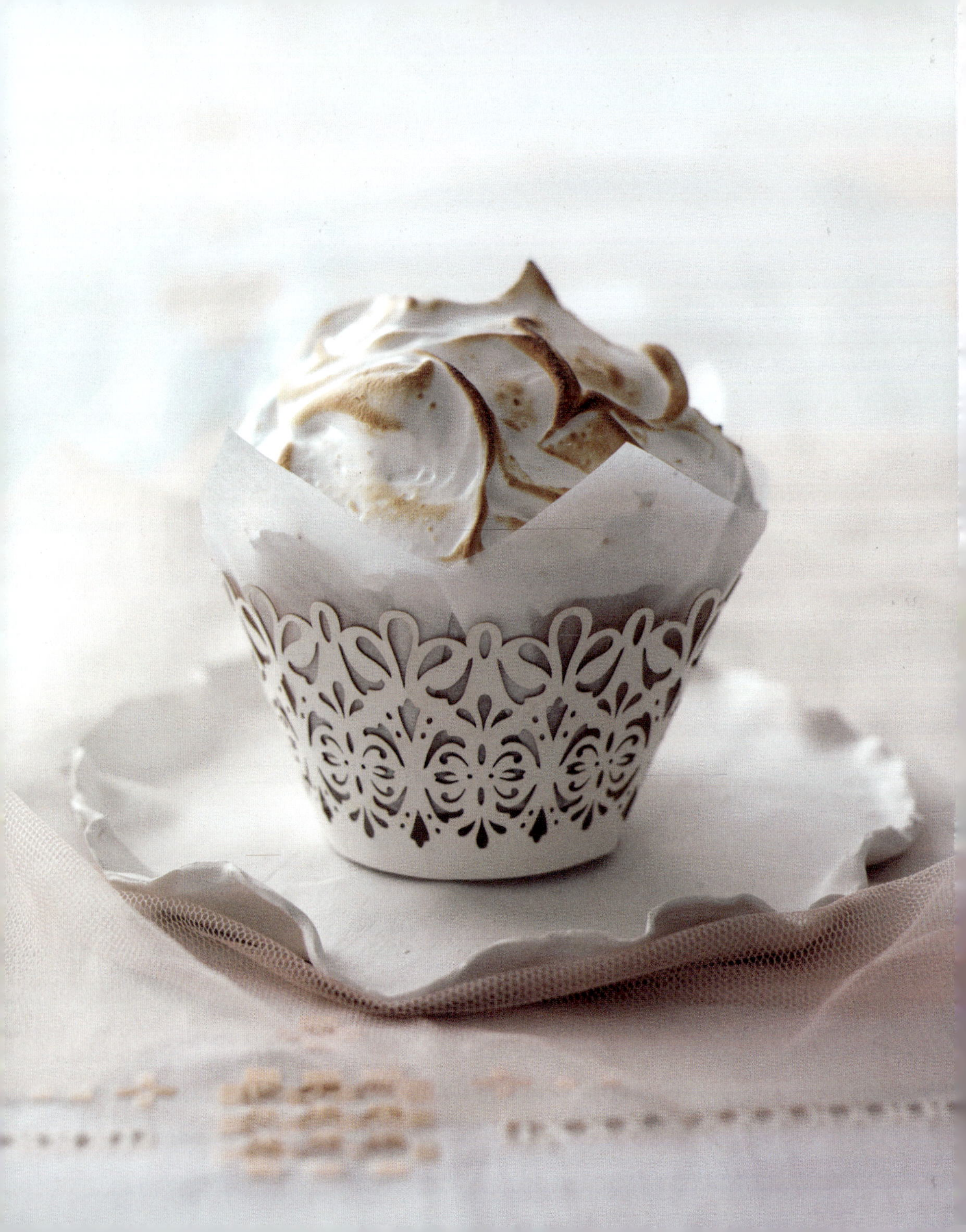

SWEET
DELIGHTS

The Australian Women's Weekly

SWEET DELIGHTS

TRIPLE TESTED — THE AUSTRALIAN WOMEN'S WEEKLY TEST KITCHEN

CONTENTS

SCONES 6

MACAROONS & MERINGUES 30

BISCUITS & BISCOTTI 50

PUFFS & PASTRIES 76

SLICES 106

TARTS & TARTLETS 124

LITTLE CAKES 152

BIG CAKES 176

CLASSIC CAKES 178
SYRUP CAKES 196
TEA CAKES 214
LAYERED CAKES 234

SHOWING OFF 256

glossary 288
conversion chart 291
index 292

SCONES

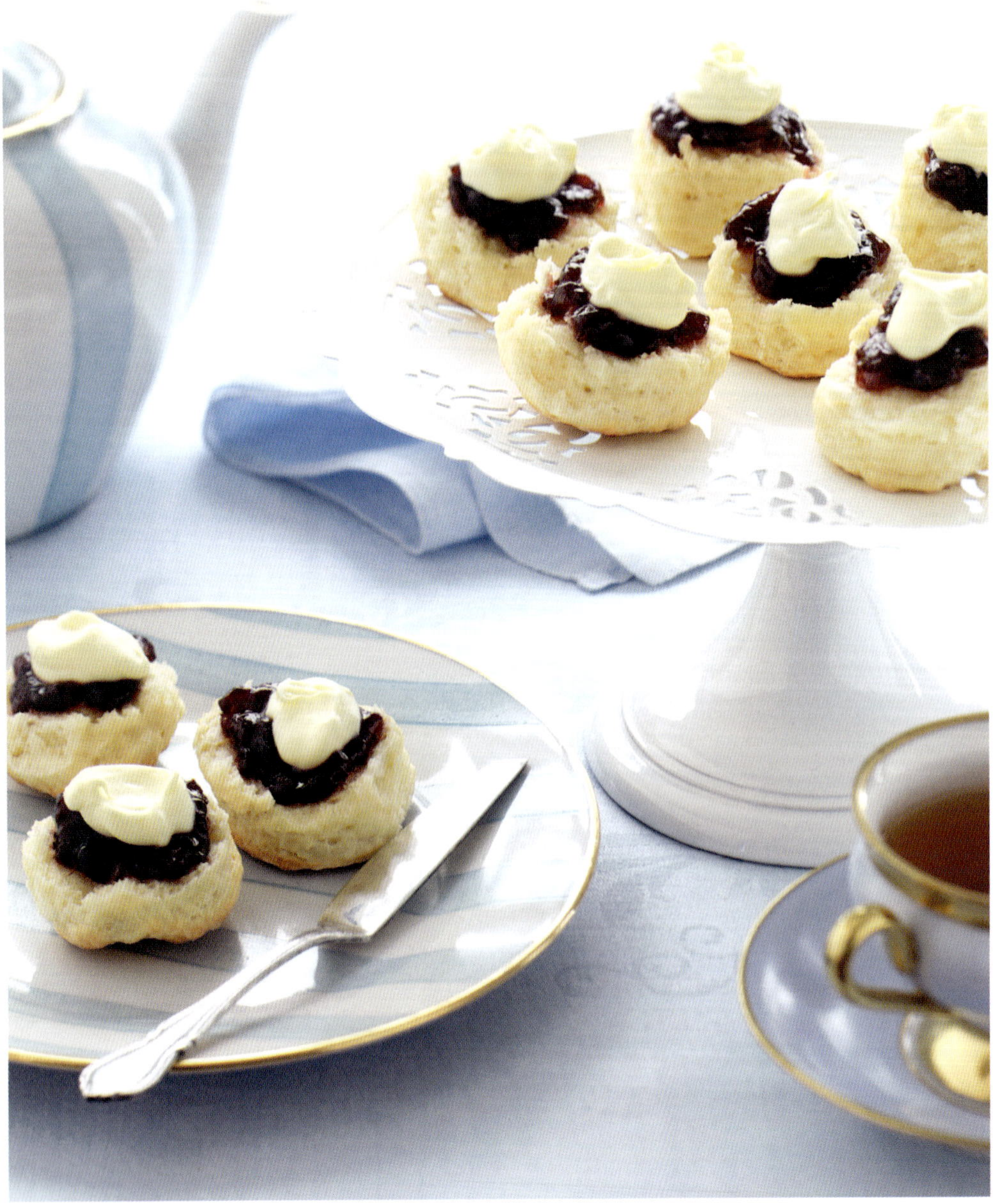

Scones
with jam & cream

prep + cook time 35 MINUTES *makes* 25

2½ cups (375g) self-raising flour
1 tablespoon caster (superfine) sugar
30g (1oz) butter, chopped
1¼ cups (310ml) buttermilk, plus extra
¾ cup (240g) black cherry jam
1 cup (250ml) thick (double) cream

1 Preheat oven to 220°C/425°F. Grease a 22cm (9in) square cake pan.
2 Sift flour and sugar into a large bowl; rub in butter.
3 Add buttermilk. Use a flat-bladed knife to cut the buttermilk through the flour mixture to make a soft, sticky dough. Turn dough onto a floured surface, knead gently until smooth.
4 Press dough out to 2cm (¾in) thickness, cut out 4cm (1½in) rounds. Place scones, just touching, in pan. Gently knead scraps of dough together; repeat process. Brush scones with a little extra buttermilk.
5 Bake scones for 15 minutes or until golden. Serve scones warm with jam and cream.

tip You could substitute the thick cream for clotted cream or whipped thickened cream.
keeps Scones are best made on the day of serving. They can be frozen for up to 3 months. Thaw in oven, wrapped in foil.

GINGERBREAD SCONES
WITH LEMON GLACÉ ICING

prep + cook time 40 MINUTES *makes* 16

30g (1oz) butter, softened
¼ cup (55g) firmly packed brown sugar
1 egg yolk
2½ cups (375g) self-raising flour
3 teaspoons ground ginger
1½ teaspoons ground cinnamon
¼ teaspoon ground cloves
1 cup (250ml) buttermilk, plus extra
2 tablespoons treacle or golden syrup
2 tablespoons shredded lemon rind, optional

LEMON GLACÉ ICING
1 cup (160g) icing (confectioners') sugar
15g (½oz) butter, melted
1 tablespoon lemon juice, approximately

1 Preheat oven to 220°C/425°F. Grease a 22cm (9in) square cake pan.

2 Beat butter, sugar and egg yolk in a small bowl with an electric mixer until light and fluffy. Transfer mixture to a large bowl; add sifted dry ingredients and combined buttermilk and treacle. Use a flat-bladed knife to cut the buttermilk mixture through flour mixture to make a soft, sticky dough. Turn dough onto a floured surface, knead gently until smooth.

3 Press dough out to 2cm (¾in) thickness, cut into 5cm (2in) rounds. Place rounds, just touching, in pan. Gently knead scraps of dough together; repeat process. Brush scones with a little extra buttermilk.

4 Bake scones for 20 minutes or until golden brown. Cool for 10 minutes.

5 Meanwhile, make lemon glacé icing.

6 Serve warm scones drizzled with lemon icing and decorated with shredded lemon rind.

LEMON GLACÉ ICING Sift icing sugar into a small heatproof bowl; stir in butter and enough juice to make a thick paste. Place bowl over a small saucepan of simmering water; stir until mixture is smooth.

tip Use a zester to shred lemon rind.

KEEPS
Scones are best made on the day of serving. They can be frozen for up to 3 months. Thaw in oven, wrapped in foil.

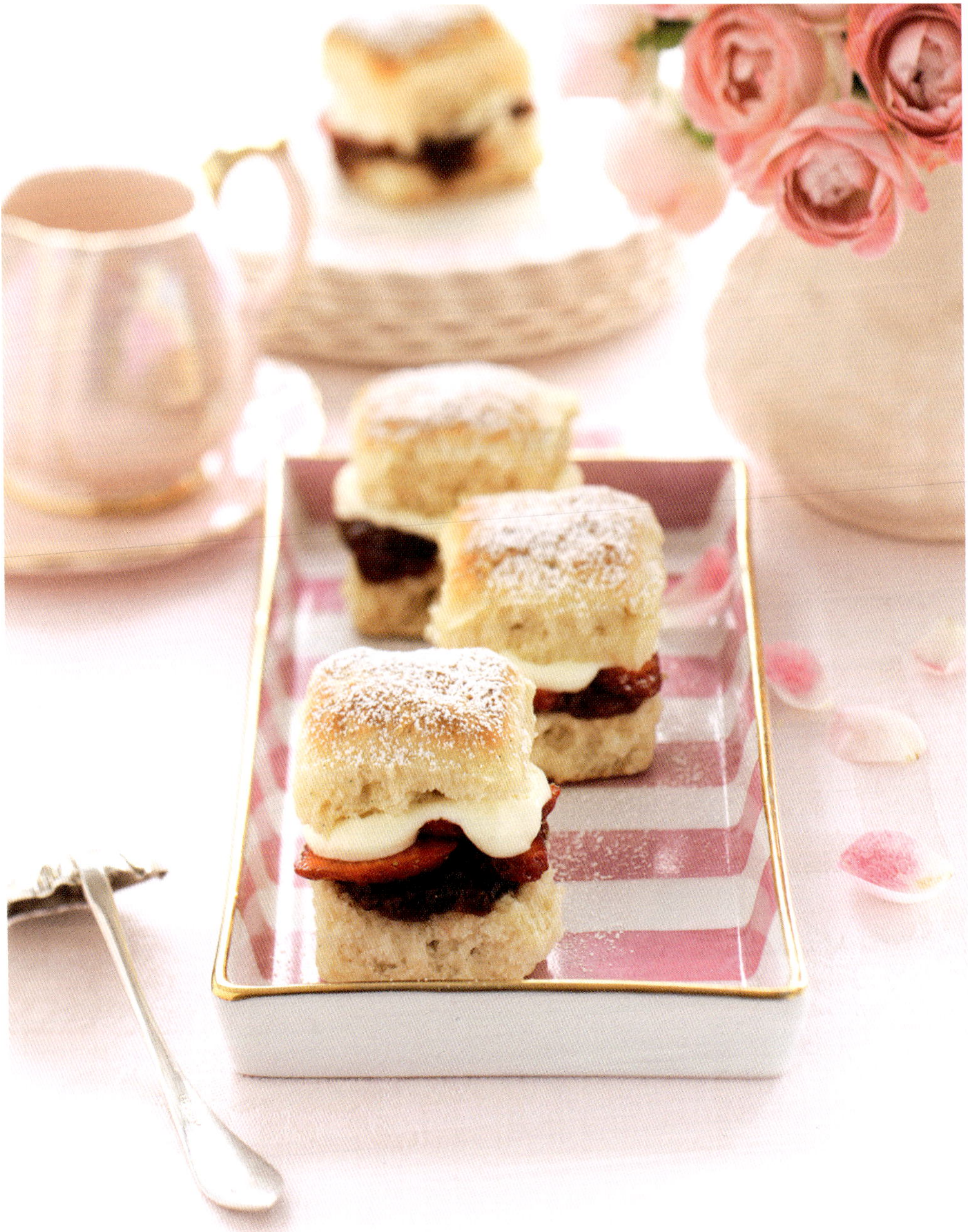

VANILLA BEAN
SCONES

prep + cook time 40 MINUTES ❧ *makes* 16

2½ cups (375g) self-raising flour
1 tablespoon caster (superfine) sugar
30g (1oz) butter, chopped
¾ cup (180ml) milk, plus extra
½ cup (125ml) water
1 vanilla bean
300ml thickened (heavy) cream
2 tablespoons icing (confectioners') sugar
¾ cup (240g) strawberry jam
250g (8oz) strawberries, sliced thinly

1 Preheat oven to 220°C/425°F. Grease a 22cm (9in) square cake pan.
2 Sift flour and caster sugar into a large bowl; rub in butter.
3 Combine milk and the water in a medium jug. split vanilla bean open and scrape seeds into the milk mixture; discard bean. Add milk mixture to flour mixture; use a flat-bladed knife to cut the milk mixture through the flour mixture to make a soft, sticky dough. Turn dough onto a floured surface, knead gently until smooth.
4 Press dough out to 20cm (8in) square, cut into 16 squares using a floured knife. Place squares, just touching, in pan. Brush with a little extra milk.
5 Bake scones for 20 minutes or until golden.
6 Meanwhile, beat cream and half the sifted icing sugar in a small bowl with an electric mixer until soft peaks form.
7 Sandwich warm scones with jam, strawberries and cream; serve dusted with remaining icing sugar.

keeps Scones are best made on the day of serving. They can be frozen for up to 3 months. Thaw in oven, wrapped in foil.

STRAWBERRY BLISS SCONES

prep + cook time 40 MINUTES ✽ *makes* 12

3½ cups (525g) self-raising flour
150g (5oz) white chocolate, cut into 5mm (¼in) pieces
1 cup (250ml) chilled carbonated lemonade (see tips)
1 cup (250ml) pouring cream
150g (5oz) strawberries, cut into 5mm (¼in) pieces
1 tablespoon icing (confectioners') sugar
1 cup (320g) strawberry jam
¾ cup (180ml) thick (double) cream

1 Preheat oven to 220°C/425°F. Grease two oven trays; line with baking paper.
2 Sift flour into a large bowl; stir in chocolate. Combine lemonade and pouring cream in a jug; pour evenly over the flour mixture. Using a knife, cut liquid through flour mixture until it starts to clump. Add strawberries; continue to combine until the mixture comes together forming a dough. (Don't over work the mixture or the dough will be tough.)
3 Divide dough in half. Shape one half into an 18cm (7¼in) round on one tray with floured hands. Mark the round into six wedges, using the back of a floured knife. Repeat with the remaining dough and tray.
4 Bake scone rounds for 25 minutes, swapping trays on shelves halfway through cooking time, or until tops are golden brown. Dust scones with sifted icing sugar; serve warm with jam and cream.

tips Use a clear, carbonated lemonade for this recipe for a light-textured scone. Many a scone maker has come undone when it comes to kneading and cutting out the dough, so baking the mixture as two large rounds saves time and angst – it also happens to look spectacular.

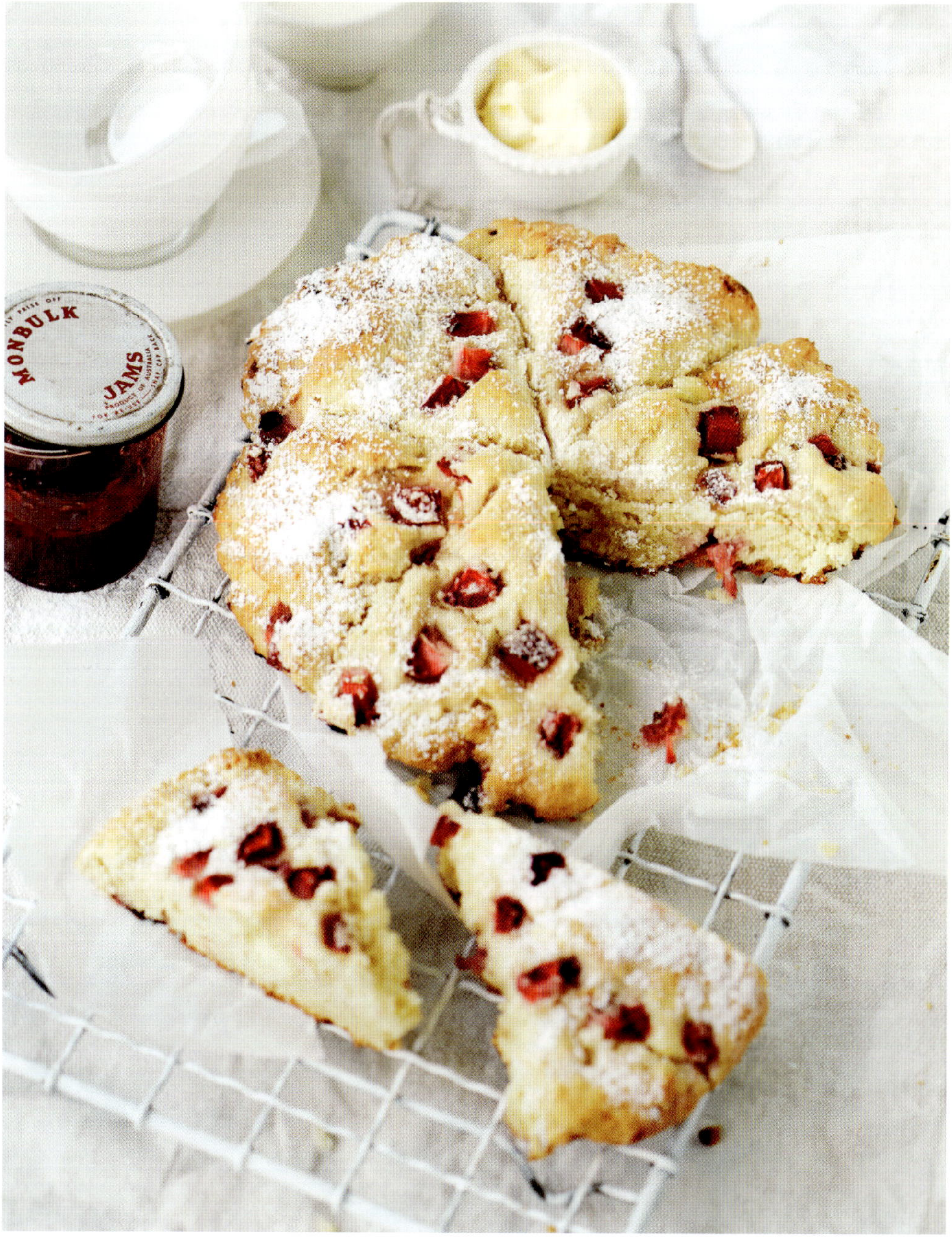
MONBULK
JAMS
PRODUCT OF AUSTRALIA

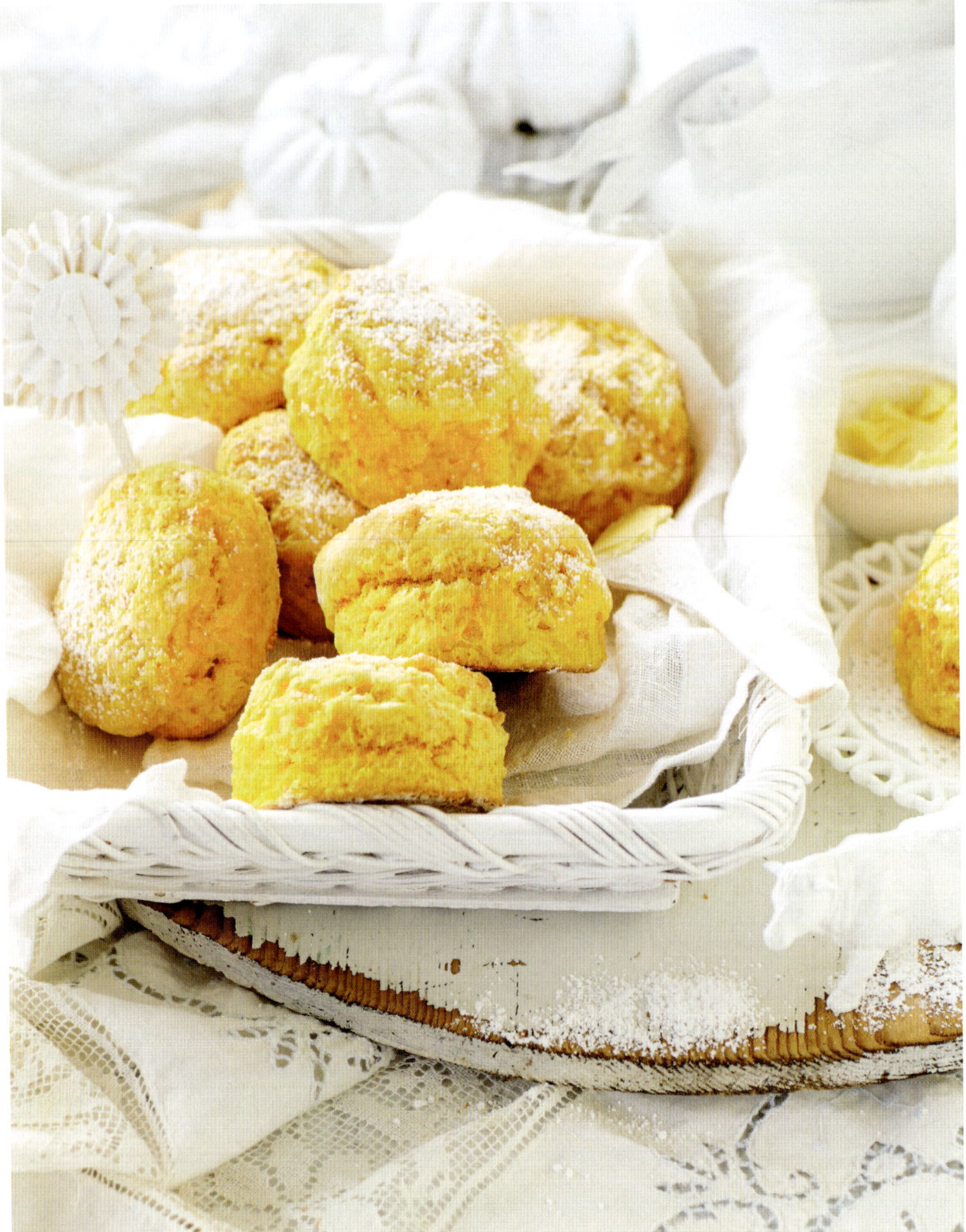

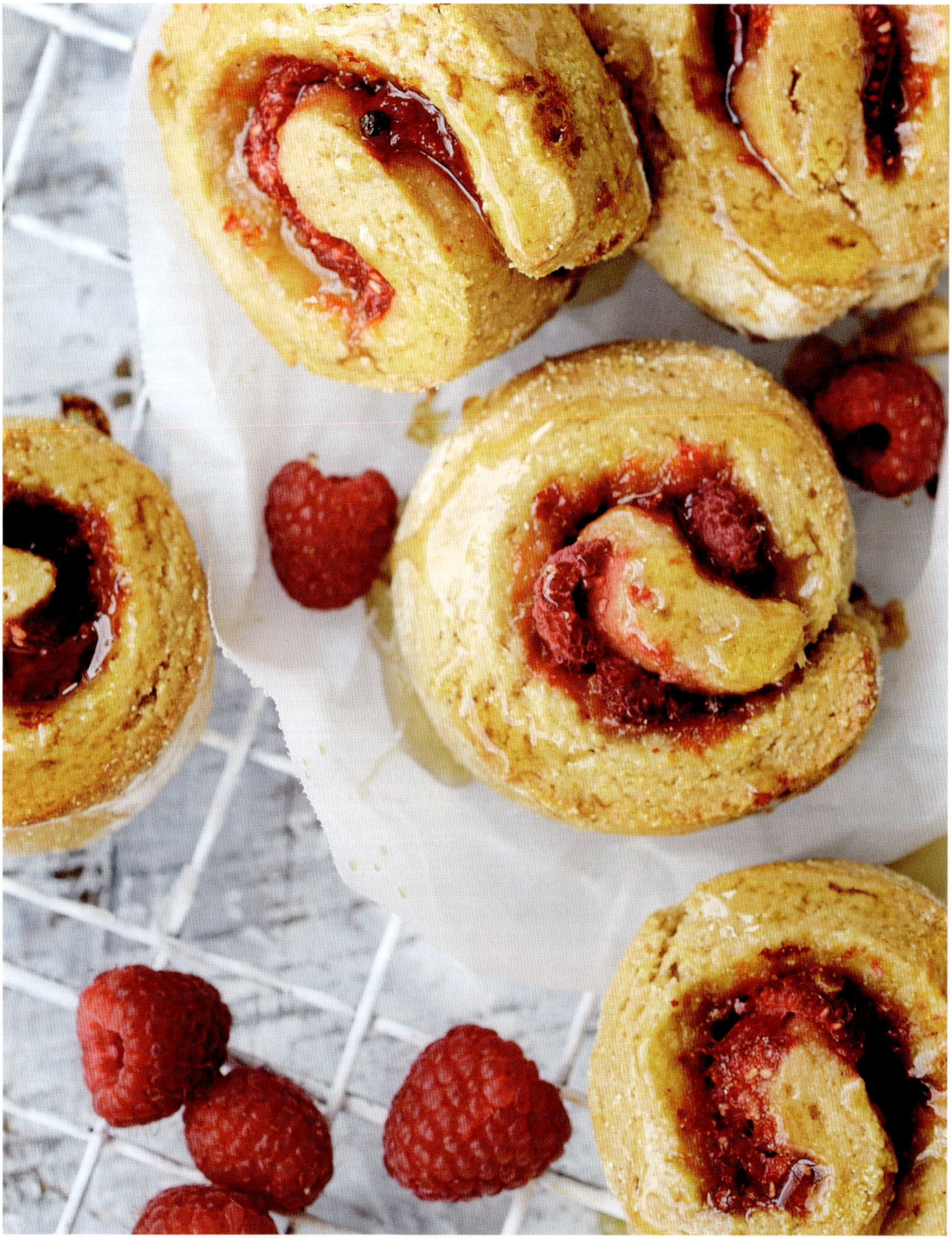

PRIZE-WINNING
PUMPKIN SCONES

prep + cook time 30 MINUTES ✽ *makes* 8

- 60g (2oz) butter, softened
- ¼ cup (55g) caster (superfine) sugar
- 1 egg yolk
- 1 cup (250g) cooked, cold mashed pumpkin
- 2½ cups (355g) self-raising flour
- ½ teaspoon salt
- ¼ teaspoon bicarbonate of soda (baking soda)
- 2 tablespoons milk, approximately
- 2 teaspoons icing (confectioners') sugar

This is the recipe that long-time show competitor Graham Weir used for his pumpkin scone entry in the 2008 Sydney Royal Easter Show – he won 1st prize.

1 Preheat oven to 240°C/475°F. Grease a baking tray; line with baking paper.

2 Beat butter, sugar and egg yolk in a small bowl with an electric mixer until combined. Transfer to a large bowl. Stir in mashed pumpkin. Sift over flour, salt and bicarbonate of soda. Using a flat-bladed knife, cut the flour mixture through the pumpkin mixture to make a soft dough.

3 Place on a floured surface and knead lightly. Roll or pat dough out to approximately 2cm (¾in) thick. Cut scones out using a 6cm (2½in) floured cutter. Place on tray; brush tops with a little milk.

4 Bake for 14 minutes or until golden and hollow sounding when tapped. Transfer, top-side up, to a wire rack to cool. Dust with sifted icing sugar.

tips You will need to cook 300g (9½oz) pumpkin. If you like, add 1 teaspoon finely grated lemon rind and a pinch of ground nutmeg to the butter mixture in step 2. The trick to beautiful light scones is to handle the mixture as little as possible. To ensure scones rise evenly with straight sides, cut out the scones using a sharp metal cutter; remove the cutter in an upward, rather than a twisting motion.

raspberry & pink peppercorn
POLENTA SCROLLS

Raspberry & Pink Peppercorn Polenta Scrolls

prep + cook time 45 MINUTES ✻ *makes* 8

2 cups (300g) white spelt flour, plus extra, for dusting
½ cup (85g) fine polenta
1½ teaspoons baking powder
pinch of salt
½ cup (125ml) buttermilk
¼ cup (85g) rice malt syrup
1 teaspoon pink peppercorns
1 teaspoon vanilla extract
1 tablespoon finely grated blood orange rind
¼ cup (85g) rice malt syrup, extra
75g (2½oz) fresh raspberries

1 Preheat oven to 180°C/350°F. Grease an oven tray; line with baking paper.
2 Combine flour, polenta, baking powder and salt in a large bowl. Make a well in the centre. Add buttermilk and syrup. Using a flat-bladed knife, cut liquid through dry ingredients until it forms a rough dough.
3 Crush pink peppercorns using a mortar and pestle. Stir in vanilla, rind and 1 tablespoon of the extra syrup.
4 Turn dough onto a floured surface; knead lightly. Press out into a 18cm x 28cm (7¼in x 11¼in) rectangle; spread with peppercorn mixture. Tear raspberries into smaller pieces; arrange on dough.
5 Starting from one long side, roll up dough to form a log. Cut log into 8 slices. Place slices 5cm (2in) apart, cut-side up, on tray.

6 Bake scrolls for 25 minutes or until risen and lightly golden. Brush hot scrolls with remaining extra syrup. Serve warm.

tips These scrolls are egg-free, nut-free and sugar-free. Pink peppercorns are not related to black peppercorns, they carry no heat and have a pine-like taste slightly similar to juniper berries. If you can't find them, simply omit them from the recipe; the scrolls will still have plenty of flavour without them. If blood oranges are not in season, use regular oranges.
keeps These scrolls are best made on the day and served warm. If you make them ahead of time on the day, be sure to reheat them in the oven before serving.

HOT CROSS BUN
SCONES

prep + cook time 45 MINUTES (+ STANDING) *makes* 28

1 cup (160g) dried currants
2 tablespoons dark rum
3½ cups (525g) self-raising flour
2 teaspoons mixed spice
1 teaspoon ground cinnamon
1 cup (250ml) chilled carbonated lemonade
1 cup (250ml) pouring cream, plus extra
½ cup (80g) icing (confectioners') sugar
3 teaspoons lemon juice

1 Combine currants and rum in a medium bowl. Cover; stand for 2 hours.
2 Preheat oven to 220°/425°F. Grease a 20cm x 30cm (8in x 12in) rectangular pan.
3 Sift flour and spices into a large bowl. Make a well in centre; add lemonade, cream and currant mixture. Using a flat-bladed knife, cut the liquid and currants through the flour mixture, mixing to a soft, sticky dough. Knead dough gently on a floured surface until smooth.
4 Press dough out to 2.5cm (1in) thickness. Dip a 4cm (1½in) round cutter in flour; cut as many rounds as you can from dough. Place rounds, side-by-side, just touching, in pan. Gently knead scraps of dough together; repeat pressing and cutting of dough, place in same pan. Brush tops with a little extra cream.
5 Bake scones for 20 minutes or until browned lightly and scones sound hollow when tapped.
6 Combine sifted icing sugar and juice in a small bowl; spoon icing into a small piping bag fitted with a 5mm (¼in) plain tube. Pipe a cross onto each scone.

serving suggestion Serve warm scones with butter.

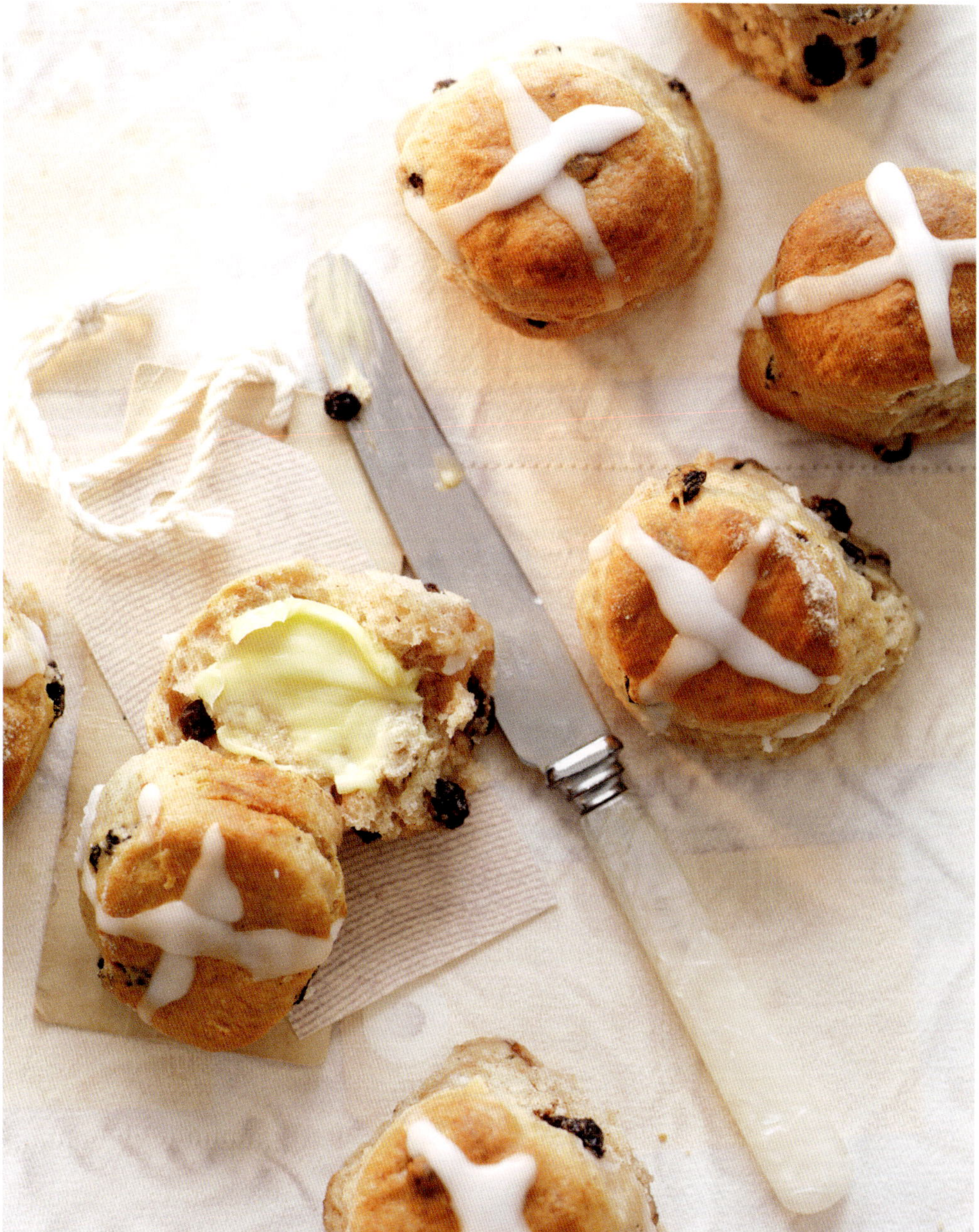

SERVING SUGGESTION
Serve warm rock cakes with butter.

MINI DATE & GINGER
ROCK CAKES

prep + cook time 35 MINUTES *makes* 30

- 2 cups (300g) self-raising flour
- 1 teaspoon ground ginger
- ⅓ cup (75g) caster (superfine) sugar
- 90g (3oz) butter, chopped
- 1 cup (140g) coarsely chopped dried dates
- ¼ cup (45g) finely chopped glacé ginger
- 2 teaspoons finely grated orange rind
- 1 egg, beaten lightly
- ½ cup (125ml) milk
- 1 tablespoon caster (superfine) sugar, extra

1 Preheat oven to 180°C/350°F. Grease oven trays.
2 Sift flour, ground ginger and sugar into a large bowl; rub in butter. Stir in dates, glacé ginger and rind, then combined egg and milk (do not overmix).
3 Drop level tablespoons of mixture, about 5cm (2in) apart, onto trays; sprinkle with extra sugar.
4 Bake rock cakes for 15 minutes or until golden brown. Cool on trays.

keeps These rock cakes are best made and eaten on the same day.

ROCK CAKES

prep + cook time 30 MINUTES *makes* 18

2 cups (300g) self-raising flour
¼ teaspoon ground cinnamon
⅓ cup (75g) caster (superfine) sugar
90g (3oz) cold butter, chopped
1 cup (160g) sultanas
1 egg, beaten lightly
½ cup (125ml) milk
1 tablespoon caster (superfine) sugar, extra

1 Preheat oven to 200°C/400°F. Grease oven trays.
2 Sift flour, cinnamon and sugar into a medium bowl; rub in butter. Stir in sultanas, egg and milk. Do not overmix.
3 Drop rounded tablespoons of mixture about 5cm (2in) apart onto trays; sprinkle with extra sugar.
4 Bake for 15 minutes or until golden brown. Cool cakes on trays.

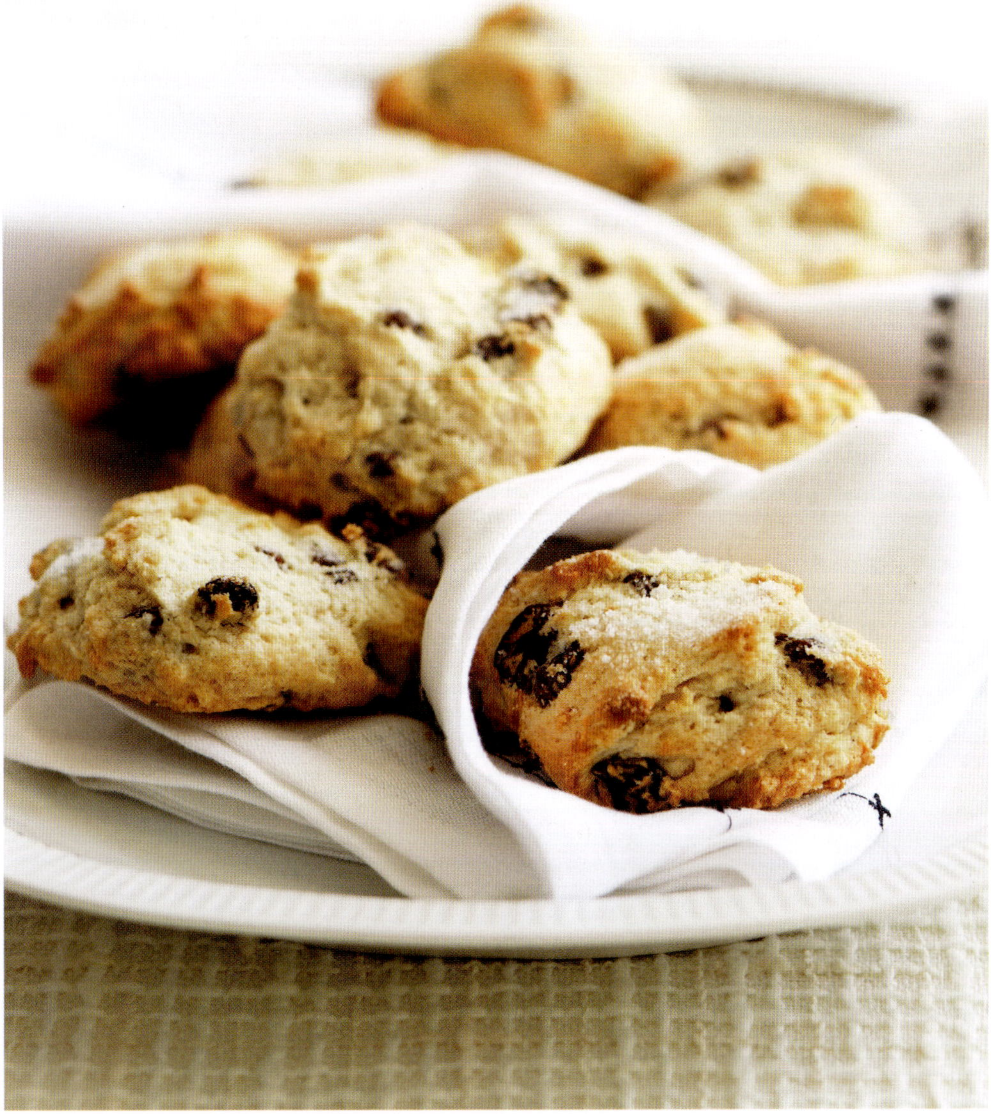

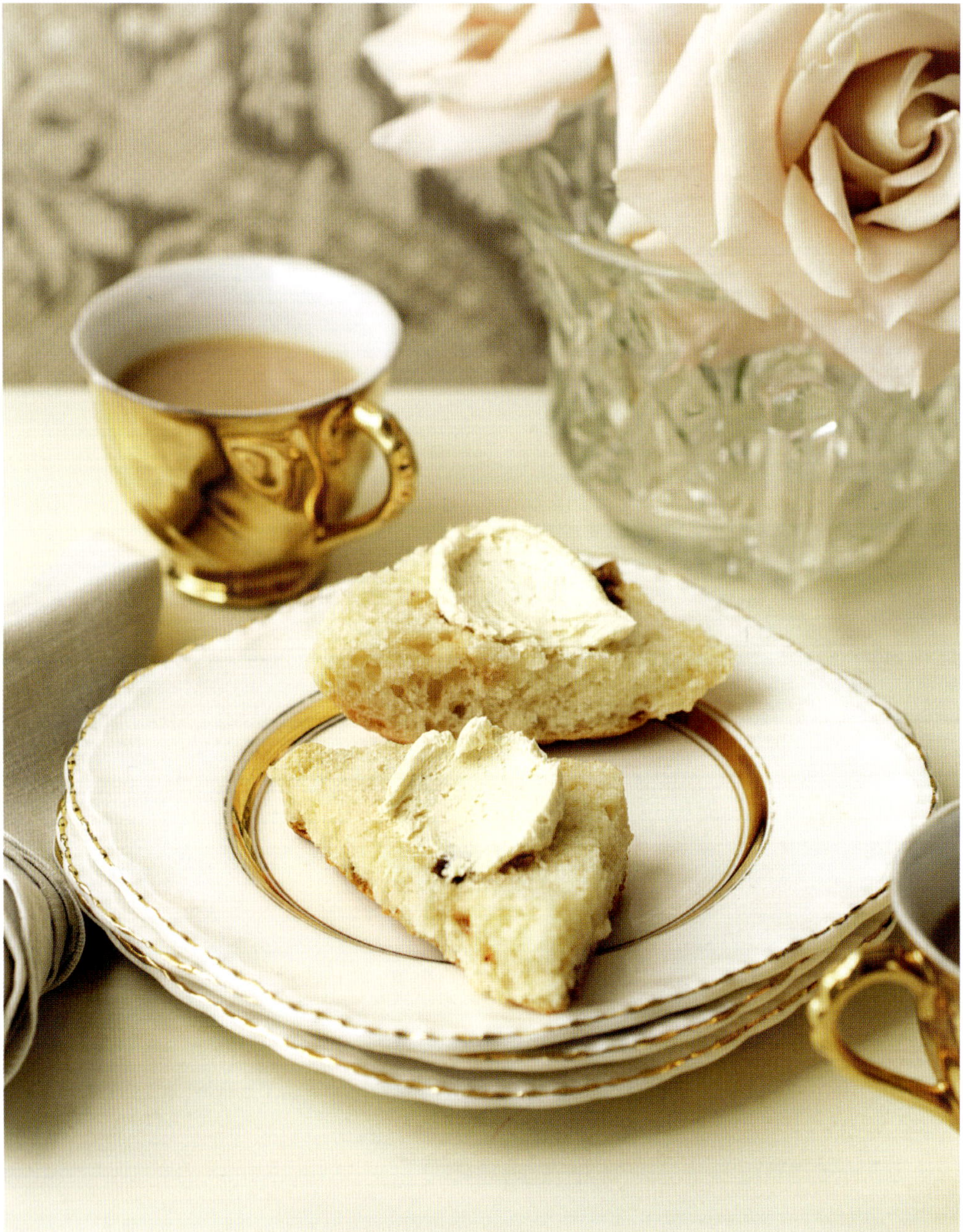

Date Scones
with whipped caramel butter

prep + cook time 40 MINUTES ❊ *makes* 18

30g (1oz) butter, softened
¼ cup (55g) firmly packed brown sugar
1 egg yolk
2½ cups (375g) self-raising flour
⅓ cup (50g) finely chopped seeded dried dates
1¼ cups (310ml) buttermilk, plus extra

WHIPPED CARAMEL BUTTER

150g (5oz) unsalted butter, softened
¼ cup (55g) firmly packed brown sugar
2 teaspoons vanilla extract

1 Preheat oven to 220°C/425°F. Grease a 22cm (9in) square cake pan.
2 Beat butter, sugar and egg yolk in a small bowl with an electric mixer until light and fluffy. Transfer mixture to a large bowl; add sifted flour, dates and buttermilk. Use a flat-bladed knife to cut the buttermilk through the flour mixture to make a soft, sticky dough. Turn dough onto a floured surface, knead gently until smooth.
3 Press dough out to 20cm (8in) square, cut into nine squares, using a floured knife, then cut each square in half diagonally. Place scones side-by-side, just touching, in pan. Brush with a little extra buttermilk.
4 Bake scones for 20 minutes or until golden brown.
5 Meanwhile, make whipped caramel butter.
6 Serve warm scones with whipped caramel butter.
WHIPPED CARAMEL BUTTER Beat ingredients in a small bowl with an electric mixer until light and fluffy.

keeps Scones are best made on the day of serving. They can be frozen for up to 3 months. Thaw in oven, wrapped in foil.

MACAROONS & MERINGUES

TIP
Push 6 fresh or thawed frozen raspberries through a fine sieve to make raspberry puree.

Raspberry Macaroon Dreams

prep + cook time 40 MINUTES (+ STANDING & REFRIGERATION) *makes* 16

3 egg whites
¼ cup (55g) caster (superfine) sugar
pink food colouring
1¼ cups (200g) icing (confectioners') sugar
1 cup (120g) almond meal
1 tablespoon raspberry puree (see tip)
1 tablespoon icing (confectioners') sugar, extra
¼ cup (60ml) pouring cream
150g (5oz) white chocolate, chopped coarsely
1 tablespoon raspberry jam, warmed, sieved

1 Grease oven trays; line with baking paper.
2 Beat egg whites in a small bowl with an electric mixer until soft peaks form. Add caster sugar and a few drops of colouring, beat until sugar dissolves; transfer mixture to a large bowl. Fold in sifted icing sugar, almond meal and raspberry puree, in two batches, until mixture is glossy.
3 Spoon mixture into a piping bag fitted with a 2cm (¾in) plain tube. Pipe 4cm (1½in) rounds about 2cm (¾in) apart onto trays. Tap trays on bench so macaroons spread slightly. Dust macaroons with extra sifted icing sugar; stand for 30 minutes.
4 Meanwhile, preheat oven to 150°C/300°F.
5 Bake for 20 minutes or until macaroons can be gently pushed without breaking. Cool on trays.
6 Bring cream to the boil in a small saucepan, remove from heat; add chocolate, stir until smooth. Stir in jam and a few more drops of colouring. Refrigerate until spreadable.
7 Sandwich macaroons with white chocolate filling.

keeps Unfilled macaroons will keep in an airtight container for about a week. Fill macaroons just before serving.

COFFEE HAZELNUT
MERINGUES

prep + cook time 1 HOUR (+ COOLING) *makes* 30

2 egg whites
½ cup (110g) caster (superfine) sugar
2 teaspoons instant coffee granules
½ teaspoon hot water
3 teaspoons coffee-flavoured liqueur
¼ cup (35g) roasted hazelnuts

1 Preheat oven to 120°C/250°F. Grease oven trays; line with baking paper.
2 Beat egg whites in a small bowl with an electric mixer until soft peaks form. Gradually add sugar, beating until dissolved after additions.
3 Meanwhile, dissolve coffee in the water in a jug; stir in liqueur. Fold coffee mixture into meringue mixture.
4 Spoon mixture into a piping bag fitted with a 5mm (¼in) fluted tube. Pipe meringues onto trays 2cm (¾in) apart; top each meringue with a hazelnut.
5 Bake for 45 minutes. Cool meringues in oven with door ajar.

keeps Store in an airtight container for up to 4 days.

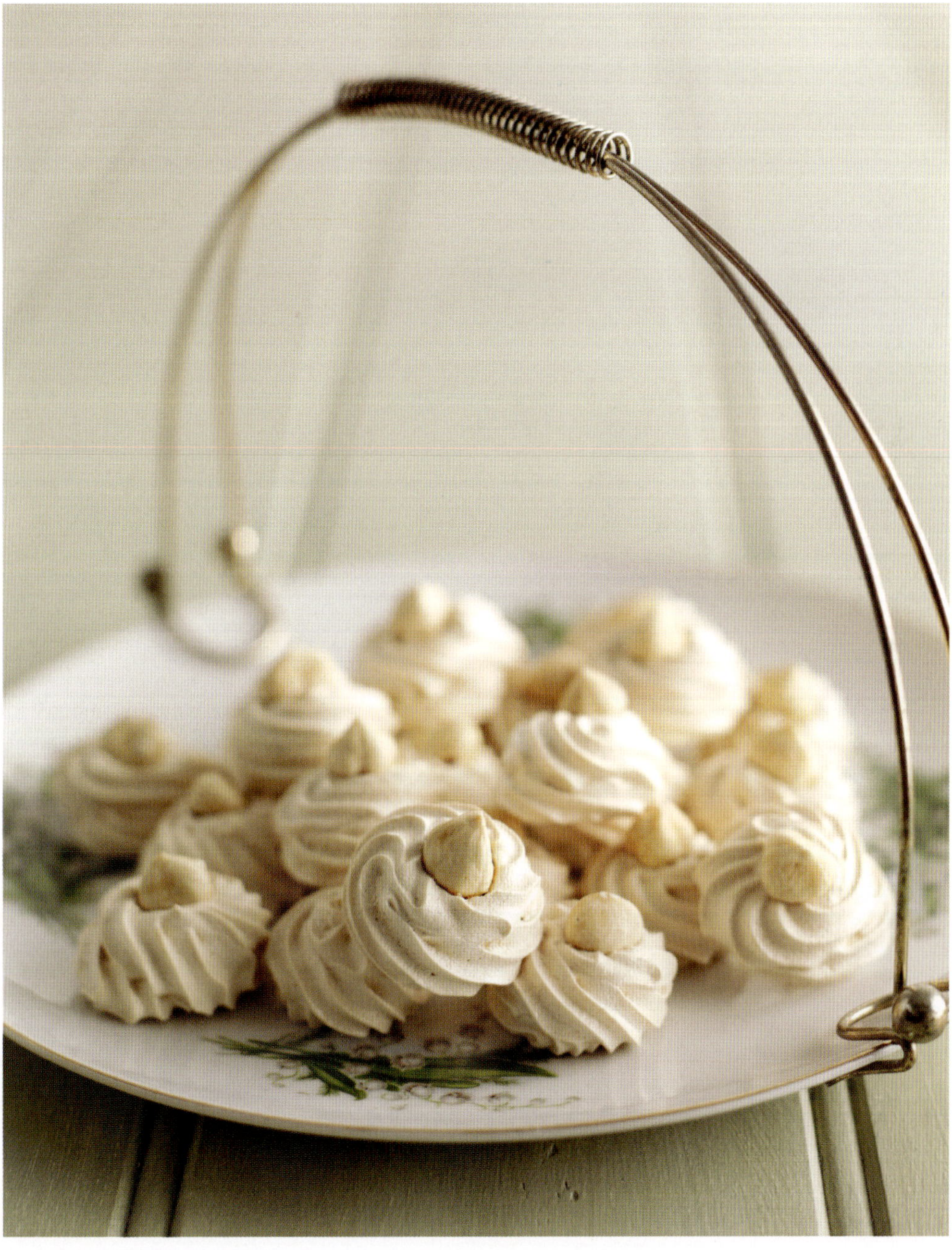

TIP
Limoncello is an Italian lemon-flavoured liqueur made from the peel only of fragrant lemons, which is steeped in clear alcohol then diluted with sugar and water.

Lemon Liqueur
MACAROONS

prep + cook time 40 MINUTES (+ STANDING) ❋ *makes* 16

3 egg whites
¼ cup (55g) caster (superfine) sugar
yellow food colouring
1¼ cups (200g) icing (confectioners') sugar
1 cup (120g) almond meal
2 teaspoons finely grated lemon rind
1 tablespoon icing (confectioners') sugar, extra
¼ cup (60ml) pouring cream
150g (5oz) white chocolate, chopped coarsely
4 teaspoons limoncello liqueur (see tip)

1 Grease oven trays; line with baking paper.
2 Beat egg whites in a small bowl with an electric mixer until soft peaks form. Add caster sugar and a few drops of colouring, beat until sugar dissolves; transfer mixture to a large bowl. Fold in sifted icing sugar, almond meal and rind, in two batches, until mixture is glossy.
3 Spoon mixture into a piping bag fitted with 1cm (½in) plain tube. Pipe 4cm (1½in) rounds about 2.5cm (1in) apart onto trays. Tap trays on bench so macaroons spread slightly. Dust with extra sifted icing sugar; stand for 30 minutes or until dry to touch.
4 Meanwhile, preheat oven to 150°C/300°F.
5 Bake for 20 minutes or until macaroons can be gently pushed without breaking. Cool on trays.
6 Bring cream to the boil in a small saucepan, remove from heat; add chocolate, stir until smooth. Stir in liqueur; stand at room temperature until spreadable. Sandwich macaroons with white chocolate filling.

keeps Store unfilled macaroons in an airtight container for about a week. Fill macaroons just before serving.

CAPPUCCINO MACAROONS

prep + cook time 1 HOUR (+ STANDING) ❋ *makes* 16

1¼ cups (240g) icing (confectioners') sugar
¾ cup (75g) hazelnut meal
2 teaspoons instant coffee granules
1 teaspoon boiling water
3 egg whites
2 tablespoons caster (superfine) sugar
2 teaspoons cocoa powder

WHITE CHOCOLATE GANACHE
⅓ cup (80ml) pouring cream
180g (5½oz) white chocolate, chopped finely

1 Grease oven trays; line with baking paper.
2 Blend or process icing sugar and hazelnut meal until fine. Sift mixture; discard any coarse pieces in sifter.
3 Combine coffee and the boiling water in a bowl.
4 Beat egg whites in a small bowl with an electric mixer until soft peaks form. Add caster sugar, beat until sugar dissolves; transfer mixture to a large bowl. Fold in sifted icing sugar and hazelnut meal mixture and coffee mixture, in two batches, until glossy.
5 Spoon mixture into a piping bag fitted with a 1cm (½in) plain tube. Pipe 4cm (1½in) rounds, about 2.5cm (1in) apart, on trays. Tap trays on bench so macaroons spread slightly; stand for 30 minutes or until macaroons feel dry to touch.
6 Preheat oven to 150°C/300°F.
7 Bake for 20 minutes or until macaroons can be gently pushed without breaking. Cool on trays.
8 Meanwhile, make white chocolate ganache.
9 Sandwich macaroons with ganache. Serve dusted with sifted cocoa powder.

WHITE CHOCOLATE GANACHE Bring cream to the boil in a small saucepan. Remove from heat; add chocolate, stir until smooth. Stand at room temperature until spreadable.

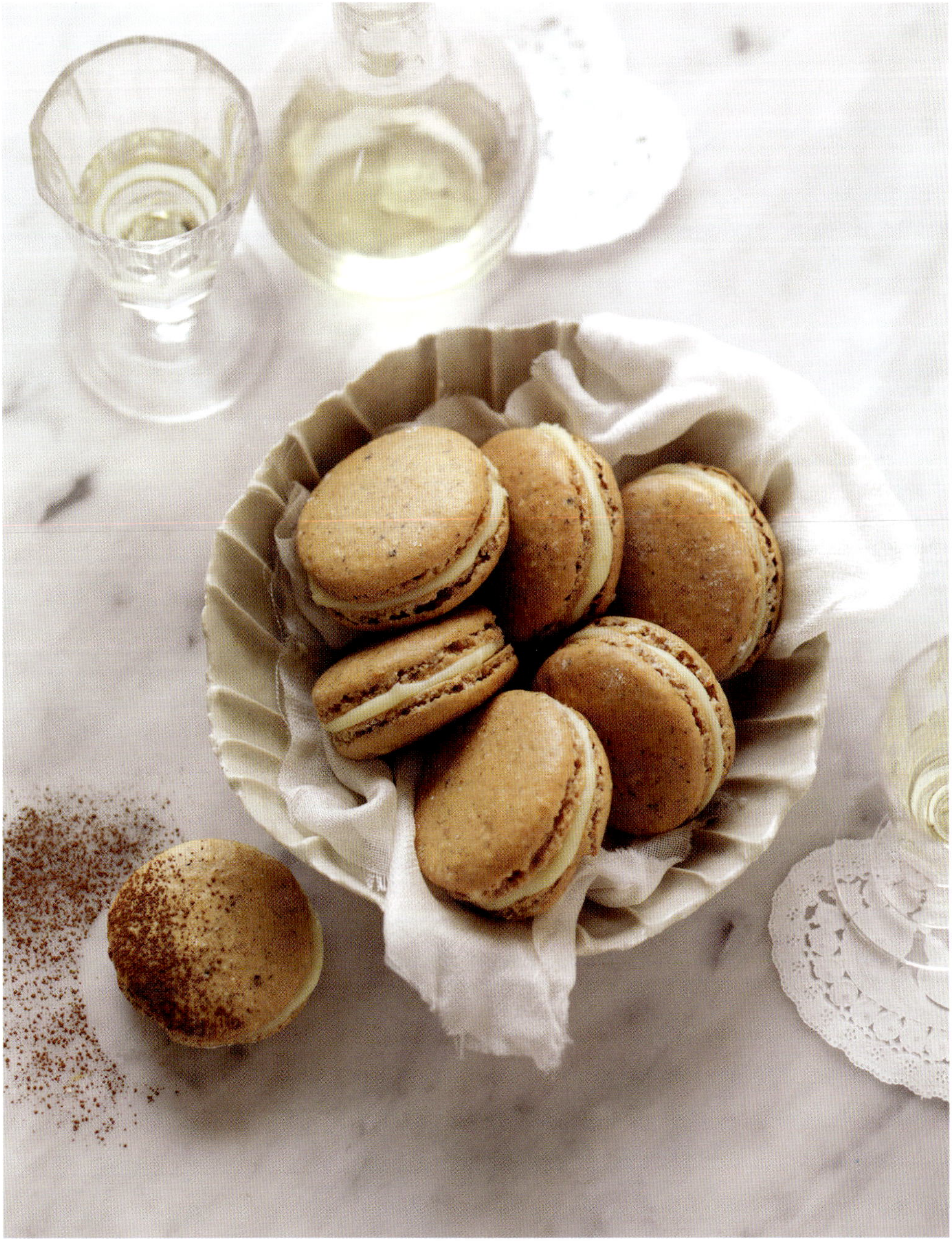

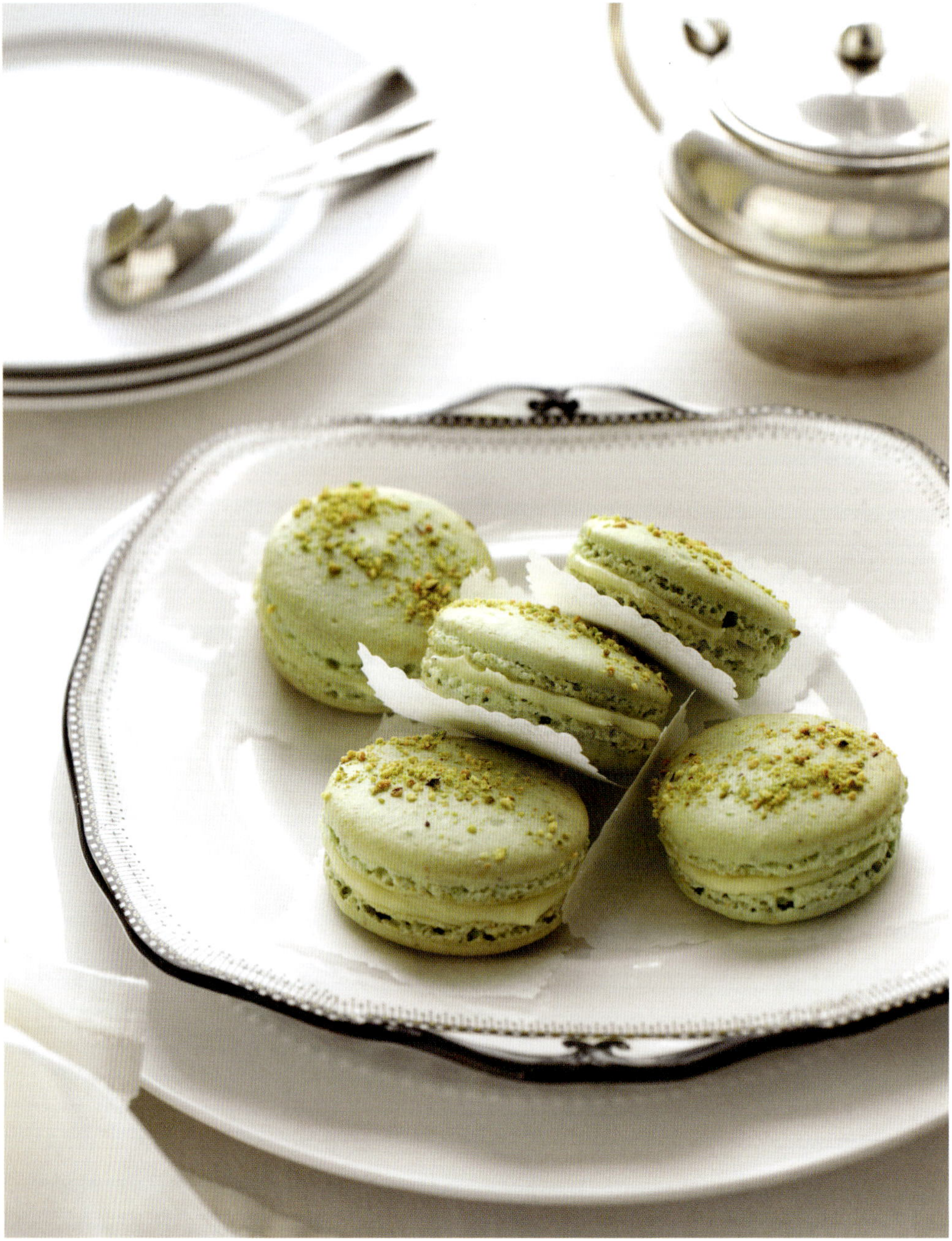

Pistachio & White Chocolate Macaroons

prep + cook time 45 MINUTES (+ STANDING)   *makes* 16

⅓ cup (45g) unsalted, roasted, shelled pistachios
3 egg whites
¼ cup (55g) caster (superfine) sugar
green food colouring
1¼ cups (200g) icing (confectioners') sugar
¾ cup (90g) almond meal

HONEYED WHITE CHOCOLATE GANACHE
¼ cup (60ml) pouring cream
155g (5oz) white chocolate, chopped coarsely
2 teaspoons honey

1 Grease oven trays; line with baking paper.
2 Process pistachios until finely ground.
3 Beat egg whites in a small bowl with an electric mixer until soft peaks form. Add caster sugar and a few drops of colouring, beat until sugar dissolves; transfer mixture to a large bowl. Fold in ¼ cup of the ground pistachios, sifted icing sugar and almond meal, in two batches, until mixture is glossy.
4 Spoon mixture into a piping bag fitted with a 1cm (½in) plain tube. Pipe 4cm (1½in) rounds about 2.5cm (1in) apart onto trays. Tap trays on bench so macaroons spread slightly. Sprinkle macaroons with remaining ground pistachios; stand for 30 minutes.
5 Meanwhile, preheat oven to 150°C/300°F.
6 Bake for 20 minutes or until macaroons can be gently pushed without breaking. Cool on trays.
7 Meanwhile, make honeyed white chocolate ganache.
8 Sandwich macaroons with ganache.

HONEYED WHITE CHOCOLATE GANACHE
Bring cream to the boil in a small saucepan. Remove from heat; pour over chocolate and honey in a small bowl, stir until smooth. Stand at room temperature until spreadable.

Coconut Macaroons

prep + cook time 45 MINUTES (+ STANDING) *makes* 16

3 egg whites
¼ cup (55g) caster (superfine) sugar
½ teaspoon coconut essence
1¼ cups (200g) icing (confectioners') sugar
¾ cup (90g) almond meal
¼ cup (20g) desiccated coconut
1 tablespoon icing (confectioners') sugar, extra

WHITE CHOCOLATE GANACHE
¼ cup (60ml) pouring cream
155g (5oz) white chocolate, chopped coarsely
2 teaspoons coconut-flavoured liqueur

1 Grease oven trays; line with baking paper.
2 Beat egg whites in a small bowl with an electric mixer until soft peaks form. Add caster sugar and essence, beat until sugar dissolves; transfer mixture to a large bowl. Fold in sifted icing sugar, almond meal and coconut, in two batches, until mixture is glossy.
3 Spoon mixture into a piping bag fitted with 1cm (½in) plain tube. Pipe 4cm (1½in) rounds about 2.5cm (1in) apart onto trays. Tap trays on bench so macaroons spread slightly. Stand for 30 minutes.
4 Meanwhile, preheat oven to 150°C/300°F.
5 Bake for 20 minutes or until macaroons can be gently pushed without breaking. Cool on trays.
6 Meanwhile, make white chocolate ganache.
7 Sandwich macaroons with ganache. Serve dusted with extra sifted icing sugar.

WHITE CHOCOLATE GANACHE Bring cream to the boil in a small saucepan. Remove from heat; pour over chocolate in a small bowl, stir until smooth. Stir in liqueur. Stand at room temperature until spreadable.

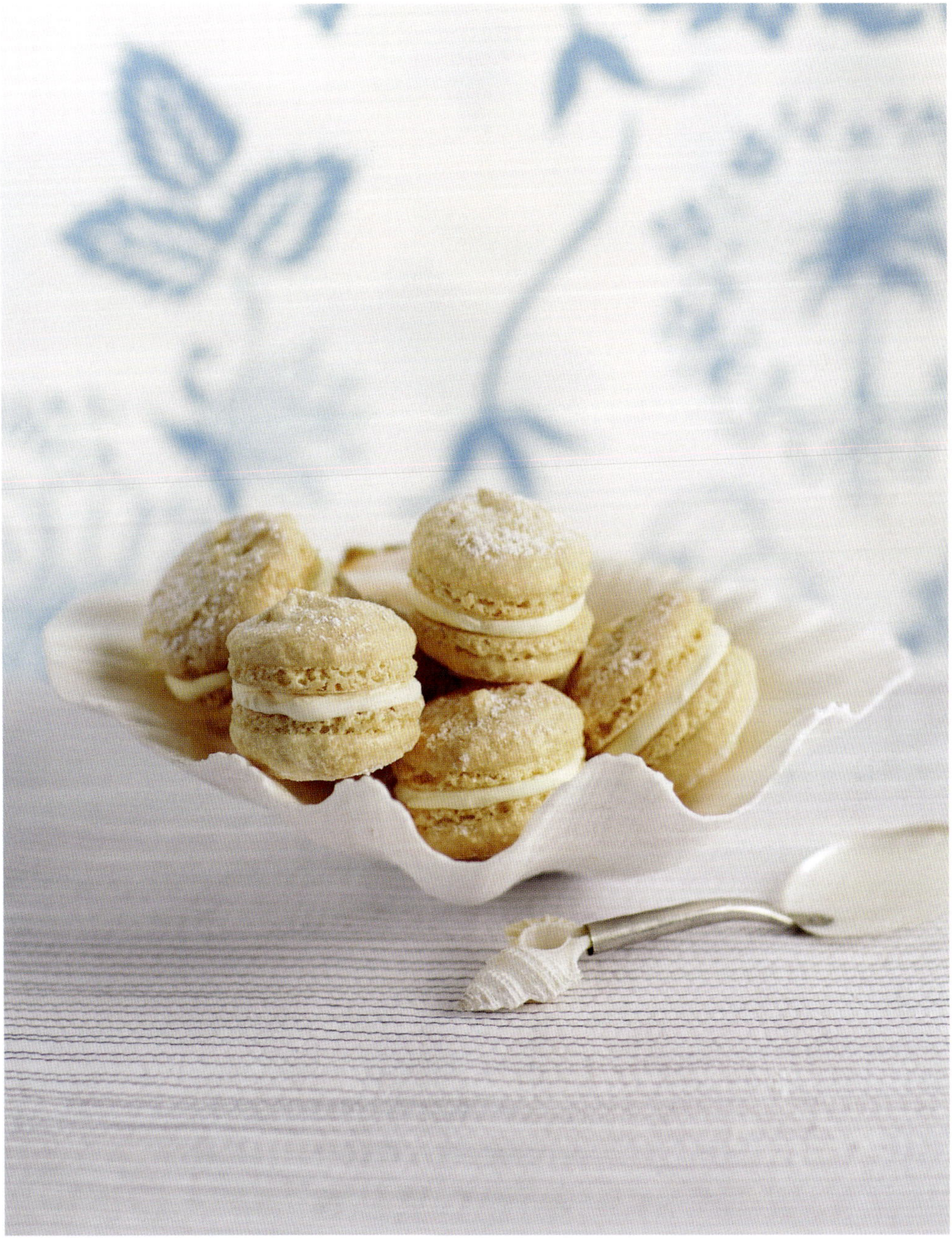

KEEPS
Unfilled macaroons will keep in an airtight container for about a week. Fill macaroons just before serving.

Chocolate Almond Macaroons

prep + cook time 40 MINUTES (+ STANDING & REFRIGERATION) *makes* 16

3 egg whites
¼ cup (55g) caster (superfine) sugar
1 cup (160g) icing (confectioners') sugar
¼ cup (25g) cocoa powder
1 cup (120g) almond meal
2 teaspoons cocoa powder, extra
¼ cup (60ml) pouring cream
150g (5oz) dark (semi-sweet) chocolate, chopped finely

1 Grease oven trays; line with baking paper.
2 Beat egg whites in a small bowl with an electric mixer until soft peaks form. Add caster sugar, beat until sugar dissolves; transfer mixture to a large bowl. Fold in sifted icing sugar and cocoa, and almond meal, in two batches, until mixture is glossy.
3 Spoon mixture into a piping bag fitted with a 2cm (¾in) plain tube. Pipe 4cm (1½in) rounds about 2cm (¾in) apart onto trays. Tap trays on bench so macaroons spread slightly. Dust macaroons with extra sifted cocoa; stand for 30 minutes.
4 Meanwhile, preheat oven to 150°C/300°F.
5 Bake for 20 minutes or until macaroons can be gently pushed without breaking. Cool on trays.
6 Bring cream to the boil in a small saucepan, remove from heat; add chocolate, stir until smooth. Refrigerate for 20 minutes or until spreadable.
7 Sandwich macaroons with chocolate filling.

LEMON MERINGUE
KISSES

prep + cook time 1 HOUR 50 MINUTES (+ REFRIGERATION)　*makes* 24

- 90g (3oz) unsalted butter, chopped
- 1 egg, beaten lightly
- ¼ cup (55g) caster (superfine) sugar
- ½ teaspoon finely grated lemon rind
- 2 tablespoons lemon juice
- 2 egg whites
- ½ cup (110g) caster (superfine) sugar, extra
- 1 teaspoon lemon juice, extra

1 Combine butter, egg, sugar, rind and juice in a small heatproof bowl. Stir over small saucepan of simmering water for 10 minutes or until mixture coats the back of a spoon. Refrigerate curd for 3 hours or overnight.
2 Preheat oven to 120°C/250°F. Grease oven trays; line with baking paper.
3 Beat egg whites, extra sugar and extra juice in a small bowl with an electric mixer for 15 minutes or until sugar is dissolved.
4 Spoon mixture into a piping bag fitted with a 2cm (¾in) fluted tube; pipe 4cm (1½in) stars onto trays 2cm (¾in) apart. Bake meringues for 1 hour. Cool on trays.
5 Sandwich meringues with lemon curd; dust with sifted icing (confectioners') sugar before serving, if you like.

keeps Store unfilled meringues in an airtight container for up to 4 days. Fill meringues just before serving.

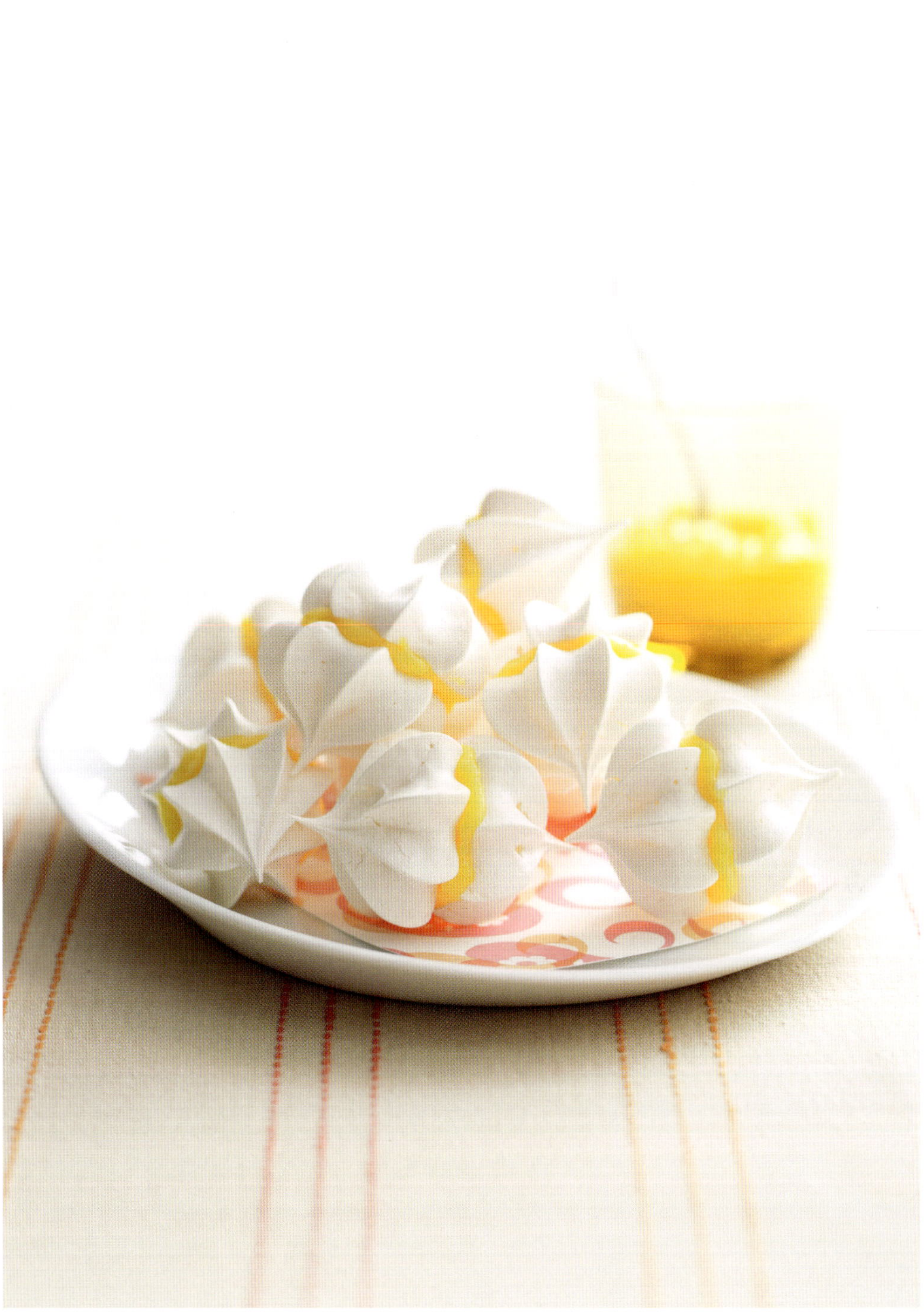

TIP

Keep sheets of paper towel within easy reach when brushing the raspberry puree onto the meringues; wipe the brush between each stroke to keep the bristles clean.

ROSEWATER & RASPBERRY SWIRL MERINGUES

prep + cook time 1 HOUR (+ COOLING) ❈ *makes* 12

150g (5oz) frozen raspberries, thawed
⅓ cup (55g) icing (confectioners') sugar
⅓ cup (80ml) water
4 egg whites
1 cup (220g) caster (superfine) sugar
1 teaspoon white wine vinegar
2 teaspoons rosewater
¾ cup (180ml) thickened (heavy) cream
125g (4oz) fresh raspberries

1 Preheat oven to 150°C/300°F. Grease a large oven tray; line with baking paper.
2 Process raspberries, 2 tablespoons of the icing sugar and the water until smooth. Push raspberry puree through a fine sieve over a small bowl; discard seeds.
3 Beat egg whites in a large bowl with an electric mixer until soft peaks form. Gradually add caster sugar, beating until glossy and stiff. Beat in vinegar and rosewater on low speed until just combined (overbeating at this stage will cause the meringue to deflate).
4 Drop large serving-spoon-sized amounts of meringue mixture (about ⅓ cup each) onto the tray, 5cm (2in) apart. Using a pastry brush, brush a little of the raspberry puree on the meringues, swirling gently to create a brush stroke effect.
5 Reduce oven to 120°C/250°F; bake meringues for 45 minutes or until dry to touch. Cool in oven with door ajar.
6 Meanwhile, place remaining raspberry puree in a small saucepan with the remaining icing sugar. Bring to the boil. Reduce heat; simmer for 3 minutes or until thickened slightly. Cool.
7 Beat cream in a small bowl with the electric mixer. Serve meringues with cream, drizzled with raspberry sauce, and topped with fresh raspberries.

keeps Meringues can be made a day ahead; store them in an airtight container at room temperature.

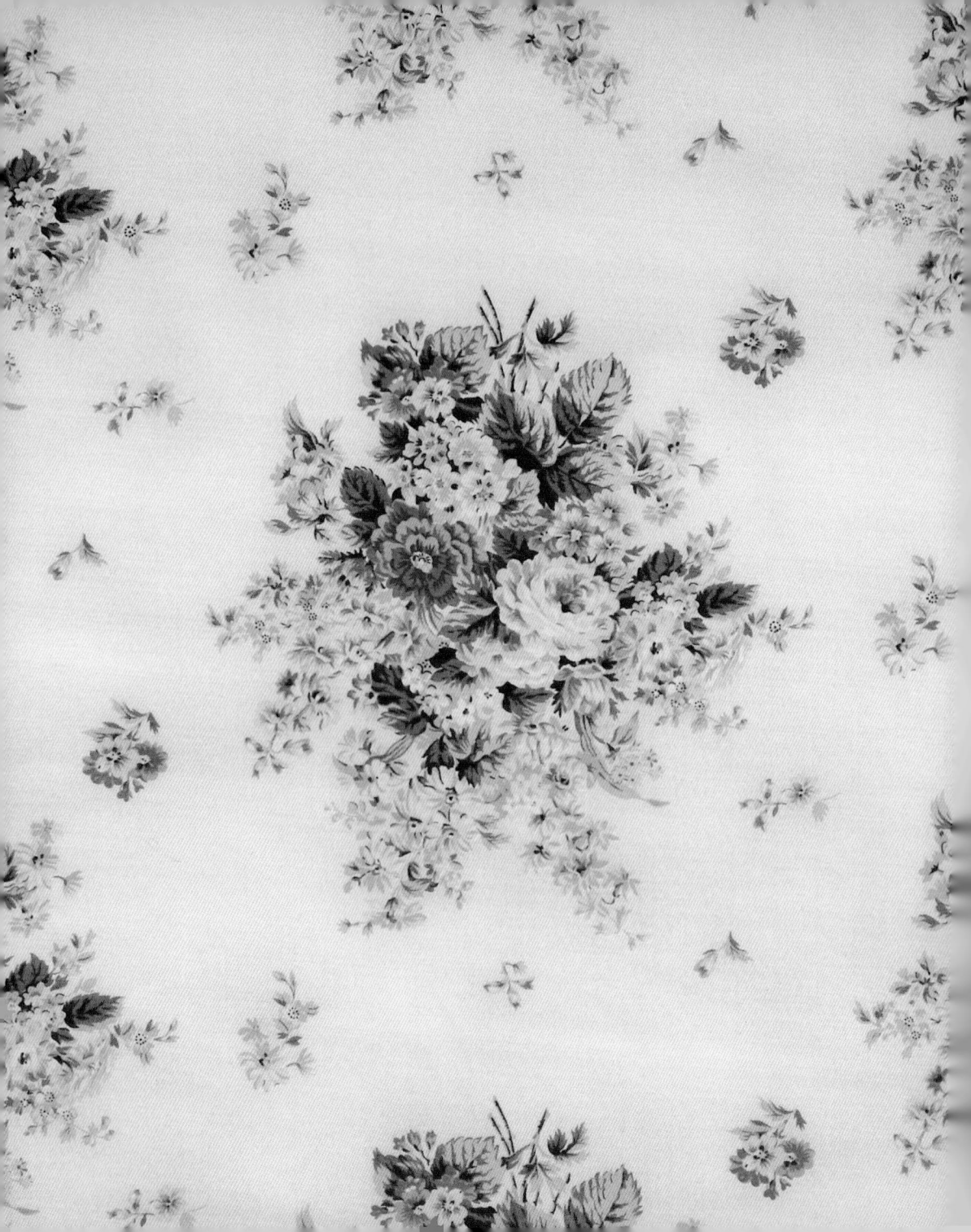

BISCUITS & BISCOTTI

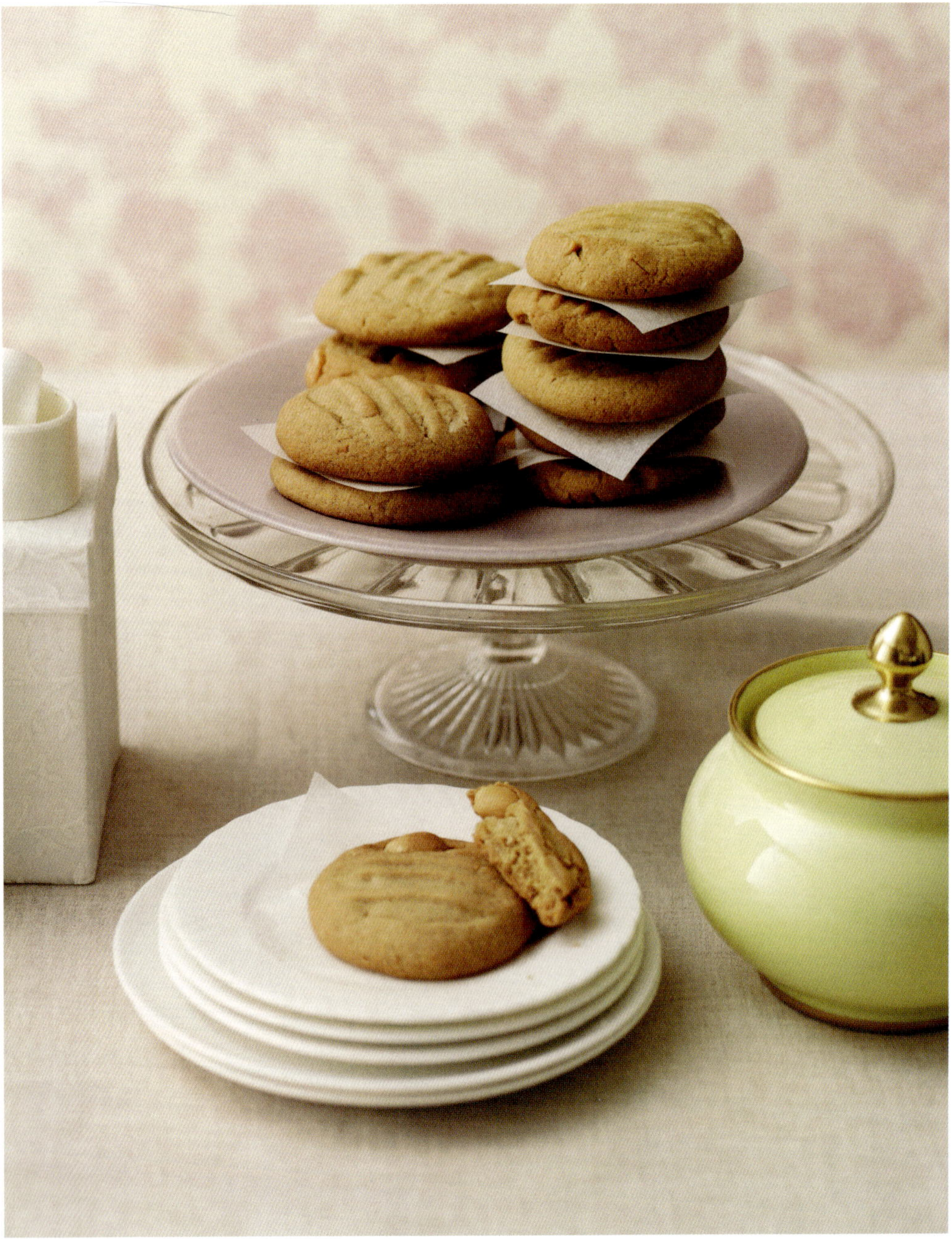

PEANUT BUTTER COOKIES

prep + cook time 25 MINUTES ✻ *makes* 30

125g (4oz) butter, softened
¼ cup (70g) crunchy peanut butter
¾ cup (165g) firmly packed brown sugar
1 egg
1½ cups (225g) plain (all-purpose) flour
½ teaspoon bicarbonate of soda (baking soda)
½ cup (70g) roasted unsalted peanuts, chopped coarsely

1 Preheat oven to 180°C/350°F. Grease oven trays; line with baking paper.
2 Beat butter, peanut butter, sugar and egg in a small bowl with an electric mixer until smooth (do not over-mix). Transfer mixture to a medium bowl; stir in sifted flour and bicarbonate of soda, then peanuts.
3 Roll level tablespoons of mixture into balls; place 5cm (2in) apart on trays and flatten with floured fork.
4 Bake cookies for 12 minutes or until golden brown. Cool on trays.

keeps Store in an airtight container for up to a week.

PASSIONFRUIT CREAM
BISCUITS

prep + cook time 45 MINUTES (+ REFRIGERATION & COOLING)   *makes* 25

You need about 6 passionfruit for this recipe.

125g (4oz) butter, softened
2 teaspoons finely grated lemon rind
⅓ cup (75g) caster (superfine) sugar
2 tablespoons golden syrup or treacle
1 cup (150g) self-raising flour
⅔ cup (100g) plain (all-purpose) flour
¼ cup (60ml) passionfruit pulp

PASSIONFRUIT CREAM
2 tablespoons passionfruit pulp
90g (3oz) butter, softened
1 cup (160g) icing (confectioners') sugar

1 Beat butter, rind and sugar in a small bowl with an electric mixer until light and fluffy. Add golden syrup, beat until combined. Stir in sifted dry ingredients and passionfruit pulp.
2 Turn dough onto a floured surface, knead gently until smooth. Cut dough in half; roll each portion between sheets of baking paper to 5mm (¼in) thickness. Refrigerate for 30 minutes.
3 Preheat oven to 180°C/350°F. Grease oven trays; line with baking paper.
4 Cut 24 x 4cm (1½in) fluted rounds from each portion of dough; place about 2.5cm (1in) apart on trays.
5 Bake biscuits for 10 minutes or until golden. Cool on trays.
6 Meanwhile, make passionfruit cream.
7 Spoon passionfruit cream into a piping bag fitted with a 5mm (¼in) fluted tube. Pipe cream onto half the biscuits; top with remaining biscuits. Serve dusted with a little extra sifted icing sugar, if you like.
PASSIONFRUIT CREAM Strain passionfruit pulp through fine sieve into small jug, discard seeds. Beat butter and sugar in a small bowl with an electric mixer until light and fluffy. Beat in passionfruit juice.

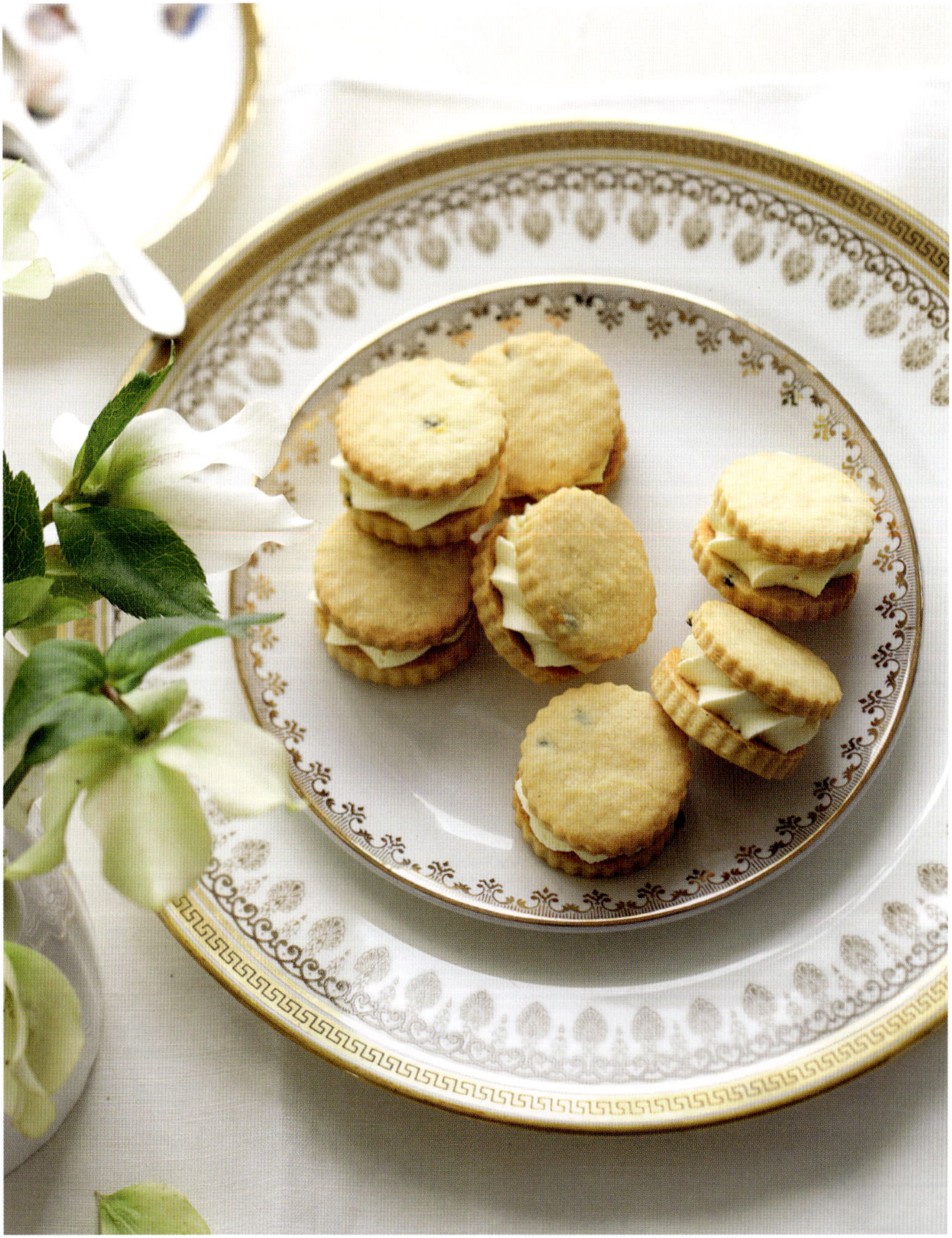

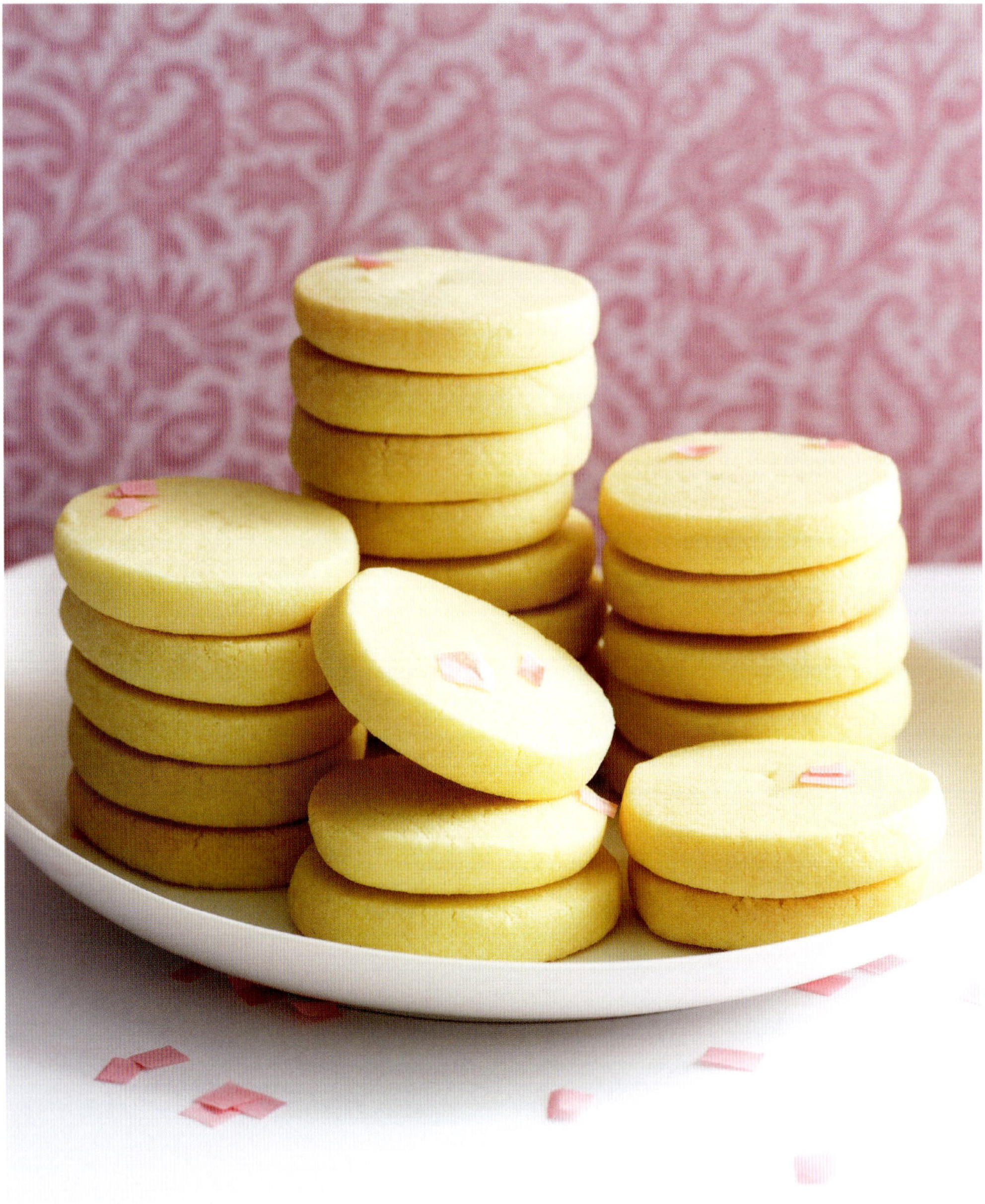

REFRIGERATOR
SLICE-AND-BAKE COOKIES

prep + cook time 30 MINUTES (+ REFRIGERATION) *makes* 50

250g (8oz) butter, softened
1 cup (160g) icing (confectioners') sugar
2½ cups (375g) plain (all-purpose) flour

1 Beat butter and sifted icing sugar in a small bowl with an electric mixer until light and fluffy. Transfer to a large bowl; stir in sifted flour, in two batches.
2 Knead dough lightly on a floured surface until smooth. Divide dough in half; roll each half into a 25cm (10in) log. Enclose logs in plastic wrap; refrigerate for 1 hour or until firm.
3 Preheat oven to 180°C/350°F. Grease oven trays.
4 Cut logs into 1cm (½in) slices; place 2.5cm (1in) apart on trays.
5 Bake cookies for 10 minutes or until lightly golden. Cool on trays.

tip These basic cookies can be topped with nuts before baking or, once cooked, iced then dipped into various sprinkles, or simply dusted lightly with sifted icing sugar. If you want to flavour the dough, beat any essence or extract of your choice with the butter and sugar mixture, or beat in a teaspoon or two of finely grated citrus rind.
keeps The cookies will keep in an airtight container for at least a week.

LIME & GINGER
KISSES

prep + cook time 35 MINUTES (+ COOLING) ※ *makes* 18

125g (4oz) butter, softened
½ cup (110g) firmly packed brown sugar
1 egg
¼ cup (35g) plain (all-purpose) flour
¼ cup (35g) self-raising flour
¾ cup (110g) cornflour (cornstarch)
2 teaspoons ground ginger
½ teaspoon ground cinnamon
¼ teaspoon ground cloves

LIME BUTTERCREAM
60g (2oz) butter, softened
2 teaspoons finely grated lime rind
¾ cup (120g) icing (confectioners') sugar
2 teaspoons milk

1 Preheat oven to 180°C/350°F. Line oven trays with baking paper.
2 Beat butter, sugar and egg in a small bowl with an electric mixer until smooth. Stir in the sifted dry ingredients.
3 Roll heaped teaspoons of mixture into balls; place balls about 5cm (2in) apart on trays.
4 Bake biscuits for 10 minutes or until golden brown. Loosen biscuits; cool on trays.
5 Meanwhile, make lime buttercream.
6 Sandwich cooled biscuits with buttercream.
LIME BUTTERCREAM Beat butter and rind in a small bowl with the electric mixer until as white as possible. Beat in sifted icing sugar and milk, in two batches.

keeps Unfilled biscuits will keep in an airtight container for up to a week. Filled biscuits will keep for a few days in an airtight container in the fridge.

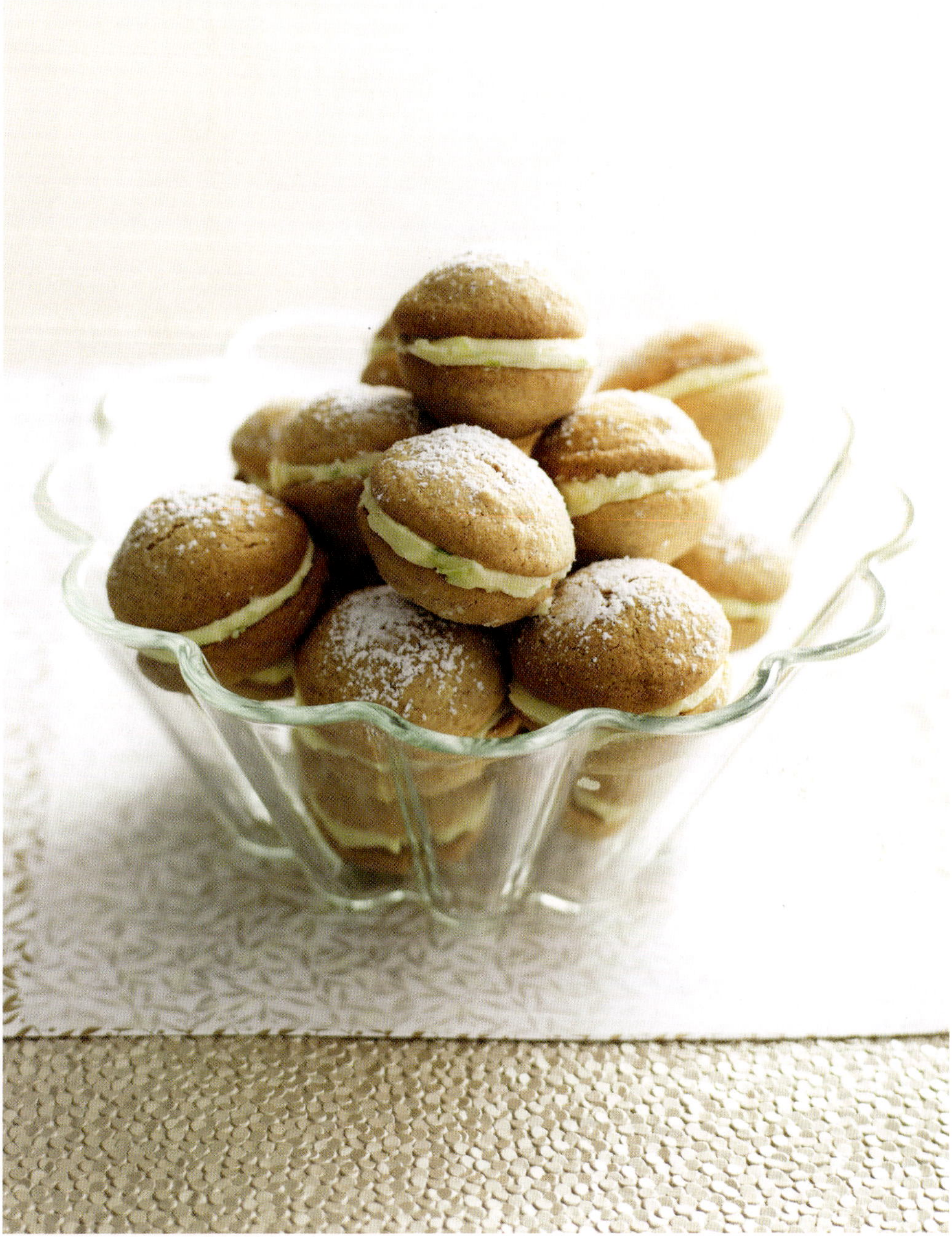

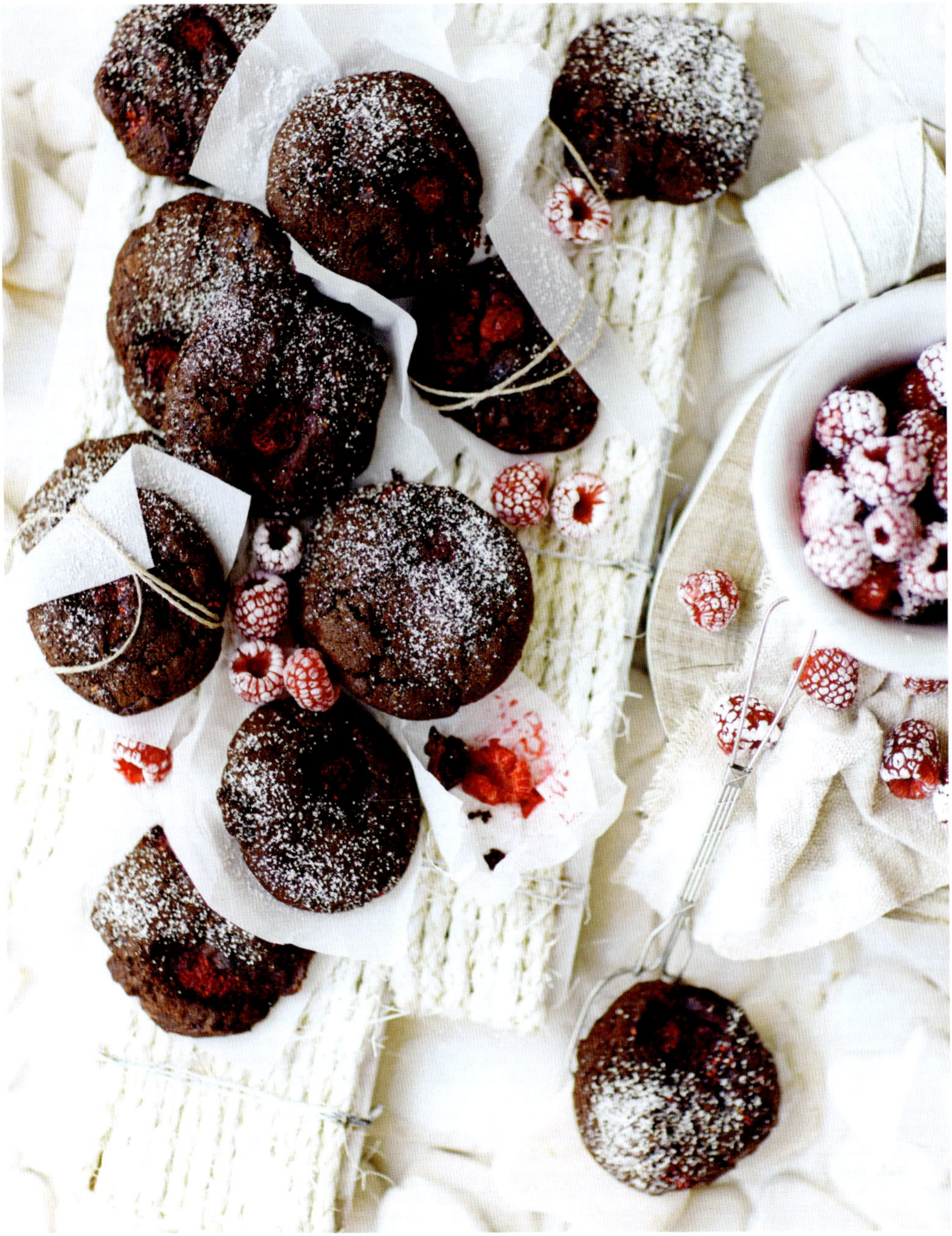

CHOCOLATE CHUNK & RASPBERRY COOKIES

prep + cook time 35 MINUTES *makes* 24

125g (4oz) butter, softened
¾ cup (165g) firmly packed brown sugar
1 egg
1 teaspoon vanilla extract
1 cup (150g) plain (all-purpose) flour
¼ cup (35g) self-raising flour
⅛ cup (35g) cocoa powder
½ teaspoon bicarbonate of soda (baking soda)
90g (3oz) dark (semi-sweet) chocolate, chopped coarsely
125g (4oz) frozen raspberries

1 Preheat oven to 180°C/350°F. Line oven trays with baking paper.
2 Beat butter, sugar, egg and vanilla in a small bowl with an electric mixer until combined. Stir in sifted flours, cocoa and soda, in two batches, then stir in chocolate and raspberries.
3 Drop tablespoons of mixture 5cm (2in) apart onto trays; flatten slightly.
4 Bake cookies for 12 minutes or until a biscuit can be gently pushed without breaking. Leave cookies on trays for 5 minutes before transferring to a wire rack to cool.

tips Mix and match different coloured chocolate with different types of berries if you like. Biscuits generally feel soft in the oven and become firmer as they cool. If they are very soft, loosen with a palette knife or spatula and lift onto a wire rack to cool.
keeps These cookies can be made a day ahead; store in an airtight container in the fridge.

LAVENDER SHORTBREAD

prep + cook time 40 MINUTES *makes* 32

250g (8oz) unsalted butter, softened
⅓ cup (75g) caster (superfine) sugar
1 tablespoon water
2 cups (300g) plain (all-purpose) flour
½ cup (100g) rice flour
2 tablespoons dried edible lavender, chopped coarsely
2 tablespoons demerara sugar, plus extra

1 Preheat oven to 160°C/325°F. Grease oven trays.
2 Beat butter and caster sugar in a small bowl with an electric mixer until light and fluffy; transfer to a large bowl. Stir in the water, sifted flours and half the lavender, in two batches.
3 Turn dough onto a floured surface, knead gently until smooth. Shape dough into two 6cm x 20cm (2¼in x 8in) rectangular logs; cut into 1cm (½in) slices. Place about 2.5cm (1in) apart on oven trays; sprinkle with demerara sugar and remaining lavender.
4 Bake shortbread for 10 minutes or until light golden. Stand for 5 minutes; transfer to a wire rack to cool. Sprinkle shortbread with extra demerara sugar before serving.

TIP
Dried edible lavender is available from specialist cooking stores.

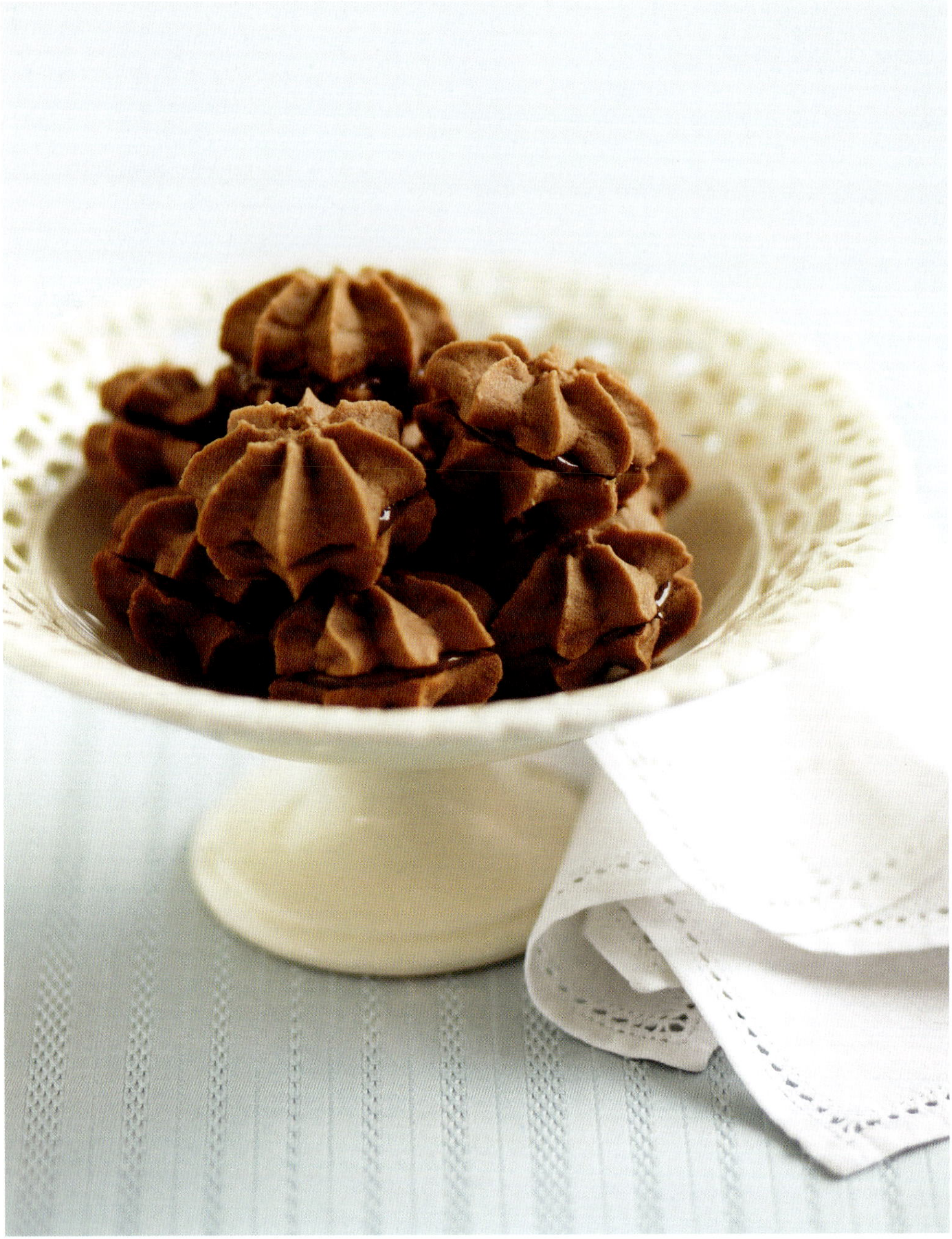

CHOCOLATE
MELTING MOMENTS

prep + cook time 25 MINUTES (+ COOLING)   *makes* 20

- 125g (4oz) butter, softened
- 2 tablespoons icing (confectioners') sugar
- ¾ cup (110g) plain (all-purpose) flour
- 2 tablespoons cornflour (cornstarch)
- 1 tablespoon cocoa powder
- ¼ cup (85g) chocolate hazelnut spread

1 Preheat oven to 180°C/350°F. Grease oven trays; line with baking paper.
2 Beat butter and sifted icing sugar in a small bowl with an electric mixer until light and fluffy. Stir in sifted dry ingredients.
3 Spoon mixture into a piping bag fitted with 1cm (½in) fluted tube. Pipe stars about 3cm (1¼in) apart on trays. Bake for 10 minutes or until just firm; cool on trays. Sandwich biscuits with hazelnut spread.

keeps Store unfilled biscuits in an airtight container for up to a week. Store filled biscuits in an airtight container, in the refrigerator, for up to 3 days.

CITRUS COCONUT BISCOTTI

prep + cook time 1 HOUR 25 MINUTES (+ COOLING) ✳ *makes* 60

1 cup (220g) caster (superfine) sugar
2 eggs
1⅓ cups (200g) plain (all-purpose) flour
⅓ cup (50g) self-raising flour
1 cup (80g) desiccated coconut
2 teaspoons finely grated lemon rind
2 teaspoons finely grated lime rind
2 teaspoons finely grated orange rind

1 Preheat oven to 180°C/350°F. Grease oven trays; line with baking paper.
2 Whisk sugar and eggs in a medium bowl until combined; stir in sifted flours then coconut and rinds.
3 Knead dough on a floured surface until smooth. Divide dough in half, roll each portion into a 30cm (12in) log; place logs on tray. Bake for 30 minutes. Cool on trays for 10 minutes.
4 Reduce oven temperature to 150°C/300°F.
5 Using a serrated knife, cut logs diagonally into 5mm (¼in) slices. Place slices, in a single layer, on ungreased oven trays. Bake biscotti for 30 minutes or until dry and crisp, turning halfway through baking. Cool on wire racks.

KEEPS
Store in an airtight container for up to 1 month.

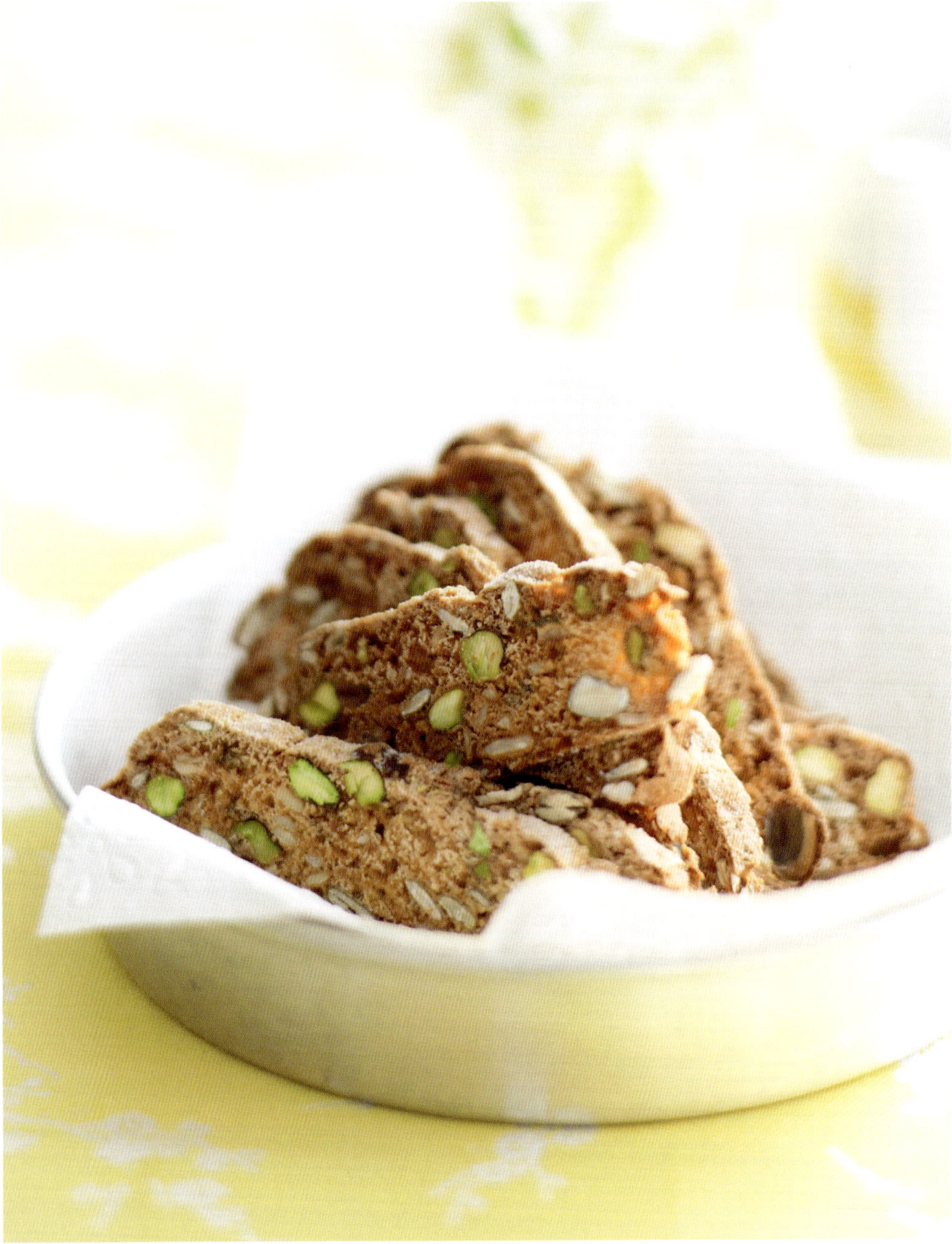

Lemon, Honey & Pistachio Biscotti

prep + cook time 1 HOUR 10 MINUTES (+ COOLING) *makes* 40

½ cup (110g) caster (superfine) sugar
1 egg
½ cup (75g) plain (all-purpose) flour
¼ cup (35g) self-raising flour
2 teaspoons finely grated lemon rind
½ cup (70g) roasted unsalted pistachios
¼ cup (50g) pepitas (pumpkin seed kernels)
¼ cup (35g) sunflower seeds
1 tablespoon honey
2 teaspoons caster (superfine) sugar, extra

1 Preheat oven to 180°C/350°F. Grease oven trays; line with baking paper.

2 Whisk sugar and egg in a medium bowl; stir in sifted flours and rind, then pistachios, seeds and honey. Shape dough into a 20cm (8in) log; place on tray. Sprinkle with extra sugar; bake for 30 minutes. Cool on trays for 10 minutes.

3 Reduce oven temperature to 150°C/300°F.

4 Using a serrated knife, cut log diagonally into 5mm (¼in) slices. Place slices, in a single layer, on ungreased oven trays. Bake biscotti for 20 minutes or until dry and crisp, turning halfway through baking. Cool on wire racks.

keeps Store in an airtight container for up to 1 month.

TRIPLE CHOCOLATE & HAZELNUT BISCOTTI

prep + cook time 1 HOUR 10 MINUTES (+ REFRIGERATION & COOLING) *makes* 30

30g (1oz) butter, softened
½ cup (110g) firmly packed brown sugar
1 teaspoon vanilla extract
3 eggs
¾ cup (110g) plain (all-purpose) flour
¼ cup (35g) self-raising flour
⅓ cup (35g) cocoa powder
1 cup (140g) roasted hazelnuts, chopped coarsely
60g (2oz) dark (semi-sweet) chocolate, chopped finely
30g (1oz) milk chocolate, chopped finely
60g (2oz) white chocolate, chopped finely

1 Beat butter, sugar and vanilla in a small bowl with an electric mixer until combined. Add eggs, beat until combined (mixture will curdle at this stage, but will come together later). Stir in sifted dry ingredients, then hazelnuts and chocolates. Cover mixture, refrigerate for 1 hour.
2 Preheat oven to 180°C/350°F. Grease oven trays; line with baking paper.
3 Divide dough in half, roll each portion into a 15cm (6in) log; place logs on tray. Bake for 25 minutes. Cool on trays for 10 minutes.
4 Reduce oven temperature to 150°C/300°F.
5 Using a serrated knife, cut logs diagonally into 1cm (½in) slices. Place slices, in a single layer, on ungreased oven trays. Bake biscotti for 30 minutes or until dry and crisp, turning halfway through baking. Cool on wire racks.

KEEPS
Store in an airtight container
for up to 1 month.

NOTES
Almond bread is an excellent accompaniment to desserts such as mousse, sorbet or ice-cream.

ALMOND BREAD

prep + cook time 1 HOUR 35 MINUTES (+ COOLING & STANDING) *makes* 40

3 egg whites
½ cup (110g) caster (superfine) sugar
1 cup (150g) plain (all-purpose) flour
¾ cup (120g) almonds

1 Preheat oven to 180°C/350°F. Grease a 10cm x 20cm (4in x 8in) loaf pan.
2 Beat egg whites in a large bowl with an electric mixer until soft peaks form. Gradually add sugar, beating until dissolved between additions.
3 Fold sifted flour and almonds into egg white mixture, spread mixture into pan; bake for 30 minutes. Cool bread in pan. Remove bread from pan, wrap in foil; stand overnight.
4 Preheat oven to 150°C/300°F.
5 Using a sharp serrated knife, cut bread into wafer-thin slices; place, in a single layer, on ungreased oven trays. Bake for 45 minutes or until dry and crisp. Cool on a wire rack.

keeps Store in an airtight container for up to 1 month.

Apple, Cranberry & White Chocolate Biscotti

prep + cook time 1 HOUR 25 MINUTES (+ COOLING)   *makes* 60

1 cup (220g) caster (superfine) sugar
2 eggs
1⅓ cups (200g) plain (all-purpose) flour
⅓ cup (50g) self-raising flour
½ cup (35g) finely chopped dried apple
½ cup (65g) coarsely chopped dried cranberries
90g (3oz) white chocolate, grated coarsely

1 Preheat oven to 180°C/350°F. Grease oven trays; line with baking paper.
2 Whisk sugar and eggs in a medium bowl until combined; stir in sifted flours then apple, cranberries and chocolate.
3 Knead dough on a floured surface until smooth. Divide dough in half, roll each portion into a 30cm (12in) log; place logs on trays. Bake for 30 minutes. Cool on trays for 10 minutes.
4 Reduce oven temperature to 150°C/300°F.
5 Using a serrated knife, cut logs diagonally into 5mm (¼in) slices. Place slices, in a single layer, on ungreased oven trays. Bake biscotti for 30 minutes or until dry and crisp, turning halfway through baking. Cool on wire racks.

KEEPS
Store in an airtight container for up to 1 month.

PUFFS & PASTRIES

PARIS BREST

prep + cook time 1 HOUR 10 MINUTES (+ COOLING) ✤ *makes* 12

½ cup (125ml) water
60g (2oz) butter, chopped finely
1 tablespoon caster (superfine) sugar
½ cup (75g) strong baker's flour
3 eggs
2 tablespoons flaked almonds
1 tablespoon icing (confectioners') sugar

PRALINE CREAM
⅓ cup (75g) caster (superfine) sugar
2 tablespoons water
⅓ cup (25g) flaked almonds, roasted
2 cups (500ml) thickened (heavy) cream, whipped

1 Preheat oven to 220°C/425°F. Grease oven trays.
2 To make choux pastry, combine the water, butter and caster sugar in a medium saucepan; bring to the boil. Add flour, beat with a wooden spoon over medium heat until mixture comes away from base of pan. Transfer pastry to a medium bowl; beat in two of the eggs, one at a time. Whisk remaining egg with a fork; beat enough of the egg into the pastry until it becomes smooth and glossy but will hold its shape.
3 Spoon pastry into a piping bag fitted with a 1.5cm (¾in) fluted tube; pipe 5.5cm (2¼in) rings, about 5cm (2in) apart on trays. Sprinkle with almonds.
4 Bake rings for 10 minutes. Reduce oven to 180°C/350°F; bake for 15 minutes. Using a serrated knife, split rings in half and remove any soft centres. Return to trays, bake for a further 5 minutes or until puffs are dry. Cool on trays.
5 Meanwhile, make praline cream.
6 Spread cream into pastry bases; top with pastry tops. Dust with icing sugar to serve.

PRALINE CREAM Line a tray with baking paper. Stir sugar and the water in a small saucepan over high heat, without boiling, until sugar dissolves. Bring to the boil. Boil, uncovered, without stirring, until golden brown. Allow bubbles to subside; add almonds, but do not stir. Pour mixture onto tray; leave praline to set at room temperature. Break praline into pieces, then process until fine; fold into whipped cream.

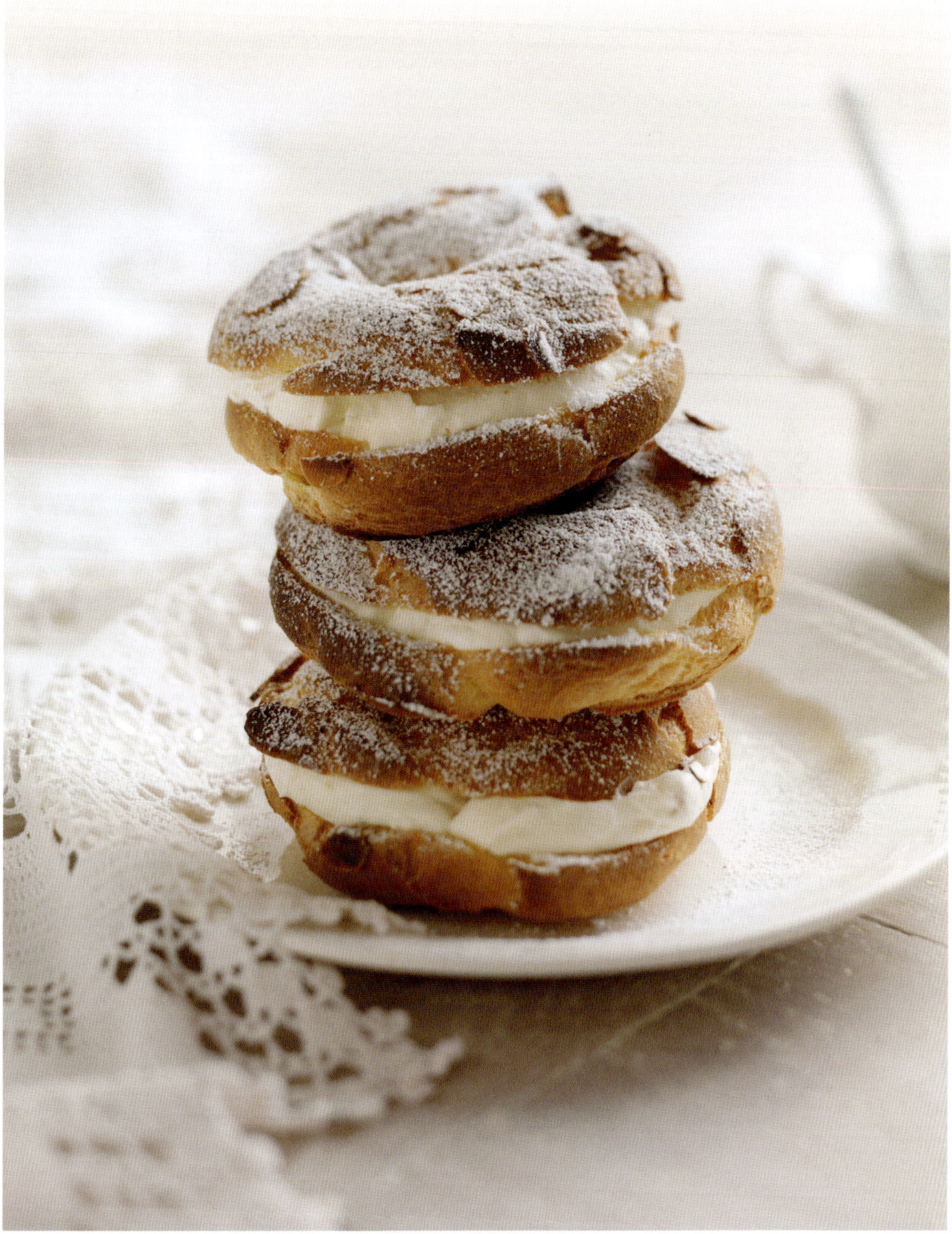

chocolate
ÉCLAIRS

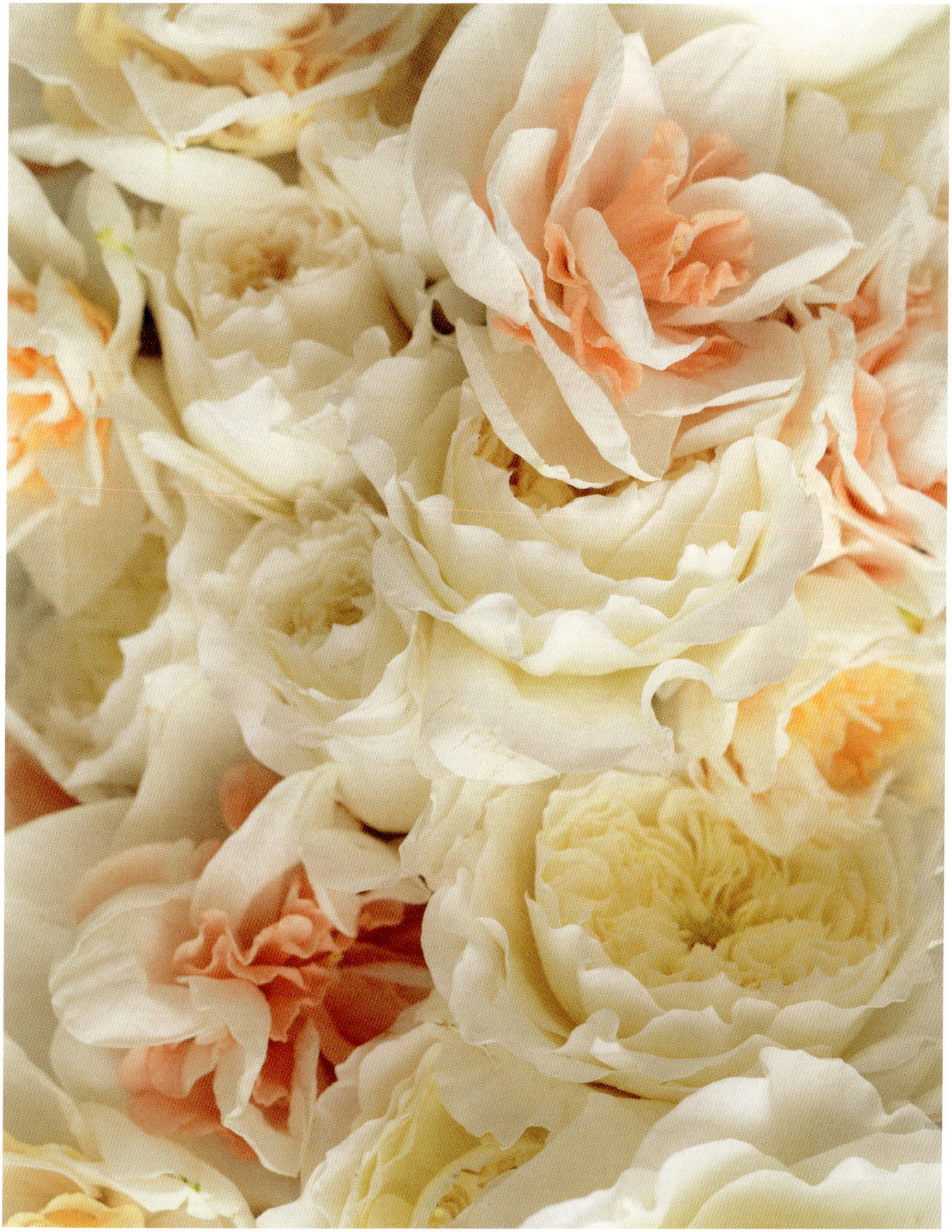

CHOCOLATE ÉCLAIRS

prep + cook time 1 HOUR (+ REFRIGERATION & COOLING) ❋ *makes* 16

15g (½oz) butter
¼ cup (60ml) water
¼ cup (35g) plain (all-purpose) flour
1 egg

CUSTARD CREAM
1 vanilla bean
1 cup (250ml) milk
3 egg yolks
⅓ cup (75g) caster (superfine) sugar
2 tablespoons pure cornflour (cornstarch)
⅓ cup (80ml) thickened (heavy) cream, whipped

CHOCOLATE GLAZE
30g (1oz) dark (semi-sweet) chocolate, chopped coarsely
30g (1oz) milk chocolate, chopped coarsely
15g (½oz) butter

1 Make custard cream.
2 Preheat oven to 220°C/425°F. Grease two oven trays.
3 Combine butter and the water in a small saucepan; bring to the boil. Add flour, beat with a wooden spoon over medium heat until mixture comes away from base and side of pan and forms a smooth ball.
4 Transfer mixture to a small bowl; beat in egg with an electric mixer until mixture becomes glossy. Spoon pastry mixture into a piping bag fitted with a 1cm (½in) plain tube. Pipe 5cm (2in) lengths about 5cm (2in) apart on trays; bake for 7 minutes. Reduce oven temperature to 180°C/350°F; bake for a further 10 minutes. Using a serrated knife, cut éclairs in half and remove any soft centres. Return to trays, bake for a further 5 minutes or until dry to touch. Cool on trays.
5 Make chocolate glaze.
6 Spoon custard cream into a piping bag fitted with a 5mm (¼in) fluted tube. Pipe custard cream into 16 pastry bases, top with pastry tops. Spread éclairs with chocolate glaze.

CUSTARD CREAM Split vanilla bean, scrape seeds into milk in a small saucepan (discard bean); bring to the boil. Meanwhile, beat egg yolks, sugar and cornflour in a small bowl with an electric mixer until thick. With motor operating, gradually beat in hot milk mixture. Return custard to pan; stir over medium heat until mixture boils and thickens. Cover surface of custard with plastic wrap; refrigerate 1 hour. Fold cream into custard in two batches.

CHOCOLATE GLAZE Stir ingredients in a small heatproof bowl over a small saucepan of simmering water until smooth. Use while warm.

keeps Éclairs and custard cream can be made and stored separately, 2 days ahead; fold the cream into custard just before using. Assemble and serve the éclairs as close to serving time as possible – about an hour is good.

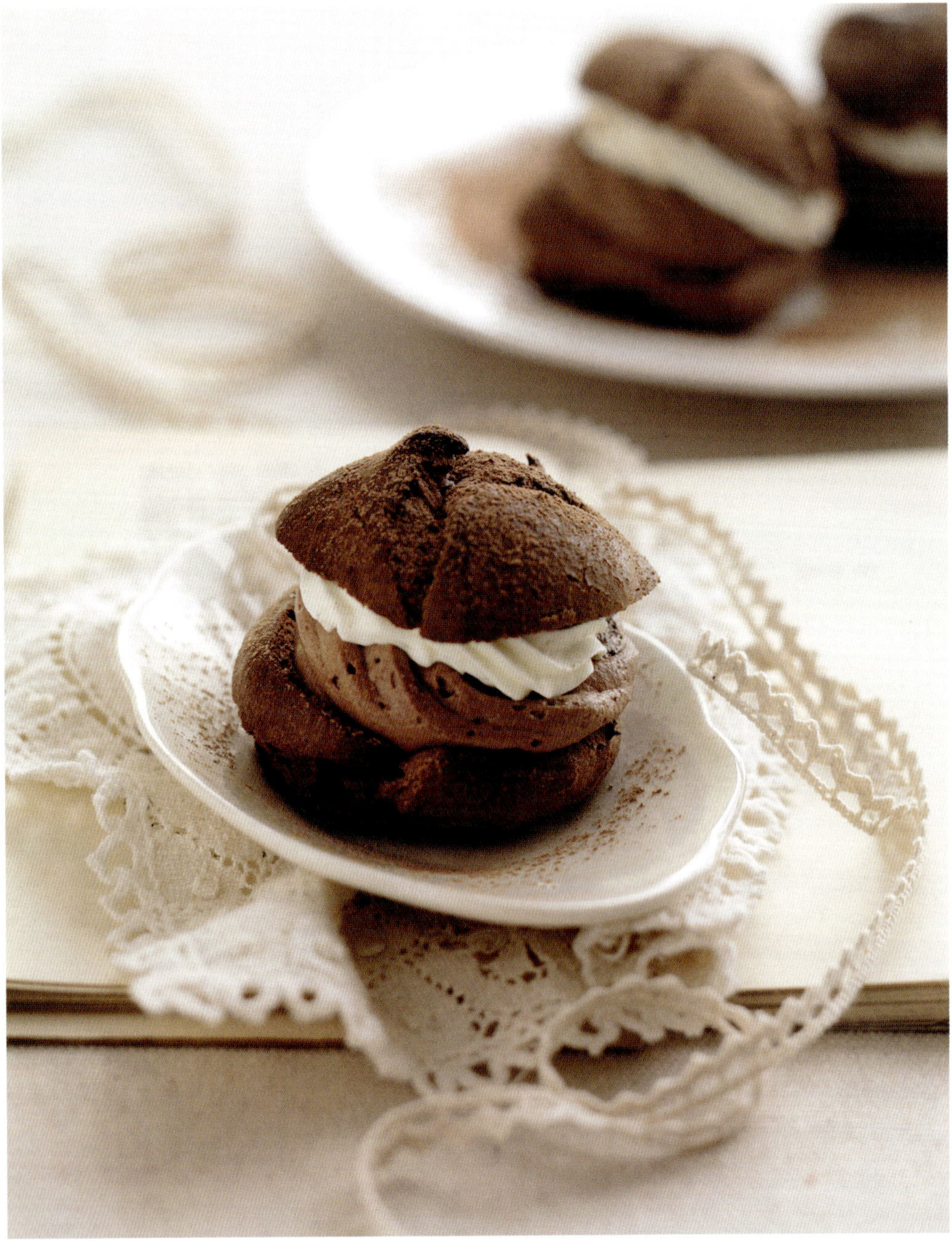

DOUBLE CHOCOLATE PUFFS

prep + cook time 1 HOUR 20 MINUTES (+ REFRIGERATION) *makes* 10

½ cup (125ml) water
60g (2oz) butter, chopped finely
1 tablespoon caster (superfine) sugar
½ cup (75g) strong baker's flour
2 tablespoons cocoa powder
3 eggs
1 cup (250ml) thickened (heavy) cream, whipped

CHOCOLATE MOUSSE

90g (3oz) dark (semi-sweet) chocolate, chopped coarsely
⅔ cup (160ml) thickened (heavy) cream
1 egg, separated
1 tablespoon caster (superfine) sugar

1 Make chocolate mousse.
2 Preheat oven to 220°C/425°F. Grease two oven trays.
3 To make choux pastry, combine the water, butter and sugar in a medium saucepan; bring to the boil. Add sifted flour and cocoa, beat with a wooden spoon over medium heat until mixture comes away from base of pan. Transfer pastry to a medium bowl; beat in two of the eggs, one at a time. Whisk remaining egg with a fork; beat enough of the egg into the pastry until it becomes smooth and glossy but will hold its shape.
4 Drop rounded tablespoons of pastry, about 5cm (2in) apart, on trays.
5 Bake puffs for 10 minutes. Reduce oven to 180°C/350°F; bake for 15 minutes. Using a serrated knife, split puffs in half, remove any soft centres; return to trays, bake for a further 5 minutes or until puffs are dry. Cool on trays.
6 Spoon chocolate mousse into a piping bag fitted with a 1.5cm (¾in) fluted tube; pipe mousse into pastry bases. Top with whipped cream then pastry tops. Dust with a little extra sifted cocoa.

CHOCOLATE MOUSSE Place chocolate and half the cream in a medium heatproof bowl over a medium saucepan of simmering water; stir until smooth. Cool mixture 5 minutes, then stir in egg yolk. Beat remaining cream in a small bowl with an electric mixer until soft peaks form. Beat egg white in another small bowl with electric mixer until soft peaks form; add sugar, beat until sugar dissolves. Fold cream into chocolate mixture, then fold in egg white. Cover; refrigerate overnight.

MARBLED RASPBERRY MASCARPONE PUFFS

prep + cook time 1 HOUR 15 MINUTES ✤ *makes* 14

½ cup (125ml) water
60g (2oz) butter, chopped finely
1 tablespoon caster (superfine) sugar
½ cup (75g) strong baker's flour
3 eggs
200g (6½oz) fresh raspberries
icing (confectioners') sugar, for dusting

MASCARPONE CREAM

250g (8oz) cream cheese, softened
250g (8oz) mascarpone
600ml thickened (heavy) cream
½ cup (160g) raspberry jam

RASPBERRY GLACÉ ICING

2 fresh raspberries
1 cup (160g) icing (confectioners') sugar
10g (½oz) soft butter
2 teaspoons hot water, approximately

1 Preheat oven to 220°C/425°F. Grease two oven trays.
2 To make choux pastry, combine the water, butter and sugar in a medium saucepan; bring to the boil. Add flour, beat with wooden spoon over medium heat until mixture comes away from base of pan. Transfer pastry to a medium bowl; beat in two of the eggs, one at a time. Whisk remaining egg with a fork, beat enough of the egg into the pastry until it becomes smooth and glossy but will hold its shape.
3 Drop level tablespoons of pastry, about 5cm (2in) apart, on trays.
4 Bake for 10 minutes. Reduce oven to 180°C/350°F; bake for 15 minutes. Using a serrated knife, split puffs in half, remove any soft centres; return to trays, bake for a further 5 minutes or until dry. Cool on trays.
5 Meanwhile, make mascarpone cream and raspberry glacé icing.
6 Spoon mascarpone cream into pastry bases; top with pastry tops. Drizzle puffs with icing, top with raspberries. Dust with icing sugar to serve.

MASCARPONE CREAM Beat cream cheese and mascarpone in a bowl with an electric mixer until smooth. Fold in cream, then jam for marbled effect.

RASPBERRY GLACÉ ICING Push raspberries through a fine sieve into a small heatproof bowl; discard seeds. Sift icing sugar into raspberry puree; stir in butter and enough of the water to make a thick paste. Place bowl over a small saucepan of simmering water; stir until icing is spreadable.

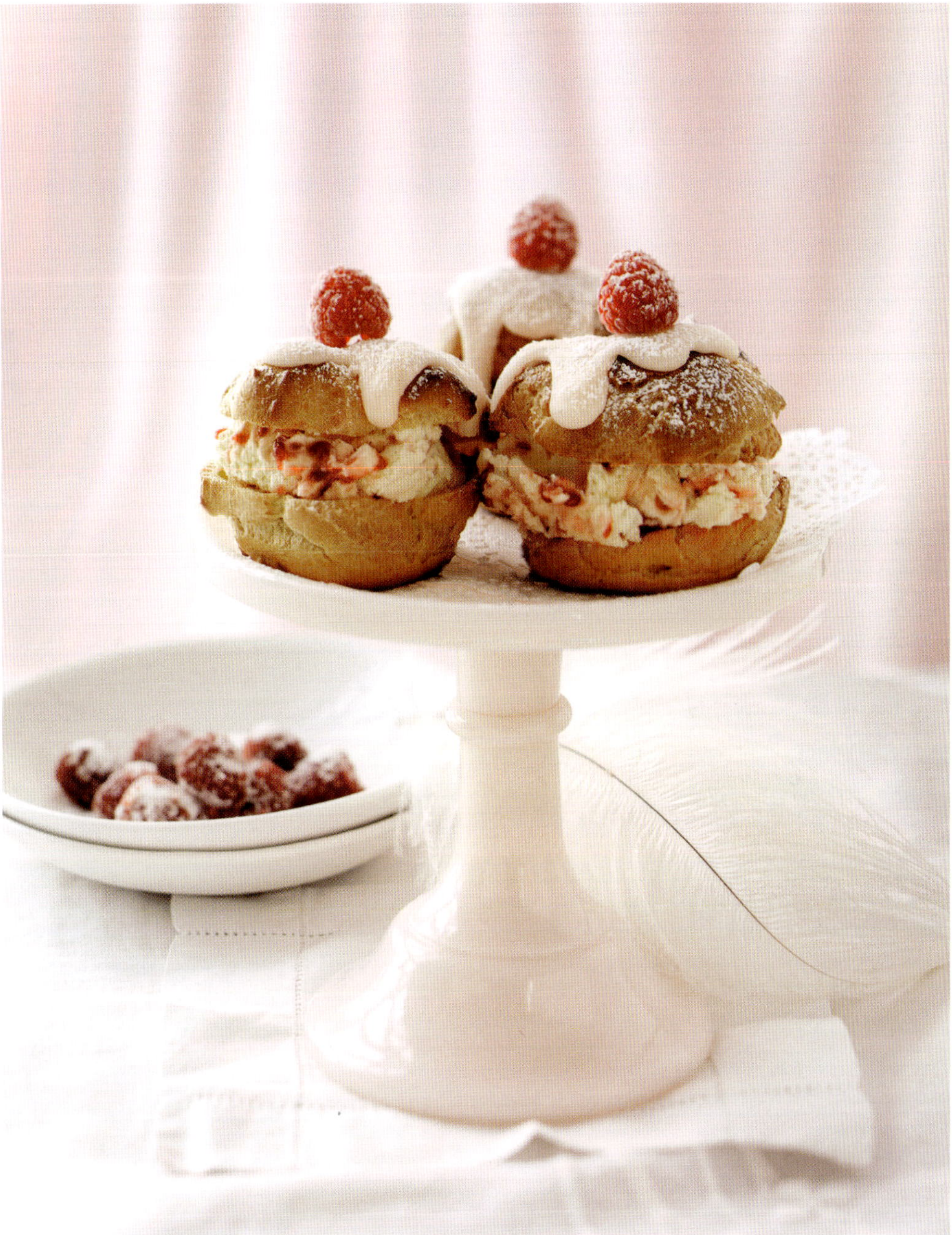

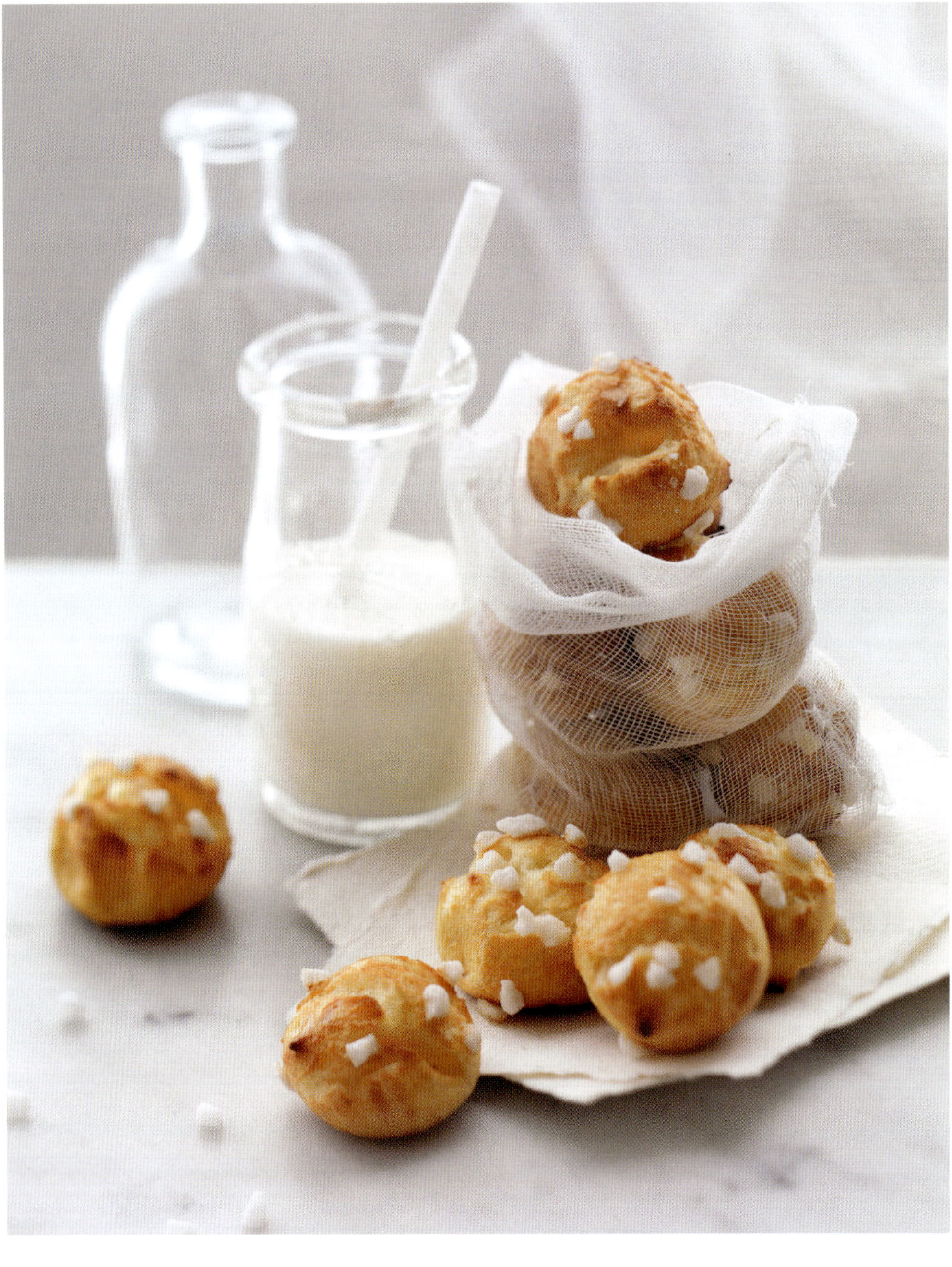

CHOUQUETTES
(sugar puffs)

prep + cook time 30 MINUTES *makes* 40

½ cup (125ml) water
60g (2oz) butter
1 tablespoon caster (superfine) sugar
½ cup (75g) strong baker's flour
4 eggs
¼ cup (45g) pearl sugar

1 Preheat oven to 220°C/425°F. Grease two oven trays.
2 To make choux pastry, combine the water, butter and caster sugar in a small saucepan; bring to the boil. Add flour, stir over medium heat until mixture comes away from base and side of pan and forms a smooth ball. Transfer dough to a medium bowl; beat in three of the eggs, one at a time, until dough becomes smooth and glossy.
3 Spoon pastry into a piping bag fitted with a 1cm (½in) plain tube. Pipe small rounds, about 5cm (2in) apart, on trays; brush all over with lightly beaten remaining egg, sprinkle with pearl sugar.
4 Bake puffs for 20 minutes or until golden and puffed. Serve warm.

tips These puffs are best eaten soon after baking. They are a traditional French afternoon snack for kids after school. They are sold at bakeries by the weight in paper bags. Pearl sugar is a coarse white sugar which keeps its shape when heated or exposed to moisture; it's available at specialist food stores.

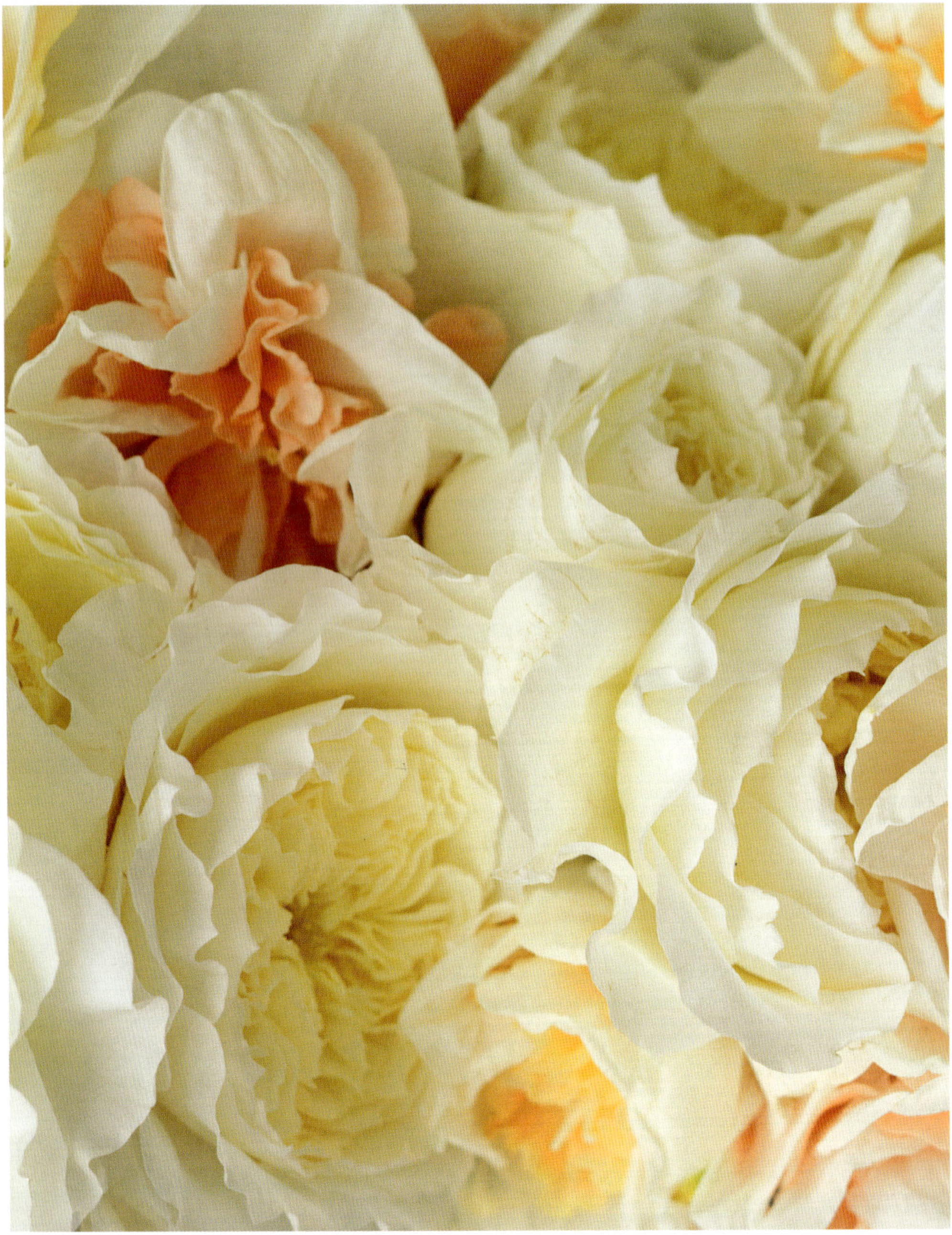

popcake
PUFFS

POPCAKE
PUFFS

prep + cook time 1 HOUR 30 MINUTES (+ COOLING & REFRIGERATION) *makes* 34

⅓ cup (80ml) water
40g (1½oz) butter, chopped finely
3 teaspoons caster (superfine) sugar
⅓ cup (50g) strong baker's flour
2 eggs

CRÈME PÂTISSIÈRE

1⅓ cups (330ml) milk
⅓ cup (75g) caster (superfine) sugar
1 teaspoon vanilla extract
2 tablespoons cornflour (cornstarch)
3 egg yolks

TOFFEE

2 cups (440g) caster (superfine) sugar
1 cup (250ml) water

1 Make crème pâtissière.
2 Preheat oven to 220°C/425°F. Grease three oven trays.
3 To make choux pastry, combine the water, butter and sugar in a small saucepan; bring to the boil. Add flour, beat with a wooden spoon over medium heat until mixture comes away from base of pan. Transfer pastry to a medium bowl; beat in eggs, one at a time, until pastry becomes glossy.
4 Drop rounded teaspoons of pastry, about 5cm (2in) apart, on trays.
5 Bake the puffs for 10 minutes. Reduce oven to 180°C/350°F; bake for 15 minutes. Cut small opening in base of each puff; bake for a further 10 minutes or until puffs are dry. Cool on trays.
6 Spoon crème pâtissière into a piping bag fitted with a 3mm (⅛in) plain tube; pipe through cuts into puffs.
7 Make toffee.
8 Push one paddle pop stick into each puff. Working quickly, dip puffs in toffee; place on baking-paper-lined oven tray. Stand at room temperature until set.

CRÈME PÂTISSIÈRE Combine milk, sugar and vanilla in a small saucepan; bring to the boil. Meanwhile, combine cornflour and egg yolks in a medium heatproof bowl; gradually whisk in hot milk mixture. Return mixture to pan; stir over medium heat until custard boils and thickens. Cover surface of custard with plastic wrap; cool for 20 minutes. Refrigerate for 4 hours.

TOFFEE Stir sugar and the water in a medium saucepan over medium heat, without boiling, until sugar dissolves. Bring to the boil; boil, uncovered, without stirring, until small amount of toffee dropped into cold water sets hard and can be snapped with fingers.

tips You will need 17 paddle pop sticks (halved) for this recipe. When dipping the puff popcakes in toffee, tilt the pan of toffee to one side, so the toffee is deep enough to completely coat the popcakes and a bit of the stick in toffee; this will ensure the popcakes don't fall off the sticks.

LEMON CURD & BLUEBERRY MILLE FEUILLE

prep + cook time 1 HOUR 10 MINUTES *makes* 6

3 sheets fillo pastry
1 egg white, beaten lightly
¼ cup (40g) icing (confectioners') sugar
185g (6oz) ghee (see tips)
500g (1lb) blueberries
LEMON CURD
2 egg yolks
¼ cup (55g) caster (superfine) sugar
1 teaspoon finely grated lemon rind
2 tablespoons lemon juice
60g (2oz) cold unsalted butter, chopped coarsely

1 Make lemon curd.
2 Brush one sheet of pastry with a little of the egg white; top with remaining two pastry sheets, brushing between each with more egg white. Cut 18 x 4cm x 10cm (1½in x 4in) rectangles from pastry. Dust both sides of rectangles with 2 tablespoons of the sifted icing sugar.
3 Heat ghee in a medium frying pan; cook pastry, in batches, until browned lightly and crisp. Drain on absorbent paper.
4 Drop one teaspoon of lemon curd onto centre of six serving plates; top each with one pastry piece. Divide half the lemon curd and half the berries over pastry. Top each with another pastry piece, then remaining curd and berries; top with remaining pastry. Serve dusted with remaining sifted icing sugar.
LEMON CURD Whisk egg yolks and sugar in a small heatproof bowl until pale and thickened slightly. Whisk in rind and juice; stir over small saucepan of simmering water for 12 minutes or until mixture coats the back of a spoon. Remove from heat; gradually whisk in butter until combined. Cool.

tips Ghee, also called clarified butter is available from the refrigerated section of large supermarkets. To make clarified butter, place 185g (6oz) of unsalted butter in a small saucepan; melt butter over low heat until it separates into three layers. Remove saucepan from heat and stand for 5 minutes. Skim off the top layer of white foam (the whey proteins) and discard. The milk solids will drop to the bottom of the saucepan and form a milky layer of sediment. What's left in the middle is clarified butter. Strain the mixture through muslin-lined sieve and discard milk solids.

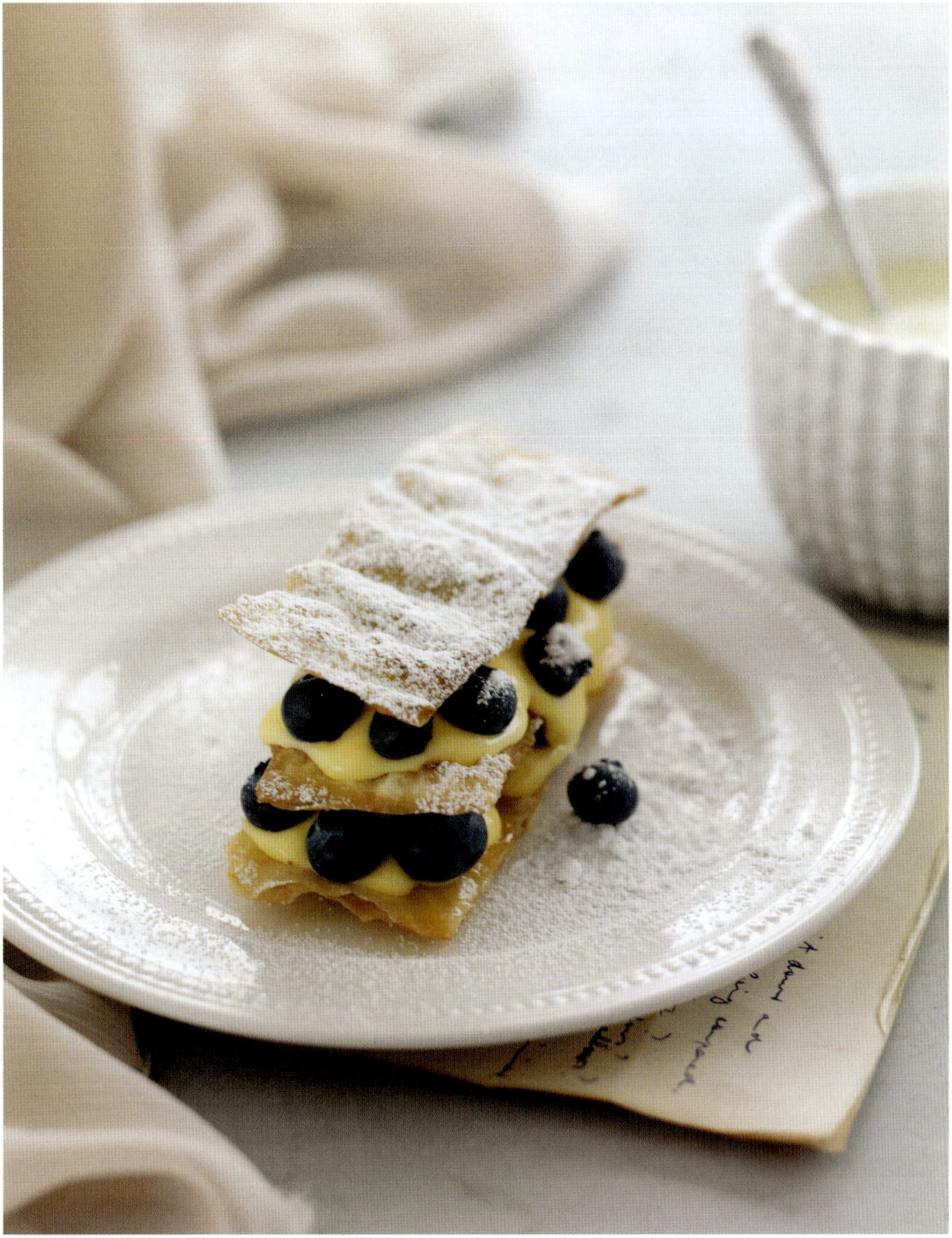

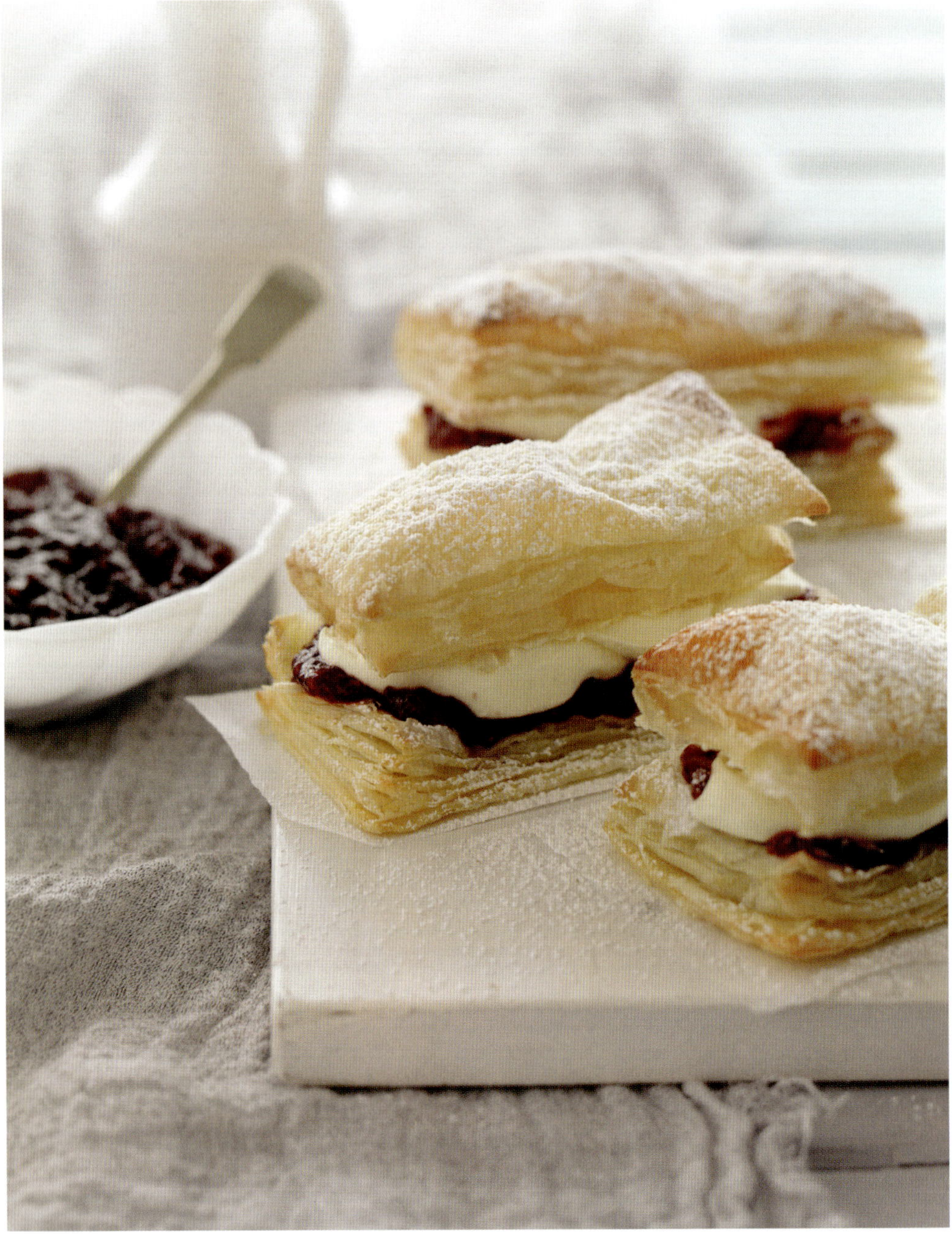

MASCARPONE MATCHSTICKS

prep + cook time 20 MINUTES *makes* 4

½ sheet butter puff pastry, thawed
¼ cup (40g) icing (confectioners') sugar
200g (6½oz) mascarpone
½ cup (125ml) thickened (heavy) cream
⅓ cup (110g) raspberry jam

1 Preheat oven to 220°C/425°F. Line oven tray with baking paper.
2 Cut pastry sheet into four rectangles. Place on oven tray. Dust pastry with 2 teaspoons of the sifted icing sugar.
3 Bake pastry for 10 minutes or until golden brown. Cool. Using a serrated knife, carefully split each rectangle horizontally.
4 Beat mascarpone, cream and 2 tablespoons of the remaining sifted icing sugar in a small bowl with an electric mixer until soft peaks form.
5 Spread jam then mascarpone mixture between pastry pieces. Serve dusted with remaining sifted icing sugar.

MOCHA PUFFS

prep + cook time 1 HOUR (+ REFRIGERATION) *makes* 24

15g (½oz) butter
¼ cup (60ml) water
¼ cup (35g) plain (all-purpose) flour
1 egg

MOCHA PASTRY CREAM

2 teaspoons instant coffee granules
2 teaspoons hot water
1 cup (250ml) milk
60g (2oz) dark (semi-sweet) chocolate, chopped finely
3 egg yolks
⅓ cup (75g) caster (superfine) sugar
1 tablespoon cornflour (cornstarch)

TOFFEE

½ cup (110g) caster (superfine) sugar
¼ cup (60ml) water

1 Preheat oven to 220°C/425°F. Grease two oven trays.
2 Combine butter and the water in a small saucepan; bring to the boil. Add flour, beat with a wooden spoon over medium heat until mixture comes away from base and side of saucepan and forms a smooth ball.
3 Transfer mixture to small bowl; beat in egg with an electric mixer until mixture becomes glossy. Spoon pastry mixture into a piping bag fitted with a 1cm (½in) plain tube. Pipe small rounds, about 5cm (2in) apart, on trays; bake for 7 minutes. Reduce oven temperature to 180°C/350°F; bake for a further 10 minutes. Cut small opening in side of each puff; bake for a further 5 minutes or until dry to touch. Cool on trays.
4 Meanwhile, make mocha pastry cream and toffee.
5 Spoon pastry cream into a piping bag fitted with a 5mm (¼in) plain tube, pipe through cuts into puffs. Place puffs on foil-covered tray; drizzle with toffee.

MOCHA PASTRY CREAM Dissolve coffee in the hot water in a small jug. Combine milk, chocolate and coffee mixture in a small saucepan and stir over medium heat, until smooth. Bring to the boil. Meanwhile, beat egg yolks, sugar and cornflour in a small bowl with an electric mixer until thick. With motor operating, gradually beat in hot milk mixture. Return custard to pan; stir over medium heat until mixture boils and thickens. Cover surface of custard with plastic wrap; refrigerate for 1 hour.

TOFFEE Combine sugar and the water in a small saucepan; stir over medium heat, without boiling, until sugar dissolves. Bring to the boil. Boil, uncovered, without stirring, until golden brown.

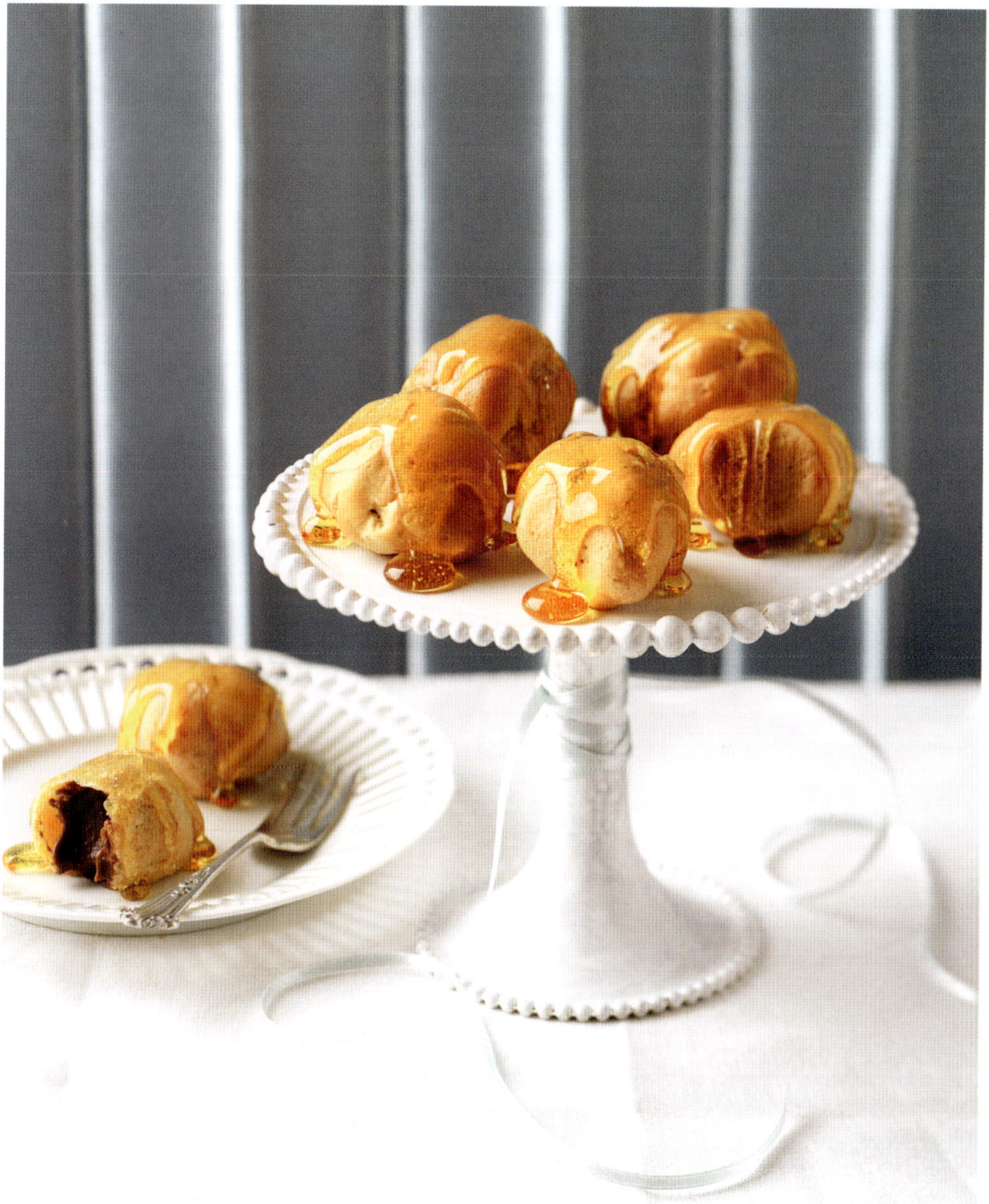

SERVING SUGGESTION
Serve warm with crème anglaise (custard), cream or ice-cream.

Plum & Almond Turnovers

prep + cook time 1 HOUR 10 MINUTES (+ COOLING) *makes* 30

825g (1¾lb) canned whole plums in natural juice
¼ cup (55g) caster (superfine) sugar
3 cardamom pods, bruised
2 tablespoons cornflour (cornstarch)
1 tablespoon water
250g (8oz) marzipan, chopped
⅓ cup (80ml) thickened (heavy) cream
6 sheets puff pastry
1 egg, beaten lightly
¼ cup (20g) flaked almonds
1 tablespoon demerara sugar
1 tablespoon icing (confectioners') sugar

1 Drain plums over small bowl, reserving ½ cup of juice. Cut plums into quarters; discard seeds.
2 Place plums, reserved juice, caster sugar and cardamom in a medium saucepan; stir over medium heat, without boiling, until sugar dissolves. Bring to the boil; boil, uncovered, for 5 minutes or until thickened slightly. Blend cornflour with the water in a jug, add to the pan and cook, stirring, until mixture boils and thickens. Cool 2 hours. Discard cardamom.
3 Meanwhile, blend or process marzipan and cream until smooth.
4 Preheat oven to 200°C/400°F. Grease oven trays; line with baking paper.
5 Cut 30 x 9cm (3¾in) rounds from pastry sheets. Spread rounded teaspoons of marzipan mixture over each pastry round, leaving 1cm (½in) border. Divide plum mixture between the centres of pastry rounds. Brush edges with egg; fold rounds in half to enclose filling and pinch edges to seal. Place on trays, about 5cm (2in) apart.
6 Brush turnovers with egg; sprinkle with almonds, then demerara sugar. Use a small sharp knife to cut two small slits in the top of each turnover.
7 Bake turnovers for 25 minutes or until golden brown. Cool on trays. Serve warm, dusted with sifted icing sugar.

mini apple
TARTE TATINS

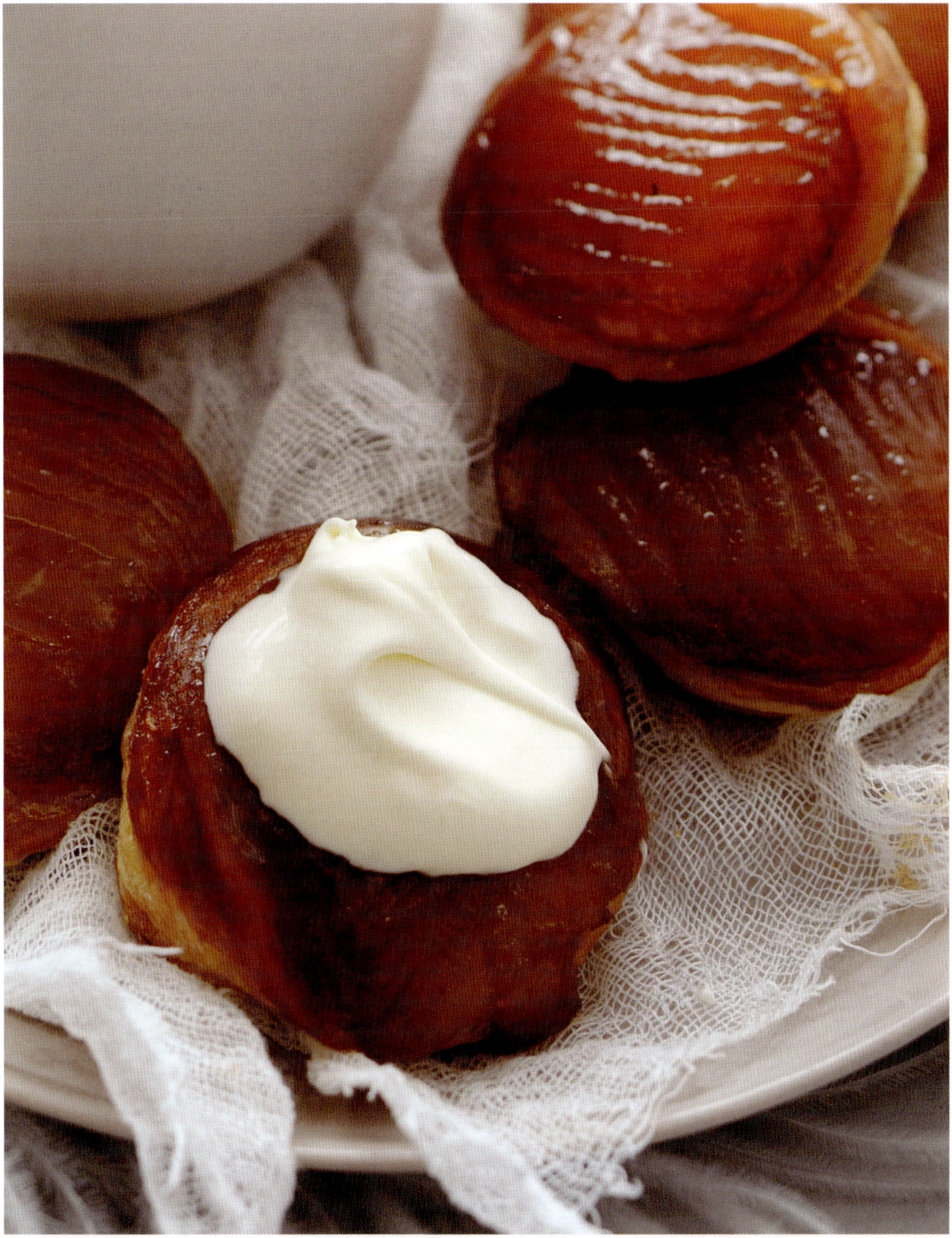

MINI APPLE TARTE TATINS

prep + cook time 1 HOUR 20 MINUTES (+ REFRIGERATION & STANDING) makes 12

1 cup (150g) strong baker's flour
150g (5oz) butter, at room temperature, chopped coarsely
⅔ cup (160ml) iced water, approximately
¼ cup (60ml) thick (double) cream

CARAMELISED APPLE
3 small apples (390g)
2 tablespoons lemon juice
½ cup (110g) caster (superfine) sugar
50g (1½oz) unsalted butter, chopped coarsely
2 tablespoons water

1 To make pastry, sift flour into medium bowl; rub in butter until mixture is crumbly and you can still see small chunks of butter. Make a well in the centre. Stir in enough of the iced water to make a firm dough. Knead the dough on a floured surface until smooth; shape into a rectangle. Enclose pastry in plastic wrap; refrigerate for 20 minutes.
2 Roll pastry on a floured surface into a 20cm x 40cm (8in x 16in) rectangle, keeping edges straight and even. Fold the top third of pastry down until two-thirds of the way down the rectangle, then fold the bottom third up and over. Turn the dough a quarter-turn clockwise; repeat rolling and folding once more. Enclose pastry in plastic wrap; refrigerate 1 hour.
3 Meanwhile, make caramelised apple.
4 Roll pastry on a floured surface until 3mm (⅛in) thick. Cut 12 x 6cm (2½in) rounds from pastry. Place rounds on top of apples in pan, tucking pastry down side of pan holes.
5 Bake tarts for 30 minutes. Stand tarts in pan 20 minutes before turning onto a baking-paper-lined tray. Serve topped with cream.

CARAMELISED APPLE Preheat oven to 200°C/400°F; grease a 12-hole (1½-tablespoon/30ml) shallow round-based patty pan. Peel, core and quarter apples; slice thinly, without cutting through the apple quarter. Combine apples and juice in a medium bowl. Stir sugar, butter and half the water in a small frying pan, over medium heat, without boiling, until sugar dissolves. Bring to the boil. Reduce heat; simmer, uncovered, without stirring, for 8 minutes, shaking pan occasionally, until dark caramel in colour. Allow bubbles to subside, then carefully spoon caramel into pan holes. Add remaining water to hot frying pan; reserve caramel liquid. Position one apple quarter, trimmed to fit, rounded-side down, in each pan hole; brush apples with reserved caramel liquid. Cover patty pan with foil, place on oven tray; bake for 10 minutes. Remove foil.

tips The butter should be at room temperature but not soft. Leftover trimmings of pastry should be stacked up and chilled for another use. Don't press scraps together in a ball as the flaky layers of pastry will be spoiled.

SLICES

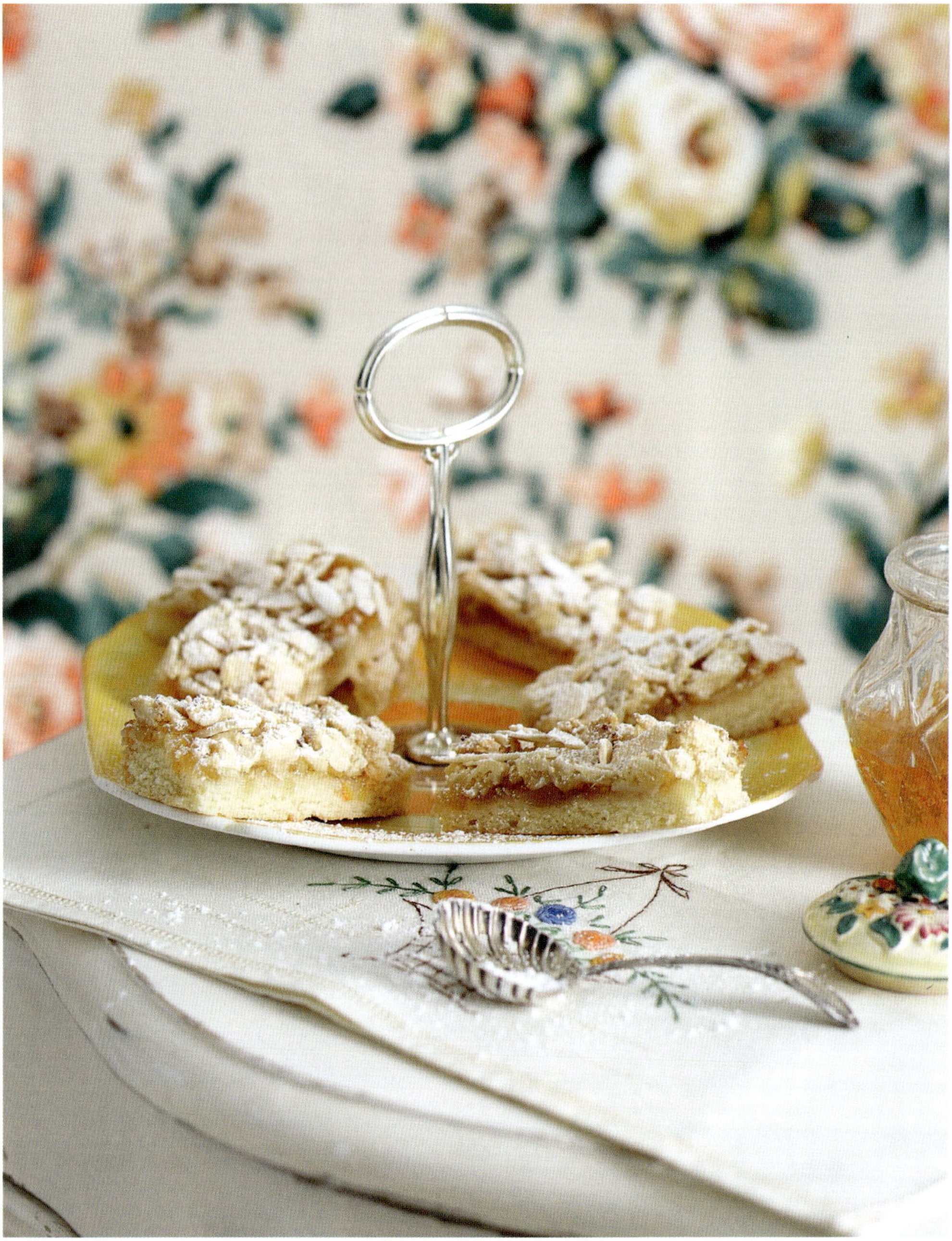

MARMALADE, GINGER & ALMOND SLICE

prep + cook time 1 HOUR *makes* 24

90g (3oz) unsalted butter, softened
½ cup (110g) caster (superfine) sugar
1 egg
⅔ cup (100g) plain (all-purpose) flour
⅓ cup (50g) self-raising flour
1 cup (340g) orange marmalade
⅓ cup (60g) finely chopped glacé ginger
1 egg, beaten lightly, extra
1½ cups (120g) flaked almonds
½ cup (60g) almond meal
1 tablespoon icing (confectioners') sugar

1 Preheat oven to 160°C/325°F. Grease a 20cm x 30cm (8in x 12in) rectangular pan; line base and long sides with baking paper, extending the paper 5cm (2in) over sides.
2 Beat butter, caster sugar and egg in a small bowl with an electric mixer until light and fluffy. Stir in sifted flours. Spread dough into pan. Combine marmalade and ginger in a small bowl; spread over dough.
3 Combine extra egg, 1 cup (80g) of the flaked almonds and the almond meal in a medium bowl. Spread almond mixture over marmalade; sprinkle with remaining flaked almonds.
4 Bake slice for 40 minutes. Cool slice in pan. Dust with sifted icing sugar before cutting.

keeps This slice will keep in an airtight container for up to a week.

APPLE STREUSEL SLICE

prep + cook time 1 HOUR (+ FREEZING & COOLING) ❊ *makes* 12

220g (7oz) unsalted butter, softened
1 cup (220g) caster (superfine) sugar
2 egg yolks
1⅓ cups (200g) plain (all-purpose) flour
½ cup (75g) self-raising flour
2 tablespoons custard powder
4 large apples (800g), sliced thinly
1 tablespoon honey
1 teaspoon finely grated lemon rind

STREUSEL TOPPING

½ cup (75g) plain (all-purpose) flour
¼ cup (35g) self-raising flour
⅓ cup (75g) firmly packed brown sugar
½ teaspoon ground cinnamon
90g (3oz) unsalted butter, chopped coarsely

1 Make streusel topping.
2 Preheat oven to 180°C/350°F. Grease a 20cm x 30cm (8in x 12in) rectangular pan; line base and long sides with baking paper, extending the paper 5cm (2in) over sides.
3 Beat butter, sugar and egg yolks in a small bowl with an electric mixer until light and fluffy. Transfer mixture to a large bowl; stir in sifted flours and custard powder. Press mixture into pan.
4 Bake base for 25 minutes. Cool for 15 minutes.
5 Meanwhile, cook apple, honey and rind, covered, in a medium saucepan, stirring occasionally, for 5 minutes or until apples are tender. Remove from heat; drain. Cool for 15 minutes.
6 Spread apple mixture over base; coarsely grate streusel topping over apple.
7 Bake slice for 20 minutes. Cool slice in pan.
STREUSEL TOPPING Process ingredients until combined. Enclose in plastic wrap; freeze 1 hour or until firm.

keeps Slice will keep in an airtight container in the fridge for up to 3 days.

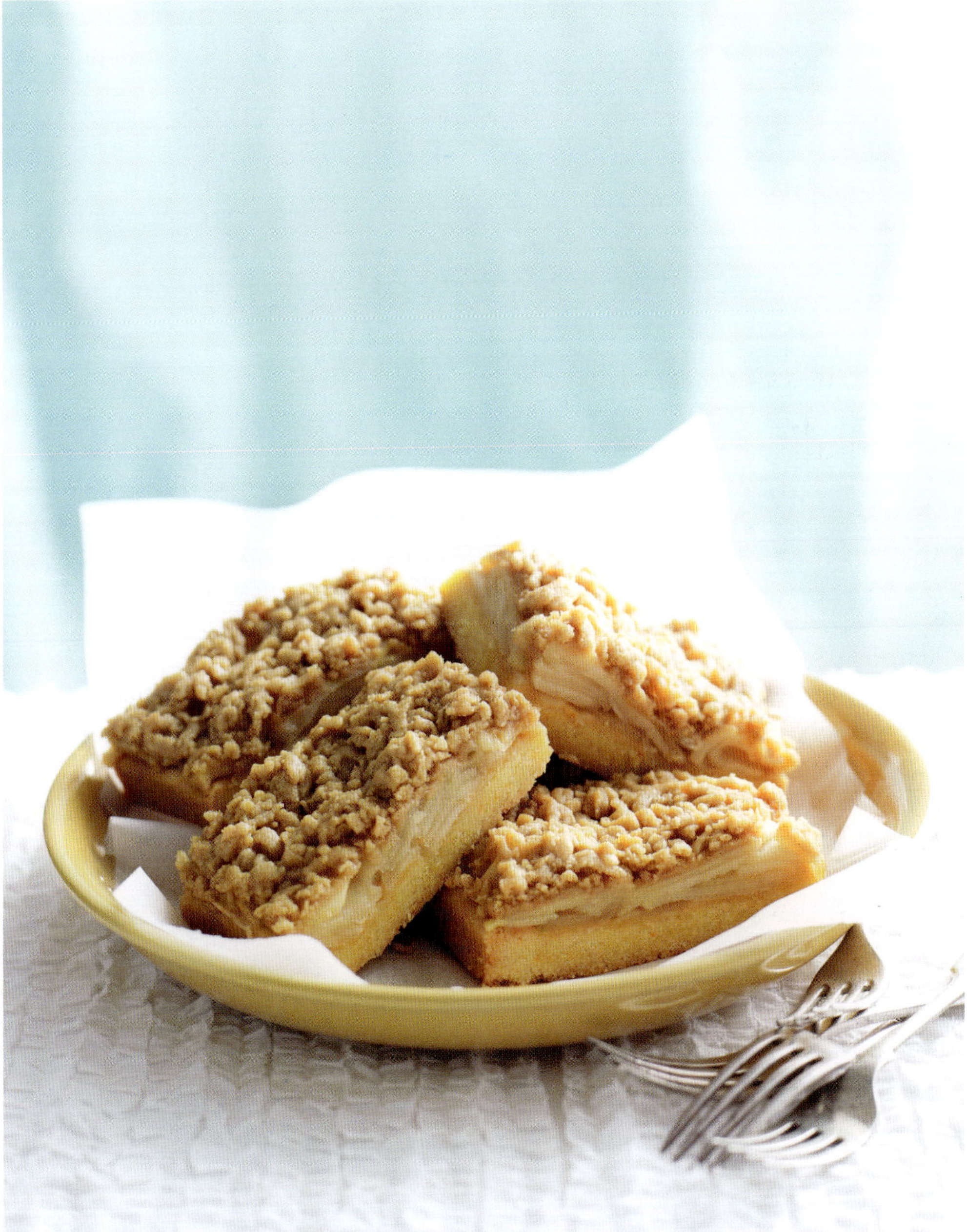

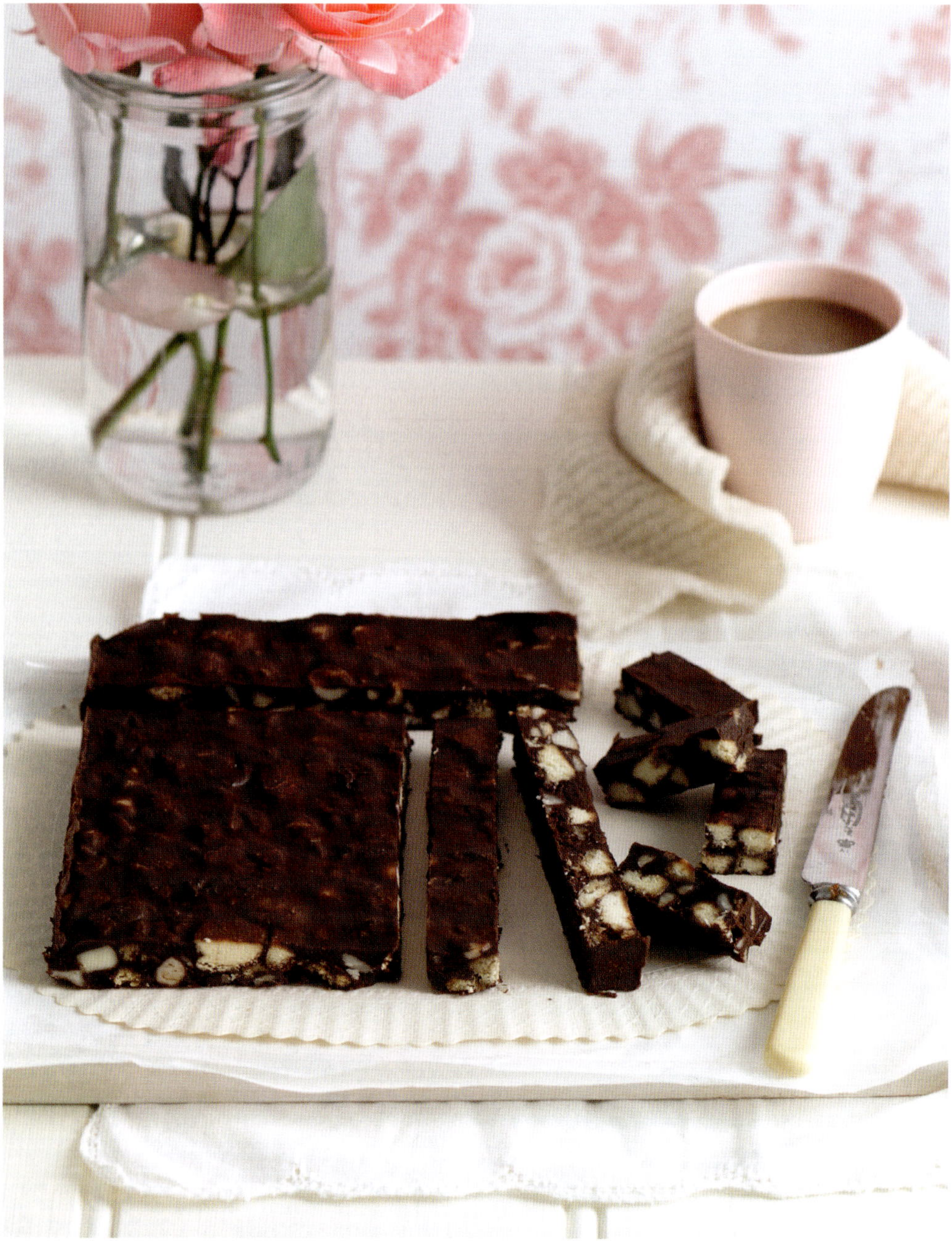

Mocha
Hedgehog Slice

prep + cook time 20 minutes (+ standing & refrigeration) • makes 40

⅓ cup (50g) raisins
¼ cup (60ml) hot strong coffee
400g (12½oz) dark (semi-sweet) chocolate, chopped coarsely
155g (5oz) butter, chopped
1 egg
¼ cup (55g) caster (superfine) sugar
185g (6oz) shortbread biscuits, chopped coarsely
1 cup (140g) unsalted macadamias, roasted, chopped coarsely

1 Combine raisins and coffee in a small bowl; stand for 1 hour.
2 Grease a 20cm x 30cm (8in x 12in) rectangular pan; line base and long sides with baking paper, extending the paper 5cm (2in) over sides.
3 Stir chocolate and butter in a medium heatproof bowl over a medium saucepan of simmering water until smooth.
4 Beat egg and sugar in a small bowl with an electric mixer until thick and doubled in volume. Stir into chocolate mixture. Fold coffee mixture and remaining ingredients into egg mixture.
5 Spread mixture into pan. Cover surface with plastic wrap, smooth surface with spatula or hands. Refrigerate for 3 hours or overnight before cutting into pieces to serve.

keeps This slice will keep in an airtight container in the refrigerator for up to a week. Serve straight from the fridge.

VANILLA
PASSIONFRUIT SLICE

prep + cook time 30 MINUTES (+ COOLING & REFRIGERATION) *makes 8*

1 sheet ready-rolled puff pastry
¼ cup (55g) caster (superfine) sugar
¼ cup (35g) cornflour (cornstarch)
1½ tablespoons custard powder
1¼ cups (310ml) milk
30g (1oz) butter
1 egg yolk
½ teaspoon vanilla extract
PASSIONFRUIT ICING
¾ cup (110g) icing (confectioners') sugar
1 tablespoon passionfruit pulp
1 teaspoon water, approximately

1 Preheat oven to 240°C/475°F. Grease a 20cm (8in) square cake pan; line base and long sides with baking paper, extending the paper 5cm (2in) over sides.
2 Place pastry sheet on oven tray. Bake for 15 minutes or until puffed; cool. Split pastry in half horizontally; remove and discard any uncooked pastry from centre. Flatten pastry pieces gently with hand; trim both to fit pan. Place top half in pan, top-side down.
3 Meanwhile, combine sugar, cornflour and custard powder in a medium saucepan; gradually stir in milk. Stir over medium heat until mixture boils and thickens. Reduce heat; simmer, stirring, for 3 minutes or until custard is thick and smooth. Remove pan from heat; stir in butter, egg yolk and vanilla.
4 Spread hot custard over the pastry in pan; top with remaining pastry, bottom-side up, pressing down gently. Cool to room temperature.
5 Meanwhile, make passionfruit icing.
6 Spread icing over pastry; set at room temperature. Refrigerate for 3 hours before cutting.
PASSIONFRUIT ICING Sift icing sugar into a small heatproof bowl; stir in passionfruit and enough water to make a thick paste. Stir over a small saucepan of simmering water until icing is spreadable.

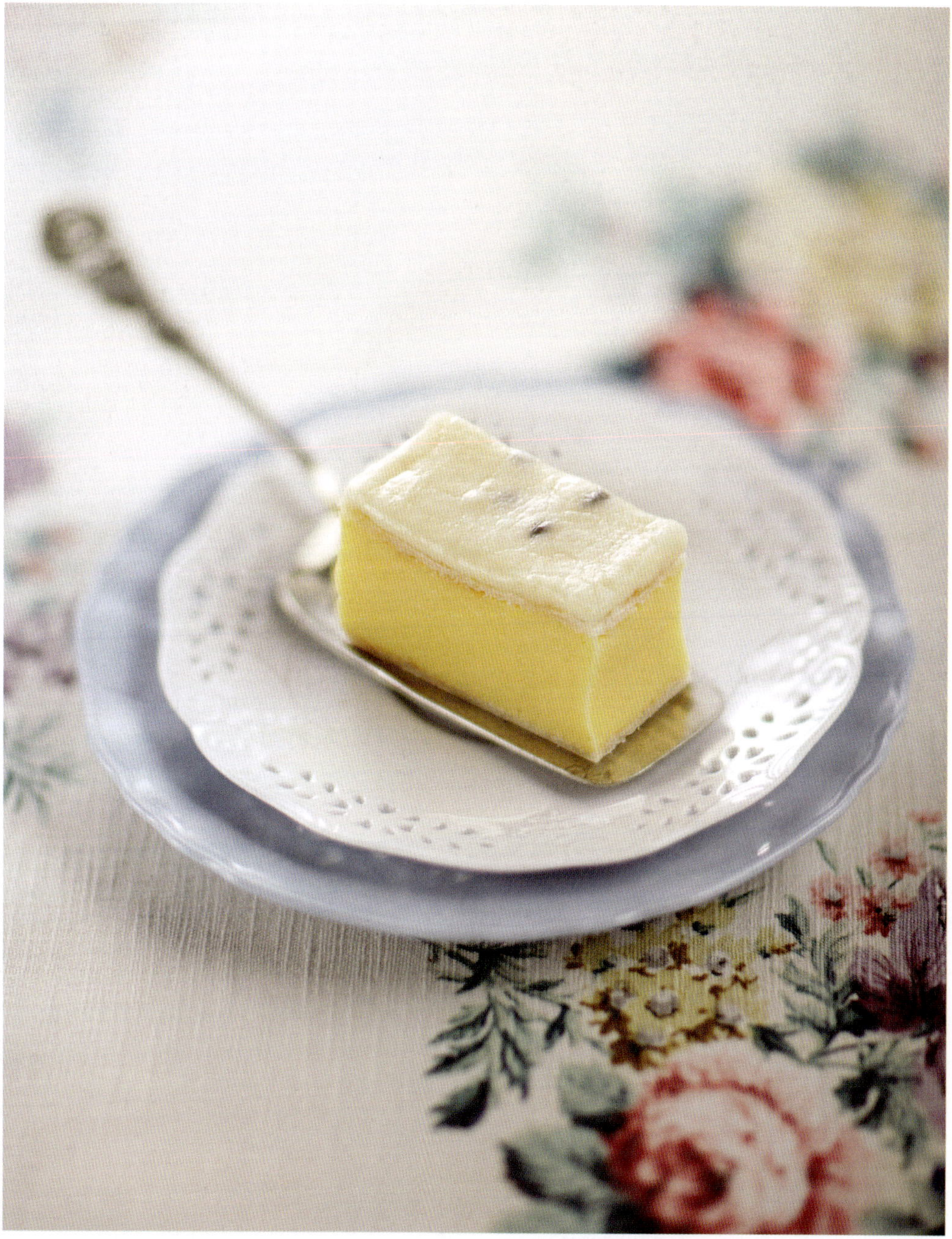

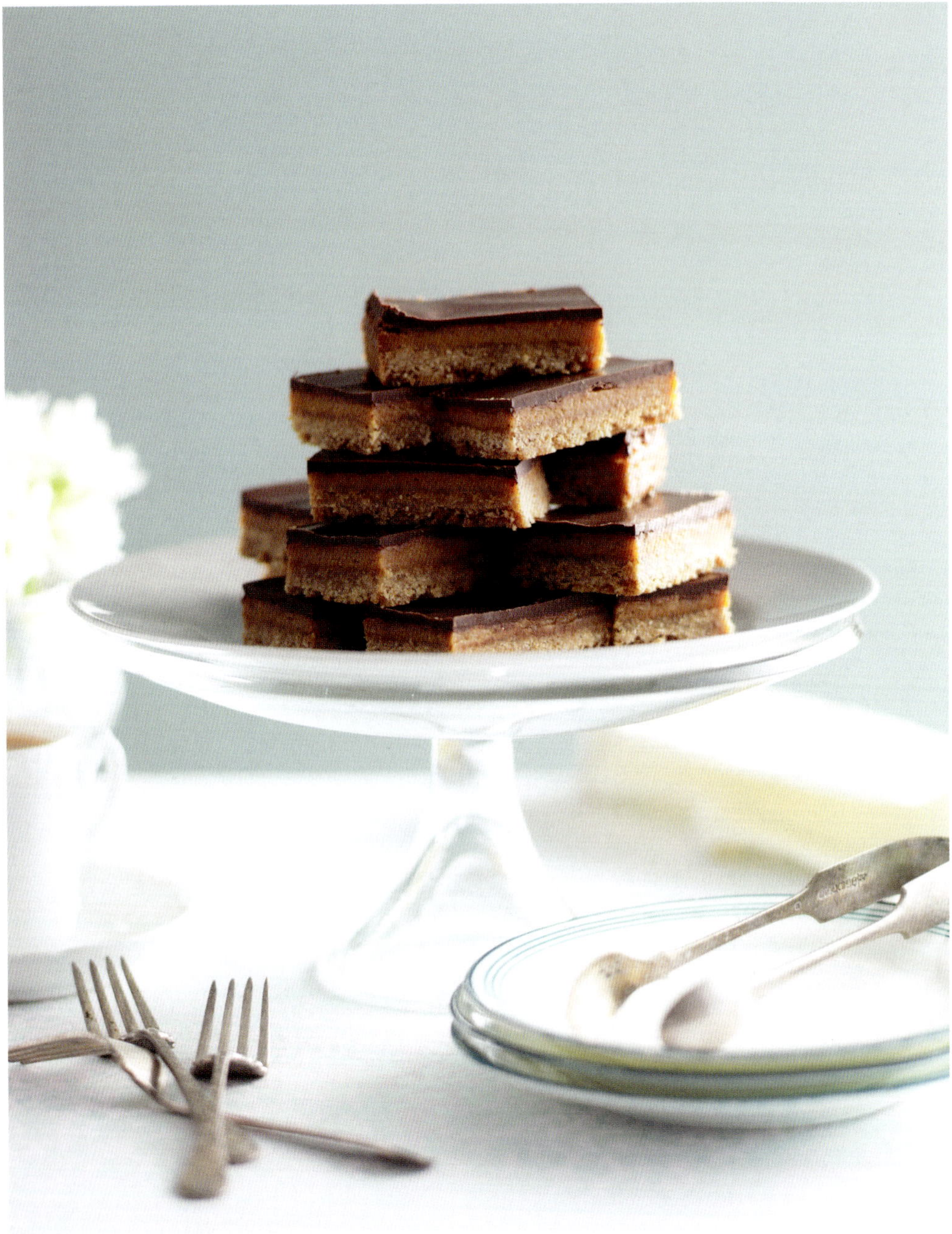

CHOCOLATE CARAMEL SLICE

prep + cook time 45 MINUTES (+ COOLING & REFRIGERATION) *makes* 24

½ cup (75g) self-raising flour
½ cup (75g) plain (all-purpose) flour
1 cup (80g) desiccated coconut
1 cup (220g) firmly packed brown sugar
125g (4oz) butter, melted
395g (14oz) canned sweetened condensed milk
30g (1oz) butter, extra
2 tablespoons golden syrup or treacle
185g (6oz) dark (semi-sweet) chocolate, chopped coarsely
2 teaspoons vegetable oil

1 Preheat oven to 180°C/350°F. Grease a 20cm x 30cm (8in x 12in) rectangular pan; line base and long sides with baking paper, extending the paper 5cm (2in) over sides.
2 Combine sifted flours, coconut, sugar and butter in a medium bowl; press mixture evenly over base of pan.
3 Bake base for 15 minutes or until browned lightly.
4 Meanwhile, stir condensed milk, extra butter and golden syrup in a small saucepan over medium heat for 15 minutes or until caramel mixture is golden brown; pour over base.
5 Bake slice for 10 minutes; cool.
6 Stir chocolate and oil in a small saucepan over low heat until smooth. Pour warm topping over cold caramel. Refrigerate for 3 hours or overnight.

keeps The slice will keep in an airtight container in the fridge for up to 4 days.

TURKISH DELIGHT SLICE

prep + cook time 1 HOUR (+ STANDING) ✤ *makes* 24

185g (6oz) unsalted butter, softened
⅓ cup (75g) caster (superfine) sugar
1 teaspoon vanilla extract
1½ cups (225g) plain (all-purpose) flour
⅓ cup (50g) self-raising flour
4 teaspoons gelatine
2 tablespoons water
⅓ cup (80ml) water, extra
1½ cups (330g) white (granulated) sugar
⅓ cup (50g) cornflour (cornstarch)
2 tablespoons rosewater
red food colouring
2 tablespoons icing (confectioners') sugar

1 Preheat oven to 180°C/350°F. Grease a 20cm x 30cm (8in x 12in) rectangular pan; line base and long sides with baking paper, extending the paper 5cm (2in) over sides.

2 Beat butter, caster sugar and vanilla in a small bowl with an electric mixer until combined. Stir in sifted flours. Press mixture evenly over base of pan; using a fork, rough up the surface. Bake base for 20 minutes or until golden brown. Cool.

3 Sprinkle gelatine over the water in a small heatproof jug; stand jug in a small saucepan of simmering water and stir until gelatine dissolves.

4 Reserve 1 tablespoon of the extra water. Stir the remaining extra water and white sugar in a medium saucepan over low heat, without boiling, until sugar dissolves; bring to the boil. Boil, without stirring, until temperature reaches 116°C/240°F on a sugar thermometer. Reduce heat; simmer, for 5 minutes, without stirring, regulating heat to maintain temperature at 116°C/240°F. Remove from heat.

5 Blend cornflour with the reserved 1 tablespoon water, gelatine mixture, rosewater and a few drops of food colouring until smooth; stir into sugar syrup. Return to heat; simmer, stirring, for 3 minutes or until mixture is opaque. Strain mixture over slice base, skim any scum from surface; stand for 3 hours or overnight at room temperature.

6 Dust slice with sifted icing sugar to serve.

keeps The slice will keep in an airtight container in the fridge for up to 4 days.

TIPS

It's important to use a sugar thermometer for guaranteed success with this recipe. Use a hot wet knife to cut the slice.

SERVING SUGGESTION
This recipe is best served warm and would be delicious as a dessert with ice-cream.

PEAR & RASPBERRY
STREUSEL SLICE

prep + cook time 1 HOUR 10 MINUTES (+ FREEZING & COOLING) *makes* 12

3 medium pears (700g), peeled, cored, sliced thinly
¼ cup (55g) caster (superfine) sugar
¼ cup (60ml) water
90g (3oz) butter, softened
⅓ cup (75g) caster (superfine) sugar, extra
1 egg
1 cup (150g) self-raising flour
⅓ cup (80ml) milk
155g (5oz) fresh or frozen raspberries
¼ cup (30g) finely chopped walnuts

STREUSEL TOPPING
⅓ cup (50g) plain (all-purpose) flour
2 tablespoons self-raising flour
¼ cup (55g) firmly packed brown sugar
1 teaspoon mixed spice
90g (3oz) cold butter, chopped

1 Make streusel topping.
2 Preheat oven to 180°C/350°F. Grease a 20cm x 30cm (8in x 12in) rectangular pan; line base and long sides with baking paper, extending the paper 5cm (2in) over sides.
3 Combine pear, sugar and the water in a large saucepan; cook, covered, stirring occasionally, for 10 minutes or until pear softens. Drain, then cool.
4 Beat butter and extra sugar in a small bowl with an electric mixer until light and fluffy. Add egg; beat until combined. Stir in sifted flour and milk, in two batches. Spread mixture into pan.
5 Bake base for 15 minutes. Remove from oven.
6 Increase oven to 200°C/400°F.
7 Working quickly, arrange cooked pear over base; sprinkle with raspberries and walnuts. Coarsely grate streusel over fruit mixture.
8 Bake slice for 20 minutes. Stand slice in pan 10 minutes before transferring, top-side-up, onto a wire rack to cool. Serve warm or cold.

STREUSEL TOPPING Process ingredients until combined. Enclose in plastic wrap; freeze for 1 hour or until firm.

CHOCOLATE BROWNIE SLICE

prep + cook time 1 HOUR ✻ *makes* 25

125g (4oz) butter, chopped
185g (6oz) dark (semi-sweet) chocolate, chopped coarsely
½ cup (110g) caster (superfine) sugar
2 eggs
1¼ cups (185g) plain (all-purpose) flour
155g (5oz) white chocolate, chopped
90g (3oz) milk chocolate, chopped

1 Preheat oven to 180°C/350°F. Grease a deep 20cm (8in) square cake pan; line base with baking paper, extending the paper 5cm (2in) over sides.
2 Stir butter and dark chocolate in a medium saucepan over low heat until smooth. Cool for 10 minutes.
3 Stir in sugar and eggs, then sifted flour, white chocolate and milk chocolate. Spread mixture into pan.
4 Bake brownie for 35 minutes. Cool in pan.

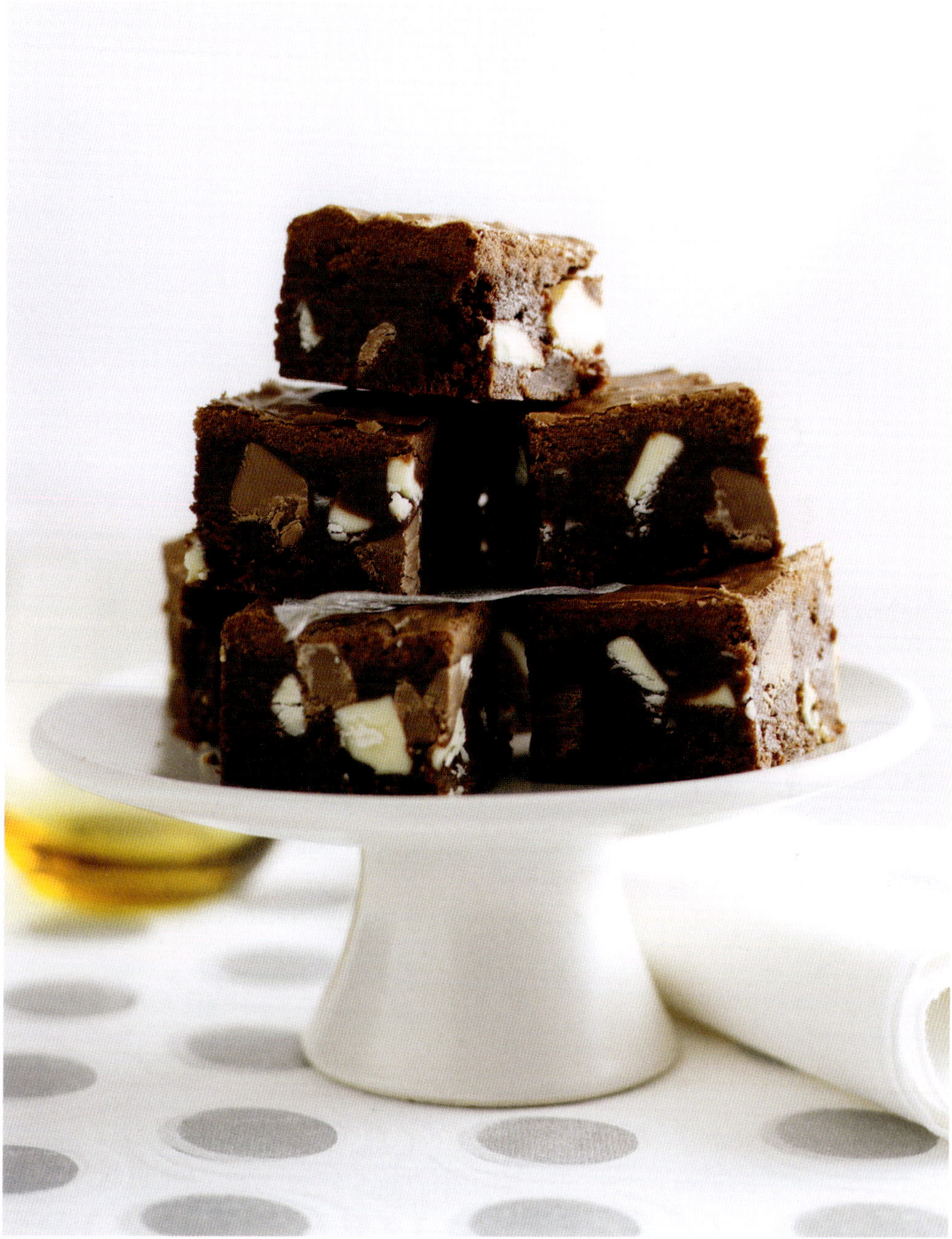

TARTS & TARTLETS

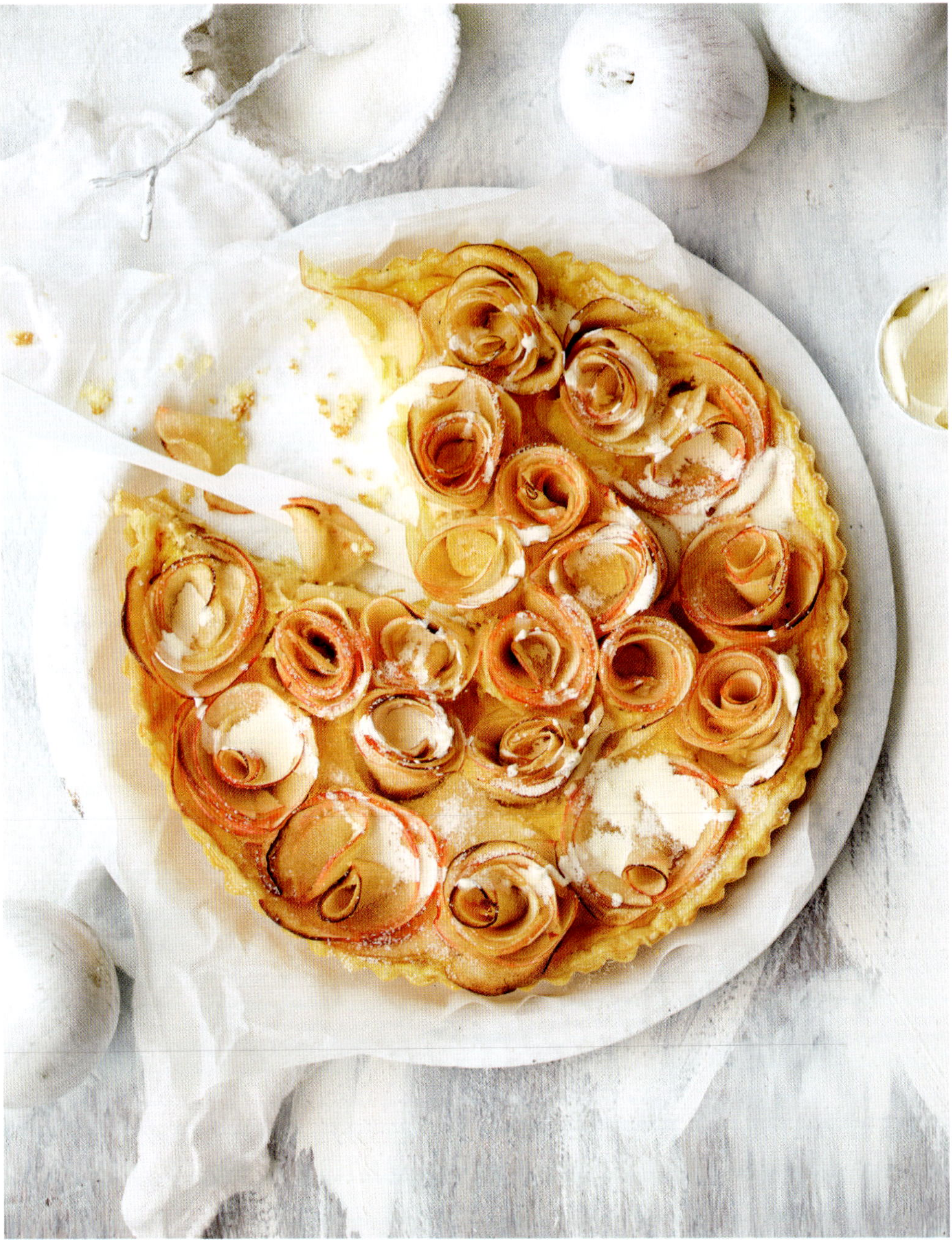

Apple & Cardamom Tart

prep + cook time 1 HOUR 15 MINUTES (+ REFRIGERATION) *serves* 6

2 sheets butter puff pastry
1¼ cups (310g) ready-made vanilla custard
200g (6½oz) mascarpone
2 egg yolks
1 teaspoon vanilla bean paste
¼ teaspoon ground cardamom
4 medium red-skinned apples (450g)
1 tablespoon caster (superfine) sugar
1 tablespoon lemon juice
1 tablespoon white (granulated) sugar
pouring cream, to serve

1 Grease a 24cm (9½in) round loose-based fluted tart tin. Roll pastry between sheets of baking paper until large enough to line the tin. Lift pastry into tin, press into base and sides; trim excess pastry. Prick base with a fork. Cover; refrigerate for 20 minutes.
2 Preheat oven to 180°C/350°F.
3 Meanwhile, whisk custard, mascarpone, egg yolks, vanilla and cardamom in a small bowl until combined. Cover; refrigerate until chilled.
4 Core and halve apples; slice thinly. Combine apple slices, caster sugar and juice in a medium bowl. Spread custard mixture into pastry case. Arrange apple slices slightly overlapping into rosette shapes, on custard mixture. Drizzle with any juices.
5 Bake tart for 50 minutes or until pastry and apples are golden. Cool. Refrigerate for 1 hour. Serve tart sprinkled with white sugar and drizzled with cream.

tip Vanilla bean paste contains real vanilla bean seeds. It is highly concentrated, with 1 teaspoon of paste equalling 1 whole vanilla bean. It is sold in tubes or small jars from most supermarkets.
keeps The tart shell can be made a day ahead; keep refrigerated. The tart is best cooked on day of serving.

Jam Tarts

prep + cook time 45 MINUTES (+ REFRIGERATION) *makes* 24

1¾ cups (260g) plain (all-purpose) flour
¼ cup (40g) icing (confectioners') sugar
185g (6oz) cold unsalted butter, chopped coarsely
1 egg yolk
2 teaspoons iced water, approximately
2 tablespoons strawberry jam
2 tablespoons apricot jam
2 tablespoons raspberry jam
2 tablespoons black cherry jam
2 teaspoons icing (confectioners') sugar, extra

1 Process flour, sugar and butter until crumbly. With motor operating, add egg yolk and enough of the water to make ingredients come together. Turn dough onto a floured surface; knead gently until smooth. Roll half the pastry between sheets of baking paper until 3mm (⅛in) thick. Repeat with remaining pastry. Place on trays; refrigerate for 30 minutes.
2 Grease two 12-hole (1-tablespoon/20ml) mini muffin pans. Cut 24 x 5.5cm (2¼in) rounds from pastry; press rounds into pan holes. Prick bases of cases well with a fork. Refrigerate for 30 minutes.
3 Re-roll scraps of pastry between baking paper until 3mm (⅛in) thick. Refrigerate for 30 minutes.
4 Preheat oven to 220°C/425°F.
5 Bake pastry cases for 8 minutes. Divide strawberry jam into six cases; repeat with remaining jams and cases. Cut 12 x 3.5cm (1½in) rounds from remaining pastry; cut rounds in half. Top tarts with pastry halves.
6 Bake tarts for 10 minutes; cool. Refrigerate for 30 minutes. Serve tarts dusted with sifted extra icing sugar.

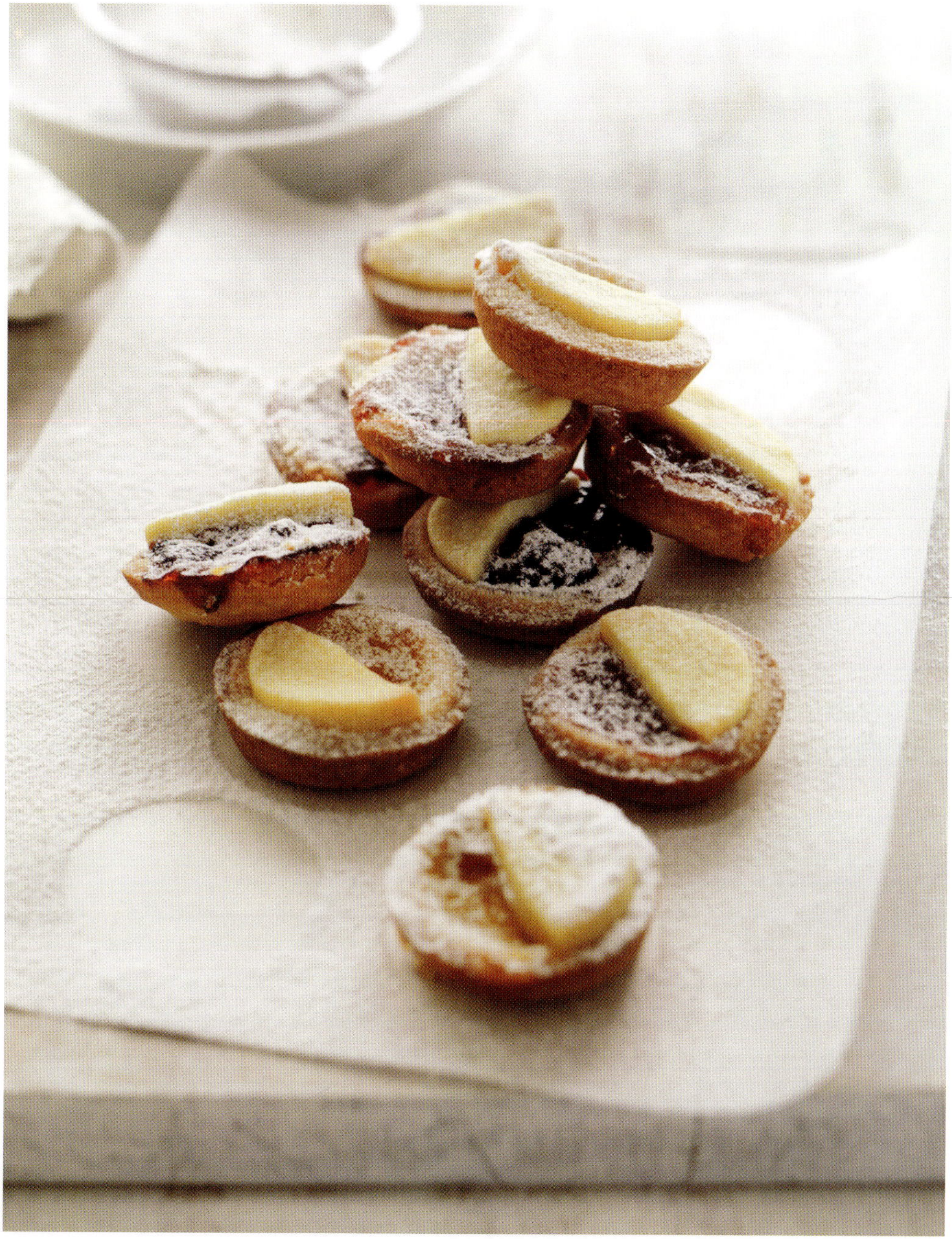

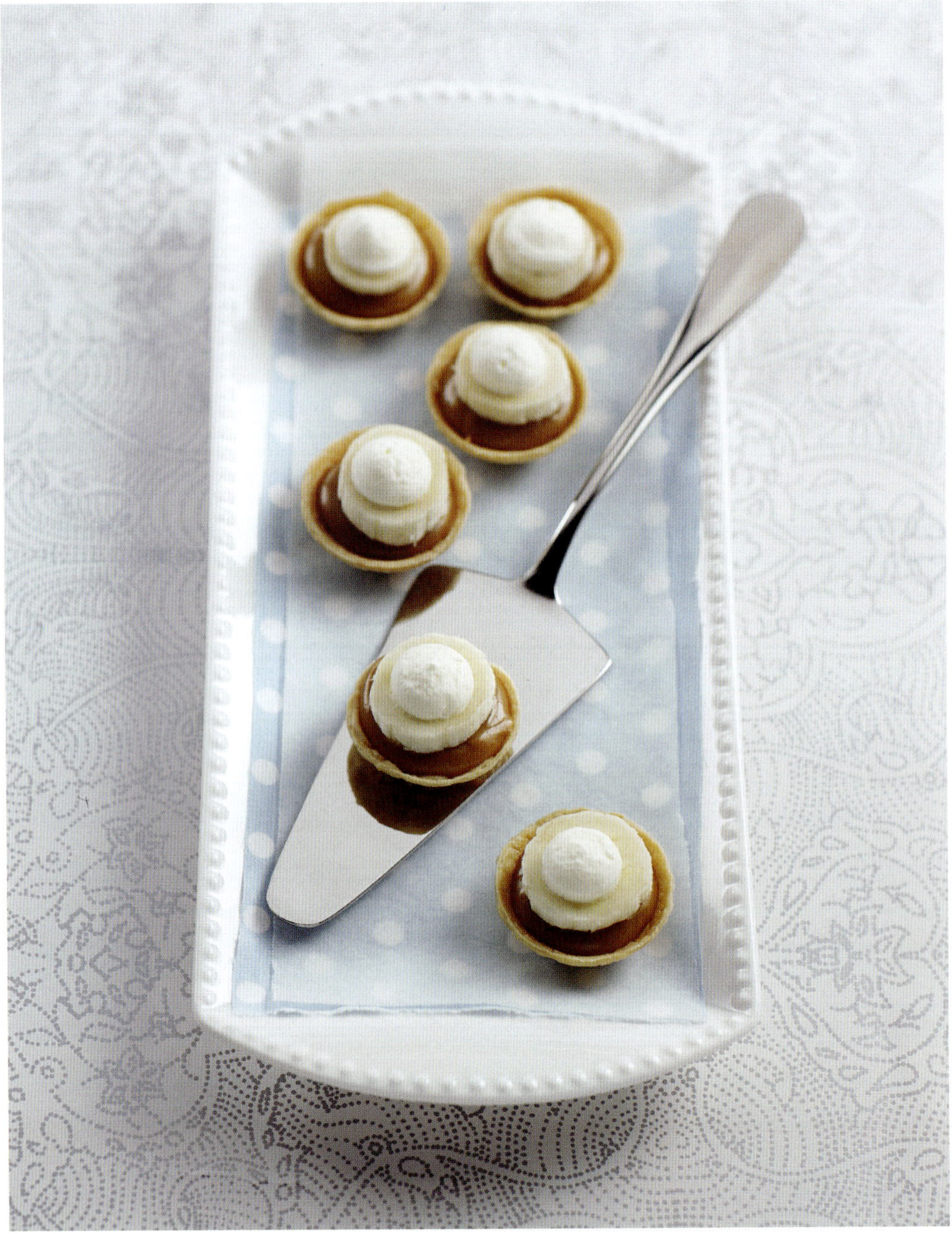

BANOFFEE TARTLETS

prep + cook time 30 MINUTES *makes* 24

395g (14oz) can sweetened condensed milk
2 tablespoons golden syrup
60g (2oz) unsalted butter
24 x 4.5cm (1¾in) diameter baked pastry cases
1 large banana (230g)
½ cup (125ml) thickened (heavy) cream, whipped

1 Combine condensed milk, golden syrup and butter in a small heavy-based saucepan; stir over medium heat until smooth.
2 Bring mixture to the boil; boil, stirring, for 10 minutes or until mixture is thick and dark caramel in colour. Remove pan from heat; cool.
3 Fill pastry cases with caramel; top with a slice of banana, then a dollop of cream.

*lemon
crème brûlée*
TARTS

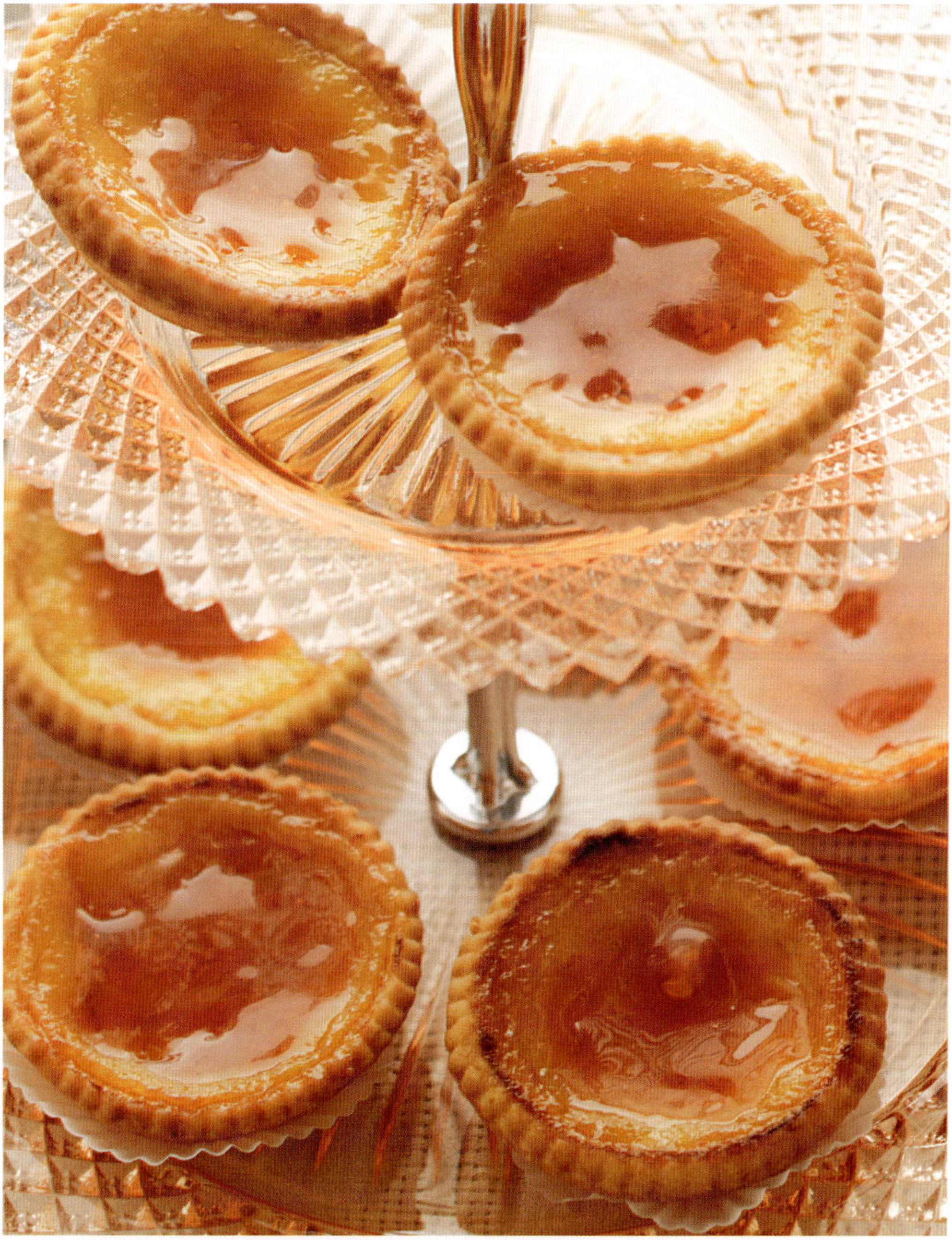

LEMON CRÈME BRÛLÉE TARTS

prep + cook time 1 HOUR 10 MINUTES (+ REFRIGERATION & COOLING) ❊ *makes* 24

1¼ cups (300ml) pouring cream
⅓ cup (80ml) milk
4 x 5cm (2in) strips lemon rind
4 egg yolks
¼ cup (55g) caster (superfine) sugar

PASTRY
1¾ cups (260g) plain (all-purpose) flour
¼ cup (40g) icing (confectioners') sugar
2 teaspoons finely grated lemon rind
185g (6oz) cold butter, chopped
1 egg yolk
2 teaspoons iced water, approximately

TOFFEE
1 cup (220g) caster (superfine) sugar
½ cup (125ml) water

1 Make pastry.
2 Grease two 12-hole (1½-tablespoons/30ml) shallow round-based patty pans. Roll half the pastry between sheets of baking paper to 3mm (⅛in) thickness. Cut out 12 x 6cm (2¼in) fluted rounds; press rounds into holes in pans. Prick bases of cases well with a fork. Repeat with remaining pastry. Refrigerate for 30 minutes.
3 Preheat oven to 160°C/325°F.
4 Combine cream, milk and rind in a small saucepan; bring to the boil. Beat egg yolks and sugar in a small bowl with an electric mixer until thick and creamy. Gradually beat hot cream mixture into egg mixture; allow bubbles to subside. Strain custard into a medium jug, divide between cases; bake for 25 minutes. Cool. Refrigerate tarts for 2 hours.
5 Make toffee.
6 Remove tarts from pan; place on an oven tray. Sprinkle custard with toffee; using a blowtorch, heat until toffee caramelises.

PASTRY Process flour, sugar, rind and butter until crumbly. With motor operating, add egg yolk and enough of the water to make ingredients come together. Turn dough onto a floured surface, knead gently until smooth. Enclose pastry in plastic wrap; refrigerate for 30 minutes.

TOFFEE Stir sugar and the water in a medium saucepan over medium heat, without boiling, until sugar dissolves. Bring to the boil. Boil, uncovered, without stirring, until golden brown. Pour toffee on a greased oven tray to set. Break toffee into large pieces; process until chopped finely.

tip Blowtorches are available from kitchenware and hardware stores.

KEEPS
These cheesecakes are best eaten within 2 days of making them. Keep them in an airtight container in the fridge.

MINI BAKED LEMON CHEESECAKES

prep + cook time 50 MINUTES (+ REFRIGERATION) *makes* 12

100g (3½oz) plain sweet biscuits
45g (1½oz) butter, melted
500g (1lb) cream cheese, softened
2 teaspoons finely grated lemon rind
½ cup (110g) caster (superfine) sugar
2 eggs

APRICOT BRANDY GLAZE
⅔ cup (220g) apricot jam
2 tablespoons brandy

1 Preheat oven to 150°C/300°F. Line a 12-hole (⅓-cup/80ml) muffin pan with paper cases.
2 Blend or process biscuits until fine. Add butter; process until just combined. Divide mixture into paper cases; press down firmly. Refrigerate for 30 minutes.
3 Beat cream cheese, rind and sugar in a small bowl with an electric mixer until smooth. Beat in eggs. Pour mixture into paper cases.
4 Bake cheesecakes for 25 minutes. Stand in pan for 5 minutes; turn, top-side up, onto a wire rack to cool.
5 Make apricot brandy glaze. Pour glaze evenly over cheesecake tops; refrigerate 2 hours or until glaze is set.
APRICOT BRANDY GLAZE Heat ingredients in a small saucepan over low heat; strain.

MIXED BERRY & RICOTTA TART

prep + cook time 1 HOUR 30 MINUTES (+ REFRIGERATION) *serves* 10

- 1½ cups (225g) plain (all-purpose) flour
- ⅓ cup (80g) chilled coconut oil
- 2 tablespoons sesame seeds, toasted lightly
- ¼ cup (60ml) iced water, approximately
- 500g (1lb) soft ricotta
- ⅓ cup (95g) Greek-style yoghurt
- ⅓ cup (75g) caster (superfine) sugar
- 3 eggs
- 1 tablespoon finely grated lemon rind
- 200g (6½oz) strawberries
- 125g (4oz) blueberries
- 125g (4oz) raspberries
- 2 teaspoons icing (confectioners') sugar

1 Process flour, coconut oil and sesame seeds until combined. With the motor operating, pour in enough of the water until mixture just comes together. Knead dough lightly on a floured surface until smooth. Shape pastry into a disc, enclose in plastic wrap; refrigerate for 30 minutes.

2 Grease a 24cm (9½in) round loose-based fluted tart tin. Grate chilled pastry into tin; press over base and side. Prick base all over with a fork. Refrigerate for 30 minutes.

3 Preheat oven to 200°C/400°F.

4 Place tin on an oven tray. Line pastry with baking paper; fill with dried beans or rice. Bake for 15 minutes. Remove paper and beans; bake a further 15 minutes or until browned lightly and crisp. Remove from oven; cool.

5 Reduce oven to 180°C/350°F.

6 Meanwhile, process ricotta, yoghurt, caster sugar, eggs and rind in a small bowl with an electric mixer until smooth. Pour ricotta mixture into tart shell.

7 Bake tart for 35 minutes or until filling is just set. Cool. Refrigerate until cold.

8 Slice or halve strawberries. Just before serving, top tart with all the berries and dust with icing sugar.

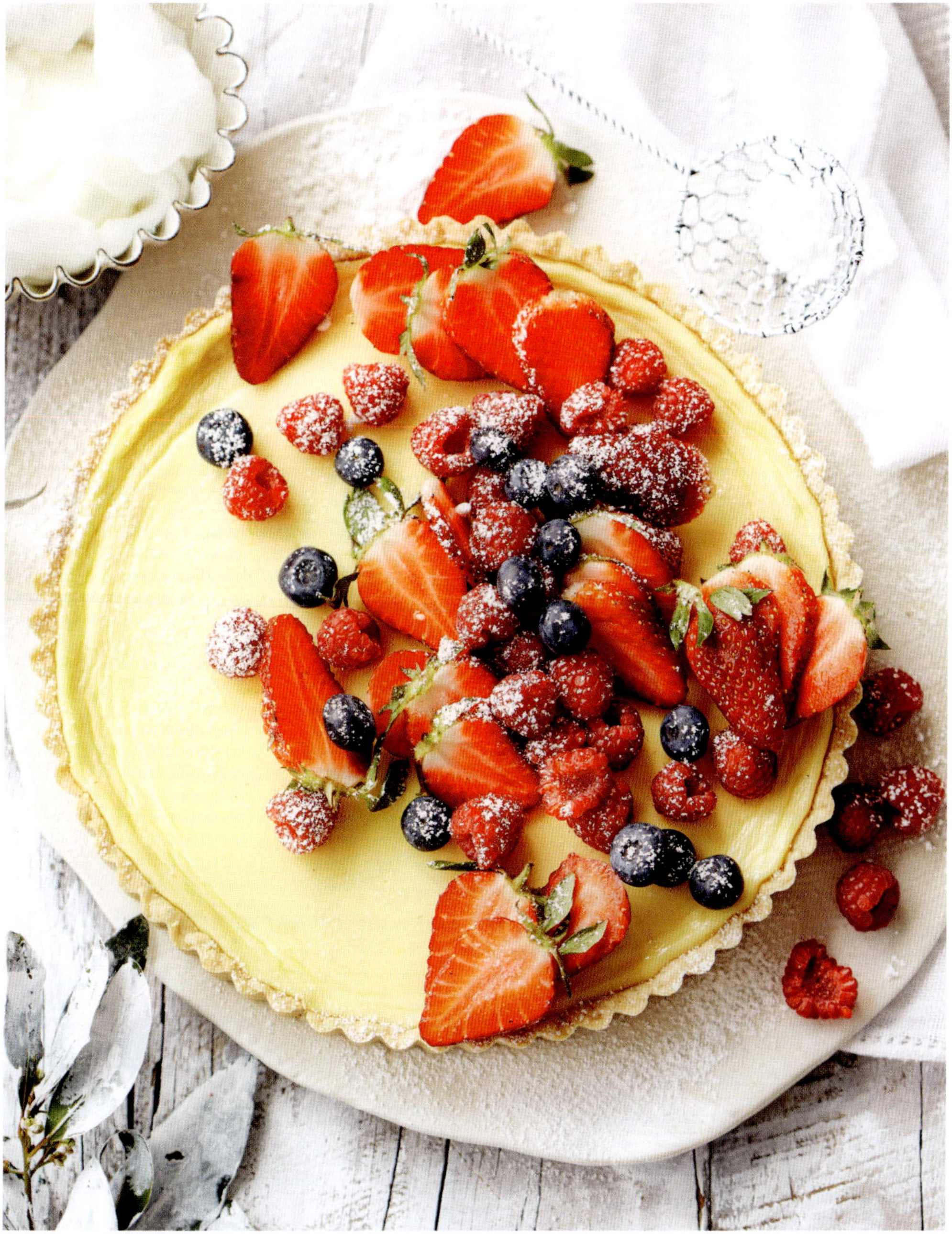

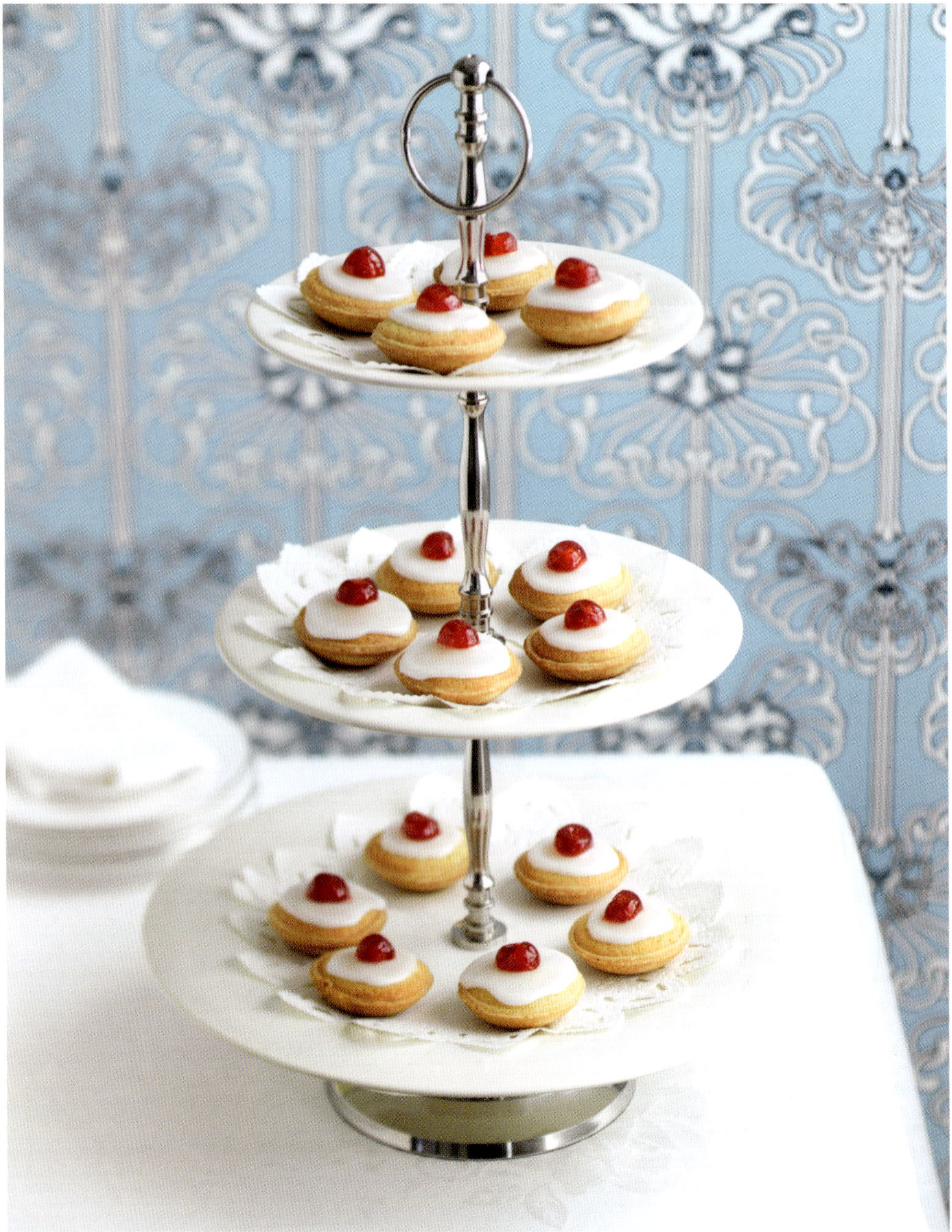

CHERRY BAKEWELL TARTS

prep + cook time 1 HOUR (+ REFRIGERATION)   *makes* 24

90g (3oz) unsalted butter, softened
2 tablespoons caster (superfine) sugar
1 egg yolk
1 cup (150g) plain (all-purpose) flour
½ cup (60g) almond meal
2 tablespoons strawberry jam
12 red glacé cherries, halved

ALMOND FILLING
125g (4oz) unsalted butter, softened
½ teaspoon finely grated lemon rind
½ cup (110g) caster (superfine) sugar
2 eggs
¾ cup (90g) almond meal
2 tablespoons plain (all-purpose) flour

LEMON GLAZE
1 cup (160g) icing (confectioners') sugar
2 tablespoons lemon juice, approximately

1 Beat butter, sugar and egg yolk in a small bowl with an electric mixer until combined. Stir in sifted flour and almond meal in two batches. Turn dough onto a floured surface, knead gently until smooth. Enclose in plastic wrap; refrigerate for 30 minutes.
2 Preheat oven to 220°C/425°F.
3 Make almond filling.
4 Grease two 12-hole (1½-tablespoons/30ml) shallow round-based patty pans. Roll pastry between sheets of baking paper until 3mm thick. Cut 24 x 6cm (2¼in) rounds from pastry; gently press rounds into holes in pans. Divide jam then almond filling into cases; bake for 20 minutes. Stand tarts for 10 minutes; turn, top-side up, onto a wire rack.
5 Meanwhile, make lemon glaze.
6 Spoon glaze over warm tarts; top with halved cherries. Cool.

ALMOND FILLING Beat butter, rind and sugar in a small bowl with an electric mixer until light and fluffy. Beat in eggs, one at a time. Stir in almond meal and flour.

LEMON GLAZE Sift icing sugar into small bowl, stir in enough juice to make glaze pourable.

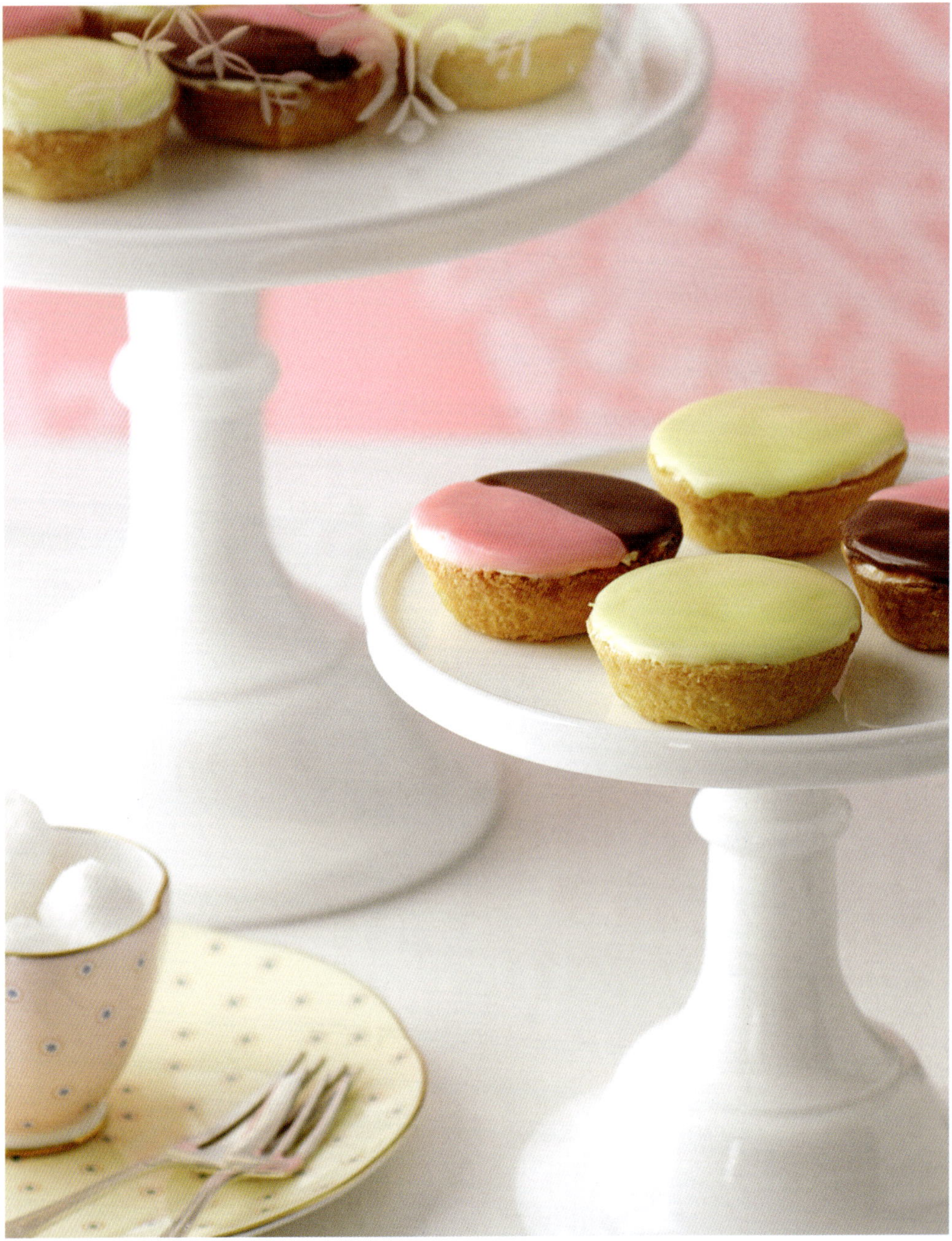

neenish & pineapple
TARTS

NEENISH & PINEAPPLE TARTS

prep + cook time 1 HOUR 10 MINUTES (+ REFRIGERATION & COOLING) makes 24

1¾ cups (260g) plain (all-purpose) flour
¼ cup (40g) icing (confectioners') sugar
185g (6oz) cold butter, chopped coarsely
1 egg yolk
2 teaspoons iced water, approximately
2 tablespoons strawberry jam
2 tablespoons finely chopped glacé pineapple

MOCK CREAM

¾ cup (165g) caster (superfine) sugar
⅓ cup (80ml) water
1½ tablespoons milk
½ teaspoon gelatine
185g (6oz) unsalted butter, softened
1 teaspoon vanilla extract

GLACÉ ICING

1½ cups (240g) icing (confectioners') sugar
15g (½oz) unsalted butter, melted
2 tablespoons hot milk, approximately
yellow and pink food colouring
½ teaspoon cocoa powder

1 Process flour, sugar and butter until crumbly. With motor operating, add egg yolk and enough of the water to make ingredients come together. Turn dough onto a floured surface, knead gently until smooth. Enclose pastry in plastic wrap; refrigerate for 30 minutes.
2 Grease two 12-hole (2-tablespoons/40ml) deep flat-based patty pans. Roll out half the pastry between sheets of baking paper until 3mm (⅛in) thick. Cut out 12 x 7.5cm (3in) rounds; press rounds into holes of one pan. Prick bases of cases well with a fork. Repeat with remaining pastry. Refrigerate for 30 minutes.
3 Preheat oven to 220°C/425°F.
4 Bake cases for 12 minutes. Stand cases 5 minutes before transferring to a wire rack to cool.
5 Meanwhile, make mock cream and glacé icing.

6 Divide jam between half the cases and pineapple between remaining cases. Fill cases with mock cream, level tops with a spatula. Spread yellow icing over pineapple tarts. Spread pink icing over half of each jam tart; cover remaining half with chocolate icing.

MOCK CREAM Stir sugar, ¼ cup of the water and milk in a small saucepan over low heat, without boiling, until sugar dissolves. Sprinkle gelatine over remaining water in a small jug; stir into milk mixture until gelatine dissolves. Cool to room temperature. Beat butter and vanilla in a small bowl with an electric mixer until as white as possible. While motor is operating, gradually beat in cooled milk mixture; beat until light and fluffy.

GLACÉ ICING Sift icing sugar into medium bowl; stir in butter and enough of the milk to make a thick paste. Place ⅓ cup of the icing in a small heatproof bowl; tint with yellow colouring. Divide remaining icing between two small heatproof bowls; tint icing in one bowl with pink colouring and the other with sifted cocoa. Stir each bowl over small saucepan of simmering water until icing is spreadable.

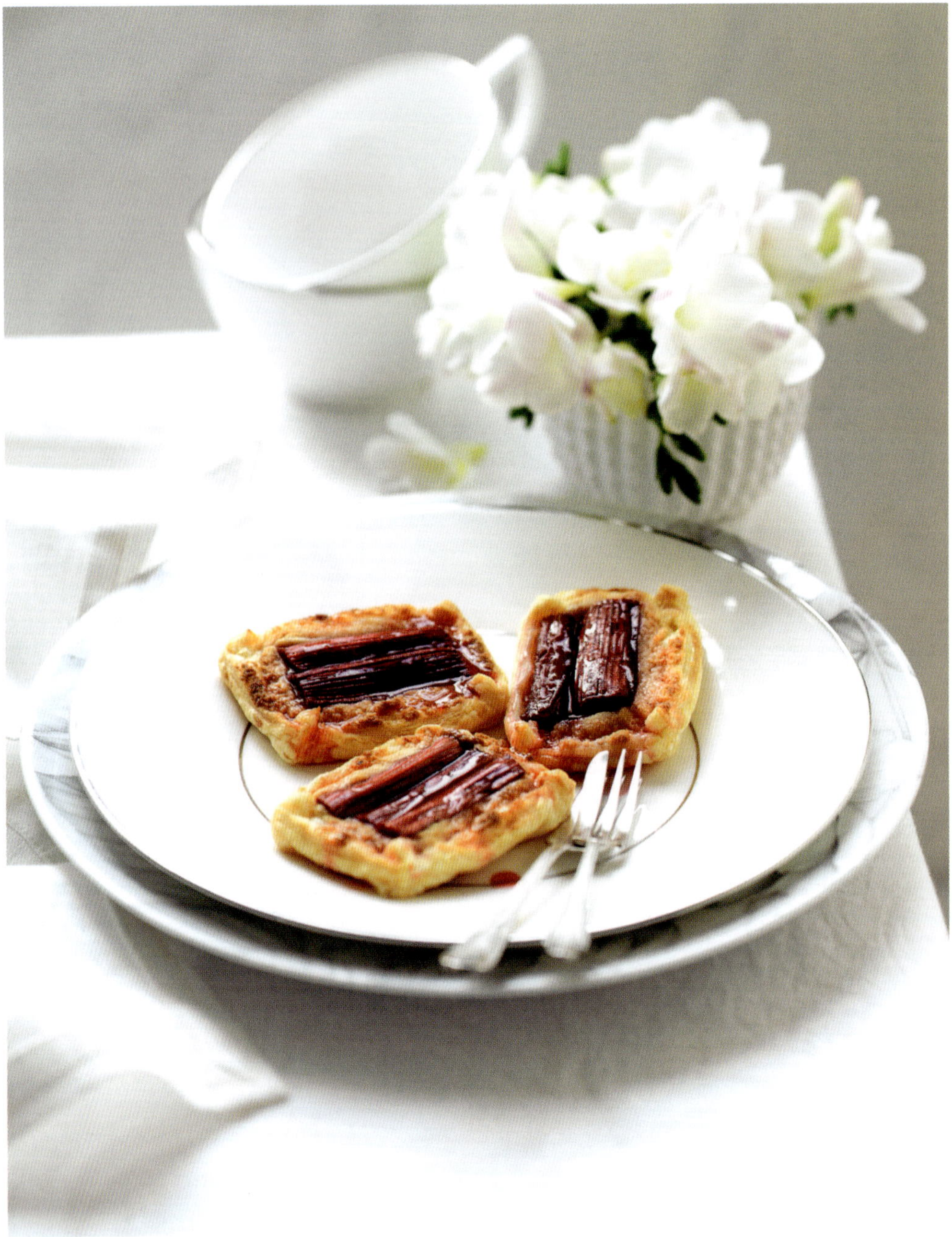

RHUBARB FRANGIPANE TARTS

prep + cook time 1 HOUR 10 MINUTES (+ COOLING) makes 12

1 vanilla bean
½ cup (110g) caster (superfine) sugar
¼ cup (60ml) water
10 stalks trimmed rhubarb (300g), cut into 4cm (1½in) lengths
40g (1½oz) butter, softened
2 tablespoons caster (superfine) sugar, extra
½ teaspoon vanilla extract
1 egg yolk
½ cup (60g) almond meal
2 teaspoons plain (all-purpose) flour
1 sheet butter puff pastry

1 Preheat oven to 180°C/350°F. Grease two oven trays.
2 Split vanilla bean, scrape seeds into a small saucepan; discard bean. Add sugar and the water to the pan. Stir over medium heat, without boiling, until sugar dissolves. Combine rhubarb and syrup in a medium baking dish; bake for 15 minutes or until rhubarb is tender. Cool. Drain rhubarb; reserving syrup.
3 Meanwhile, beat butter, extra sugar, vanilla and egg yolk in a small bowl with an electric mixer until light and fluffy. Stir in almond meal and flour.
4 Cut pastry into quarters; cut each quarter into three rectangles. Place pastry rectangles about 5cm (2in) apart on trays; spread rounded teaspoons of almond mixture over each rectangle, leaving a 5mm (¼in) border. Top with rhubarb; fold pastry edges in towards centre to form raised border.
5 Bake tarts for 25 minutes.
6 Serve tarts warm, brushed with reserved syrup.

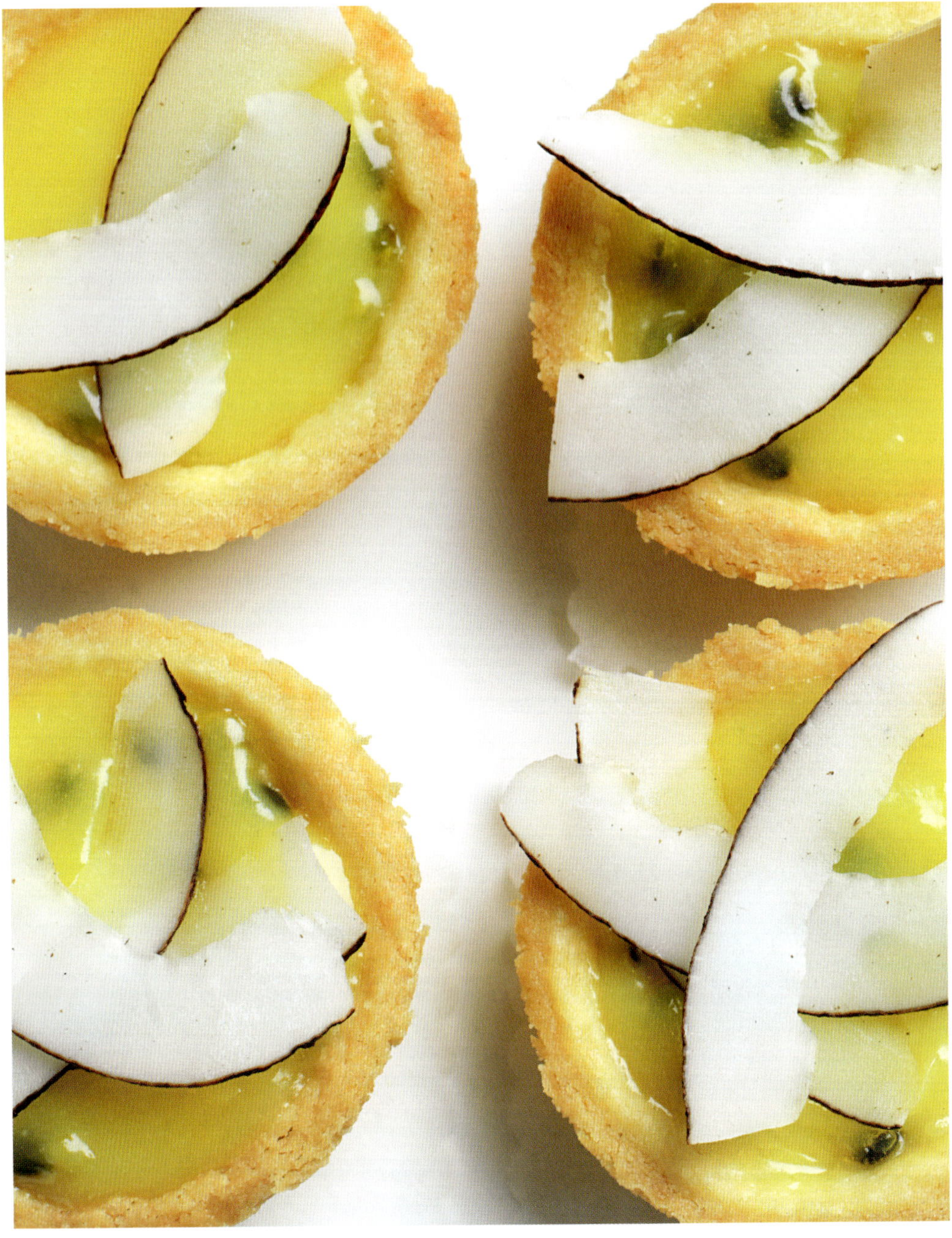

passionfruit curd &
COCONUT TARTS

PASSIONFRUIT CURD & COCONUT TARTS

prep + cook time 1 HOUR 10 MINUTES (+ REFRIGERATION & COOLING) *makes* 24

1¾ cups (260g) plain (all-purpose) flour
¼ cup (40g) icing (confectioners') sugar
¼ cup (20g) desiccated coconut
185g (6oz) cold unsalted butter, chopped coarsely
1 egg yolk
2 teaspoons iced water, approximately
1 small coconut (700g)

PASSIONFRUIT CURD

⅓ cup (80ml) passionfruit pulp
½ cup (110g) caster (superfine) sugar
2 eggs, beaten lightly
125g (4oz) unsalted butter, chopped coarsely

1 Make passionfruit curd.

2 Process flour, sugar, desiccated coconut and butter until crumbly. With motor operating, add egg yolk and enough of the water to make ingredients come together. Turn dough onto a floured surface, knead gently until smooth. Enclose pastry in plastic wrap; refrigerate for 30 minutes.

3 Grease two 12-hole (2-tablespoons/40ml) deep flat-based patty pans. Roll out half the pastry between sheets of baking paper until 5mm (¼in) thick. Cut out 12 x 7.5cm (3in) rounds; press rounds into holes of one pan. Prick bases of cases well with a fork. Repeat with remaining pastry. Refrigerate for 30 minutes.

4 Preheat oven to 220°C/425°F.

5 Bake cases for 12 minutes or until browned. Stand cases for 5 minutes before transferring to a wire rack to cool.

6 Increase oven temperature to 240°C/475°F. Pierce one eye of the coconut using a sharp knife; drain liquid from coconut. Place coconut on an oven tray; bake for 10 minutes or until cracks appear. Carefully split the coconut open by hitting with a hammer; remove flesh. Using vegetable peeler, slice coconut into curls; reserve ½ cup coconut curls for this recipe and keep remaining for another use. Roast reserved coconut on oven tray for 5 minutes or until lightly browned.
7 Divide passionfruit curd between cases; top with coconut curls.

PASSIONFRUIT CURD Stir ingredients in a medium heatproof bowl over a medium saucepan of simmering water for 10 minutes or until mixture coats the back of a wooden spoon. Cover surface with plastic wrap; refrigerate overnight.

LITTLE CAKES

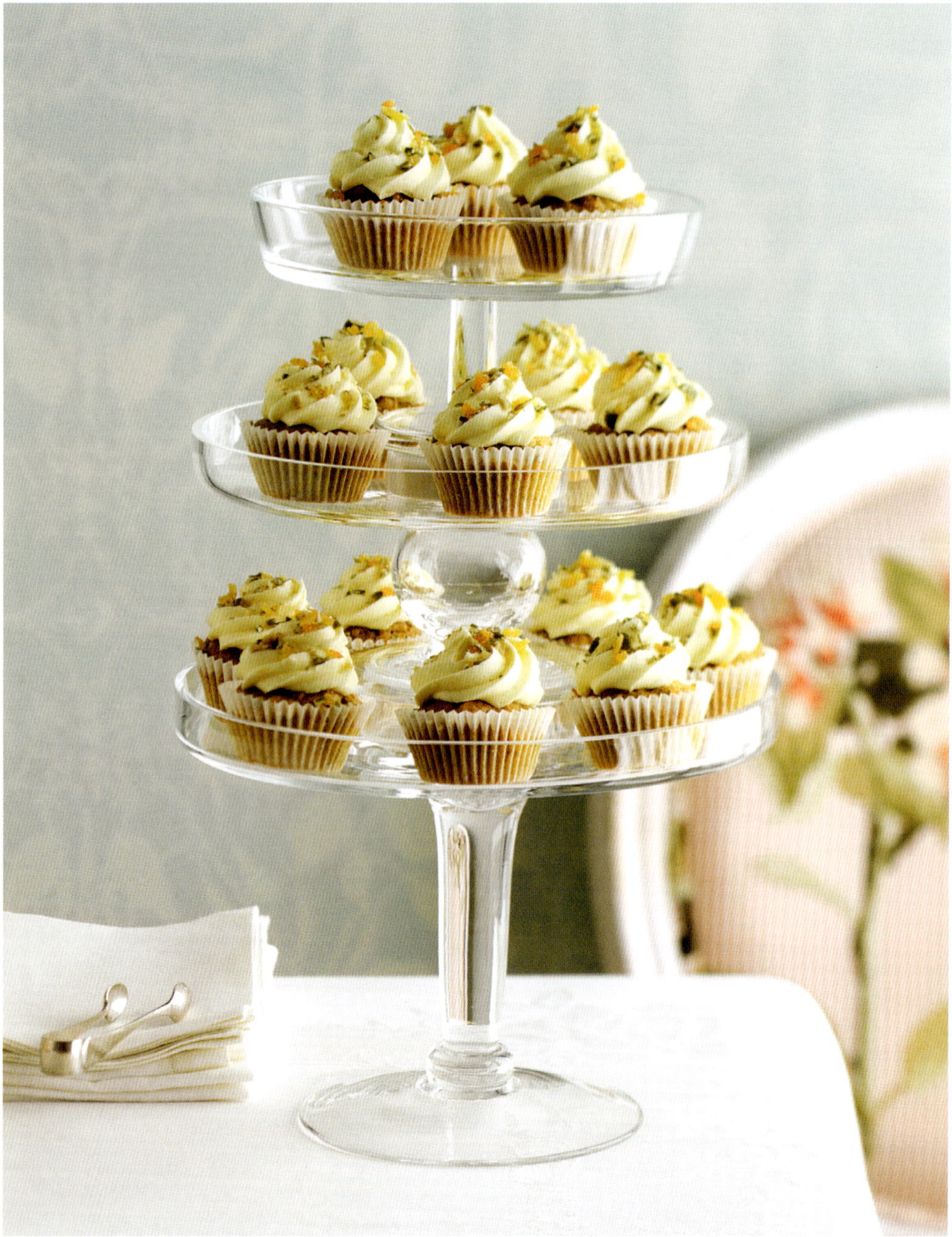

CARROT CAKES

prep + cook time 45 MINUTES (+ COOLING) makes 18

⅓ cup (80ml) vegetable oil
½ cup (110g) firmly packed brown sugar
1 egg
1 cup firmly packed coarsely grated carrot
⅓ cup (40g) finely chopped walnuts
¾ cup (110g) self-raising flour
½ teaspoon mixed spice
1 tablespoon pepitas (pumpkin seed kernels), chopped finely
1 tablespoon finely chopped dried apricots
1 tablespoon finely chopped walnuts, extra

LEMON CREAM CHEESE FROSTING
90g (3oz) cream cheese, softened
30g (1oz) unsalted butter, softened
1 teaspoon finely grated lemon rind
1½ cups (240g) icing (confectioners') sugar

1 Preheat oven to 180°C/350°F. Line 18 holes of two 12-hole (2-tablespoon/40ml) deep flat-based patty pans with paper cases.
2 Beat oil, sugar and egg in a small bowl with an electric mixer until thick and creamy. Stir in carrot and walnuts, then sifted flour and spice. Divide mixture into paper cases.
3 Bake cakes for 20 minutes. Stand cakes 5 minutes before turning, top-side up, onto a wire rack to cool.
4 Meanwhile, make lemon cream cheese frosting.
5 Spoon lemon cream cheese frosting into a piping bag fitted with a 2cm (¾in) fluted tube; pipe frosting onto cakes. Sprinkle cakes with combined pepitas, apricots and extra walnuts.
LEMON CREAM CHEESE FROSTING Beat cream cheese, butter and rind in a small bowl with an electric mixer until light and fluffy; gradually beat in sifted icing sugar.

white chocolate
RASPBERRY
LAMINGTONS

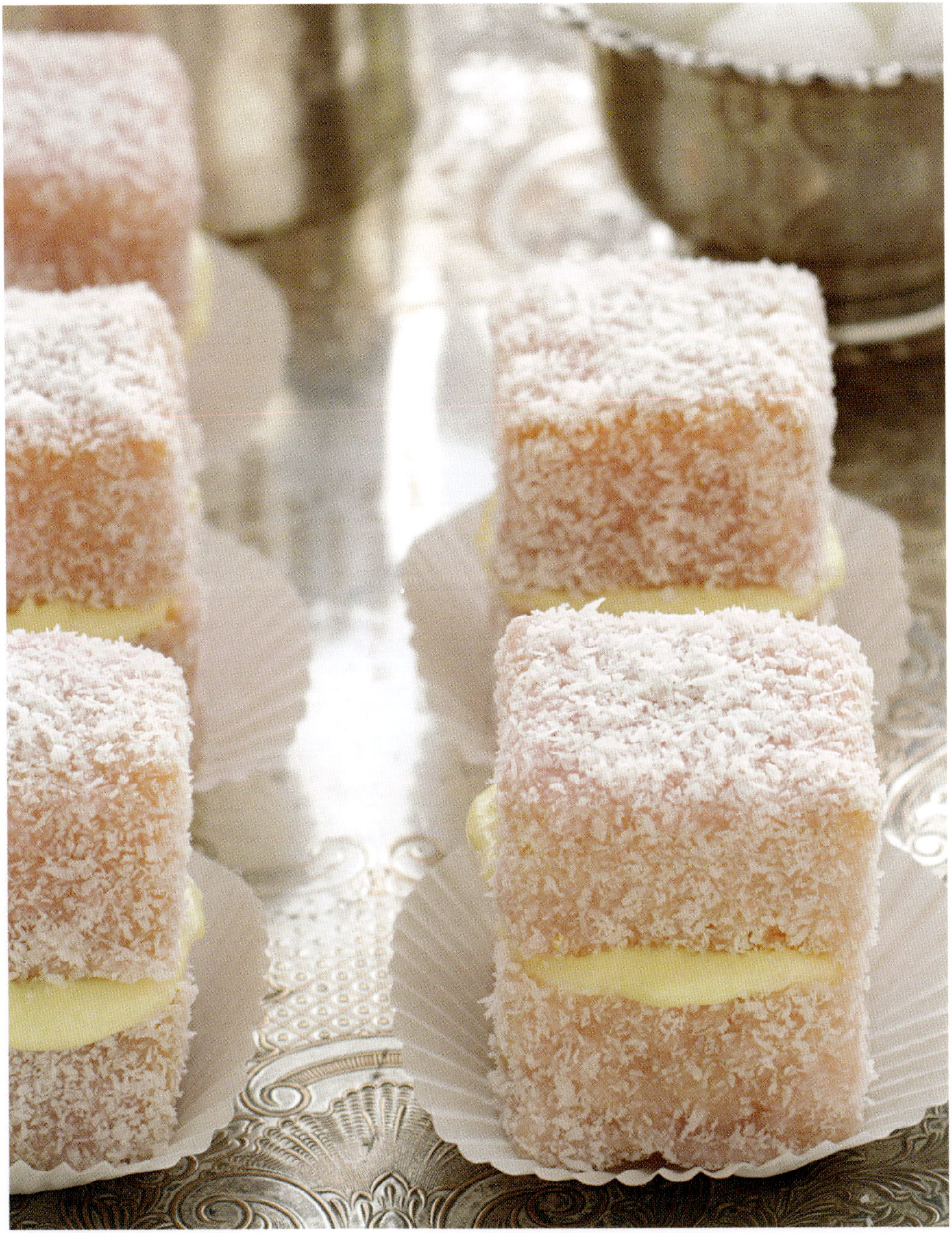

WHITE CHOCOLATE
RASPBERRY LAMINGTONS

prep + cook time 1 HOUR 20 MINUTES (+ REFRIGERATION & COOLING) *makes* 25

6 eggs
⅔ cup (150g) caster (superfine) sugar
½ cup (75g) plain (all-purpose) flour
½ cup (75g) self-raising flour
¼ cup (35g) cornflour (cornstarch)
60g (2oz) fresh raspberries
4 cups (640g) icing (confectioners') sugar
½ cup (125ml) milk
2 cups (160g) desiccated coconut

WHITE CHOCOLATE MOUSSE
125g (4oz) white chocolate, chopped finely
2 tablespoons thickened (heavy) cream
10g (½oz) unsalted butter, chopped
1 egg
1 tablespoon caster (superfine) sugar
¼ cup (60ml) thickened (heavy) cream, whipped, extra

1 Make white chocolate mousse.
2 Preheat oven to 180°C/350°F. Grease a deep 22cm (9in) square cake pan well with butter; line base and sides with baking paper, extending the paper 5cm (2in) above sides.
3 Beat eggs and caster sugar in a bowl with the electric mixer for 10 minutes or until thick and creamy.
4 Meanwhile, sift flours twice, then sift a third time over egg mixture; fold ingredients together. Spread mixture into pan.
5 Bake sponge for 35 minutes. Turn the sponge immediately onto a baking-paper-covered wire rack, then turn, top-side up, to cool.

6 Blend or process raspberries until smooth. Strain through a fine sieve into a medium heatproof bowl; discard solids. Sift icing sugar into bowl with raspberry puree; stir in milk. Stir over a medium saucepan of simmering water until icing is of a coating consistency.

7 Cut sponge into 25 squares. Dip a square of sponge into icing, drain off excess; toss sponge in coconut. Place lamington on a wire rack to set. Repeat with remaining sponge, icing and coconut.

8 Split each lamington in half; sandwich with mousse.

WHITE CHOCOLATE MOUSSE Stir chocolate and cream in a small heatproof bowl over a small saucepan of simmering water until smooth. Remove from heat; stir in butter. Beat egg and sugar in a small bowl with an electric mixer until pale and thick; fold egg mixture then extra cream into chocolate mixture. Cover; refrigerate overnight.

FIG & WALNUT FRIANDS

prep + cook time 35 MINUTES ❦ *makes* 12

1¼ cups (125g) roasted walnuts
6 egg whites
185g (6oz) unsalted butter, melted
1½ cups (240g) icing (confectioners') sugar
½ cup (75g) plain (all-purpose) flour
2 teaspoons finely grated orange rind
1 tablespoon orange juice
4 dried figs (85g), sliced thinly

1 Preheat oven to 200°C/400°F. Grease a 12-hole (½-cup/125ml) oval friand pan.
2 Process walnuts until ground finely.
3 Place egg whites in a medium bowl; whisk lightly with a fork until combined. Add butter, sifted icing sugar and flour, rind, juice and ground walnuts; stir until combined. Divide mixture into pans, top with slices of fig.
4 Bake friands for 20 minutes. Stand friands for 5 minutes before turning, top-side up, onto a wire rack to cool. Serve dusted with a little sifted icing sugar.

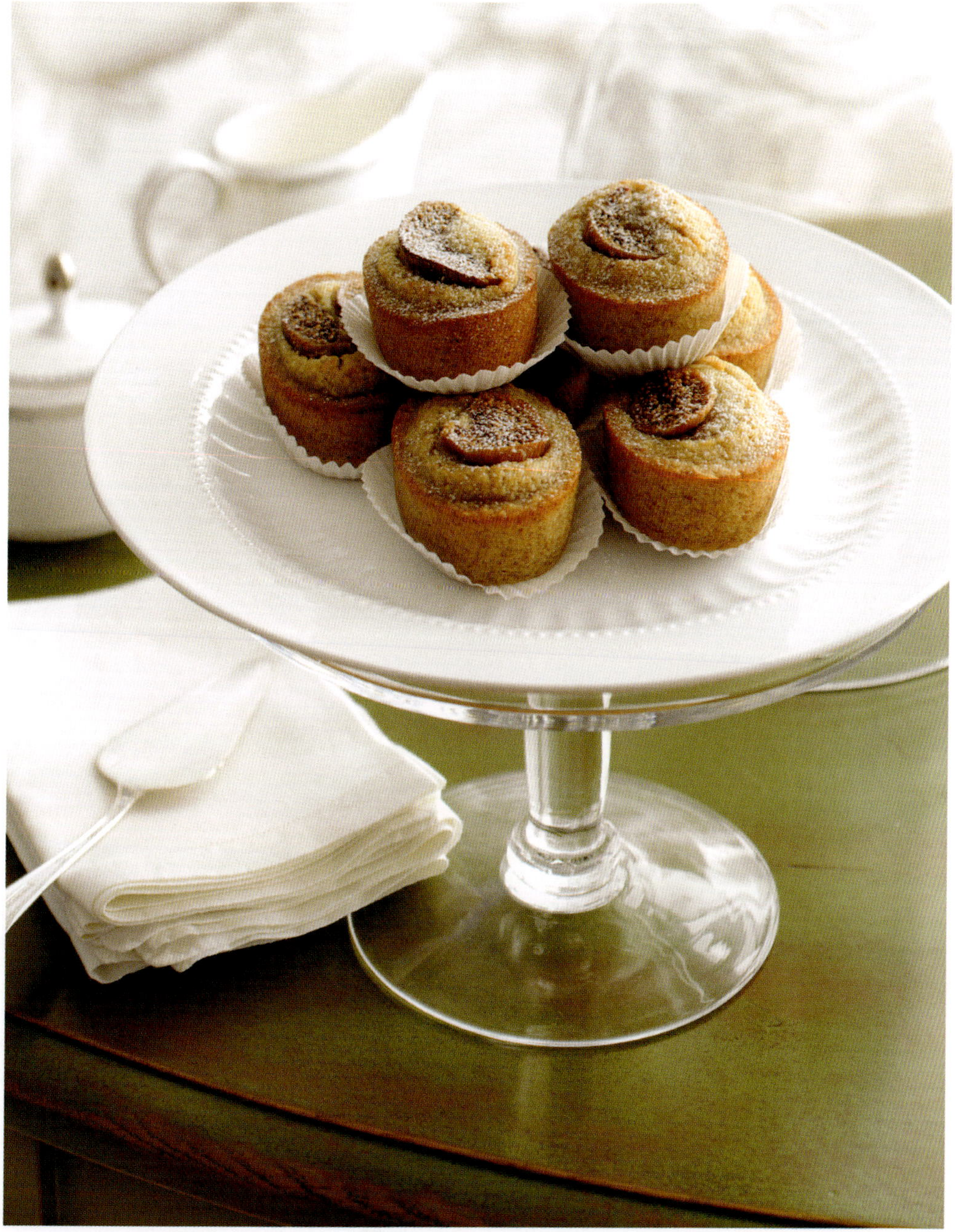

TIP
You can use any fresh berries you like in this recipe.

RASPBERRY POWDER PUFFS

prep + cook time 1 HOUR *makes* 14

2 eggs
⅓ cup (75g) caster (superfine) sugar
2 tablespoons pure cornflour (cornstarch)
2 tablespoons plain (all-purpose) flour
2 tablespoons self-raising flour
½ cup (125ml) thickened (heavy) cream
2 tablespoons icing (confectioners') sugar
1 cup (120g) fresh raspberries, chopped coarsely

1 Preheat oven to 180°C/350°F. Butter and flour 28 holes from three 12-hole (1½-tablespoon/30ml) shallow round-based patty pans.
2 Beat eggs and caster sugar in a small bowl with an electric mixer for 4 minutes or until thick and creamy.
3 Sift flours twice onto baking paper, then sift a third time over egg mixture; fold flour into egg mixture. Drop level tablespoons of mixture into pan holes.
4 Bake puffs for 12 minutes; immediately turn puffs onto wire racks to cool.
5 Beat cream and half the icing sugar in a small bowl with an electric mixer until soft peaks form; fold in raspberries.
6 Sandwich puffs with raspberry cream just before serving. Dust with sifted remaining icing sugar.

COCONUT ICE CAKES

prep + cook time 1 HOUR (+ COOLING) *makes* 18

60g (2oz) butter, softened
½ teaspoon coconut essence
½ cup (110g) caster (superfine) sugar
1 egg
¼ cup (20g) desiccated coconut
¾ cup (110g) self-raising flour
½ cup (120g) sour cream
2 tablespoons milk

COCONUT ICE FROSTING
1 cup (160g) icing (confectioners') sugar
⅔ cup (50g) desiccated coconut
1 egg white, beaten lightly
pink food colouring

1 Preheat oven to 180°C/350°F. Line 18 holes of two 12-hole (2-tablespoons/40ml) deep flat-based patty pans with paper cases.
2 Beat butter, coconut essence, sugar and egg in a small bowl with an electric mixer until light and fluffy. Stir in the coconut, sifted flour, sour cream and milk, in two batches. Divide mixture into paper cases.
3 Bake cakes for 20 minutes. Stand cakes for 5 minutes before turning, top-side up, onto a wire rack to cool.
4 Meanwhile, make coconut ice frosting.
5 Drop alternate rounded teaspoons of white and pink frosting onto cakes; marble over the top of each cake.

COCONUT ICE FROSTING Sift icing sugar into medium bowl; stir in coconut and egg white. Place half the mixture in a small bowl; tint with pink food colouring.

TIP
Use a hot wet palette knife to spread the frosting over cakes.

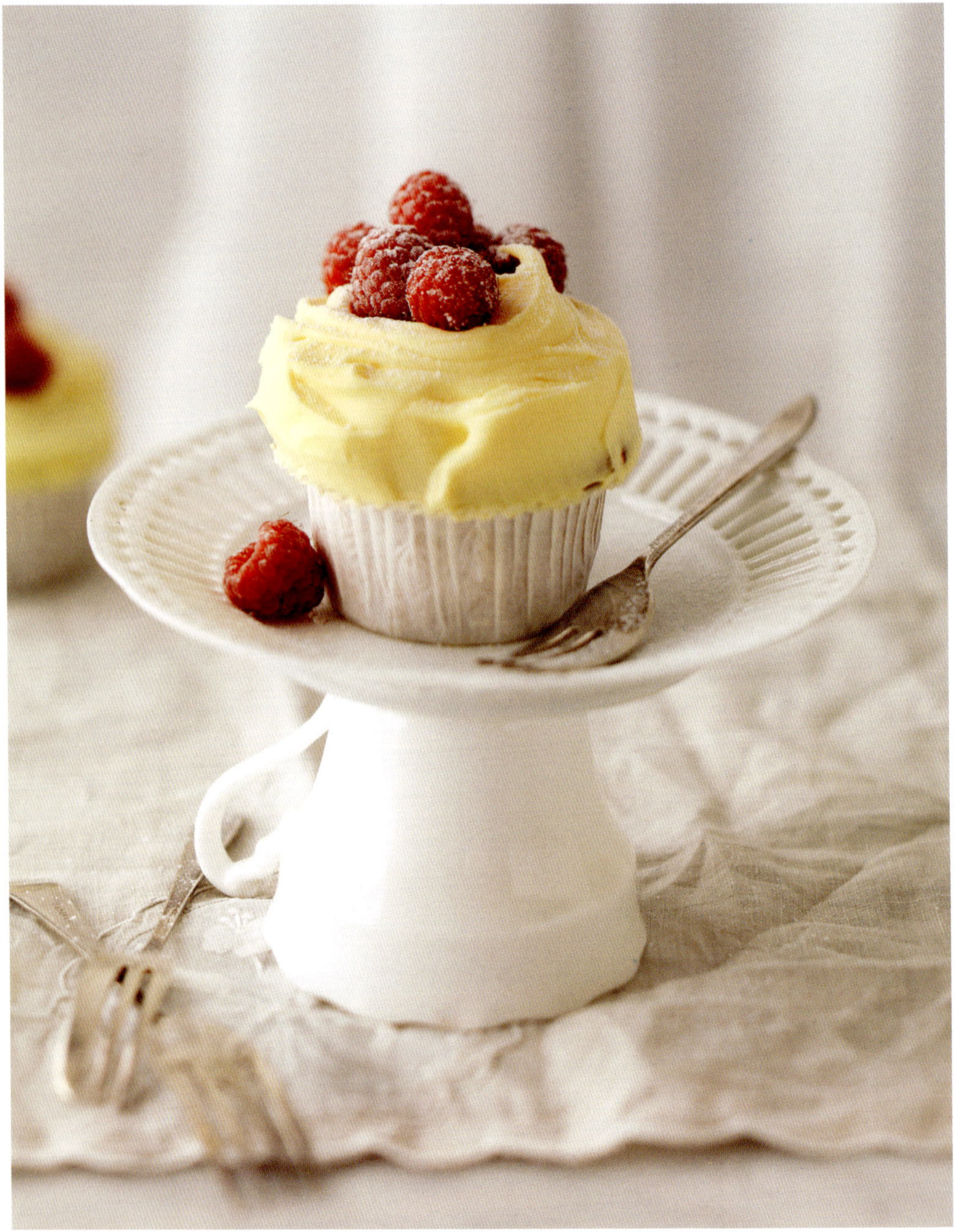

RASPBERRY
TRIFLE CUPCAKES

prep + cook time 1 HOUR 10 MINUTES (+ COOLING & REFRIGERATION) *makes* 12

90g (3oz) unsalted butter, softened
½ teaspoon vanilla extract
½ cup (110g) caster (superfine) sugar
2 eggs
1 cup (150g) self-raising flour
2 tablespoons milk
⅔ cup (100g) frozen raspberries
2 tablespoons sweet sherry
125g (4oz) fresh raspberries

WHIPPED CUSTARD ICING
2 tablespoons custard powder
2 tablespoons caster (superfine) sugar
1 cup (250ml) pouring cream
1 cup (250ml) thickened (heavy) cream

1 Make whipped custard icing.
2 Meanwhile, preheat oven to 180°C/350°F. Line 12-hole (⅓-cup/80ml) muffin pan with paper cases.
3 Beat butter, vanilla, sugar, eggs, sifted flour and milk in a small bowl with an electric mixer on low speed until ingredients are combined. Increase speed to medium; beat until mixture changes to a paler colour. Fold in frozen raspberries. Divide mixture into paper cases; smooth surface.
4 Bake cakes for 30 minutes. Stand cakes in pan for 10 minutes before turning, top-side up, onto a wire rack to cool. Brush warm cakes with sherry.
5 Top cakes with whipped custard icing and fresh raspberries. Dust with a little extra sifted icing sugar.
WHIPPED CUSTARD ICING Blend custard powder and sugar with pouring cream in a small saucepan; stir over medium heat until mixture boils and thickens. Remove from heat. Cover surface of custard with plastic wrap; cool for 20 minutes. Refrigerate 1 hour. Beat cold custard in a small bowl with an electric mixer until smooth. Add thickened cream; beat until soft peaks form.

MADELEINES

prep + cook time 25 MINUTES *makes* 24

2 eggs
2 tablespoons caster (superfine) sugar
2 tablespoons icing (confectioners') sugar
1 teaspoon vanilla extract
¼ cup (35g) self-raising flour
¼ cup (35g) plain (all-purpose) flour
75g (2½oz) butter, melted
1 tablespoon hot water
2 tablespoons icing (confectioners') sugar, extra

1 Preheat oven to 200°C/400°F. Grease two 12-hole (1½-tablespoon/30ml) madeleine pans with a little butter.
2 Beat eggs, caster sugar, icing sugar and vanilla in a small bowl with an electric mixer until thick and creamy.
3 Meanwhile, sift flours twice. Sift flours a third time over egg mixture; pour combined butter and the water down side of bowl then fold ingredients together.
4 Drop rounded tablespoons of mixture into pan holes.
5 Bake madeleines for 10 minutes. Tap hot pan firmly on bench to release madeleines then turn immediately onto baking-paper-covered wire racks to cool. Serve dusted with extra sifted icing sugar.

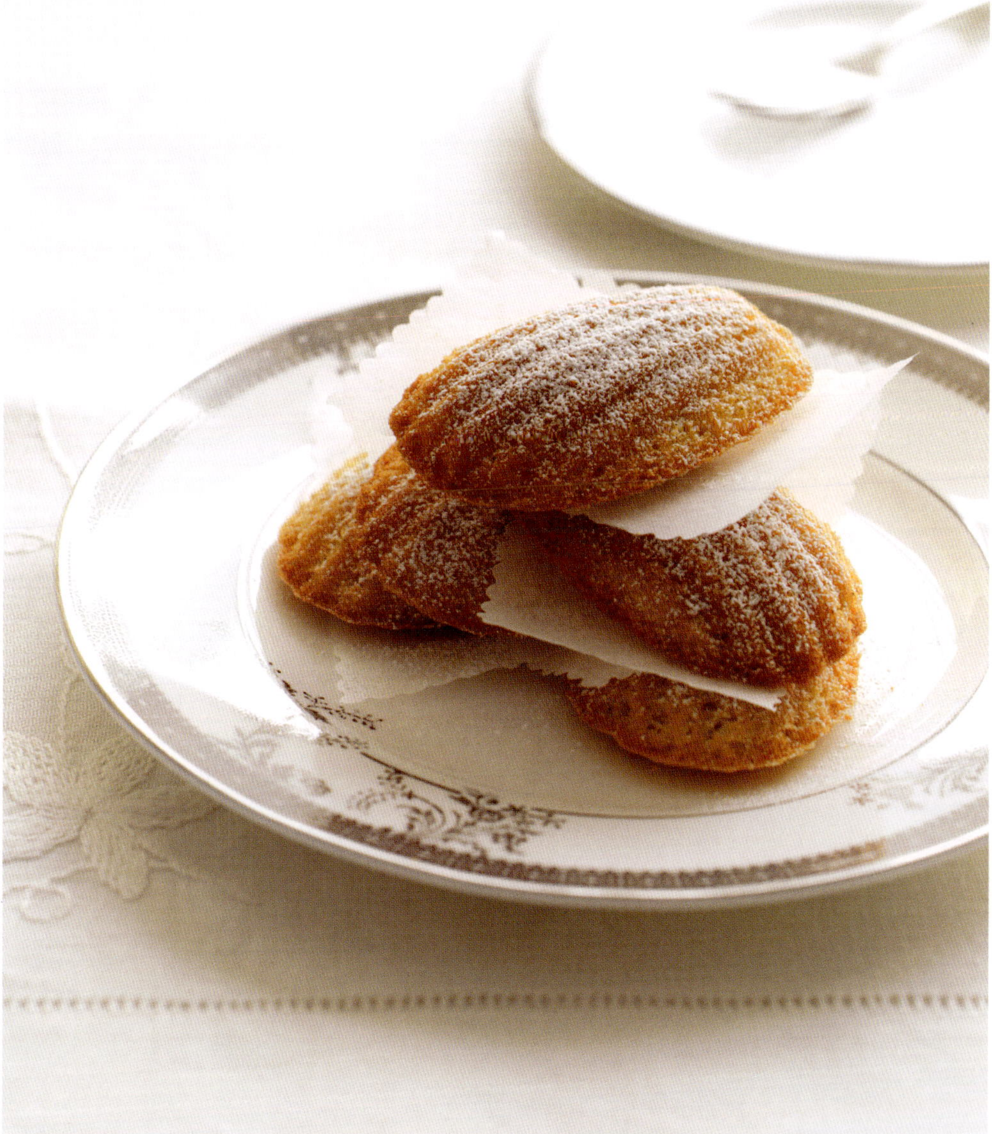

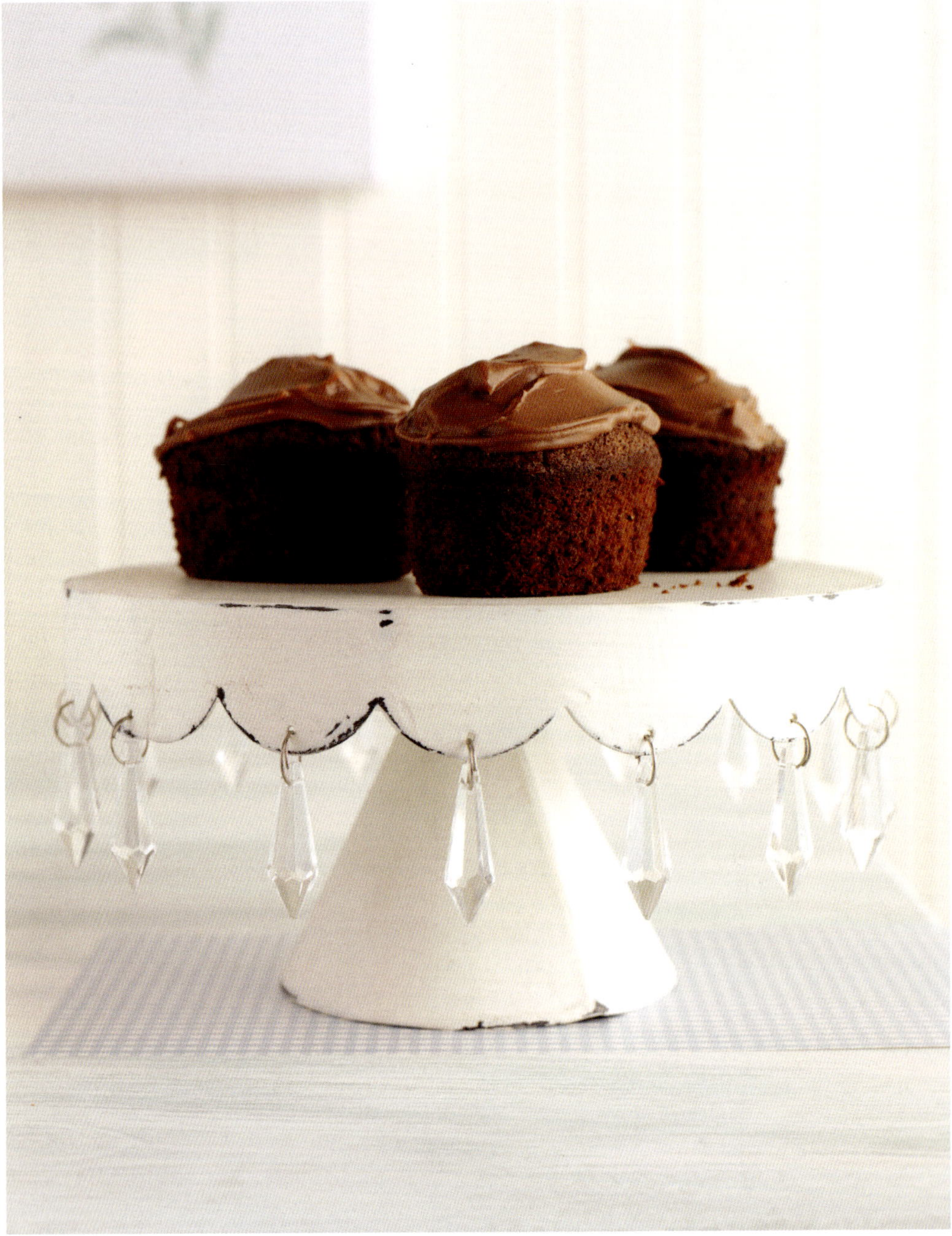

MINI CHOCOLATE HAZELNUT CAKES

prep + cook time 1 HOUR (+ STANDING) makes 12

100g (3oz) dark (semi-sweet) chocolate, chopped coarsely
¾ cup (180ml) water
100g (3oz) butter, softened
1 cup (220g) firmly packed brown sugar
3 eggs
¼ cup (25g) cocoa powder
¾ cup (110g) self-raising flour
⅓ cup (35g) hazelnut meal

WHIPPED HAZELNUT GANACHE
⅓ cup (80ml) thickened (heavy) cream
185g (6oz) milk chocolate, chopped finely
2 tablespoons hazelnut-flavoured liqueur

1 Preheat oven to 180°C/350°F. Grease a 12-hole (½-cup/125ml) oval friand pan.
2 Make whipped hazelnut ganache.
3 Meanwhile, combine chocolate and the water in a medium saucepan; stir over low heat until smooth.
4 Beat butter and sugar in a small bowl with the electric mixer until light and fluffy. Add eggs, one at a time, beating until just combined between additions (mixture might separate at this stage, but will come together later); transfer mixture to a medium bowl. Stir in warm chocolate mixture, sifted cocoa and flour, and hazelnut meal. Divide mixture into pan holes.
5 Bake cakes for 20 minutes. Stand for 5 minutes; turn cakes, top-side up, onto a wire rack to cool. Spread ganache over cakes.

WHIPPED HAZELNUT GANACHE Combine cream and chocolate in a small saucepan; stir over low heat until smooth. Stir in liqueur; transfer mixture to a small bowl. Cover; stand for 2 hours or until just firm. Beat ganache in a small bowl with an electric mixer until mixture changes to a pale brown colour.

Raspberry Almond
Petit Fours

prep + cook time 55 minutes (+ standing) ✽ *makes 32*

125g (4oz) butter, softened
¾ cup (165g) caster (superfine) sugar
3 eggs
½ cup (75g) plain (all-purpose) flour
¼ cup (35g) self-raising flour
½ cup (60g) almond meal
⅓ cup (80g) sour cream
150g (5oz) fresh raspberries
32 ready-made icing flowers

ICING

2½ cups (400g) icing (confectioners') sugar
2 tablespoons lemon juice
1½ tablespoons boiling water, approximately

1 Preheat oven to 180°C/350°F. Grease a 20cm x 30cm (8in x 12in) rectangular pan; line base and sides with baking paper, extending the paper 5cm (2in) over sides.
2 Beat butter and sugar in a small bowl with an electric mixer until light and fluffy. Beat in eggs, one at a time. Stir in sifted flours, almond meal, sour cream and raspberries. Spread mixture into pan.
3 Bake cake for 40 minutes. Stand cake in pan for 10 minutes; transfer to a wire rack to cool. Using a serrated knife, trim and discard edges of cooled cake. Cut cake into 32 squares.
4 Make icing.
5 Place cake squares on a wire rack over a baking-paper-lined tray; spread or drizzle icing over squares. Top with icing flowers; stand until set.

ICING Stir ingredients in a medium bowl to a smooth paste (add a little extra water for a thinner consistency if you like).

tips You can serve petit fours in patty paper cases. You could top the petit fours with fresh raspberries instead of the icing flowers. Petit fours are best made on the day of serving.

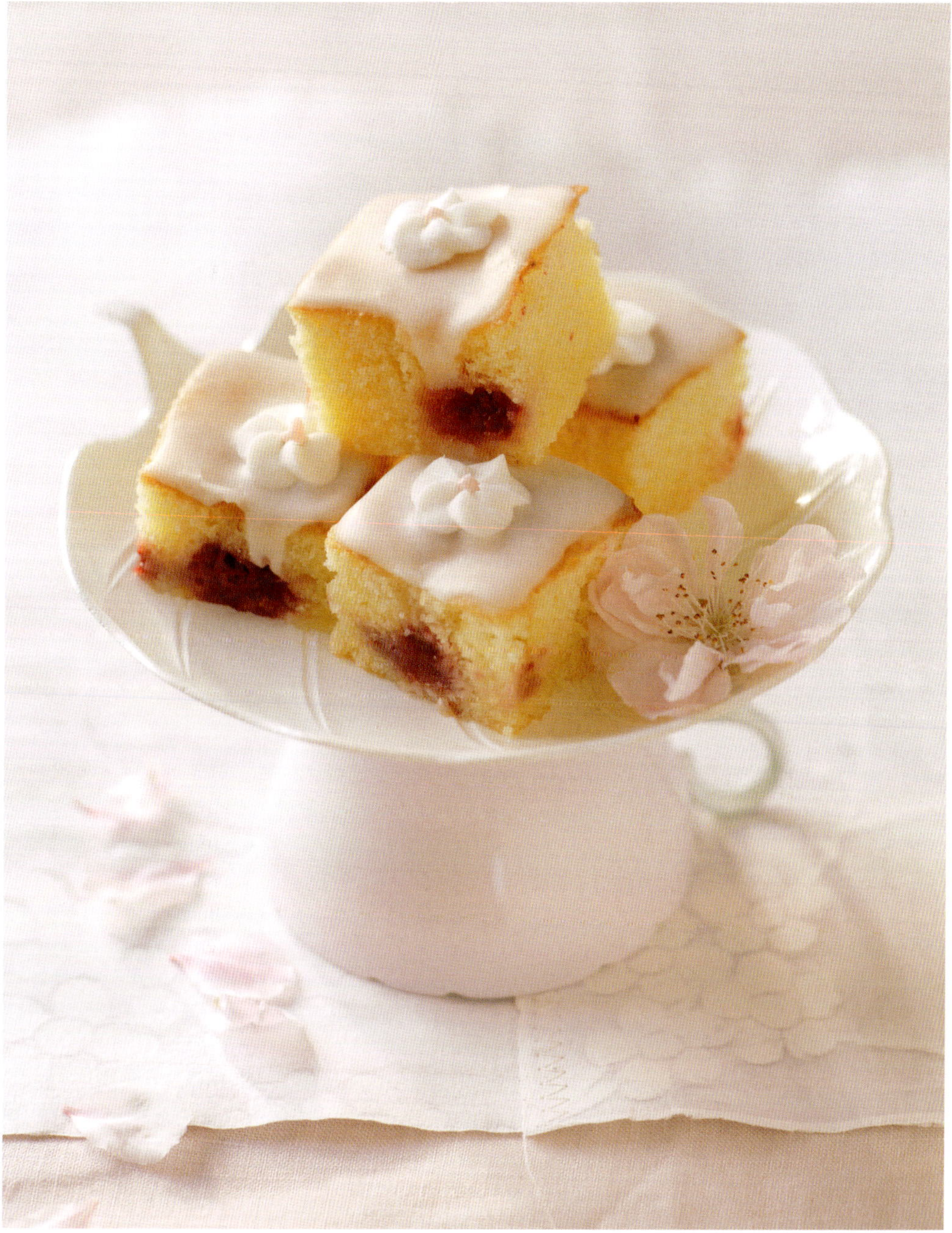

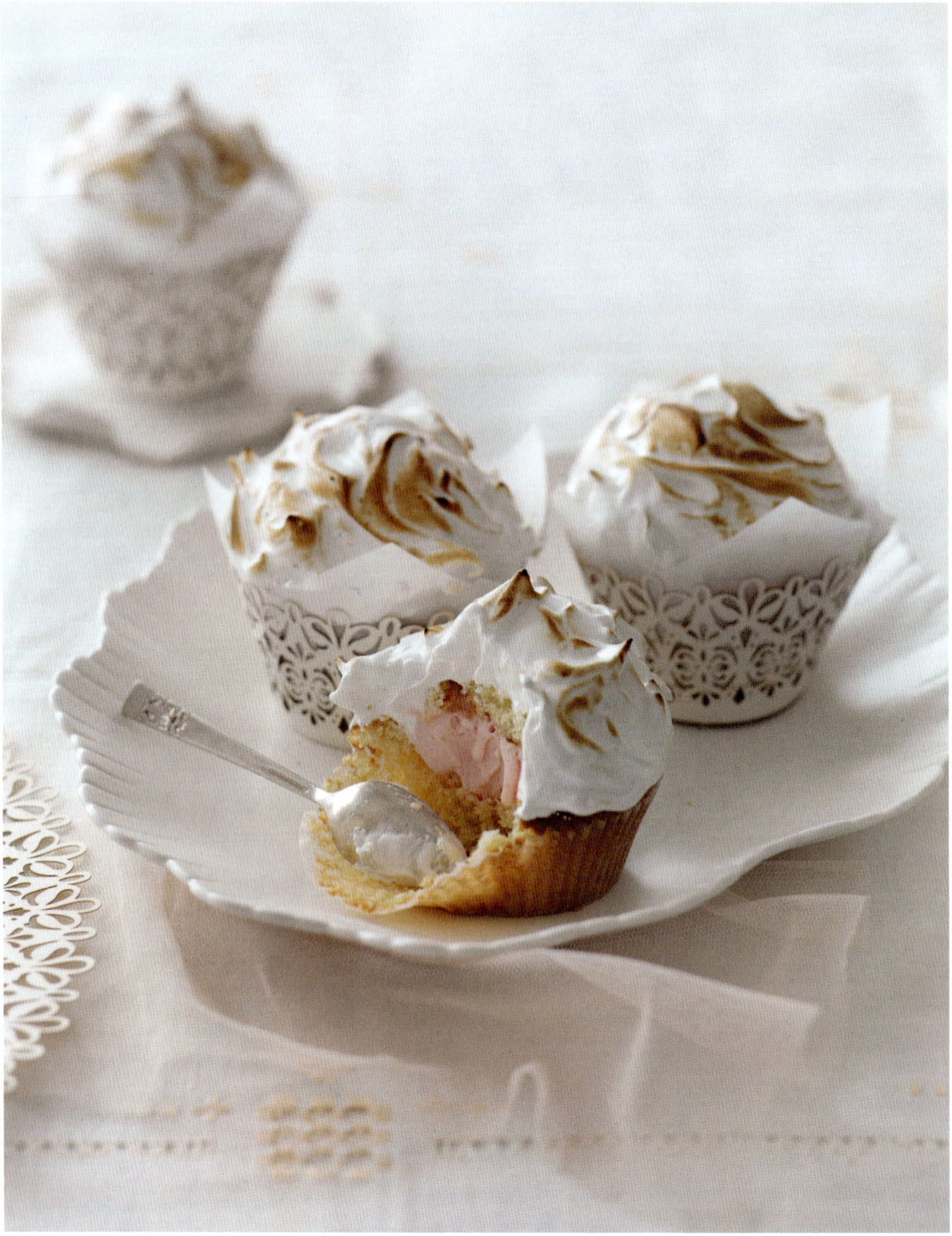

Neapolitan Meringue Cupcakes

prep + cook time 1 HOUR 10 MINUTES (+ COOLING & FREEZING)   *makes* 12

125g (4oz) unsalted butter, chopped coarsely
80g (2½oz) white chocolate, chopped coarsely
1 cup (220g) caster (superfine) sugar
½ cup (125ml) milk
½ cup (75g) plain (all-purpose) flour
½ cup (75g) self-raising flour
1 egg
1 cup (250ml) neapolitan ice-cream

MERINGUE
3 egg whites
¾ cup (165g) caster (superfine) sugar

1 Preheat oven to 180°C/350°F. Line a 12-hole (⅓-cup/80ml) muffin pan with paper cases.
2 Stir butter, chocolate, sugar and milk in a small saucepan over low heat until smooth. Transfer mixture to a medium bowl; cool for 15 minutes.
3 Whisk in sifted flours, then egg. Divide mixture into cases.
4 Bake cakes for 30 minutes. Stand cakes in pan for 10 minutes before turning, top-side up, onto a wire rack to cool.
5 Using a sharp pointed knife, cut a deep hole in the centre of each cake; reserve cut out cake. Fill each hole with a level tablespoon of ice-cream, top with reserved cake. Place cakes on a tray; freeze.
6 Preheat oven to 220°C/425°F.
7 Meanwhile, make meringue.
8 Top cakes with meringue. Bake for 2 minutes or until meringue is browned lightly. Serve immediately.

MERINGUE Beat egg whites and sugar in a small bowl with an electric mixer until sugar is dissolved.

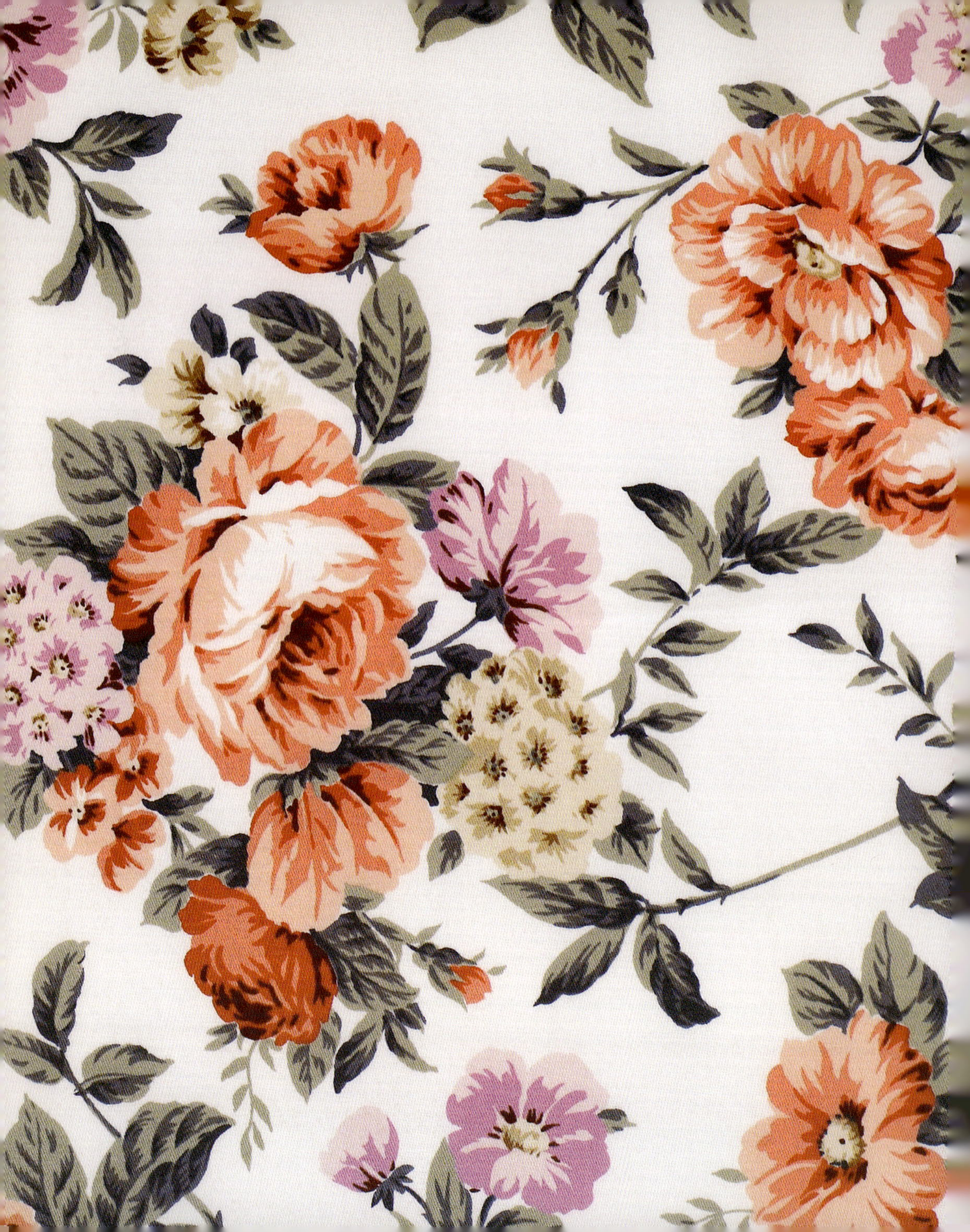

BIG CAKES

CLASSIC CAKES

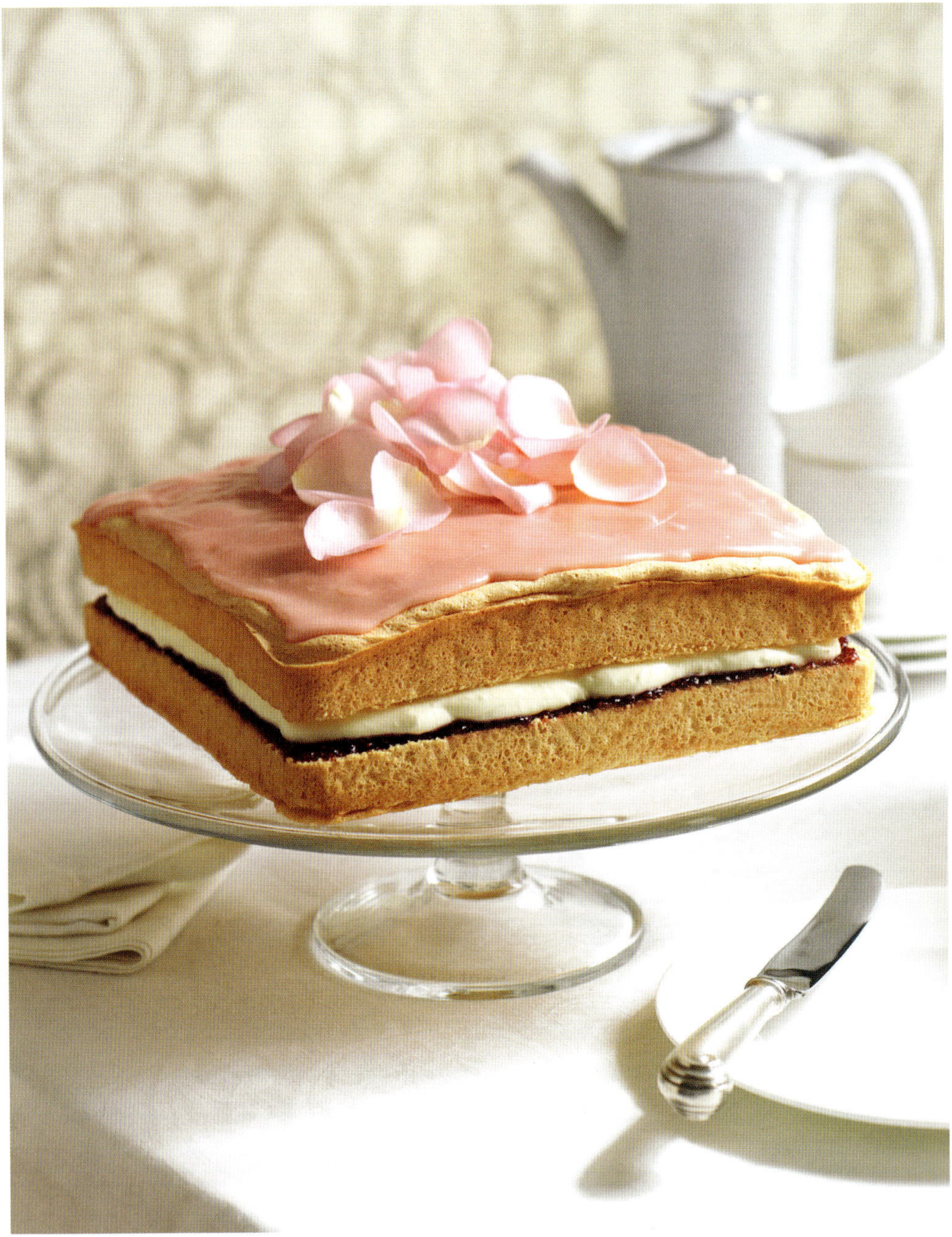

RASPBERRY CREAM SPONGE

prep + cook time 50 MINUTES (+ COOLING) *serves* 16

4 eggs
¾ cup (165g) caster (superfine) sugar
⅔ cup (100g) wheaten cornflour
¼ cup (30g) custard powder
1 teaspoon cream of tartar
½ teaspoon bicarbonate of soda (baking soda)
¾ cup (240g) raspberry jam
1½ cups (375ml) thickened (heavy) cream, whipped
fresh rose petals, to decorate (optional)

RASPBERRY GLACÉ ICING
45g (1½oz) fresh raspberries
2 cups (320g) icing (confectioners') sugar
15g (½oz) butter, softened
2 teaspoons hot water, approximately

1 Preheat oven to 180°C/350°F. Grease a deep 22cm (9in) square cake pan with butter.
2 Beat eggs and sugar in a small bowl with an electric mixer for 10 minutes or until thick and creamy and sugar has dissolved; transfer to a large bowl.
3 Sift dry ingredients twice, then sift a third time over egg mixture; fold dry ingredients into egg mixture. Spread mixture into pan.
4 Bake sponge for 25 minutes. Turn the sponge immediately onto a baking-paper-covered wire rack, then turn, top-side up, to cool.
5 Meanwhile, make raspberry glacé icing.
6 Split sponge in half. Sandwich with jam and cream. Spread the top of sponge with icing, sprinkle with fresh rose petals, if using.

RASPBERRY GLACÉ ICING Push raspberries through a fine sieve into a small heatproof bowl; discard solids. Sift icing sugar into the same bowl; stir in butter and enough of the water to make a thick paste. Place bowl over a small saucepan of simmering water; stir until icing is spreadable.

tips Use a serrated knife to split and cut the sponge. If you can't find wheaten cornflour, you can use regular corn (maize) cornflour.

COFFEE & WALNUT CAKE

prep + cook time 1 HOUR 15 MINUTES (+ COOLING) serves 8

30g (1oz) butter
1 tablespoon brown sugar
2 teaspoons ground cinnamon
2 cups (200g) roasted walnuts
½ cup (125ml) milk
1 tablespoon instant coffee granules
185g (6oz) butter, softened, extra
1⅓ cups (300g) caster (superfine) sugar
3 eggs
1 cup (150g) self-raising flour
¾ cup (110g) plain (all-purpose) flour

TOFFEE
½ cup (110g) caster (superfine) sugar
2 tablespoons water
3 teaspoons pouring cream

1 Preheat oven to 160°C/325°F. Butter a 22cm (9in) baba cake pan well; dust with flour, shake out excess.
2 Melt the butter in a small saucepan; stir in brown sugar, cinnamon and walnuts. Cool.
3 Combine milk and coffee in a small bowl; stir until coffee dissolves.
4 Beat extra butter and caster sugar in a bowl with an electric mixer until light and fluffy. Beat in eggs, one at a time. Stir in sifted flours, then coffee mixture.
5 Spread one-third of the cake mixture into base of pan; sprinkle with half the walnut mixture. Top with remaining cake mixture. Bake for 45 minutes. Stand in pan 5 minutes; turn onto a wire rack over an oven tray to cool.
6 Make toffee.
7 Working quickly, drizzle some of the toffee on top of cake, press on remaining walnut mixture; drizzle with remaining toffee.

TOFFEE Stir sugar and the water in a small saucepan over medium heat, without boiling, until sugar dissolves; bring to the boil. Reduce heat; simmer, uncovered, until toffee becomes caramel in colour. Add cream; stir 1 minute or until thickened slightly.

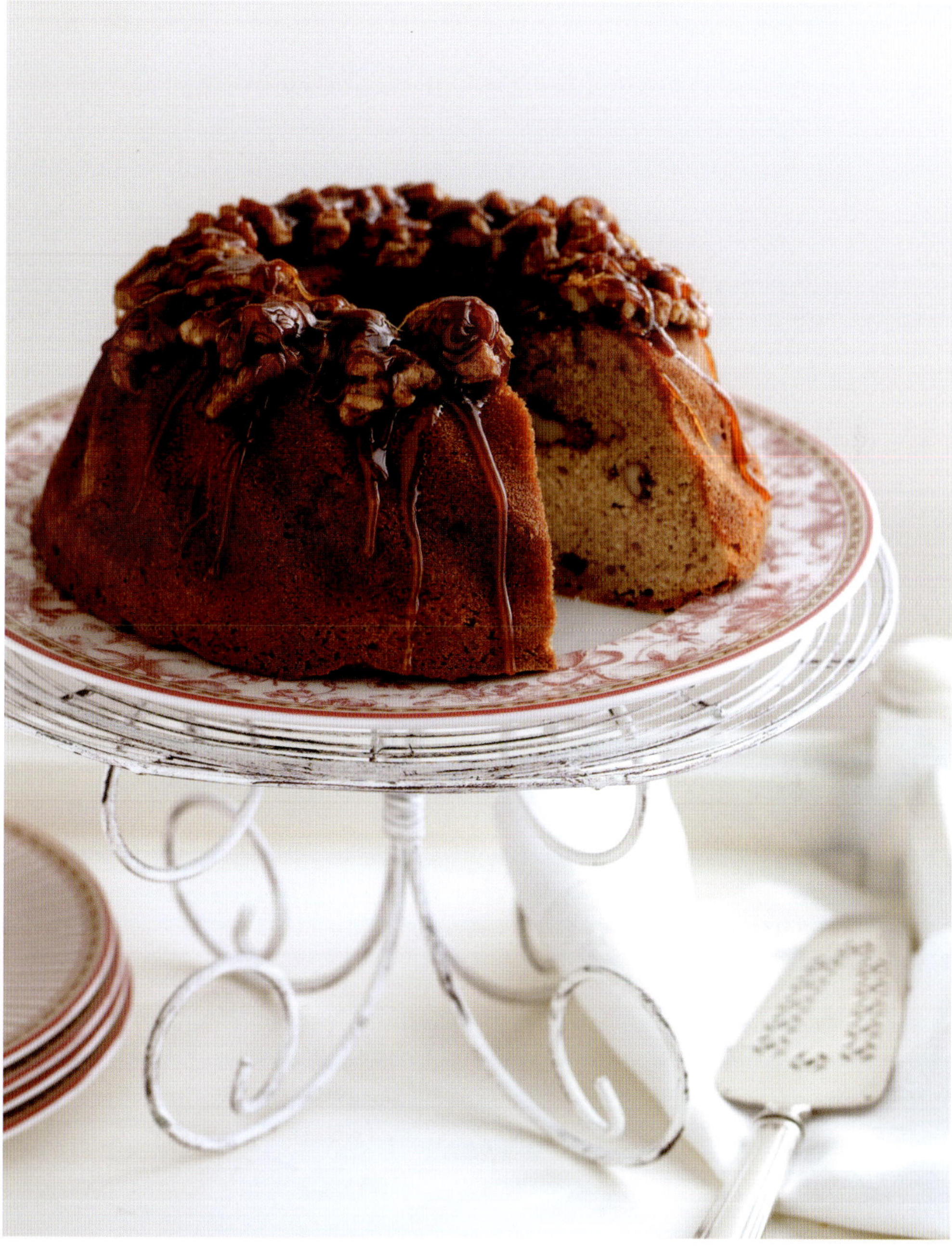

TIPS

The traditional colours for a marble cake are chocolate brown, pink and white, but you can use any food colouring you like. Make the colours fairly strong for maximum impact, as they may fade during baking.

MARBLE CAKE

prep + cook time 1 HOUR 40 MINUTES ❈ *serves* 12

250g (8oz) butter, softened
1 teaspoon vanilla extract
1¼ cups (275g) caster (superfine) sugar
3 eggs
2¼ cups (335g) self-raising flour
¾ cup (180ml) milk
pink food colouring
2 tablespoons cocoa powder
2 tablespoons milk, extra

BUTTER FROSTING
125g (4oz) butter, softened
2 cups (320g) icing (confectioners') sugar
2 tablespoons milk

1 Preheat oven to 180°C/350°F. Grease a deep 22cm (9in) round cake pan; line base with baking paper.
2 Beat butter, vanilla and sugar in a medium bowl with an electric mixer until light and fluffy. Beat in eggs, one at a time. Stir in sifted flour and milk, in two batches.
3 Divide mixture into three bowls; tint one mixture pink. Blend sifted cocoa with extra milk in a cup; stir into second mixture. Leave remaining mixture plain. Drop alternate spoonfuls of mixtures into pan. Pull a skewer backwards and forwards through cake mixture to create a marble effect.
4 Bake cake for 1 hour. Stand in pan for 5 minutes; turn, top-side up, onto a wire rack to cool.
5 Meanwhile, make butter frosting.
6 Spread frosting all over cooled cake.
BUTTER FROSTING Beat butter in a small bowl with an electric mixer until light and fluffy; beat in sifted icing sugar and milk, in two batches.

keeps This cake will keep in an airtight container, at room temperature, for up to 3 days. Un-iced cake can be frozen for up to 3 months.

MISSISSIPPI MUD CAKE

prep + cook time 1 HOUR 45 MINUTES (+ COOLING & STANDING) *serves 16*

250g (8oz) butter, chopped
150g (5oz) dark (semi-sweet) chocolate, chopped
2 cups (440g) caster (superfine) sugar
1 cup (250ml) hot water
⅓ cup (80ml) coffee liqueur
1 tablespoon instant coffee granules
1½ cups (225g) plain (all-purpose) flour
¼ cup (35g) self-raising flour
¼ cup (25g) cocoa powder
2 eggs, beaten lightly

DARK CHOCOLATE GANACHE
½ cup (125ml) pouring cream
200g (6½oz) dark (semi-sweet) chocolate, chopped coarsely

1 Preheat oven to 160°C/325°F. Grease a deep 20cm (8in) round cake pan; line base and side with baking paper.

2 Combine butter, chocolate, sugar, the hot water, liqueur and coffee granules in a medium saucepan. Using a wooden spoon, stir over low heat until chocolate melts.

3 Transfer chocolate mixture to a large bowl; cool for 15 minutes. Whisk in combined sifted flours and cocoa, then egg. Pour mixture into prepared pan.

4 Bake cake for 1½ hours. Stand cake in pan for 30 minutes before turning, top-side up, onto a wire rack to cool.

5 Meanwhile, make dark chocolate ganache; spread over top of cake.

DARK CHOCOLATE GANACHE Bring cream to the boil in a small saucepan. Pour hot cream over chocolate in a medium heatproof bowl; stir until smooth. Stand at room temperature until spreadable.

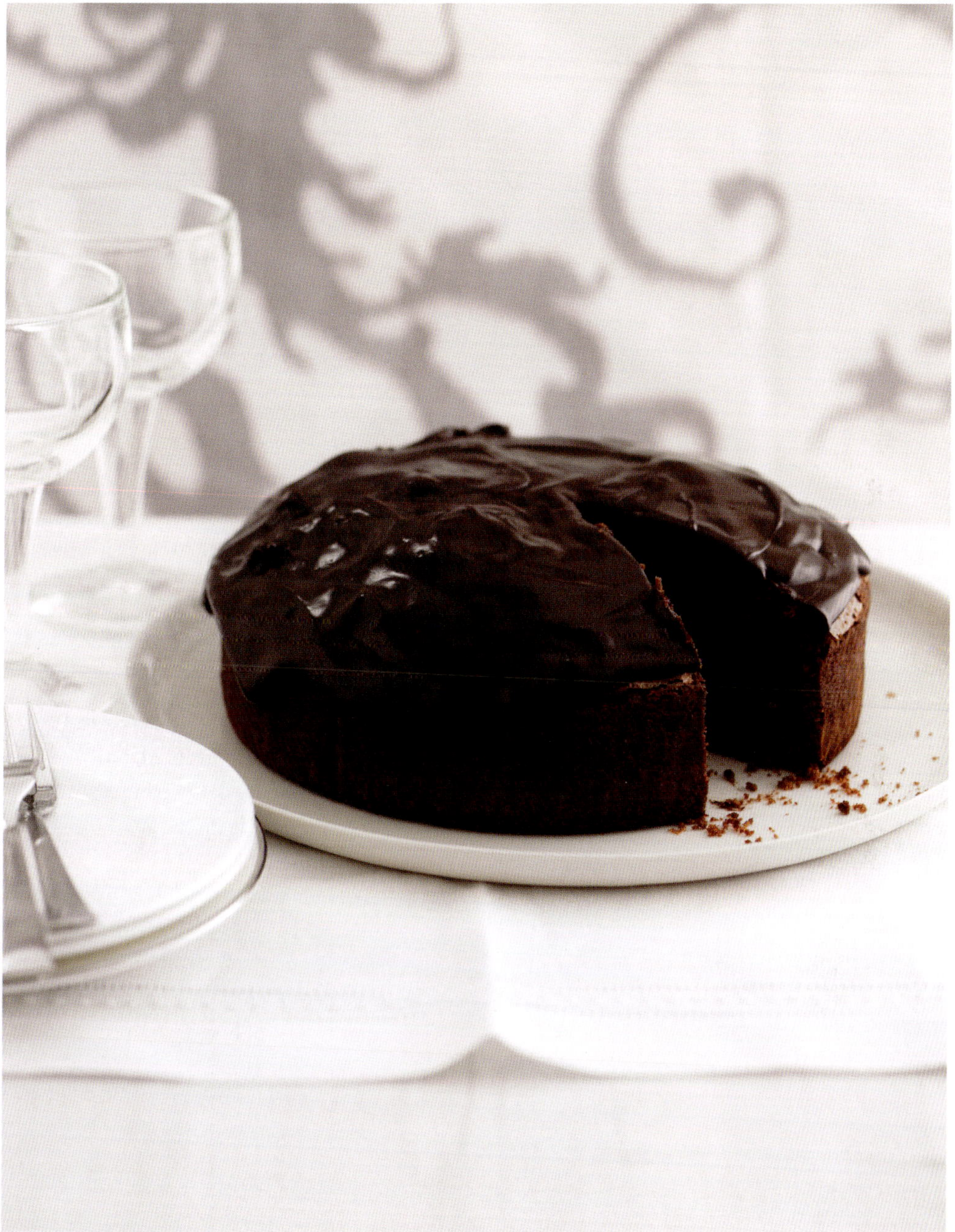

ZESTY LEMON SOUR CREAM CAKE

prep + cook time 1 HOUR 15 MINUTES (+ STANDING) *serves* 10

125g (4oz) butter, chopped
1 tablespoon finely grated lemon rind
1 cup (220g) caster (superfine) sugar
2 eggs
1½ cups (225g) self-raising flour
½ cup (125ml) sour cream
1 tablespoon icing (confectioners') sugar

LEMON CURD MASCARPONE
250g (8oz) mascarpone
½ cup (125ml) pouring cream
350g (11oz) bottled lemon curd

1 Preheat oven to 180°C/350°F. Grease a 22cm (9in) ring pan.

2 Beat butter, rind, caster sugar, eggs, flour and sour cream in a medium bowl with an electric mixer on low speed until just combined. Increase speed to medium; beat until mixture is smooth and changed in colour. Spoon mixture into pan; smooth surface.

3 Bake cake for 50 minutes or until a skewer inserted in cake comes out clean. Leave in pan for 10 minutes before turning out onto a wire rack to cool.

4 Make lemon curd mascarpone.

5 Dust cooled cake with sifted icing sugar; serve with spoonfuls of lemon curd mascarpone.

LEMON CURD MASCARPONE Stir mascarpone and cream in a small bowl until smooth and combined. Using a metal spoon, gently fold lemon curd through mascarpone mixture until just swirled through.

tip Bottled lemon curd is available in the jams and spreads aisle at most supermarkets.
keeps Cake can be made a day ahead; store in an airtight container.

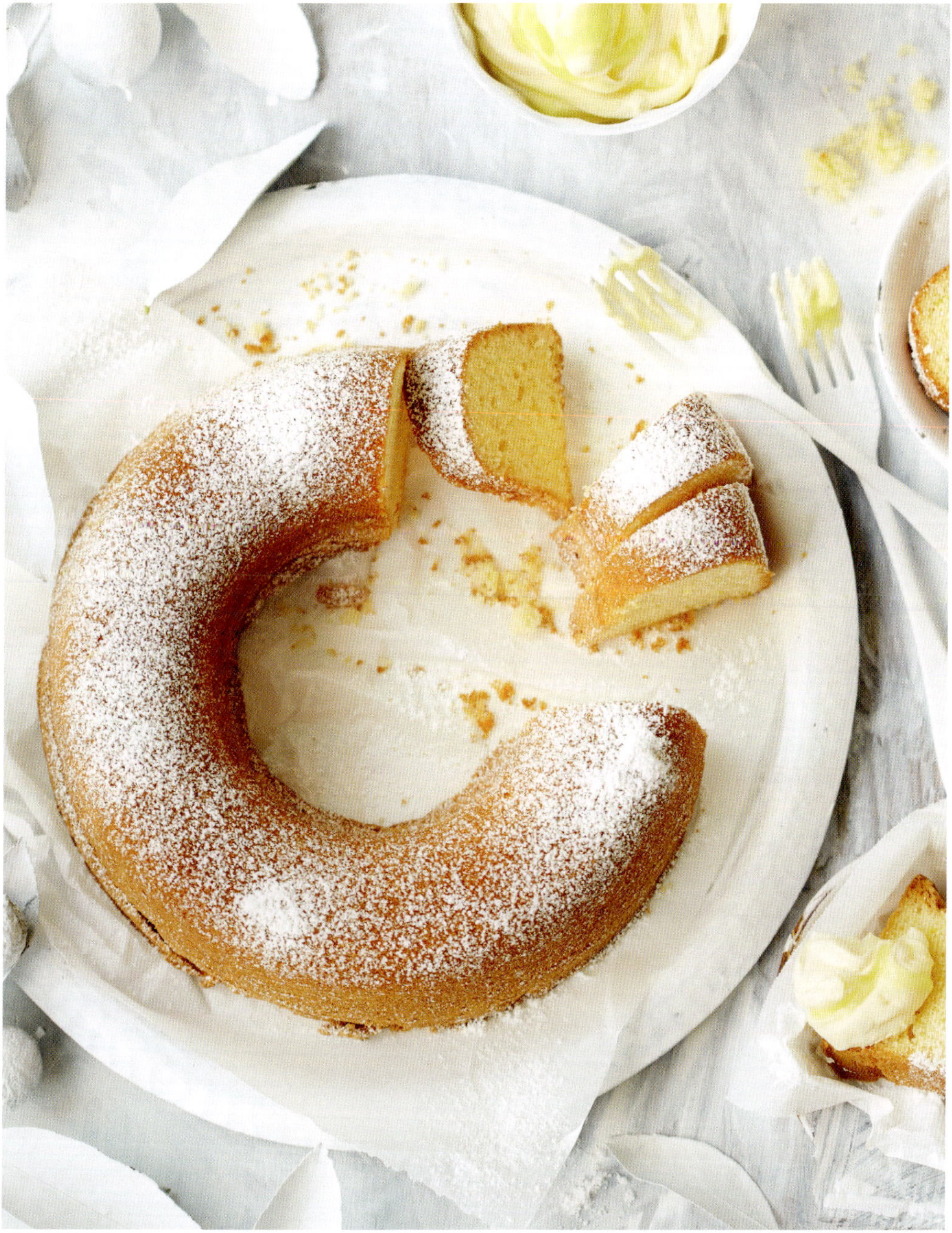

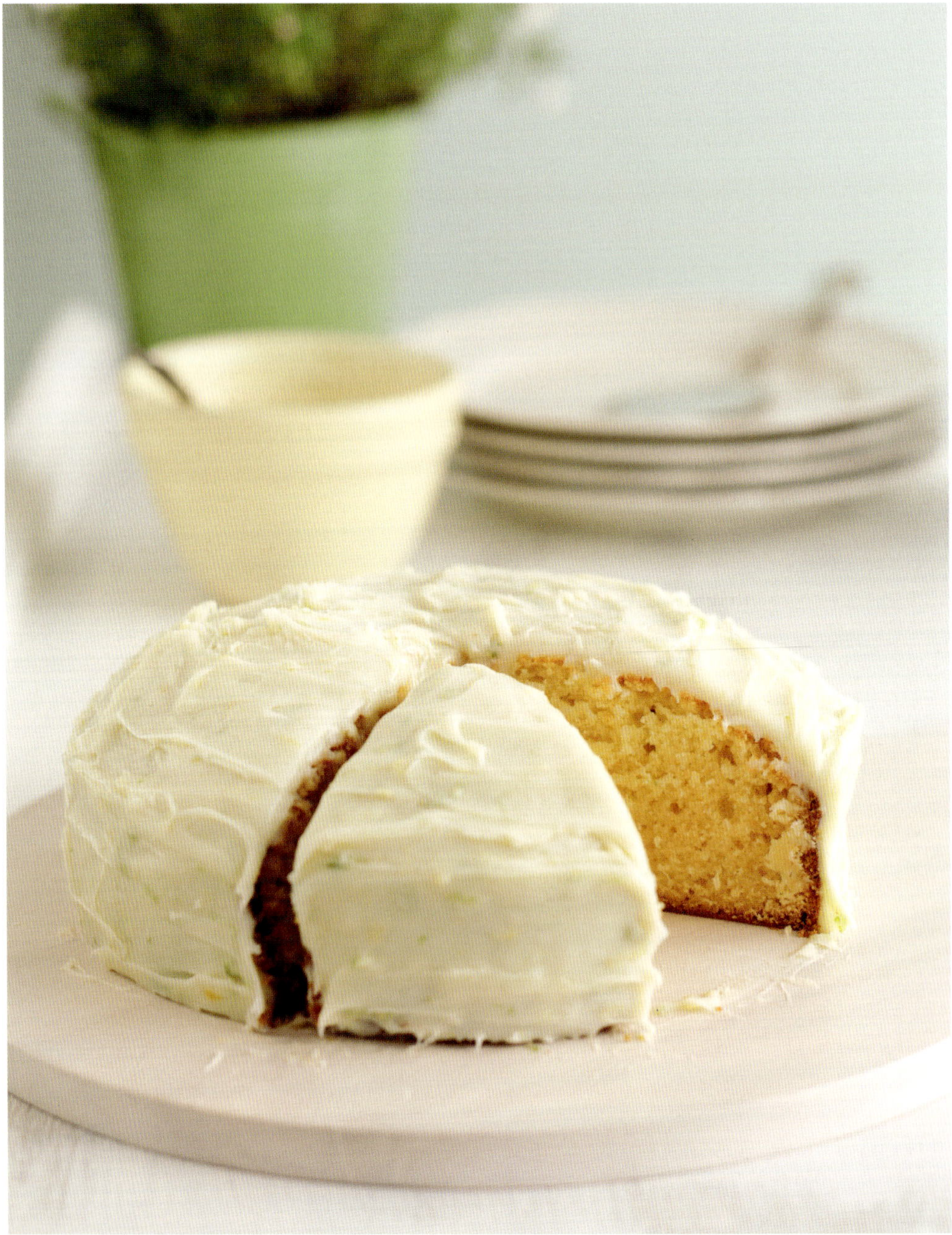

Lemon & Lime White Chocolate Mud Cake

prep + cook time 2 HOURS 20 MINUTES (+ COOLING & REFRIGERATION)   *serves 10*

250g (8oz) butter, chopped
2 teaspoons finely grated lemon rind
2 teaspoons finely grated lime rind
180g (5½oz) white chocolate, chopped coarsely
1½ cups (330g) caster (superfine) sugar
¾ cup (180ml) milk
1½ cups (225g) plain (all-purpose) flour
½ cup (75g) self-raising flour
2 eggs, beaten lightly

COCONUT GANACHE
360g (11½oz) white chocolate, chopped finely
1 teaspoon finely grated lemon rind
1 teaspoon finely grated lime rind
½ cup (125ml) coconut cream

1 Preheat oven to 170°C/340°F. Grease a deep 20cm (8in) round cake pan; line base with baking paper.
2 Stir butter, rinds, chocolate, sugar and milk in a medium saucepan over low heat until smooth. Transfer mixture to a large bowl; cool for 15 minutes.
3 Stir in sifted flours and egg; pour mixture into pan.
4 Bake for 1 hour 40 minutes; cool cake in pan.
5 Meanwhile, make coconut ganache.
6 Turn cake, top-side up, onto serving plate; spread ganache over cake.

COCONUT GANACHE Combine chocolate and rinds in a medium bowl. Bring coconut cream to the boil in a small saucepan; pour over chocolate mixture, stir until smooth. Cover bowl; refrigerate, stirring occasionally, for 30 minutes or until ganache is spreadable.

tips Grate the citrus rind called for here then save the fruit to extract the juice for another use. Without this protective "skin", the fruit will become dry and hard, so they should be juiced, say for a salsa or salad dressing, within a day or two.

lemon & earl grey
CHIFFON CAKE

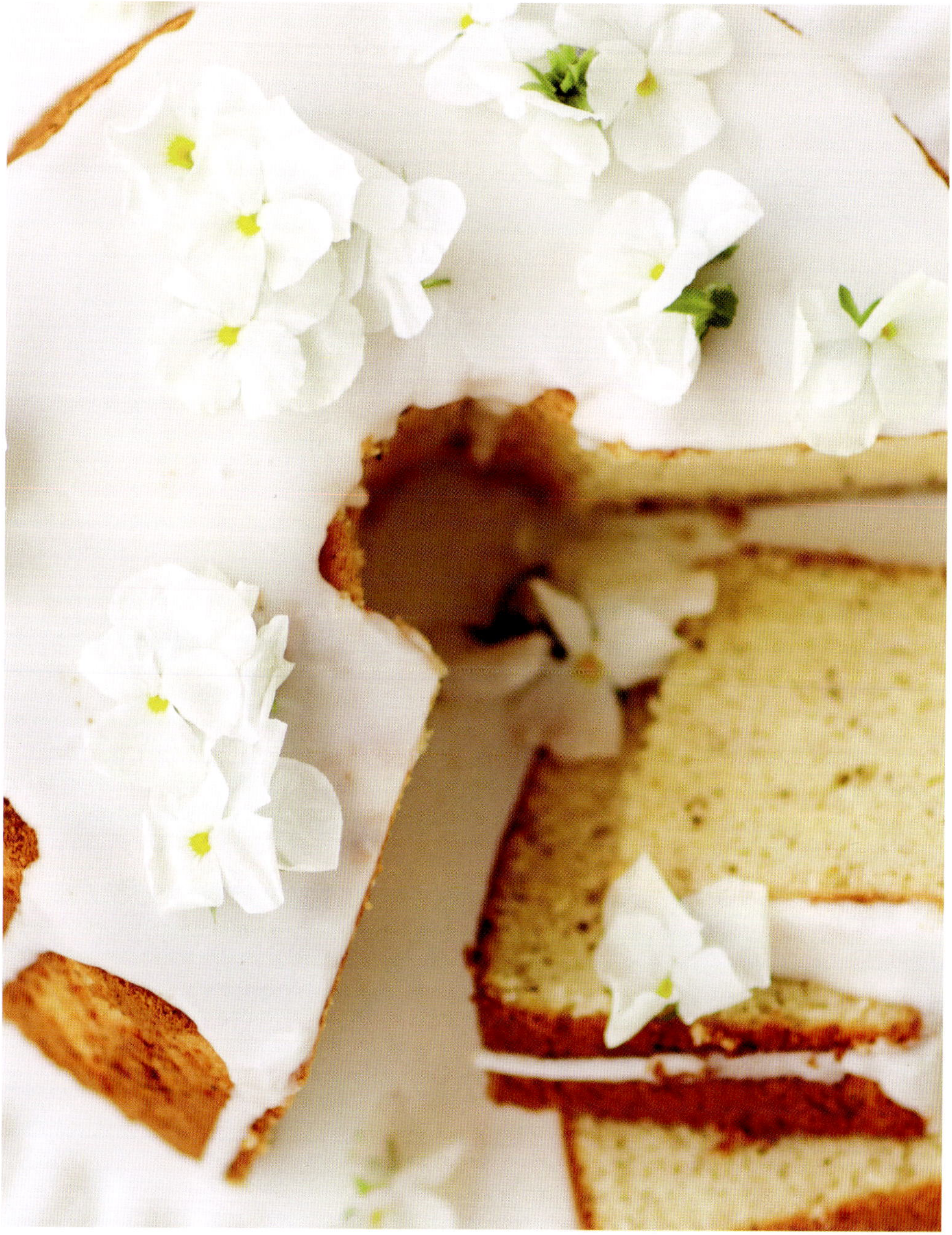

Lemon & Earl Grey Chiffon Cake

prep + cook time 1 HOUR 20 MINUTES (+ COOLING & STANDING) *serves* 12

2 cups (300g) self-raising flour
2 teaspoons earl grey tea leaves
1½ cups (330g) caster (superfine) sugar
7 eggs, separated
¾ cup (180ml) strained lemon juice
½ cup (125ml) extra virgin olive oil
1 tablespoon finely grated lemon rind
½ teaspoon cream of tartar
white edible flowers, to decorate (optional)

LEMON ICING
2 cups (320g) icing (confectioners') sugar
¼ cup (60ml) strained lemon juice

1 Adjust oven shelf to lowest position; place an oven tray on the shelf. Preheat oven to 180°C/350°F.
2 Triple-sift flour into a medium bowl.
3 Process tea leaves and ¾ cup (165g) of the sugar until leaves are finely chopped. Transfer mixture to a small bowl of an electric mixer fitted with the whisk attachment, add egg yolks; beat for 5 minutes or until thick and pale. Gradually add juice, oil and half the rind, beating until well combined. Sift flour over mixture, then fold in with motor operating on low speed until just incorporated.
4 Beat egg whites in a large bowl with electric mixer until soft peaks form. Add cream of tartar, then gradually add remaining sugar, beating until mixture is thick and glossy. Fold egg white mixture into yolk mixture, in two batches, until just combined. Spoon mixture into an ungreased 25cm (10in) angel food cake pan with a removable base; smooth the surface.

5 Place cake pan on heated oven tray; bake cake for 50 minutes or until a skewer inserted into the centre comes out clean (cover with foil if necessary to prevent over-browning). Place a piece of baking paper, just larger than the pan on a work surface. Immediately turn hot pan upside-down on the paper; leave to cool completely in this position.
6 Meanwhile, make lemon icing.
7 Carefully run a small knife around the edge of cake and the tube to help release cake from pan (you may also need to run a knife or spatula between the base and the cake).
8 Place cake on a cake plate or stand. Spoon icing on top of cake, allowing it to drip down over the edge a little. Stand for 20 minutes or until icing is set. Decorate with flowers, if you like.
LEMON ICING Sift icing sugar into a medium bowl. Gradually add juice, stirring until icing is the consistency of thickened cream.

keeps The cake can be made a day ahead; store in an airtight container at room temperature. Decorate with lemon icing on the day of serving.

SYRUP CAKES

LIME SYRUP BUTTERMILK CAKE

prep + cook time 1 HOUR 30 MINUTES *serves* 8

250g (8oz) butter, softened
1 tablespoon finely grated lime rind
1 cup (220g) caster (superfine) sugar
3 eggs, separated
2 cups (300g) self-raising flour
1 cup (250ml) buttermilk

LIME SYRUP
⅓ cup (80ml) lime juice
¾ cup (165g) caster (superfine) sugar
¼ cup (60ml) water

1 Preheat oven to 180°C/350°F. Grease a 20cm (8in) baba pan (or grease a deep 20cm (8in) round cake pan and line base and side with baking paper).
2 Beat butter, rind and sugar in a small bowl with an electric mixer until light and fluffy; beat in egg yolks, one at a time, until combined. Transfer mixture to a large bowl; stir in sifted flour and buttermilk, in two batches.
3 Beat egg whites in a small bowl with an electric mixer until soft peaks form; fold into flour mixture, in two batches. Spread mixture into pan; bake for 1 hour.
4 Meanwhile, make lime syrup.
5 Stand cake in pan for 5 minutes before turning onto serving plate. Gradually pour hot lime syrup evenly over hot cake. Serve cake sprinkled with thinly sliced lime rind, if you like.

LIME SYRUP Combine ingredients in a small saucepan; stir over medium heat, without boiling, until sugar is dissolved. Bring to the boil; remove from heat.

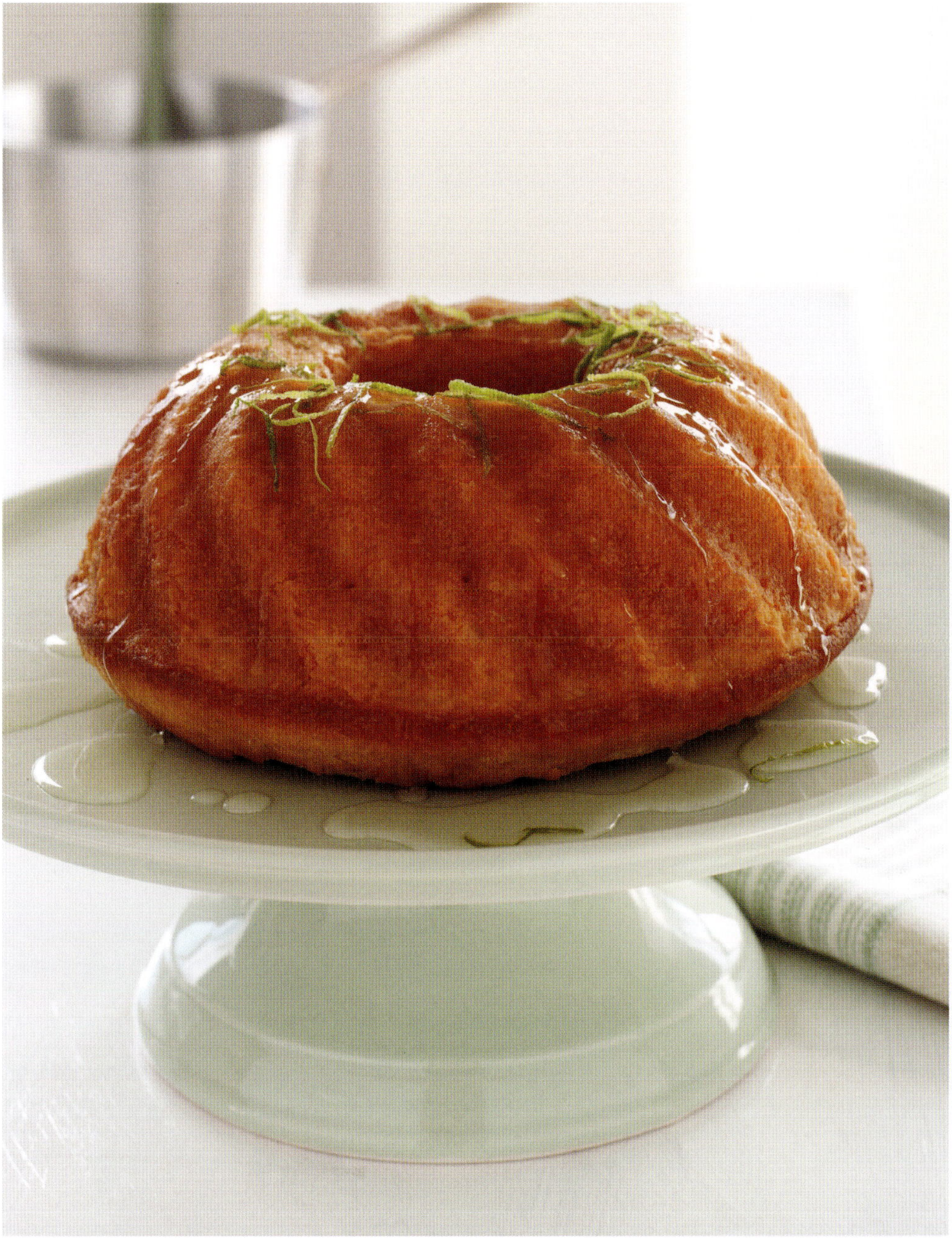

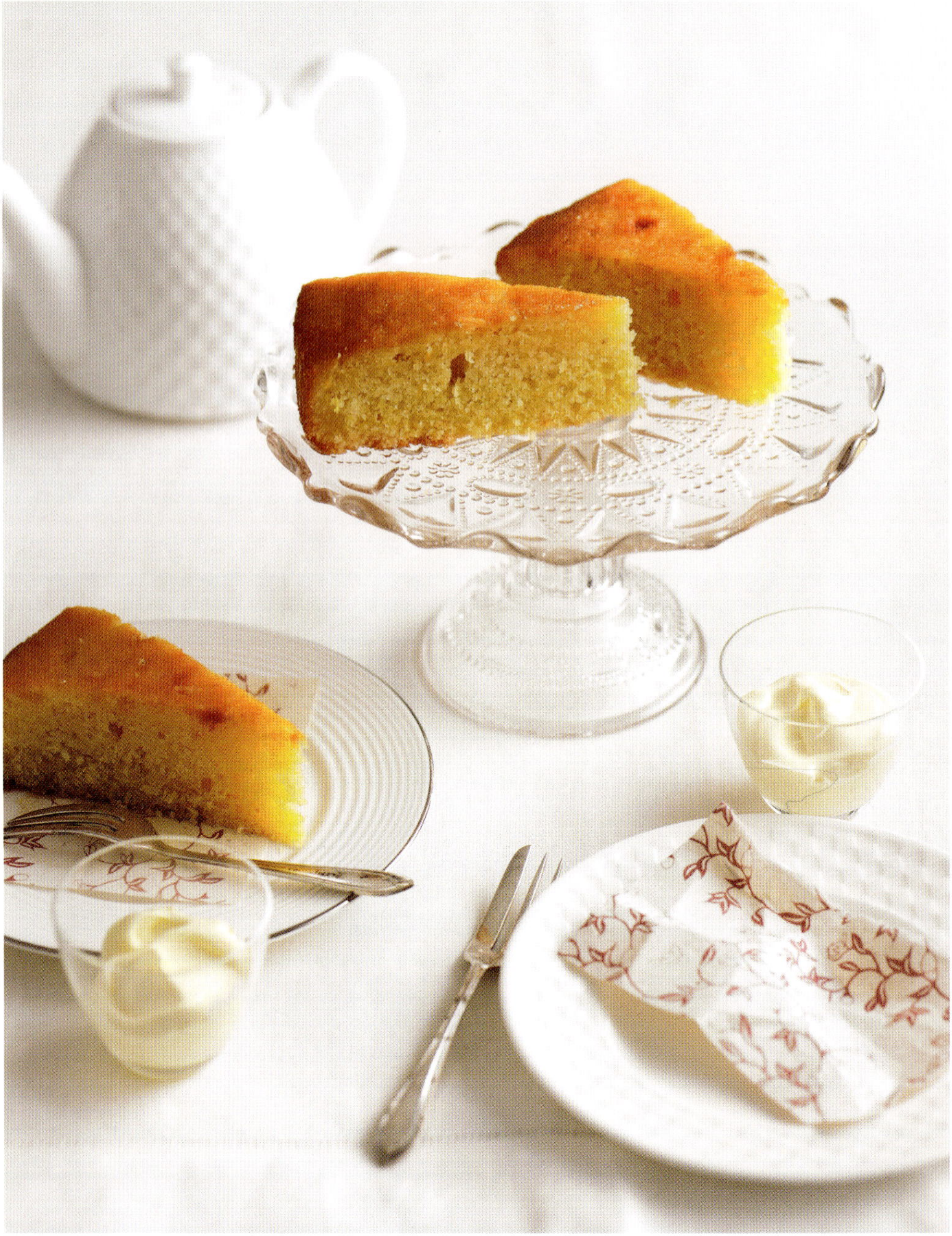

ORANGE ALMOND HALVA CAKE

prep + cook time 1 HOUR 15 MINUTES *serves* 10

125g (4oz) butter, softened
2 teaspoons finely grated orange rind
½ cup (110g) caster (superfine) sugar
2 eggs
1 teaspoon baking powder
1 cup (180g) semolina
1 cup (120g) almond meal
¼ cup (60ml) orange juice
1 cup (250ml) thick (double) cream

ORANGE & BRANDY SYRUP
1 cup (250ml) orange juice
½ cup (110g) caster (superfine) sugar
1 tablespoon brandy

1 Preheat oven to 180°C/350°F. Grease a deep 20cm (8in) round cake pan; line base and side with baking paper.
2 Cream butter, rind and sugar in a small bowl with an electric mixer until light and fluffy. Beat in eggs, one at a time, until combined. Transfer mixture to a large bowl; stir in the dry ingredients and juice, in two batches. Spread mixture into pan; bake for 40 minutes.
3 Meanwhile, make orange and brandy syrup.
4 Turn cake, top-side up, onto a wire rack set over an oven tray; brush half the hot syrup over hot cake. Bake cake, on the wire rack, for a further 5 minutes. Remove from oven; brush with remaining hot syrup. Serve cake warm or cold with cream.
ORANGE & BRANDY SYRUP Combine juice and sugar in a small saucepan; stir constantly over medium heat, without boiling, until sugar is dissolved. Bring to the boil; reduce heat, simmer, uncovered, without stirring, for 5 minutes. Stir in brandy.

Gluten-Free Raspberry & Lemon Syrup Cake

prep + cook time 1 HOUR 15 MINUTES *serves* 8

dairy-free spread, for greasing
rice flour, for dusting
125g (4oz) dairy-free spread, extra
¾ cup (165g) caster (superfine) sugar
1 tablespoon finely grated lemon rind
3 eggs
1¾ cups (235g) gluten-free self-raising flour
¼ cup (60ml) soy milk
¾ cup (100g) frozen raspberries
vanilla bean soy yoghurt and fresh raspberries, to serve

LEMON SYRUP
½ cup (110g) caster (superfine) sugar
4 x 5cm (2in) strips lemon rind
¼ cup (60ml) lemon juice
¼ cup (60ml) water

1 Preheat oven to 190°C/375°F. Grease a 22cm (9in) ring pan well with dairy-free spread; dust with rice flour, shake out excess.

2 Beat extra dairy-free spread, sugar and rind in a medium bowl with an electric mixer until light and fluffy. Beat in eggs, one at a time, until just combined after each addition. Stir sifted flour and soy milk alternately, in batches, into mixture; stir in frozen raspberries. Spread mixture into pan.

3 Bake cake for 45 minutes or until a skewer comes out clean. Leave cake in pan for 5 minutes before turning onto a wire rack over a tray.

4 Meanwhile, make lemon syrup.

5 Pour hot lemon syrup over hot cake. Serve cake with soy yoghurt and fresh raspberries.

LEMON SYRUP Stir ingredients in a small saucepan over medium heat, without boiling, until sugar dissolves. Bring to the boil. Reduce heat; simmer, for 5 minutes or until syrup thickens slightly.

keeps This cake is best made on the day of serving. Reheat cold cake slices individually in the microwave oven on MEDIUM (50%) until warmed through.

This cake is also dairy-free and nut-free.

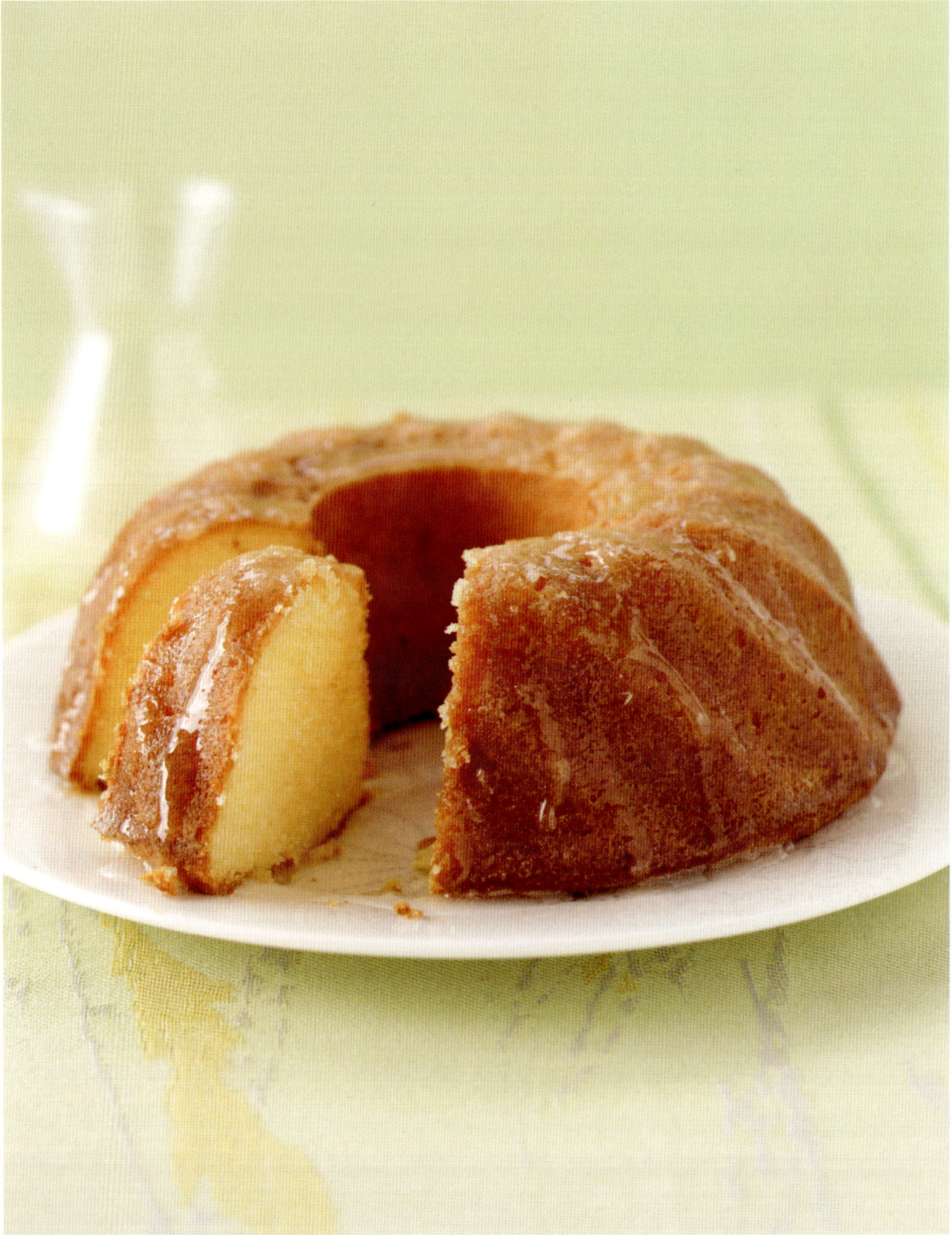

Semolina & Yoghurt Syrup Cake

prep + cook time 1 HOUR 10 MINUTES *serves* 8

250g (8oz) butter, softened
1 tablespoon finely grated lemon rind
1 cup (220g) caster (superfine) sugar
3 eggs, separated
1 cup (150g) self-raising flour
1 cup (180g) semolina
1 cup (280g) yoghurt

LEMON SYRUP
1 cup (220g) caster (superfine) sugar
⅓ cup (80ml) lemon juice

1 Preheat oven to 180°C/350°F. Grease a 20cm (8in) baba pan (or grease a deep 20cm (8in) round cake pan and line base and side with baking paper).

2 Beat butter, rind and sugar in a small bowl with an electric mixer until light and fluffy. Beat in egg yolks. Transfer mixture to a large bowl; stir in sifted flour, the semolina and yoghurt.

3 Beat egg whites in a small bowl with an electric mixer until soft peaks form; fold egg whites into cake mixture, in two batches. Spread mixture into pan; bake for 50 minutes.

4 Meanwhile, make lemon syrup.

5 Stand cake in pan 5 minutes before turning onto a wire rack over a tray. Pierce cake all over with skewer; pour hot lemon syrup over hot cake.

LEMON SYRUP Combine ingredients in a small saucepan; stir over medium heat, without boiling, until sugar dissolves. Bring to the boil, without stirring, then remove from heat.

LIME & POPPY SEED
SYRUP CAKE

prep + cook time 1 HOUR 40 MINUTES *serves* 16

Before grating the lime, make sure it is at room temperature and roll it, pressing down hard with your hand, on the kitchen bench. This will help extract as much juice as possible from the fruit. You can use any other citrus fruit – lemons, mandarins, oranges, blood oranges – instead of the limes if you wish.

¼ cup (40g) poppy seeds
½ cup (125ml) milk
250g (8oz) butter, softened
1 tablespoon finely grated lime rind
1¼ cups (275g) caster (superfine) sugar
4 eggs
2¼ cups (335g) self-raising flour
¾ cup (110g) plain (all-purpose) flour
1 cup (240g) sour cream

LIME SYRUP
½ cup (125ml) lime juice
1 cup (250ml) water
1 cup (220g) caster (superfine) sugar

1 Preheat oven to 180°C/350°F. Grease base and sides of a deep 22cm (9in) square cake pan.
2 Combine poppy seeds and milk in a small jug; soak for 10 minutes.
3 Beat butter, rind and sugar in a small bowl with an electric mixer until light and fluffy. Add eggs, one at a time, beating until combined between additions; transfer mixture to a large bowl. Stir in sifted flours, sour cream and poppy seed mixture, in two batches. Spread mixture into pan.
4 Bake cake for 1 hour.
5 Meanwhile, make lime syrup.
6 Stand cake for 5 minutes, turn onto a wire rack over a tray. Pour hot lime syrup over hot cake.
LIME SYRUP Stir ingredients in a small saucepan over medium heat, without boiling, until sugar dissolves. Simmer, uncovered, without stirring, for 5 minutes.

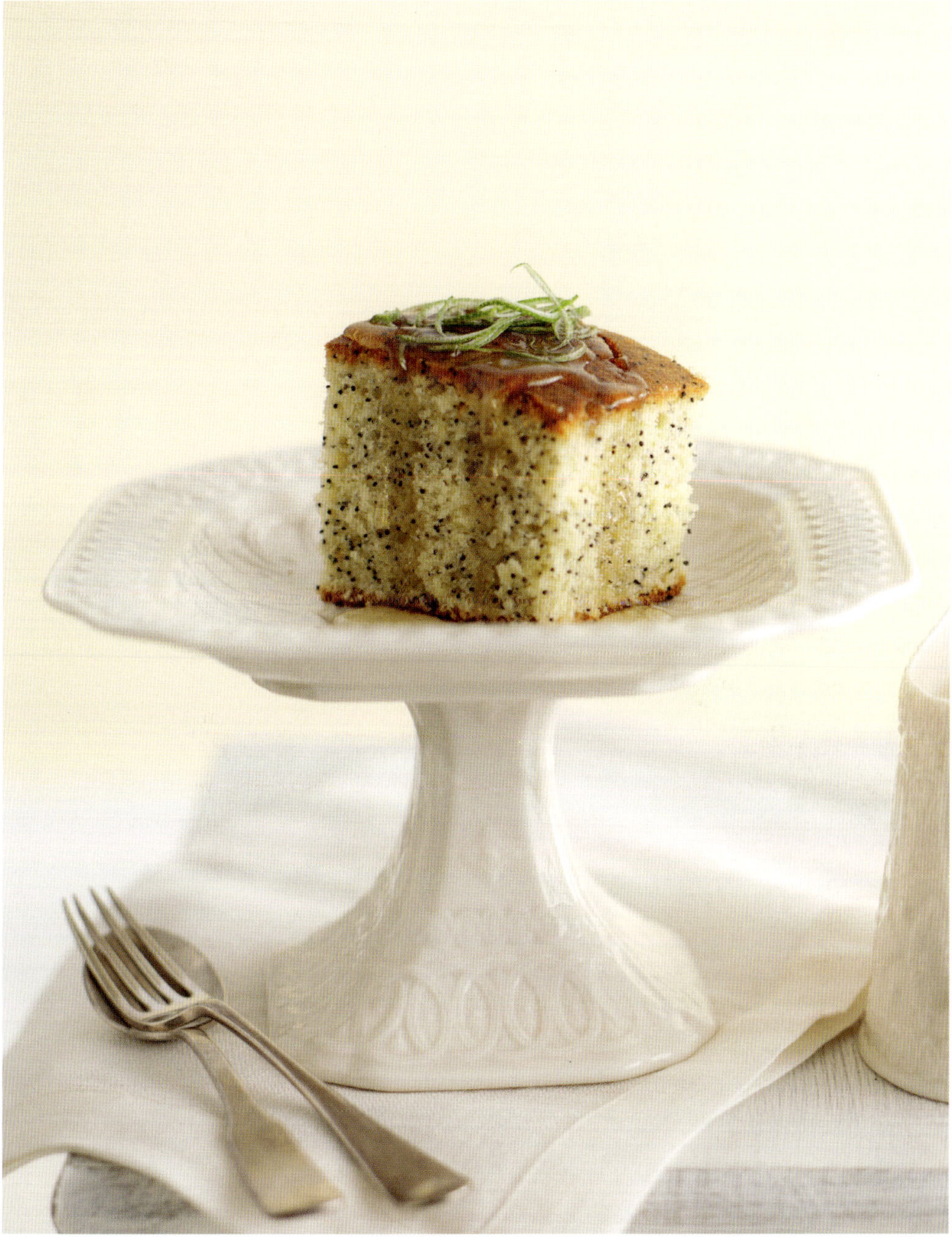

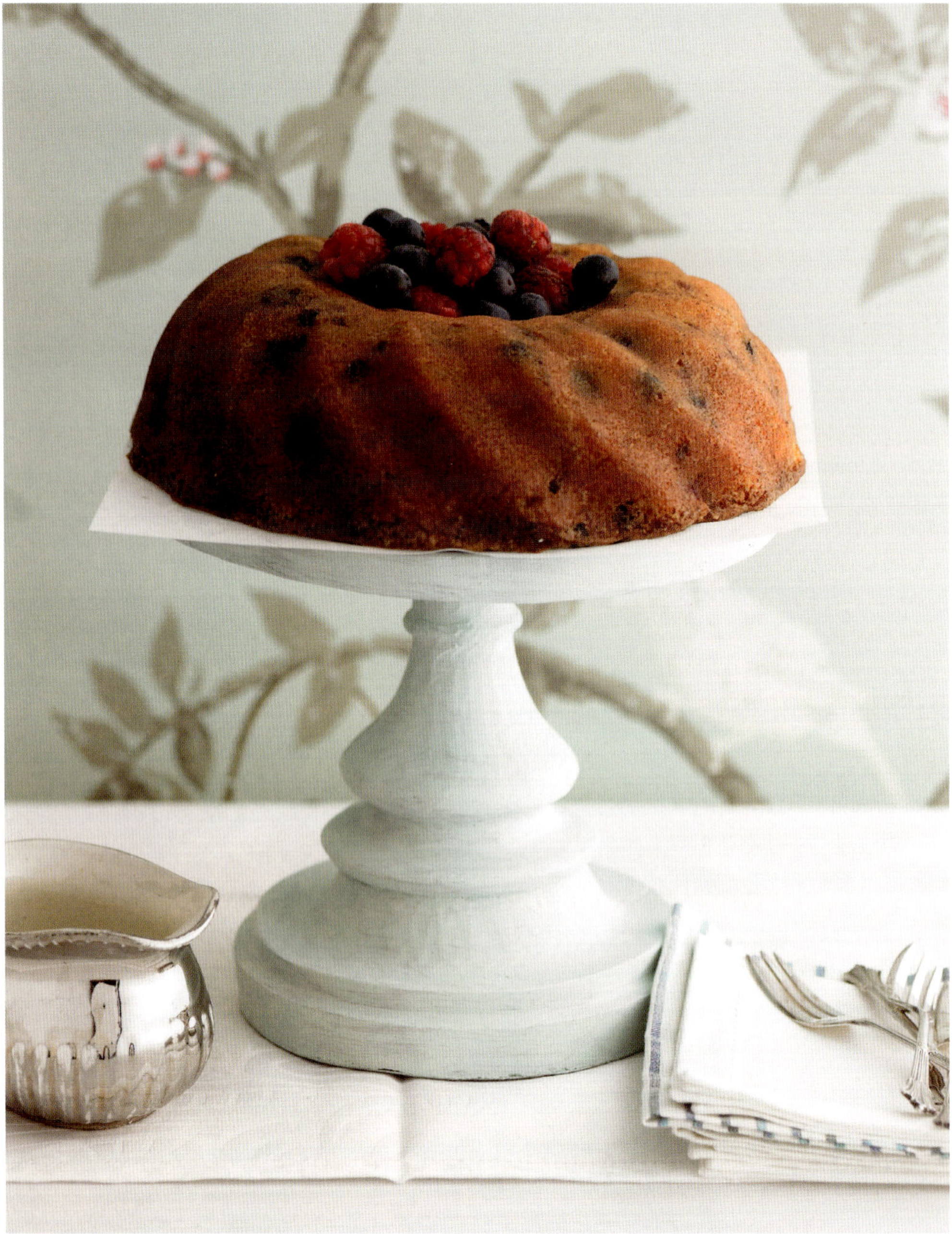

MIXED BERRY CAKE
WITH VANILLA BEAN SYRUP

prep + cook time 1 HOUR *serves* 8

125g (4oz) butter, softened
1 cup (220g) caster (superfine) sugar
3 eggs
½ cup (75g) plain (all-purpose) flour
¼ cup (35g) self-raising flour
½ cup (60g) almond meal
⅓ cup (80g) sour cream
1½ cups (225g) frozen mixed berries
½ cup (100g) drained canned seeded black cherries
fresh blueberries and raspberries, to serve

VANILLA BEAN SYRUP
½ cup (125ml) water
½ cup (110g) caster (superfine) sugar
2 vanilla beans

1 Preheat oven to 180°C/350°F. Grease a 21cm (8½in) baba pan (or grease a deep 20cm (8in) round cake pan and line base and side with baking paper).
2 Beat butter and sugar in a small bowl with an electric mixer until light and fluffy. Beat in eggs, one at a time. Transfer mixture to a large bowl; stir in sifted flours, almond meal, sour cream, berries and cherries. Pour mixture into pan; bake for 40 minutes.
3 Meanwhile, make vanilla bean syrup.
4 Stand cake in pan 5 minutes before turning onto a wire rack over a tray. Pour hot syrup over hot cake. Serve with fresh berries.

VANILLA BEAN SYRUP Combine the water and sugar in a small saucepan. Split vanilla beans in half lengthways; scrape seeds into pan then place pods in pan. Stir over medium heat, without boiling, until sugar dissolves. Simmer, uncovered, without stirring, for 5 minutes. Using tongs, remove pods from syrup.

ORANGE & RHUBARB
SEMOLINA SYRUP CAKE

prep + cook time 1 HOUR 30 MINUTES *serves* 10

- 185g (6oz) butter
- 1 tablespoon finely grated orange rind
- ⅔ cup (150g) caster (superfine) sugar
- 3 eggs
- 1 cup (150g) self-raising flour
- ½ cup (80g) fine semolina
- ¼ cup (60ml) buttermilk
- 200g (6½oz) trimmed rhubarb stalks, cut diagonally into 3cm (1¼in) lengths
- 1 tablespoon demerara sugar
- 2 teaspoons icing (confectioners') sugar

ORANGE RHUBARB SYRUP
- 1 cup (110g) coarsely chopped rhubarb
- ½ cup (110g) caster (superfine) sugar
- 1 cup (250ml) orange juice
- ½ cup (125ml) water

1 Preheat oven to 180°C/350°F. Grease a deep 20cm (8in) round cake pan; line base and side with baking paper.
2 Beat butter, rind and caster sugar in a small bowl with an electric mixer until light and fluffy. Beat in eggs, one at a time. Fold in sifted flour, the semolina and buttermilk. Spread mixture into pan; top with rhubarb and sprinkle with demerara sugar.
3 Bake cake for 1 hour. Leave cake in pan for 5 minutes before turning, top-side up, onto a wire rack to cool.
4 Meanwhile, make orange rhubarb syrup.
5 Before serving, place cake on a plate; dust with sifted icing sugar. Serve cake with orange rhubarb syrup and, if you like, whipped cream.

ORANGE RHUBARB SYRUP Stir ingredients in a small saucepan over high heat, without boiling, until sugar dissolves. Bring to the boil. Reduce heat; simmer for 10 minutes or until syrup has thickened slightly.

tips You will need a bunch of rhubarb with about 8 thin stalks. Use the red parts of the stalks for the best flavour. You need 2 large oranges for this recipe.
keeps The cake and the syrup can be made a day ahead. Store the cake in an airtight container at room temperature, and the syrup in the fridge. Add the finishing touches just before serving.

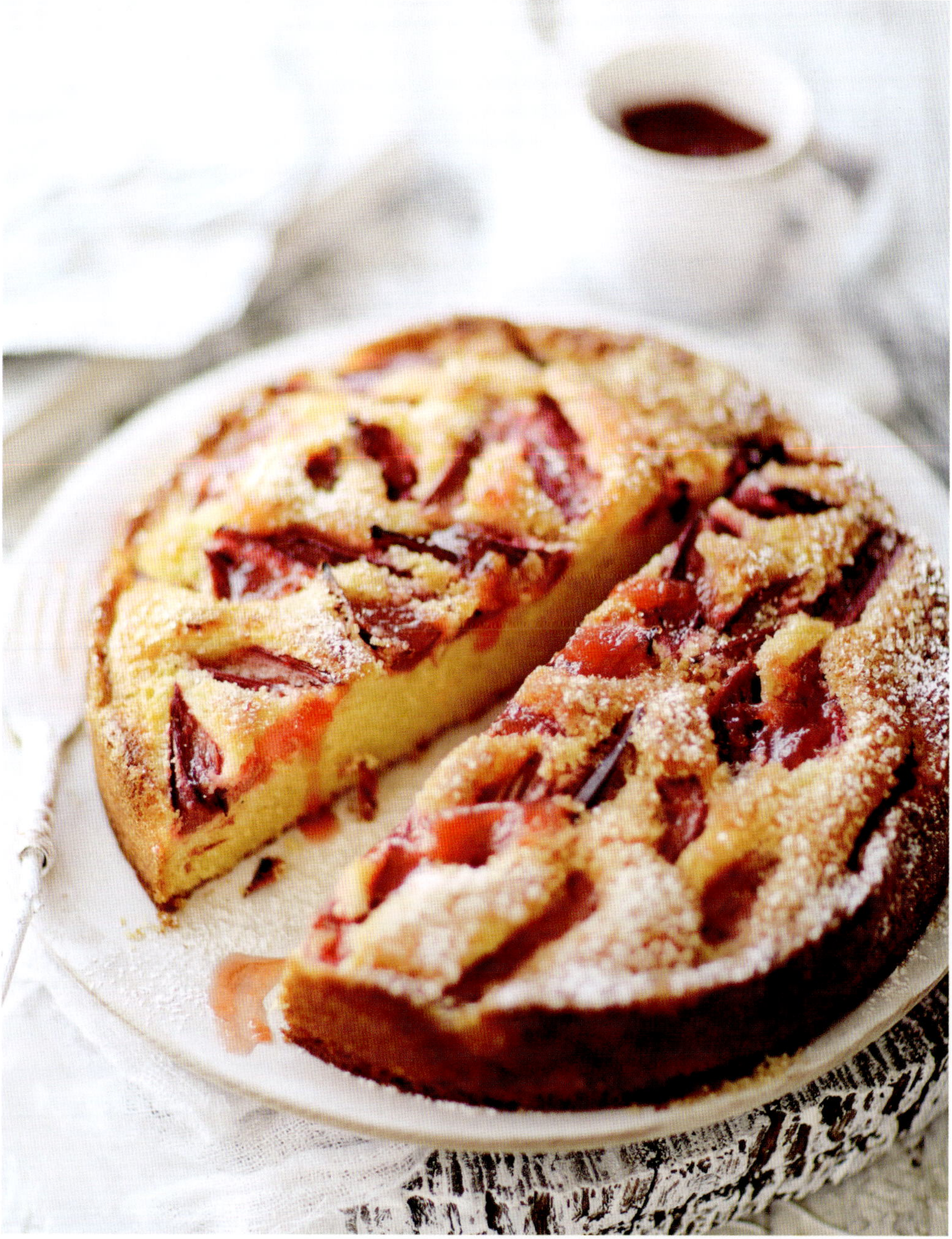

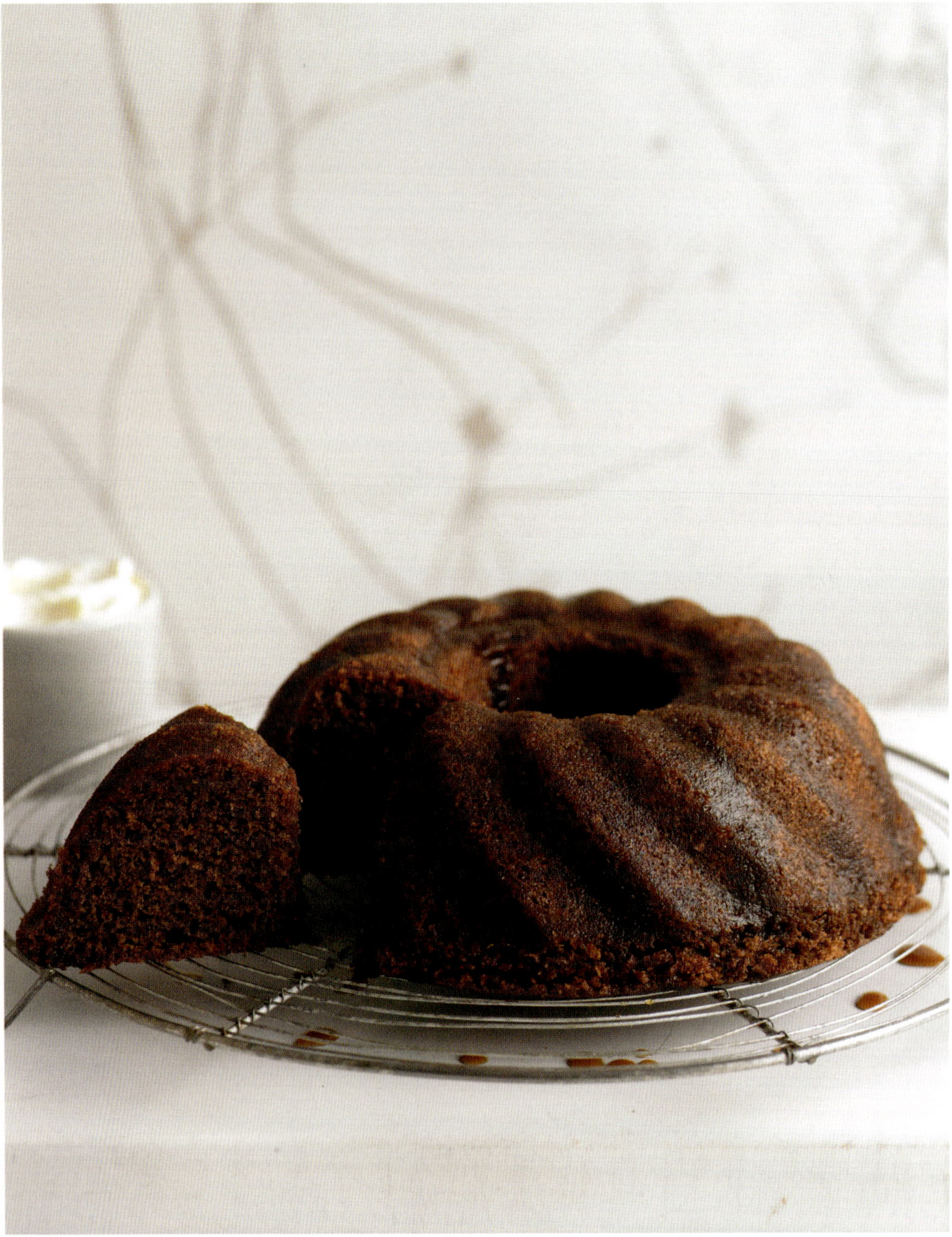

ESPRESSO SYRUP CAKE

prep + cook time 1 HOUR *serves* 8

3 teaspoons instant coffee granules
1 tablespoon hot water
3 eggs
¾ cup (165g) caster (superfine) sugar
1 cup (150g) self-raising flour
1 tablespoon cocoa powder
150g (5oz) butter, melted

ESPRESSO SYRUP
¾ cup (165g) caster (superfine) sugar
¾ cup (180ml) water
3 teaspoons instant coffee granules

1 Preheat oven to 180°C/350°F. Grease a 20cm (8in) baba pan (or grease a deep 20cm (8in) round cake pan and line base and side with baking paper).
2 Combine coffee and the hot water in a small jug; stir until dissolved.
3 Beat eggs in a small bowl with an electric mixer for 8 minutes or until thick and creamy; gradually add sugar, beating until dissolved between additions. Fold in sifted flour and cocoa, then butter and coffee mixture. Pour mixture into pan; bake for 40 minutes.
4 Meanwhile, make espresso syrup.
5 Stand cake in pan 5 minutes before turning onto a wire rack placed over a tray. Reserve ¼ cup espresso syrup; drizzle remaining hot syrup over hot cake. Serve with reserved syrup.

ESPRESSO SYRUP Combine ingredients in a small saucepan; stir over medium heat, without boiling, until sugar dissolves. Bring to the boil then remove from heat.

TEA CAKES

ORANGE TEACAKE

prep + cook time 50 MINUTES ✻ *serves* 12

150g (5oz) butter, softened
1 tablespoon finely grated orange rind
⅔ cup (150g) caster (superfine) sugar
3 eggs
1½ cups (225g) self-raising flour
¼ cup (60ml) milk
¾ cup (120g) icing (confectioners') sugar
1½ tablespoons orange juice

1 Preheat oven to 180°C/350°F. Grease a deep 20cm (8in) round cake pan; line base with baking paper.
2 Beat butter, rind, caster sugar, eggs, flour and milk in a medium bowl on low speed with an electric mixer until just combined. Increase speed to medium; beat for 3 minutes or until mixture is smooth and pale in colour.
3 Spread mixture into pan; bake for 40 minutes. Stand cake in pan 5 minutes before turning, top-side up, onto a wire rack to cool.
4 Meanwhile, combine sifted icing sugar and juice in a small bowl; stir until smooth. Spread icing over cooled cake.

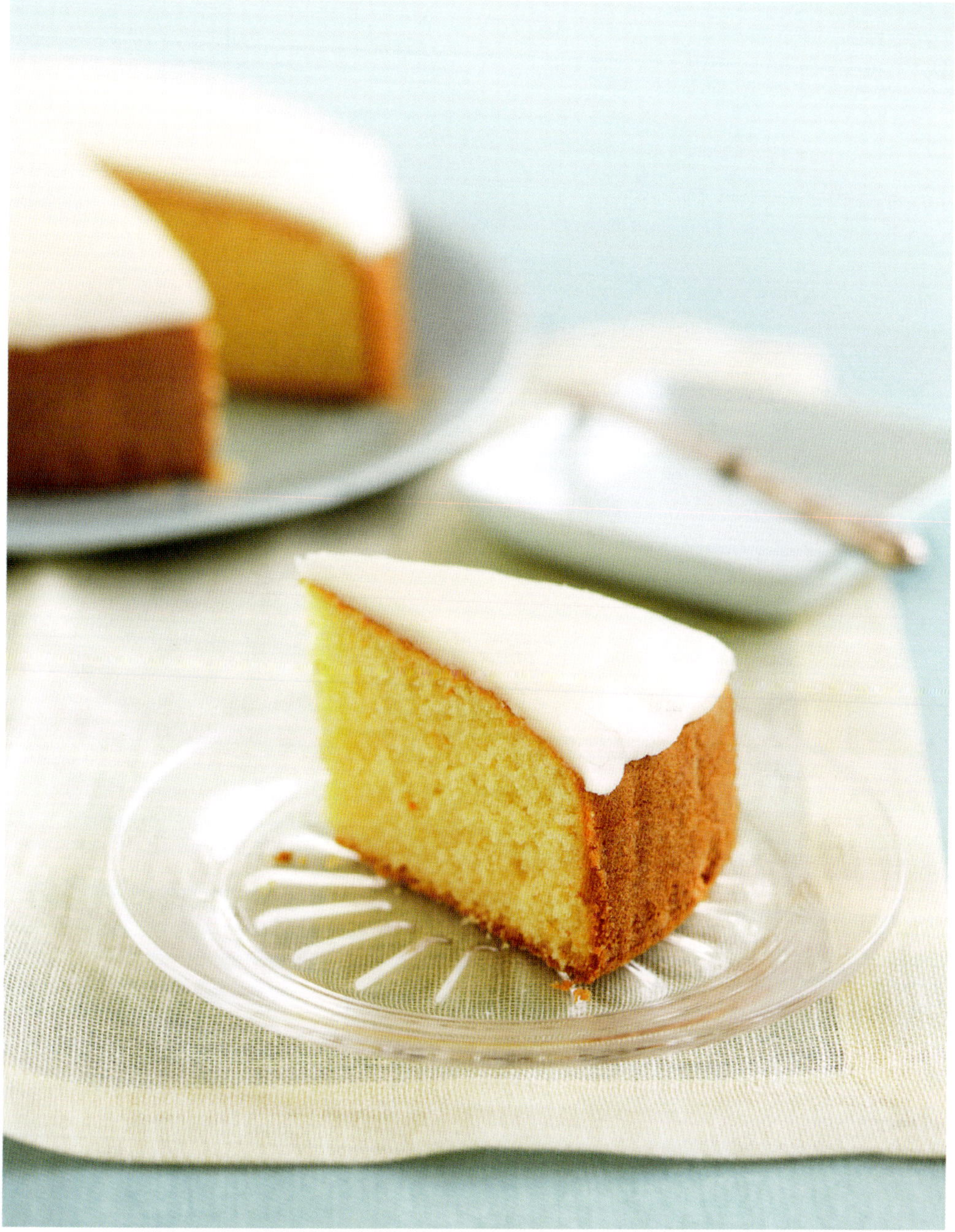

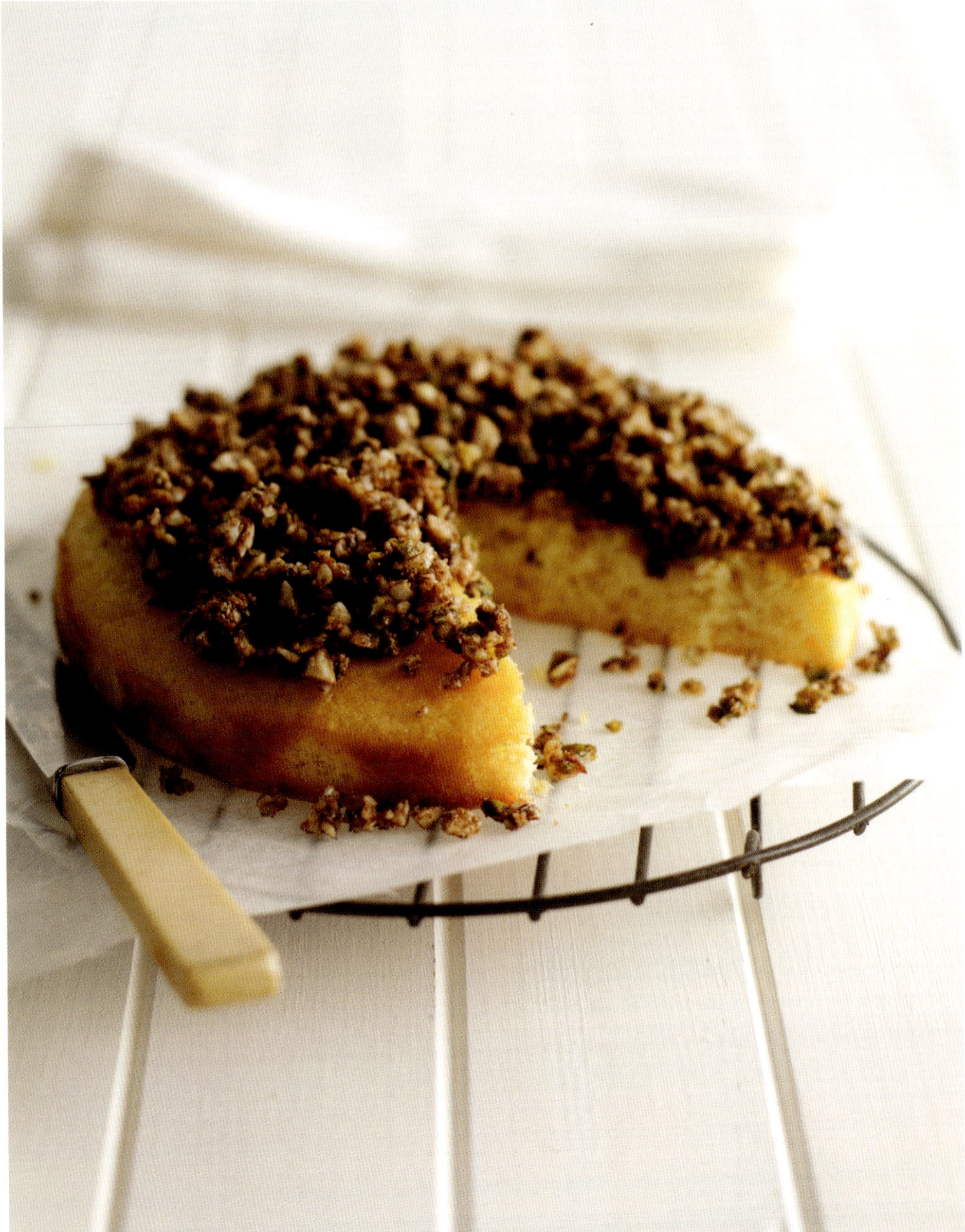

SPICED NUT TEACAKE

prep + cook time 1 HOUR *serves* 10

60g (2oz) butter, softened
1 teaspoon vanilla extract
½ cup (110g) caster (superfine) sugar
1 egg
1 cup (150g) self-raising flour
⅓ cup (80ml) milk
20g (¾oz) butter, melted, extra

SPICED NUTS
2 tablespoons shelled pistachios, chopped finely
2 tablespoons blanched almonds, chopped finely
2 tablespoons pine nuts, chopped finely
¼ cup (40g) icing (confectioners') sugar
1 teaspoon ground cinnamon
½ teaspoon ground allspice
½ teaspoon ground cardamom

1 Preheat oven to 180°C/350°F. Grease a 20cm (8in) round cake pan.
2 Beat butter, vanilla, sugar and egg in a small bowl with an electric mixer until light and fluffy. Stir in sifted flour and milk. Spread mixture into pan.
3 Bake cake for 25 minutes. Stand cake 5 minutes; turn, top-side up, onto a wire rack to cool.
4 Meanwhile, make spiced nuts.
5 Brush cooled cake with extra butter; sprinkle with spiced nuts. Serve warm.

SPICED NUTS Place nuts in strainer; rinse under cold water. Combine wet nuts in a large bowl with icing sugar and spices; spread mixture onto oven tray, roast in oven for 10 minutes or until nuts are dry.

The secret to a successful teacake lies in the beating of the sugar, egg and butter – the mixture must be very light in colour and full of air.

Apple Custard Teacake

prep + cook time 2 HOURS (+ COOLING) *serves* 8

200g (6½oz) butter, softened
½ cup (110g) caster (superfine) sugar
2 eggs
1¼ cups (185g) self-raising flour
⅓ cup (40g) custard powder
2 medium green-skinned apples (300g), peeled, cored, sliced thinly
1 tablespoon butter, melted
2 teaspoons caster (superfine) sugar, extra
½ teaspoon ground cinnamon

CUSTARD
2 tablespoons custard powder
¼ cup (55g) caster (superfine) sugar
1 cup (250ml) milk
20g (¾oz) butter
2 teaspoons vanilla extract

1 Make custard.
2 Preheat oven to 180°C/350°F. Grease a deep 22cm (9in) round cake pan; line base with baking paper.
3 Beat butter and sugar in a small bowl with an electric mixer until light and fluffy. Beat in eggs, one at a time. Stir in sifted flour and custard powder.
4 Spread half the mixture into the pan, top with custard. Top custard with spoonfuls of remaining teacake mixture; gently spread with a spatula to completely cover custard. Arrange apples on top; brush with melted butter, then sprinkle with combined extra sugar and cinnamon.
5 Bake teacake for 1¼ hours; cool in pan. Sprinkle with a little more caster sugar, if you like.
CUSTARD Combine custard powder and sugar in a small saucepan; gradually add milk, stirring over medium heat until mixture thickens slightly. Remove from heat; stir in butter and vanilla. Transfer to a small bowl, cover surface with plastic wrap to prevent a skin forming; cool. Whisk until smooth just before using.

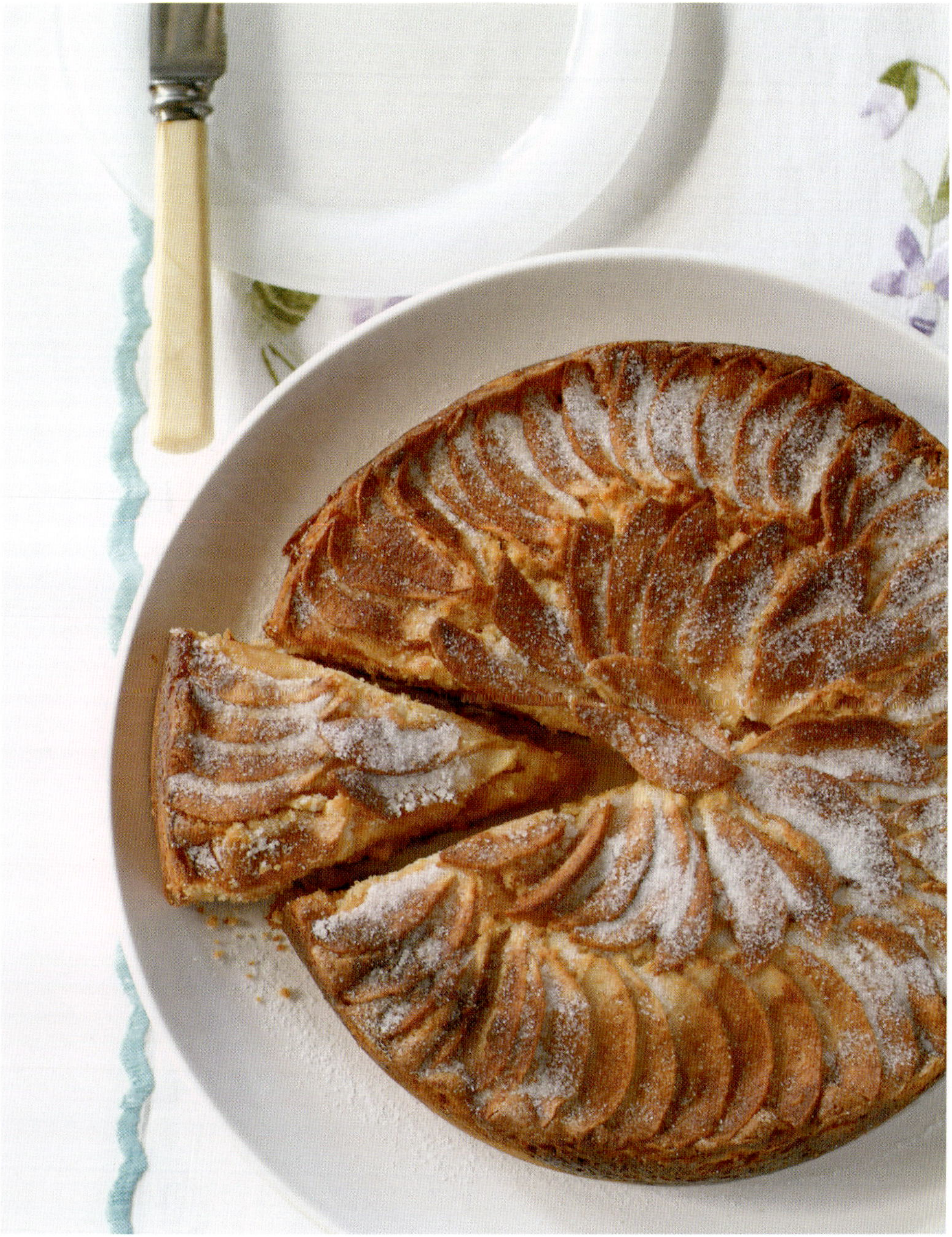

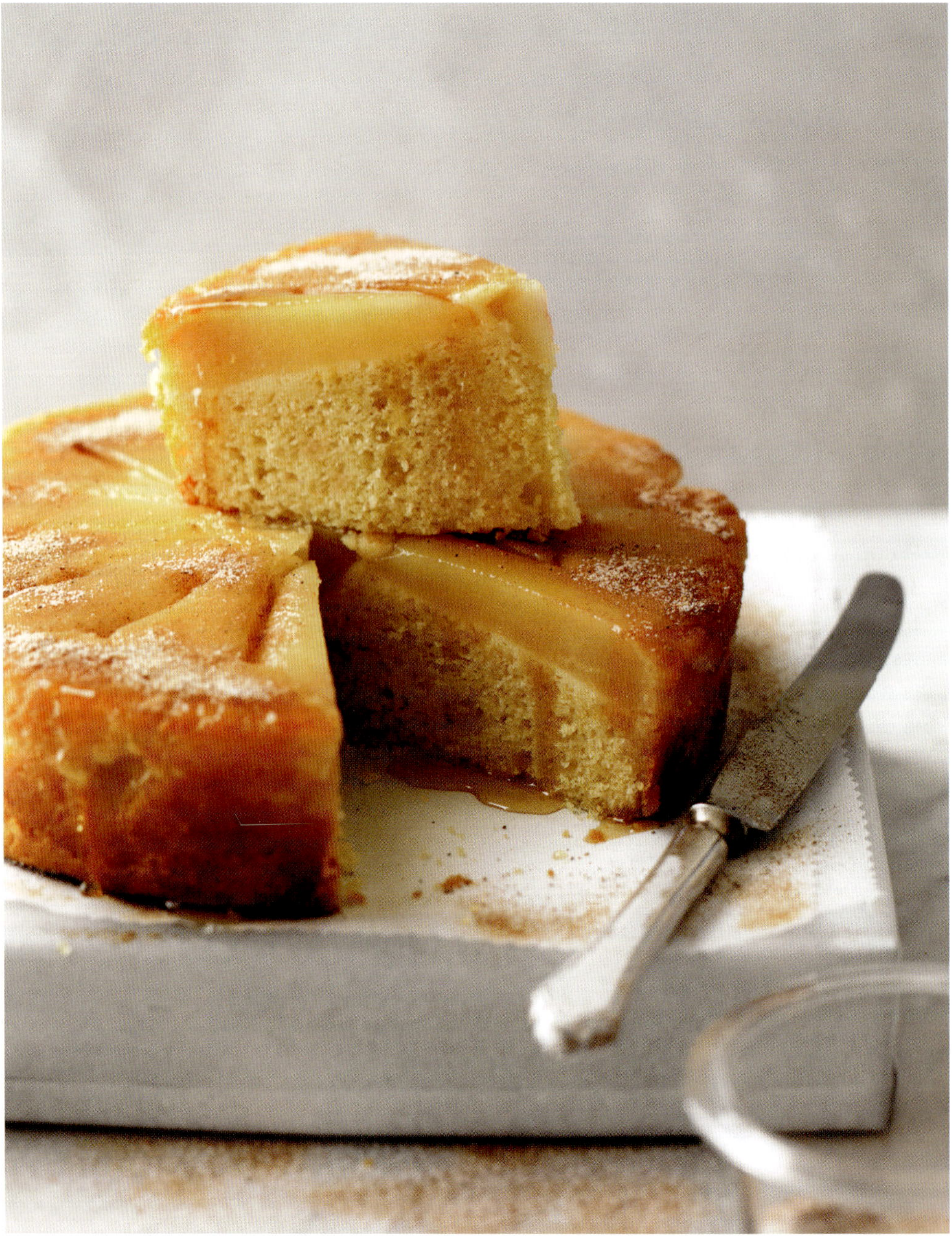

Poached Pear & Nutmeg Teacake

prep + cook time 2 HOURS 45 MINUTES ❊ *serves* 10

200g (6½oz) butter, softened
¾ cup (150g) caster (superfine) sugar
2 teaspoons vanilla extract
2 eggs
2 cups (300g) self-raising flour
⅔ cup (160ml) buttermilk
30g (1oz) butter, melted
1 tablespoon caster (superfine) sugar, extra
½ teaspoon ground cinnamon
½ teaspoon ground nutmeg

POACHED PEARS
4 medium beurre bosc pears (950g)
1 cup (220g) caster (superfine) sugar
2 cups (500ml) dry white wine
2 cups (500ml) water
1 medium lemon (140g), halved
2 dried bay leaves

1 Make poached pears.
2 Preheat oven to 180°C/350°F. Grease a deep 22cm (9in) round cake pan; line base and side with baking paper.
3 Arrange the poached pears on base of pan, rounded-side down.
4 Beat butter, sugar and vanilla in a small bowl with an electric mixer until light and fluffy. Beat in eggs, one at a time. Stir in sifted flour and buttermilk, in two batches. Spread mixture over pears in pan.
5 Bake teacake for 1 hour 10 minutes. Stand in pan for 10 minutes; turn onto a wire rack.
6 Brush pears with melted butter; sprinkle with combined extra sugar and spices. Serve teacake warm with syrup.

POACHED PEARS Peel, quarter and core pears. Place pears in a large saucepan with sugar, wine, the water, lemon and bay leaves; bring to the boil. Reduce heat; simmer, covered, for 25 minutes or until pears are tender. Using a slotted spoon, remove pears from syrup; cool. Remove and discard lemon halves; simmer remaining syrup, uncovered, over low heat, for 20 minutes until reduced.

serving suggestion Serve with whipped cream.

CHERRY TEACAKE

prep + cook time 1 HOUR 20 MINUTES *serves* 10

200g (6½oz) butter, softened
¾ cup (150g) firmly packed brown sugar
2 teaspoons vanilla extract
2 eggs
2 cups (300g) self-raising flour
⅔ cup (160ml) buttermilk
425g (13½oz) canned pitted black cherries in syrup, drained
30g (1oz) butter, melted

VANILLA SUGAR

1 vanilla bean
½ cup (110g) white (granulated) sugar

1 Preheat oven to 180°C/350°F. Grease a deep 22cm (9in) round cake pan; line base and side with baking paper.

2 Beat softened butter, sugar and vanilla in a small bowl with an electric mixer until light and fluffy. Beat in eggs, one at a time. Stir in sifted flour and buttermilk, in two batches. Spread mixture into pan; top with cherries.

3 Bake teacake for 1 hour. Stand in pan for 10 minutes; turn, top-side up, onto a wire rack.

4 Meanwhile, make vanilla sugar.

5 Brush warm teacake with melted butter; sprinkle with reserved vanilla sugar. Serve warm.

VANILLA SUGAR Split vanilla bean in half lengthways; scrape seeds into blender or processor. Add sugar; process until fine. Reserve 2 tablespoons for this recipe; store unused sugar in an airtight container for another use.

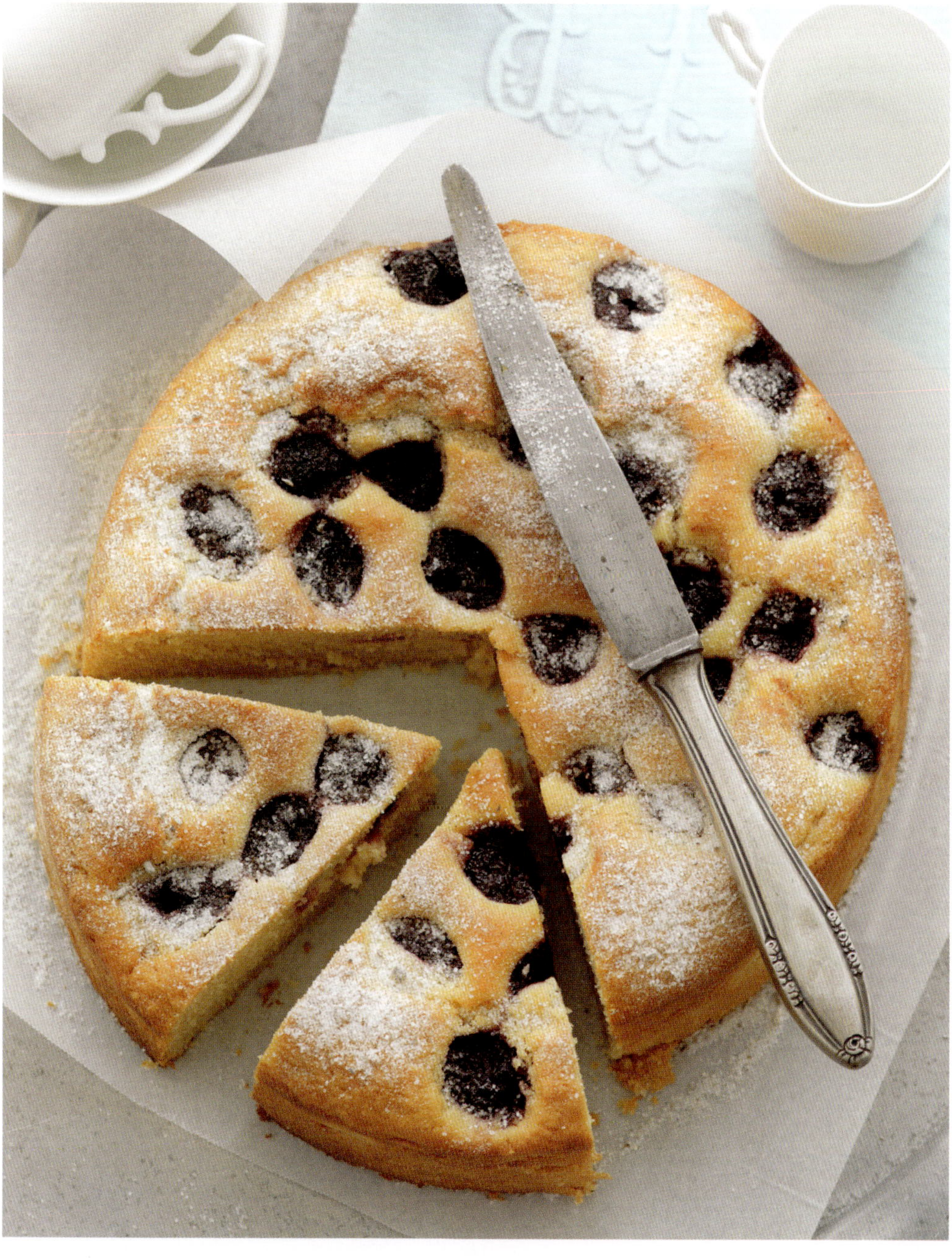

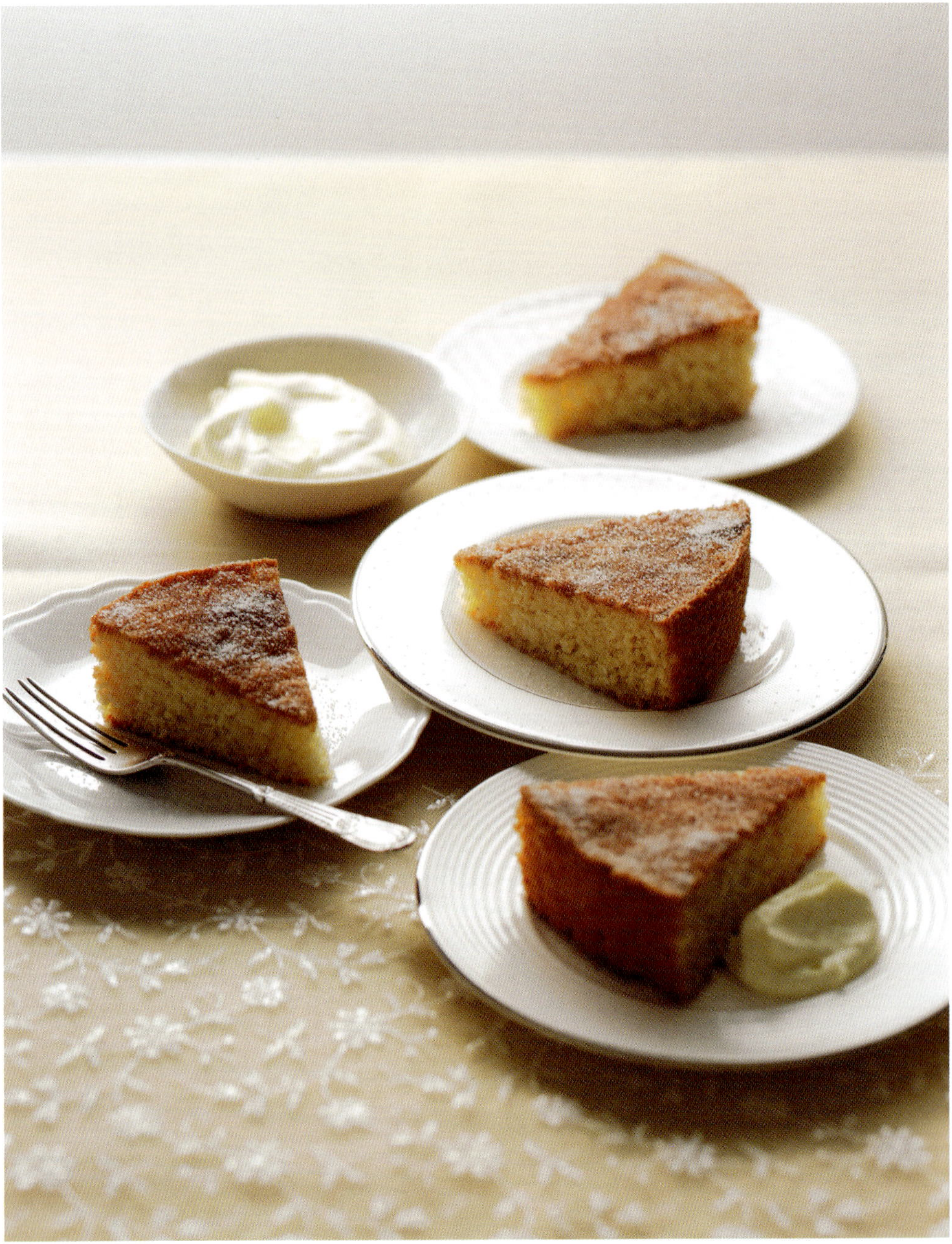

CINNAMON TEACAKE

prep + cook time 50 MINUTES *serves* 10

- 60g (2oz) butter, softened
- 1 teaspoon vanilla extract
- ⅔ cup (150g) caster (superfine) sugar
- 1 egg
- 1 cup (150g) self-raising flour
- ⅓ cup (80ml) milk
- 10g (½oz) butter, extra, melted
- 1 teaspoon ground cinnamon
- 1 tablespoon caster (superfine) sugar, extra

1 Preheat oven to 180°C/350°F. Grease a deep 20cm (8in) round cake pan; line base with baking paper.

2 Beat butter, vanilla, sugar and egg in a small bowl with an electric mixer until light and fluffy. Stir in sifted flour and milk.

3 Spread mixture into pan; bake for 30 minutes. Stand cake in pan 5 minutes before turning, top-side up, onto wire rack. Brush top of cake with melted butter; sprinkle with combined cinnamon and extra sugar. Serve warm with whipped cream or butter.

Almond, Lemon & Pine Nut Teacake

prep + cook time 45 MINUTES ❋ *serves* 8

- **125g (4oz) butter, softened**
- **½ cup (110g) caster (superfine) sugar**
- **3 eggs**
- **1 tablespoon finely grated lemon rind**
- **2 tablespoons milk**
- **1 cup (120g) almond meal**
- **¼ cup (35g) self-raising flour**
- **2 tablespoons pine nuts**
- **1 tablespoon flaked almonds**

1 Preheat oven to 180°C/350°F. Grease a shallow 13.5cm x 24cm (5½in x 9½in) loaf pan; line base with baking paper.

2 Beat butter, sugar, eggs and rind in a small bowl with an electric mixer until light and fluffy. Stir in milk, almond meal and sifted flour. Spread mixture into pan; smooth surface. Sprinkle with nuts.

3 Bake for 35 minutes. Stand in pan 5 minutes; turn cake, top-side up, onto a wire rack to cool. Serve warm or at room temperature.

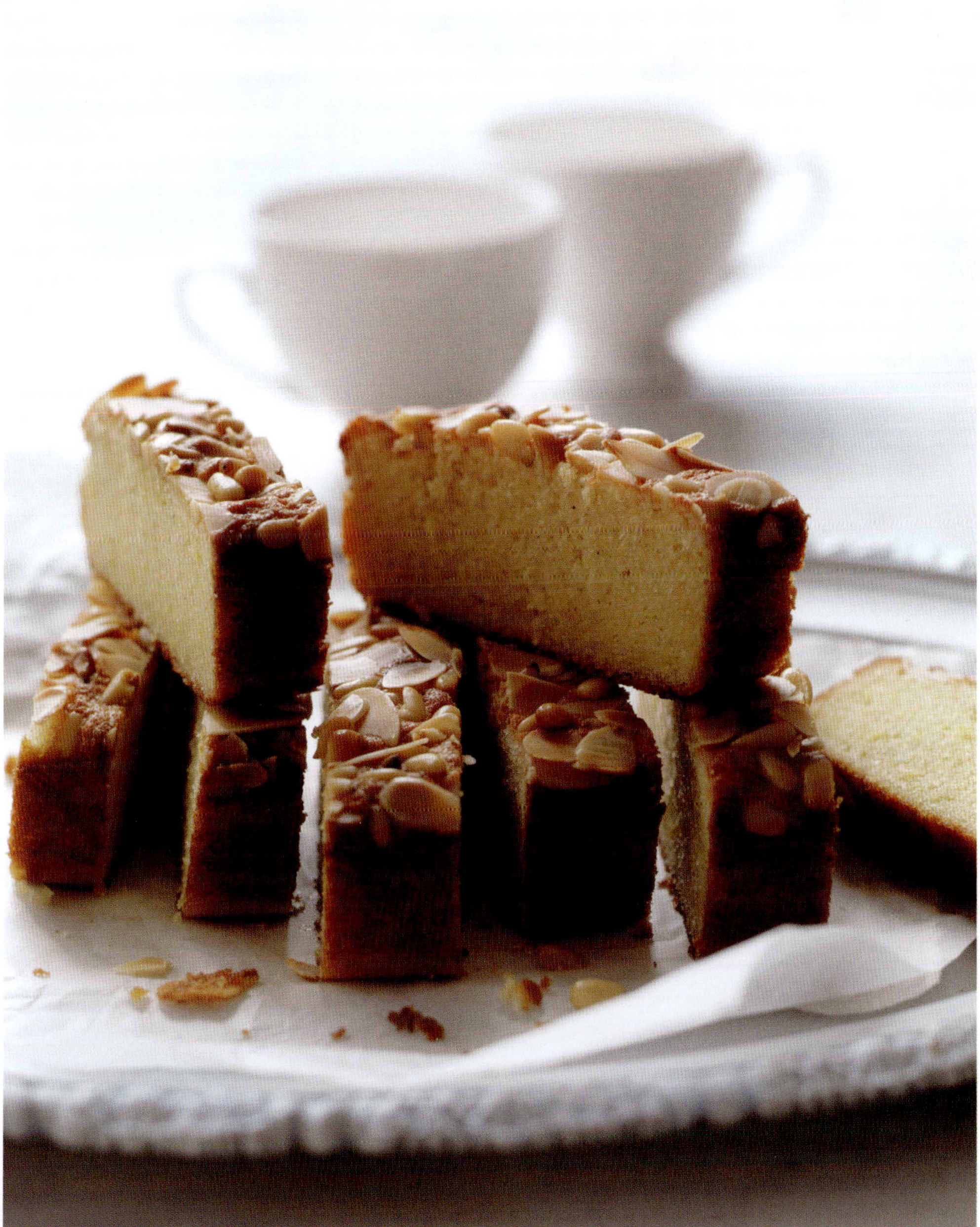

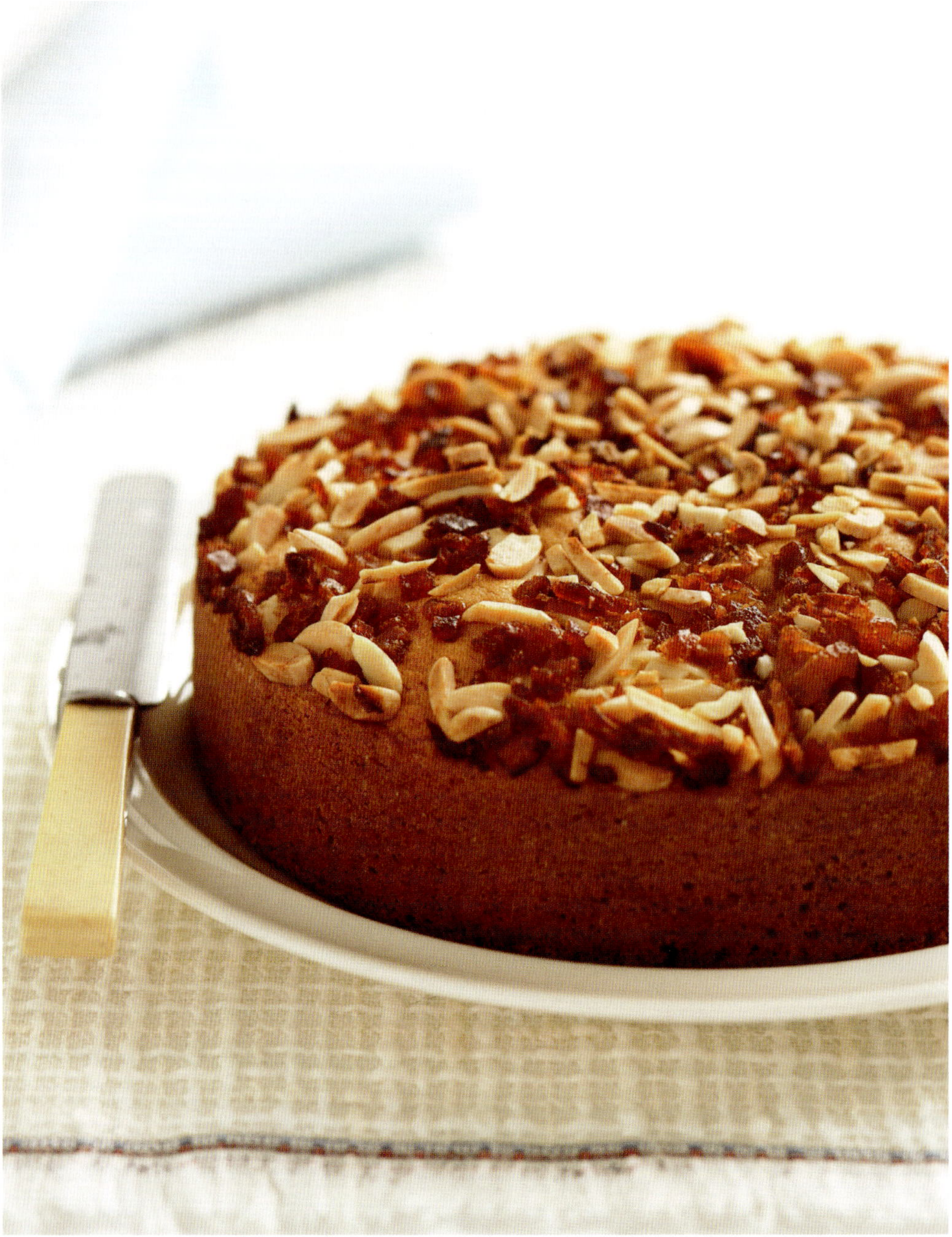

MADEIRA CAKE

prep + cook time 1 HOUR 15 MINUTES serves 12

180g (5½oz) butter, softened
2 teaspoons finely grated lemon rind
⅔ cup (150g) caster (superfine) sugar
3 eggs
¾ cup (110g) plain (all-purpose) flour
¾ cup (110g) self-raising flour
⅓ cup (55g) mixed peel
¼ cup (35g) slivered almonds

1 Preheat oven to 160°C/325°F. Grease a deep 20cm (8in) round cake pan; line base with baking paper.
2 Beat butter, rind and sugar in a small bowl with an electric mixer until light and fluffy; beat in eggs, one at a time. Transfer mixture to a large bowl, stir in sifted flours.
3 Spread mixture into pan; bake for 20 minutes. Remove cake from oven; sprinkle with peel and almonds. Return cake to oven; bake for 40 minutes. Stand cake in pan for 5 minutes before turning, top-side up, onto a wire rack to cool.

MAPLE & CASHEW LOAF

prep + cook time 1 HOUR 10 MINUTES (+ STANDING)   *serves* 10

125g (4oz) butter, softened, chopped
¾ cup (150g) firmly packed brown sugar
2 eggs
1 cup (150g) self-raising flour
½ cup (75g) plain (all-purpose) flour
½ teaspoon mixed spice
½ cup (120g) sour cream
2 tablespoons pure maple syrup
1 cup (150g) unsalted roasted cashews, chopped coarsely
2 teaspoons icing (confectioners') sugar
sour cream and pure maple syrup, extra, to serve

1 Preheat oven to 180°C/350°F. Grease a 15cm x 25cm (6in x 10in) loaf pan; line base and two long sides with baking paper, extending the paper 2cm (¾in) above the sides.

2 Beat butter, brown sugar, eggs, flours, spice, sour cream and maple syrup in a medium bowl with an electric mixer on low speed until combined. Increase speed to medium, beat until mixture is smooth and changed to a lighter colour. Spoon mixture into pan; smooth the surface. Sprinkle with cashews.

3 Bake loaf for 50 minutes or until a skewer inserted into the centre comes out clean. Leave loaf in pan for 20 minutes before turning, top-side up, onto a wire rack to cool. Dust with sifted icing sugar; serve with extra sour cream and maple syrup.

tips Make sure you use pure maple syrup in this recipe; maple-flavoured syrup is made from sugar cane and is not an adequate substitute for the real thing. You could replace the cashews with pecans or walnuts if you like.

keeps This loaf can be made a day ahead; store in an airtight container.

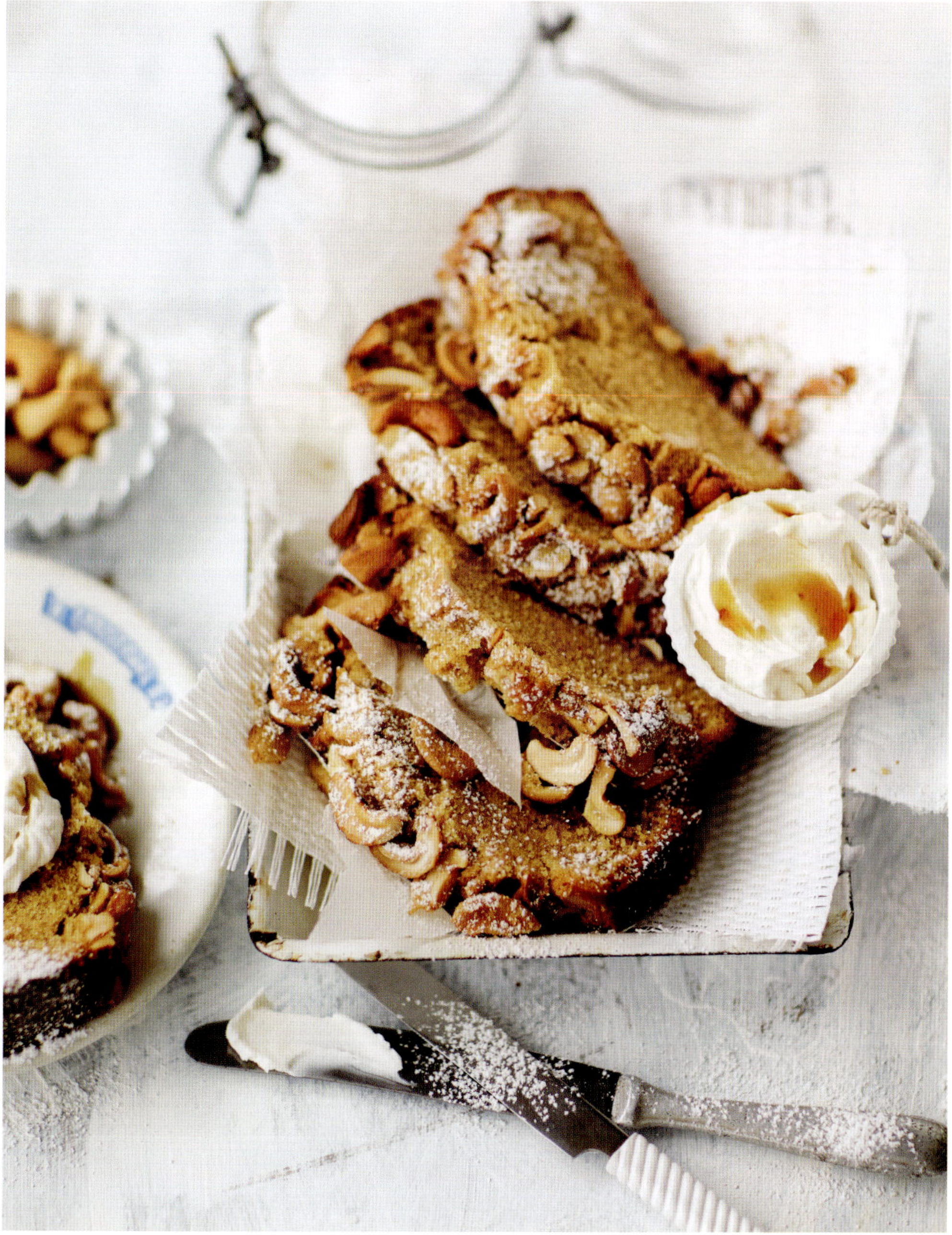

LAYERED CAKES

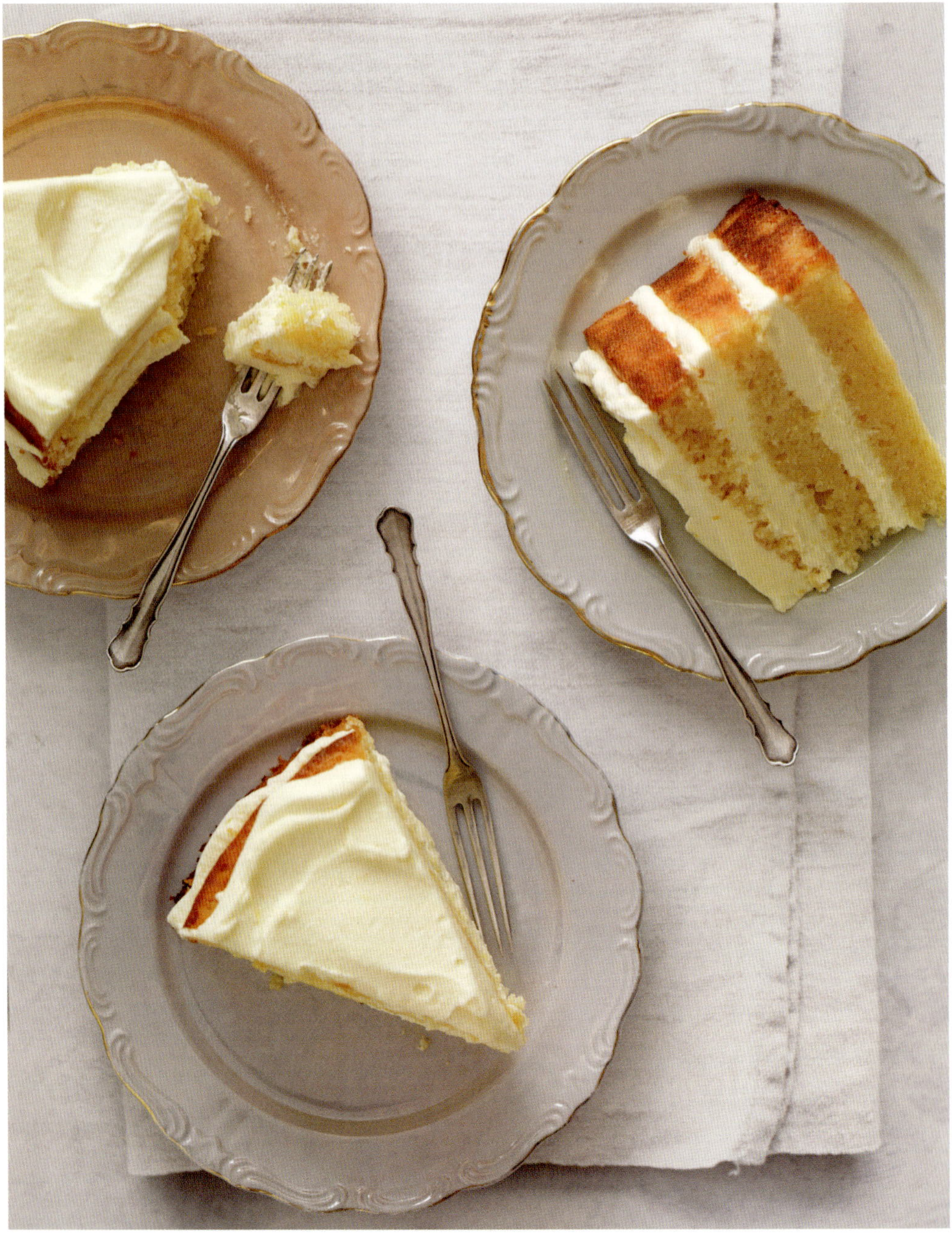

LEMON MASCARPONE
LAYER CAKE

prep + cook time 1 HOUR 20 MINUTES *serves* 8

125g (4oz) butter, softened
2 teaspoons finely grated lemon rind
1¼ cups (275g) caster (superfine) sugar
3 eggs
1½ cups (225g) self-raising flour
½ cup (125ml) milk
¼ cup (60ml) lemon juice

LEMON MASCARPONE FROSTING

1 cup (250ml) thickened (heavy) cream
½ cup (80g) icing (confectioners') sugar
2 teaspoons finely grated lemon rind
⅔ cup (170g) mascarpone

1 Preheat oven to 180°C/350°F. Grease a deep 20cm (8in) round cake pan; line base with baking paper.
2 Make lemon mascarpone frosting. Refrigerate, covered, until required.
3 Beat butter, rind and sugar in a small bowl with an electric mixer until light and fluffy. Beat in eggs, one at a time (mixture might separate at this stage, but will come together later); transfer mixture to a large bowl. Stir in sifted flour, milk and juice, in two batches. Pour mixture into pan.
4 Bake cake for 50 minutes. Stand cake in pan for 5 minutes before turning, top-side up, onto a wire rack to cool.
5 Split cooled cake into three layers, place one layer onto serving plate, cut-side up; spread with one-third of the frosting. Repeat the layering process, finishing with the frosting.

LEMON MASCARPONE FROSTING Beat cream, sifted icing sugar and rind in a small bowl with an electric mixer until soft peaks form. Fold cream mixture into mascarpone.

keeps Frosted cake will keep in an airtight container, in the fridge, for up to 3 days.

Banana Caramel Layer Cake

prep + cook time 1 HOUR 10 MINUTES ❋ *serves* 8

You need 2 large overripe bananas (460g) for this amount of mashed banana.

185g (6oz) butter, softened
1¼ cup (175g) caster (superfine) sugar
3 eggs
2¼ cups (335g) self-raising flour
½ teaspoon bicarbonate of soda (baking soda)
1¼ cups mashed banana
⅓ cup (80ml) milk
380g (13½oz) can caramel Top 'n' Fill
¾ cup (180ml) thickened (heavy) cream, whipped
1 large banana (230g), sliced thinly

1 Preheat oven to 180°C/350°F. Grease a 24cm (9½in) bundt pan or 24cm (9½in) patterned silicone pan well.

2 Beat butter and sugar in a small bowl with an electric mixer until light and fluffy. Beat in eggs, one at a time. Transfer mixture to a large bowl; stir in sifted dry ingredients, mashed banana and milk.

3 Spread mixture into pan; bake for 40 minutes. Stand cake in pan for 5 minutes before turning onto a wire rack to cool.

4 Split cake into three layers. Spread bottom layer of cake with half the caramel, top with half the cream then half the banana slices. Repeat next layer using remaining caramel, cream and banana slices. Replace top of cake. Dust with icing (confectioners') sugar before serving, if you like.

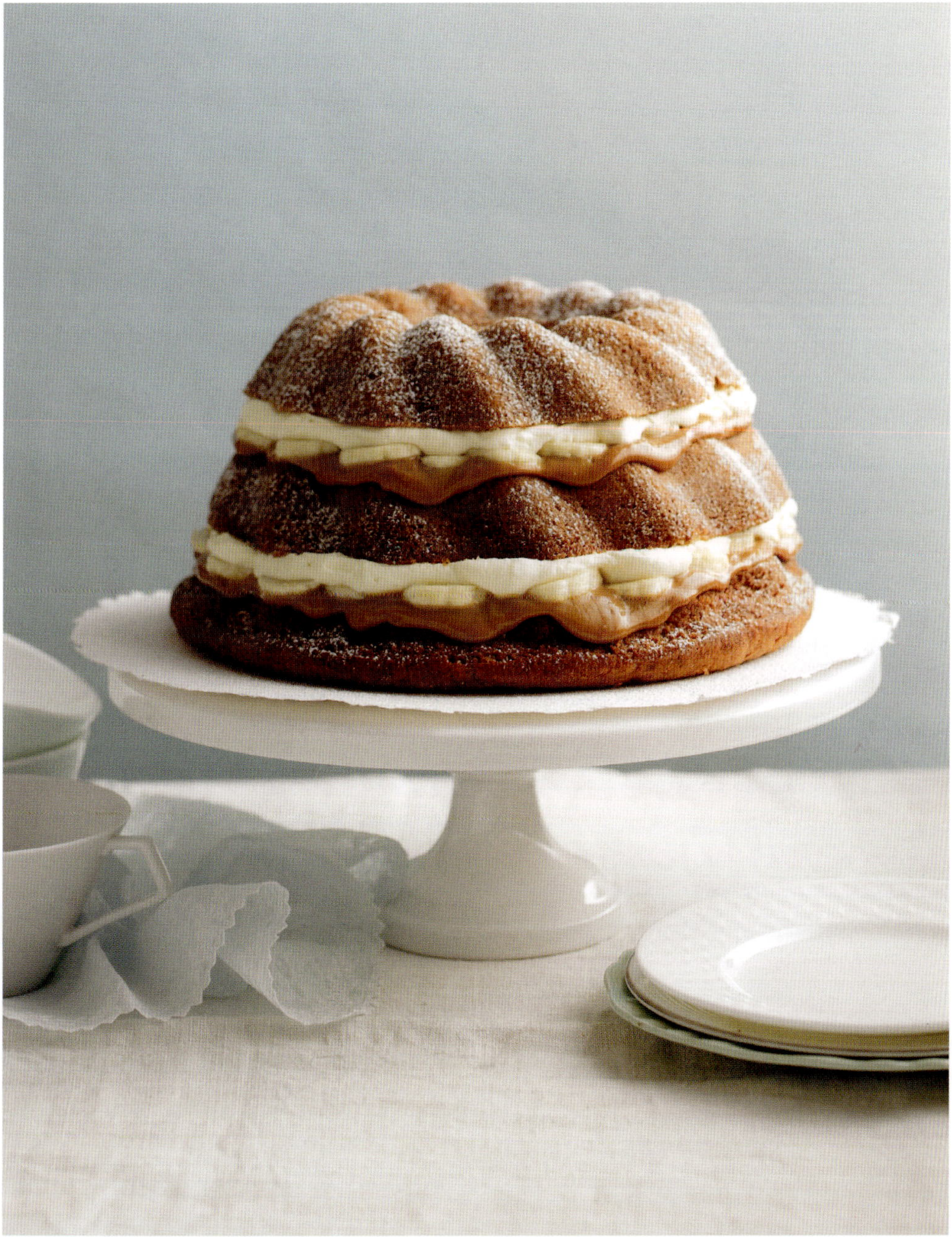

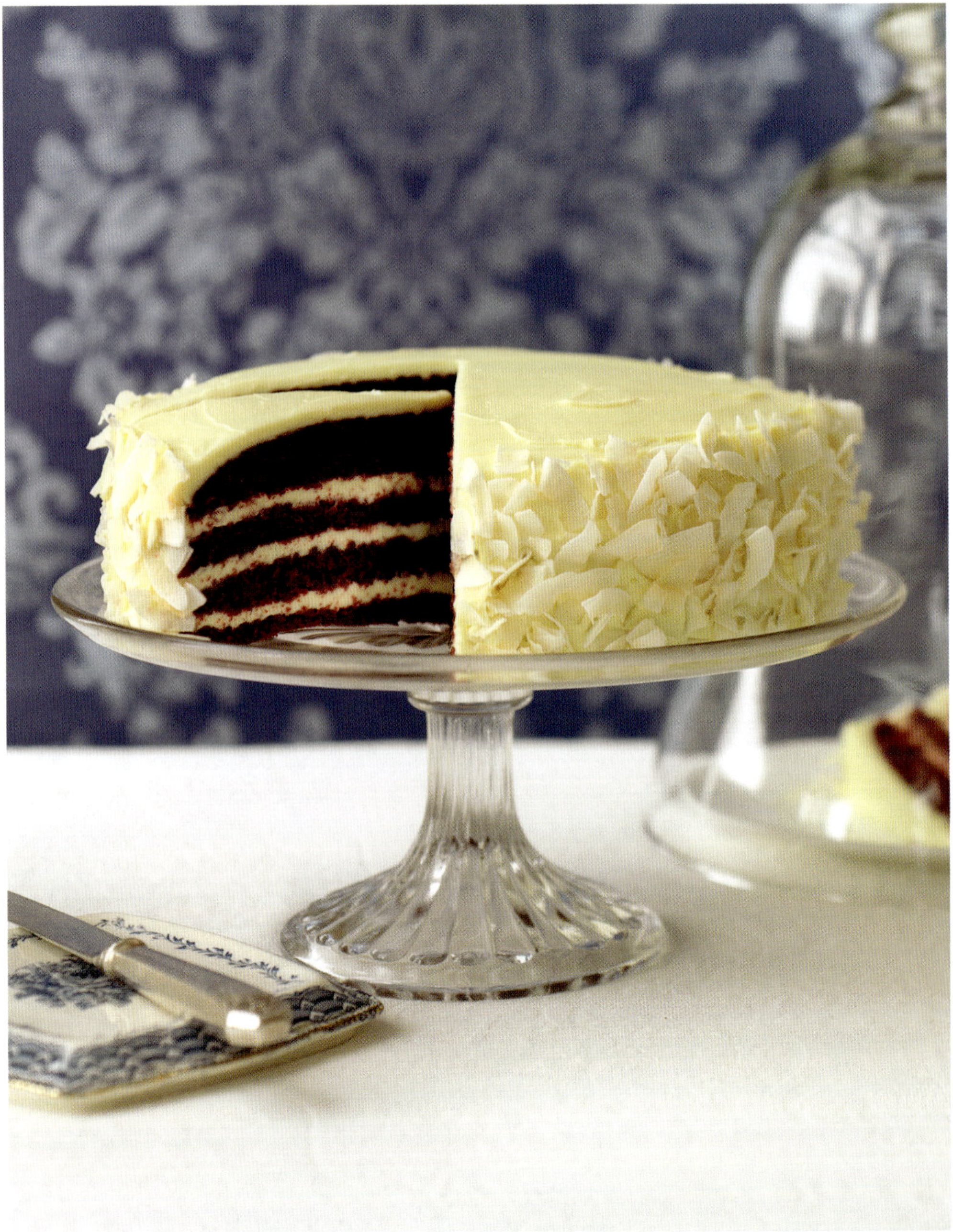

PINK VELVET CAKE

prep + cook time 1 HOUR (+ STANDING & FREEZING) — *serves* 12

125g (4oz) butter, softened
1 teaspoon vanilla extract
1½ cups (330g) caster (superfine) sugar
2 eggs
1½ cups (225g) plain (all-purpose) flour
2 tablespoons cornflour (cornstarch)
2 tablespoons cocoa powder
1 cup (250ml) buttermilk
1 tablespoon rose pink food colouring
1 teaspoon white vinegar
1 teaspoon bicarbonate of soda (baking soda)
1 cup (50g) flaked coconut

MASCARPONE FROSTING
250g (8oz) cream cheese, softened
250g (8oz) mascarpone
1 cup (160g) icing (confectioners') sugar
1 teaspoon vanilla extract
300ml thickened (heavy) cream

1 Preheat oven to 180°C/350°F. Grease two deep 23cm (9in) round cake pans; line bases and sides with baking paper.
2 Beat butter, vanilla, sugar and eggs in a small bowl with an electric mixer until light and fluffy. Transfer mixture to a large bowl; stir in sifted flours and cocoa and the combined buttermilk and food colouring, in two batches.
3 Combine vinegar and bicarbonate of soda in a cup; allow to fizz then fold into cake mixture. Divide mixture between pans.
4 Bake cakes for 25 minutes. Stand for 10 minutes before turning top-side up onto a wire rack to cool. Wrap cakes in plastic; freeze for 40 minutes.
5 Meanwhile, make mascarpone frosting.
6 Split cold cakes in half. Place one layer on serving plate, cut-side up; spread with ⅔ cup frosting. Repeat layering, finishing with remaining frosting spread over top and side of cake; press coconut onto side of cake.

MASCARPONE FROSTING Beat cream cheese, mascarpone, sugar and vanilla in a small bowl with an electric mixer until smooth. Beat in cream.

tip To make your own buttermilk equivalent, combine 1 tablespoon fresh lemon juice with enough reduced-fat milk to make 1 cup. Stand a few minutes until thickened; stir.

TIRAMISU TORTE

prep + cook time 1 HOUR 10 MINUTES (+ COOLING & REFRIGERATION)   *serves* 12

3 eggs
½ cup (110g) caster (superfine) sugar
¼ cup (35g) plain (all-purpose) flour
¼ cup (35g) self-raising flour
¼ cup (35g) pure cornflour (cornstarch)
2 tablespoons instant coffee granules
¾ cup (180ml) boiling water
⅓ cup (80ml) marsala
2 tablespoons coffee-flavoured liqueur
500g (1lb) mascarpone
⅓ cup (55g) icing (confectioners') sugar
300ml thickened (heavy) cream

1 Preheat oven to 180°C/350°F. Grease a deep 22cm (9in) square cake pan with butter.

2 Beat eggs in a small bowl with an electric mixer for 10 minutes or until thick and creamy; gradually add caster sugar, one tablespoon at a time, beating until sugar dissolves between additions. Transfer to a large bowl.

3 Sift flours twice. Sift flours a third time over egg mixture; fold ingredients together. Spread into pan.

4 Bake sponge for 25 minutes. Turn the sponge immediately onto a baking-paper-covered wire rack, top-side up, to cool.

5 Meanwhile, dissolve coffee in the water in a small heatproof jug. Stir in marsala and liqueur; cool.

6 Beat mascarpone and icing sugar in a small bowl with an electric mixer until smooth. Beat in cream and ⅓ cup of the cooled coffee mixture.

7 Split sponge in half vertically then each sponge in half horizontally. Place one of the cake rectangles on serving plate, cut-side up; brush with a quarter of the remaining coffee mixture then spread with ⅔ cup of mascarpone mixture. Repeat layering process finishing with the cake, cut-side down, and remaining mascarpone mixture spread on top and sides of cake. Refrigerate cake for 2 hours.

8 Decorate torte with coarsely chopped vienna almonds, if you like.

TIP

Alternate the sponge pieces when layering so that the cut side of the sponge is on different sides on each layer; this will ensure the torte is even and does not lean to one side.

KEEPS
This cake will keep in an airtight container for up to 3 days.

PISTACHIO & ROSEWATER LAYER CAKE

prep + cook time 2 HOURS (+ COOLING) *serves* 12

200g (6½oz) roasted unsalted shelled pistachios
250g (8oz) butter, softened
1½ cups (330g) caster (superfine) sugar
2 teaspoons finely grated lemon rind
4 eggs
1 cup (150g) plain (all-purpose) flour
½ cup (75g) self-raising flour
¾ cup (200g) Greek-style yoghurt

ROSEWATER BUTTERCREAM
250g (8oz) butter, softened
2 teaspoons rosewater
3 cups (480g) icing (confectioners') sugar

1 Preheat oven to 170°C/340°F. Grease a deep 22cm (9in) round cake pan; line base and side with baking paper.
2 Blend or process pistachios until finely ground.
3 Beat butter, sugar and rind in a medium bowl with an electric mixer until light and fluffy. Beat in eggs, one at a time. Stir in sifted flours, yoghurt and 1 cup of the ground pistachios. Spread mixture into pan.
4 Bake cake for 1 hour 10 minutes. Stand in pan for 5 minutes; turn, top-side up, onto a wire rack to cool.
5 Make rosewater buttercream.
6 Split cooled cake in half. Place bottom layer, cut-side up, onto a serving plate; spread with one-third of the buttercream, top with remaining cake layer. Spread remaining buttercream over top and side of cake. Sprinkle with remaining ground pistachios.

ROSEWATER BUTTERCREAM Beat butter and rosewater in a medium bowl with the electric mixer until as white as possible. Gradually beat in sifted icing sugar until smooth.

tip Rosewater will vary in strength between brands. Start adding a small amount at a time and adjust to your taste. If you're using rosewater essence, start with 1 teaspoon.

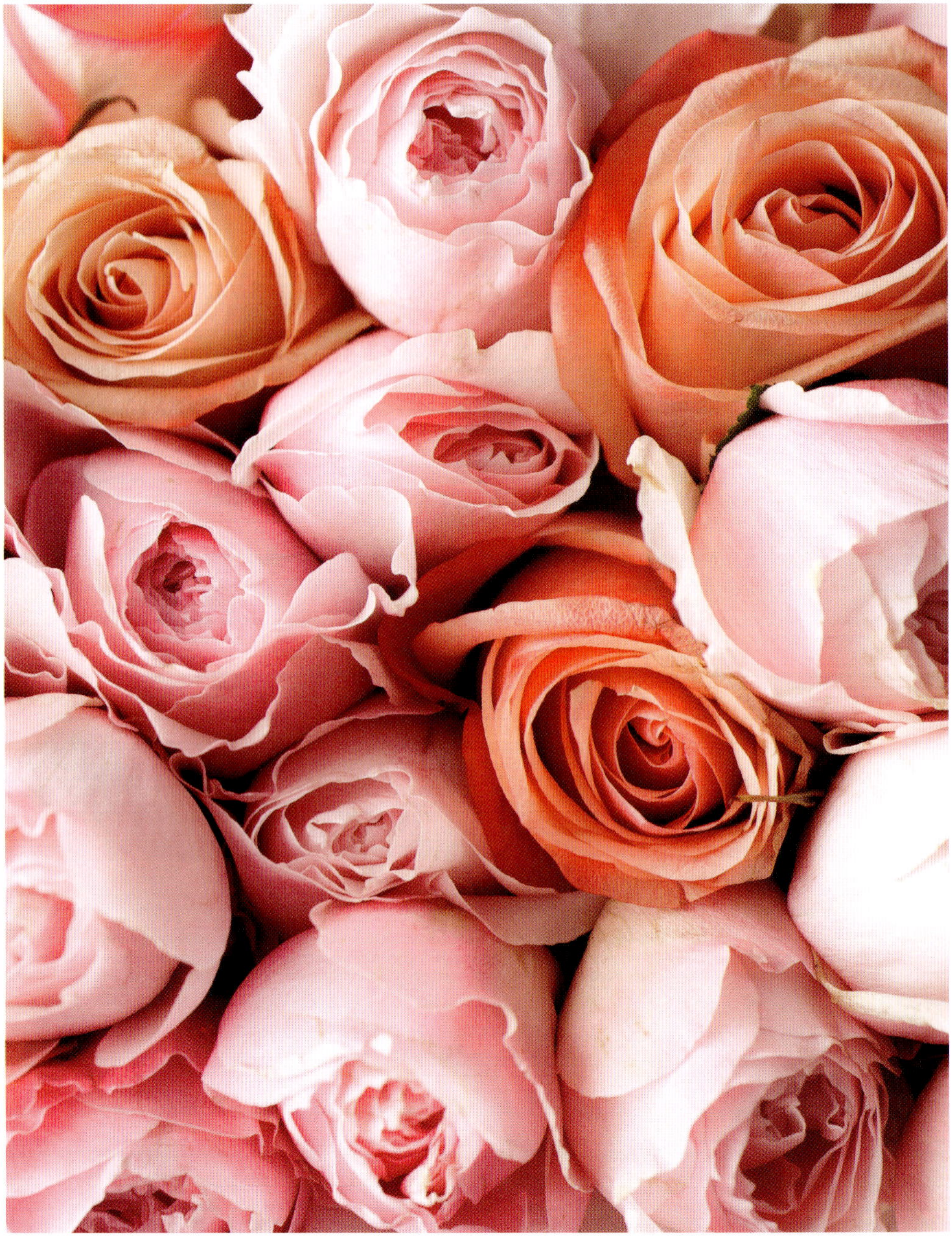

opera
GATEAU

OPERA GATEAU

prep + cook time 1 HOUR (+ COOLING & REFRIGERATION) *serves* 24

4 eggs
1¼ cups (150g) almond meal
1 cup (160g) icing (confectioners') sugar
⅓ cup (50g) plain (all-purpose) flour
25g (1oz) unsalted butter, melted
4 egg whites
1 tablespoon caster (superfine) sugar

COFFEE BUTTERCREAM

¼ cup (60ml) milk
¼ cup (55g) firmly packed brown sugar
2 teaspoons instant coffee granules
1 egg yolk
125g (4oz) unsalted butter, softened

COFFEE SYRUP

⅓ cup (80ml) boiling water
2 tablespoons caster (superfine) sugar
1 tablespoon instant coffee granules

GANACHE

160g (5½oz) dark (semi-sweet) chocolate, chopped coarsely
⅓ cup (80ml) pouring cream

GLAZE

50g (1½oz) unsalted butter, chopped
75g (2½oz) dark (semi-sweet) chocolate

1 Preheat oven to 220°C/425°F. Grease two 25cm x 30cm (10in x 12in) swiss roll pans; line bases with baking paper, extending the paper 5cm (2in) over long sides.

2 Beat eggs, almond meal and sifted icing sugar in a small bowl with an electric mixer until creamy; beat in flour. Transfer mixture to a large bowl; stir in butter. Beat egg whites in a small bowl with the electric mixer until soft peaks form; add caster sugar, beating until sugar dissolves. Fold into almond mixture, in two batches. Divide mixture between pans. Bake for 7 minutes. Cool.

3 Make coffee buttercream, coffee syrup and ganache.

4 Cut each cake into a 20cm x 25cm (8in x 10in) rectangle and a 10cm x 25cm (4in x 10in) rectangle. Place one of the large cake rectangles on a baking-paper-lined tray; brush with half the coffee syrup then spread cake with half the buttercream. Refrigerate for 10 minutes. Top buttercream with the two small cake rectangles, side-by-side. Brush tops with the remaining coffee syrup then spread with ganache. Top with remaining cake; refrigerate for 10 minutes. Spread remaining buttercream over top of cake; refrigerate for 3 hours.

5 Make glaze. Quickly spread glaze evenly over cake. Refrigerate 30 minutes or until set.

COFFEE BUTTERCREAM Stir milk, sugar and coffee in a small saucepan, over low heat, until sugar dissolves. Whisk yolk in a small bowl; gradually whisk in hot milk mixture. Return custard to pan; stir over medium heat, without boiling, for 5 minutes or until thickened slightly. Cool. Beat butter in a bowl with an electric mixer until light and fluffy; beat in custard.

COFFEE SYRUP Combine ingredients in a small bowl.

GANACHE Stir ingredients in a small heatproof bowl over small saucepan of simmering water until smooth. Refrigerate until ganache is spreadable.

GLAZE Stir ingredients in a small heatproof bowl over small saucepan of simmering water until smooth. Use while warm.

CREAMY COCONUT CAKE

prep + cook time 2 HOURS (+ COOLING) *serves* 16

250g (8oz) unsalted butter, softened
1½ cups (330g) caster (superfine) sugar
½ cup (125ml) coconut cream
4 eggs, separated
1½ cups (225g) plain (all-purpose) flour
1 cup (150g) self-raising flour
1 cup (250ml) buttermilk
2 cups (100g) flaked coconut

COCONUT FROSTING
375g (12oz) cream cheese, softened
100g (3oz) unsalted butter, softened
2 teaspoons coconut extract
2 cups (320g) icing (confectioners') sugar
⅓ cup (80ml) coconut cream
1 cup (80g) desiccated coconut

1 Preheat oven to 170°C/340°F. Grease two deep 22cm (9in) round cake pans.
2 Beat butter, sugar and coconut cream in a small bowl with an electric mixer until light and fluffy. Beat in eggs yolks until combined. Transfer mixture to a large bowl; stir in sifted flours and the buttermilk, in two batches.
3 Beat egg whites in a small bowl with an electric mixer until soft peaks form. Fold egg whites into cake mixture, in two batches. Divide mixture between pans.
4 Bake cakes for 50 minutes. Stand cakes in pan for 10 minutes before turning, top-side up, onto a wire rack to cool.
5 Meanwhile, make coconut frosting.
6 Split cakes in half. Place one layer on serving plate, cut-side up; spread with ⅔ cup of frosting. Repeat layering, finishing with remaining frosting spread over top and side of cake. Press flaked coconut all over cake.
COCONUT FROSTING Beat cream cheese, butter and extract in a large bowl until smooth. Beat in sifted icing sugar and coconut cream, in three batches; stir in desiccated coconut.

tip If you want to make your own flaked coconut, buy a small brown-husked coconut (700g). Preheat oven to 220°C/425°F. Pierce eyes of the coconut, drain and discard liquid. Place coconut on oven tray; bake for 10 minutes or until cracks appear. Carefully split the coconut open by hitting with a hammer; remove flesh. Using vegetable peeler, slice coconut flesh into curls.

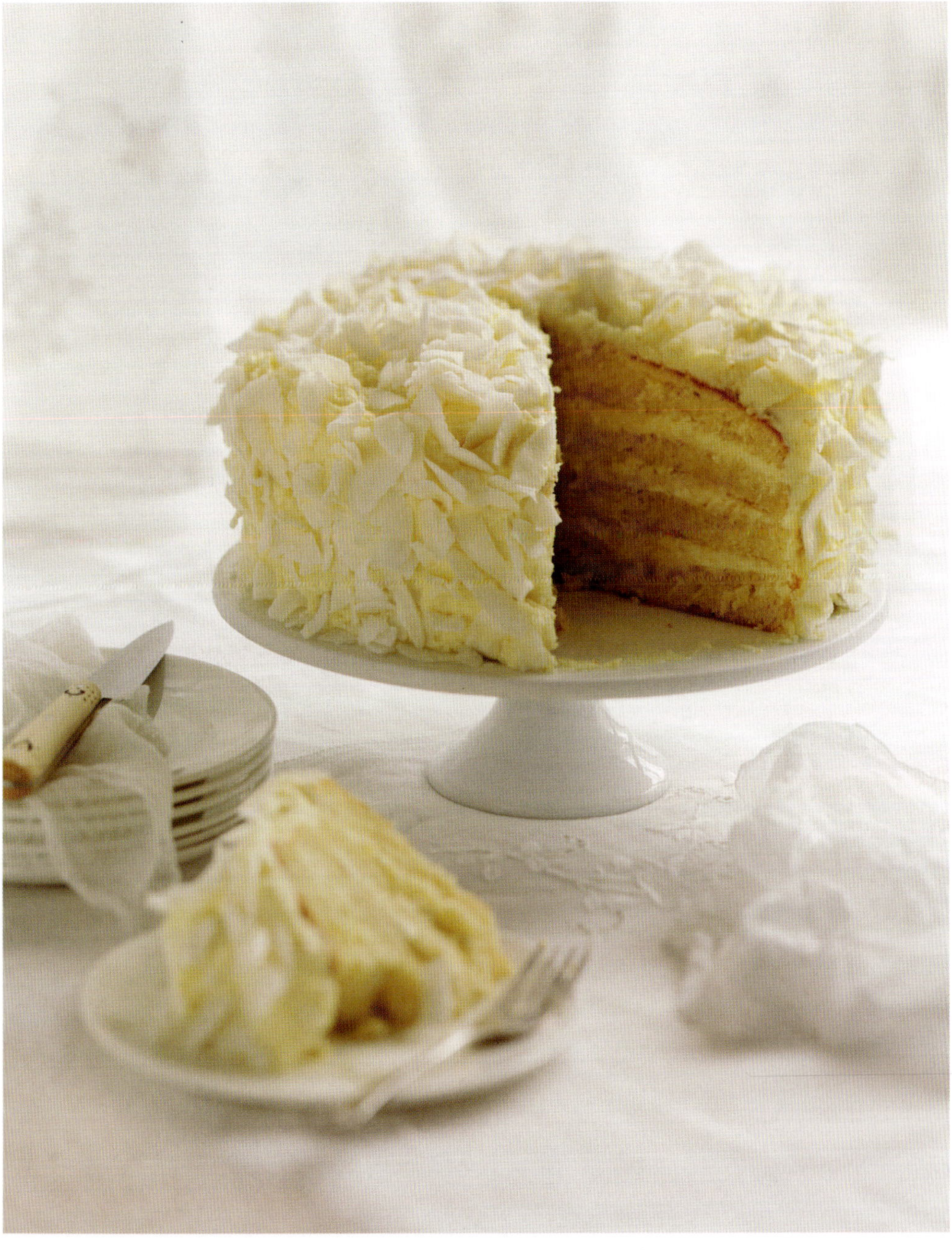

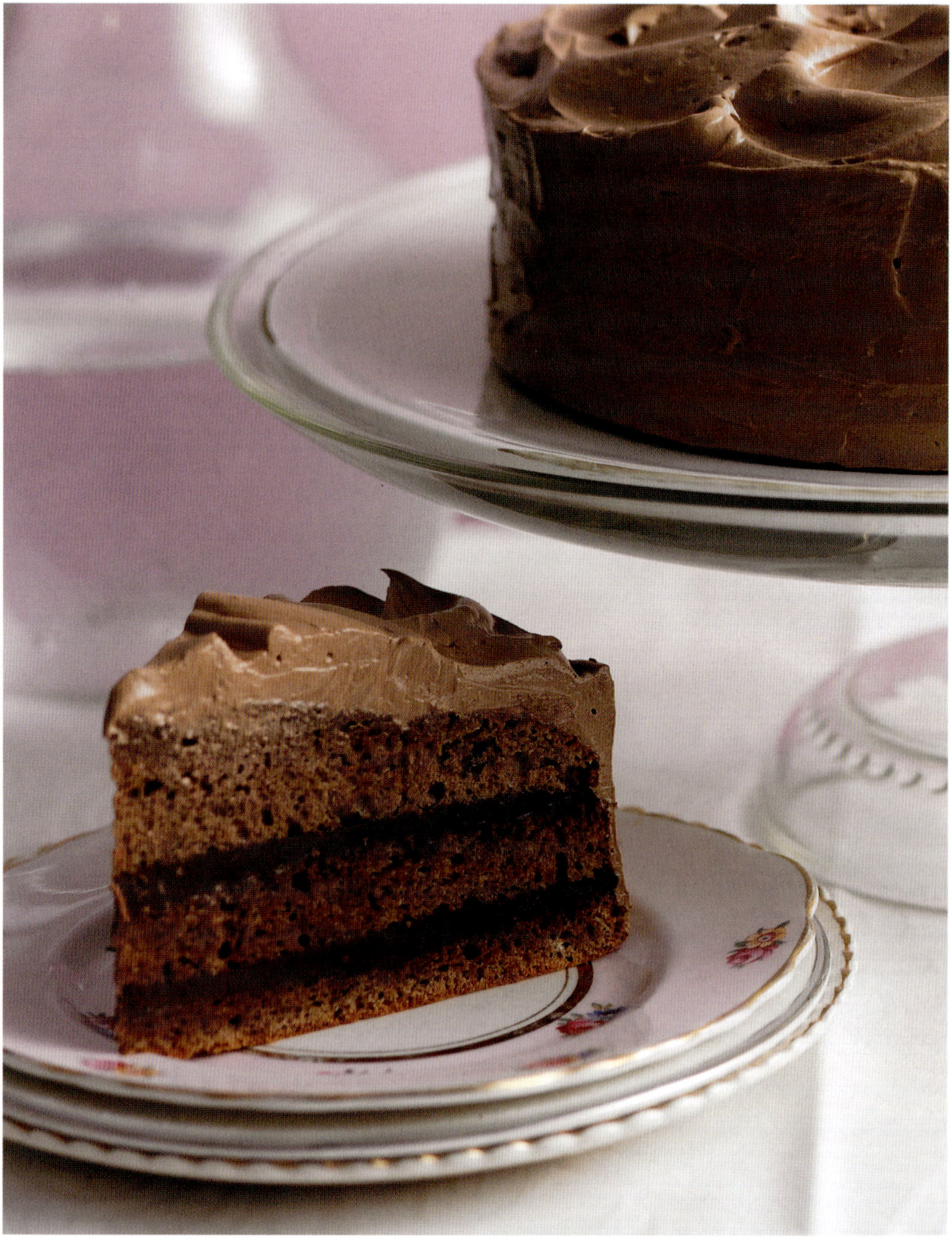

rich mocha
GATEAU

Rich Mocha
Gateau

prep + cook time 1 HOUR 15 MINUTES (+ STANDING & REFRIGERATION) *serves 12*

½ cup (125ml) Cointreau liqueur
2 teaspoons finely grated orange rind
150g (5oz) milk chocolate, melted
90g (3oz) unsalted butter, melted
6 eggs, separated
¾ cup (110g) self-raising flour
⅓ cup (75g) caster (superfine) sugar

MOCHA FILLING

2 teaspoons instant coffee granules
2 tablespoons hot water
300g (9½oz) dark (semi-sweet) chocolate, melted
6 egg yolks

CHOCOLATE BUTTERCREAM

2 tablespoons instant coffee granules
¼ cup (60ml) hot water
200g (6½oz) dark (semi-sweet) chocolate, melted
4 egg yolks
¼ cup (55g) caster (superfine) sugar
185g (6oz) unsalted butter, softened

1 Preheat oven to 180°C/350°F. Grease a deep 22cm (9in) round cake pan; line base with baking paper.
2 Stand liqueur and rind in a bowl for 30 minutes. Strain; reserve rind and liqueur separately.
3 Combine chocolate, butter and rind in a large bowl. Stir in 3 teaspoons of the reserved liqueur, the egg yolks and sifted flour.
4 Beat egg whites in a large bowl with an electric mixer until soft peaks form; gradually add sugar, beating until dissolved between additions. Fold whites into chocolate mixture, in two batches.
5 Pour mixture into pan; bake for 35 minutes. Stand cake in pan for 5 minutes before turning, top-side up, onto a wire rack to cool.

6 Meanwhile, make mocha filling and chocolate buttercream.

7 Split cake into three layers. Place the bottom layer on a serving plate; spread with half the mocha filling. Refrigerate for 15 minutes. Top with second cake layer; spread with remaining mocha filling. Top with third cake layer; refrigerate for 30 minutes. Spread buttercream over top and side of cake; refrigerate for 30 minutes.

MOCHA FILLING Combine coffee and the water in a large bowl; stir in melted chocolate, then yolks and ⅓ cup of the remaining liqueur. Refrigerate until set.

CHOCOLATE BUTTERCREAM Combine coffee and the water in a large bowl; stir in the chocolate and remaining liqueur. Beat yolks and sugar in a small bowl with an electric mixer until thick and creamy; beat in butter in several batches until smooth. Gradually beat in chocolate mixture; refrigerate for 10 minutes or until spreadable.

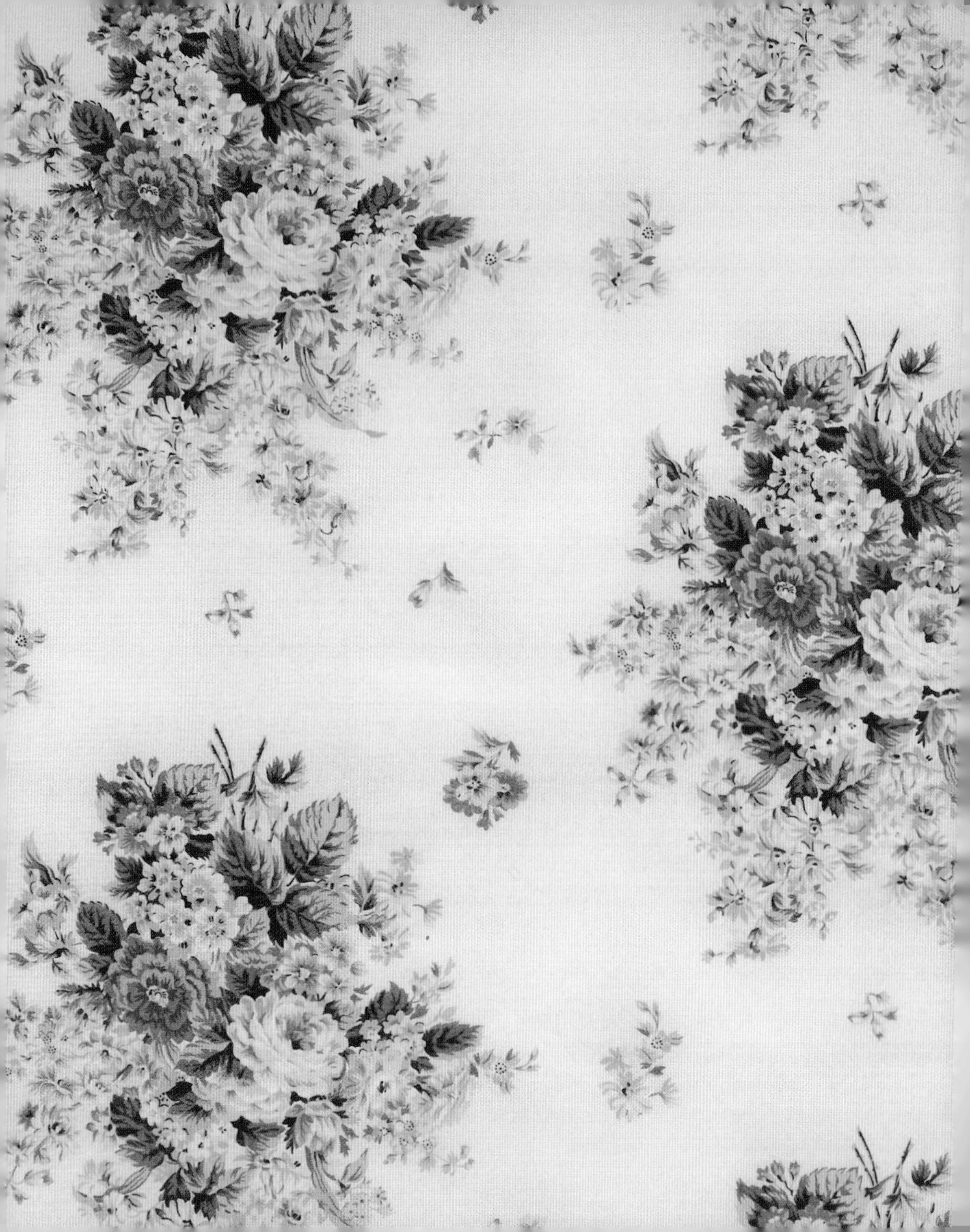

SHOWING OFF

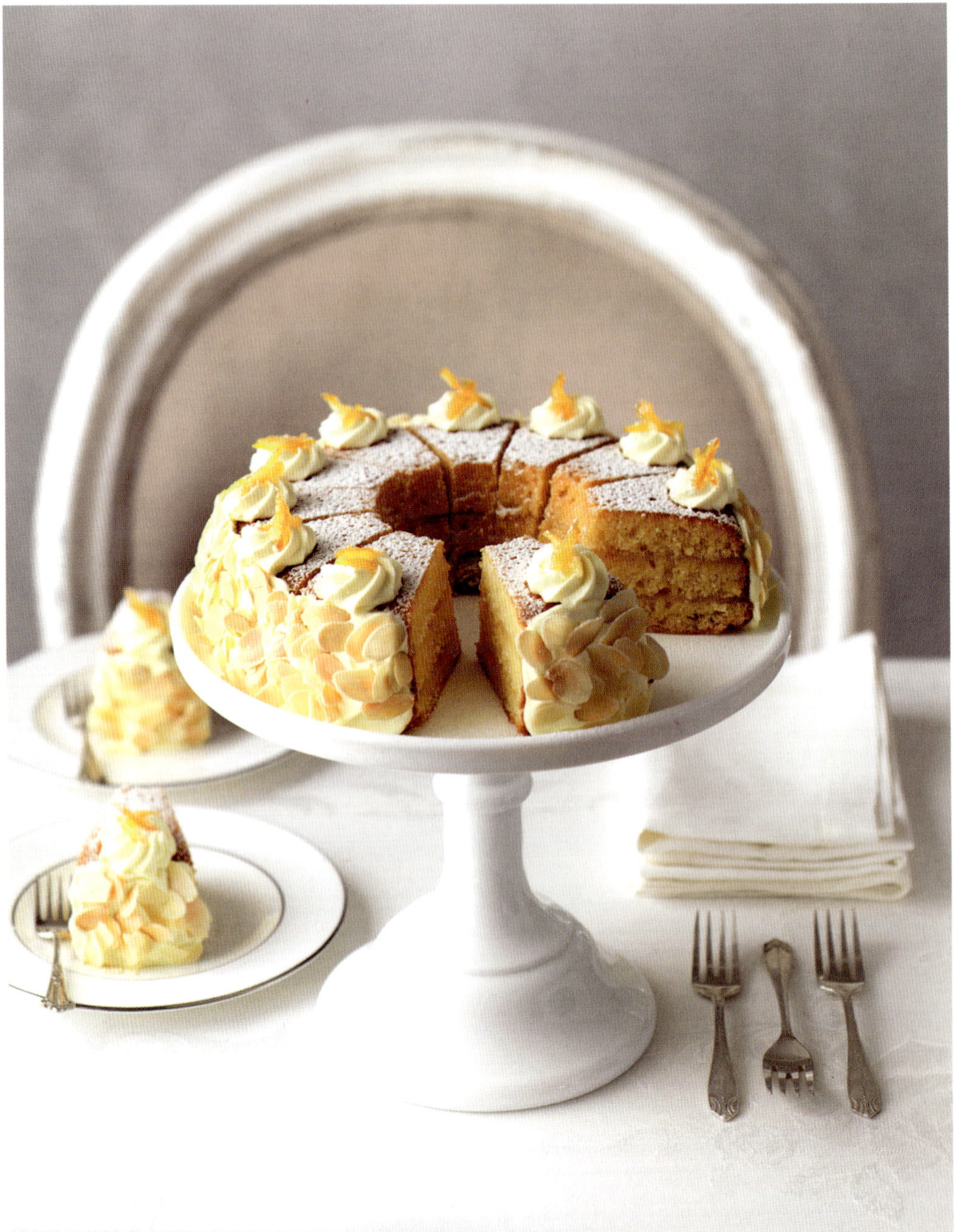

Orange Almond Victoria Sponge

prep + cook time 55 MINUTES (+ COOLING) *serves* 12

185g (6oz) unsalted butter, softened
1 teaspoon vanilla extract
¾ cup (165g) caster (superfine) sugar
3 eggs
¼ cup (60ml) milk
1½ cups (225g) self-raising flour
1 cup (320g) orange marmalade, warmed
300ml thickened (heavy) cream
2 tablespoons icing (confectioners') sugar
½ cup (40g) flaked almonds, roasted

1 Preheat oven to 180°C/350°F. Grease a deep 20cm (8in) ring pan well with butter.

2 Beat butter, vanilla, and caster sugar in a small bowl with an electric mixer until light and fluffy. Beat in eggs, one at a time. Stir in milk and sifted flour, in two batches.

3 Spread mixture into pan; bake for 30 minutes. Turn sponge immediately onto baking-paper-covered wire rack, top-side up, to cool.

4 Meanwhile, strain marmalade through fine sieve; reserve syrup and rind separately.

5 Beat cream and half the icing sugar in a small bowl with an electric mixer until soft peaks form.

6 Split sponge into three layers. Place one layer onto serving plate, cut-side up; spread with half of the marmalade syrup. Top with another layer of sponge and remaining syrup; top with remaining layer of sponge. Cut sponge into twelve pieces, keeping cake in ring shape.

7 Spread two-thirds of the cream around side of sponge; press almonds into cream. Spoon remaining cream into a piping bag fitted with 1cm (½in) fluted tube. Pipe rosettes on top of cake; top with some of the reserved rind. Serve sponge dusted with remaining icing sugar.

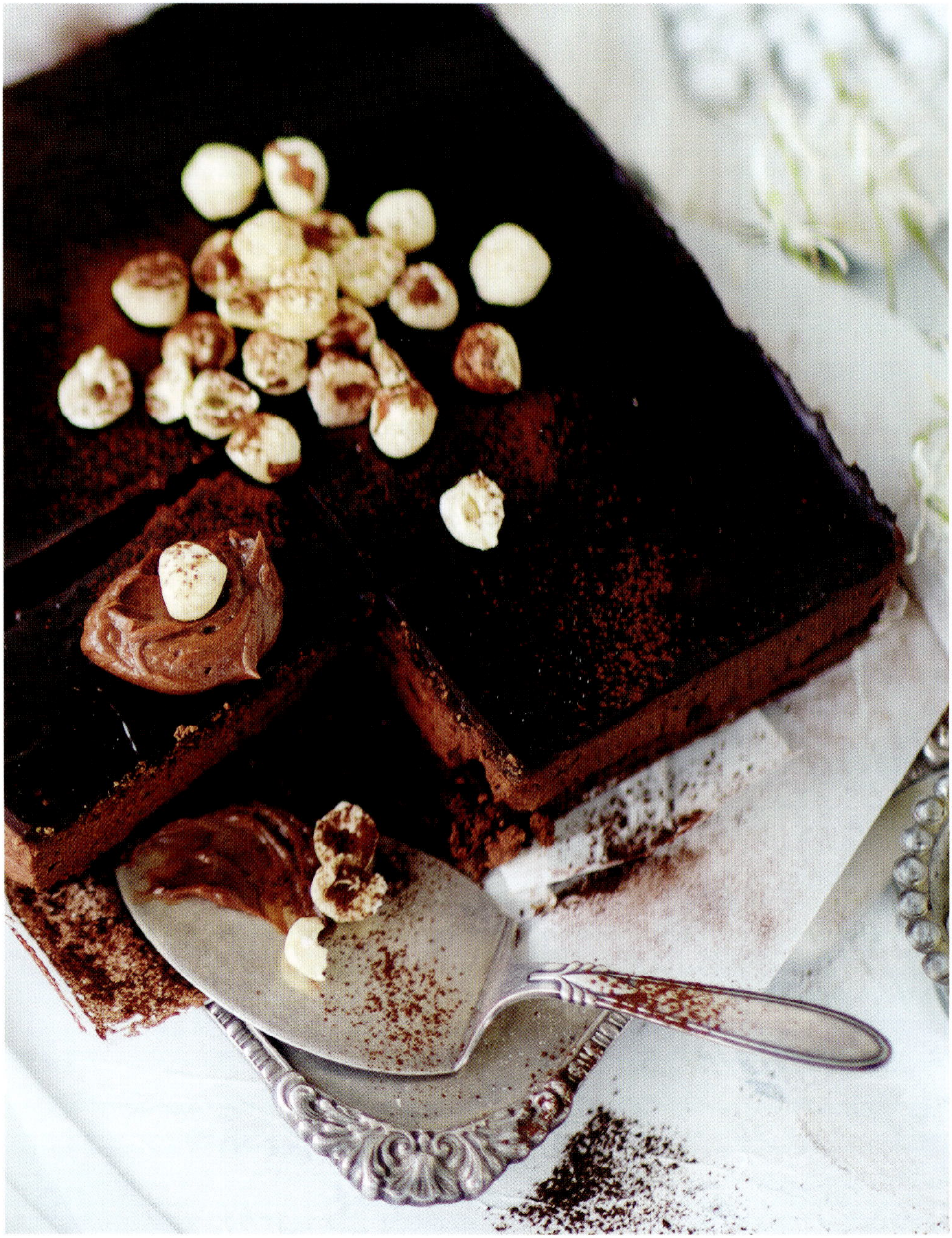

chocolate hazelnut
MOUSSE CAKE

Chocolate Hazelnut Mousse Cake

prep + cook time 1 HOUR 45 MINUTES (+ COOLING & REFRIGERATION) *serves* 8

360g (12oz) dark (semi-sweet) chocolate
2 eggs, separated
¼ cup (55g) caster (superfine) sugar
2 tablespoons cocoa powder
300ml thickened (heavy) cream
¼ cup (40g) icing (confectioners') sugar
2 teaspoons cocoa powder, extra
roasted peeled hazelnuts, to serve

SATIN GLAZE
¼ cup (25g) cocoa powder
2 tablespoons water
80g (2½oz) dark (semi-sweet) chocolate
¼ cup (55g) caster (superfine) sugar
10g (½oz) butter
¼ cup (60ml) pouring cream

HAZELNUT MASCARPONE
⅔ cup (170g) mascarpone
⅓ cup (110g) chocolate-hazelnut spread

1 Preheat oven to 180°C/350°F. Grease a deep 20cm (8in) square cake pan; line base with baking paper.
2 Break 60g (2oz) of the chocolate into a small heatproof bowl. Place bowl over a small saucepan of simmering water (don't let water touch base of bowl); stir until smooth. Cool until just warm.
3 Beat egg whites and caster sugar in a small bowl with an electric mixer until sugar is dissolved. Beat in egg yolks. Fold in sifted cocoa, then melted chocolate. Spread mixture into pan. Bake cake for 10 minutes. Turn cake onto a baking-paper-covered wire rack, then peel away lining paper. Cool.

4 Clean same deep 20cm (8in) square cake pan; grease, then line base and sides with baking paper, extending the paper 5cm (2in) over the sides. Place cooled cake in pan.
5 Break remaining chocolate into a medium heatproof bowl over a medium saucepan of simmering water (don't let water touch the base of bowl); stir until melted and smooth. Cool for 10 minutes.
6 Beat cream and sifted icing sugar in a small bowl with an electric mixer until soft peaks form. Fold cream mixture into melted chocolate, in two batches. Spread mousse over cake in pan; smooth the surface. Cover; refrigerate for 4 hours or until firm.
7 Make satin glaze; spread over mousse in pan. Refrigerate for 1 hour or until firm.
8 Make hazelnut mascarpone.
9 Lift mousse cake out of the pan onto a board. Trim outside edges with a hot dry knife; cut cake into eight rectangles. Place cake pieces on plates; dust with extra cocoa then top with hazelnut mascarpone and hazelnuts.

SATIN GLAZE Blend sifted cocoa with the water in a medium saucepan until it forms a thick paste. Break chocolate into pan, then add remaining ingredients; stir over low heat until smooth. Cool to room temperature.

HAZELNUT MASCARPONE Place the mascarpone in a small bowl; fold in spread.

keeps The mousse cake can be made a day ahead; store in an airtight container in the fridge. Satin glaze and hazelnut mascarpone are best made just before serving.

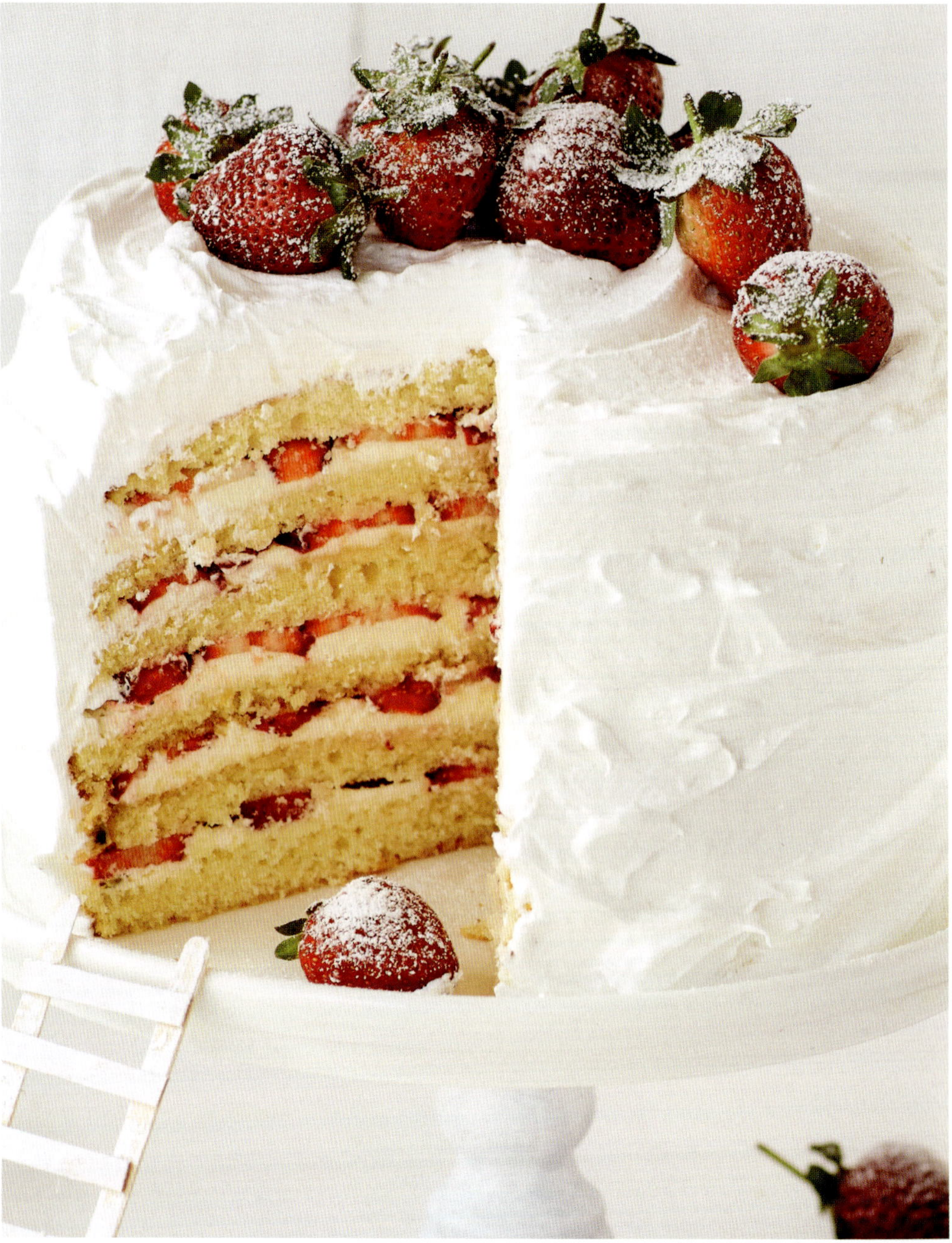

strawberry & passionfruit
MILE HIGH LAYER CAKE

STRAWBERRY & PASSIONFRUIT
MILE HIGH LAYER CAKE

prep + cook time 1 HOUR 50 MINUTES *serves* 12

250g (8oz) butter, softened
2 cups (440g) caster (superfine) sugar
1 teaspoon vanilla extract
4 eggs
2 cups (300g) plain (all-purpose) flour
¼ cup (35g) self-raising flour
¾ cup (180ml) milk
500g (1lb) strawberries
1 tablespoon icing (confectioners') sugar

PASSIONFRUIT CREAM
600ml thickened (heavy) cream
2 tablespoons icing (confectioners') sugar
⅓ cup (80ml) passionfruit pulp

MERINGUE FROSTING
1 cup (220g) caster (superfine) sugar
1 tablespoon glucose syrup
2 tablespoons water
3 egg whites
1 tablespoon caster (superfine) sugar, extra

1 Preheat oven to 160°C/325°F. Grease three 20cm (8in) round sandwich cake pans; line each base with baking paper.
2 Beat butter, sugar and vanilla in a large bowl with an electric mixer until light and fluffy. Beat in eggs, one at a time. Fold in sifted flours and milk, in two batches. Divide mixture evenly into pans.
3 Bake cakes for 35 minutes or until a skewer inserted into the centre comes out clean. Leave cakes in pans for 5 minutes before turning, top-side down, onto wire racks to cool.
4 Meanwhile, make passionfruit cream.

5 Reserve half of the strawberries; thinly slice remaining. Split cooled cakes in half. Place one cake layer on a plate or cake stand; spread with ⅔ cup of the passionfruit cream, top with one-fifth of the sliced strawberries, then another cake layer. Repeat layering, finishing with a cake layer.
6 Make meringue frosting.
7 Spread frosting over top and side of cake. Just before serving, decorate with reserved strawberries and dust with sifted icing sugar.

PASSIONFRUIT CREAM Beat cream in a small bowl with an electric mixer until soft peaks form. Stir in sifted icing sugar and passionfruit.

MERINGUE FROSTING Stir sugar, glucose and the water in a small saucepan over medium heat until sugar dissolves. Bring to the boil; boil for 3 minutes or until syrup reaches 116°C/240°F on a sugar thermometer (or when a teaspoon of syrup, dropped into a cup of cold water, forms a soft ball when rolled between your fingers). Remove from heat to allow bubbles to subside. Meanwhile, beat egg whites in a small bowl with an electric mixer until soft peaks form; beat in extra sugar until dissolved. While motor is operating, pour in hot syrup in a thin steady stream; beat on high speed for 5 minutes or until the mixture is thick.

keeps You can make the cakes a day ahead. Complete the recipe to the end of step 5, then refrigerate for several hours or overnight. Cover the layered cake with meringue frosting no more than 3 hours before serving.

CHOC-STRAWBERRY MERINGUE GATEAU

prep + cook time 1 HOUR 30 MINUTES *serves* 12

125g (4oz) butter, softened
4 eggs, separated
¾ cup (165g) caster (superfine) sugar
1 cup (150g) self-raising flour
⅓ cup (35g) cocoa powder
½ teaspoon bicarbonate of soda (baking soda)
1 cup (250ml) buttermilk
⅓ cup (75g) caster (superfine) sugar, extra
¼ cup (30g) coarsely chopped roasted hazelnuts
⅔ cup (160ml) thickened (heavy) cream
1 tablespoon icing (confectioners') sugar
250g (8oz) strawberries, halved

1 Preheat oven to 160°C/325°F. Grease two 20cm (8in) round cake pans; line bases and sides with baking paper.
2 Beat butter, egg yolks and caster sugar in a medium bowl with an electric mixer until light and fluffy. Stir in combined sifted flour, cocoa and soda, then buttermilk. Divide mixture between pans.
3 Beat egg whites in a small bowl with the electric mixer until soft peaks form; gradually add extra caster sugar, a tablespoon at a time, beating until sugar dissolves between additions.
4 Divide meringue mixture over cake mixture in pans; using a spatula, spread meringue so cake mixture is completely covered. Sprinkle hazelnuts over meringue mixture on one of the cakes.
5 Bake cakes for 25 minutes. Cover pans loosely with foil; bake for a further 20 minutes. Leave cakes in pans for 5 minutes before turning, top-side up, onto wire racks to cool.
6 Beat cream and icing sugar in a small bowl with the electric mixer until soft peaks form. Place the cake without hazelnuts on serving plate; spread with cream mixture. Top with strawberries, then remaining cake.

TIP
This recipe is best made on the day of serving.

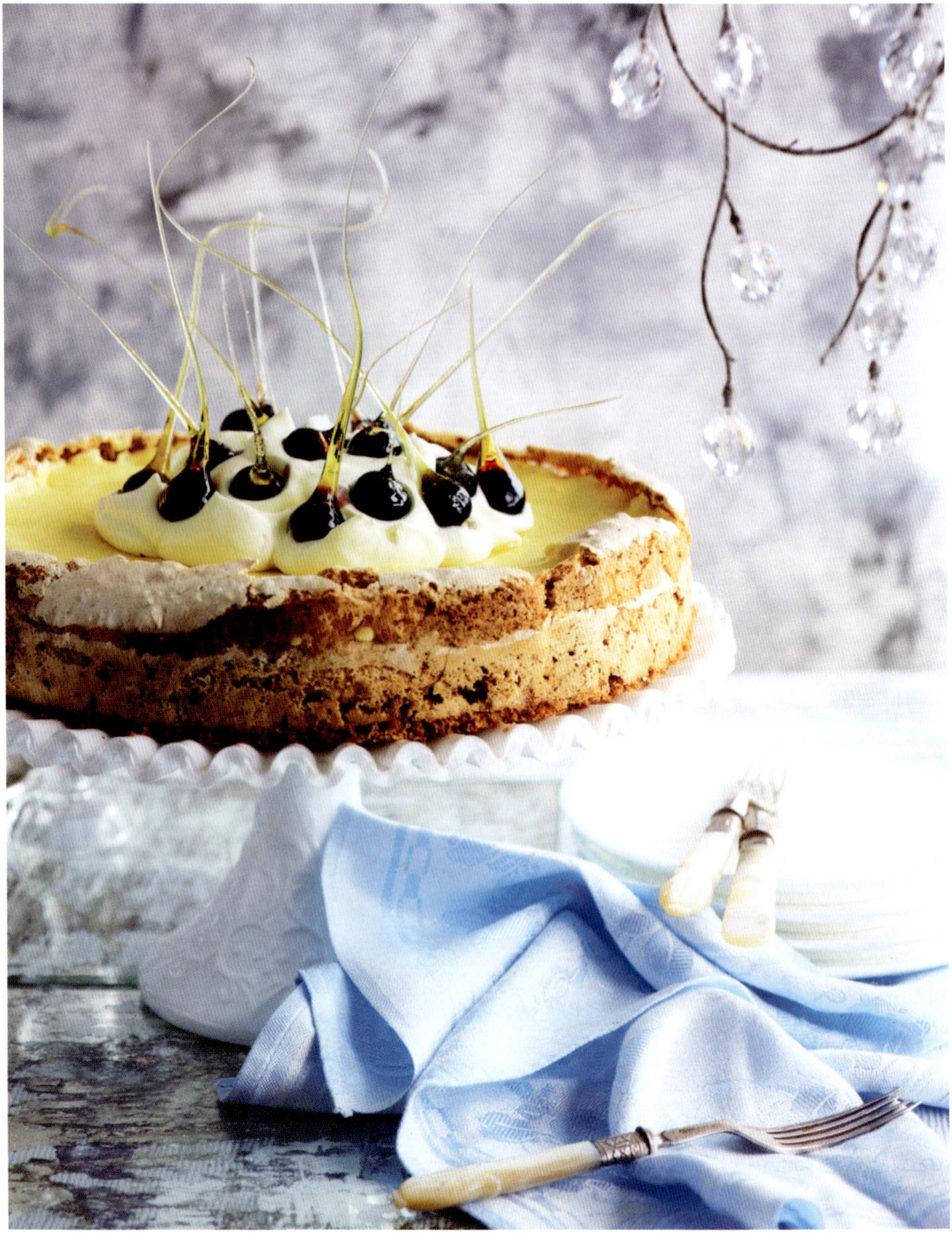

lemon curd meringue cake
WITH TOFFEE-DIPPED
BLUEBERRIES

LEMON CURD MERINGUE CAKE
WITH TOFFEE-DIPPED BLUEBERRIES

prep + cook time 1 HOUR 45 MINUTES (+ COOLING & REFRIGERATION) *serves* 12

1 cup (150g) almonds
4 egg whites
1 cup (220g) caster (superfine) sugar
125g (4oz) white chocolate, grated coarsely
600ml thick (double) cream

LEMON CURD
250g (8oz) cold butter, chopped coarsely
2 eggs, beaten lightly
2/3 cup (160ml) lemon juice
1 1/3 cups (300g) caster (superfine) sugar
2 egg yolks

TOFFEE-DIPPED BLUEBERRIES
1 cup (220g) white (granulated) sugar
1/2 cup (125ml) water
125g (4oz) fresh blueberries

1 Make lemon curd.
2 Preheat oven to 160°C/325°F. Grease a 24cm (9½in) springform pan; insert base of pan upside down to make cake easier to remove. Line base with baking paper.
3 Spread almonds, in a single layer, on an oven tray; roast, uncovered, for 12 minutes or until skins begin to split. Cool. Chop almonds finely.
4 Beat egg whites and ¼ cup of the sugar in a small bowl with an electric mixer until firm peaks form. Add remaining sugar; beat on high speed for 5 minutes or until sugar is dissolved. Fold in chocolate and chopped almonds. Spread mixture into pan.
5 Bake meringue for 40 minutes. Cool in pan.
6 Beat half the cream in a small bowl with an electric mixer until soft peaks form; fold in curd. Spoon curd mixture onto meringue. Refrigerate for several hours or overnight until firm.
7 Before serving, make toffee-dipped blueberries. Spoon remaining cream onto cake; top with toffee-dipped berries. Serve immediately.

LEMON CURD Place butter in a medium saucepan; strain egg into pan. Add remaining ingredients; stir over low heat, without boiling, for 10 minutes or until mixture thickly coats the back of a spoon. Transfer curd to a medium heatproof bowl; refrigerate until cold.

TOFFEE-DIPPED BLUEBERRIES Stir sugar and the water in a small saucepan over medium heat until sugar is dissolved. Bring to the boil; boil, without stirring, until sugar has thickened and turns a caramel colour. Push a wooden toothpick into each blueberry. Remove toffee from heat; allow bubbles to subside. Working with one blueberry at a time, holding by the toothpick, dip berry into thickened toffee. Hold berry above toffee so a trail of toffee falls from the berry. Hold upside down until starting to set. You may need to reheat the toffee if it starts to thicken too much.

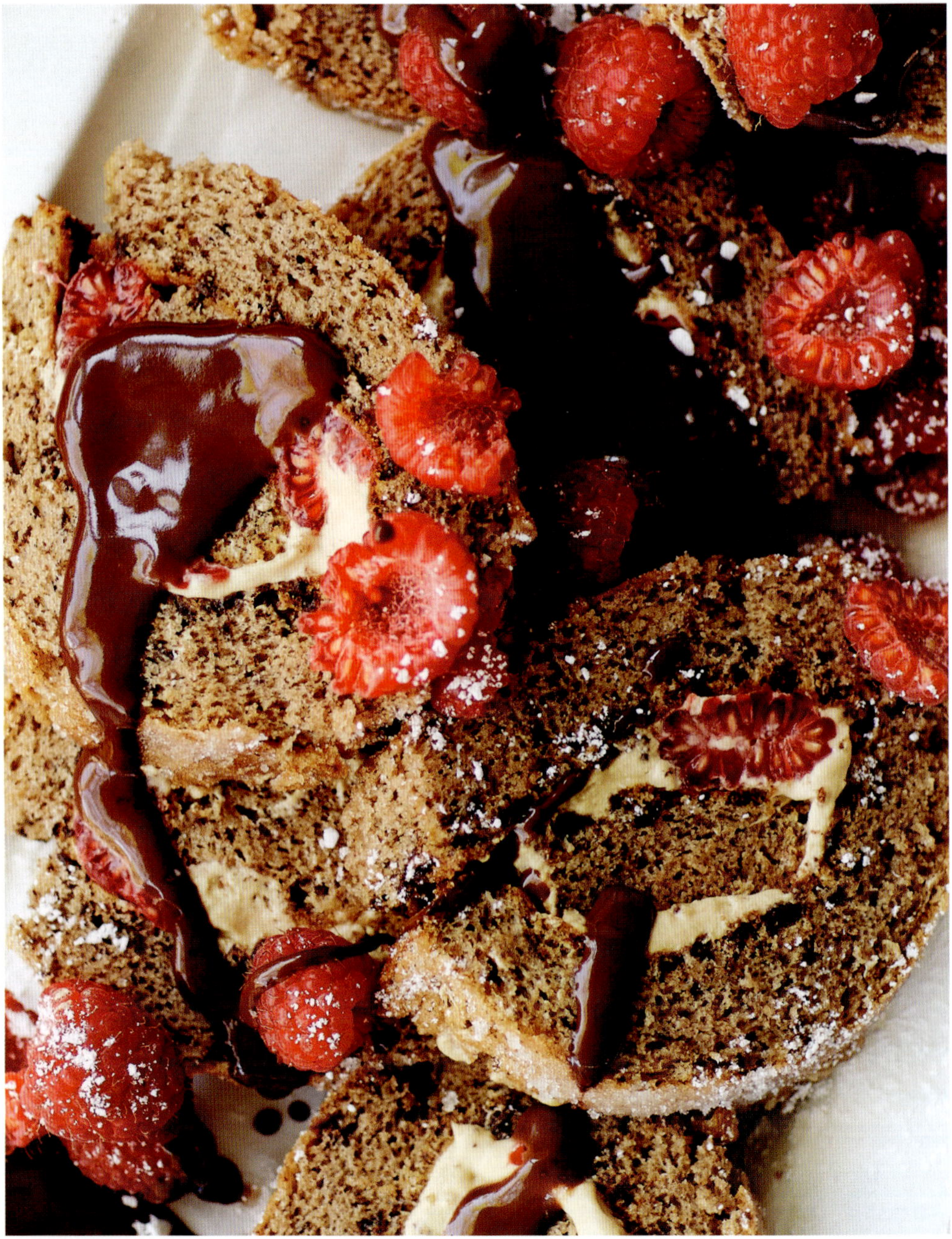

chocolate raspberry &
COFFEE CREAM ROULADE

Chocolate Raspberry & Coffee Cream Roulade

prep + cook time 45 MINUTES (+ COOLING) *serves* 10

5 eggs, separated
⅔ cup (150g) caster (superfine) sugar
1½ tablespoons hot water
80g (2½oz) dark (semi-sweet) chocolate, grated finely
⅔ cup (100g) self-raising flour
¼ cup (55g) caster (superfine) sugar, extra
125g (4oz) raspberries
125g (4oz) raspberries, extra

CHOCOLATE SAUCE

1 cup (250ml) thickened (heavy) cream
150g (5oz) dark (semi-sweet) chocolate, chopped finely

COFFEE CREAM

2 teaspoons instant coffee granules
2 tablespoons boiling water
¾ cup (180ml) thickened (heavy) cream
¼ cup (40g) icing (confectioners') sugar

1 Preheat oven to 200°C/400°F. Grease a 26cm x 32cm (10½in x 12¾in) swiss roll pan; line base with baking paper, extending the paper 5cm (2in) over the long sides.

2 Beat egg yolks and sugar in a medium bowl with an electric mixer for 5 minutes or until very thick. Pour the hot water down the inside of the bowl, then add chocolate; gently fold in sifted flour until just combined. Transfer mixture to a large bowl.

3 Beat egg whites in a medium bowl with an electric mixer until soft peaks form. Fold egg whites into chocolate mixture, in two batches, until just combined. Spread mixture into pan.

4 Bake cake for 12 minutes or until golden and sponge springs back when pressed lightly with a finger.

5 Meanwhile, place a piece of baking paper, cut just larger than the pan, on a work surface; sprinkle evenly with extra sugar. Turn hot sponge onto sugar-covered-paper, peel away lining paper. Working quickly, and using paper as a guide, roll sponge up from a long side. Cool for 5 minutes. Unroll sponge, remove paper; reroll, cover with a clean tea towel. Leave to cool.

6 Meanwhile, make chocolate sauce, then make coffee cream.
7 Unroll sponge; spread with coffee cream leaving a 2.5cm (1in) border. Top with raspberries. Reroll sponge to enclose filling. Serve roulade drizzled with chocolate sauce and scattered with extra raspberries.
CHOCOLATE SAUCE Bring cream almost to the boil in a small saucepan. Add chocolate; remove from heat, stand for 5 minutes. Stir mixture until melted and smooth. Transfer to a serving jug.
COFFEE CREAM Stir coffee and boiling water in a small heatproof cup until dissolved. Cool. Beat cream, sifted icing sugar and cooled coffee in a small bowl with an electric mixer until firm peaks form.

Syrup of honey and sugar, spiked with the juice and rind of citrus, drench a nut-rich layer cake reminiscent of Middle-Eastern baklava.

BAKLAVA TORTE

prep + cook time 1 HOUR 15 MINUTES (+ COOLING) *serves* 12

250g (8oz) butter, softened
½ teaspoon almond extract
1 cup (220g) caster (superfine) sugar
4 eggs
⅓ cup (80ml) milk
1½ cups (225g) self-raising flour
½ cup (60g) almond meal
1 cup (70g) slivered almonds
1 cup (140g) coarsely chopped pistachios
1 cup (110g) coarsely chopped walnuts
250g (8oz) mascarpone
½ cup (125ml) thickened (heavy) cream
½ teaspoon ground cinnamon

HONEY LEMON SYRUP
¾ cup (165g) caster (superfine) sugar
¾ cup (180ml) water
⅓ cup (115g) honey
5cm (2in) strip lemon rind
¼ cup (60ml) lemon juice

1 Preheat oven to 180°C/350°F. Grease two deep 22cm (9in) round cake pans; line bases with baking paper.
2 Beat butter, almond extract and sugar in a medium bowl with an electric mixer until light and fluffy. Beat in eggs, one at a time, until combined. Stir in milk, sifted flour and the almond meal, in two batches.
3 Spread mixture evenly between pans; top with combined slivered almonds, pistachios and walnuts, pressing down lightly.
4 Bake cakes for 35 minutes or until a skewer inserted into the centre comes out clean.
5 Meanwhile, make honey lemon syrup.
6 Using a skewer, pierce hot cakes a few times, then drizzle ¼ cup hot syrup over each hot cake. Cool cakes in pan. Cool remaining syrup.
7 Combine mascarpone, cream and cinnamon in a small bowl.
8 Place one cake on a cake stand or plate; spread with mascarpone cream, then top with remaining cake. Serve cake topped with remaining syrup.
HONEY LEMON SYRUP Stir sugar, the water, honey and rind in a small saucepan over medium heat, without boiling, until sugar dissolves. Bring to the boil. Remove from heat; stir in juice.

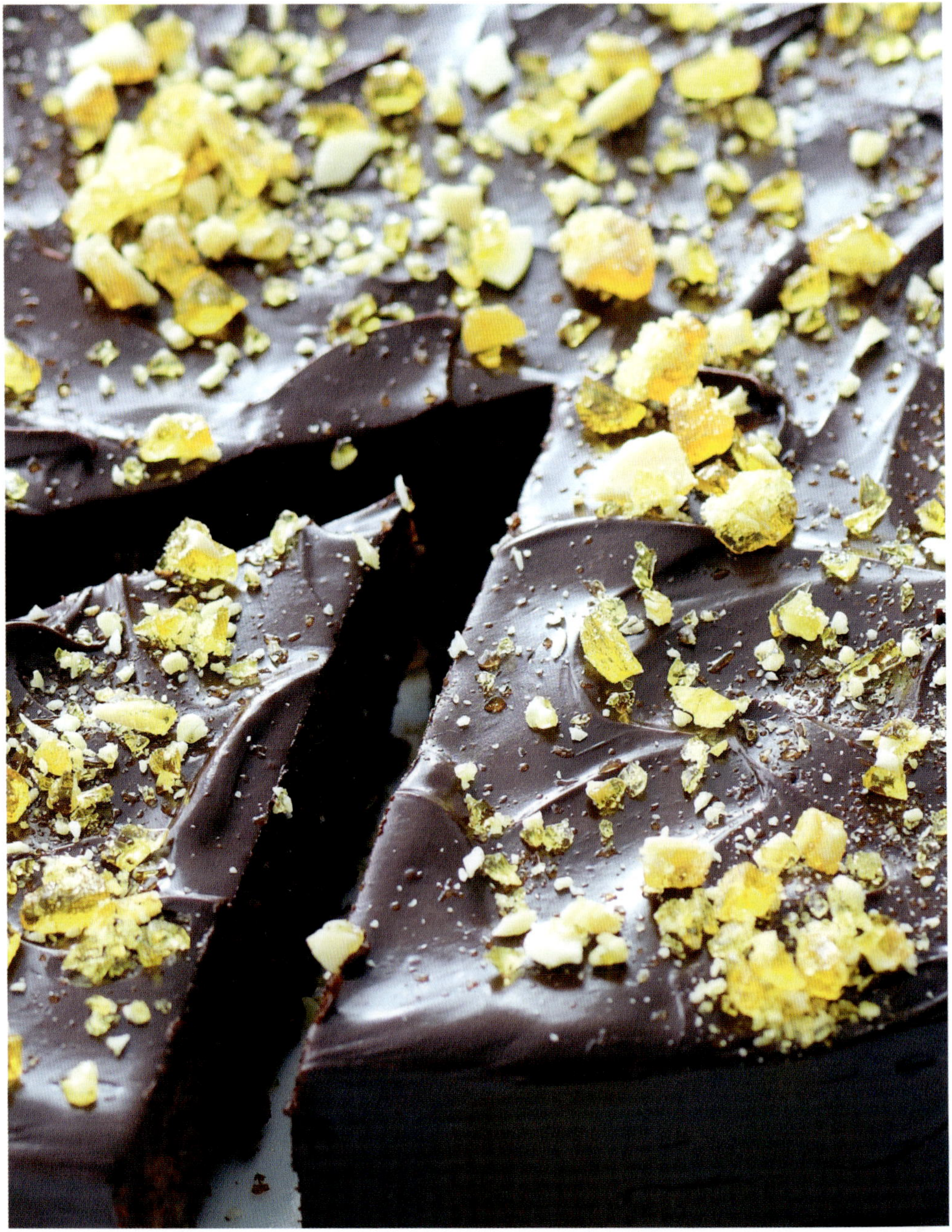

chocolate &
ROASTED ALMOND
TORTE

Chocolate & Roasted Almond Torte

prep + cook time 1 HOUR 15 MINUTES (+ COOLING & STANDING) serves 12

1¼ cups (200g) blanched almonds, roasted
185g (6oz) butter, chopped
200g (6½oz) dark (semi-sweet) chocolate, chopped coarsely
6 eggs, separated
1 cup (220g) caster (superfine) sugar
1 cup (250g) thick (double) cream

ALMOND PRALINE
⅔ cup (50g) flaked almonds
1 cup (220g) caster (superfine) sugar
⅓ cup (80ml) water

CHOCOLATE GLAZE
½ cup (125ml) pouring cream
200g (6½oz) dark (semi-sweet) chocolate, chopped coarsely

1 Preheat oven to 180°C/350°F. Grease a 24cm (9½in) springform pan; line the base and side with baking paper.
2 Blend or process almonds until fine.
3 Stir butter and chocolate in a medium saucepan over low heat until smooth. Cool.
4 Beat egg yolks and sugar in a large bowl with an electric mixer until combined. Beat egg whites in a medium bowl with an electric mixer until soft peaks form.
5 Fold chocolate mixture and almonds into egg yolk mixture; fold in egg white mixture, in two batches. Pour mixture into pan.
6 Bake cake for 40 minutes. Stand in pan for 10 minutes; transfer to a wire rack over an oven tray to cool.
7 Meanwhile, make almond praline, and then chocolate glaze.
8 Spread glaze over top and side of cake; sprinkle top with crushed praline. Serve cake with thick cream and praline shards.

ALMOND PRALINE Preheat oven to 180°C/350°F. Place almonds on a baking-paper-lined oven tray; roast for 5 minutes or until browned lightly. Meanwhile, stir sugar and the water in a small frying pan over medium heat without boiling, until sugar dissolves; bring to the boil. Boil, uncovered, without stirring, until mixture is caramel in colour. Pour toffee over almonds on tray; stand at room temperature until set. Break about one-third of the praline into pieces; place in a resealable plastic bag, seal tightly. Smash praline with a rolling pin or meat mallet until crushed finely. Break remaining praline into large shards.

CHOCOLATE GLAZE Bring cream to the boil in a small saucepan. Remove from heat; stir in chocolate until smooth.

keeps This cake will keep in an airtight container for up to 3 days.
serving suggestion Serve with vanilla ice-cream.

toffee
TUMBLES

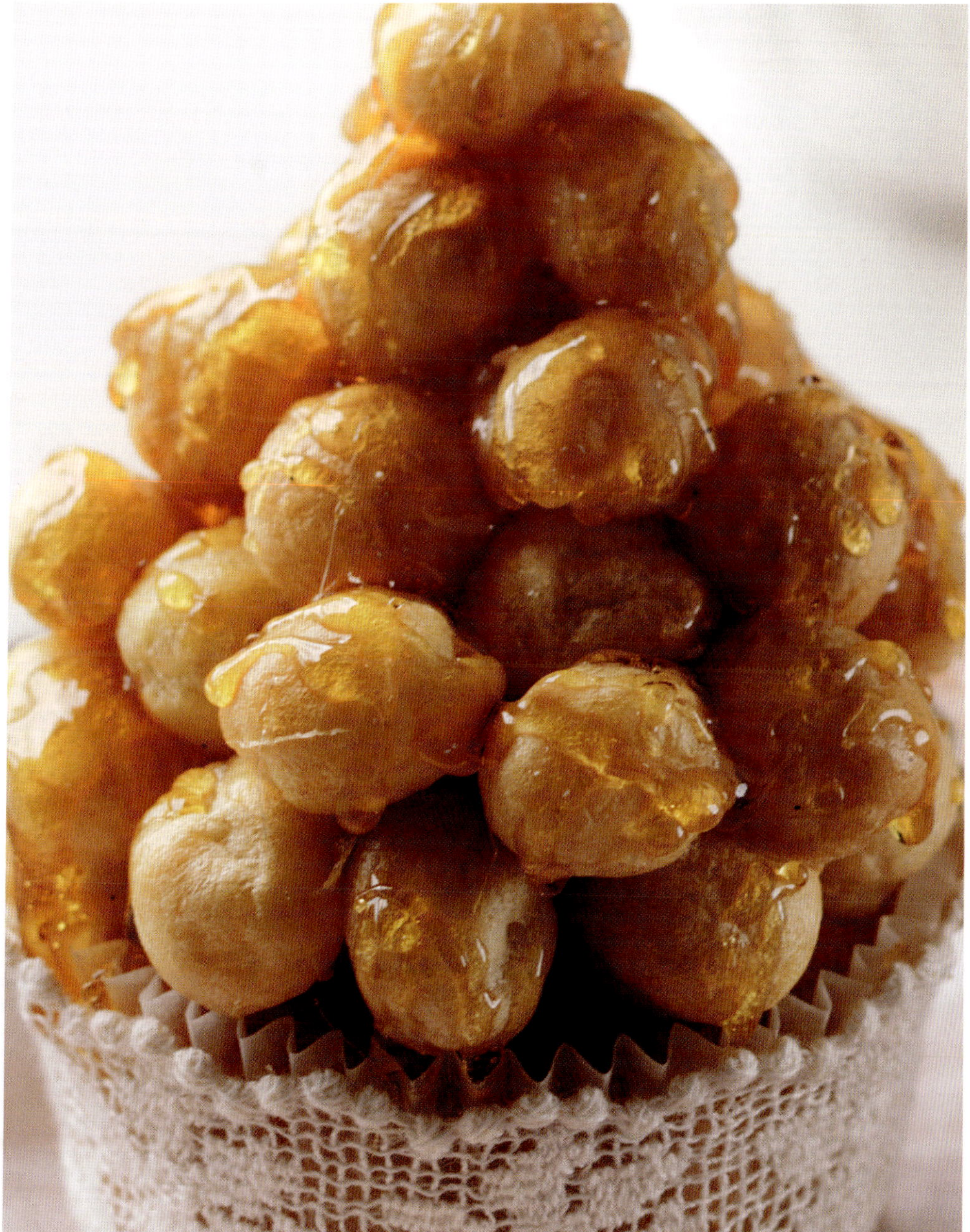

TOFFEE TUMBLES

prep + cook time 3 HOURS 30 MINUTES (+ COOLING) ❋ *makes* 12

155g (5oz) butter, softened
½ teaspoon almond extract
⅔ cup (150g) caster (superfine) sugar
2 eggs
⅓ cup (50g) self-raising flour
½ cup (75g) plain (all-purpose) flour
½ cup (60g) almond meal

CHOUX PUFFS
60g (2oz) butter
¾ cup (180ml) water
¾ cup (105g) plain (all-purpose) flour
3 eggs, beaten lightly

VANILLA CUSTARD
1¼ cups (310ml) milk
1 vanilla bean, split
4 egg yolks
½ cup (110g) caster (superfine) sugar
¼ cup (40g) cornflour (cornstarch)

TOFFEE
1 cup (220g) caster (superfine) sugar
½ cup (125ml) water

1 Make choux puffs; make vanilla custard.
2 Line 12-hole (⅓-cup/80ml) muffin pan with paper cases.
3 Beat butter, almond extract, sugar and eggs in a small bowl with an electric mixer until light and fluffy. Stir in sifted flours and almond meal, in two batches. Divide mixture into paper cases; smooth surface.
4 Bake for 20 minutes at 180°C/350°F. Stand cakes in pan for 5 minutes before turning, top-side up, onto a wire rack to cool.
5 Cut 2cm (¾in) deep hole in centre of cooled cakes, fill with custard; replace lid. Spread cakes with a little more custard; top with a layer of puffs. Stack remaining puffs on cakes, dipping each in a little custard to hold in place.
6 Make toffee; drizzle over puffs.

CHOUX PUFFS Preheat oven to 220°C/425°F. Grease oven trays, line with baking paper. Combine butter and the water in a medium saucepan; bring to the boil. Add flour; beat with a wooden spoon over medium heat until mixture forms a smooth ball. Transfer mixture to small bowl; beat in egg with an electric mixer, in about six batches, until mixture becomes glossy. Spoon mixture into a piping bag fitted with a 1cm (½in) plain tube. Pipe about 300 tiny dollops of pastry (about ¼ level teaspoon), 2cm (¾in) apart, onto trays; bake for 7 minutes. Reduce oven temperature to 180°C/350°F; bake puffs a further 5 minutes or until crisp (see tip). Leave oven on to bake cupcakes.

VANILLA CUSTARD Boil milk and vanilla bean in a small saucepan; remove from heat, discard bean. Beat egg yolks, sugar and cornflour in a small bowl with an electric mixer until thick. Gradually beat in warm milk; return to pan. Stir over medium heat until mixture boils and thickens. Cover surface of custard with plastic wrap; cool.

TOFFEE Combine sugar with the water in a small heavy-based saucepan. Stir over medium heat, without boiling, until sugar dissolves. Boil, then simmer, uncovered, without stirring, until mixture is golden. Remove from heat; stand until bubbles subside before using.

tip Puffs must be baked for the total cooking time before the next batch can be baked.

GLOSSARY

allspice also known as pimento or jamaican pepper; so-named because it tastes like a combination of nutmeg, cumin, clove and cinnamon. Available whole or ground.
almonds
blanched brown skins removed.
flaked paper-thin slices of blanched or natural almonds.
meal also known as ground almonds; powdered to a coarse flour-like texture.
slivered small pieces cut lengthways.
vienna toffee-coated almonds.
baking powder a raising agent consisting mainly of two parts cream of tartar to one part bicarbonate of soda (baking soda).
bicarbonate of soda (baking soda) a raising agent used in baking.
butter use salted or unsalted (sweet) butter; 125g is equal to one stick (4oz) of butter.
buttermilk in spite of its name, buttermilk is actually low in fat. Originally the term given to the slightly sour liquid left after butter was churned from cream, today it is made from low-fat milk to which bacterial cultures have been added during the manufacturing process.

cardamom a spice native to India; can be purchased in pod, seed or ground form. Has a distinctive aromatic and sweetly rich flavour.
cheese
cream commonly known as Philadelphia or Philly, a soft cow's-milk cheese with a fat content of at least 33%. Sold at supermarkets in bulk or in smaller-sized packages.
mascarpone an Italian fresh cultured-cream product made similarly to yoghurt. Soft, creamy and spreadable, it is used in Italian desserts and as an accompaniment to fresh fruit.
ricotta a soft, sweet, moist, white cow-milk cheese with a low fat content and a slightly grainy texture. The name roughly translates as 'cooked again' and refers to ricotta's manufacture from a whey that is itself a by-product of other cheese making.
cherries, glacé also called candied cherries; boiled in a heavy sugar syrup then dried.
chocolate
dark (semi-sweet) also called luxury chocolate; made of a high percentage of cocoa liquor and cocoa butter, and a little added sugar.
milk the most popular eating chocolate, mild and very sweet; similar to dark with the difference being the addition of milk solids.
white contains no cocoa solids but derives its sweet flavour from cocoa butter. Is very sensitive to heat, so watch carefully when melting.
chocolate hazelnut spread also known as Nutella; made of cocoa powder, hazelnuts, sugar and milk.
cinnamon dried inner bark of the shoots of the cinnamon tree; available in stick (quill) or ground form.
cloves dried flower buds of a tropical tree; can be used whole or in ground form. Has a distinctively pungent and 'spicy' scent and flavour.
cocoa powder also known as cocoa; dried, unsweetened, roasted then ground cocoa beans (cacao seeds).
coconut
cream obtained commercially from the first pressing of the coconut flesh alone, without the addition of water. Available from most supermarkets.
desiccated concentrated, dried, unsweetened and finely shredded coconut flesh.

flaked dried flaked coconut flesh.
oil is extracted from the coconut flesh so you don't get any of the fibre, protein or carbohydrates present in the whole coconut.
cornflour (cornstarch) available made from 100% corn (maize) or wheat; used as a thickening agent.
cream
pouring also called fresh, single or pure cream. It has no additives and a minimum fat content of 35%.
sour a thick cultured soured cream. Minimum fat content of 35%.
thick (double) a dolloping cream with a minimum fat content of 45%.
thickened (heavy) a whipping cream containing a thickener; has a minimum fat content of 35%.
cream of tartar the acid ingredient in baking powder; added to confectionery mixtures to help prevent sugar from crystallising. Keeps frostings creamy and improves volume when beating egg whites.
custard powder instant mixture used to make pouring custard; it is similar in texture and flavour to North American instant pudding mixes.

essence/extract an essence is either a distilled concentration of a food quality or an artificial creation of it. Coconut and almond essences are synthetically produced. An extract is made by extracting the flavour from a food product. In the case of vanilla, pods are soaked, usually in alcohol, to capture the authentic flavour. Essences and extracts keep indefinitely if stored in a cool dark place.
flour
plain (all-purpose) unbleached wheat flour is the best for baking: the gluten content ensures a strong dough, which produces a light result.
rice very fine, almost powdery, gluten-free flour; made from ground white rice.
self-raising plain flour that has been sifted with baking powder in the proportion of 1 cup flour to 2 teaspoons baking powder.
strong baker's also known as gluten-enriched, baker's or bread-mix flour. Produced from a variety of wheat that has a high gluten content and is best suited for pizza and bread making.
food colouring dyes that can be used to change the colour of various foods; are edible and do not change the taste to a noticeable extent.

gelatine if using gelatine leaves, three teaspoons of powdered gelatine (8g or one sachet) is roughly equivalent to four gelatine leaves.
ghee clarified butter; with the milk solids removed, this fat has a high smoking point so can be heated to a high temperature without burning.
ginger
glacé fresh ginger root preserved in sugar syrup.
ground also called powdered ginger; used as a flavouring but cannot be substituted for fresh ginger.
glucose syrup also known as liquid glucose, made from wheat starch; used in jam and confectionery making.
golden syrup a by-product of refined sugarcane; pure maple syrup or honey can be substituted.
liqueurs
cointreau citrus-flavoured liqueur.
Grand Marnier orange liqueur based on cognac-brandy.
hazelnut-flavoured we use frangelico.
limoncello Italian lemon-flavoured liqueur; originally made from the juice and peel of lemons grown along the Amalfi coast.

rum we use a dark underproof rum (not overproof) for a more subtle flavour in cooking.

maple syrup, pure distilled from the sap of sugar maple trees. Maple-flavoured syrup or pancake syrup is not an adequate substitute for the real thing.

marsala a fortified Italian wine; recognisable by its intense amber colour and complex aroma.

marzipan made from ground almonds, sugar and glucose. Similar to almond paste but is not as strong in flavour; is finer in consistency and more pliable. Cheaper brands often use ground apricot kernels and sugar.

milk we use full-cream homogenised milk unless stated otherwise.

caramel top 'n' fill a canned milk product consisting of condensed milk that has been boiled to a caramel.

soy rich creamy 'milk' extracted from soya beans that have been crushed in hot water and strained. It has a nutty flavour.

sweetened condensed a canned milk product consisting of milk with more than half the water content removed and sugar added to the remaining milk.

oil
coconut see *Coconut*
olive made from ripened olives. Extra virgin and virgin are the first and second press, respectively, of the olives; "light" refers to taste not fat levels.

vegetable any of a number of oils sourced from plant rather than animal fats.

orange blossom water also called orange flower water; concentrated flavouring made from orange blossoms. Available from Middle-Eastern food stores, delicatessens and some supermarkets.

pastry
fillo paper-thin sheets of raw pastry; brush each sheet with oil or melted butter, stack in layers, then cut and fold as directed.
sheets packaged ready-rolled sheets of frozen puff and shortcrust pastry.

polenta also known as cornmeal; a flour-like cereal made of ground corn (maize). Also the name of the dish made from it.

rice malt syrup also known as brown rice syrup or rice syrup; is made by cooking brown rice flour with enzymes to break down its starch into sugars from which the water is removed.

rosewater extract made from crushed rose petals; used for its aromatic quality in many sweetmeats and desserts.

semolina coarsely ground flour milled from durum wheat; the flour used in making gnocchi, pasta and couscous.

sugar
brown an extremely soft, finely granulated sugar retaining molasses for its characteristic colour and flavour.
caster (superfine) also called finely granulated table sugar.

demerara a granulated, golden coloured sugar with a distinctive rich flavour; often used to sweeten coffee.
icing (confectioners') also known as powdered sugar; granulated sugar crushed together with a little added cornflour (cornstarch).
icing pure (confectioners') also known as powdered sugar, but has no added cornflour (cornstarch).
pearl also called nib or hail sugar; a product of refined white sugar, it is very coarse, hard, opaque white, and doesn't melt during baking. Available from specialist food stores.
white (granulated) also called crystal sugar; coarse, granulated table sugar.

treacle a concentrated, refined sugar syrup with a distinctive flavour and dark black colour.

vanilla
bean dried, long, thin pod from a tropical golden orchid; the minuscule black seeds inside the bean are used to impart a luscious vanilla flavour.
extract obtained from vanilla beans infused in water; a non-alcoholic version of essence.
paste made from vanilla beans and contains real seeds. Is highly concentrated: 1 teaspoon replaces a whole vanilla bean.

yoghurt, Greek-style plain yoghurt that has been strained in a cloth (muslin) to remove the whey and to give it a creamy consistency.

CONVERSION CHART

MEASURES

One Australian metric measuring cup holds approximately 250ml; one Australian metric tablespoon holds 20ml; one Australian metric teaspoon holds 5ml.

The difference between one country's measuring cups and another's is within a two- or three-teaspoon variance, and will not affect your cooking results. North America, New Zealand and the United Kingdom use a 15ml tablespoon.

All cup and spoon measurements are level. The most accurate way of measuring dry ingredients is to weigh them. When measuring liquids, use a clear glass or plastic jug with metric markings.

We use large eggs with an average weight of 60g.

DRY MEASURES

metric	imperial
15g	½oz
30g	1oz
60g	2oz
90g	3oz
125g	4oz (¼lb)
155g	5oz
185g	6oz
220g	7oz
250g	8oz (½lb)
280g	9oz
315g	10oz
345g	11oz
375g	12oz (¾lb)
410g	13oz
440g	14oz
470g	15oz
500g	16oz (1lb)
750g	24oz (1½lb)
1kg	32oz (2lb)

LIQUID MEASURES

metric	imperial
30ml	1 fluid oz
60ml	2 fluid oz
100ml	3 fluid oz
125ml	4 fluid oz
150ml	5 fluid oz
190ml	6 fluid oz
250ml	8 fluid oz
300ml	10 fluid oz
500ml	16 fluid oz
600ml	20 fluid oz
1000ml (1 litre)	32 fluid oz

LENGTH MEASURES

3mm	⅛in
6mm	¼in
1cm	½in
2cm	¾in
2.5cm	1in
5cm	2in
6cm	2½in
8cm	3in
10cm	4in
13cm	5in
15cm	6in
18cm	7in
20cm	8in
23cm	9in
25cm	10in
28cm	11in
30cm	12in (1ft)

OVEN TEMPERATURES

These are conventional temperatures. If you have a fan-forced oven (ie. not conventional), decrease temperatures by 10-20 degrees.

	°C (celsius)	°F (fahrenheit)
Very slow	120	250
Slow	150	300
Moderately slow	160	325
Moderate	180	350
Moderately hot	200	400
Hot	220	425
Very hot	240	475

INDEX

A

apple
  apple & cardamom tart 127
  apple, cranberry & white chocolate biscotti 74
  apple custard teacake 220
  apple streusel slice 110
  caramelised 104–5
  mini apple tarte tatins 104–5
apricot brandy glaze 137

B

baklava torte 279
banana caramel layer cake 238
banoffee tartlets 131
berries
  mixed berry & ricotta tart 138
  mixed berry cake with vanilla bean syrup 209
blueberries
  lemon curd & blueberry mille feuille 94
  toffee-dipped blueberries 272–3

C

cappuccino macaroons 38
caramel
  banana caramel layer cake 238
  caramelised apple 104–5
  chocolate caramel slice 117
  whipped caramel butter 29

carrot cakes 155
cheesecake, mini baked lemon 137
cherries
  cherry bakewell tarts 141
  cherry teacake 224
chocolate
  apple, cranberry & white chocolate biscotti 74
  buttercream 254–5
  choc-strawberry meringue gateau 268
  chocolate almond macaroons 45
  chocolate & roasted almond torte 282–3
  chocolate brownie slice 122
  chocolate caramel slice 117
  chocolate chunk & raspberry cookies 61
  chocolate hazelnut mousse cake 262–3
  chocolate raspberry & coffee cream roulade 276–7
  dark chocolate ganache 186
  double chocolate puffs 85
  éclairs 82–3
  glaze 82–3, 282–3
  honeyed white chocolate ganache 41
  lemon & lime white chocolate mud cake 191
  melting moments 65
  mini chocolate hazelnut cakes 171
  mousse 85
  pistachio & white chocolate macaroons 41

(*chocolate* continued)
  sauce 276–7
  triple chocolate & hazelnut biscotti 70
  white chocolate ganache 38, 42
  white chocolate mousse 158–9
  white chocolate raspberry lamingtons 158–9
chouquettes 89
choux puffs 286–7
cinnamon teacake 227
citrus coconut biscotti 66
coconut
  citrus coconut biscotti 66
  coconut ice cakes 164
  coconut ice frosting 164
  coconut macaroons 42
  creamy coconut cake 250
  frosting 250
  ganache 191
  passionfruit curd & coconut tarts 150–1
coffee
  buttercream 248–9
  chocolate raspberry & coffee cream roulade 276–7
  coffee & walnut cake 182
  coffee hazelnut meringues 34
  cream 276–7
  syrup 248–9
cranberries
  apple, cranberry & white chocolate biscotti 74
custard 220
  apple custard teacake 220
  cream 82–3
  vanilla 286–7

D

date
  mini date & ginger rock cakes 25
  scones with whipped caramel butter 29

E

espresso syrup cake 213

F

fig & walnut friands 160
fillings
  almond 141
  chocolate mousse 85
  crème pâtissière 92–3
  custard cream 82–3
  lime buttercream 58
  mascarpone cream 86
  mocha pastry cream 98
  mock cream 144–5
  passionfruit cream 54
  praline cream 78
  white chocolate mousse 158–9
friands
  fig & walnut 160

G

ganache 248–9
  coconut 191
  dark chocolate 186
  honeyed white chocolate 41

(*ganache* continued)
  whipped hazelnut 171
  white chocolate 38, 42
gateau
  choc-strawberry meringue 268
  opera 248–9
  rich mocha 254–5
ginger
  gingerbread scones with lemon glacé icing 10
  lime & ginger kisses 58
  marmalade, ginger & almond slice 109
  mini date & ginger rock cakes 25
glaze 248–9
  apricot brandy 137
  chocolate 82–3, 282–3
  lemon 141
  satin 262–3
gluten-free raspberry & lemon syrup cake 202

H

honey
  honey lemon syrup 279
  honeyed white chocolate ganache 41
  lemon, honey & pistachio biscotti 69

I

icing 172 *see also* ganache
  butter frosting 185

(*icing* continued)
  chocolate buttercream 254–5
  coconut frosting 250
  coconut ice frosting 164
  coffee buttercream 248–9
  coffee cream 276–7
  glacé 144–5
  lemon 194–5
  lemon cream cheese frosting 155
  lemon glacé 10
  lemon mascarpone frosting 237
  lime buttercream 58
  mascarpone frosting 241
  meringue frosting 266–7
  mocha filling 254–5
  passionfruit 114
  passionfruit cream 266–7
  raspberry glacé 86, 181
  rosewater buttercream 245
  whipped custard 167

J

jam tarts 128

L

lamingtons
  white chocolate raspberry 158–9
lemon
  almond, lemon & pine nut teacake 228
  curd 94
  curd mascarpone 188
  glacé icing 10

(*lemon* continued)
  glaze 141
  gluten-free raspberry & lemon syrup cake 202
  honey lemon syrup 279
  icing 194–5
  lemon & earl grey chiffon cake 194–5
  lemon & lime white chocolate mud cake 191
  lemon cream cheese frosting 155
  lemon crème brulee tarts 134–5
  lemon curd & blueberry mille feuille 94
  lemon curd meringue cake with toffee-dipped blueberries 272–3
  lemon, honey & pistachio biscotti 69
  lemon liqueur macaroons 37
  lemon mascarpone frosting 237
  lemon mascarpone layer cake 237
  lemon meringue kisses 46
  mini baked lemon cheesecakes 137
  syrup 202, 205
  zesty lemon sour cream cake 188
lime
  buttercream 58
  lemon & lime white chocolate mud cake 191
  lime & ginger kisses 58
  lime & poppy seed syrup cake 206
  lime syrup buttermilk cake 198
  syrup 198, 206

M

madeira cake 231
madeleines 168
maple & cashew loaf 232
marble cake 185
marmalade, ginger & almond slice 109
mascarpone
  cream 86
  frosting 241
  hazelnut 262–3
  lemon mascarpone frosting 237
  lemon mascarpone layer cake 237
  marbled raspberry mascarpone puffs 86
  matchsticks 97
meringue 175
  choc-strawberry meringue gateau 268
  coffee hazelnut 34
  frosting 266–7
  lemon curd meringue cake with toffee-dipped blueberries 272–3
  lemon meringue kisses 46
  rosewater & raspberry swirl meringues 49
mocha
  filling 254–5
  hedgehog slice 113
  pastry cream 98
  puffs 98
  rich mocha gateau 254–5
mud cake, Mississippi 186

N

Neapolitan meringue cupcakes 175
neenish & pineapple tarts 144–5
nuts
  almond bread 73
  almond filling 141
  almond, lemon & pine nut teacake 228
  almond praline 282–3

(*nuts* continued)
  chocolate almond macaroons 45
  chocolate & roasted almond torte 282–3
  chocolate hazelnut mousse cake 262–3
  coffee & walnut cake 182
  fig & walnut friands 160
  hazelnut mascarpone 262–3
  lemon, honey & pistachio biscotti 69
  maple & cashew loaf 232
  marmalade, ginger & almond slice 109
  mini chocolate hazelnut cakes 171
  orange almond halva cake 201
  orange almond victoria sponge 259
  pistachio & rosewater layer cake 245
  pistachio & white chocolate macaroons 41
  plum & almond turnovers 101
  raspberry almond petit fours 172
  spiced nut teacake 219
  spiced nuts 219
  triple chocolate & hazelnut biscotti 70

O

opera gateau 248–9
orange
  orange almond halva cake 201
  orange almond victoria sponge 259
  orange & brandy syrup 201
  orange & rhubarb semolina syrup cake 210
  orange rhubarb syrup 210
  teacake 216

P

Paris brest 78
passionfruit
   passionfruit cream biscuits 54
   passionfruit curd & coconut tarts 150–1
   strawberry & passionfruit mile high layer cake 266–7
   vanilla passionfruit slice 114
peanut butter cookies 53
pear
   pear & raspberry streusel slice 121
   poached 223
   poached pear & nutmeg teacake 223
pineapple
   neenish & pineapple tarts 144–5
pink velvet cake 241
pistachio & white chocolate macaroons 41
plum & almond turnovers 101
popcake puffs 92–3
praline
   almond 282–3
   cream 78
pumpkin scones, prize-winning 17

R

raspberry
   chocolate chunk & raspberry cookies 61
   chocolate raspberry & coffee cream roulade 276–7
   gluten-free raspberry & lemon syrup cake 202
   macaroon dreams 33
   marbled raspberry mascarpone puffs 86

(*raspberry* continued)
   pear & raspberry streusel slice 121
   raspberry almond petit fours 172
   raspberry & pink peppercorn polenta scrolls 20–1
   raspberry cream sponge 181
   raspberry glacé icing 86, 181
   raspberry powder puffs 163
   raspberry trifle cupcakes 167
   rosewater & raspberry swirl meringues 49
   white chocolate raspberry lamingtons 158–9
refrigerator slice-and-bake cookies 57
rhubarb
   orange & rhubarb semolina syrup cake 210
   orange rhubarb syrup 210
   rhubarb frangipane tarts 147
ricotta
   mixed berry & ricotta tart 138
rock cakes 26
mini date & ginger 25

S

scones
   date scones with whipped caramel butter 29
   gingerbread scones with lemon glacé icing 10
   hot cross bun 22
   prize-winning pumpkin 17
   scones with jam & cream 9
   strawberry bliss 14
   vanilla bean 13
scrolls
   raspberry & pink peppercorn polenta 20–1
semolina
   orange & rhubarb semolina syrup cake 210

(*semolina* continued)
   semolina & yoghurt syrup cake 205
shortbread, lavender 62
sponge
   orange almond victoria 259
   raspberry cream 181
strawberry
   choc-strawberry meringue gateau 268
   strawberry & passionfruit mile high layer cake 266–7
   strawberry bliss scones 14
streusel topping 110, 121

T

tiramisu torte 242
toffee tumbles 286–7
torte
   baklava 279
   chocolate & roasted almond torte 282–3
Turkish delight slice 118

V

vanilla
   custard 286–7
   sugar 224
   vanilla bean scones 13
   vanilla bean syrup 209
   vanilla passionfruit slice 114
velvet cake, pink 241

Y

yoghurt
   semolina & yoghurt syrup cake 205

PUBLISHED IN 2019 BY BAUER MEDIA BOOKS, AUSTRALIA.
BAUER MEDIA BOOKS IS A DIVISION OF BAUER MEDIA PTY LIMITED.

BAUER MEDIA GROUP
Chief executive officer Paul Dykzeul
Chief financial officer Andrew Stedwell

BAUER MEDIA BOOKS
Publisher Sally Eagle
Editorial & food director Sophia Young
Creative director Hannah Blackmore
Senior designer Jeannel Cunanan
Designer Amy Daoud
Managing editor Stephanie Kistner
Junior editor Amanda Lees
Food editor Kathleen Davis
Operations manager David Scotto

International rights manager
Simone Aquilina
saquilina@bauer-media.com.au
Ph +61 2 8268 6278

Cover photographer James Moffatt
Cover stylist Bhavani Konnings
Cover photochef Sam Coutts
Cover recipe Lemon and Earl Grey Chiffon Cake, pages 194 and 195.

Printed in China by 1010 Printing International.

A catalogue record for this book is available from the National Library of Australia.

ISBN: 978-1-74245-995-0

Published by Bauer Media Books,
a division of Bauer Media Pty Ltd,
54 Park St, Sydney; GPO Box 4088,
Sydney, NSW 2001, Australia
phone +61 2 9282 8685; fax +61 2 9126 3702
www.awwcookbooks.com.au

© Bauer Media Pty Limited 2019

ABN 18 053 273 546
This publication is copyright. No part of it may be reproduced or transmitted in any form without the written permission of the publishers.

To order books
Phone 136 116 (within Australia) or
Order online at www.awwcookbooks.com.au
Send recipe enquiries to:
recipeenquiries@bauer-media.com.au